DRAGON
FIRE

DRAGON FIRE

S T E P H E N   F R A N C I S   M O N T A G N A

Copyright © 2022 by Stephen Francis Montagna

All rights reserved. No part of this publication may be reproduced, distributed, or transmitted in any form or by any means, including photocopying, recording, or other electronic or mechanical methods, without the prior written permission of the copyright owner and the publisher, except in the case of brief quotations embodied in critical reviews and certain other noncommercial uses permitted by copyright law. For permission requests, write to the publisher, addressed "Attention: Permissions Coordinator," at the address below.

ARPress
45 Dan Road Suite 5
Canton MA 02021

Hotline: 1(888) 821-0229
Fax: 1(508) 545-7580

Ordering Information:
Quantity sales. Special discounts are available on quantity purchases by corporations, associations, and others. For details, contact the publisher at the address above.

Printed in the United States of America.

| ISBN-13: | Softcover | 979-8-89389-255-0 |
| | eBook | 979-8-89389-256-7 |

Library of Congress Control Number: 2024907147

Table of Contents

This novel is written to honor all veterans.
A Veteran is someone who at one point in his or her life
wrote out a blank check made payable to the United States of
America for an amount up to and including, his or her life.
God bless all veterans.

PROLOGUE

THE AL-MASADA MOSQUE: THE LION'S DEN, NEW YORK CITY.

General Abdulaziz al-Wahhad, an ex-Iraqi Military Intelligence Officer, was granted a special visa to attend certain schools in the United States by Central Command Operations in Iraq. The Iraqi Officer set his eyes on the al-Masada Mosque of New York City for his religious beliefs. He was in search of assistance from other Arab men and women attending the Mosque. Ever since he first came to the United States, al-Wahhad had one thought locked in his mind. That thought was to get even with anyone living in the United States. Most of his anger was directed at the American soldiers destroying Iraq with their continuing occupation of his nearly destroyed country. Al-Wahhad at one point in his military life was sent to Pakistan by his President of Iraq, to undergo specialized training at the hands and direction of selected al-Qa'eda fighters and trainers. Iraqi General al-Wahhad also went through certain training at the guidance of the once feared Republican Guard of President Saddam Hussein.

During the second invasion of Iraq in Operation Iraqi Freedom carried out by Coalition Forces headed by the United States. General al-Wahhad realized the days of Saddam Hussein's iron-fisted rule over his country were number. Being of the sharp military mind, he started to work for the American troops in hopes of getting better treatment from them, once the Coalition Forces drove Saddam Hussein out of command of the nation. As the American soldiers entered the village where he was hiding, the General approached the Coalition Troops armed with a fistful of secret documents he stole from his military command center. That move won him the respect of the American Army Units who took over his village.

General al-Wahhad assisted the American Forces in Iraq and was instrumental in helping to maintain the peaceful transition of Coalition Forces over the Iraqi village, and the local population of where al-Wahhad called home. He was so helpful the American Troops started to search him out whenever they had to investigate a suspected home in the village for possible hidden weapons, or al-Qa'eda propaganda or fighters. Or if the Coalition Forces wanted help controlling the citizens. For a full year al-Wahhad helped the American Forces and was well paid for his services that also came with the offer to become a translator for the Coalition Troops. Al-Wahhad ended up working for the Americans for the full time of the Coalition occupation of Iraq until he showed interest in going to the United States for schooling.

The American Command developed in Iraq was impressed by the assistance of General al-Wahhad. The Commander of Allied Forces of Iraq offered al-Wahhad the ability of going to the United States for schooling and learning the English language, along with understanding the ways and beliefs of America. But there was another reason in the back of American Command's decision to offer this Iraqi ex-intelligence soldier to go to the United States for this special training. The CIA displayed an interest in this Iraqi in hopes of turning him, and then having him work for them, and maybe even use him to infiltrate the leadership of the al-Qa'eda terrorist organization system in the Iraq network.

It took three years for the offer to be approved by American Command in Iraq and General al-Wahhad was offered the ability to go to the United States in 2008. The Iraqi ex-military officer spent the next year attending schools and living like he truly enjoyed life in the United States. He settled in New Jersey, and in the latter part of 2008, decided to move to New York City, after searching the Mosques spread throughout the tri-state area. He was in search of one Imam, because this fiery Arab preacher spoke openly of his hatred for the United States, and all she and her people stood for. This angry Imam was practically ordering the young men of the Mosque to think about different ways of attacking, and causing problems for the United States leaders, police, and civilians.

The new Democratic Presidency installed in the United States in 2009, caused countless problems for the CIA and FBI, and the other intelligence gathering communities of the country. Consumed with political correctness, and the growing fear of lawsuits brought of racial profiling against the new Administration, forced our intelligence communities to duck. Instead of forcing the Islamic extremists to duck for fear of being caught in the crosshairs of justice dealt out by the United States.

With the threat of reveling newly discovered pictures of torture of the captured Arab terrorists being waterboarded, deprived of sleep and other torture programs employed against the terrorists being held at Guantanamo Bay, released to the civilian community and world. Coupled with the mounting fear of CIA Agent's identities being compromised over the threat of releasing these pictures and conditions to the public. Also, with cuts in funding too many of the Intel Communities, coupled with a mess of stifling presidential orders, severely limiting the abilities of the Intel Community to carry out wiretaps, and the employment of what was called racial profiling of Muslims in the United States.

These new laws and stifling restrictions caused the eleven intelligence networks of the United States empowered by law to protect the lives of the civilians, to begin to crumble. This crumbling of the intelligence networks caused future terrorist threats leveled against the United States, to start to slip through the cracks of this protection our hard-pressed intelligence peoples constructed over the years. Since the Islamic terrorist sneak attack carried out against the Twin Towers on Nine, One, One in New York City, and the Pentagon attack in Washington.

The no-fly list was severely neglected because of an endless list of new presidential regulations, and ongoing threats of the Attorney General investigating and prosecuting any Intel personnel who employed torture techniques against any Arab terrorist prisoners. Soon to be terrorists followed in other nations by our diligent intelligence personnel and placed on the terrorist no fly watch lists, were stopped being held under tight surveillance over the passing years. As the once fear of another devastating Nine, One, one terrorist attack started to fade from the memories of the civilians and politicians of the United States.

The American Civil Liberties Union was having a field day and making a fortune bringing one lawsuit after the other against our intelligence communities and personnel, while trying to force the release of the ugly pictures of torture of Arab terrorists held in Iraq to the world's attention. The ACLU lawyers coupled this request to release the horrific pictures of the enhanced interrogations with the demand to close the detention center stationed at Guantanamo Bay on the Island of Cuba. Along with the countless lawsuits came the ever-growing fear by our intelligence community personnel, threatened to be brought to public trial, to detain any thought of tracking down newly discovered Muslim terrorists. Because these brave intelligence people we trusted with our security, were severely handicapped and crippled while trying to carry out their duties. To keep the civilians of the United States safe with their hands tied behind their backs by the lawyers of America and their demands.

The ACLU was trying to force the new Democratic Administration to have the Arab terrorists being held at the Guantanamo Bay prison, transferred to the mainland of the United States. So, the Islamic terrorists order to stand trial for terrorist crimes committed against humanity in the civilian courts of New York City. ACLU lawyers and other liberal lawmakers failed to consider trying the terrorists as what they were, saboteurs. By labeling the captured Muslim terrorists as saboteurs, would remove all rights they would enjoy to legal protection in the civilian courts of law throughout the world. Saboteurs were solely the problem of the military units of the country affected by the actions of the terrorists, and once the military courts were done with them. The saboteurs were to be put to death by firing squad.

This demand of trying the Islamic radicals in civilian courts in the very heart of where they carried out their sneak attack in New York was met with strong resistance from not only the civilians, especially from the peoples of New York City. But even Congress grew upset and stood and put their backs up and was set against this demand from the ACLU to try the terrorists on mainland United States soil.

The Democratic Administration was wavering back and forth with the thought of bringing the Muslim extremist held at Guantanamo Bay to the United States. The Islamic prisoners was scheduled to be held in a special prison in Illinois, and their trials would be held in New York City right under the shadow that would have been cast by the Twin Towers, if the building still stood in the City.

The governor withdrew his support of trying the terrorists in the New York court system, by complaining bitterly about the staggering monetary costs for security such trials would cause the people of New York City and

State. The governor added the insult and slap in the face to the civilians of New York, to have the terrorists brought to New York to stand trial for their crimes of terror so near where they destroyed the buildings and killed so many civilians. This resistance from many people, police offices and officials, forced the new Administration to change course in mid-stream, and allow the isolated detention center at Gitmo to stand and remain opened, and carry out the military criminal war trials aimed against the Islamic terrorists held on the Island.

But the constant and widening attacks aimed at the unrecognized and belittled intelligence warriors on guard and standing their watches both day and night for the United States and her civilians, continued by the horde of bleeding hearts and ACLU lawyers. This action caused larger cracks to develop in the security systems designed to keep all known and wanted terrorists out of the United States, and the civilians to be safe and free in their own lands.

The "no fly list" was left up to being monitored by poorly trained and heavily overworked civilian airliner flight attendants, while they worked on checking the passengers in for their flights to wanted destinations. In many instants, by the time a wanted or person of interest mistakenly checked in with the airlines, whose names never made it on the no-fly list. When the list was updated and checked again, the wanted terrorist was already on board the airliner, and he or she was on their way to their destinations. This caused the airline personnel to recall the aircraft so they could remove the wanted criminal or person of interest.

Captains of the aircraft while in flight, were ordered to reroute to the nearest airport capable of taking their aircraft and land or fly back to their original airport. Once on the ground, a terrorist or person of interest was removed from the flight and placed in custody. Then the aircraft and her passengers were allowed to get on with its flight.

The severe lapse of keeping known and wanted terrorists and people of concern under constant surveillance was surfacing. This stunning discovery caught up to, and it forced Congress to correct this extremely troubling situation. Especially after the attack on a civilian aircraft while in flight by the so-called underwear bomber on Christmas Day, where the man tried to blow a plane while in flight, out of the air over Detroit.

The members of both sides of Congress started to pick up their error, and the country's leaders began to band together, and they decided to get off the backs of our intelligence and security communities and their elite personnel and allow them to do their work unmolested. Congress even reapplied the withheld monies to the intelligence communities. This change in political policy aimed at our intelligence communities, allowed the important guardians to our security and safety within the borders of the United States, to carry out their important and dangerous work in secret. Using all assets available, to accomplish their work carried out against the cowardly murderers against the free world, who work their evil and death aimed at the innocent civilians of all peace-loving nations of the world.

CHAPTER ONE

CAMP LEJEUNE, JACKSONVILLE NORTH CAROLINE
JANUARY 3rd, 2009

The elite troopers from several different countries, who made up the Multi-National Rapid Response Force, (MNRRF) on loan to the United States to round out the specialized soldiers' units. These highly trained soldiers were gathered on Camp Lejeune at Jacksonville in North Carolina. The soldiers recently return from Iraq, where they engaged in the search for the designer biological weapon discovered being developed in Iraq, under the command of the madman who once controlled that nation.

The Special Forces offered to the United States were the best their countries had to offer for defense against the continuing threat of terrorism carried out by the radical followers of Islam against any other nations of the world. During their operation in Iraq, the soldiers killed the Iraqi woman in possession of the biological weapon they were sent there to locate. Many of the elite soldiers were beat up from the feet up and were trying to heal countless cuts and minor wounds received from the mission in the troubled Arab nation of Iraq.

The specialized warriors were given three days no work while resting on the military base. So, the exhausted soldiers could catch up on rest, and regain some of their strength. The mix batch of male and female soldiers was as usual, riding each other to get control over their spirits. The young commander of the highly trained soldiers was Captain Robert Walker, and he was flanked by his girlfriend and fellow soldier, Sergeant Dorothy Ramirez. Along with his best friend, Lieutenant Frank Hall, better known to the group of Tier One soldiers as the Mutt because he was blessed with a black father and a white mother.

The other soldiers gathered around their commander was Sergeant Robert Abbott, his unit's name was No Neck, because his body was so large it looked like his head rested right on his shoulders. Sergeant Vincent Lambardo, branded Buckethead because his head was so large, the service had to have his helmet specially designed for his noggin. Sergeant Regina Raphael, on loan to the United States' Special Unit from France and was the girlfriend of the Mutt. Also, there was Sergeant Teri Dorland, known as Baby Tee because of the small size of her breasts, and she was kind of interested in Buckethead in a romantic way. She was with Sergeant Diane Morrison who the unit nicknamed "Ice". Because she was as cold as ice whenever she was on a mission, she was sort of dating No Neck off and on for the past few months.

Both units' extremely dangerous point men and snipers, or Vampires to the unit were with the rest of the close netted troops gathered by Captain Walker. Sergeant Walter Casper, known as Casper or the Ghost, because he moved like a ghost whenever he was working on an operation and was operating in the field along with his partner the Hunter, the second point man of the unit. Sergeant Frank Whitcomb rounded out the group of soldiers.

The troops were packed in the private quarters in the barracks of Walker. The soldiers were complaining about their latest mission in Iraq when Sergeant David Nirajima, branded McNip because he had a Japanese mother and an American father. Entered Walker's private living quarters in the barracks, rushed in and warned the soldiers gathered in the room. "Hey Grunts, Colonel hot shit is making a fucking beeline straight at our stinking barracks. I guess the big growl's gonna get on our asses for something we did wrong someplace along the line."

"Shit, I was wondering when the number ten prick was gonna get on our fucking asses for something he thinks we did wrong on this last operation. Okay, everyone outta here until I find out what the fuck the resident pricks want from our asses. Mutt, you and Raz stick with my ass, the rest of you ball sacks get the hell outta my quarters!" Walker waited until the troops left.

"Okay Mutt I want you with me, but I want your ass shut down tight while I speak to the major prick. I don't need you setting off old whatsisface and he goes off on us because of…"

"It's whatsisface Sir to your fucking ass, mister! Walker, just because you're a fucking Captain now, it doesn't mean you don't have to respect my ass when you're employing my name in any conversation you're engaged in, pissant! And you!" Colonel Bruce Leadbetter, the Commandant of the Marine Training base growled at the Mutt, as he turned his attention on him.

"Arrrr… fuck it, I'm not even going to waste my fucking breath on the likes of your ass. There's no fucking hope for you in this world or the next, scumbag. Sergeant Ramirez, it's a pleasure to see you again as always. For the life of me Ramirez, I can't understand why on God's green earth, you'd waste your time or exquisite body on this shitbird you're balling, sister. Look at the piece of shit, girl. He's ugly as hell, he smells worse than my grandmother did when we buried her, and she was five days dead when we finally dumped her off in the damn grave. He's stupid as shit, disrespectful as all hell, he eats like a pig in slop, and he'd screw a three-day old corpse of a female if he got half a chance to. He's constantly hanging around with this other jewel we call the Mutt, who tries to pass himself off as a specialized soldier of my beloved Marine Corps? C'mon Raz, use your head…"

"And they're the best soldiers we have in the Unit, Colonel Leadbetter." Ramirez offered as she dared to interrupt the steaming commander of the base.

"Yeah…yeah, I guess you got a good point there, Sergeant. They are good soldiers at that but remember you didn't hear that shit coming from my puss, sister. Arrr…all kidding aside you three jackrabbits, the reason I came to your barracks was so I could inform you screaming squirrels as of Oh, Four, Thirty-Five Hundred Hours. You'll have your troops mustered on the damn grinder before my quarters, and we're going to do the first full day's work since you pack of lunatics showed back up on my beloved base. Now before you start crying in the fucking breast milk Walker. I have no idea how long this next training program will be, and I have no idea when your crazy ass people will get any fucking leave time, so don't bother to ask…"

"C'mon will ya for crap's sake Colonel Leadbetter we just got back from I fucking raq not a month ago, from one helluva suck ass bug hunt mission, sir. I can't believe you're gonna forced our stinking asses to go through some kinda added training crap you dreamed up, before you'd begin to discuss any leave for my troops, Colonel." Walker grumbled as he locked up his commanding office in his glare while waiting his reply.

"Sniff, sniff, single fucking tear running down the side of my puss, buster. I just told you I didn't want to hear any crying in the breast milk, didn't I? Captain, I haven't the foggiest idea what the hell to do with the rest of you people, because I haven't heard jack shit from Command about the status of our specialized units. So, until I get confirmation on what to do with your wild ass pack of popping jays. We're remaining on base, and we will fill our time usefully while here. We're going to go over any new training scenarios to keep the razor on the edge on the blades of you group of damn pissants, buster. Besides Walker, how many times do I have to pound into that damn noggin of yours, these sweat warriors are not your people, buster?

"Walker, everything's going to hell in a damn handbag as fast as shit through a fucking goose, until the new President is finally sworn in and he takes command on the twentieth of this month of our country, Captain. I guess that's why we didn't hear squat shit from General White, because he doesn't know if the new Administration is going to keep his ass on as the Chairman of the Joint Chiefs of Staff.

"Everyone in fucking Washington's keeping their heads low to the ground until they see what the new President's going to do, and how he's going to shape his upcoming Administration. Until that shit happens, and we know what direct this damn new Administration is going to go off in. We're stuck on base until that time arrived, Captain. Unless, before he leaves office, President Cole somehow remembers us, and he sends us on leave until the new government is up and running. That's why my hands are tied, and we're going to remain on base until I get word on what to do with your puds.

"I can tell you this about the new Presidential Administration, Captain. From the bullshit the new President was spouting off during his campaign run for the office. This man's going to be a serious problem for us to deal with. The President has his eyes leveled on our Intel communities and according to his own words while running for office. This Boss is going to go after our Intel people harder than he intends to go after the fucking radicals we have to deal with. This guy obviously doesn't want to understand the fucking terrorists are rewriting the rules of engagement in the field, which forces us to rewrite the rules of interrogation, and how we handle and treat the damn terrorists being held at Gitmo and elsewhere. If we treat the terrorist with kid gloves like this new guy wants, and he wants to offer them protect and lawyers to defend these animals.

"Walker, we're no longer going to get much useful information from the sacks of shit still being held in special prisons spread throughout the world. I don't understand why our people don't call these ball sacks what the fuck they truly are. These bastards are nothing more than goddamn saboteurs. Because once we label the animals as saboteurs, all bets are off the table for these fucking guys, because even under the Geneva rules of war. Saboteurs are not given any legal rights of protections. If an animal is classified as a saboteur, that animal's questioned strictly by the military. The terrorist's interrogation would be carried out in any manner the military inquisitor wants to question and treat the god damn saboteur.

"Once the inquisitor has gleaned all the information he wants and needs and feels he can get from the fucking animal. The creeps get quick marched out to the back courtyard and shot by firing squad; it's that fucking simple Captain. That way there's no burden to the taxpayers of any country the lousy saboteur was working his evil ways in.

"With the death of the damn saboteur, there's no need for any costly trials, no victims will be forced to go through the torture of speaking or hearing how their loved ones met their deaths at the hands of the terrorist slash saboteurs. The trial lawyers won't make a damn fortune dragging out a trial trying to save the lives of these fucking animals. So, we'll be forced to deal with the rat bastards in the future once they're released and come back at us a second time as a saboteur. What a hell of a mess we have on our hands trying to deal and stop a future terrorist catastrophic attack on the United States homeland, operating with our damn hands tied behind our backs. We need another Republican Leader who'll give us power to work over the terrorists, so they keep their damn heads down. Instead of this Administration forcing our Intel communities to keep their heads down while trying to stop a terrorist attack with their damn eyes blindfolded."

Colonel Leadbetter stopped speaking and drew in a huge gulp of air. He remained silent for a few seconds to see if Walker wanted to say something during this conversation. When he realized, the captain was going to hold his tongue, he added to his bitch. "Walker, I understand this shit sucks the big one, and I wish there was something I could do about this damn situation of leave for your troops. But I don't have the power or authority to cut our troops any leave on my own, mister. That order has to come from the front office, and until we know how this guy's going to run that office, we can't do a damn thing about shit, Captain."

"Shit Colonel, we got our stinking asses caught between the shit and sweat, sir. Why wasn't this last mission held up until this new stinking President took office. Crap what am I talking about? We hadta do our act when we hadta do it, sir. Or that fucking bug crap we went afta in Iraq, mighta been released and the world would be paying the price with a biological situation, and we'd be burying civilians by the fucking truckload, Colonel. I only wish the old President kept us in mind, and he cut leave orders before this uther guy took command of the country, sir. We did our act so the least the brain thrust can do is remember us..."

"Wait a minute Captain you just gave me an idea and a mission to go off on, mister. Sure, I can approach General White and request he gives you jerks some leave. He's still the current Chairman of the Joint Chiefs of Staff, and as such he has the power to cut any unit leave time he wants to issue. I'm going to contact the General and breach the question of leave, before there are any changes in the command structure of the country, Captain. Knowing the General, he'd be willing to cut leaves, and he'd deal with the new President if this guy has a hardon for what he did before the other guy took command of the country. Dammit! It's Saturday and I was informed General White was going to be out of his office until Monday at his usual time of arrival. So, it looks like we're stuck on base until at least that long, sir."

THE PENTAGON, ZERO, EIGHT TWENTY HOURS
MONDAY, JANUARY 5th, 2009

General John White, the current Chairman of the Joint Chiefs of Staff, was getting comfortable in his office and motioned CIA Director John Raincloud to take a seat. The General arrived a little late at his office because he took time to pick up the Director, because he wanted to have a conversation with him. General White was able to smell the coffee perking and knew Mary; his secretary followed them to his office. He could not nor did he try to hide the smile, knowing Mary was at her post and she was his right hand.

John Raincloud, a full-blooded Sioux Native American, noticed the General's smile, and he figured he was in a good mood. But that thought disappeared quickly the moment the powerful General spoke.

"Goddammit John, with this new President taking command of the country, his actions already have my balls tied up in a fucking knot for Christ's sake. I don't know what to do. I don't know for certain if I'm going to have my job once this new guy shapes up his Administration. This shit having a new President move in and take command of our country every four or eight years, rips apart the good we accomplished over the years we worked together, Director Raincloud. I don't know how you people at the damn Agency keep things running like you do. I'm having one helluva time trying to keep…Dammit, now what for Christ's sake?"

General White grumbled angrily as he answered the phone. He was taken back because the call was put through to his office by his secretary. She knew he was entertaining the Director, and that meant this call had to be extremely important. He glanced at the caller ID and realized it was coming from the Commandant of Camp Lejeune. He found himself wondering what Colonel Leadbetter wanted with him so early in the morning as he answered the call. "Yeah, Colonel Leadbetter, General White here, what's up your ass this morning, sir? I can't believe you're busting my damn horns so early in the fucking morning, Colonel. I'm involved in an important meeting with Director Raincloud, so you have to make this damn call short and sweet and right to the fucking point, sir."

"Sorry for interrupting your meeting with the Director, General White Sir. The reason for this call is, I have a mess of extremely exhausted and seriously grumpy Tier One soldiers on my hands, and the troops are wondering what the hell's going on and what's happening with them, sir. My troops want to head home for some leave time, General. They're riding my ass to hell and back, to see if you'd allow them to go home for some relaxation. The troops don't want to get stuck sitting on base until we know what this new President's going to do with the armed services, sir. You know whenever a Democratic gets in office, the first thing they do is want to cut the military down to the damn bone…"

"I hear you there, Colonel Leadbetter, but I have no idea what I'm doing myself, sir. Hell, I don't know if I'm going to have a fucking job when the new guy takes command of the office, sir. Colonel, if I'm removed as Chairman, I'm going to retire. I have no intention of working with my hands tied behind my back with this guy running the country.

"Arrr…. we have a few days left with the old Republican President before he leaves office. We're going to have to hold our breath, and see what this President's going to do, and how he's going to run the country. Colonel Leadbetter, you raised a good point here though, I'll tell you what I'm going to do. When I end this conversation sir, I'll put my meeting with Director Raincloud off for a few minutes, and I'll call the President and see if he'll allow me to send your troops home on leave. I'm almost positive he'll allow me to authorize the requested leave, Colonel Leadbetter Sir."

"Outstanding General White, I'm certain if anyone can get my troops some leave time, you're the man for the job, sir. I'll end this conversation so you can finish up with Director Raincloud, and then speak to the President on our behalf, sir. Hell, General White, I'm sure going to miss this man when he leaves office, sir. If there was one thing a soldier could count on, was this last President was one hundred percent behind his troops, sir. Please give my regards to Director Raincloud, I hope this new President's going to keep you both on, and he'll be shooting himself in the damn foot if he replaces either of you two, sir. Good luck with the President, General."

"Thanks for bringing this situation up to my attention Colonel Leadbetter, and I'm ordering you to standby because I'll be back to you the first moment I get, when I'm finished speaking with the outgoing President over this matter of leave for your specialized troops, sir." General White replied as he broke off the connection with his Colonel, and then looked at the Director for a moment before offering.

"John that was Colonel Leadbetter, he's sucking around for some leave time for his troops who he's worried will be stuck on the base until this new President takes command of the country. I'm going to speak to the outgoing President and see if he'll authorize my releasing these kids on leave. So, hang onto your thoughts for a few moments until I'm finished speaking to our Command in Chief, sir." The General warned the CIA Director.

"Don't worry about me General White I can amuse myself while you speak to the President. Heaven knows after what these kids just pulled off in Iraq for our country. They deserve leave, with our blessings and we are paying for it, General White."

"Thanks for understanding Director Raincloud, excuse me while I make this call sir." General White offered as he picked up the phone while acknowledging the nod from Raincloud with one of his own. The General allowed a smile as he dialed the President's number.

After the third ring, a pleasant but exhausted sounding voice reported. "This is the President's Chief Aide Peter Walters; how may I direct this call please?"

"Yeah, Pete this is General White, son. I know it must be a real nut house over there, but I need to speak to your Boss PDQ, young man. It's important Peter."

"Boy General White you said a mouth full there, sir. The First Lady is supervising the packing of their personal property, and we have a flood of people walking all over the place trying to help with the moving, sir. It seems everyone is coming over and wants to say their goodbyes to our President. I know the President's busy, but I'm certain he'd be pleased to speak with you General. Please hold on while I locate the Boss, I know he's somewhere on the second floor of the White House, the last time I saw him he was speaking with Senator Mullins, sir."

The General did not reply as he settled in to wait for the President's aide to locate his boss.

President Albert Cole was busy speaking to Senator Mullins and Vice President Mary Hirshfield. Peter could see the hurt look etched in Mary's eyes as she watched the President walking around, and it seemed like he was taking his last look around the mansion. Peter walked over to and then stood silently behind the President and waited to be addressed by his boss.

The President picked up the man standing behind him out of the corner of his eye, and rushed his words with the elderly Senator, and the first moment he got, he offered with a smile. "Senator Mullins, will you be so kind as to give me a moment please, sir? I see my Aide and he must have an important message I have to handle. Mary, will you show Senator Mullins to the Johnson room and wait there with him. Have some warm brandy sent in for us." President Cole remarked as he watched Mary lead the elderly Senator away then he turned to Peter and asked.

"What's up Pete, you seem to be in a bit of a rush, young man?" The President offered as he rested his hand gently on the young aide's shoulder, and he leaned his head a bit close to hear what his aide wanted to speak to him over.

"Please excuse me for interrupting you and the Senator, Mr. President. But General White's waiting on the line and wants to speak with you at your earliest convenience, Sir. I can have the call transferred to the phone line in the Special Agent's security closet, if you want privacy while speaking with the General, Mr. President."

"That's a good idea Peter you have the call transferred to the security room while I inform Mary and the Senator I'll be engaged for a few moments." The President left Peter to carry out his orders and by the time he got to the security room, the call was waiting for him.

The exhausted American Leader took the receiver and said in a pleasant tone. "Ahhh…General White it's a pleasure and you're not going to believe this for a minute, sir. But I was planning to place a call to you later in the day when I got a few moments to myself, sir. You beat me to the punch with this call, what's on your mind General White?"

"Please excuse me for interrupting you Mr. President. I know you must be going through hell wrapping up all the loose ends to your Administration, sir…"

"General White we known each other and worked together for eight years now, sir. So, I think you earned the right to call me Albert or Al, and let's skip this "Sir" shit while we're at it, John." The outgoing President remarked as he cut off the General in mid-sentence.

"I thank you for that honor and pleasant words, Mr. President, err… Al." General White was having a hard time trying to get used to addressing the well-respected President by his first name. "Mr. Pres… err… Al, the reason I bothered you with this call, is I just received a call from my Colonel stationed at Camp Lejeune, sir. He's concerned he was going to get stuck keeping his elite troops stuck on base until the new err… excuse me sir, President takes command of the office, sir. Mr. President, the Tier One soldiers Colonel Leadbetter's in command of, are the troops who tracked down and took possession of the…"

"John, I know who the soldiers this Colonel is in command of. I also know what these kids did for this country and my Administration in Iraq, sir. I understand the concerns of your Colonel, General White. I also understand where this conversation's heading, and I'll make it simple for you John. I'll make my way to the Oval Office by early afternoon, and I'll cut orders for leave for the soldiers. If it's the last order I give while I'm holding command, sir.

"John, General White, I'll leave the extent of leave for the soldiers for you to fill in later, sir. I'm pleased you brought this situation up to my attention before these kids were forgotten by us, General. With all the crap I'm going through getting the House cleared out for the new President and finishing up the loose ends I have to look after, is taking up most of my damn time. I'm sure going to miss being in command, General. But I'm looking forward to getting back to my civilian life with my dear lady and kids at my side, sir."

"I bet you're looking forward to getting back to the civilian lifestyle, Mr. President."

"Look John when my wife and I are settled in on the ranch. Why don't you and your lady make plans to come down to Texas for an extended weekend, and you can get some serious relaxation in with me and the wife? We can get in some fishing and hunting while you're there, and there's always plenty of crap to keep us busy we can get involved in. It'd help getting my better half back in the swing of entertaining normal company on a much smaller scale than what she grown accustomed to at the big house these eight years, General White."

"I'll keep the offer in mind and once I see you're settled in, I'll pay you an extended visit, Mr. President. I'll await your return call sir. I thank you for remembering my troops, Mr. President. I'll leave you so you can get back to your visitors and what you must handle, sir. Good luck and I think it sucks you can't stay on for another four years, sir. With the nuts we've been forced to deal with in the past eight years, sir. I hope the new guy is up to snuff..."

"General White, John the new President needs you and Director Raincloud more than you'll know sir and knowing how you are General. I understand you and Mr. Raincloud will help the new President like you helped me throughout my eight-year Administration. I hope you hear what

I'm telling you General?" The outgoing President interrupted his chairman and ordered his officer to help the new administration as if the General was still working for him.

"I read you loud and clear Mr. President and rest assured we'll take care of the new guy like we took care of you and stopped you from walking on any land minds along the way during your very successful Administrations, sir." General White replied with a slight laugh as he broke off the connection with the President.

Director Raincloud shifted his weight in the chair and then offered the powerful military officer. "Well, that conversation was pleasant enough, and it seems to have gone in your favor, General White. How was the President taking leaving the White House?"

"It went as well as it could have, I guess, John. The President seemed to be operating in pretty good spirits, and he's going to draft the order for leave for my Tier One troops stationed at Lejeune, sometime today. The President said if that was his last order before leaving the Presidency, he'd make certain to draft the orders for leave for my troops personally, Mr. Raincloud." General White replied as he made himself comfortable, just as Mary came in the office carrying a tray with coffee and cakes for all to enjoy.

THE CHANGING OF COMMAND IN THE UNITED STATES

General John White, along with CIA Director John Raincloud, was present at the swearing in of the new and liberal Democratic President, Mark Otomer. It was a great ceremony and good for the nation to have a new leader, what with unemployment running ramped and banks starting to crash along with the housing and stock markets. But this day was for welcoming in the new President and his command structure. General White with Director Raincloud and two Republican Senators was surprised when the new President specifically searched him out. The President took him by the arm and offered to him as he skillfully led the powerful military officer away from his friends.

"General White, please allow me to say I have no intention of replacing either you or Director Raincloud in my upcoming Administration, sir. I read your history with the outgoing President, General. I'll pray you'll be of the same outstanding service and value to me, as you were to the prior President and his Administration, sir. General White, if I feel for one moment your heart and soul are not with my best interests, and the interests of the country. I'll not hesitate for one second to have you replaced, or anyone else I decided to keep on from the past Administration. General White, there'll be many changes in my Administration. Many people you dealt with over the last eight years will be replaced, by people I believe will be in better command of the situations we'll be forced to deal with in the coming future, sir." The President stopped speaking to allow the military officer a chance to respond to his words.

"With all due respect Mr. President, if you're here to test my loyalty. Then you'll find yourself only testing my patience, sir. I need no one to direct me on how to better assist any Presidential Administration I have sworn my life to serve, sir. I hope I have set your mind at ease over my intentions to serve your Administration, Mr. President. On the other hand, sir, if you ever find yourself feeling the least bit uncomfortable with me for any reason, Mr. President, it's at your pleasure to have me replaced. In fact, Mr. President, if I make you feel I'm not working one hundred and fifty percent for your sake, and for the sake of your Administration and our country. I demand you have me replaced immediately, Mr. President." General White looked hard and long into the staring eyes of the youngish President. The officer held that contact until the President allowed a smile, and then he added to his words.

"I thank you for those reassuring words, and I'll remember this conversation for the length of my Administration, General White. I'll bring it up to your attention if I ever feel threatened or neglected by your actions while under my command, sir. I thank you much for your honesty and obvious backing of my upcoming Administration, sir. General White, I know we're likely going to butt heads together on several situations I'll be forced to deal with in the future during my Administration, sir. I need you to be always honest with me over any problems we might face together, no matter the outcome of these situations, sir. General, I know damn well I made many promises during my exhausting campaign run for the White House over the past year and a half, sir.

"General White, some of those promises I intend to keep, others I'll pray the public have short memories, and they forget I made them. So,

I'm not forced to have to explain why I'm not going to keep some of those promises, and we can get on with the matters facing the civilians of the United States, sir. General White, one reason I wanted to speak privately with you sir. Is because I need a detailed report on the situation at the Detention Center at Guantanamo Bay, the first chance you get to file that report, sir. That request comes with a deadline attached to it sir. General, I expect that report to cross my desk by no later than February 6th, sir. Because that's one promise I made I intend to keep, closing that nightmare of a hellish place down as soon as humanly possible, and…"

General White decided to test the President's metal by daring to interrupt him as he remarked. "Mr. President, I understand you promised to close down Guantanamo during your campaign run, sir. I find myself having to caution you to look at all sides of that problem, before you act against the damn Detention Center, sir. There are many reasons for keeping the center at Guantanamo operating for as long as we must deal with any terrorists. It's a necessary evil we must live with sir. Mr. President, I believe now is not the time for this conversation to be taking place, sir. Why don't you sit back and enjoy your special day of honor and respect, because this day belongs to you. After you had some time sitting in the big chair, and seeing how things work around here, we can meet again at our leisure and speak about the reasons to close, and to keep Gitmo operating, sir."

The President stepped back while allowing a slight smile to cross his lips as he stared at the General and quickly collected his thoughts, and then offered. "General White, I see I was correct with wanting to keep you staying on as my Chairman of the Joint Chiefs of Staff, sir. You are correct sir, now is not the time for this conversation to take place, General. I'll take your advice and get used to my office before we tackle the countless problems this damn Detention Center is causing to the conscious of man, sir."

"Thank you for understanding Mr. President and I hope you'll take the rest of my advice and enjoy your day of celebrations, sir." The respected military officer remarked to the smiling President He wanted to end this conversation so he could get back to Director Raincloud. He was trying to ditch the President because the situation of Gitmo was a sore subject to him. The Chairman knew he was going to lock horns with the man over the Detention Center in the future, and he was prepared to go to the wall over the subject. He knew the value and reasons of keeping Gitmo operating.

"Very well General White Sir, I guess I must get back to my people as you suggested, sir. Please remember General White, I'll be expecting that report from you by February the 6th, sir." The President nodded to the officer and then he quickly disappeared into the madness taking over the heart of Washington.

The moment the President left his side, General White turned and headed for Director Raincloud and catching up to him; the Director hit him with the first question. "What was that shit all about sir? Hell, General White, your meeting with the President had his secret service personnel thinking you might harm the poor man, sir. You had a flood of Democrats from the masses trying to figure out why their guy was interrupting his celebrations to speak privately with you, sir. General, my radio was teaming with questions about your conversation, and what the security guards should do about it." Raincloud stopped speaking and smiled at the General.

"Sorry for causing you problems John and for the stuff shirts under your command, and their fucking concerns can kiss my damn ass for all I care. I wasn't the one who took the President aside to engage in conversation, he was the one who approached me. John, he stated the obvious, he was going to keep us on board until he can find people to replace us, even though he didn't outright say he was going to replace us. John, you know I'm not much for these Washington big ass parties. I think I'm going to head back to my office and fill out the request for Colonel Leadbetter's crew to head home for leave. Cover me while I'm gone."

"Will do General, all celebrations are going to be Democrats enjoying themselves and Washington knows I'm a conservative, so you can guess how many parties I was invited to."

"About as many as I was, I guess, Director. You want to follow me back to my office? I'm certain there's something there we can party with. I have a bottle of Rye hidden in the bottom drawer of my desk, and once I finish my draft of the leave order for the soldiers stationed at Lejeune, I intend to get blind ass fucking drunk. I'm going to salute the outgoing President for the job well done keeping the United States safe, and his backing of my people when they were in harm's way." The General offered then waited for the director's reply.

"Lead the way because I'm right behind you. It's going to be hell getting out of downtown Washington as long as all the celebrating is going on, sir." Raincloud offered with concern.

"That's where you're dead wrong Director Raincloud. I had the smarts to have my driver remain on duty while we met with the President. I had him park where all he has to do is hit the siren, and we'll be picked up by a police escort that'll get us out of here in no time, sir." General White placed a smile of triumph on as he headed for his car with the Director right on his heels.

Three and a half hours later, General White and Director Raincloud exhaustedly entered the General's private office at the Pentagon with the Director complaining. "Well General White that was sure some fucked up idea you had of having your damn driver park where he was, sir. Hell John, if it wasn't for some of my people coming by to see what all the commotion you were causing was about, sir. I'd bet the damn bank on it that we'd still be stuck sitting in the middle of the mess of downtown Washington for who knows how long, sir."

"Ahhhh…I see you're nagging your way to ecstasy today, John. One of these days you're going to make someone a helluva damn good fucking wife, what with the way you keep nagging my damn ass all the fucking time, my friend. Don't get a breeze up; didn't we get here safe and sound sir?" General White bitched at the Director.

"We certainly got here, but I was afraid I was going to die of old age first, General."

"Keep going mister, you're going to keep that fucking flapjack of the damn grill a while longer I see, Director. Sit your ass down and make yourself comfortable, while I get in contact with my Colonel cooling his heels at Lejeune. But so, you don't get bored, have yourself a drink, sir. Say when." General White remarked as he pulled the bottle of whisky from the bottom drawer and poured them a stiff belt of the harsh liquid.

"When your fingers get wet will do just fine for me, General. Boy, downtown Washington is a helluva mess today. Every mother's son was out and about today, sir." Director Raincloud replied as he took the drink and saluted the General with the glass to the tip of his brow and added.

"Here's to the outgoing Republican President, may this new guy be half as good as the old one was, and our country might get over this nightmare we're mired in."

"Here, here John, I agree and hope this new guy's going to be half as good a President as the last one was." The General added as he joined the Director in his salute to the old President, and then he dialed Colonel Leadbetter's office. General White just got comfortable when a voice over the phone replied.

"This is Colonel Bruce Leadbetter, the Commandant of Camp Lejeune's office, sir. Who is calling and how may I direct this call for you please, sir? This is Sergeant John Kirkpatrick manning the Colonel's desk in his absence, and I'll handle any questions you may have, sir." The Sergeant offered politely over the phone.

"Sergeant Kirkpatrick this is General White, I need to speak to your Commander A-SAP." The powerful General snorted in the phone, upset the Colonel was not at his office.

"Good evening General White Sir, it's a pleasure to speak with you sir. General White, I figured you'd be making the rounds to the countless parties we heard about down here, sir. What with the new President taking command today, and the wild celebrating that's still raging sir…"?

"Well son you guessed wrong didn't ya? Let's cut to the chase with you, Sergeant. I don't have the time or the luxury to get involved in a long-winded conversation I have no intention of getting involved in, Sergeant. Just find your damn Colonel and inform him I need to speak to him immediately, Sergeant." General White grumbled in the phone.

"Yes, Sir General White, General, Colonel Leadbetter's engaged, and he has…"

"I don't give a flying fuck if the Colonel's married. I ordered you to get him on this damn phone, before you find yourself checking the stockpile of One Fifty-Five cannon rounds for duds with a fucking hammer, mister. Do you read me loud and clear son?" General White growled.

"Yes, Sir General White, I read you loud and clear and understand your orders, sir. I'll carry them out immediately, sir. I'll get Colonel Leadbetter on the horn as quickly as possible General White. Sorry I caused you delay, sir. I assure you General White, it'll not happen…"

"What the hell's going on with you, Sergeant? Why are you stalling my ass over getting the damn Colonel on the damn horn for me, mister? Sergeant, if you keep stalling me like you're obviously doing for your Colonel. Both you and your damn Commander are going to be feeling my anger tonight. What the hell's the story and why are you running interference for your Commander, Sergeant?" General White interrupted the Sergeant and roared in the phone. Then he looked at the Director smiling at him.

"I'm sorry to offer General White, but Colonel Leadbetter figured you'd be engaging in a number of parties today and tonight he was certain would be going on in Washington, sir. Colonel Leadbetter left the base to have a few drinks and some downtime, sir. He informed me he was planning to return to base by Twenty-Three Hundred Hours tonight, sir. General White, if it's that important to speak with Colonel Leadbetter, sir. I can call the local watering holes and find the Colonel, and order him back to base for you, General." Sergeant Kirkpatrick replied with concern lacing his tone.

General White had to laugh as he responded. "Sergeant I'd love to see you try and order your Commander for any reason, mister. I'm certain there wouldn't be much left of your ass if you tried if I know the Colonel, son. Sergeant, I'd never place my NCO (Non-Commissioned Officer) in a situation as to order his Commander. I'll not interfere with your Colonel's relaxation. I see I'm forced to wait until your Commander places a call back to my ass, mister. Sergeant, I'll be waiting for his call back, I better not be forced to wait after Twenty-Three Hundred Hours though, son."

"General White, the Colonel said he'd be back by that time, and he will, sir."

CHAPTER TWO

General John White broke off the communication with the young Marine Sergeant by merely hanging upon him. It was one of the General's power plays, and the Sergeant was the one he aimed his game at this time. He then sat back and looked at the CIA Director, who seemed to be amused over the slight confrontation that just went down between the two military personnel, as he offered with a smirk. "I see you're having yourself one helluva good time enjoying the crap I have to put up with when I'm forced to deal with the pain in the ass Sergeant, my friend. What say John you need another drink or are you still fine sir?"

"I can stand for another drink if you don't mind, General. That's if you're joining me. I hate to drink alone sir. How soon before your Colonel is going to get back to you, General?" The Director remarked as he held out his glass then waited for the General to fill it.

The General let out his breath as he filled his glass and then remarked. "The damn desk Sergeant stated the Colonel was due back by Twenty-Three Hundred Hours. It seems the Colonel decided to do a little celebrating of his own, John. The Sergeant mentioned the Colonel felt I'd be doing the rounds at some of the parties taking place in Washington. My Officers don't know me as well as I thought they did. Arrr…if it wasn't for Colonel Leadbetter getting permission for some leave time for his troops from the President, I'd never been bothering the man, John. I hate to interrupt my people when they decide to let their hair down and enjoy a night. My damn Officers deserve all the enjoyment time they can get, John."

"Sounds about right to me General, err…John do you want me to hang around until your Colonel calls in, or is it okay if I take off for a little while? You might want to be a stick in the mud, but I happen to enjoy hitting some of the wild-ass Washington parties scheduled to take place for tonight, sir. Besides, I have a hundred and fifty Agents prowling around downtown Washington trying to protect the new President. I should be out there making certain nothing happens without my knowledge." The concerned Director smiled again.

"You don't have to waste time hanging with my ass and being bored to death, mister. I'm a big boy and I can handle my time very well for myself, sir. I know you want to get out of here to hit some of these damn parties. You ain't fooling me for a second, I assure you, sir. You want to get the hell out there and check some of the skirts and try to look down some blouses while you're at it, you dirty old man you. Get the hell out of here will ya please. After all, you drank half my damn booze, and now you're horny as hell and need some loving." General White looked at the Director, and then gave him one of his well-noted smiles.

The General's smirk made the Director smile and he replied. "What can I tell you General, I am a dirty old man, and I'm going to be a dirty old man until the day I die, sir. I better be on my way and check on my Agents in the field, and make certain they're on their damn toes, sir. Good luck with your Colonel when he finally checks in with you, General. Do you want me to come back to your office when I finish with my Agents and check out some of these damn parties, General White Sir?"

"And the chicks hanging all over Washington and celebrating the new Administration moving in the White House. Naw, no sense returning here tonight, John, by the time you hit a few of these damn parties, you ain't going to be in any shape to have an intelligent conversation with anyhow. If anything happens with my Colonel, I'll contact you, and if any shit hits the fan with this new guy. Call and I'll get military help out…"

"General White Sir, I almost forgot. Your troops looked sharp as a razor with that twenty-one-gun salute they gave the new President, sir. Your soldiers looked first class, real classy General White." The Director offered as he interrupted the General.

"Thanks for the kind words, every once in a while, it's great to hear a compliment about the troops under your command, Director." The General responded as he nodded.

Director Raincloud rose and then offered the General his hand, and after shaking it he walked out of the General's office. The General never allowed anyone to walk around his office unless his secretary was in the outer office, so she could keep an eye on anyone leaving or entering his office. The men stopped when they came face to face with Mary, as she worked making a pot of coffee. She snuck into the outer office shortly after the two men entered the office.

General White shook his head and slapped the Director on the back as he offered with a huge grin. "Hello John, I should've known my little hawk here would be on her toes, and she followed us so she could look after us like we were two kids sneaking into the movies. Jesus Mary, how the hell did you know John and I returned to the damn office, young lady? Hell lady, you should be getting stewed to the gills instead of wasting your time being stuck here with the two of us old goats."

"For your information General White, I was enjoying myself that was until I saw you two fools trying to get through the maddening crowds of downtown Washington. Running your siren and sticking your head out the window and screaming at any poor soul guilty of enjoying themselves and might have been in your way. I was so embarrassed when you screamed at that poor woman who wouldn't get out of your way fast enough for your likes, General White. I tried to hide my face, so no one recognized I worked for such a crazy acting person, sir. You Director, you're no better than the General is, sir. I saw you screaming at some people trying to enjoy themselves as well, mister. Can't you two learn to let your hair down and enjoy yourselves occasionally for Pete's sake? I feel sorry for the two of you." Mary stopped speaking and glared at the two men, but she could not hold it for long and smile.

General White let his breath out as he moaned. "Whew honey, for a moment there I thought you were pissed off at us. Mary, the Director's heading out to check on his people in the field. I'm afraid I'm stuck in my office waiting for Colonel Leadbetter to check in with me. What are you doing here anyway, girl?"

"I told you I saw you two leaving downtown Washington, and I knew you guys were heading for your office. Why are you waiting for Colonel Leadbetter to check in with you, General White? I'd think your Colonel would be using the confusion in Washington to have some time off for himself, sir." Mary replied as she allowed herself to relax.

"Mary, Colonel Leadbetter's checking in, because while you were out there having yourself a blast, young lady. The Colonel requested I investigate getting some leave time in for his troops at his base. It was a good call because if we didn't settle the leave question tonight with the outgoing President. His troopers would've been stuck sitting on base until the new President found the time to address some left for the soldiers."

"General White, I can't believe you were able to get a hold of the outgoing President, and able to breach the subject of leave for your outstanding troops, and you got it, sir?" Mary cried, stunned the General contacted the President on his last day in office, and received permission for leave for the General's soldiers at Lejeune.

"Look lady, when it comes down to my troops, and they request some leave time. I'd move heaven and earth to get that request fulfilled for them. You know how I am honey if I must get hold of someone no matter who he might be, or where he is. I'm going to get his damn ear one way or the other, young lady." General White replied smugly as he placed a smile of victory as Director Raincloud left his office.

Mary and the Chairman of the Joint Chiefs of Staff watched as Director Raincloud left the office, and then Mary offered to the General with a smile. "I'll have coffee for you in five minutes General. You worry about your troops, sir. Go in your office and wait for Colonel Leadbetter's call back, sir. I'll bring us in coffee when it's ready, sir."

"Please." General White replied as he took his secretary's advice and returned to his office to wait for his Colonel's call. It seemed like he just got comfortable when his phone rang, and Mary walked into his office carrying a tray with cups of coffee and cheesecakes at the same time.

"Goddammit, I should've known the damn Colonel would call when we were going to share a few moments and coffee." General White complained to his secretary as he reached for the phone and watched Mary place his cup in front of him.

General White smiled as she made herself comfortable. Once she was comfortable, he picked up the phone and barked. "Colonel Leadbetter, this better be you I'm speaking with!"

"General White, why are you busting my damn horns like this tonight, sir? Jesus Christ and miracles General White Sir, you should be hitting some of the damn parties smoking in that stinking town up there, instead of getting on my fricking ass like this, sir." The Colonel replied, and the way he was speaking, General White was easily able to tell he had a few drinks, and they were affecting his speech and manner.

"Are you okay to carry on an intelligent fucking conversation with my damn ass, Colonel Leadbetter Sir? You sure sound like you're three sheets to the god damn wind, mister." General White snapped at the Marine Colonel.

"Hell, General White, just put a damn weapon in my hands then point me in the direction of our enemy, and you'll see how much I'm in control of my ass, sir. I might sound like I had a few which I surely did, sir. But I'm cocked, locked, and ready to fucking rock, General White."

"Yes, I see by the way you're daring to speak to me that you had a few drinks, mister. Colonel Leadbetter Sir, listen up, the reason for my call is, I was able to get the outgoing President's ear, and I breached the subject of leave for your troops, sir. President Cole assured me he'll make it to his office before he leaves the White House and draft order for leave. I was hoping I would've received the damn order before we spoke tonight, sir. The outgoing President is going to have a currier deliver the damn order personally to my ass, and that won't happen until tomorrow morning at the earliest, Colonel. Hell, the way the streets of Washington are crawling with pain in the ass wild acting civilians. It took me half the damn day to get back to my office when I left Washington, Colonel." General White took a break.

Colonel Leadbetter was amazed the powerful Chairman of the Joint Chiefs of Staff was able to speak with the outgoing President and to get the man to take the time to write an order for leave for his troops before he left office. He knew his place in this conversation and held his tongue and if the General wanted to take the bows for speaking with the President. The General would have to bring it up in this conversation.

"I'm pleased you had the smarts to hold your damn tongue for a minute Colonel Leadbetter, that's going to make this conversation go a helluva lot smoother for the both of us, mister. I'm expecting the order to cross my desk by sometime tomorrow morning at the latest. The moment that order is in my hands, I'll execute it and have the first of your troops heading home by Wednesday afternoon, on January 7th. Colonel, I'm going to keep your troopers on leave until I see which way this new President's going to handle them. From his mouthing when he was running for office, the guy made it known he was going to be hunting military heads. I have it from reliable people that this President isn't going to be very friendly with us military types. Colonel Leadbetter, I hope I still have your god damn attention, mister?"

"Yes, you do General White, Sir. I'm listening to your every word sir."

"Very well mister, I was warned this President was going to be aiming his eyes at our Intelligence Communities, and our military personnel. Therefore, I intend to keep your troops on leave for as long as I can, sir. With that pack of live wires of yours down there, I can ill afford to have any of them bumping into this President by accident or on purpose, Colonel. With the way my luck's been running lately, the President would probably run into your Captain Walker, and the next thing I'd know. He'd be demanding to disband our Rapid Response Forces. He made it quite clear to my ass he still intends to close Gitmo no matter how bad an idea it is, Colonel. This President has a lot to learn about these fucking threats facing our nation, and how to handle them properly, and get along with his people ready to help.

"From what I've seen of this guy, he's going to make a living out of attacking our Intelligence Communities, and military. I hate when we must break in a new guy. They always come with such a damn hardon for anything the prior Administration accomplished, and to destroy the bipartisan relationships the past Administration established with the offices the President must rely on and deal with if he wants to be a great leader of our country. Colonel Leadbetter Sir, I can't tell you how many Generals and Colonels warned me if this President tries to make their lives a living hell. Many of them will entertain retiring and going into private work, dammit. I can't believe what some of my Officers…"

"To be quite frank with you General White Sir, I also considered retiring." Colonel Leadbetter offered in a slightly slurred tone of voice as he went on with his worlds. "It's quite easy to see this President isn't in love with the military services, sir. I have not wanted to be driven crazy with a Commander in Chief whose only want is to drive my ass fucking nuts, sir. Our line of work is hard enough without the main man not backing our damn actions, General White." The Colonel offered while interrupting his commander.

"Allow me to inform you of something you might not be aware of, Colonel Leadbetter. You might as well place any thoughts of your retiring out of your fucking mind once and for all, mister. You might request to retire, but certainly, I'll not entertain any such request from you. The only way you'll get out of the service Colonel, is when I'm no longer in command of you." General White warned his lesser military officer.

"General White, the day you leave command, is the day I'll be walking out right behind you sir. There could never be another Chairman I'd ever want to work under, sir."

"Colonel Leadbetter, you don't have to blow any god damn smoke up my ass, mister. You'll do what is good for our country, and the first time I see you slipping from that order. Is the day I'll drum your sagging ass right the hell out of the service faster than a keg of beer disappears at a fucking college party, sir." General White retorted as he allowed a smile for the first time since the start of this conversation.

"You got it, General." He replied, reinforcing his wish to leave if the general left.

The Chairman's chest swelled with pride over the fact he commanded such loyalty from his lesser officers as he replied. "Colonel Leadbetter, be that as it may, right now we're not considering either of us leaving the services. Getting back to the reason for this call Colonel, once you send your troops home on leave, I'm ordering you to take a hundred and eighty-days leave yourself, sir. It's time you go home and let your wife know you're still alive and kicking. I'm planning to take thirty days myself and contemplate my future with the service. Colonel, if this President's planning to attack people under my command, he's in for one helluva fight. I have no intentions of sitting on my tongue while anyone, especially a President tells the world any servicemen or women, are not living up to the oath they took when they entered the services.

"Colonel, I went through working with a President who didn't like the personnel charged with keeping the United States a free country, when I was in the service for five years. I was forced to eat a lot of crows and sit on my damn tongue and watch the fool make a first-class ass of himself, Colonel. I have no intention of biting my tongue while someone takes jabs at my personnel. It's an entirely different world now, and we have all sorts of fucking nuts coming out of the damn woodwork looking to kill American civilians. Since I'm the Chairman, that makes me the most powerful military officer in the country, and as such, it falls on my fucking shoulders to protect those who serve under me, and that's what I intend to do, sir.

"Arrr…I bored your ass long enough already I guess Colonel Leadbetter, as I said when I receive the order from the President, I'll execute that order then get your troops home on leave. Well, Colonel, that's all I have for you currently, sir. I wanted you to be informed your troops will be heading home for leave by Wednesday. Errr…good luck with that damn hangover I'm certain you'll be entertaining tomorrow morning, Colonel Leadbetter." The General laughed as he broke off the communication. He enjoyed his smile as he raised his feet and plopped them down on his desk and locked his fingers together behind his head, seeing the thought of sending his troops home for an extended leave.

Colonel Leadbetter hung up and looked at Sergeant Kirkpatrick hovering over his shoulder, listening in on the conversation while trying to see if he was getting any leave. The Colonel maintained an ice-cold stare, causing the young Sergeant to think he was unable to get the requested leave for the troops. Letting his breath out in a rush, he snapped at the worried Sergeant. "Well mister, it looks like you're going to be working your fingers to the bone writing many leave orders in the next few days, Mister."

"Outstanding Colonel Leadbetter, I can't believe General White was able to get leave from the new President so quickly, sir." He replied while fishing for any information.

"I got a news flash for your ass mister. General White didn't get leave from the new President. He was able to get it from the outgoing President."

"Shit, the General must have some pull with the outgoing President, to get the man to sign a leave order so close to the end of his Administration, Colonel. I hope General White's going to work with the new President as he did with the outgoing one." Kirkpatrick offered.

"You can forget that wish Sergeant. The General and I discussed we'd go in retirement if the new President goes after our people. He told me he thinks this new guy's going to be on a witch hunt against the Intelligence Communities and Military Commanders. So, you can forget about the General working with this new guy. Crap, you better get what you have to prepare to send our troops home on leave, Sergeant." Leadbetter ordered then waited for him to leave.

TUESDAY, JANUARY 6th, 2009, ZERO FOUR HUNDRED HOURS CAMP LEJEUNE, JACKSONVILLE, NORTH CAROLINA

Colonel Bruce Leadbetter found himself doing what General White warned him about over the phone the night before, nursing a pounding hangover. He was not very pleasant to be anywhere near throughout the entire day, and everyone in command gave the suffering military officer a wide berth. All the hubbub of yesterday settled down, and Washington was slowly getting back to near normal, with a new President standing at the helm of the country.

GENERAL WHITE'S PRIVATE OFFICE AT THE PENTAGON, 11:30 A.M, JANUARY 6th, 2009

True to his word, the outgoing President sent a special currier out to deliver the leave order for his troops currently stationed at Camp Lejeune. The currier handed the envelope to Mary and when he left, she rushed the large envelope to her boss, knowing what it was. The secretary handed the General the envelope and he tore it apart and read the order. Then he handed the stack of papers back to Mary and ordered her to get the document out to his Marine Colonel. All the while, he was smiling from ear to ear over his respect and admiration for the well-respected outgoing Republican President.

Colonel Leadbetter was resting in his office with his head in his arms as he tried to still the pounding ripping the top of his head off. Sergeant Kirkpatrick entered the office like he was walking his last mile with the order locked in his hand. He tipped toed into the office and snuck up to the suffering colonel and whispered. "Colonel Leadbetter, please sir, I have an important dispatch from General White's office addressed to you, sir. Please, you must see what it's about, sir." He could not remove the grin from his lips, for he knew it was the leave order.

"Huh, what, what the hell do you want and why the hell are you talking to my damn ass for, mister? Didn't I threaten you with a fucking firing squad if you bothered me today, Sergeant?" The suffering Colonel moaned as he lifted his head and blinked his eyes and that effort drove the pounding headache wild inside his skull.

Sergeant Kirkpatrick smiled at his commander as he added. "Gees sir, are you able to see out of those eyes, sir? I've never seen eyes so bloodshot, Colonel."

"Sergeant my whole fucking body's bloodshot, buster. What the hell do you want from my ass anyhow, mister?" The officer grumbled at his Sergeant.

"Colonel Leadbetter Sir, I just received a dispatch from General White, sir. I believe it's the leave papers, sir." He replied with excitement in his tone to his commanding officer.

"You know it is, so give me the damn things will ya, mister." Leadbetter took the envelope and opened it. Then he looked at his Sergeant and growled at him. "Here's the damn paperwork, get on writing up the fucking orders for the troop's leave. You're instructed to start with the soldiers living the furthest from the base, and it'll take them the longest to get home. Once you have the distant soldiers on their fucking way, start on the next furthest living troops. Then so on and so forth until you have the whole pack of lunatics on their fucking way off my base, and things can get back to normal around here."

Sergeant Kirkpatrick straightened his stance and then asked his commanding officer. "Colonel Leadbetter Sir, will you be heading off base for leave along with our other soldiers, sir? It's about time you took some time off, sir."

"Yes Sergeant, I'll be heading home for a thirty-dayer myself, mister. Then I'm going to report back to base and start work on several new training scenarios for this pack of screaming eagles to work through, and trip them up on their training if possible. So, they're better prepared to protect their country from attacks by any flaming assholes constantly circling our country and looking for ways to hurt our civilians. Yeah, Sergeant, and before you ask my ass, you'll be heading home for a thirty-day leave yourself, and then your ass will report back to base on the same day I return to base, mister. I see by the shitty look planted on the damn puss that you wanted more time off than I'm offering you, Sergeant.

"But they are the fucking breaks when you work for my ass around here, mister. If I must find my damn ass stuck back on base then so will you, Sergeant. Get on with your damn orders and get these sick twists the fuck off my damn base before I order every one of them shot on general purposes. Sergeant, even though you'll report back to base on the same day I do. I'll set it up that you pull every weekend off duty. That way you can spend a little extra time with your wife and kids. Better yet, why don't you have the family move on base, that way you can spend every night and weekend with them? I'll set it up and clear the way so your family can join us on base, Sergeant. That's the least I can do for you and the loyalty you offer to my ass, Sergeant." He stared his Sergeant in the eyes while waiting for his reply.

"Colonel Leadbetter Sir, it's funny you bring this subject up to my attention sir, because for the past few months I was considering the same thought but didn't know how to breach the subject with you, sir. Lately, my wife's been giving me all sorts of problems being away from her and the kids so much. I was even considering leaving the service and getting a job near home, so I could spend some more time with her and the kids, sir. Lately, Colonel, my wife's been straddled rearing the children, and she wasn't enjoying it. The boy's getting to be quite the handful, and the wife demanding my help getting the kid under control. It's been tough trying to calm down the boy and threatening him over the damn phone, sir. I hang up and the kid's right back at it with my lady and I…"

"Sergeant, I didn't ask about your damn home life, mister. All I did was suggest you move your family on base so you can spend a little more time with them, son. Huh, if you need any help with your boy, I'd be glad to lend you a hand with his little ass." Leadbetter offered with a sort of sarcastic smirk.

Sergeant Kirkpatrick knew what the Colonel meant, although he would normally ask help with the boy. He would never allow his commanding officer to work with his son for one day. All he needed was the Colonel to treat his son like he did the troops, and the kid would run away from home and never be seen again.

The Colonel read the look on his Sergeant's face and grumbled at the man. "You're damn right Sergeant, its better you raise your damn kid, mister. Get on with your orders and get the damn troops heading home for leave. You better remind every swinging dick and bouncing tits out there that they're subject to call back on a moment's notice if the shit goes down while the soldiers are on leave, Sergeant. I also want a weekly call-in by every soldier on leave, so they know if we need them. Warn them even though they're on fucking leave, I'll call them in once in a while, to go over some new tactics I devised for their ongoing education with defeating terrorism in the States, or aboard. Carry on with your orders and get out of my office, I have my fucking work to do Sergeant." He stared at his Sergeant.

WEDNESDAY, JANUARY 7th, 2009.
THE AL-MASADA (THE LION'S DEN) MOSQUE,
NEW YORK CITY, 7:30 A.M. EST

The ex-Iraqi General Abdulaziz al-Wahhad spent three days working with and trying to separate the Muslim men and women he felt were the more radical ones of the Mosque membership. He was pleased to find Mohsen al-Gasim, a man of twenty-three years who made no qualms about his hatred for the Western world. Twice since joining the Mosque did, he listen to the man as he went off on all the non-believers of the world to the sacred words written in the Holy Qur'an and of his religious beliefs. Listening to the young Arab warrior's complaints made the future leader of a terrorist cell believe he found his second in command. Even though he was working without backing, or the blessings of his leader, Usama bin Laden. Al-Wahhad's every thought was in correlation with bin Laden's wants to destroy the Western civilization, especially America and her interests throughout the world.

After al-Gasim's latest cursing fit against the United States, caused other members of the Mosque to complain bitterly over the threatening statements made by this young Islamic radical. It caused al-Wahhad to approach the man, to see if he truly believed what he was complaining about in the United States to the others.

Before he approached al-Gasim, he looked around the rest of the gathering of the Mosque. He was surprised and a little disappointed over how many older members of the Mosque were condemning al-Gasim's angry words aimed at the United States and her people. The gathering was largely against the radical's heated words, and some members were even cursing the anger locked in the young Arab man's heart. But al-Wahhad noticed a certain another group of men and women separated from the others condemning al-Gasim's words of hatred.

When al-Gasim calmed down and the other members of the Mosque left to examine their minds and pray for the young man's misguided ways of hatred. The soon-to-be the leader of the terrorist cell he was planning to develop, decided to throw caution to the wind and approach the angry young man. Resting his hand lightly on al-Gasim's shoulder and he led the man away from the center of the room, so he could speak to al-Gasim in private. When he led him to a corner of the large room, al-Wahhad offered calmly to the young man. "Allahu Akhbar al-Gasim, Salaam Alaikum, (peace be upon you) please allow me to introduce myself to you, son. I am Abdulaziz al-Wahhad, and I come to this Mosque to…"

"Allahu Akhbar Abdulaziz al-Wahhad. Yes, I noticed you when you first joined the Mosque, stranger to my world. I see in your eyes the hatred I harbor for these cursed infidels who pollute the air Allah has allowed his faithful to enjoy, which is the same as I feel. What is it you want of me? Why do you approach me with your hand resting on my shoulder like you are my father? Do I know you? Are you somehow related to me and I'm unaware of that fact? I don't know you, so I don't owe you anything but my hand in friendship, and an ear to listen to your words if they speak the truth to me. Speak, what is troubling your mind, and get it done so I can get on with the rest of my day. I have much I have to look after today." Al-Gasim allowed his eyes to narrow and turn harsh as he glared at the stranger speaking to him.

Al-Wahhad did not pick up the others who separated themselves from the older ones of the Mosque who were cursing al-Gasim moment before. Had worked their way nearer to them, and they circled the two and took a protective stance of their fellow young Arab brother.

"I see the impatience of youth was not wasted upon your soul, my young friend from the land of our great ancestors. I have dared to approach you in the name of peace and understanding, and that is why I have rested my hand upon your shoulder in friendship. I studied you and your actions and words since I joined the Lion's Den Mosque. I have also listened to what you had to say about the god-cursed lowly infidels of the land of Satan they dwell within. I happen to agree with everything you said against the non-believers and lowly jackals of this cursed land. But I have intentions to do a lot more than just talking out against these filthy people who have no right to continue to live in Allah's good graces…"

"Exactly what is it you intend to do against the foul ones who live in the land of Satan, al-Wahhad?" Reemabdel Aziz al-Rowaili, al-Gasim's pretty girlfriend snapped in a heated tone.

It was at this point al-Wahhad realized he was suddenly cut off from fleeing by a few young Arab men and women, as they cautiously circled and were glaring at him. He swallowed as he studied the concerned young faces staring at him as they waited for his reply to Reemabdel's question. His mind raced because he wanted to speak privately with al-Gasim before he dared speak to anyone else from the gathering of the Mosque. He wanted to make certain of al-Gasim's true feelings, along with his hatreds and want to attack the United States as he growled moments ago before he tried to enlist him in his future.

His eyes wandered from face to young face as he searched the small crowd for the one who just asked him the question. He did not see the woman walk over to al-Gasim's side, and she took his hand in hers. She waited for al-Wahhad to say why he approached her lover, and what he wanted from al-Gasim and the rest of his following.

"Al-Wahhad, it was I who asked what you want from al-Gasim, and I repeat that question to you a second time. What is it you want from him, al-Wahhad?" The beautiful woman stared into the eyes of al-Wahhad. She was making no hidden feelings of how she loved the man she held the hand of, and she displayed no fear of al-Wahhad and what he had on his mind.

Shaking his head slightly he gave into his concerns, because he realized he had to speak to the group now if he wanted to enlist their aide to destroy the United States from within her borders. He continued to stare at the young woman and then he finally responded to her question. "Young fool to the old ways of the Arab man. How dare you allow a lowly worthless woman to speak to me in this foul manner? I thought I had discovered a true Arab man in this land of sin. I see you allow a cursed woman to command your actions, al-Gasim. What has become of the manly ways of an Arab leader? How do I respond to your girlfriend's question? Do I address her, or do I address you with my response, fool of fools?"

"Al-Wahhad, how dare you to bring the old and oppressive ways of our country to this land of crime, you must understand we Arabs who live in this evil land, have become equal and as an equal, I back al-Gasim with my life. As do the rest of those who believe so as al-Gasim and me, al-Wahhad. Now you were asked a question twice. You will address your reply to me, and if you have a problem with that demand. Then you can leave me and my friends in the name of Allah and peace, al-Wahhad." Reemabdel Aziz al-Rowaili allowed her eyes to narrow and blaze with the anger she had in her heart for al-Wahhad, who wanted to treat women the way they do in their oppressive homeland. Reemabdel felt she progressed and was not going to allow herself to be dragged back to the ways of the old and suppressed.

CAMP LEJEUNE, JACKSONVILLE, NORTH CAROLINA; WEDNESDAY, JANUARY 7th, 2009. ZERO SIX-THIRTY HOURS

The activity throughout the massive Marine Base was at a fever pitch, as a horde of over-excited young soldiers from the elite Rapid Response Forces, prepared to go on leave for the first time in over seven months since the last reporting to base. The soldier's last mission was carried out in Iraq when the troops dispatched to locate an Iraqi woman in possession of a newly developed and extremely dangerous designer biological weapon. The troops were able to locate and stop the Iraqi female from releasing the weapon against the world population. Their action ended costing the Iraqi her life because she would not listen to Walker's command for her to stop opening the biological weapon to the air.

Sergeant Kirkpatrick did a masterful effort with getting the leave papers written up and prepared for the troops heading home in a short time. The Sergeant had to enlist Walker's assistance to control the charged up elite soldiers under his command.

Colonel Leadbetter stood on the side with Captain Walker as they both watched the amped-up troops head for the paymaster, so they could leave the base with a fistful of cash. It was mayhem at best, with the excited specialized soldiers shoving each other out of the way, as they jockeyed for position before the Paymaster Sergeant. The troops paid off mounted the buses to be transported to the civilian airport for transportation home. Not only did Sergeant Kirkpatrick work on writing up the papers, but he also set up air flights for each soldier not driving home.

The troops scheduled to leave the base the next day dropped their draws and started to moon the soldiers on the buses. Some female soldiers flashed the soldiers mooning them from the buses, and this caused all sorts of hoots and hollers from the troops hanging around the platform, along with the soldiers stacked up on the buses. The mayhem and merriment continued as a few female soldiers stuck on the base, responded by flashing the soldiers trapped on the buses.

A horde of MPs started to work into the group of excited soldiers. The MPs were looking for some women and males flashing and mooning the other soldiers on the buses. Two MPs tried to push onto a bus to get one woman soldiers they locked eyes on, that had her breasts pressed against the window, and a few male soldiers were trying to cop a feel from her.

The MPs way was blocked from getting on the bus by the male troops who knew what they wanted, and there was no way the troops were going to get out of the military police's way, so they could arrest one of their own. The MPs working the platform were fairing no better because they were being shoved and harassed by the flood of soldiers still stuck on base. Colonel Leadbetter noticed things were starting to get out of hand with his troops getting heavier handed with the MPs, and he growled at his young Marine Captain.

"Walker, you better get some kind of fucking control of your pack of flaming assholes before some Colonel or General takes an interest in their childish actions, and orders all troops held in the fucking Brig for who knows how long, mister. Walker, I could see it now if that shit happened. This base would be torn a fucking apart by your pack of screaming squirrels because they couldn't take off on leave. You get after the males, and Ramirez, you get control over the damn females before they find their asses caught in a sling."

Both Walker and Ramirez responded quickly by jumping into the maddening crowd of overly excited soldiers. The two started to shove the certain soldiers creating all the problems out of the group, and ordering them back to their barracks before the MPs caught them, and they had the troublemakers arrested and moved to the base Brig. The first soldier Walker went after was Lieutenant Frank Hall. Catching up to him, Walker dragged the Mutt by the collar until he found, No Neck and Buckethead. Controlling these three wild soldiers brought most of the mayhem and craziness taking place on the platform to a quick end, because these few soldiers were trying to get the female soldiers to flash or otherwise create mayhem on the platform, or the troops on the buses.

Finally, the buses containing fifty-three of the one hundred and ninety-seven elite troops pulled away from the curb. The second the buses moved; the mayhem returned in all its passion. The troops waiting on the platform started to give the soldiers on the buses the finger, and several other crude motions. That caused another wave of flashing by the female soldiers, and that started another wave of hoots and hollers from the soldiers still on base.

This time it got so wild that Colonel Leadbetter had to get involved in the mess. He grabbed soldiers by their collars and warned them if they did not get off the platform and head back for the barracks, they were going to be placed on report. Slowly, the soldiers started to head for the barracks. When it was only Colonel Leadbetter, Walker and Ramirez, and Kirkpatrick with twelve angry MPs standing on the platform, the Colonel grumbled at his Captain and Sergeants.

"Well, that was fucking exciting I say in a way I don't mean. You better get a fucking handle on the rest of the god damn troops, Walker. Or I'm going to have the lot of them neutered and spayed, to protect the population of our country from their misgivings and troublemaking, mister. I have to admit I never saw so many tits except for when I went to the local titty bar. Some of your women soldiers are hotter than the damn strippers, mister. Well, we have over a hundred and forty Tear One soldiers we still have to get off the damn base and hope things go a helluva lot smoother than this latest fiasco went down, Captain. Sergeant Kirkpatrick!" Colonel Leadbetter turned and growled at his NCO.

"Yes, Sir Colonel Leadbetter Sir, I'm standing behind you, sir. What do you need, Colonel?" The Sergeant replied as he snapped to attention and saluted his commander briskly and then waited for the Colonel's next orders.

"Ahhh...as I live and breathe, it's good to see a real soldier every once and a while on this base who knows how to properly salute his Commanding Officer. You see Walker, that's the right way soldiers are supposed to show proper respect for their Commander. It's not the way you and the rest of your damn misfits respect my ass around here for Christ's sake. The only salute I get from your pack of dumb shits is the one-finger salute. One of these days I'm going to get the respect I worked for and deserve from you and your pack of damn Squids, Captain." Leadbetter griped in a heated tone as he held Walker in his angry gaze and then waited for his reply.

"Yeah, sure Colonel anything you say, sir, if my fricking people saluted you as this fucking guy does, you won't recognize us any longer, sir. Colonel Leadbetter, what the hell do you want from life, sir? My troops saluting your ass like a pack of stinking mindless robots. Or do you want the best fighting fucking troop in the damn world under your command, sir? You can't have both you know Colonel it's one or the uther sir. You can't have us elite troops wasting their time saluting you while knocking out any fucking terrorists attacking our country or allies anywhere in the world, sir." Walker replied with a snap in his voice.

"Yeah, right, okay Captain fucking Wiseass. I guess I'll have to take things the way they are for the time being, but I won't like it buster. Until you, damn Squids get under my skin, and I have to take to shooting a whole lot of your damn shit sacks on general principles, Walker. Sergeant Kirkpatrick, I'm changing the way we'll be releasing the next batch of fucking troops from the base. Judging by all the fucking mayhem created by the damn troops here today, Sergeant. We'll not and I repeat, we will not be releasing another god damn batch of fools on leave the same way, Sergeant.

"The next time we go through this kind of God damn nightmare on this base will be the last time I assure you because we'll release a whole lot of the assholes at the same damn time. Sergeant, you get the damn Paymaster to pay the soldiers off for the rest of the day, and then get transportation set up for the troops we're still holding back on base. When everything's set for a go with the remaining troops, get this crap the fuck off my beloved base. If I have any further trouble from this pack of fucking lunatics, it's going to be your ass I'll be chewing on, fella. Walker, you'll have your damn troops available for the Paymaster if they want any fucking leave. No pay, no leaving the damn base, period Captain." The angry acting Colonel turned and snapped at his young Captain.

"You got it Colonel Leadbetter, and I'll start my troops drifting over to the Paymaster's office in alphabetical order throughout the rest of the stinking day until the troops are paid off and then they can prepare to leave the base on their off time, sir. And yes, I'll stay on top of them to make certain there's no further trouble from any of them, sir." Walker replied to his commanding officer as he shot him a smile.

"Stick your damn smile up your stinking ass, Captain. You and your pack of shit sacks shorten my damn life span by years, with this constant shit you guys keep pulling off against my damn command, mister. I'm done with the likes of your troops, Captain. If any troops were arrested in this mess that went down today, I'll cut orders and have the asses released when they cool off a bit from their crap. Sergeant Kirkpatrick, you have the rest of this cream of the crap to take control of. It's your job to get the flaming assholes the hell off my base ten minutes ago if you catch my drift, mister. I wash my damn hands off a lot of the damn shit sacks, Sergeant." The Colonel headed for his office.

Walker and Kirkpatrick watched the angry Colonel stomp away with smirks on their lips. They knew he would go against the wall for the troops under his command.

Walker stayed away from the barracks because he knew he was going to be flooded with a ton of questions and complaints from the other troopers wanting off base. Ramirez, along with Lieutenant Hall was as always, standing by their Captain's side. Walker assigned the two large soldiers, Neck and Buckethead, to make certain the other soldiers made their way over to the Paymaster to pick up their back pay. Walker and Ramirez were concerned about getting home, while they were on the mission. The Island of Marathon in the Florida Keys was hit by a powerful force three hurricanes, and they were worried about what they might be heading home to find left of their place, boats, and property.

Lieutenant Frank Hall also owned a home on the tiny Island, and he was sharing it with the French soldier Sergeant Regina Raphael, who was on loan from France to their elite group of soldiers. He was likewise aware of the hurricane, but he was not so concerned about his home. This was because he was getting a little bored with living on the Island of late. It was too small a patch of land in the over one hundred miles of Islands making up the Florida Key Chain, and if you were not hitting the bars or fishing.

There was not very much left to do on the Island that interested him. The Mutt was planning to speak to Walker about his concerns and see if he might be interested in heading for a more populated area of Florida.

The Lieutenant was interested in looking at Clearwater, or the Safety Harbor area in Pinellas County, about midway of Florida. He read many interesting things about the area and found out it had a helluva lot more to offer and had three seasons, and the area could be hit by a hard freeze, and he liked the cold weather now and then.

The Mutt heard the people living in this area of Florida were not nearly as transient as the ones living or visiting Marathon for the few good months of the year. He began to feel he and Regina, Walker, and Ramirez would be able to make long-lasting and better friends who would be around them all year long. Instead of having friends for what was called the busy or season of the year to visit or play in the Keys. Lieutenant Hall breached this subject with Regina about his plans, and she was for anything he was going to do if it also included her in his plans.

Regina was eyeing the thought of getting married to the good-looking young soldier. She was so proud to be part of such an elite group of specialized troops who respected her as much as she respected them.

CHAPTER THREE

WEDNESDAY JANUARY 7th, 2009. THE Al-MASADA (THE LION'S DEN) MOSQUE, NEW YORK CITY, 8:25 A.M. EST

Abdulaziz al-Wahhad did not respond to Reemabdel's so angry words, he only continued to stare at the young Mohsen al-Gasim. With his eyes displaying the anger buried in his heart, as if his eyes demanded from the young man the reason why he was allowing a woman to dare speak to him in such a disrespectful manner. Reemabdel Aziz al-Rowaili picked up the look al-Wahhad aimed at her lover, and she added angrily to her words.

"Don't dare to look at al-Gasim in such a cursed fashion, al-Wahhad! It's me who challenged you to speak with him, not him. You didn't answer me so I repeat, if you cannot act civil and respect, we women the same as you do any males of this Mosque. Bow your foul head politely, and then make your excuses to Allah and Muhammad, and leave our sight at once, al-Wahhad. Fool of fools you are you must remember we're living in the United States now. We, women, had our eyes opened by the customs of this lowly land of sin, and we have discovered it's wise and correct for the males to respect women and give them equality in dealing with you filthy males when you want and need our help, al-Wahhad."

Al-Wahhad was forced to turn to place Reemabdel in his glare, and then he allowed a slight but ugly sneer to slowly cross his lips as he bowed slightly to the woman. He wanted nothing more in life than to be allowed to open the nasty woman's back with the sting of the lash and ignore her and her words aimed at him. He was trapped because he knew he needed al-Gasim and his young friends if he intended to attack the civilians of the United States. Softening his stare, a bit, he straightened and sought forgiveness from the Arab female by offering in a contrite tone of voice to her. "Woman, you must forgive my rudeness, because it seems I must have forgotten time is marching on, and the old customs of our past are rapidly fading from our minds. I stand before you and beg absolution for the insults I have leveled at your person, a woman who I don't know your name. Ahhh…you see it's not only I who suffers rudeness."

"Yes, al-Wahhad, you're correct and most wise at that. I beg forgiveness for the rudeness I have allowed to insult you with. Allahu Akhbar al-Wahhad, allow me to introduce myself to you. My name is Reemabdel Aziz al-Rowaili, and I like my lover, come from the lands of Iraq. We left our country when it came under attack a second time by the invading Crusaders mostly from this god-cursed country. We joined this Mosque in hopes of finding other men and women, who want to seek vengeance on the country that has destroyed so many Arab countries of the Middle East. We have successfully amassed several other followers who more…"

Burning with sudden anger, al-Gasim steamed at the pretty and young Arab woman in a controlled rage. "Reemabdel, you have allowed your god-cursed tongue to wag without control. Your wandering tongue has placed us and our friends in danger in this country of Satan. When will you ever learn to hold your foul tongue in check, and speak only when it's the proper time to do so, woman? If I was angry enough and believed in what our fathers felt was a woman's lot in life. I'd resort to the old ways and whip your back for what you have just exposed to this stranger to our Mosque." Turning his attention back to the stranger, al-Gasim offered.

"Al-Wahhad, please forgive me for allowing this worthless woman to address you in such a foul manner she chose to speak before you. Al-Wahhad I'll straighten her out once I have a chance to speak with her in private. But I must agree with her question of you, and I wonder why it was you have approached to speak with me privately. What do you have in your mind, and how can I help you, Abdulaziz al-Wahhad?"

Al-Wahhad nodded ever so slightly for the first time since starting a conversation with him. He felt he now held the upper hand in his request to speak with this man and those who follow him. He was no fool and he instantly seized on the anger taking place between the two young lovers, as he offered in a calm voice. "Al-Gasim, I forgive the way your woman spoke to me, and all she allowed to cross her foul lips about your young Arab friends. Al-Gasim; I am no threat to you or your friends. My friend, it seems we both are in search of the same reasons for joining this Mosque. You see I seek ways to repay the horror and evil this foul nation has released against our country, and I need help..."

"Al-Wahhad, what makes you believe for one moment on Allah's earth, either I or any of my friends harbor ill will against this country of sinners we share life with? I don't remember anyone saying anything like we're looking to seek any kind of revenge against the United States or her worthless civilians. If you're banking on the foolish words that came forth from a lowly woman's mouth to hang your wants and desires upon. Then I suggest you go to another Mosque in your search for allies to help with you harm the United States." He ended up staring into the eyes of al-Wahhad.

They want to be the leader of a terrorist cell understood why al-Gasim offered no one from his group of future terrorists, was interested in harming anyone from the United States as he cast a quick look at the woman who started this conversation. He agreed with the way al-Gasim reacted to his words, because who knew how many ears might be listening to their conversation, and ears and wagging tongues could spell disaster to his plans he was going to aim at the United States. Drawing in a deep breath, he finally replied.

"Yes, al-Gasim your wisdom and caution are much needed in all conversations we engage in. I have no desire to harm anyone living in the world. I'm so weary of all the death and destruction that has been visited upon the Arab world in the last fifteen years of my unworthy and foul life. But alas I desire to speak further with you and your group of young friends. To see if I could be of some assistance to you and your future living in this foreign country of sin. But on the other hand, I wanted to see if you might also be of any assistance to my future of living in the United States.

"I feel it's a shame we were forced to leave the country of our ancestors we love and hold dear to our hearts, because of the constant invaders to our lands, and the cursed looting of our sacred history of thousands of years. Since we were forced to leave our country, we did, and we have gathered in the very heart of the invader's land. We Arabs must stick together and assist each other to survive until all foreigners and Crusaders against our country leave our lands. Then we can return home in peace in hopes of rebuilding our lives and homes, al-Gasim. It'll be a task to remember the old ways and bring them back to our country and beliefs. That is why I believe Allah has demands we remain in constant contact until we can return to our homeland to rebuild the sacred land of Allah." The wise al-Wahhad stopped speaking and waited to see how al-Gasim was going to react to his words and want to continue speaking.

"Yes al-Wahhad and that's why we have joined this Mosque. So, we could remain in constant contact and hold dear the ancient customs and beliefs of our country. While we can't live within our homeland and bless the sacred sands of the vast desert Allah has given us to dwell upon. Al-Wahhad, allow me to welcome another lost Arab into the fold of us lost brothers and sisters, who have fled to this land of non-believers to the written words of Muhammad. It's important we as you offered, stick together until we can return to our homeland free of all lowly infidels and invaders for all times to come." Now it was al-Gasim's turn to stop speaking.

Al-Wahhad shook hands with al-Gasim, and that seemed to relieve the tension between them. Al-Gasim leaned his head close to al-Wahhad and whispered. "I fear this is not the proper place or time to carry out the conversation that needs to cross our lips. So, we know the true reason for you being in this evil land of sin. I have a safe place where I live free of unwanted ears and lips, where we may speak our minds and have no fear of betrayal. Please, allow me to guide you to my home, where we'll be free to speak in peace without interruptions."

He turned to the others of his group and offered. "My invite to our new brother includes the rest of my followers. I want everyone to hear the words al-Wahhad must share with us. If we all attend his words, then it'll not be necessary for me to repeat his words to you fools. I believe he'll speak the words we only dared to believe and want to be held deep within our hearts. Shall we leave this Mosque so we may speak in private and secure in a safer place?"

Mohsen sidestepped and one by one, the rest of his group passed and headed out the Mosque. Al-Gasim smiled because he noticed the smirk on the lips of many of his friends as they walked by him, and he realized they held no animosity towards him for calling them fools. Al-Gasim was pleased to see his friends gathered outside the Mosque and once together. Mohsen led the way speaking with al-Wahhad as they headed for his place a mile from the place of worship.

All the while al-Wahhad walked and spoke with al-Gasim. His eyes scanned the way and committed it to memory, in case he was walking into a trap and al-Gasim and his young friends wanted to harm him. He had to know the way out safely because he trusted no one in the world but himself. It took the group nearly fifteen minutes to walk over to al-Gasim's apartment in a rundown hotel that looked like it was on the verge of collapsing in on itself. Al-Wahhad was surprised to see a building in such a terrible state of disrepair. He had no way of knowing the building was damaged in the Nine, One, One terrorist attack, and the city put off repairing the building. The city decided to condemn the structure and tear it down in the future and replace the building with a thirty-five-story office building in hopes of rejuvenating the area.

When the small group of future terrorists reached the apartment, they waited for al-Gasim to open the door, and then they quickly filed into the small two-bedroom apartment. Bandur Ibn Saud, a Saudi who had training in constructing explosive devices, and was accepted by the group as the second in command under al-Gasim. Walked to the fridge as if he owned the apartment and removed a beer for each of the males, the women were not allowed any alcohol. This much of the old ways were accepted and still practiced by them. The group included twenty-seven members, nineteen males, and eight females.

Awadh al-Awajy was an Iraqi national and the third member of the group, and he was followed by Abdullah al-Mutairi, another Iraqi. He stood by another Iraqi, Adelah al-Faiz. Seated was Adelah al-Faiz an Iranian. He was seated with Talal bin al-Ahmady, a mix of Iraqi by his mother's side and a Saudi by his father. Seated with these men was the only Afghanistan member of the group, Mustafa Saleh. Standing behind this group was a second Iranian male, Esmatullah Basir. He was with Ali Abdullah Tlas, an Iraqi, and they were standing with Mohammed al-Maluk, an Iraqi, and Abdel al-Ahmar a Saudi. Also in the room was Nizar Hamdoon, Bashia al-Beidh, Morteza Dastjerdi, Bassam Abu Fallahi, Hussein Ali Soruch, Mohammed Taborzadi, Morteza Mohammedi and the last man was Farideh Karbaschi. These men were Iraqi and moved to the United States during the first Gulf War.

The eight women of the group were gathered because they did not trust any Arab men. They were concerned over the presence of the stranger to their group, al-Wahhad who joined the males. The women were surrounding their leader and settled in and waited for al-Wahhad to explain further why he chose this Mosque to display his respect to Muhammad and Allah. And, what he had on his mind, and what he wanted to commit against the United States as revenge for what their hated soldiers were doing to their country.

Standing by Reemabdel Aziz al-Rowaili's side was her closest friend, a young Saudi female, Sultana Abunaja, and she was with a second Saudi, Maha Ajwad al-Fassi and she was with another Saudi, Hatoon Al-Muneef. Farima Ebadi an Iraqi-born American was standing with two other Iraqi-born legal Americans, Leila Alibabic and Shirin Zarabi, and they were with the only Jordanian member of the group, Nazira Zayn Abbus.

All of them except for al-Wahhad were naturalized American citizens, and they are living in the United States legally with papers, or they were waiting for papers to go through to become legal American citizens holding green cards, and legal licenses, and Social Security cards. Al-Wahhad was aware of this, and it was a major reason why he searched out this gathering of young Arabs he hoped to radicalize. From the looks of the situation, that feat was not going to be hard to accomplish. He knew most of this group of Arabs were classified as citizens of the United States. This fact was going to keep them off the radar from the FBI, and other investigating arms of the Homeland Defense Systems of this country, making them much harder to track, and get legal wiretaps on, or order them to be followed.

As far as al-Wahhad was concerned, his plans to attack targets of high value and cause uncountable deaths and destruction in New York City and Washington were shaping up well for him. Under his breath, he was thanking Allah for placing al-Gasim and the rest of his young friends in his path. With this group of Arabs under his command, his attacks were certainly to draw al-Qaeda and their leadership's eyes to his efforts. In his mind's eye, he saw himself being elevated to a high standing with the terrorist group and sharing a Haqqah, the water pipe with the leader, Usama bin Laden. As he phases his attacks against the sworn enemy of Arab lands, the United States, and he handed him the ancient Kashmir rifle as his reward for the attacks.

Al-Wahhad's thoughts were interrupted by al-Gasim when the man loudly cleared his throat. This action forced his mind back to the problems at hand. Al-Gasim was interested in what he had to offer him and his future radical terrorists, as the younger man asked al-Wahhad with concern lacing his voice. "Al-Wahhad, I'm certain you didn't request to speak privately with me and the rest of my friends, just so we could watch you standing in the center of my room thinking and daydreaming. What was the true reason you wanted to speak with me and my friends? My time and patience are hard-pressed for time, and I have little of both to waste on things that don't concern us."

THE ISLAND OF MARATHON IN THE FLORIDA KEYS

It did not take Sergeant Kirkpatrick long to set up leave for the Tier One troops remaining on base at Camp Lejeune. Captain Robert Walker, along with Sergeant Dorothy Ramirez, Lieutenant Frank Hall, and Sergeant Regina Raphael, piled into Walker's car, and they drove for the Island and homes, the moment they were handed their leave papers. When his car crossed the Vaca Cut Bridge to Marathon, Walker was able to see the storm damage still marring the small Island. His mind went wandering, wondering what kind of damage he was going to discover at his and Ramirez's home.

Pulling his car on the road to his home, Walker noticed several tree stumps. The trees cut down, obvious damage from the hurricane that attacked the Island while he was stationed in Iraq. He stopped his car in front of the Mutt's home and dropped him and Regina off. He scanned the property and noticed some more damage to the side of his home, and now he was in a rush to get home to check his place out. He backed his car onto the narrow road, dropped it in gear, and took off for his place. His home was closer to the ocean, and he expected to see more damage to his place than what was obvious at the Mutt's place.

Turning in his driveway, he cursed when he noticed the blue tarp draped over his roof. Ramirez was out of the car before the vehicle came to a complete stop, tears were already building in her eyes when she noticed plywood nailed over two windows and many of her plants dead or ripped out of the ground.

Walker got out of the car and ran around the home to check his boat. The boat was dragged on the property, a large hole ripped in the side of one of the pontoons, his tuna tower was twisted, and one motor was missing from the boat's stern. He was able to tell his boat was deposited on his property from the force of the flood surge, as it ripped apart the Island. Much of his fishing gear was missing, which could have been caused by the storm. Or by thieves who picked his boat clean of anything worth taking from her.

His electronics were still in place, but they were damaged and useless and had to be replaced. The saltwater and exposure to the elements had taken their toll on the sensitive equipment. He figured in his mind how much it was going to cost to repair his boat. He knew the World Cat Company would fix the hole in the pontoon or change it. His fishing gear fried his anger though, all his hooks, lures, weights, and extra reels, and the likes were gone. Even many tackle boxes were taken, which made him believe someone stole the items from his disabled boat.

Ramirez opened the house up and she picked up water damage caused by the roof being ripped from the home during the storm. This discovery made her cry as she ran from one room to another to check on their belongings and furniture.

Walker spat and headed for the home. As he walked towards his place, his cell phone rang. It was the Mutt, and he wanted to know what kind of damage he received from the storm. Walker informed him his boat was trashed, and he would have to check with the insurance company to see if they would total the boat or repair it. He was still on the phone as he entered the home and cursed. That made the Mutt offer. "Hey, Bro, I'm on my way to your place."

He dropped his cell phone on the marble Island countertop, and then he went off looking for Ramirez. He found her in their bedroom sorting through their clothes. Many were mildew and ruined and she was crying as she went through the clothes. He moved up and grabbed her hand and grumbled. "What the fuck are you doing and what the hell are you crying about, baby? The stinking insurance company will take care of most of that crap. C'mon baby, I'm taking you out for lunch. The stinking Mutt and his lady are on their way over here and when they get here, we'll head out for Herbies to chow down some, sister. We didn't come back to the stinking Island just to get upset over what happened to our crap by the damn hurricane, let's go and enjoy ourselves a little, baby."

"What about Robert Jr., Bobby? We must pick him up from the babysitter. Damn, I hope he still recognizes us as his parents, we've been away so long on this mission…"

"Will you get hold of yourself for crap's sake baby? If I know the sitter, she and Robert were long gone off the damn Island before the fucking storm hit. She probably has him fat as a house and in school. C'mon baby, that has to be the Mutt and his lady." Walker offered when he heard someone moving around in the kitchen.

Walker and Ramirez walked into the kitchen and Ramirez bolted from her lover's side. She charged for her son with Cathy holding his hand. Cathy was the babysitter they used when the Tier One soldiers were ordered to report to base. On seeing his mother, Robert Jr. ran and slammed into her arms. She picked her son up and smothered his face and neck with a flood of sloppy kisses, which made the child laugh with glee. Walker went to Cathy and smiled.

"Mr. Walker, I took Robert from the Island, and we went and visited my mother in Clearwater before the storm hit. We were safe there Mr. Walker. When we came back to the Island so Robert could go to school, I checked your home. I started to clean up the mess, but the next-door neighbor came by and told me the insurance agency had to check the damage before I could clean up. I tried to get the Agent to come over, but they kept telling me the owner of the home had to contact them, and he or she had to be there when the Agent came to view the damage.

"I did all of what I could do for you, I contacted a builder and had the workers put the protective cover over your roof to stop any further damage to the home and your furniture. I'm sorry I couldn't do more than I did for you, Mr. Walker. I'm sorry, it must be very upsetting to see all the damage done to your beautiful home by the storm, especially after what you and your lady done for our country…"

"Look, honey, you did great with getting Robert to safety before the storm hit the damn Island. All this uther crap that's damaged can be thrown out or replaced easily enuf. How much do I owe ya for the roof cover?" Walker asked while smiling at the babysitter.

"Nothing, that much the insurance company took care of. They were protecting their interest in the home I guess, Robert." The babysitter offered as she looked over her shoulder as the Mutt and his lady entered the home and started to look around the place.

"Fuck that shit I wanna take Raz and the kid out for lunch. Are you shitbirds up for something to eat?" Walker asked as he looked at the Mutt.

"Does Hoody Doody have wooden balls? Hell, yes, I can do with some civilian food for a stinking change, instead of the damn slop we always get on base, man. Where the hell are we heading for man?"

"I was kinda figuring to take everyone to over Herbies for a chow down and after that. I'll get in touch with the insurance company and see what they're gonna do about this stinking mess."

"Sounds like a plan to my ass, Walker. I checked out the boat, tough luck on that one man." The Mutt offered as he shook his head and cursed under his breath because they were away when the storm hit the Island. The damage to both homes was amplified because they could not look after the storm damage properly.

"That crap can be replaced easy enuf man. I got Raz and the kid and you two turds in my corner, and that's all I need to survive anywhere on the face of the earth." Walker replied as he turned to the babysitter and asked her. "Hey, Cathy, what say are you up for something to eat?"

"Please Mr. Walker. I hate to admit it, I'm starving."

"Then you're with us, we're getting the hell outta here and chow down some. Then I'm gonna look for a stinking place to stay while the insurance company does their damn act with our home. I'm not gonna live under these conditions, not after spending so much stinking time on base and running around in the desert of Iraq. I need some damn pampering and so do Raz and my kid. I'm gonna rent a boat and get some fishing in…"

"Maybe we can see if Toby wants to come to the Island and do some fishing, Robert. I'd like to see him again, and maybe we can get him to sing his new songs while he's visiting us. I've been keeping an eye on his songs, and he has three new ones out since the last time we were with him, Robert." Ramirez remarked, she loved country music with a passion, and Toby Keith was one of the best singers she enjoyed because he was so patriotic and a blast to be around. Another country singer was working over the charts that drew her attention. He was Chris Young, and he had a great voice and sang fantastic songs, especially "Tomorrow".

"I got news for your purdy little ass that's gonna make you forget all about that country and western boyfriend of yours, baby. Buckethead and the Neck are coming to the stinking Island after they stop off at their parents' homes for a quick visit. They're gonna bring Baby Tee and Ice along with them." Walker smiled at his lady, but the smile left when he noticed Ramirez standing with her hands on her hips, and she was glaring at him.

Ramirez hissed, "Again with the boyfriend shit I see buster. What happened the last time you called Toby my boyfriend, mister? Let me refresh your warped memory for you buddy, you went two weeks without any good loving from me, mister. I love his singing but you're the only lover I'm interested in, stupid."

"Huh, hey what about me Raz? Don't tell me all the time I've known ya, you were leading me on and taking advantage of my body and feelings, baby sister. I thought we have something going on between us, honey." The Mutt cried as he put a terrible pout on his lips, and he stared at the female Sergeant.

Ramirez smiled as she walked over to the Mutt and cupped his face in both hands then planted a kiss that would melt the butter as she purred at the soldier. "Besides Walker, you'd be the only other man in the world I could ever be interested in, Frankie dear."

"I can take that to the bank, baby sister?" The Mutt asked as he smiled this time.

"To the bank and lock it in the vault, mister." Ramirez purred as she wiggled her hips at the Mutt, and then she went back to Walker's side and rested her hand on Jr.'s shoulder.

Robert Jr. was grinning from ear to ear as he listened to the bantering going on between the adults, even though he did not understand most of what was going on. He was hanging on to his father's leg for dear life and was not letting go for love or money.

Walker had enough of conversations and piped up. "C'mon people, I'm getting older and more hungry listening to this crap. I'll get the car, Raz you get the insurance agent's number. I'll call his ass from Herbies after I had something to eat. I got Robert Jr., and we're heading for the car. You get the number and meet us outside and leave this uther crap for the damn insurance company to deal with. We did enuf shit to last us a lifetime, baby."

She nodded at Walker as she took off for the bedroom. She had the insurance policy locked in the safe Walker stored the extra weapons and ammunition in, to protect them from their son getting in trouble with them. By the time Walker had the car turned around. She rushed out of the home after she opened the windows to get some of the mildew smell out of the home. She locked the front door and rushed for the car and friends.

When she was in the car, Walker took off for the restaurant so they could eat then get on with the rest of the things he had to look after. The meal was great as always, and after Walker set up a meeting with the agent, he stopped at three motels and one hotel on the Island. Settling on the hotel and connecting rooms to stay until their home was squared away.

When Walker spoke to the agent, he suggested he and his family take rooms until their home was repaired. The boat was going to be another story, and Walker had to go through a different agency. He knew the boat was not going to be a big problem because he carried more than enough insurance coverage on the boat and tackle.

The Mutt went down to the lobby and ordered a room right next to Walker's until his home was repaired by the insurance company. He returned to Walker's room and showed him and the others the key to the room on the other side of Walker's which opened into his room employing a side door. Walker grumbled at his friend. "Gees man, you're like a fucking spot of tar on my damn foot, my friend. I can't get rid of your stinking ass for a damn moment I see, buddy. Can't you find another place to hang your stinking hat until your place is fixed up again, man?"

"What the hell's that shit everything about man, you making an ethnic slur on my ass or sumthin? If you ain't more careful, you're gonna hurt my damn feelings you know, man." The Mutt retorted while grinning.

Walker allowed his eyes to narrow as he stared at the Mutt while trying to figure out if he was serious about his last bitch. Seeing his smile, he knew the Mutt was just busting his horns, and he grumbled at his lifelong friend. "You know mutherfucker, one of these stinking days I'm gonna take your crap serious, and then I'm gonna dump you right on your fricking ass. Besides my friend, you must have a stinking conscious to have feelings to be hurt, buster. You, buddy, haven't heard jack squat from your stinking conscious in all the years I've known your sagging ass. So don't give me any of that crap about hurting your stinking feelings with anything I say." Walker turned to Ramirez and complained at her.

"Hey baby, it looks like we're gonna be stuck with this pain in the ass as usual until our homes are fixed up. Are you gonna be able to put up with his stinking ass that long, baby? Or should we start to look for another hotel to hide in until we can go home and start living in our place again, honey?"

She turned from Walker and looked into the concerned eyes of the Mutt. Seeing he was really worried about her looking for another hotel to stay at and she knew she had to set his mind at ease. She understood what Walker was doing. He was paying the Mutt back for the slug about him making a racial slur at him. But Ramirez was not going to allow the Mutt to get off the hook that easily. She was going to make him wiggle on the line for a while longer, as she looked at Regina and noticed her smiling.

Knowing she was not fooling the Mutt's lady; Ramirez knew she had to let Mutt down and she complained at the wild soldier. "You know dog man, Robert's right about you joking all the time, mister. One of these days someone is going to take you seriously and work you can over good and proper. Oh, what the hell, I believe I can put up with your ugly puss and sexual antics for a little while. I guess if Robert can put up with you hanging around as much as it looks like we're going to be stuck together until we can finally go home and live a..."

"Cool deal sister and we can party and have a good time with each uther while we're at it, baby sister." The Mutt responded in an excited tone.

"Never mind any of that stuff, mister. If you think for one moment, I'm going to allow one of your sex parties to take place between us with Robert Jr. staying right next door to us, you're out of your mind my friend. I can't afford to have my child walk in the room and see us going at it on the floor like a dog pack in heat. I should've known that was what was in the back of your filthy and evil mind when you went downstairs and paid for the hotel room right next to ours. You'll never change your filthy ways will you dog man?" Ramirez complained as she held the Mutt in her angry gaze.

"What the hell's the diff does it make if your kid's next door or the kid's sleeping in your home, baby sister? It never stopped us from partying before you know, girl. Why the hell does it matter now, Raz? C'mon baby sister, we always have a good and crazy party whenever we get back home from a stinking mission. It's the only way for us to break up the damn stress we're always suffering from our crazy-ass missions and lifestyle. Why are you changing things around now for, sister?" The Mutt cried as he started at Ramirez, hoping she was not serious about not allowing a party to take place.

Ramirez continued to stare at the Mutt. By the way, he was almost begging her, and the sorry look he had on his face, forced her to smile though she fought desperately not to allow the smile. Then she laughed as she gave in to the Mutt's twisted mind, and then warned him in no uncertain terms. "You see mister this is exactly what Walker meant by his bitch about being you being serious occasionally, dog man. How do you like it when someone busts your horns for a change? Mutt, I'm sorry but we do have to watch how we speak and party, especially around my son. Now with Robert Jr. getting a little older and he starting to understand more than you give him credit for when we're speaking about such things before him. If we party, we're going to have to make certain Robert Jr. is well protected from seeing anything we do."

"You know sumthin Raz, you're starting to become a reality you lately, you know. Damn girl, you know what you are, baby sister. I don't like it when you go screwing around with my stinking emotions like that. You know how much I like partying with you and butthead over there, Raz. You had me going there for a little while, girl. Hey girl, I'm gonna take Regina back home so she can pack up some clothes and uther crap we're gonna need while staying at this stuffy ass stinking dump we just rented. We gotta lock up the damn place and make our calls to our stinking insurance company and get a fricking agent to come out to the house to check out our damage from the stinking storm. Though we didn't get hit half as bad as you and numbnuts behind you did and…"

Walker cut his friend off in mid-sentence as he snapped angrily at him. "Hey stupid, I allowed the first slug you shot off at my stinking ass to go by unchallenged. But you just took a second shot at my ass for no good fucking reason, buddy. This time I'm warning you if you take another fucking shot at me for the rest of the damn day. I'm gonna pick you up by the fucking ears, and then I'm gonna pitch your ass outta the frigging window and see if you can fly on your way to the ground, buddy. I bout had it with you and all your damn bitches, man."

"Gees, what the hell's going on with you two lately for fuck's sake? I've never known you slobs to be so damn thin-skinned bout anything I said to either one of you two birds. If you keep this shit up, I'm gonna be afraid to open my damn mouth for fear of making you crybabies start crying in the breast milk for crap's sake. You two guys gotta come back down to fucking earth and let things work out the way they usta do all the time and stop looking to jump on my fricking ass all of a sudden now. Hell people, we just came back from a lousy bug hunt in I am stinking Raq, and we always party when we completed a successful operation.

CHAPTER FOUR

WEDNESDAY, NOVEMBER 17th, 2010. WASHINGTON D.C.

Passing days quickly turned into weeks, and the weeks turned into months, with the new American President taking firm control of the White House and the command of the country. Appointing the key people, he believed he needed and wanted the most to help him run the country. Most people appointed to assist the new President were liberal in mind, and some were working with a hidden agenda designed to attack the previous Republican President, his past Administration, along with the loyal people the last President had working with or for him on the unending war against terrorism.

Some liberals were hell-bent on making the past Administration look bad, they even went after the Intelligence Communities, threatening to place some agents on trial for their harsh handling of the Islamic terrorists still being held as prisoners at Camp Justice, Guantanamo Bay, Cuba. The new Democratic Administration went after members of the Red Cell Unit from SEAL Team Six or NSDG, the Naval Special Development Group once known as SEAL Team Six.

The new Democratic President was sending out mixed signals to the Intelligence Communities, by remarking he would not allow his Attorney General to bring any special agents before Congress. Possibly giving up their identities to the public and terrorist world or allowing the important bastions of security to be brought up on any criminal charges. In another interview, the President stated it was up to his Attorney General on how he was going to handle the special agents controlling the terrorist interrogations.

The President kept flip-flopping on the fate of the agents, sending many of them scurrying in protect your ass mode. Members of eleven different Intelligence Communities began to lose track of several well-known and wanted terrorists, while a good number of special agents kept trying to protect their identities and any criminal charges aimed at them by the Attorney General. This made the different Intelligence Agencies stop communications together, and they started to attack each other while trying to get the angry eye of the new Administration off their shoulders and aimed at another agency of protection.

The problems the Administration caused between the Intelligence Communities and the Homeland Defense people were causing growing serious problems between Director Raincloud and the Chairman of the Joint Chiefs of Staff, General White. The two men shared a close relationship for many years, spanning over three different Administrations. This new President's beliefs were causing many concerning problems between them.

It was seven thirty-five a.m. and General John White was already at his Pentagon office, fuming when he placed a call to CIA Director John Raincloud. The General was aware Raincloud had a series of late-night meetings, and he would still be sleeping. He did not care because he wanted to speak with the man. The damage to the Pentagon from the aircraft striking it during the Nine, One, one terrorist attack was repaired. It was hard to see any original damage or memory of the sneak attack. Except for the few monuments constructed to remember the attack and the ones who lost their lives. The phone ran three times before it was finally answered by an exhausted-sounding Director.

Director Raincloud knew it was General White on the line by his caller-ID system, and he grumbled in the phone. "Yeah, John what's up sir?"

"I'll tell you what's up John, only after you get your damn backside over to my office. We have to meet, and we have to meet as soon as possible today my friend." General White was having a problem keeping his rage out of his voice as he waited for Raincloud's reply.

"Shit, I knew this damn nightmare was coming, we might as well face it head-on rather than wait until later and it becomes a stalking monster against us. General, I'll get down to your office, but first I'll have to clear my calendar of several already scheduled meetings I had set up for later today, sir. Once this is accomplished, I'll head over to your office. Do you want me to bring anything with me for the meeting, sir?"

"Bring your ass and get it down here as soon as you can get here, John."

"Whew, it's good to see you're in such a good mood today, General White. You got it John and I'll get over to your office STAT." Director Raincloud replied as he broke off the connection and looked at his wife. She was in bed and up on an elbow and looking at him as he spoke on the phone. When the Director hung up, she offered with concern lacing her voice, "I'll get breakfast going while you get dressed, dear."

"Please, I have a hell of a lot of crap I must do, and precious little time to accomplish it, honey. So, any help I can get will be appreciated."

CIA Director Raincloud rushed to his office and quickly cleared his calendar. Then he informed his secretary he was heading over to the Pentagon to have a meeting with the Chairman, and she was to hold all his calls. Anyone who wanted to schedule a meeting with him was to be put off until further notice. Then he rushed out of his office leaving his secretary staring at him.

The ride to the Pentagon was uneventful, and when he pulled into the north parking lot. He pulled his car under the protective cover, and a young Marine Sergeant quickly stepped forward and opened the door for the powerful CIA Director. The Director nodded at the soldier as he replaced him in the car. He rushed into the building and headed for the elevators for the second floor of the building. He entered the outer office and smiled at the secretary, and she informed him she would notify the General he was waiting to meet with him.

As Mary suppressed the button on the intercom, Director Raincloud crossed the room and opened the door to the General's private office. He entered with the secretary smiling at his back. Because this was not the first time the Director entered the General's office without waiting to be announced first.

The moment the Chairman noticed John he barked at him. "It's about time you got your ass over here. You better sit down because we have a shitload of crap to go over, and we have to accomplish this shit today, John. The President sent word he wants us both at his office to address the National Security Council members, tomorrow morning. The man warned my secretary he was assembling the Council, and he wants a complete briefing delivered. Covering the situation, we're facing with these damn Islamic terrorists and their threats, and the trouble they and Pakistan are causing our asses. Do you want or need something to drink or eat before we get started? Because we're going to be here until we go over everything the boss wants to be briefed on at this meeting tomorrow. I'm going to give the Man this one, but the next time he demands anything from me, he better go through the proper channels first."

"A cup of coffee would do fine, General." The Director replied. Even before the General was able to hit the intercom, Mary came strolling in the office She was carrying a tray with a coffee pot, some cakes, and cups. She entered the room and went to the side table and placed the tray down and before she turned to offer them coffee. The two men were standing behind her waiting for her to move, so they could get at the coffee and cakes.

"Gees will you two allow me to get out of your way before you fool bowl me over, and step on me to get at the coffee." Mary cried and smiled at them as they grabbed cups and filled them. She knew the General wanted her to attend the meeting with Director Raincloud and take some notes so he could review their conversation later before he reported to the White House, so he was ready for the meeting.

The meeting between the Chairman of the Joint Chiefs of Staff and the powerful CIA Director lasted the entire day, and both men headed home exhausted after eight p.m. They were scheduled to meet with the Security Council at eight-thirty at the White House in the Oval Office with the President. Both men were still thoroughly exhausted as they appeared at the White House at the ordered time and waited to be escorted to the Oval Office by the White House Chief Aide.

General White was the first one to enter the Oval Office, followed by Raincloud. Both men nodded to the seated and grinning President, and to the other members of the council. General White's warning was on spot because of the other members of the council attending the meeting. The President headed the list, followed by the Vice President, Secretary of Defense, the NSA Security Advisor, the Director of the Homeland Defense and Secretary of State if available.

The President nodded at Director Raincloud and General White as he offered to the two. "Good morning gentlemen and I thank you for attending this meeting. Who'll be first to brief us on the current situation with the terrorist, and other problems facing our country, gentlemen?"

Director Raincloud stepped up and started to address the members. "Gentlemen, ladies, please allow me to offer it's a pleasure to be addressing the esteem members gathered to attend this meeting today." Turning to face the President, Raincloud continued with his words. "Good morning, Mr. President Sir, since the last discussion we had concerning the more important threats facing us in the form of terrorism. We've concluded finding terrorists and killing them is harder to accomplish than originally figured, sir.

"The main reason for this problem Mr. President is, because we find ourselves dealing with a group of loosely knitted persons who owns no home address. They own no real estate we can sink our teeth into, and aim our people and weapons at, sir." The Director made certain he refrained from calling the terrorists Islamic or Muslim terrorists, because he understood this new President was dead set against calling any terrorists, Muslim. The Director sucked in air and then went on with his briefing for the other members of the council and American President.

"Mr. President, we're stuck trying to find an extremely elusive enemy that we can't bomb or beat into submission. We're searching for people who can't be pressed into any logical way of clear thinking or actions. The Geneva Convention describes a terrorist under the word 'Perfidy' the act of terrorists or soldiers dressing as civilians or surrendering while under the protection of a white flag, and then attacking the soldiers they're deceiving. The accepted word by signature nations, 'Perfidy' identifies anyone who disguises themselves as civilians. Mr. President, this phrase will have to be questioned and changed in the upcoming small wars we'll be forced fight in the future against these damn terrorists and their bloody aims."

"How is that Mr. Raincloud?" The interested President asked as he suddenly sat forward and stared at the CIA Director while waiting for his reply.

"The reason I offer this statement Mr. President, is because even in Afghanistan, we had and continue to have our Special Forces soldiers dressed in local garb, and the soldiers grow beards in an obviously fragrant violation of stated Geneva Convention rules of engagement, sir. Our Special Forces troops were dressed in the Northern Alliance uniform, which makes it theoretically correct under these most trying instances, sir. The detainees we're still holding at Guantanamo Bay, Cuba, are being considered as essentially criminals, Mr. President. These damn detainees are terrorists without a true country or uniform to honor, and who don't carry a weapon openly, sir. So, they can't be distinguished between soldiers, or the civilians caught up in the fighting and are trying to get out of harm's way."

Even though the Director was addressing everyone at the meeting, he was aiming his words at the seated and concerned President as he went on with his presentation. "These people that make up the forces in all terrorist organizations don't respect the usual laws and accepted customs of normal warfare. The Geneva Convention offers no legal protection to these fellows in their bylaws. Mr. President, we're faced with an enemy who can't be sanctioned into abandoning the misguided quest to attack anyone living, or from the West by normal means of the word of sanctions.

"Mr. President, what we're dealing with during this ongoing and growing terrorist threat, is a bunch of fanatics who can kill or be killed in the most savage way. Here's another problem that we're faced with over this continuing terrorist situation, Mr. President. The only time we'll end up with any positive and concrete evidence a terrorist or group of terrorists, or even a rebel nation that has these deliverable weapons of mass destruction will be after the fact. And the terrorists or rebel nation has unleashed those damn weapons of mass destruction on any nation they have a beef with, sir. Mr. President, if any nation, including our own might I add, who suffer a terrorist attack employing a nuclear, biological, or chemical mass destruction by one of these terrorist organizations. We'll suffer a death toll uncountable, sir. Needless to add to this present conversation Mr. President, once a terrorist organization or rebel nation such as North Korea, or even Iran for that matter has unleashed an attack employing a weapon of mass destruction, it'll be too late to try and stop them then, Mr. President Sir."

"That's an extremely concerning and threatening portrait you're painting for us, Director Raincloud. It seems like we're fighting the terrorist situation alone by the sounds of it, sir." The President complained in a harsh tone, as he held Director Raincloud in his angry glare.

Staring back at the upset looking President, Director Raincloud slowly shook his head, and then he added to his words of warning for the group.

"With all due respect Mr. President, you have to keep in mind the United States alone, was the country attacked by a group of Middle East terrorists who employed civilian aircraft on the Nine, One, One, sneak attack aimed against our nation, sir. It's more than likely the United States alone will be the future target in the next such unprovoked major terrorist attack perpetrated by the next group of wannabe terrorists, aimed at our country by their commanders or their warped ideals and minds, sir.

"But the next attack could very well be carried out against us with the terrorists employing some form of a weapon of mass destruction, Mr. President. A President and Congress' main obligation are to protect the shores of our country and her civilians. Regardless of how many other nations approve or disapprove on how we go about attacking and defending ourselves, and our shores against a terrorist cell that has dared to harm our civilians, either in the United States or abroad, sir. When did standing alone become such a curse to carry out for our country, sir? Our founding Fathers stood alone in 1776. I also recall Sir Winston Churchill, when he proclaimed to the world in 1940, that Britain was fighting the Nazi horde 'by ourselves' sir. Mr. President, we're not fighting this war for ourselves in the least, sir. We have every other nation of the free world who wants to continue living free, standing behind us sir.

"Mr. President, I have to ask this question of you, sir. How many French, Italians, Belgians, and Brits are buried on our soil after giving the ultimate sacrifice to defend our country against the enemies of the world, sir? Not even one, sir. The count is one hundred and four thousand, three hundred and sixty-six dead brave American soldiers who paid the ultimate price of freedom with their lives, to free Europe of Nazism, and the Japanese Empire. Hell Mr. President, we never once asked for any kudos for our sacrifices…but we have absolutely no reason whatsoever to apologize to Europe or the Middle East, or any other nation of the world for that matter, because our country is thought of as being 'arrogant'. Dammit to hell and back sir. Apologize to no one and remind these narrow-minded asses of our soldier's great sacrifices, and don't go confusing arrogance for world leadership, sir…"

Again, the President interrupted the Director's briefing, as he snapped angrily at him, because he took the stinging words of Raincloud as a serious affront against his leadership. "Director Raincloud, I know you're a holdover from the previous Republican Administration, sir. So, I suggest you take a few moments to examine where your loyalties truly lay, sir. This is not the time to do any campaigning for another office you might have an interest in, Director. I don't need you going off on that worn out platform that we have terrorists hiding behind every tree and in every shadow. We must be ready to attack with all assets available to us, if some nation or group of people looks at us cross-eyed. I know how you feel, and if it wasn't for my pressing need for your outstanding services to my Administration. I would've had you replaced when I took the office of the Presidency, Mr. Raincloud."

There was dead silence, and the tension was so thick it could be cut with a knife in the Oval Office. With everyone attending the meeting, shocked at how the President just dressed down the powerful CIA Director in front of them. General White was fuming over how the President spoke to Raincloud, and he was having a hard time trying to hide his outrage over the situation.

The President ignored the silence as he asked the Director in a heated tone. "Mr. Raincloud, I believe we're going to leave this part of the briefing for a moment, and you'll answer my next question. What about Pakistan? What's the situation with that country? Is that nation becoming a serious threat to our country's security, and the soldiers operating in Afghanistan?"

Gathering his composure while continuing to hide his anger, Director Raincloud replied confidently to the new American Leader. "With all due respect Mr. President, it's our belief that Pakistan's sleeping with a wide array of different enemies to our country, and to India and including a few others ally nations in the region, sir. It's further believed that Pakistan's actively engaged to try and undermine the stability we have successfully established in neighboring Afghanistan. Pakistan's further trying to keep the region in a constant state of turmoil, unrest and outright war, Mr. President.

"We've been able to gather quite a bit of evidence that Pakistan is flirting with a pending disaster of creating a new age of war on the subcontinent, by harboring numbers of militants fighting India over the disputed Kashmir region. Pakistan's using the situation raging with the al-Qaeda terrorist organization and the Taliban, to hide the fact she's in contention for sole ownership over Kashmir. We must ask what role

Pakistan is playing in the proliferation of nuclear weapons worldwide also, Mr. President? We're quite confident that for a long time, Pakistan and North Korea have active roles in Iran's quest to become a nuclear threat against the Middle East and the world. There are many other questions over Pakistan for our concerns, and where her alliances lay.

"We have massed hard evidence proving beyond a shadow of a doubt that Pakistan's backdoor supporting the Taliban movement and al-Qaeda operatives working against our interests in this region, Mr. President. She's constantly running heavy interference with our main efforts to hunt down and kill the leading terrorists of these rather troublesome organizations, using that country as a platform to mobilize their operation, and attack our forces operating in Afghanistan from. Pakistan's also blocking our use of unmanned drone strikes in that country's borders, sir. That fact is helping to extend our stay in Afghanistan and the surrounding regions, and it's forcing our defenses to remain on a much stronger alert status, Mr. President. Because we can't get at the damn terrorist leadership hiding in the Tribal controlled region of that country sir…"

"Director Raincloud, that shit is about to change drastically for Pakistan I assure you. I intend to dramatically expand our use of unmanned drone strikes operating inside Pakistan, and Yemen. I'm growing sick and tired of seeing the most wanted and extremely dangerous terrorist threats to the world, hiding and being protected in these lawless countries and regions, and the damn terrorist leaders thumbing their damn noses at us, sir. Director Raincloud, I want bin Laden and al-Awlaki's heads resting on a stick, and I want them now." The President growled as he rose and leaned over his desk after resting his hands on the surface of the antique desk, and he outright glared at the Director.

General White realized this conversation was going south fast, and he decided to place an end to it before one or the other man said something not going to work out well for either during this tense meeting. The General rose and cleared his throat, instantly ending the confrontation raging between the President and the well-seasoned CIA Director.

President Otomer ripped his eyes away from Raincloud's face, and he aimed his angry glare at General White, as the fuming American Leader roared at the military officer. "Yes, General White, do you have something to add to this damn conversation, sir?"

"Yes, I certainly do Mr. President Sir, I believe we should take a step back here and draw in a breath, and then we can get back to the matters that concern the security of the United States and our allies, with more level heads and sensible decisions, sir." The General tried one of his best smiles on the new American Leader. The smile did the trick and the President dropped back in his chair. Then he went in thought for a few moments while making a steeple of his fingers and rested his pointer fingers against his lips.

Everyone at the security meeting remained silent to give the new American Leader the silence and time to sort out his thoughts for a few moments. Suddenly the President grumbled at the gathered. "Gentlemen, ladies, I believe we had enough of this meeting. I'm quite certain all of you have already scheduled meetings for this day as do I, you that we must attend to. I'm of the mind to end this meeting for the time being, and we'll reconvene later of my choosing to finish this briefing. I'll have my people inform each of you on the next date I'll pick to carry on with this meeting. Director Raincloud, I trust I made my point with you, sir?"

"Yes Sir Mr. President, I'm at your service both day and night twenty-four seven, sir." Director Raincloud offered to the concerned looking President.

"That's better Mr. Raincloud, do me a favor and remember that last remark, any time we're at another meeting, sir. If I feel you're a disruptive force in my Administration for one moment of time, Director Raincloud. I'll not hesitate in the least to have you immediately replaced at the drop of a hat, sir." The President snapped and then rose to his feet, this time he marched out of the Oval Office in a huff.

Director Raincloud remained standing and silent in the center of the room, and only relaxed when the General came up to him, and he rested his hand lightly on his shoulder. Three other members from the meeting gathered around the CIA Director. All tried to comfort him and make excuses for the way the new President snapped so angrily at him.

When General White felt the fuming CIA Director had enough bull from the others. He led the obviously shaken Director out of the White House to their vehicles and drivers. The General ordered the Director's driver to take Raincloud to the Pentagon, so they could share a drink together. To get him over the severe dressing down the President just aimed at him.

When the two men reached the General's office, they walked past the secretary and entered the office without words for anyone they passed. General White removed the bottle of whisky from the drawer and poured them both a stiff hit, and they downed the harsh liquid without tasting it. Mary rushed in the office because she could tell something was wrong with both men. She carried a pot of coffee and two cups, but when she noticed them drinking the hard stuff, she placed the coffee down on the side table.

Director Raincloud nodded kindly to Mary, but it was the upset General who offered in a kind of angry voice. "Christ Almighty John, I can't believe the way the Boss came down on your ass at the fucking meeting, my friend. Hell, the old President would've never done anything like that, especially in front of the other members of the damn council. The old President would've waited until after the meeting was concluded, and if he had a beef with you. He would've gone after you hot and heavy in private. This new guy even upset some of his own people at the damn meeting and I don't even think he realized what he did."

"Yeah, but I said what many others at the meeting wanted to stay from the get-go, General." Raincloud offered as he helped himself to another drink.

"Gees John, I can't believe you had the moxie to bring up that part about his apologizing to everyone he comes across, ever since he took over his damn office. That took some fucking Bravo's (balls) I tell you, my friend. It's a good thing I didn't tell you what my Colonel told me the other day, sir." General White offered with a grin as he settled in his chair.

"What was it, John? I always want to know what our ground pounders have to offer us, General. They always seem to see things in an entirely different light than we see the problems. I've learned a lot from my lesser people under my command, sir." The CIA Director asked as he allowed himself to relax a bit as the booze hit him.

"So do I John, I listen close to what my lesser Officers have to offer me, sir. Well John, I don't know if I should add to your ammunition and anger for this new guy, but what the hell. My Colonel said he got in a rather heated conversation with some of his troops on base the other day, and it came out in our search for the Muslim terrorists, especially the king rat bastard himself, bin Laden. Colonel Leadbetter growled at his Captain that the Islamic terrorists are rewriting the usual rules of engagement written under the Geneva Convention which in essence, is forcing us to rewrite the rules of interrogation, and how we're handling the Islamic terrorists we're still holding down at Gitmo. I didn't want you to bring up the subject of Gitmo to the new President.

"Not after the fucking black eye he received when he first stated he wanted to close that facility down when he took over the Presidency, and it's still in operation and screwing with his mind. Boy, if you think you got out of the Oval Office with your Bravos still intact, mister. If you were foolish enough and even dared to mention the word Gitmo to him, the President would've cut them off for your ass." Again, the General smiled at the Director.

"Yes, General and I understand how your soldiers must feel over the way this new guy is screwing around with our security and Intelligence Communities, sir. Ever since he became President, he's been spending his spare time attacking and blocking and taking away something from our Intelligence people for doing their damn job here in the States. His Administration's people are getting so bad that the damn fools can't tell the fucking, sorry Mary." The Director offered as he turned to the General's secretary and nodded before he went on with his complaint.

"General White, the people working with this new Administration are getting so bad they can't tell the difference between the damn arsonist, and the firefighter. The Muslim terrorists are the arsonists, and what matters the most too any terrorist. Isn't the technological complexity of the explosive device they're planting; these damn animals are more interested in how many innocent people that device will kill and maim. The rudimentary makeup of the damn explosive device is necessarily the simpler the device is the better possibility of success for the lousy animals. The terrorist could be either a sophisticated failure or an amateurish murderer, General. General, so many of my people are ducking their heads in the sand for fear of being dragged before Congress and questioned in open session if they gave a terrorist a bloody damn nose, or a crack in the back of their damn heads. Or if one of my Agents tried to teach one of the bastards how to surf on a water board for Christ's sake."

"Say Chief." General White offered because he was the only man in all Washington who could dare call Raincloud Chief and live to speak further. "You know what they say sir. 'The Ark was built by an armature, and the damn Titanic built by fucking professionals." The General gave a quick glance to Mary because of his curse, and then he went on with his words. "That's why we have to keep a close eye on everything happening around the world. Or the armatures are going to become the damn professionals in this ongoing drama. Director, if you feel some of your people are burying their fricking heads in the sand then I think it's time for you to start replacing some of these people you're obviously concerned about.

"If we allow our guard to drop for one lousy moment during these trying and dangerous times, we're going to find ourselves covered dick deep in a bunch of crazy asses screaming Muslim terrorists and buried in dead and dying civilians." General White glared at the Director, and he did not bother to apologize to his secretary for his colorful words he used in front of her in his conversation with the Director.

Raincloud allowed the nasty words to go over his head as he fired back at the concerned looking military officer. "John, I can't help but feel this new Administration and Democratic controlled Congress and House, are more concerned with protecting the rights of the damn terrorists. Then they are with protecting the lives of the American people. John, how the hell can we make this new President understand we're after people who represent the purest manifestation of immorality the world has ever come across? General White, I was told while growing up that America will never be destroyed from the outside. If we falter and lose our freedom, it'll be because we have been foolish enough to destroy ourselves from the inside, sir."

"Are you telling me this President's trying to destroy our country from the inside out?"

"Arrrr…shit, I don't know what the hell I'm trying to tell you at this point, General White. All I know is I keep finding myself asking the same damn question if whether political correctness, or the desire to protect the diversity of our country. Prevented our Intelligence and Security Communities from recognizing and dealing with a problem in our midst, it's a problem hiding in plain sight right before our eyes, dammit. We have a horde of civilians afraid to come forward and challenge someone's ideology. Because they fear of getting an equal opportunity complaint leveled against them, and a lawsuit for racial profiling hammered on their asses that can end careers or jobs. General White Sir, homegrown terrorists are the largest threat to America's security to detect and stop. Simply because the homegrown terrorist's plot to harm America and her people can't be stopped in time, because it's hatched in a fanatic's head, and leaves no trail to follow until the trail is left in innocent blood and death.

"General White, you have to understand what I and all other Intelligence personnel are fighting. This new Administration is obviously more concerned that every citizen in our country must prove they're carrying medical insurance. But the people don't have to prove they're legalized citizens. Talk about an odd hypocrisy, sir. I and other security and Intelligence Communities are fighting a stone wall trying to secure our borders. Sooner or later some terrorist cell is going to cross our border from Mexico, and they'll do some serious damage to our country before we can get our damn hands on the sonofabitches.

"Hell General, it's getting so bad lately that I read a report from ICE. (Immigration and Customs Enforcement) It stated two border agents stopped who they conceived an Islamic terrorist member at the border from Mexico. Because of the present Administration's policies, the Agents believed the person might be an illegal alien. So, one Agent said, 'Don't ask him if he's an illegal, let him go before we get our asses sued and fired over a racial profiling charge'.

"God dammit General White, this is what I and other Directors of the Intelligence and Security Communities are face with. Yet the public demand and expect we make and keep them safe in their beds at night from further terrorist attacks. I no longer have my civilian contractors assisting my people with special interrogation of the captives still being held at Guantanamo. The reason for this is because I can't get the access I once enjoyed while carrying out interrogations of the radical followers of Islam prisoners. Coupling that with the orders and countless regulations where we're no longer allowed to engage in any form of enhanced interrogations of the damn prisoners. Has severely degraded my ability to gather current information from the terrorists, and the orders has my hands tied behind by back, General.

"General White, during the past series of enhanced interrogations of the prisoners still being held at Gitmo, we've been able to gleam crucial information that led to the capture or elimination of some top al-Qaeda and Taliban leaders. The information made it possible to stop at least three separate Muslim terrorist attacks that would've been carried out against us, General.

"John, you know the next smoking gun a terrorist organized attack will level at our country, sooner or later is going to be a mushroom cloud right in the heart of our country, if we don't stay on top of these damn animals, we call terrorists. To risk that would be more than irresponsibility of our leadership it'd be just plain nuts, sir. Yet at every twist and turn any Intelligence Community makes, it seems our damn path is being blocked by the current Administration's policies. Also, by the Army of lawyers it has released to examine everything we do or done to keep an eye on the damn terrorists, whether they're of the homegrown variety, or trying to sneak into our country to harm our civilians. General, a terrorist state can expand without a terrorist network in place. But the terrorist networks find it hard to exist without the terrorist states such as North Korea, Pakistan, and Iran, allowing the terrorists a haven to operate from sir…"

"I agree with everything you just stated, Director Raincloud. You have to stay on top of your people no matter what, or we're going to get hit and hit hard soon by another serious terrorist attack I can tell ya, sir." The Chairman of the Joint Chiefs of Staff offered, as he interrupted the rather upset CIA Director. Then he offered as if an afterthought. "We have to make the Kill Chain a hell of a lot shorter, Director."

"Kill Chain General White Sir? That's a new one on me sir, I never heard that phase used before, sir." The Director offered in a concerned tone of voice.

"Yes, the Kill Chain Director. The kill chain is the time it takes between finding a terrorist target such as this bastard bin Laden or this other al-Awlaki fella, and I don't give a fuck this second guy is an American citizen or not, dammit. He's a fucking enemy target as far as I'm concerned and destroying those two targets once we discover where the hell these two pricks are hiding. The Kill Chain, sir."

"You have a good point there, General White, and I agree with you completely sir. We have to start killing some of these threats the moment we get them locked up in our sights, General."

"Director Raincloud, if I were in command of the damn interrogations being carried out against the gullible lunatics being held at Gitmo. I swear to the good Christ Child, I'd have every one of those sonofabitches begging to surfing on a water board. I'd have the damn asses believing it was an exhilarating experience by the time I was done with their asses I tell you, sir. Director, I'd also know everything I want to know about their internal organization and command structure, and future intended targets the terrorists were planning to hit, Director Raincloud."

"That's a great statement General White. But your hands are not being tied behind your back by this current Administration as mine, and the other leaders of the Intelligence and Security Agencies are, sir. Our ability to track and deal with known and wanted terrorists, especially within the borders of the United States, has seriously been degraded by this new Administration and its crazy ass policies. I don't know how the hell this new President wants us to deal with known terrorists, sir. I think the man wants us to sneeze on their damn assholes and give the terrorists the fucking flu, General White."

The Director's comment made both men laugh, and the General got right on it by remarking. "Yeah Director, and it's like the old saying goes, 'you can lead a man to Congress, but you can't make him think'. I know your Agents are getting the short end of the shit stick from this new Administration. But our country's future is at stake, and we must keep on the damn terrorists' asses, if we intend to keep our civilians safe and secure in their own country. Director, I need a straight answer from you on the next questions. What's the true state of the damn no fly list, and how the hell are we handling keeping an eye on possible new terrorists trying to sneak into our country, or knock one of our aircraft out of the fucking air?"

"General White, I have to admit that the no-fly list is one helluva mess at this time sir. We're having a hell of a pack of trouble with getting any newly discovered terrorists added to the lists, rapidly enough for discovery and tracing their efforts, sir. We're being forced to allow the ticket tenders to monitor the damn list for us, and keeping their eyes opened for any wanted and known terrorists and keep them from getting on the aircraft.

Then they must alert my people and try and detain this person until my Agents can arrive on site and question the man, and then possibly take him or her into custody, dammit.

"In the past General White, we, and by we, I mean my Agents and other Intelligence personnel were able to monitor the list and keep their eyes opened for any wanted or known terrorists, so we can trace their steps and see what the hell these sonofabitches are up to sir. That's why the underwear bomber was able to get on board the aircraft the damn jackass tried to knock out of the air against us, sir. A ticket taker missed his damn name even though it was plainly added to the no-fly list well in advance of his attempted act of terrorism, and she allowed the nut to board the flight. General White, that's how that Army Major was able to get past our damn radar, because of the want to display how tolerant the United States can be at the cost of our own civilian's safety, sir. We have to drop back and protect our civilians the way President Reagan would have. While he was President, no terrorist would dare try and harm any Americans anywhere in the world, let alone in our cou…"

"C'mon Director Raincloud, you're starting to drift away from the questions I just asked you, sir. Get back to that damn no fly list crap, and what the hell you're doing to try and correct the short comings on the damn system, my friend. That's what concerns my ass more than you are crying about this new damn Administration, and how the President's people are tying your hands behind your back. You know many other ways to carry out your duties successfully, no matter how hard the new Boss is leaning on you and your damn Agents, Director Raincloud." General White snarled as he interrupted the Director a second time.

"Back off my ass will ya General! I'm having a hard enough damn time dealing with this new President, and his people and screwed up policies. I don't need you getting on my ass telling me how to run my damn office or salute the flag. I can handle that all by myself. General, I believe…" Raincloud offered in a heated tone and added.

"Despite the heavy pressure this new Administration's placing on my ass. I ordered my Agents to come out from the backrooms and concentrate their efforts with monitoring the twenty-two nations we're most concerned with that their terrorists would try and sneak into the United States against us. General White Sir, without securing the damn border with Mexico,

I'm under the assumption that it's only a matter of time before a terrorist cell uses that avenue, to sneak into the country to attack our citizens and our interests here in the States. That scenario will stretch my assets to the absolute limit, and I can only pray to God we discover the damn assholes before they're able to carry out their intended mission. This Administration is acting like they're just hell bent on blocking our efforts of securing the damn border. General White, they're going after the border states as they try and adopt laws to secure the border."

"Director Raincloud, what do you attribute this desire to stop the southern states from securing the damn borders themselves with Mexico?" General White asked with concern.

"You want the truth, General White?"

"For your future information Director Raincloud, any question I ask of you, I want the fucking truth about it, sir. I won't stand for any pussy footing around when I want a straight answer from you, sir." General White replied with acid lacing his tone.

"General White, remember you asked this question, and you're the one who demanded the answer to what I believe is the reason why this new Administration refuses to secure our border with Mexico while blocking the southern states from adopting laws to secure the border on their own accord, sir. General White, it's my belief this new Administration is blocking the securing of our border with Mexico, because he and every Democrat in our country will be relying heavily on the Latino vote, especially when the President runs for a second term in office. Before you interrupt me, please allow me to finish my statement sir. I'm not suggesting the President is selling out his country for the Latino vote, General. But he's aware if he gave the assets to secure the damn border, the growing Latino vote will evaporate rapidly for him…"

"Gees Christ John, I need some of the shit you're smoking for Pete's sake, man. Director, I can't believe you believe the kind of crap you're offering me today. What are you basing your decision on? I know he's fighting the southern states from adopting laws to protect the damn border, but that's a far cry from doing it just to get the Latino vote though, sir." General White remarked as he smirked at the concerned Director.

"General White, look at the evidence before you sir. Christ General, with the poor shape our economy is in, the President's offering to extend unemployment benefits for a third time, at the cost to the taxpayers of over one hundred and forty billion dollars. If you add the three extensions, it amounts to four hundred and twenty billion dollars, that's nearly a half a trillion dollars, General. Yet the President refuses to secure the damn border with Mexico. So, in essence General White, the President's paying our people to stay home, and he's allowing the damn illegal aliens to work on good paying construction jobs most of our people would jump at the chance to work on. General, I was in Tampa, Florida the other day, and I drove by two commercial buildings under construction.

"For some reason I'm now aware of, I got out of my car and stood for a while, and I studied the buildings under construction. I noticed at least a hundred men working on the two large commercial buildings. All the while I was there a few other men were standing outside the large construction site main gate. One man said he was out of work for over seven months, and then he asked me. 'Hey buddy, you wanna see something really interesting?'

"He didn't wait for me to reply, and he suddenly bellowed out in Mexican the words meaning 'Immigration Officers' were coming to check out the construction site. General, I'm not shitting you sir. Nearly all the worker disappeared like their asses were shooting out sparks. The only thing I can take from that was most of the damn workers on the site was illegal aliens. They were not taking jobs our unemployed American workers refused to do, General White. They were taking good paying jobs at rock bottom prices, and undermining our workers who are stuck on unemployment, sir.

"The large group of illegal aliens was working on good high paying construction jobs, while American workers are forced to stay home and collect unemployment. So, if you look at it the way I do sir, the government is paying our people to stay home and allowing illegals to work in our country and beat us out of taxes the illegal aliens won't pay, or the companies they were working for won't pay either. I see it as another form of welfare, we pay our people to stay home, and pay illegals to work in their stead on jobs our unemployed workers would jump at the chance to work on, sir."

General White let out with a weak laugh and then he remarked. "I have nothing to do with the economic conditions facing our country, thank God for that much Director. I leave that shit up to the people better off trying to figure that crap out. My job is to supply soldiers and military equipment that'll keep our nation and interests abroad, safe, and free from attacks by terrorists or other nations. Chief, I suggest you forget about this crap and worry about keeping on the asses of your damn Agents and make certain they're doing their jobs to the best of their abilities, sir. Sooner or later the people of this nation will see who is responsible for the woes we're facing with our economy, and the other nightmares haunting us. John, they'll go to the polls and vote the ones they believe are not doing their jobs properly, out of office…"

"General White, I'm afraid you're starting to sound much like a politician here, sir. I know the American public is the ones who'll get a handle on straightening out this country of our sir, as they did one way or the other in the past. The only thing I'm somewhat worried about this time is General White. Is if it takes the civilians too long to react and then vote out the ones screwing up everything so badly on us."

CHAPTER FIVE

CAMP LEJEUNE NORTH CAROLINA, MONDAY JANUARY 3rd, 2011

Colonel Bruce Leadbetter received a direct order originating from Central Command Center stationed at MacDill Airforce Base, situated on the very tip of Tampa Bay, Florida. The report ordered the Colonel to pull in all his Special Forces troops from left, for added special training in the latest adopted Urban Warfare tactics. Colonel Leadbetter was concerned because of where the order had originated from. Usually, it was General White who would issue orders for the Multi-National Rapid Response Force to activate. Nevertheless, he activated the radios his troops were ordered to always keep on their person while on leave. He smiled because, in his mind's eye, he was able to see his troops fuming over the order to report back to base in twenty-four hours.

MARATHON, THE FLORIDA KEYS, MONDAY, JANUARY 3rd, 2011. ZERO, SIX HUNDRED HOURS

Captain Robert Walker was sound asleep with Sergeant Dorothy Ramirez at their recently repaired home on Marathon. He did not hear the radio send out the signal ordering him to contact his Commanding Officer. It was Ramirez who heard the signal and she lazily reached over Walker and took the radio, and then read the screen informing her he was ordered to call the base. Instantly the phone rang, and she answered, it was the concern of Mutt, and he was asking in an excited voice if the signal to report to base was a joke, or were they ordered back to base in the next twenty-four hours.

She tried to keep her voice low because she did not want to wake Walker until the last possible moment, as she replied. "Frankie, I don't know what's up yet, Robert's screen is ordering him to contact the Colonel at Lejeune. We'll not know for certain if this is a call-up until he calls in and sees what the orders are about. I'm going to wake him so he can contact Colonel Leadbetter. Wait a moment Frankie, I have another call coming in."

She checked the number on the caller ID system and noticed it was Sergeant Vincent Lambardo calling in. She did not take the call as she went back to speaking with the Mutt. "Frankie, that was Buckethead, I didn't take his call because he's probably calling in to see if this is a call back to base or not. I'm going to wake Bobby and have…"

"You don't gotta wake my ass up fur nuthin, not with all the fucking noise you're making on the damn phone, sister. I'm up for Pete's sake, baby sister. But if you're expecting bright-eyed and bushy-tailed then, you should betta go out and catch yourself a fucking squirrel, baby. What the hell's going on and what's got everyone going crazy?" Walker grumbled as he got up on an elbow and he smiled at his lover and blinked the sleep out of his eyes.

"Bobby, we have an alert call over the handheld for us to respond to immediately, honey."

"Give me the damn thing so I can beep whatshis stinking puss and see what the fuck he wants from us. I see no reason for our call back to base. Nothing's heating up in Afghanistan or Iraq I'm aware of. Maybe he's lonely and wants someone to talk with, baby." Walker replied as he took the radio and pressed the button and instantly, the Colonel's voice came in growling at him.

"What the hell's wrong with you soldier? You're under direct orders to always have this fucking radio on your damn person while on live, buster! You're to check in with my ass the moment I send out the damn signal, Captain."

"Take it easy Colonel after all I was only put together with one screw, sir."

"Ha, ha Mr. Wiseass, here you are joking a fucking round with twenty thousand comedians out of work, and you want to be one, buster. I sent out the signal and you and your pack of misfits are ordered to report back to base within the next twenty-four hours. I have confirmations from more than half the Tier One troops already, Captain. I want you, Ramirez, and that poor excuse for an Officer, Hall, and any other soldiers hiding on that tiny fucking Island of yours up here, before the other soldiers report to base." The Colonel ordered his lesser officer.

"I'm closing the place up as we speak, Colonel Leadbetter Sir." Captain Walker replied with a sharp snap in his voice, as he got out of bed. He looked at his lady that caused her to jump into action. She got the Mutt off the phone after ordering him to their home with Sergeant Raphael A-SAP. Then she placed a call to their babysitter and getting her on the phone, she asked Cathy to come to their place as soon as possible.

Walker continued speaking with the Colonel as he quickly got dressed while holding the small radio to his ear with his shoulder. "Colonel Leadbetter Sir, what's going down? Did the shit hit the fan and I'm not aware of it, sir? Are we going hot after someone, sir?"

"Calm down a little soldier, as far as my orders go and I understand them. I was instructed to call in the troops to go over some new UCT, or Urban Combat Training crap some other Officer dreamed up for our sagging asses. These orders didn't come from the usual desk though, they originated from CENCOM. So, I'm not classifying these orders as top secret currently, Captain. There's no need for concern, this is a secured communication Captain."

"Crap, I had plans for the next few days, and if this isn't a stinking emergency, Colonel. Can't you see if you can have these orders change to a more appropriate time, sir?"

"Christ's sake Walker, I have a single tear running down the side of my puss over your fucking plans, mister. What is this shit from your ass anyhow, Captain? Central Command must check with your ass and make certain we're not interfering with any of the fucking plans of my Captain? Walker, you have your fucking orders mister, and I expect you to carry them out as received, buster! Or you're going to have my ass to contend with. I'm dispatching a VIP military aircraft out to pick you and the other asses with you up on that damn Island of yours, Captain. Expect that aircraft to land at Marathon by Zero Ten Hundred Hours today, and the Commander has orders to lift off at exactly Zero Ten Twenty Hours, with or without you people on board. I'm warning you, mister if your carcasses are not on board that fucking aircraft when it takes off. You better find another country to hide in. Do you catch my drift, Captain?"

"Loud and clear Colonel and my people will be on board the aircraft when it takes off sir."

"Good" Was all the Colonel replied as he broke off the communication?

"Well, that's that. It looks like we have to report back to base, honey."

"Walker don't tell me we're going on another mission so soon. I'm getting a little sick and tired of placing my life on the front of the dime all the time. I want to enjoy the rest of my life with you and Robert Jr. I want to…"

"Relax baby, according to the stinking Colonel, this isn't a call to active duty, we're being pulled in for some kinda special urban warfare training some uther fricking Officer dreamed up for us. I know the stinking Colonel wasn't pulling my pud with the orders because he told me General White didn't cut the damn orders for this new mess. The orders were cut by CENCOM, and we know it's only the General who orders our specialized units out on a new mission, baby. This is going to be just a stinking nuisance call-up, but we should be home within the next thirty to sixty days I bet. How the heck are you doing with getting the home all squared away for us, and the babysitter here to look after our kid?"

She let her breath out in a rush and then she replied to her lover. "Bobby, the house is fine, and I have the babysitter on the way over already. The Mutt and Blind Date are also heading over as we speak, honey. I guess they plan to leave our home this time around, Bobby. When do we have to get going, Robert?"

"The king shit's sending a small VIP aircraft out for our asses at Zero Ten Hundred Hours today, so that's the time we have to be at the damn airport, honey. He wants us on base before the rest of our troops show up, so we can control them for the stinking Colonel. What can I tell ya?" Walker replied as he fired off a reaffirming smile at his lady.

"Tell me you love me, and you'll keep me and our son safe, Robert." She offered as she moved into her lover's arms and melted against his powerful chest as Walker hugged her to him.

MONDAY JANUARY 3rd, 2011, ZERO NINE FIFTY-FIVE AM, THE MARATHON ISLAND AIRPORT

Walker, Ramirez, the Mutt, Blind Date, Buckethead, Baby Tee, No Neck, Ice, and the Ghost were all visiting Walker when the call-in order came from Colonel Leadbetter. Was standing in the small Island Airport dressed in their travel military uniforms. The soldiers were carrying duffle bags crammed full of extra military uniforms, boots, and everything else they were going to need at Camp Lejeune for this special training gig. Most of the soldiers were sort of daydreaming, but Ramirez was on the lookout through the large plate glass window. She was the first one to see the small jet coming in, and she called out to the others.

"Let's look alive people, the transportation's arriving." Ramirez picked up her duffle bag and slung it over her shoulder, the weight forced her to take a step back and grunt. Walker reached out and steadied her with his hand and followed her out the doors onto the tarmac. The small twin engine military jet tore down the long runway and turned off the main landing strip and circled back towards the waiting soldiers. The aircraft came across the turning strip and stopped fifteen feet from the troops. The pilot lined the aircraft up with the longer runway and was set up for a fast takeoff.

The engines were left idling, and the co-pilot lowered the ladder and the soldiers quickly piled into the aircraft. The moment the pilot realized the soldiers were settled in he asked permission to take off and received the okay from the small control tower. In less than a heartbeat, the small aircraft shot in the air then banked right and headed for Fort Bragg at full power. So, they could be picked up by military transportation and driven to Camp Lejeune.

MONDAY, JANUARY 3rd, 2011 AT ZERO TWELVE OH ONE P.M. CAPTAIN ROBERT WALKER AND HIS GROUP WERE ENTERING THE MILITARY BASE OF CAMP LEJEUNE

Captain Walker was seated in the passenger seat of the extended Chevy suburban carryall truck staring ahead. He noticed Colonel Bruce Leadbetter with Sergeant John Kirkpatrick, standing in front of the barrack his troops usually shared, every time while they were occupying the massive military base. Walker smiled as he shook his head, Sergeant Dorothy Ramirez noticed his action and she leaned forward and whispered to him. "What's up Robert?"

"Arrr… the friggin resident penis is waiting for our asses in front of the stinking barracks, Raz. He's standing with that sneaky little shit of his, Sergeant Kirkpatrick. I guess he's gonna get right on our stinking asses even before we're settled in."

The truck pulled up before the barracks and parked. As always, Walker was the first one out of the vehicle, he snapped to attention and shot off a sharp salute at his Commanding Officer. The Colonel did not bother to return the salute as he offered with a snap in his voice. "Never mind that crap, come with me, mister! We have some important shit to go over, so you understand the fucking reason for this damn call-in."

The Colonel led Walker to his barracks with the other soldiers following them. When the soldiers entered Walker's private sleeping quarters, the Colonel looked behind and noticed the other troops. He ignored the group as he sat down on the edge of Walker's desk. He waited for his Captain to be seated before he spoke to him and the other soldiers. "Okay, you pack of assholes better be fucking quiet, if you want to sit in on this damn briefing! One peep out of any of you shit sacks, and you'll find your asses hauled the fuck out of there faster than a beer keg disappears at a damn frat party. Walker, I know I told you your screaming squirrels were called back to base to absorb a shitload of new tactics in urban warfare shit. Well, that was only half the truth, and the reason for this sudden call-up, I'm…"

Ramirez put her hands to her lips and cried softly "Oh no" just loud enough for the Colonel to hear her words, and he snapped his head around and glared at her as he snorted. "Dammit Ramirez, didn't I just fucking warn you I didn't want to hear a fucking another peep from the damn peanut gallery? What's your malfunction, Sergeant?"

"I knew we were being called in for another mission, Colonel Leadbetter."

"Jesus H. Christ is that what's bugging your purdy little ass, Ramirez. Well, sister, that's not what's happening in this case, and if you would've kept your damn mouth shut tight, and your ears open. You would've known what the fuck I was about to tell my damn Captain here. Again,

I'm going to warn you and the other swinging dicks and bouncing tits in this fucking room. You, people, are classified as Tier One Assets which means you're no fail operators. Walker, I know I told you your pack rats were ordered to base for some new urban warfare tactics, that's only half the damn truth, mister. I got wind something big is in the fucking works, and yes, we're going to be running several certain scenarios on how to run urban warfare. We're also going to work on supporting some other specialize military units during their actions…"

"What the hell's this shit about Colonel? Since when do we run fucking support for any other stinking conventional soldiers? We're always the lead attack group on any stinking action we're sent out on we're never the slack ass backup soldiers for any Special Forces Operation, Colonel!" Walker growled as he interrupted and stared at his Commander.

"You got some pair of fucking brass balls hanging between your stinking legs mister, to dare interrupt my ass while I'm speaking to the bunch of you ball sacks, buster. Make sure the damn things don't get tarnished or in your way on your ass, mister. Walker, because of the present situation I'll give you this one fucking interruption, but I'm warning you in no uncertain terms. Don't try it again, or you're going to find out how good the damn hospitalization your government offers you is.

"As I was saying before you interrupted me Walker, nothing is written in stone on any mission we're sent out on. I happened to have picked up some scuttlebutt something huge, maybe one of the largest operations ever pulled off by our country, might be in the works. Your people are called back to base in case this operation needs some expert support and backup for this possible future operation. Before you ask my ass, I have no fucking idea what this mission might be about, Captain. All I know for certain is if it goes down, it's going to be big Captain." The Colonel paused to allow Walker to ask questions.

Walker let out his breath in a low hiss as he bitched at his Commanding Officer. "Colonel Leadbetter, have you been able to pick up who this uther Unit is, we might get stuck making certain they don't get caught with their stinking asses swinging out in the breeze, sir?"

"That was a good question Walker, and it does my heart good to know you're fucking paying attention to my briefing, buster. Yes Captain, I was able to pick up the Unit or Units in command of this supposed upcoming operation. Red Cell which is a special Unit from SEAL Team Six of JSOC (Joint Special Operations Command) Units branded NSDG. (Naval Special Development Group) If Red Cell is involved in this fucking future operation, this mission is going to be one hell of an action going down, soldier.

"If our Units are picked to run support of this specialized group, you and your pack rats better take it as a fucking privilege to be their backup, soldier. Walker, these damn troops are every bit as good as we are, mister." Colonel Leadbetter snarled, not stepping back an inch dealing with his young military officer.

Colonel Leadbetter took his attention away from Walker for a moment, and he looked at the other soldiers in Walker's quarters, and instantly hissed at them. "Do any of you fucking lunatics have anything to add to this damn conversation? You have any complaints or gripes working with Red Cell SEAL Team Units? You people better air the bitches now, so I know who I'm going to dump from my Units, people. Speak up if you have the balls to gripe to my face."

The soldiers diverted their eyes and acted like he did not ask them any questions, which caused the angry Colonel to growl at the troops. "I didn't think so, there's not a brass ball or ovary between the lot of you damn Squids. Walker, I'm having your people ordered to base, organizing in front of my office on the marching grinder. Your knuckle draggers and cave sweepers (women soldiers) will remain on the damn grinder until I'm done with you pack of jackrabbits. Then you and I will address the flaming asses and then I'll turn the mess over to you for processing. I'm going to give you the rest of this day and all of tomorrow to get your troops on base and settled in. That means Wednesday, I'll expect your full complement of troops to muster on the grinder at exactly Zero Six Hundred Hours, ready to get on with this urban training shit you were called back to base to learn.

"Walker I'm warning you straight from the fucking shoulder on this one, mister. If any of your flaming assholes can't learn the new tactics we're going to drum into their damn noggins. They'll find their asses drummed out of my Units, and the failures will be shipped back to their original Units we originally drafted the pack of asses from. So, the failures can rot there and only dream about being a member of the Special Forces soldiers.

"You better warn the assholes I'm certain somewhere along the line, General White will show up on base and get his ass involved in the urban warfare tactics training, or this mission. You better believe he's keeping his eyes glued on your people's every move. After all Captain you people are his pet project. The General stuck his dick in a fucking blender more than once to keep you jackrabbits together and operating as trained. Any complaints about your troops always end up on his fricking desk and die there. But guess who the damn General dumps on when one of your fucking gun bunnies gets in trouble?"

"Yours Colonel!" Walker remarked trying to be smart.

"You are god damn right my ass the General gnarls on, any time you damn Squids get in fucking trouble anywhere on this earth. Here's another question for your wiseass. Can you guess whose stinking ass I'll be chewing on, if the stinking General gets on my ass for something one of your god damn puppets gets into?" The Colonel turned his head and stared directly at the Mutt, who immediately pointed to his chest and grumbled.

"What the hell are you looking at my ass for Colonel? I didn't do nuthin wrong sir."

"I didn't do nuthin wrong yet, you mean asshole." The Colonel mimicked the Mutt's voice, and then added to his angry words at the Lieutenant. "No Mutt, you never do anything fucking wrong do you mister? How come any complaint that comes sliding across my desk? It usually states the soldier in the write up is you, you fucking idiot?"

"That's because none of the uther Officers like me. I think they're against me because I'm half black and half white." The Mutt smirked because he was trying to get under the Colonel's skin.

The Commanding Officer glared hard at the Mutt as he slowly shook his head, and then he grinded his teeth before responding to the young soldier. "One of these fucking days mister, I'm going to get rid of your ass one way or the other, Mutt. What would make me the happiest in life is if I'm able to stand your ass up against a wall, and I'm allowed to use the two halves of your mixed-up ass, as target practice, soldier. Arrr...enough of this bickering around crap for Christ's sake, I ordered you fricking people to stand there and keep your damn mouths shut while I'm running over your damn orders, and that's exactly what you're going to do. If you Squids know what's good for the lot of your lazy asses that is, people."

The Colonel took a quick breath and then he turned to his Captain and grumbled at him this time. "Walker, all goofing aside, you have to retain complete control over your people, and make damn certain the Squids absorb this training crap we're going to spoon feed the assholes. I don't know how long your damn Squids are going to get stuck on base, so you better prepare them for a possible extended stay. That way we'll cover any duration the troops get stuck with, if what I was able to pick up about this operation is true that is. It's going to take Red Cell a while to study their target and get to know the surrounding terrain like the back of their damn hands.

"Captain Walker Sir, preparing for a special operation could take the troops up to six months or longer, before the soldiers involved in the operation understand what they're doing, and the mission goes operational. So, you better figure on staying on base for at least that long a period. Well, I guess we better walk over to my office and see how many shit sacks have showed up back on base as ordered, Captain. There better be at least half the flaming assholes waiting on the grinder by this time, or else Walker."

Walker did not reply to the Colonel's last threat aimed at him as he and the other group of elite soldiers followed them to his office and quarters. He noticed at least three dozen soldiers were standing at parade rest on the grinder. The other soldiers stared at the troopers entering the area and noticed Colonel Leadbetter enter his private office, leaving Walker and the other soldiers outside. Instantly, the troops on the grinder surrounded the other troopers, and began flooding Walker with a ton of questions and demands.

Not being able to think with the flood of words being fired at him one after the other, Walker had to put his hands in the air, and then he barked at the excited group of soldiers. "Will you people shut the fuck up for a stinking minute and give me a god damn chance to think for Pete's sake. I can't hear one question with all you people talking at the same damn time for the love of the Christ child. If you one of you people ask a question I can understand, I might be able to answer it intelligently for you slobs."

The other soldiers quieted down and once they were silent, Walker picked one trooper and he asked him. "You, Blood Clot (Sergeant Richard Burmbach) I'll start with your stinking ass, mister. Maybe with you I can answer the rest of these guys fucking questions for them in one shot. Don't ask me, I'll tell you what's going on and why you people were called back to base. We're called in to learn some new stinking tactics some uther flaming asshole dreamed up about urban warfare, and that's the only reason we're stuck here, plain, and simple. Does that answer yours and the questions of the uther guys?"

"That answers my question good enuf I guess, Captain." Blood Clot, the Unit's medic replied calmly, as he shrugged and had a grin on his lips.

"Well, that might answer one fucking question for his stinking ass, but it sure doesn't answer my fucking concerns, man!" CoCo-G, (Sergeant Milton Pettibone) snarled as he held Walker in his angry glare before he went on with his complaint. "I wanna know how fricking long we're gonna be stuck staying on this dump, man."

"I shoulda known your black ass would make a damn fool of yourself and let me warn you buster. No matter how much of a friend I am to you stinking people, you better take the damn vinegar outta your tone whenever addressing my lousy ass. Or you're gonna live just long enuf to regret your stinking mistake, buster. If you wanna keep the heat in your tone, you betta add, "Sir" at the beginning and end of your stinking gripe. Now stupid to answer your fucking bitch, I don't know the stinking answer to that question. But you betta be prepared to hang around base for a short time, or a long one. How is that for a fucking answer, buster?" The captain stared at the angry looking soldier bitching at him.

"What! What the hell was that load of shit about you just popped off with, Walker?"

"Walker what mister?" He growled at the soldier who just snapped at him.

"Yeah, right, okay Walker, Sirrr." CoCo replied with a snap as he rolled his eyes.

"That's betta spudhead. I'm sorry, but it's the best I can give ya for the time being, until I'm betta informed on what this crap's all about, dammit. All I know for certain is, we're called in for this added special training crap, and that's all I know fur now, guys. If you think there's more to know, you can ask old whatshispuss when he comes outta his stinking office, and make sure you ask him in the same fucking way you just asked me, pal." Walker smirked as he dared CoCo to snap at the Colonel like he did to him.

"Errr...no thanks Walker, I kinda like my dick swinging where it is, thank you..."

"Ask whatshispuss what Walker, and its 'Sir Whatshispuss Sir' to you. What the fucks going on out here, and how come you don't have these slobs standing at attention when their Commander is waiting to address the pack of shit? You're beginning to fuck up Walker! Am I going to be forced to have you retrained, so you know how to properly handle your damn troops and respect Officers again, dammit? Look, here comes another load of shit we call elite soldiers. Here comes the cream of the crap I see.

"Walker, I'm going to go and get myself something to eat. You can waste your damn time with getting this shit all in order, mister. When I return, I'll address this mess and once I'm done with these flaming assholes, maybe I'll allow them to chow down and relax for the rest of the damn day. Get it done soldier, I should be back here in a half an hour or so, mister." Colonel Leadbetter snarled as he halfassed saluted his young Captain, and then headed off for the mess hall. All the while the Colonel was walking away from the formation, he was smirking at himself about his outstanding soldiers.

By the time the well-respected Colonel returned to the grinder area and his troops. Most of Walker's soldiers were assembled and waiting for his return. The moment he stood by Walker's side, the soldiers immediately went to full attention, and they saluted their Commander.

"Ahhhhhh... that's much fucking better you damn Squids, I see there's still some hope turning this bunch of rip rap into full blooded tried and true Marines." The Commander remarked as he returned the salute to the troops. After taking a few moments to collect his thought, the angry Colonel informed the troops what was expected of them during this new training secession. "Okay Squids," the Colonel used the derogatory term for new recruits while addressing his well-seasoned troops as he continued with his orders.

"The reason why you're here is because I was getting a little lonely being here all by myself, and I decided I wanted some fucking company. I'm giving you slobs the rest of this fucking day off and tomorrow as well. On Friday we'll assemble and be ready for some real fucking work by Zero Six Hundred Hours. That's all I have to say to you Squids. Okay slugs, pick up your Duffle bags and follow your Captain to the barracks you shit sacks will occupy for your duration on my beloved military base. Move it out people, move it, move it, move it."

The specialized soldiers fell in line with Walker, and they followed him to their assigned barracks. He stopped in front of his barrack and began counting heads and concluded he was eighteen soldiers shy of his full complement of troops. The next day the eighteen missing soldiers dribbled on base, and by Fourteen Hundred Hours, all his troops were present on the complex.

WEDNESDAY MORNING JANUARY 5th, 2011
ZERO SIX HUNDRED HOURS

Colonel Bruce Leadbetter stormed out of his office acting like a bear being chased by a swarm of angry Hornets, as he charged to the front of the formation of specialized troops. He stopped before Walker and growled nastily at his Captain. "It seems like your fucking rat pack is all present and accounted for, mister. At least that better be the damn situation I'm seeing standing before my fucking eyes, Captain."

"Yes, Sir Colonel Leadbetter, all troops are present and accounted for as ordered, sir." Walker replied as he smartly saluted his Commander, and then went silent.

Colonel Leadbetter did not bother to return Walker's salute as he started in on his troops. "Well, well as I live and fucking breathe. I see you Squids were able to remain alive long enough to return to my beloved Marine Base when your country calls for your asses to report. Are there any fricking complaints that needed to be addressed, a sick call, anyone suffering from hangovers, woman problems, or fucking hang nails that might stop you pack of stinking crybabies from beginning their training on this fucking day?" The Commander did not wait for a reply from any of the troops as he continued ripping into the soldiers. "Okay you ball sacks and bouncing tits, the reason you people were called back to base. Is so we can start to go over the new tactics Command has adopted regarding UCRT, (Urban Combat Readiness Training) for you, assholes. I want each one of you shits to pay attention to everything I tell you damn pukes.

"I'll not repeat anything I have to offer you shitbirds, so if any of you Squids miss something I said, your assholes better be able to read my fucking mind, because I have no intentions of repeating an order to you people. Okay here we go, ever since that nightmare action that went down in Mogadishu where we lost eighteen of our best fucking Chocks. (Army Rangers) The military has significantly improved its Urban Combat Readiness Training Programs, for the betterment of their soldiers to employ on how to engage enemy combatants in any claustrophobic civilian environments. Believe it or not, it's estimated by the brain thrusts who keep their asses on top of this type of statistics. Over ninety percent of our future enemy targets will be engaged in less than fifty yards from you people trying to control the damn situation you were sent in to get a fucking handle on. Or hunt down a pack of fucking terrorists we want to neutralize.

"I'm telling every one of you people, nothing this side of judgment day can properly prepare a soldier for the relentless hell of the real thing, when the shit hits the fan on your troops! When you're faced with life threatening situations out in the field, where you must make a snap decision on whether the guy you got locked up in your sights is a damn terrorist, or a fucking civilian puke mistakenly caught out of place. Most urban engagements we've been involved in the past few years had historically resulted in around thirty percent causality rates on both sides of the damn coin. I intend to cut that number down to less than ten percent causalities on our side and increase the fucking causality rate on the enemy side dramatically for the lousy piss asses who dare to cross swords with any of you pukes. Or I'll take asses my damn self around here, you pack of asswipes.

"You people are classified as Tier One Troops, the phase we're dealing with 'Urban Warfare' means armed and hunting soldiers going in civilian areas or cities. Looking for a bunch of snot nose terrorists enjoying protection of said civilians given to the terrorists willingly, or who was terrorized into protecting these fucking criminals we want. Urban warfare, what a fucking nightmare in the making we're forced to deal with now and in the damn future. Christ Almighty, even our weapon technological advantages are less important to our troops in the field under these circumstances. When combat comes to a face-to-face confrontation with a pack of screaming lunatics who could be a riled-up bunch of confused civilians and fighting takes place in the middle of civilian neighborhoods more familiar to the fucking enemy and their control.

"This supposed situation is where our intelligence capabilities will be extremely crucial to our operation and put to the test during an urban control operation. Detailed blueprints of the infrastructure, combined with up-to-date satellite photos and live updates from unmanned drones constantly roaming over the fucking target area for the duration of the operation. To better help identify any enemy movements and possible ambushes setup against our moving troops, will help dramatically as will specially design urban combat gear and training.

"We have a damn leg up on the fucking assholes thanks to a Company calling itself Zebra Imaging, commissioned by our Defense Advanced Research Projects Agency. This system known as Urban Photonic Sandtable Display, UPSD is a holographic map system showing actual building and surrounding terrain in full living color, and in three clear dimensions. I'm happy to inform you people that you won't need glasses to see this detailed dimensional map. The map is put together after the town and surrounding landscape is swept over every inch by unobtrusive lasers mapped out by an unmanned drone. After this part of the project is completed, a special set of lenses display the buildings, even damn people caught out in the open, and the surrounding land features to heights up to 30 centimeters tall. Which gives us a much better feel of the entire area in question we're about to invade or attack.

"Arrr…getting back to why we're ordered to base. The urban response soldiers which will more than likely be you sacks of madness in most cases will carry special equipment on your persons in the name of a lightweight ladder, fifty feet of rope with a grappling hook attached to one end of the coil. A portable light, tape, or spray paint for marking out targets, prisoners and secured buildings, so follow on forces don't waste their time checking an already secured building. Night vision goggles will be carried, along with GPS tracker units that will help troops navigating much easier through the inner-city labyrinth, while trying to root out the enemy combatants from non-combatant civilians.

"A small mirror will also be included and carried by you people, to help you see around corners or under fucking doors and of course, weapons and ammunition. The invading troops searching the area in question for hidden enemy combatants or terrorists will learn to travel in small groups of no more than six to eight soldiers. If you must do a hard entry into an unsecured room or fucking building you want to check out, the first man in will immediate clear the fucking door, and then that soldier will immediately move to the back of the damn room being inspected by these inserting troops.

"The second soldier entering the room in question will rapidly cross the doorway, and he or she will then move to a diagonal corner of the room. That trooper will hunker down and help secure the room for the follow-on troops on any operation you people are sent out on. While the third soldier entering the damn room follows the first soldier's path, and that trooper will move to the nearest corner of the room, and he'll then assume a security stance at that point, and he will cover all four corners of the room. The fourth soldier entering a forced room, will follow the second soldier's path, and that soldier will turn and secure the doorway to the room. He'll not move from the doorway until he's certain the room is secured, and there are no enemy combatants hidden in the damn room.

"Our snipers or Vampires from the invading insertion teams will break off the main force, and they begin to search out their perches of opportunity high enough from the ground, to afford said snipers the widest clear fire range of the entire compromised area. The Vampires will be used to protect boots on the ground, and if we go against a possible terrorist unit. You can bet the fucking bank on it that the fricking enemy combatants would sure as hell setup their own gun firing positions in the most densely civilian populated areas we want secured. While capitalizing on our normal reluctance as soldiers with a conscious and not a god damn terrorist, to inflict the lowest possible numbers of causalities on the innocent civilians of the area we're investigating. We must be on constant guard in case the enemy releases weapons of mass destruction in the form of chemical or biologics against our asses in the field while searching the area in question.

"If that type of fucking nightmare comes true and is employed against us during any operation we're involved with. The first responsibility of our troops is to protect themselves and each other, and rapidly get into your protective NBC (Nuclear, Chemical, Biological) gear, you people will always carry on your person, if that such attack is possible against us. Once this shit is accomplished, your next responsibility is to render whatever possible aide you can give to any civilian causalities you might come across out in the field of action.

"You people will have to be on full alert at all times while n any mission for any possible man traps set out against us by the insurgents in operation, you're trying to root out of the fucking compromised urban area. The traps are usually placed in doorways or in other building entry points, to hit you while you're making a hard entry into any suspected structure. Also remember to keep a fucking eye out for sewers or tunnels that could easily hide a number of insurgents aiming to kill you people. Until they can act and hurt your advance patrols, remember to stay away from any windows where an enemy combatant can hit you from inside the damn building. Or shooting through a window into the window you might be crossing. Also be on the alert for any possible mines which could take out troops or support vehicles, and unsuspecting follow-on forces setup by retreating enemy units.

"If we must go after Arab nations suffering hostile insurgent activity or terrorist preparing to attack the nation in question, or the damn asses are aiming their future attacks against our country, and that government's requesting assistance with the damn situation. Remember any place and remarkable landmarks the enemy units might use as traps and ambushes against your advancing units. The enemy more than likely will take advantage of religious Mosques, civilian hospitals, schools, and any number of historical and ancient buildings we'd prefer not to demolish the structures if they attack us from said areas. These structures could hide enemy soldiers, snipers or munitions for insurgent use. The enemy could hide tanks, weapons, and explosives in civilian garages, or behind brick walls, or in parked cars, trucks, shit any vehicles.

"During an urban engagement, the insurgents will more than likely hide themselves among non-combatants or stupid civilians of the area. The combatants would sure as hell dress like and disguise themselves as civilians of that area we're interested in. The terrorists would more than likely resort to using civilians as human shields, if the situation comes down to that kind of response employed against our advancing troops and equipment. You people better always keep your damn noggins on a fucking swivel during any urban engagement's you people might be involved in. If you corner an enemy combatant, the motherfucker might make like he's surrendering to your asses. The moment you shits let down your guard for the slightest moment, he'll go hot and end up putting a cap in your damn asses. The fricking enemy combatants that we have branded terrorists instead of saboteurs will employ all sorts of hell against our inserting troops in the field.

"During an enemy engagement, you'll enjoy a good number of different air support platforms in any urban action our troops are engaged in. That support will come in the form of different types of rotary aircraft. The close in go fast aircraft such as the A-10 Warthogs, and Spectre gunships, will likewise assist on many missions with us, along with the Predator unmanned and armed hellfire missiles drones. Once the enemy combatants realize you're enjoying air support systems. They'll likely employ rocket and grenade launchers against your air cap protection that will pose a serious threat against our low and slower flying helicopters and other close in support platforms." Colonel Leadbetter took a second to draw in some needed air and stopped speaking and looked at some troops in the eyes. He did not like what he saw, and he suddenly roared to try and wake the groggy acting soldiers up and get their minds back on what he was talking about.

"Eyes!" The boiling angry Marine Colonel bellowed out because he was trying to wake up his troops, so they paid closer attention to his instructions. That scream made most of the elite soldiers jump, and they turned their attention to the Colonel as he went back to addressing them.

"That's better you pack of fucking lunatics. When I call for eyes, all eyes better be looking directly at my fucking ass, and you people better be clear and your minds absorbing everything I'm telling you people. Or I'll rip out any glazed over eyes I deem not looking at me properly and the owner not listening to my words. Then I'll place the damn things on the floor at the offender's feet, so I'll know for certain at least his eyes are paying attention to my ass. I looked at a number of you killers supposed to be the point of the spear for the services protecting our country, and what the fuck did I see? You so called specialized troops suffering serious eye glaze over. I didn't know if you people were sleeping on your damn feet or not. I know this shit's boring as hell, and in most cases many of you already went over this bullshit in the past.

"I feel bad for you Squids, but I have orders to go over a certain set of instructions from CENCOM. That's exactly what I'm going to do, and there's nothing you pack of gun jugglers can do but suck it up and enjoy my fucking little speech. We must keep ahead of the ever-mutating tactics of the damn terrorists and enemy combatants, and how they'll more than likely attack their next possible target. I don't know if you people want to believe this shit or not. The crap I'm going to go over is important, and maybe someday what I'm teaching you Squids during these new training programs will possibly save you damn lives. So, when you people are old enough you can retire and again live off your government tab." The crafty Marine Colonel stopped speaking so he could suck up more air, but this time he smirked at his captive audience while enjoying a little breather.

One troop called out then lowered his head so the Commander could not see who just called out at him. "Colonel Leadbetter, we're never gonna get a stinking handle on fucking terrorism until we secure the damn borders of this country. Why the hell isn't that our main objective, securing the border of our country, sir?"

Colonel Leadbetter knew the soldier who just called out was right, so he did not bother to see who yelled out at him as he added to his words. "You got that right trooper, but if you're referring to the border with Mexico, you're only half right soldier. We have other borders in the States that must be secured. We must secure the entire Peninsular of Florida, especially securing the over one hundred little Islands that make up the Florida Keys from waterside invasions by boats into our country, ferrying all sorts of troublemakers to the States. We've suffered two terrorist cells that successfully made it to the United States, both groups entered through the damn waters surrounding the Islands of the Florida Keys.

"One fucking cell attacked the damn Indian Point Nuclear Power Plant up there in New York State. The second terrorist cell tried to hit the Miami Sea Port before we put a quick end to their damn dream of harming the United States and her civilians. By sheer dumb luck might I add, we had a few of our specialized troops who just happened to intercept the followers of Islam as they inserted on the Island of Marathon in the Keys. Those elite troops trailed the small group of Muslim terrorists up to fucking Miami area where they got the drop on the fucking group of extremists, and you know the outcome of that engagement." Colonel

Leadbetter turned and gave Captain Walker a quick glance, he and a few soldiers staying or living on Marathon, were the troops who intercepted and stopped the terrorists that made it into the United States from Cuba. When Walker nodded to recognize the Colonel's look he went on with his words.

"We have to also secure the West Coast of California from boats ferrying illegals and possible Islamic radicals into our country. We have to defend ourselves against boatloads of fucking drugs, before we have to deal with another group of fricking terrorists making it to our damn shore using that route. There are many other threats and ways for the damn terrorists to get into the United States undetected, so they can hit us, is forcing us to run all over our country trying to keep a fucking handle on the lousy cocksuckers. That's another reason for our being called back to base to learn this urban warfare training crap. So, we can keep a lid on any shit a terrorist cell might cause in the United States, before they have a change to pull it off against us…"

"Say, Colonel, why the hell don't we just bomb the shit outta any stinking host nations we suspect are harboring and giving terrorists a safe stinking haven to operate from, sir? So, we don't get to put any boots on the fucking ground and in harm's way, sir." A second soldier called out while interrupting the Colonel briefing.

This time the Colonel got angry because he did not want this briefing to break down to where the soldiers just call out their gripes and stop him from getting his message across to them. Colonel Leadbetter drew in air and then he bellowed at his troops. "Look here you pack of assholes, I gave the first soldier who called out a fucking break and what do I find? I have a second one of you ball sacks calling out without requesting permission to speak first. I'm warning you shitbirds, if another one of you people tries to call out whatever the hell's bugging his or her ass. A lot of your troops will rule the fucking day your papa's ever porked your mamas. I'm running this fucking briefing, and you're here to listen and absorb every damn word I say and try and learn from my instructions, and obey my orders as issued to you shit sacks."

Taking another break, he walked halfway down the front line of the assembled troops as he quickly formulated the rest of his thoughts. When he had them organized, he stopped in front of Walker, standing at the head of the formation of troops and barked at them.

"The only reason you damn Squids weren't called back to base before this time. Is because of the sorry ass shape our damn Intel people are in. They're more screwed up than you jerks who think you're Tier One killers. From the damn scuttlebutt I picked up about our damn Intelligence Communities, most of the overseas Agents are sticking their damn heads in the sand trying to protect themselves. Mainly because they're fearful they might get called before Congress and have their asses grilled by the supposed intelligent people in open secessions.

"It's not the grilling the damn Agents are so concerned with. They're more concerned about their damn identities being compromised by some sack of shit news reporter taking a picture of them, and then posting it in their rag newspaper. I remember what my father once told me about nosy ass reporters. He said this and it's a truism worthy of note by you pack of dumb ass Squids, 'Don't fear the enemy, because they can only destroy your life. Fear the damn media because they'll destroy your honor and reputation at all costs'.

"Enough of this bullshit for Pete's sake, we understand the condition this Administration has placed the Security and Intelligence Agencies of our country in. It's going to take far more than a few years until our damn Intel Communities are back to operating up to snuff and tracking the shits, they have to keep their damn eyes glued on around the world, and in the States. But that's the only reason you weren't pulled back on base for this new training crap you're about to engage in. Well shit sacks, this training crap's going to cover a whole mess of other shit, some of it new to you people and a lot of it old hat, and we have already studied it to hell and back. But we're going to go over it again and even again, until I'm damn certain you people know this shit like the back of your damn hands.

"Regard the new crap you're being trained in as a refresher course for your asses. As you can see, we have three buildings constructed on site. One is a ground floor structure, the second one is a two-story building, and the third structure is a four-story construction that has fifteen rooms on each floor. That's to simulate a compromised office building you'll have to work through during this new training crap, people. We have a half a mile stretch of area with twelve smaller buildings constructed on each side of the damn supposed road. We tried to cover about any possible situation you might stumble across during an urban situation you're set out on to control, or for any nation who requests help from our country.

"The half mile stretch we constructed for this training course once you're allowed to work on the damn thing. Will have groups of our people dressed in different kinds of garb, the first scenario on the strip we call the half mile stretch of death. This area will have two separate groups of our soldiers dressed like wild ass acting A-rabs, or any other nation's crap having trouble with rebels or insurgents. The acting soldiers will have instructions to threateningly confront you people when you first enter the damn area. I'm warning you people, they'll try and make you react violently against their actions and threats. How you people react against a supposed irate group of civilians with a hardon for your ass will be your grade for the exercise.

"If any of you fucking asses fail on the training courses too many times, you'll be dropped from the Unit, and make no bones about it, people. Your failures will be sent back to wherever the hell you came from before your butts invaded my beloved base and Specialized Units. I have a second warning for you fucking pack of armatures. One group of supposed A-rabs harassing your asses might have a simulated detonation vest strapped on their asses. It'll be up to you and your damn spotters to detect these slugs before the carrier has a chance to detonate the simulated vest against your troops.

"If this fucking detonation is allowed to take place against your invading troops, those troops entering the training area will be classified as KIA! (Killed In Action) Believe me, if any of you slobs end up classified as a KIA in any of these training scenarios. You assholes, will wish to the good Lord above that you were truly killed in fucking action, by the time I'm done with your stinking asses. Enough of this shit for the time being, we'll continue with the fucking briefing once you Squids had a chance to chow down for breakfast. That's it for now, break ranks and reassembly on the fucking grinder at exactly Zero Eight Ten Hundred Hours, so we can continue with the special training of you Squids. Dismissed!"

CHAPTER SIX

WEDNESDAYJANUARY 5th, 2011 ZERO EIGHT
TEN HUNDRED HOURS, CAMP LEJEUNE,
JACKSONVILLE, NORTH CAROLINA

Colonel Bruce Leadbetter was standing on the tarmac of the massive training grinder, as the specialized troops rushed back from the mess hall to assemble before him. They went quickly in formation and assumed an attention stance at the time allotted, and the Colonel was pleased, but he was not going to say so to the troops. As usual, Captain Robert Walker was at the head of the formation, and he saluted the Colonel, and he returned the salute then barked. "At ease!"

The soldiers groaned as they placed their hands behind their backs and relaxed.

"It's a good thing you pack of stinking Squids got back here at the time ordered, because I would've had all fucking stragglers shot on general principals. Okay boys and girls, back to what I was saying before I allowed you people to eat at the government's expense. That one half a mile strip of structures is going to be the best training strip you'll ever step foot on, drive through, or try to discover hiding terrorists or insurgents inside the structures or hiding in the rubble piled up by the sides of the street, or control a civilian unrest situation.

"When you people are driving through the area, you'll come under attack by simulated car bombs, IED's, (Improvised Explosive Devices) ambushes involving RPG's (Rocket Propelled Grenades) and heavy weapons fire. Any hell you might stumble in while on a true operation involving a pack of irate civilians, terrorists, or enemy combatants, will be thrown at you Squids anytime you're working this strip. Why the hell am I wasting my fucking time trying to explain this crap to you Squids, everyone mounts up and follow my ass."

With that said, the Commander led the formation of specialized troops onto the training area. The elite soldiers examined the structures and the one they were most interested in, was the four-story building. The Colonel led the soldiers into the building, and it looked remarkably like a modern-day office building. Complete with rows of file cabinets and desks and cardboard computers setup in many rooms. On the third floor the soldiers saw a different setup with larger rooms laid out. The Mutt always on the hunt to make a fool of himself, noticed a door marked in red and charged at it and crashed into the door with Walker calling after him to stop. The door flung opened, and the Mutt fell three floors to the ground.

Colonel Leadbetter cursed as the Mutt disappeared from his view, and Walker charged down the stairs two at a time to check on his condition and make certain he did not get seriously hurt on the fall. The rest of Walker's troops rushed behind him. The young Captain was the first one to reach the Mutt still lying on the ground, and he was trying to get his breathing under control. His chest was killing him, and his knee was twisted and hurting bad, not to mention his back hurting him along with his pride.

Walker grabbed the Mutt by the collar of his uniform and pulled him up to a seated position. Then he snapped angrily at him. "Hey stupid, I want you to count backwards from ten while looking me in the eyes, asshole."

The Mutt opened his eyes and winced in pain as he moved his left leg, and then he fired back at his friend. "Okay Walker I admit it, I'm fucking drunk, man."

"What the fuck are you talking about, asshole? Whatdaya mean you're fucking drunk, stupid?" Walker snapped at his friend.

"Why the fuck are you asking me to count backwards from ten fur? The last time I was told to do that shit was by some stinking cop who wanted to check and see if I was fucking drunk, man." The Mutt smirked at Walker.

Colonel Leadbetter stood over Walker's shoulder, and the moment he realized his trooper was alright, he snarled at the downed soldier. "What the hell do you have for fucking brains in that damn noggin of yours,

Squid? You aren't smart enough to recognize the reason for a red painted door inside a building is to signify a damn fire door, and a way out of the structure, stupid. The door was painted red so none of you flying squirrels opened the damn thing and fell out of the damn building on your bone dome. We weren't going to construct a damn fire escape ladder for you asses to employ. I see we should've painted not an EXIT on the damn thing, or do not enter so no assholes like you did what you just done, stupid.

The irate Colonel turned to the other soldiers gathered around their fellow injured trooper and snarled at them. "You see; therefore, I keep telling you fucks you have to keep your stinking heads on a fucking swivel at all times, and your eyes opened when you're entering an unsecured building. Anything can happen to you asses by just plowing through a door that could put your asses in deep shit and compromising the rest of the troops or even the damn mission."

Walker grinned at the Mutt as he added to his worried words. "Here stupid, let me help you to your feet."

"What, I'm not on my fucking feet?" The Mutt asked, trying to be funny.

"You are flaming asshole, get back on your damn feet before I put my size eleven boot up your ass, mister. Then we'll have to wait for your morning constitutional to get my damn foot out of your backside, stupid. If I see you or any of you other people plowing through another fucking door like this lunatic just did. The enemy will be the least of your fucking problems you people will have to contend with while on a training or operation, dammit." Colonel Leadbetter growled at the group of concerned soldiers as he watched the Mutt painfully struggle to his feet. He realized the soldier was hurting so he got off his ass and allowed him some time to get back to one hundred percent as he led the rest of the troops through the half mile training strip.

Blind Date, the Mutt's girlfriend, walked up behind him and grumbled in disgust as she shoved him forward with her forearm. "So, this is man who was touched by divinity huh, that thought makes me laugh out loud, mista. I must admit it stupid American soldier. You made a first-class asshole of yourself with that stupid move inside the training building. How you get so stupid as Colonel say you are, lover?"

The Mutt turned to his lady and mumbled at her. "And the fucking hits just keep on coming? You know it's hard to kiss the stinking lips at night that has chewed on my fucking ass all day. I hate every bone in your body but mine."

Blind Date puckered her lips up sexily and made like she was kissing the Mutt.

The soldiers laughed at the Mutt's remark to Blind Date. But that ended when the fuming Colonel looked over his shoulder and barked savagely at the other troops. "Enough screwing around pissants, the fucking Mutt's working against the rotation of the damn planet. This shit is important and as you shitbirds saw already. Anything can happen to your dopey asses, and this is exactly why we're increasing your damn training in this manner. Pay attention or you'll live long enough to regret screwing around like you jerks are doing."

When the Mutt was back on his feet, he complained to Walker making certain his friend was not badly hurt. "Man, I think I mighta popped a fucking testicle on that stinking move, man."

"You wanna go on sick call?" Walker asked the hurting soldier.

"That's all I gotta do and give the stinking Colonel more fricking ammunition to get on my ass about, man." The Mutt griped as he stretched his back to get the kinks out of it.

"Forget that shit Captain. That stupid jerk isn't going on sick call, because the only sick call he'll get from my ass is being stood before a wall, and twelve soldiers using his sagging ass for target practice, Walker. Also, it's Sir Colonel Sir to you, buster. I'm demanding respect from the lot of you fucking Squids or else. Or some of you damn pukes disrespecting my ass are going to find yourselves being carried by six of your closest fucking friends by the damn handles of your coffin, you two." Colonel Leadbetter grumbled angrily at the elite group of specialized soldiers standing behind him.

Walker looked down the strip of buildings and it immediately reminded him of the streets of Iraq in the town of ar-Ramadi that he walked through on his last mission. In his mind's eye he was able to see the town, and terrible conditions he faced there. He remembered how the hot wind as jagged as broken glass wailed incisively across the barren landscape of the vast desert, and the unpaved roads of the small Iraqi town. His thoughts were interrupted as the soldiers moved a little deeper onto the makeshift training field.

The half mile strip was a pure work of genius for training purposes, the more Leadbetter pointed out to Walker and the other soldiers, the more impressed they became with the training area and setup. The Colonel showed the soldiers some of the pyrotechnics set in place to simulate different forms of weapon fire or explosions employed against them while working on the strip. Some of the explosives were shaped and placed to represent RPG rounds going off against them. Other explosives were set up to simulate an IED explosive charge, and more worked as if machine guns were being fired at the troops working on the training strip.

With each step deeper Walker took in the training area, he detected at least two different places where an enemy attacker could easily hide, and setup an ambush against his troops, when they worked down the strip. He observed several other places where he would assign a sniper to roost, to protect his troops as they moved deeper into the training area. By the time the soldiers made it through the half mile strip of exercise area, they were thoroughly impressed by the setup. The crafty Colonel was not done with the troops yet, and he grumbled at them as they gathered around their Commander to see where they were going next on the training area.

"Okay you damn pansy ass so called killers elites. I'm warning the lot of ya, once I get your lazy asses out on this fucking training sector for your first go round with this damn program. You people are going to be worked like you have never been worked before in your wasted lives. We're going to be putting in twelve to fifteen fucking hours a day, continually working this damn program to death, until we understand every possible threatening area the enemy can possibly throw at us, and when you're not out on the field sweating your damn asses off. You people will find your asses stuffed inside the damn classrooms going over other different attack and defense scenarios, until you'll be able to handle anything thrown at your asses out in the field, and save you wasted lives in the process.

"You pack of god damn criminals are going to learn the proper way to conduct our Urban Combat Operations, people. Then you're going to learn how to better avoid most civilian casualties, and if you pukes end up with non-combatant wounded on a mission. You people will learn how to administer first aide to the wounded, until real medical assistance gets on the scene. You'll pick up the accepted ways of dealing with guerrilla warfare operating aimed against you, and how to break the backs of any shits trying to attack you Squids in the field.

"You shits will be taught the proper way how to handle most humanitarian crisis's that might develop while on a mission. You'll further learn how to organize humanitarian aid to keep the misery out of the non-combatant's ranks, if at all possible, when engaging enemy actors in an urban environmental crisis. Yeah, I know and before any of you pukes start to cry in the breast milk. I told you when you first started showing up on my beloved base that these shits serious. You, lazy ass gombas will know what you're doing at all times, by the time I'm done with you asses and tits, and that much I can promise you to flame assholes."

The Colonel took a quick break to see if any troops had some questions for him. When no one asked to speak, he got on his troops again. "Okay people, I have a question to ask you guys and I want fucking answers, and don't wait to be called on to speak out. Shout out your damn response if you know the answers to my fucking questions, Squids. What are the fucking reasons you people decided to become soldiers in my Marine Corps?"

One trooper called out. "A soldier fights not because he hates what's standing in front of him, sir. He fights because of what's standing behind him…"

"What's standing behind you trooper?" The Colonel bellowed at the talker.

"My God, my country, my family and all things I love and respect, Colonel Leadbetter."

"Colonel, 'those who hammer their fucking weapons into plows will find themselves plowing for those who don't, sir." This remark from one of the soldiers got a bunch of laughs.

"The reason a soldier carries a gun is because a cop's too heavy to lug around."

More laughs as the soldiers started to get into it now, as a third soldier called out.

"If you find your ass in a fair fight then your military tactics suck the big one, Colonel."

"Colonel Leadbetter, a soldier doesn't shoot fast unless he can shoot good."

"Keep firing and make your fucking attackers force to advance through a hail of stinking bullets. You might be killed in the action with your own stinking weapon. But your attacker will have to beat you to death with an empty weapon, sir." A female warrior called out from the sloppy formation of soldiers, as some of the women entered the bantering.

"Hope is the mother of desperation, winning is the mother of confidence…"

Colonel Leadbetter held his hands in the air and then he bellowed at his troops again. "Okay people, I should've known better than to allow you damn Squids to just call out like this. We're starting to get well off the damn mark I was trying to make with you people when we first started this conversation, dammit. But I'm pleased to see the confidence you people are displaying, Squids. I want you to demonstrate to the world there is no better friend, nor worse enemy than a fucking United States Marine. Well, I'm beat and I'm going to tell you what I'm going to do.

"I'm going to call an early end of this day's instructional experience. Tomorrow morning at Zero, Five Hundred Hours, things will be much different I assure all of you screaming squirrels. There'll be no mercy displayed from my ass once we start to train, and I'll expect no one asking for mercy. Hell starts at exactly Zero Five Hundred Hours. As of this time, you people are dismissed to do whatever the hell you people do, to help you Squids survive another fucking day in my Corps. Walker!" The Commander snapped as he leveled his hot gaze at him.

"Yes, Sir Colonel Leadbetter." Walker replied as he snapped to attention and saluted.

"I'm impressed Walker, I didn't think you remembered how to respect your Commander. Walker, when you return to barracks, you'll find a new group of troops who'll joint your pack of misfits and criminals. These soldiers are good troops, I'm certain three days with your pack of damn lunatics will corrupt them good and proper, mister. Then these unsuspecting troops will be as wasted as the rest of your people are, mister. Anyway, the soldiers are your assigned EODT or Explosive Ordnance Disposal Team. I must admit Walker, you should've had an EOD team working with your troops from the get-go, but that deficiency has been corrected as of today. When you get to these troops, you'll get them up to speed on what they'll be facing with this damn new training crap and your Unit. You're dismissed so get the hell out of my sight before I decide to run a program just to punish you damn Squids."

That was all the Colonel had to say and the soldiers disappeared. Walker rushed to his barracks because he wanted to meet the new troops and see what they looked like, and if they were good enough to link up with his soldiers. He plowed into the barracks and spotted nine new soldiers waiting to see him. He walked past them as if he did not see them, and flung the door to his private quarters open, and walked into the room and barked at the FnG's. (Fucking new Guys) "You new guys betta get your stinking asses in here on the double quick if you know what's good for ya!"

The group of explosive experts followed Walker in the room, and a few other soldiers usually around him, followed the new troops in. The nine troopers took an attention stance and waited for the captain to address them. He cautiously eyed each one of them and when he felt he picked out the head cheese of the group, he barked at the man.

"Well buster who the fuck are you? What's your expertise, trooper!"

"Captain Walker Sir, I'm Colonel Frank Brettel, and I'm in command of this EOD Team, sir. I can defuse any hard-shell round without having it go off in my face I'm that good at my profession, sir."

Walker wanted to straighten this soldier out from the get-go, and he bitched at him angrily. "You only think you're in command of this fucking team, mister. That shit ended when you people walked through those damn doors into this barracks. First off Colonel don't expect to be saluted, or respected as an officer in this Unit, sir. We're all one here and that's all the damn respect you'll ever receive from any of us…"

"Excuse me Captain Walker, I've already been briefed by Command on how oddly this specialized unit's structured, and I accepted the fact sir. Captain…"

This time Walker angrily interrupted the older Colonel. "Colonel Brettel, if it's like you just said, and you were briefed about my Unit in advance. Then you know betta than to interrupt my ass if you wanna remain in one piece and on my good side. I'll give you this one Colonel Brettel, don't allow it to happen again, sir." Even though the Colonel outranked Walker, he was the accepted Commander of the Unit when Colonel Leadbetter was not working with the troops.

"Yes, Sir Captain Walker Sir, it's as you ordered, sir." The Colonel replied as he sharpened up his attention stance.

Walker cautiously eyed the new troops for a long second, and then he grumbled at the group. "Okay, I want you people to identify yourselves to my ass, where you came from, and any handles that might come with ya. Begin one after the uther."

The Colonel added for Walker and the other troopers gathered in the office, knowledge. "Captain, my handle is Gun Powder, and I work with all types of explosive devices, sir."

Walker ignored the fine-looking officer as he glared at the soldier standing next to him and waited for him to offer what he was about. "Captain Walker, I'm Major Abraham Robinowitz, and I'm on special loan to the United States from the Israeli Special Forces, the Shayetet Thirteen Unit to be exact, sir. Which is the equivalent to America's SEAL Team sir, and I was attached to the Israeli Foreign Affairs Committee that gave me the allowance to come to the United States. I'm an expert at disarming all sorts of munitions and my handle is Shadow."

Walker did not say a word back to this soldier as he digested what he just offered him, and he allowed a disgusted look to cross his eyes as he looked at the next soldier standing in the line. "Captain Walker Sir, I'm Colonel Jean Tauvy sir, and I'm on special loan to the United States from the Twenty Second Royal Mounted Regiment of Canada, sir. My handle is Snow Ball for the obvious reason, Captain."

Walker smiled as he looked at the next soldier in line.

"Captain Walker Sir, there's nothing fancy about my ass, sir. I'm Sergeant Gregory Bradford from the Army, no special hot shot branch either, sir. The Army head cheeses keep moving me around to suit their own fucking needs, sir. My handle is Moocher, and anything that can explode I can fucking defuse it safely, sir."

Again, Walker smiled, this time more to himself than at a soldier who was just speaking to him, as he turned to the remaining troops in the line and barked at them in a warning tone. "I know you three pukes already, so give me a fucking name."

"Isn't that something your mother shoulda done for you, sir? I mean give you a fucking name, Captain Walker." One of the soldiers smirked as he tried to fit in with the unit.

"Hey that was funny, real fucking funny pal. If I wasn't in such a bad fucking mood, I mighta even laugh a little over it, puke. Give me your fucking name or I'll bounce you the fuck outta here so damn quick your stinking skivvies will have a hard time with trying to keep up with your fricking ass, wiseguy." Walker growled at the new trooper.

"Yes, Sir Captain Walker. I'm Sergeant Neil Albanese, I'm from the First Marine Division Third Brigade. My handle's Shakes because I shake before working on an explosive device. Captain once I touch the damn weapon, all shaking stops and I get right down to business, sir. The soldier to my left is Sergeant Carl Butterman, from the First Marine Division, Third Brigade, and we worked together since linking up about a year and a half ago, sir.

"Most of our work was carried out in the nation of Iraq, Captain. We were part of the first unit EODs sent over to that damn nation and were employed to disarm the countless numbers of IED's our troops were constantly tangling with, sir. Captain, his moniker's Screw Loose, because you must have a fucking screw loose to be in our line of work, sir. Captain Walker, the third soldier in line is Sergeant Robert Marchman. His tag name's Left Foot because he's always screwing up thing with our outfit. All three of us come from the same unit in the service, I keep warning him he can't keep screwing up in our line of work like he keeps doing and expect to live long enuf to retire from the service. Err…, I'm afraid I don't recognize the other soldier in line sir, I have no idea who she might be, Captain." Albanese replied as he relaxed when he noticed Walker's face lighten up.

He was right he did know the three soldiers as he turned to the female soldier. She was the last trooper of the EOD team, and he locked her in his harsh stare. "Well sister, you gonna make me ask ya, or are you gonna tell me who the hell you are, and where you come from?"

The female EOD trooper replied with a snap in her voice. "Captain Walker Sir, I'm Sergeant Irene Casillas from Third Army Division, Fifth Brigade, A Company. My handle is Double Buddle and I'm proud of the name my fellow troops branded me, sir." As if to strengthen her point, she wiggled her chest and made her ample breasts sway under her shirt.

"Yeah, little sister, I see the tag works well with your ass. Okay, yeah, right, listen up you FnGs. As of this time, there's no more room in this barracks fur ya. So, you people are gonna hafta make your asses comfortable in Barracks One, Nine. That's the barracks right next door to this one, and the other troops are in that barracks. Make sure you see the soldier called Mother Flanagan. He'll make certain you settle in. Okay, get outta my quarters so I can speak to the rest of the pukes behind your backs. Dismissed!" Walker grumbled as he picked up a report and read it while ignoring the new soldiers leaving his quarters. The nine soldiers snapped to attention and ripped off a salute. Walker ignored the soldiers as he continued reading the report.

The Mutt moved up until he stood by the Colonel who bragged he was in command of the EOD team, and he mumbled at the military officer. "Hey Colonel, you puke betta get going before you piss off the captain, sir."

The EOD team moved out without another word from Walker's quarters, and they headed for their assigned barracks. The moment the EOD team was out of his office, the other troopers relaxed as a few of them lit up smokes.

THURSDAY, JANUARY 6th, 2011. ZERO
FIVE HUNDRED HOURS,
CAMP LEJEUNE NORTH CAROLINA

The start of the first day of the new training program was as Colonel Leadbetter warned the soldiers. By the end of the day, every soldier from the outfit poured themselves into their barracks. They complained of being exhausted and suffering from countless little nicks, cuts, and bruises they received in their first full day of training secession. Walker dragged himself into his quarters, and the usual soldiers at his side followed him in the room. When he plopped down in the chair, the gripes started in earnest.

"Man, what the fuck do you call that shit we were just fucking put through by the Colonel and his fucking henchmen? I think the lousy sonofabitch was outright trying to kill us off on that training field." The Mutt grumbled as he lit up a cigarette and leaned against the wall of Walker's office and blew the smoke over his head.

"I don't know about you dog man, but I call it training, buster." Walker snapped, upset that Mutt was bellyaching about their new training program.

"Man, Walker what's up your ass all of a sudden?" The Mutt retorted.

"Hey, pal you're a man waiting to happen. I'll tell you what the hell is up to my fucking ass, buddy. If you think today's training secession was tough on your ass. Wait until we get into this mess and start to work it over. I looked at the future training program, and what I read about it scared the shit out my ass. So, I can only imagine what the program is gonna do to the rest of you guys. The Colonel wasn't joking 'bout putting our asses through the stinking ringer on this new damn training crap. We're in for more hell than a little bit I tell ya, man." Walker fired at the Mutt and other troopers as he held them in his gaze.

"You know something Walker I know we're supposed to be here to learn these new urban tactics crap. But I've been picking up the feeling we're training to be some sorta fucking backup for some other stinking Units. Mind you I don't mind being the backup for any other Units, man. I always believed we were the tip of the stinking spear, and since when does the tip of the spear get held in reserve as a fucking backup for some other Unit of soldiers. Another thing I wanna get offa my stinking chest now we're speaking 'bout this crap. If we're gonna pull backup for some uther Unit that Unit betta be part of the JSOC. Or the uther soldiers can suck my dick and go off marching through the sand on their own, man. I don't do backup for some stinking conventional soldiers for nuthin." The Mutt griped as he stared at Walker angrily.

"Well dog man, you picked that shit up all by your little old self, huh? Let me set the record straight for your stinking ass, and the rest of these crybabies with ya. Mutt, if we pull the card from the bottom of the deck, and it tells us to run security for anuther Unit then that's what we'll fucking do. Whether those uther stinking soldiers happen to belong to the Special Forces or are some stinking conventional soldiers as you just put it, buddy. You betta remember something right here and now, buddy. If any soldiers wearing our stinking colors, or the colors of our allies, we'll support them like we do any uther soldiers from our Unit. Or I'm gonna take numbers and heads from you pukes, if I pick up any hesitation with our assisting any uther stinking Units no matter where the fuck they come from or what they are up to." Walker looked hard and long at his friend to drive the point home.

"Fuck you Walker, that's not what I meant by my bitch in the least, man. You know damn well if any of our stinking people get trapped in a load of shit. I'm gonna stick my nose in it with them. I just brought up the fact I was getting the feeling we're being trained to be some sorta stinking backup for uther troops, that's all. I wanted to see if the uther guys were picking up the same feeling I was getting." The Mutt shot back at Walker.

"Hey man, come to think of it, the stinking Mutt's right, Walker. What was with that last bit of training shit, where we split up and half of us did a drop back and ran as backup for the uther soldiers who entered the building we were supposed to attack?" The dangerous soldier branded Ghost (Sergeant Walter Casper) bitched hotly at Walker.

"I see I'm gonna have some fucking trouble from your ass now too, buster. I don't know what the fuck the friggin Colonel has in the back of his stinking mind, all I know is if he barks, we fucking jump. You betta jump as high as you can, or he's gonna be out for fucking blood, your blood asshole, and…" Walker's words were cut off by the Ghost.

"Man, I like the way you walked your stinking ass around the feeling we've been picking up on this new training crap, Walker. I wanna see if you were getting the same feeling the stinking Mutt, me, and the rest of us guys have."

"If it'll set your mind at ease, yes, I picked up the same feeling, and I've been operating under orders from the Colonel to train you Eagles in what the fuck you're bitching at me over…"

"Why is that Walker?" The Mutt grumbled as he displayed interest now.

"I haven't the foggiest fucking idea why the stinking Colonel wanted to train our asses in this possible backup shit. Maybe he feels we're starting to get away from the conventional ways the regular armed services operate, and he wants to get us back into the swing of things with the uther services. How the fuck do I know, the Colonel doesn't tell me everything he has on his stinking mind." Walker complained at the other soldiers hanging on his every word.

"Hey man, don't give me any of that fricking shit, man! The stinking hot shot Colonel clues you in on every fucking thing that goes down around here, and what kinda fucking training we gotta go through." Buckethead grumbled at Walker.

Walker glared angrily at the huge soldier without responding to his gripe.

"Hey Walker, the big man's right. Why don't you fucking level with us and tell us what the fuck's coming down the damn chute on us, man. I kinda like to know what's in front of my ass so I know what I gotta do 'bout it, Homes." Neck offered as he got into the conversation.

"Look, I'm fucking leveling with you pack of lunatics. If I knew why the fuck the Colonel was putting us through this backup shit, I'd let you people know immediately. I don't know what he's up to, and that's that. Okay, I'll do this much for you stinking crybabies. The first chance I get, I'll bring up your concerns to the Colonel, and see if he clues me in on what's really going on with this training crap. That's the best I can do for you guys. Mutt, you were with me when the Colonel told us we might be back up for uther stinking soldiers on a possible OP, so you know as much as I do about this shit." Walker shrugged at the soldier.

THE PENTAGON, THE CHAIRMAN OF
THE JOINT CHIEFS OF STAFF,
THURSDAY, JANUARY 6th, 2011, ZERO,
SEVEN THIRTY HOURS EST.

The Chairman of the Joint Chiefs of Staff's office was a beehive of activity because for the first time since the Nine, One, One attacks in New York City Twin Towers and the Pentagon. There was strong evidence that Usama bin Laden was located hiding in Pakistan. The powerful General was gathering up his documents for the special briefing called for by the President of the United States ordered for Zero Nine Hundred Hours, it was scheduled for a select few people.

The President ordered fewer people to know of this upcoming operation to take bin Laden as prisoner or kill him. The CIA Director informed General White he would meet him at the White House. The other people ordered to attend the briefing were the Deputy National Security Advisor, National Security Advisor and Secretary of State and Vice President. Also attending the meeting was Vice Admiral William Cantor, SiC, Second in

Command of the troops from the Joint Special Operations Command or JSOC, chosen to run this operation. No one else was considered in the loop for such an important operation.

General White was in command of the JSOC. His troops from the Rapid Response Forces were picked to run support for the mission controlled by soldiers from the Red Cell Unit. That was why the Vice Admiral was called in for the meeting.

The General charged out of his office after gathering up the reports he needed. He rushed by his secretary who smiled as he ran out of the office. He came out the north door of the Pentagon building and jumped into his waiting staff car. Without looking at his driver, he growled. "Phil, get my ass over to the damn White House ten minutes ago. You'll remain on duty until I completed my meeting with the President and his people, son."

"Yes, Sir General White, I'll wait with the car until you concluded your meeting, sir." His driver replied, proud he was driving the General around Washington.

General White was out of the car before the Lieutenant finished speaking. He rushed to the main doors of the building and was immediately greeted by a young White House aide, who ushered him through the hallway to the Oval Office. He entered the room and nodded politely to everyone seated in the room, and the President snapped when he laid eyes on him.

"Please don't take a seat General White. I want you to open this meeting."

"Yes Sir Mr. President, may I start off by saying how much of a pleasure it is for me to address such elite leaders of our country, sir. Mr. President, the latest information we gathered on our target, makes me believe over sixty percent that the 'Pacer' spotted by the watcher Director Raincloud installed in Abbottadad. The Pacer has also been picked up by our RO-170 Sentinel Stealth Bat drone, which is the latest drone in her class, seven times in the past two months, is more than likely bin Laden, sir. Believing the Pacer is bin Laden, I feel it's an absolute must operation to carry out by the JSOC SEAL Team. Sixty percent makes the call a must to do, sir."

"Excuse me General White you're that certain this Pacer is bin Laden, sir?"

"A sixty percent certainty makes it an almost positive identification of the lousy murderer, sir. Even if the Pacer isn't bin Laden, we still must go in there to make certain one way or the other if it's him or not, sir. This is the closest we've ever been to the man since Tora Bora, Mr. President. We have to operate under the assumption that the spotted Pacer is bin Laden, and we have made certain and take him out, sir. We can't take the chance of losing him again. I see this man in my damn sleep, sir."

"Okay General White, you convinced me we have to do something about this Pacer fellow. What's the next step, sir?" The President asked as he held the General in his stare.

"With all due respect Mr. President, I believe it's time to start the insertion teams on their specialized training that'll ensure the success of the operation against the Pacer. This training will be carried out by the teams making a carbon copy of the structure to be invaded by the insertion troops. Along with the complete layout of the outside structures and courtyards the inserted teams must work through, to get at our target and take him into custody or kill him, sir. The Vice Admiral will see to it his soldiers are well prepared before they set out on the mission, Mr. President…"

"What about your group of high-priced soldiers I was informed of General White? Why did you decide to use the SEAL Team soldiers instead of your Rapid Response troops?" The President fired at his officer, instantly angering the General.

"With all due respect Mr. President, it was decided to employ the outstanding services of the well-regarded SEAL Team Six soldiers for this operation, because they're better suited for this type of hard-hitting operation, sir. The reason for this is because in the rapid response soldiers, we have a good mixture of troops from other countries mixed in with troops from the United States, and for security and communication situations. Besides, we can't allow any foreign soldiers to be part of this operation, and possibly bring the anger of the terrorist organization down on their country, because their soldiers were part of, and assisted our troops in hunting down and either capturing or killing this bastard, sir. It was decided for this reason to employ the special SEAL Team soldiers, Mr. President."

"I guess I'll give you that one General White. How much time will be needed by these troops training before we can begin the operation against the so-called Pacer fellow? How do we keep our eye on the Pacer until we're ready to go after him? Another question for you General White, what happens if our target leaves the location, we discovered him staying at? What do we do if he discovers we're on to him, or he flatly decides to leave the area for who knows what reason, and we lose him in his shuffle, General White?" The President asked as he continued to hold the military officer in his angry gaze.

"We discussed all the what ifs until we were blue in the face, Mr. President. If the Pacer decides to leave the area for any reason, Director Raincloud's watcher will notify us immediately of his movements, sir. We'll either respond with a drone or B-2 bomber strike on the subject, sir. The watcher's eyes are not the only ones we have in the area in concern. The area is being blanketed by three RO-170 drones twenty-four seven, keeping the compound under constant observation both day and night under any weather conditions. If the subject moves, we'll know about it, and we'll react accordingly, Mr. President. Sir, the Vice Admiral is in a better position to inform you on the amount of time his troops will need, before they're good to go after the Pacer." General White offered at the displeased American Leader.

The President shifted his eyes away from the General and allowed them to rest on the Vice Admiral who replied to the moment the President looked at him. "Mr. President, my troops will need up to six months before they'll know the landscape and structure like the backs of their hands, sir. They'll need this amount of time to decide on how to attack the structure, sir. That much time will ensure the success of the operation, and the taking out of the subject successfully one way or the other, Mr. President."

"Very good Vice Admiral Cantor, I feel it's better if we take out the subject than to try and take him a prisoner, sir." The President replied to the Naval Commander.

Director Raincloud moved in his chair, and instantly drew the President's attention and he snap at the Director. "Director Raincloud, do you have a problem with anything being offered?"

"Yes, I do Mr. President." The Director replied as he rose and then began speaking again. "Mr. President, I for one would much rather take bin Laden a prisoner, sir. The reasons for this request are as follows. Think of the wealth of information we could gleam from this one man, if we had a half a chance to question him…"

"You want to question him how Director Raincloud, through enhanced interrogations, sir? You know how I feel about those terrible tactics." The President fired off at the Director.

"By any means necessary I'd employ in an interrogation of this man, Mr. President. If we get the information, we need to protect our citizens and interests in the States and aboard, sir. We haven't taken prisoners since we decided to lean heavily on drones taking out our enemy, Mr. President. We have no new information about the al-Qaeda terrorist organization or their ongoing operations, sir. The only information we're relying on, is what we've been able to gather through enhanced interrogations of the prisoners still being held at Guantanamo Bay, and quite frankly Mr. President. Most of that information is stagnate and old and unreliable at best. We must take new prisoners to gather more up to date information on the al-Qaeda terrorist network and their operations, sir. We're operating half blind and…"

"Director Raincloud, I told you before I'm tired of all this bellyaching from you and the rest of the Intelligence Communities. With all the money the government pays you intelligence people. I'm afraid you should have no problems with tracking down the intelligence you need, to keep us safe in our country's borders, Director Raincloud." The President snarled at the CIA Director.

Raincloud did the only thing he felt he should do to avoid increasing the anger of the President. He put his head down and did not offer another word. Inside he was fuming.

"Thank you, Director Raincloud. Well, the only thing left to answer is, Admiral Cantor. I believe it's time to assembly your people and get them training to make this operation a success. I guess that about settles what we had to meet for gentlemen. I suggest you get back to what you do to earn your living." Without adding another word, the President rose and stormed out the Oval Office. Leaving the ones ordered to the meeting waiting for the aides to walk them out.

General White walked up to Raincloud and rested his hand lightly on his shoulder and tried to lead him out of the room. It was easy for anyone who looked at the full blood Sioux Native American, to see the man was extremely upset over the way the President just spoke to him.

Director Raincloud had to shake his head to try and clear it before he allowed himself to move. He looked at the General and gave him a weak smile, as he allowed the military officer to guide him out the room. The Director began to speak once he was seated in the General's staff car, and they were heading for the Pentagon. The officer took the time to order the Director's driver to head for his office and wait until they finished the meeting as his driver took the two to the Pentagon in the General's car.

"God dammit John, I can't take the way this President disrespects his Intelligence Communities and our operatives. He acts like he hates the shit out of our asses, for Christ's sake. Doesn't the man realize what we're doing is for the sake of the United States and her civilians, for the love of God? Hell, he has me and many others in the intelligence game, concerned to move a muscle for fear of pissing him off. This guy better realize we're the ones on the front line in our ongoing war against terrorism and these damn terrorist organizations trying to destroy our country." Raincloud looked into the eyes of the General as if he was searching for a response.

"I hear you and agree with your concerns, John. You know for a fact you're never going to get the respect you're searching for from him. The only time you or anyone else working in the intelligence field will get a nod from him is when something works out, and it makes him look good in the eyes of the public. Then he'll say you're doing good work. What can I tell ya? You've been down this same road more than once in your time of service to our country, sir."

"Please, tell me you have a bottle of Rye in your office, General. I need a fucking drink to get this shitty taste out of my mouth, sir." Director Raincloud offered to the military officer.

"Hey, does Howdy Doody have wooden balls? Of course, I have Rye."

They entered the General's office together and shared a drink, even though it was early in the morning. Then General White announced to Director Raincloud he was going to contact Colonel Leadbetter stationed at Camp Lejeune. He was certain Vice Admiral Cantor was in touch with his command by this time, and he was likely ordering his SEAL Teams to start their training programs. He wanted to make certain the Marine Colonel's troops started theirs.

As usual, Sergeant Kirkpatrick was manning the Colonel's office, and he intercepted the General's call. He connected the General with his Commanding Officer.

"Yes, Sir General White, Colonel Leadbetter, sir." He offered as he settled down in his chair so he could hear what the General had to offer.

"Good morning, Colonel Leadbetter, look sir I'm going to make this short and sweet and right to the fucking point for ya, sir. I just finished meeting with the President, and he gave the green light to set Operation Neptune's Spear in motion for all troops involved in this mission. You better get your people working on their training on supporting the troops going on this operation, sir. We have a mission, and your troops are part of it as always, sir." The General snapped into the phone at is lesser officer.

"I'm on it, General White. When do you think the operation will go hot for our troops, sir?" The Colonel asked while trying to gather any information of the operation he could from his Commanding Officer.

"Vice Admiral Cantor was asked the same damn question, and he informed the President he'd need six months before his troops could jump off. That's the timeline, Colonel Leadbetter."

"General White, you give me six months and my people will be ready to support and take over any operations they're involved in, sir." Colonel Leadbetter bragged to the Chairman.

"Skip that bull Colonel, your people will be back up for the main action in this operation, sir. Your troops will be used only if this operation going tits up and our invasion teams are forced to tangle with Opfors. (Opposition Forces, in this case Pakistani troops) Colonel, your troops will be used to stop our Seals from becoming prisoners in that country and nothing more. If our target gets away, or the target is not on site when we come calling. The signal will be buster, and we'll pull our forces out of Pakistan before World War Three breaks out. We're having enough trouble with Afghanistan we sure don't need another war popping off with Pakistan, even though this operation is going to mount to an invasion with military forces against that country, Colonel."

"Hell sir, that pissant of a fucking country wouldn't stand up to our troops for a stinking week, if we go after them hot and heavy, sir." Colonel Leadbetter announced bitterly.

"I know that mister, but you have to understand that Pakistan has seventy to ninety nuclear warheads in their arsenal. In fact, Colonel Leadbetter, few are aware that the town of Abbottadad happens to be one of three storage areas for Pakistan's nuke stockpile. That information adds to the importance of this fucking operation, and why our target is obviously hanging around in this area. It has been brought up to our attention that our target wants this area so if the shit gets hot, his miserable followers could make a raid on the nuke storage facilities at Abbottadad, sir. That way they instantly become a nuclear threat to the rest of the world, Colonel."

"Shit, I see why the heat over this operation, sir. You can count on my troops, General." The Colonel offered after making certain this was a secured line they were speaking over.

"Get it done Colonel Leadbetter, and once this operation is a success, I'll take you out and get you blind stinking drunk, sir." The General offered his lesser officer and then he broke off the secured communication with the Colonel.

For the next five months, the SEAL Team troops from Red Cell, along with the Rapid Response Forces trained both day and night for up to sixteen hours a day. On March 1st, 2011, the troops from both units were transferred out to the city of Jalaladad in Afghanistan. So, the troop could place the final touches on their unending preparing for the assault into Pakistan, to destroy the largest target ever hunted by the United States troops, Usama bin Laden.

On Friday April 29th, 2011, after much soul searching, the President gave the green light to his National Security Advisor for the taking of Usama bin Laden as a prisoner or killing him outright. Instantly the NSA ordered the operation into effect.

CHAPTER SEVEN

SATURDAY, MAY 1st, 2011, SUNDAY, MAY 2nd, 2011
PAKISTANI TIME

On a dark and moonless night, the elite troops from Red Cell set out in four stealth Special Operations helicopters from Jalaladad in Afghanistan. The helicopters were heading on a loose course to avoid any possible tracking radar being emitted for the city of Abbottadad in Pakistan, on the start of Operation Neptune's Spear. Everything was set in place and all lines were drawn and rapidly coming together on their target believed to be still located in Abbottadad, the man Intelligence branded "The Pacer", Usama bin Laden.

Three quarters on their way to the target, the pair of CH-47D Chinook helicopters split away from the other two rotor aircraft, and went to assigned standoff positions, to standby in case their troops were needed in this operation. The troops in the two helicopters were support in case Red Cell troop's operation was discovered by the Pakistan Army, and the soldiers were forced to fight their way out of the city of Abbottadad. The two specialized stealth top secret UH-60L Blackhawk helicopters with twenty-three Seals, one Arab interpreter and one attack and security dog on board, continued directly for Abbottadad and their intended target.

In the United States, the concerned President along with a select number of his staff, cabinet and members of the military and intelligence field watched the live feed coming in from the hovering RO-170 Sentinel bat shaped stealth drone. Along with a secondary feed coming in from three SEAL Team members who had a video system operating from their helmets. As the President watched the live feeds his heart skipped a beat, when the first helicopter crashed inside the compound in Abbottadad.

The second helicopter landed outside the compound without placing any invaders on top of the building believed to be housing bin Laden. Everyone with the President watched the soldier's crash into the buildings, with the President staring at the feed from one soldier.

As the helicopter crashed, Vice Admiral Cantor spoke. "Mr. President, even though we just lost one of the damn helicopters, the operation is still hot and a go, sir. The soldiers will continue and at the completion of the mission, they'll pile into the surviving machine. Or I'll move in a Chinook to pick the troops up. We're employing soldiers and interpreter, and dog on the ground for this mission. So, the soldiers should have no problem loading bin Laden and the soldiers onto the surviving helicopter, sir. Yes, it'll be tight, but they'll do it Mr. President."

"Hold on a second Admiral Cantor, the soldiers are starting to head up to the third floor of the building, sir. Dammit, the troops just killed someone they caught moving on the steps. Look Admiral, did you see that, I'm certain that was bin Laden who just looked over the rail at our soldiers moving up on the staircase. Look at our soldiers go after that person. Damn Admiral, the soldiers just entered the room our target backed into, I think the soldiers have him, sir." The President offered excitedly as he cut off the report from the military officer.

Everyone seated in the Situation Room beneath the White House, leaned forward as one in their chairs as the lead SEAL Team members kicked in the door where the President believed he seen bin Laden back into. They watched as the soldier entered the room and a woman suddenly rushed in front of a tall man. They watched as the soldier fired at the women, striking her high on the leg, and she instantly dropped to the floor and was no longer a threat against the American soldiers. The tall man reacted by raising his hands before his chest, and the lead invading American soldier took it as a conscious attempt to attack him. He fired a short burst of three rounds at the tall man. Two rounds entered the man's chest, and a third entered his head through his left eye and it shattered his skull, sending bone and brain matter staining the wall he was standing before.

The female Secretary of State cried out softly as she put her hands to her mouth. Because this was the first time in her life, she witnessed the violent death of a person in real time.

The President put his finger to his lips to silence everyone in the room, so he could hear what the soldiers were saying to each other. The soldier who shot the man, pulled out a portfolio and compared the dead man's face to photos he carried. Then he had a second soldier lay down on the floor right next to the man to estimate the height of the dead one. After the soldiers examined the dead man, the lead soldier announced and the call came in over the secured radio uplink with the SEAL Operatives on the ground in Abbottadad, directly to the Situation Room. "Geronimo: E-KIA!" (Enemy-Killed in Action) We got him! We got the sonofabitch. The dead man is definitely identified as Usama bin Laden."

The soldier made several quick motions with his weapon, and the other soldiers placed the body in a bag, with the lead soldier ordering them to get the body out to the spooling helicopter. Then the lead soldier ordered the rest of the troopers to fan out and rip the building apart looking for any computers, hard drives, thumb flash drives, cell phones, and any papers with names and possible numbers printed on them, or anything else that might be of use to the intelligence gatherers.

The President and others in the room accustomed to having twelve people and few aides, intensely watched as two soldiers loaded the body of bin Laden on board the helicopter. With the rest of the assault team following closely, all soldiers carrying large bags loaded with intelligence against the al-Qaeda terrorist organization. No one in the room including the President, uttered another word until the helicopter and one of the backup helicopters that came in to pick up the rest of the soldiers who could not fit in the first helicopter, lifted off the ground and the machine headed off for the Afghan/Pakistan borders.

"Well, that's that, all that's left now is for me to address the American public and inform them of what we have successfully carried off today. The most wanted man in the history of the world has finally been brought to justice." The President announced sharply, but he was not going to address the American people for at least another seven hours, to give the assault team the time they needed to get out to the Aircraft Carrier, where the body of bin Laden was going to be examined and positively identified.

AL-MASADA MOSQUE (THE LION'S DEN) SUNDAY, MAY 2nd, 2011 NEW YORK CITY NINE THIRTY P.M. EST.

Even though the attack on Usama bin Laden in Pakistan began on Saturday, May 1st, it was May 2nd, in the United States because of the time difference. Ever since joining the ones of the al-Masada Mosque, Abdulaziz al-Wahhad was taking over the minds and hearts of the group of mixed Arab youths. Try as he might, nothing happened that would give him the power to take over the Arab cell he was trying to turn into a group of home-grown terrorists, operating in the United States. The Christmas day bomber and the terrorist attack on the soldiers stationed at Fort Hood in Texas occurred. But it was not enough of a reaction for al-Wahhad to take over the group and organize them into acting.

The day was exhaustingly long and al-Wahhad decided to turn in early for the night, thoroughly wasted from his day's unending work, and his want to harm the United States in any fashion he could attack the country. His sleep was interrupted by Mohsen al-Gasim and Reemabdel Aziz al-Rowaili, as al-Gasim began to pound wildly on al-Wahhad's apartment door.

Being startled awake by the heavy pounding on his door, al-Wahhad's hand instinctively searched for the Colt pistol he always slept with under his pillow. Finding the handle of the weapon, his eyes went to his door of his apartment, shaking from the heavy pounding. Throwing his legs off the side of the bed, he cautiously rose and slowly walked towards the door. He looked out the small peep hole as al-Gasim continued to pound wildly on the door for a second time. Seeing him outside he let out his breath as he threw the double lock open, and he pulled the door inside the room.

Al-Gasim and his girlfriend quickly entered without being invited in, and the excited Iraqi man began to speak the moment he saw al-Wahhad standing in the doorway. "I'm sorry for waking you like this. But something major has just taken place that you must be made aware of. I had to speak to you at once over this matter, al-Wahhad."

The soon to be leader of a new terrorist cell, Al-Wahhad closed the door behind the two youngsters and waved his hand out before them and offered the two the only place to sit in his apartment, his bed. Once they were seated, he asked in a calm tone as his heart demanded to know what was bothering his young friends. "Al-Gasim, your mother must have mated with a scorpion, and that mating has given you the impatience of the desert owner. What has you so upset on this foul night? I barely had time to fall asleep, and I'm certain that the world could not have come to an end in so short a period."

"Al-Wahhad, I heard some terrible news on the TV tonight. The hated American soldiers found, and they have successfully killed Usama bin Laden. Hiding in Pakistan right under the noses of the great fools searching the face of the earth for where the man was hiding, and the..."

The stunned al-Wahhad took a step back as if he had just received a hard slap in the face, as his mind tried to absorb the terrible news he was hearing of bin Laden's death, as he mumbled barely over a whisper. "What is this you speak of to me, fool? How could the man who has dealt such a lethal blow to the land of the great Satan, be captured, and killed so easily by the cursed fools? Are you quite certain what you heard on the American TV, is true? Do you think the hated American government is untrue about his death, in hopes of drawing Usama bin Laden out of hiding to reply to these lies, so they could find and kill him?" Al-Wahhad stopped speaking and stared al-Gasim while waiting for his reply.

"Everything that I have told you on this night is true, al-Wahhad. I have witnessed the cursed American President cut into the TV program. So, he could proudly announce bin Laden was killed by foul soldiers he sent to Pakistan to kill our divine leader. Everything must be true if the foolish American Leader said it was true. He had to be absolutely certain that Usama bin Laden was killed, or the great fool would never dare say so over the miserable TV to the fools of this foul country." Al-Gasim again stopped speaking and dumbly stared at the chosen leader of the group of young Arabs.

"By the sacred breath of Allah, our leader has been killed by the hated soldiers of the land of Satan." Al-Wahhad mumbled again barely over a whisper as he shook his head slowly in disbelief. But his sharp mind went into overdrive, and he announced to the two young people in his room. "You fools see how Allah works his way for us to follow His sacred word. He has allowed the Americans to kill our leader, so He could call him home to his guidance. But Allah has given us the fire to start our revenge against the hated land of Satan, and all who dwell within his land of disgust. With Usama bin Laden's death, we'll find many more Arab brothers and sisters who'll march to our sides in droves, to lend us aide with our revenge against the United States. The death of bin Laden is a God send for us, and it'll be the vehicle we'll use to run over all the god cursed followers of Satan."

Al-Wahhad quickly regained his strength as he swung his fist at the air and straightened his back and gathered his thoughts. Now he knew when he was going to aim the followers he was nurturing, since first joining the al-Masada Mosque in New York, within walking distance to Ground Zero where the Twin Towers once adorned the skyline of the great city that never slept.

Al-Wahhad turned to al-Gasim, while ignoring his pretty girlfriend as he grumbled angrily at the young man. "Al-Gasim, you must assemble our closest circle of friends immediately. We have a purpose to our madness now, revenge for the death of Usama bin Laden. Our revenge will fall upon the foul heads of the civilians who has support the soldiers of Satan. We'll teach the evil fools not to aim their god cursed soldiers at our Arab brother and sisters.

"By the time we're done with the civilians of this cursed country. They'll be afraid to lift their foul flag and wave it in the wind as their soldiers walk by them. You fools go and assemble the rest of our soldiers and friends for Allah. Have them meet at your place at eight a.m. tomorrow morning. We must start to make our plans to attack the lowly infidels in their worthless land. We'll make the attack of Nine, One, One look like it was a minor attack aimed against these dog eaters of non-believers to the sacred words in the Holy Qur'an."

Mohsen headed off with his girlfriend to follow al-Wahhad's orders to assemble the others of their soon to be terrorist cell. He knew the rest of the group must have been made aware bin Laden met his fate at the hands of the American soldiers. He wanted to speak to them before the others went off halfcocked, and they done something that would draw attention to their group living legally in the United States for years.

THE OVAL OFFICE, THE WHITE HOUSE, EIGHT TEN P.M. SUNDAY, MAY 2nd, 2011

It was just minutes after the President announced the most wanted man the world had ever known; Usama bin Laden was killed by American SEAL Team soldiers. Everyone part of the hard-hitting operation was relieved the elite troops were safely back in Afghanistan. Slowly the group was starting to break up and head home. CIA Director John Raincloud was waiting to sign off with the President, so he could look after loose ends needing his attention.

General White was waiting to get the President's attention when the American Leader suddenly turned to Raincloud and ordered him. "Director Raincloud, you made this operation the success it was. I thank you for your attention to details, and the outstanding way this operation has turned out for all involved. I know you have other items you must look after, and before I allow you to run, I'm ordering you, General White." The President turned and smiled at the military officer and then he went on with his words.

"I want the Secretary of State and National Security Director, along with Secretary of Defense and Vice Admiral Cantor, who'll join us by video feed. I want him attending this meeting, because I want to know why we lost that one damn helicopter during this operation. Something has let us down, and I demand to know the reason why we lost that machine. Getting back to you for the moment, Director Raincloud, I want a complete report on what you feel we'll be facing in the future, now that we have successfully destroyed bin Laden. I want to stay on top of this, and I don't want any grass growing under our feet, feeling with the death of bin Laden, our problems from the terrorist group of al-Qaeda are in the past."

"You'll have that report on your desk Mr. President I'll have that report completed by the time of the meeting, sir." Director Raincloud replied pleased at how well the operation went down. Once he replied to the President, he left so he could go over the report he long ago assembled when he knew Usama bin Laden was going to be killed in this last operation to get him.

Raincloud stayed up all night revamping the report for the President, and when the time came, he left his office and headed for the White

House. The Director was greeted at the main doors by a White House aide who ushered him to the Oval Office. The CIA Director was surprised to see General White already sitting in the room with the President, Vice President and the others ordered to attend the meeting. Vice Admiral Cantor's face was on the monitor facing the President. He nodded to the members and went to attention and saluted the President.

"Ahhh…good morning, Director Raincloud, I trust you have the report I requested from you sir?" The President snapped just within good manners, not caring in the least the Director was obviously up all night working on preparing the report for the meeting.

"Good morning, Mr. President, and allow me to say how honored I am at being allowed to address you and the esteem committee members assembled here today, sir." Director Raincloud offered in a pleasant tone of voice as he placed his briefcase on a table and removed a ream of papers and began to read from it. "First may I begin by offering to the members I have carried out a rather intensive workup as ordered by you, Mr. President. I concluded many Arab nations and leaders of the Middle East, such as Saudi Arabia, the reorganizing Iraqi government, and what's left of Syria.

"Lebanon, and the troublesome Persian nation of Iran, along with North Korea, China, Cuba, Venezuela and the likes are scared to death over the possible improving relations currently being carried out with the United States, by many of the nations of Europe not very pleased with us at this time, Mr. President Sir. Because without the great Satan to complain and kick around from all angles and forcing their masses of civilians to fear us and the freedom we stand for, sir.

"These usual troublesome nations would have no valid excuse for, and no way to continue to divert the world's attention from them, and the dreadful brutality of the oppressive rule they constantly maintain over their poor civilian hordes. Sort of what they don't know won't hurt them belief, Mr. President. The task of these brutal leaders is to keep their people isolated from the happening of the rest of the world, sir. It's the only way for the brutal leaders to remain in power over their depressed nation's population, and control their civilians at the same time, sir.

"Mr. President Sir, however, the command structure of the al-Qaeda terrorist organization may evolve with the death of their once leader, Usama bin Laden during Operation Neptune's Spear. The pattern of the international Islamic terrorism organization had been set in place for some time to come, by the man while he was still alive and the guiding control of the dreaded terrorist organization, sir. Ever since the destruction of terrorist training camps bin Laden constructed in Afghanistan. Many terrorists dispersed back to their home nations for protection. Or the fleeing terrorists have gathered in locations spread throughout the rest of the world, trying to cast as low a profile as possible. Always waiting for who'll next be elected to power and command over the al-Qaeda organization and lead them in their ongoing war against the West.

"Robbed of the secured advantages the terrorists once enjoyed for many years and came with having a state within a state to safely operate from inside the nation of Afghanistan. The terrorists have fallen back on the local terrorist networks and old habits, for logistical and possible financial support for their organization. They need further protection from other nations willing to turn a blind eye to their evil efforts, and the mounting deaths they constantly create with their hateful attacks aimed against the innocent of the world. Now with this latest development, doesn't imply by any means of the words that the current threat of international terrorism from the al-Qaeda terrorist organization is over, Mr. President.

"There's plenty of intelligence actively still being gathered by our Intelligence Communities by constant cell phone and computer monitoring. We're also employing several human resources along with selected Arab Agents who successfully infiltrated the terrorist organization, sir. They're testifying to the fact that the Islamic terrorist organization continues to have the capability to plan and then carry out their ongoing terrorist attacks aimed against nations they level their evil eyes upon, Mr. President. The ever expanding worldwide search for surviving terrorists is having the desired effects on the main body of the organization and weakened leadership of the al-Qaeda terrorist networks though, sir.

"The latest intelligence picked up, displayed no terrorist operatives are speaking of future organized attacks aimed against future targets at this time, Mr. President. All we're picking up is the uproar over the death of bin Laden, and the other leaders of the al-Qaeda system we have killed by drone attacks, coupled that news with the flood of recent arrests of their Arab brothers in crime when we take them down, sir. Somewhere in the shadowy and troubling landscape of the international terrorism world, there must be discussions raging over the death of their leader bin Laden, the one man who successfully turned global jihad into a reality, and a dream of the radical side of the Islamic religion.

"Mr. President, with the death of bin Laden, there's going to be one helluva a deep sigh of relief, and perhaps even some jubilation enjoyed, and spreading throughout many of the Muslim governments of the world. Once threatened by Usama bin Laden's more radical ideals and efforts of destroying all other religions of the world, and the damage threatened by his extremist followers once under his sole control. With the killing of bin Laden, it's going to enable exhausted nation leaders and their extended intelligence services and security people to breathe a little easier for a while, sir.

"Along with the worn-out police departments and military commanders who pulled countless hours of overtime work from one end of the earth to the other, to sleep easier at night. As the once recognized spiritual commander and main money man of the most omnipresent and indistinguishable terrorist organization to operate in modern day Islam, Usama bin Laden was able to climb to the panicle of the harsh leadership and control the terrorist organization known as al-Qaeda, Mr. President.

"Usama bin Laden was hailed as the hero by the oppressed and unguided and sorry to say, the unintelligent of the Muslim world, until the man represented the largest threat to droves of antiquated and stone aged surviving Muslim regimes being held together with just spit and glue. Solely by power and oppression aimed at their civilians that together, control one fifth of the world's population, and much of the natural resources of the world, Mr. President. Bin Laden's rapid rise to power over such a large terrorist organization he helped organized into a serious threat employed against security in the Muslim world, was fueled by the poor folks walking the streets of the Islamic Kingdoms.

"Mostly because the man spoke in their language and preached what they wanted to hear, and only dare to dream of, and he himself was actually one of them. The poor and the unguided understood what bin Laden said, and his words resonated and echoed in their demanding minds, hearts, and ears of the Arab listeners, both young and old alike. Bin Laden zoned in on the masses overpowering fears and wants. Their sentiments, the young's sadness and their pent-up frustrations and anger of the modern and rapidly developing world leaving them behind.

"Mr. President, it was absolutely imperative, and it was an extremely wise decision on your part, sir. To demand we didn't flash the pictures of the dead Usama bin Laden to the world at large. Because that action would've served to the further expiration of the young and misguided Muslim followers, adding to their resignation, and increasing anti-Americanism the Arab world harbors against anyone from the Western world, or is one of our allies Mr. President.

"The deeply disturbing images of bin Laden's death would've ended up as an extremely humiliating and dramatic episode that would have been infinitely emblazoned in the hearts and minds of young and old Arabs of the world alike, Mr. President. Especially relieved time and again in the generation of frustrated Arabs in their ever-ongoing search of a role model to follow, and lead them to a position to wallow in. Usama bin Laden, the once portrayed hero and believed to be savor of the Muslim world. Would've been stripped of his glorious and rebellious past and displayed in his death mask to the Arab world, as a mortal who died the same way he had lived his evil life, in violence and death, sir.

"I'm deeply concerned over the huge impact that Usama bin Laden's death will have on the countless young, and even the old of the Muslim world, who admired him and his actions. The young who waited his video tapes with bated breath, must be suffering complete devastation over his sudden death, because none of what bin Laden had promised the masses of the Muslim world, had come to past before he finally met his end at the hands of our Special Operatives, Mr. President. The dream of Palestine being liberated in an Arab nation, along with the death of the nation of Israel, had not come to past before Usama bin Laden's timely death. The Arab lands are still infested with foreign troops and countless what the Arab world refers to as infidels, are still in control in most nations of the world.

"No matter how operational and the questionable situation of his terrorist al-Qaeda organization might be left in with his death. It's going to be one helluva desperate struggle to continue to recruit young Jihadists, and spike rebellion among the discontented young Arab peoples of the Muslim world, Mr. President. With the magnetic and once feared powerful and feared leader of the al-Qaeda terrorist organization dead, his pack of murderers are currently paralyzed into inactivity, and in withdraw at least.

"Yes Sir Mr. President, Usama bin Laden's death will result in more blind hatred and violence being displayed and carried out against the United States, and many of our allies, I fear. Without the Jihadist's charismatic and soft-spoken spiritual leader to help guide the young radical wannabe terrorists on their path to Paradise, Usama bin Laden's leftovers would be unable to further capitalize on the mounting anger over his long sort after death, Mr. President. Because most of the upcoming leaders of the al-Qaeda terrorist organization are not well trusted by the youth of the Muslim world as was bin Laden in the past, sir. Besides Mr. President, the way we're focusing our attention on other members of his terrorist organization we believe would be the next in line to lead the al-Qaeda terrorist organization with drone strikes carried out in the nations of Afghanistan, Pakistan, and Yemen. And we're rapidly expanding our efforts in Somalia currently as well, Mr. President.

"We're also making efforts to find and kill the upcoming terrorist leaders like the nut job operating in the nation of Yemen, who we have to eliminate as much as we had to eliminate bin Laden. This Anwar al-Awlaki pain in the ass must meet his fate as fast as these other nuts that come to power, and surface in the al-Qaeda terrorist organization one after the other, sir. Since the unprovoked terrorist attack successfully aimed against the Twin Towers in New York, and Pentagon building here in Washington, Mr. President. We have the terrorists afraid to raise their damn heads above the wall, for fear of having their noggins blown off their damn shoulders. We finally have the terrorists ducking for a change, and it has to stay that way, Sir."

Director Raincloud's last comments made the concerned President smile as he suddenly held up his hand to silence the man so he could speak. "Director Raincloud, this report has the ring that it might have been written before the death of bin Laden. Nevertheless, it states what I wanted to hear from you. It seems we have delivered a lethal blow to the very heart of the al-Qaeda terrorist organization with the death of their leader."

"That's correct Mr. President, and we're still shifting through computer hard drives, and vast amounts of thumb drives, reams of cell phone records and an overwhelming wealth of papers, tape recordings and the likes that we have captured when we invaded bin Laden's lair in Pakistan. I caution you as I tried with my report, Mr. President." Director Raincloud offered with concern as he went on with his words for the American Leader's information.

"Even with the death of Usama bin Laden, the al-Qaeda terrorist organization is still an extremely dangerous and vigorous force we'll have to deal with for a long time to come I'm afraid, sir. Mr. President, we can't possibly allow ourselves to become the slightest bit complacent when considering the ongoing threat from this or any other terrorist organization threatening our lifestyle.

"Sir, as of this moment, the terrorists are running for their damn rat holes in droves to hide, because they understand we have obviously found a wealth of names in the intelligence we discovered at bin Laden's headquarters, identifications and leads where they're hiding at. Mr. President, when as the new wannabe leaders of the organization gets over the shock of bin Laden's death. One of these animals will surely step forward and assume control over the organization before it completely fragments into a non-entity. This leader will be looking to make a fast name for himself, by trying to carry..."

"Excuse me for interrupting you at this time Director Raincloud..." The American Leader offered as he interrupted the Director's words. "But I was under the impression if we killed bin Laden, the threat from the al-Qaeda organization was over. The terrorist organization would fragment, and no respected leader would step forward and take the damn reins of the damaged terrorist organization again. Don't get me wrong Director, I understand the al-Qaeda organization will never be completely disbanded, and the terrorists would likely be capable of carrying out pinprick operations that'd be more of a nuisance than a serious threat."

"I'm afraid that way of thinking, would give the al-Qaeda terrorist organization a stronger footprint than they currently enjoyed, Mr. President. We witnessed what happened when we relaxed our surveillance of the damn terrorists, sir. We were hit at Fort Hood where we lost thirteen fine young American soldiers, and forty-three troops were wounded in the attack. Then we suffered the failed underwear bomber attack, and that forced us to tighten our surveillance of our aircraft systems. Mr. President, we can't possibly relax our stance against the al-Qaeda organization or any other terrorist organizations that are a serious threat to our way of life and have evil intentions aimed against our country and our people and..."

"Director Raincloud, I'm not going to revisit that nightmare again and you can't force me to do so. I ordered what I thought was the right thing to do, and I ordered it done. Furthermore, Director Raincloud, I plan to announce in the upcoming weeks that our war with the al-Qaeda terrorist organization has run its course and is over with, and we successfully defeated the organization and that we are now going…"

Director Raincloud offered in haste before thinking who he was speaking with. "That's plan nuts to believe that Sir! If we announce we believe we have defeated the al-Qaeda terrorist organization, every damn nut will reorganize quicker than expected. They'll try and hit us and hit us hard, to prove they're still an operational terrorist force to be reckoned with, sir. Also Mr. President, if you dare to try and announce the death of the al-Qaeda terrorist organization, you'll open the damn flood gates for a whole new horde of damn Arab radicals to march through and offer their services to keep the al-Qaeda organization alive and well, and an ongoing threat to world peace. I'd fear a new host of domestic terrorists coming at us, sir. We know al-Qaeda is doing everything in their power to turn kids into their murderous meritocracy…"

"You'll watch your damn tone of voice when addressing me, Director Raincloud!" The President snarled angrily as he interrupted him as he continued his words. "Mr. Raincloud, I was led to believe by a number of my closest advisors that with the death of bin Laden, comes the death of the al-Qaeda organization. Now you stand before me and try and tell me my advisors were wrong. I'm going to follow my advisors' ways of thinking, and I intend to make a statement the war with al-Qaeda is over with, and the once terrorist organization is depleted and basically leaderless, and they're no longer a threat to the world peace. Don't give me that look mister, I believe our war with al-Qaeda is over and until I'm proved otherwise, that's what I'm going to believe and act."

"With all due respect Mr. President, if you make suck a rash statement to the world. You'll make a new leader for that fractured terrorist organization to step up quicker than if we don't try and taunt that damn terrorist organization into action, sir. We know who wants to lead the al-Qaeda organization in the worst way, sir. The Egyptian born Ayman al-Zawahiri, and we'll get that sonofabitch soon enough I assure you, sir. We believe this man will have a hard time with trying to take over command of the al-Qaeda leadership, because he's not well liked, and he's held in little favor by the surviving al-Qaeda brain thrust.

"Right now, we believe that the al-Qaeda terrorist organization is stepping back for the moment, and what's left of their leadership is taking a breath, sir. They're going to stay sitting on the fence while waiting for the dust to settle down, before they start making further noise against the world at large, sir. But if we say the terrorist organization is done for. One of their damn nuts will try something to display the terrorist organization is still alive and well and is still able to hit us where we live, sir. Mr. President, we in the Intelligence Communities are deeply concerned with the death of bin Laden. The al-Qaeda terrorist organization is in a scattered state of confusion, but even a scattered and confused enemy can be an extremely dangerous entity to deal with, sir.

"We're quite certain with the death of Usama bin Laden, some lone wolf, or one of their other gullible lunatic followers, or an isolated terrorist cell or even a freelancer agent might want to make a quick name for him or herself in the terrorist world, by offering to hit us under the banner of the al-Qaeda terrorist organization. Mr. President, any one of these misguided people or sleeper terrorist cells would want to prove al-Qaeda is still a well-tuned and deadly terrorist organization. Or one of them tries or a successful hit against us here in the States in retaliation for the killing of bin Laden. I believe we should take a moment to take stock of what we have accomplished with the death of their damn terrorist leader, Mr. President. Not go off halfcocked and start taunting the surviving al-Qaeda org..."

"You're free to believe whatever the devil you want to believe, and I'll believe what I want, Mr. Raincloud. I intend to do what I believe is the right thing and that's that. In fact, Director Raincloud, I'm done with this damn meeting. I'm calling this meeting to a conclusion, sir." With that said the President rose and he quickly headed out of the Oval Office.

MONDAY, MAY 3rd, 2011. NEW YORK CITY,
THE Al-MASADA MOSQUE. SEVEN A.M. EST

The ex-Iraqi General Abdulaziz al-Wahhad was the first one from his group of American Arabs to arrive at the Mosque on this day. He was that anxious to begin formulating his plans to seek revenge against the

American government, and her civilians for the assassination of Usama bin Laden. In his early morning prays to Allah, the crafty Arab Leader thanked Allah for placing him in command of the group of young Muslim students. This fact made it possible for him to turn the Arab kids to his want for harm against the United States and her people. As he finished his morning prays, both Mohsen al-Gasim and Reemabdel Aziz al-Rowaili, arrived at the Mosque as ordered by al-Wahhad last night at his apartment.

He nodded at the pair of Arabs as more of his fellow students arrived at the Mosque, and by 7:30 a.m. The entire group was gathered in the set aside meeting room al-Wahhad was allowed to hold his private meetings with the youth of the Mosque in. Everyone to the last person was upset over the death of bin Laden last night. They were harboring anger for the United States for what they thought was the slaughter of the leader of the al-Qaeda terrorist organization.

Abdulaziz was longing for something to happen where he could finally funnel the energies of this young group of angry Arab kids. But the unthinkable thought of the death of bin Laden was never once considered to be the turning point of his future leadership. Ever since he aligned himself with this Mosque, his sole purpose was to organize a few youths of the Mosque into a hard strike force he could aim at the United States. He smiled as he remembered the name the Intelligence Communities of the United States had branded a threat from within the borders of their country, 'Home Grown Terrorists'.

Al-Wahhad's chest swelled with pride as he thought now was the time the United States was going to witness what a home-grown terrorist could do to their country. He shifted his eyes from one member of his group to the other, pleased with the group as he realized he had a collection of naturalized American citizens living legally in the United States for years. None of the kids have come under the suspicious eyes of any Intelligence Community supposedly there to protect the civilians from the ones he has assembled before him. Drawing in his breath, the leader of the group addressed the youngsters.

"At last, my fellow young brothers and sisters from the land of sand, what we have longed for had finally taken place. True, it has cost us the leader picked by the Prophet Muhammad, to free the Muslim world from the hordes of non-believers who have oppresses us Muslims for so long.

Nevertheless, it is what we have prayed for, from this point forward we'll have to go by the names this cursed country has bestowed upon our foolish heads.

"Because I don't want to draw any special attention to ourselves, or our upcoming actions by addressing one another by our Arab names, while we play out our revenge against the cursed civilians of this evil nation. I shall be known to our group as Richard Erenberg. Yes, I know it's a very ugly Western name. But it'll keep the loathsome eyes of the hated FBI and CIA from my neck, until it's too late for them to react against what we have planned for this land of Satan. I'll lay my Arab name of Abdulaziz al-Wahhad to rest until it's the proper time to be addressed by my honored Arab name again. I shall ask each one of you to give me the evil Americanized name forced upon your heads by this foul government, and you shall use.

"I start with you, my second in command of our growing terrorist cell. Please Mohsen: give me and the others the name we shall know you by. Until our revenge aimed against this evil country is complete, and it has run its course and we can leave this land of sin forever. I'm waiting not so patiently for you to announce your name, so I can commit it to memory."

The Iraqi man straightened his back as he announced. "My Brother Abdulaziz…"

Abdulaziz immediately held up his hand and grumbled at the young man. "Ahhhh… my short-minded fool, I see you have already forgotten the name I just ordered you to address me by, fool."

"I beg your pardon Richard Erenberg, my Americanized name is Michael Hawkins. It's a most foul name I must employ, so I might continue to remain in this evil country. I cannot wait until I see the sands of our honored ancestors and feel it's hot sand under my feet once again." Al-Gasim, corrected for all listening to his words.

"That's better young fool, now I shall hear from you, and I'll use your given name for one last time, until our missions within the evil borders of the United States have been concluded. Reemabdel, what is the foul name this cursed government has bestowed upon your head, when you asked to be a member of this worthless country?"

"Richard, the cursed name forced upon me when I first signed the foul papers allowing me to dwell within the land of Satan, was Janet Keller. It's a most foul, ugly, and highly insulting name, and that was why I chose to continue to use my Arab name. I dread having to use this cursed name again, al-Wahhad."

"That was until today, Janet. You must use that loathsome name no matter how insulting to your Arab ancestry it might be against you." Al-Wahhad replied and flashed a smile, informing her he was pleased with her. Then he looked at the rest of his flock and complained at them. "I fear we're wasting too much time with this foolishness. From now on when I look at you, state your Arab name then your name to this cursed nation of sin."

The first one Abdulaziz looked to spoke up. "My name is Band Ibn Saud, I am a Saudi and the name given to me is Gary Fredericks, I'm a well-trained bomb expert."

"Good, that's what I want to hear from everybody as they address me. You'll state your Arab nation and what you're noted for best that would be of assistance to our sacred cause." Abdulaziz looked to the next man in the room, and he replied immediately.

"My name is Awadh al-Awajy, I'm an Iraqi and my American name is James Fisher. I have no chosen skill, so I can be whatever you want me to be, even a Martyr for our just cause."

The next member of the small group spoke when Abdulaziz looked at him. "I'm Adelah al-Faiz and I'm an Iranian skilled in many ways to bring death to my enemy. The loathsome name I'm forced with is Peter Cristofari. I always wanted to attack this worthless country for the sanctions they have forced upon my great country. But I was unable to organize the forces needed to be successful in my quest, so I was helpless to carry out an attack. This country has many roadblocks set up against my actions, and they have not given me a thing I can use on the lowly infidels to the words written in the Qur'an..."

"As I already stated, enough of this foolishness, we'll hold the names and what you're best noted for to forward our cause against the lowly infidels of this evil country, until I have need of you and your expertise. It shall be then I'll find out the names you were given from the foul ones who run this cursed land. But I want to correct the blind spot I picked up in your vision. Because I see you all have failed to see what Allah and the great Prophet, has delivered into your foolish hands, to employ as a weapon against the hated infidels.

"Adelah, you have obviously failed to take full advantage of what was given to you when you first entered this filthy nation of lowly dog eaters, and you have become a naturalized citizen in this land of non-believers and jackals. The name given you by the hated infidels will open the doors we need to travel through, during our opening attacks aimed against the hated land of Satan. We were branded with the evil American names and that'll help to surely remove the ever-watching eyes of the cursed defenders of this worthless country, until we have successfully exacted a terrible death toll upon their unsuspecting civilians of this evil nation, for what their loathsome leaders have done to the true leader of the Muslim world, Usama bin Laden. We must keep our eyes opened if we wish to exact our revenge on the non-believers and lowly infidels of the United States, for the death of Usama bin Laden."

The small group of soon to be terrorists nodded in agreement with their leaders' words.

Al-Wahhad smiled over the complete acceptance of his leadership over the small group of young people. He now fully understood he was in total control of the young ones he was going to send out against the enemy of his mind. He realized he was going to be the cause of death to the Arab men and women poised to follow his orders to their death, no matter what he ordered them to carry out for his cause. He was aware he was going to remain well out of sight of the defenders of the United States, so he did not come under their eyes as a possible terrorist. Because he had no intentions of dying for what he was instilling in the minds and hearts of the others of his group as their just cause for Allah, as he went on with his words.

"I have further words of concern that I must utter for the male fools of our believers to the sacred words written in the Holy Qur'an. We must shave the beards we grow to honor Allah, and the Prophet Muhammad. I warn you young fools, you must use great caution when shaving, especially for the first time. Because the loathsome defenders of this cursed country, have orders to detain anyone who have fresh nicks or cuts on their worthless faces. The evil ones will take this discovery as evidence the fools they search for, have shaved their honored beards, and the skin was not used to the bit of the edge of the razor.

"You women must be the ones to assist the male fools when they shave. You women are instructed to assist the great fools with the loss of their sacred beards for our just cause. You'll use scissors and cut the beards short in preparation for the razor's bite. Then shave the fools so they don't cut their own worthless throats with the foul razor. You lazy women understand what I mean by my words of attack on the fools."

Al-Wahhad's words brought a round of slight laughter from the group, and it served to relieve some of the heavy tension overtaking the group, from the youngsters listening to his words.

"Huh, laughter is good for the heart and soul, when one is planning their revenge to be played out against their enemy who successfully suppressed our lives for so long a time. Our mouths have been shut by the hot sands of a thousand years, until this great day of offered freedom for our people and faithful believers in the one true religion of the world. There are further warnings I must raise for our information; the males must get used to wearing fine suits and must walk and act like you're worried about life. Don't walk like Arab people, as if you're challenging anyone to a duel to the death by your aggressive actions.

"Yes, young ones, we Arabs don't fear death, especially like the non-believers of this foul nation who fear death every day of their worthless lives. But we must force ourselves to walk and speak like the lowly infidels of this country, and we must act like we fear the neighbor walking to our left or right. We Arabs have caused the fear of Allah to be fallen upon the shoulders of these non-believing jackal civilians of the United States. So, we must act the same way when we set out to work our ways against the foolish non-believers of this evil land. James Fisher." Abdulaziz offered to see if the fool recognized his American name.

"Yes Richard, I shall await your words of wisdom for my foolish ears." The young Arab Awadh al-Awajy replied when his American name was mentioned by their leader.

"Good, it does my heart happiness to see you have remembered, and how to react to your foolish American name when it is mentioned by someone. James, since you have no true expertise to offer our group of freedom fighters for our just cause. I shall employ you in our opening efforts against the fools of this hatful nation. I demand your beard be shaven clean, and then you'll begin to shave every night close, until I finally send you out on your sacred mission for Allah's sake and our revenge. Tomorrow morning, I want you to stop at a local jewelry store and order you to buy a medallion of the hated Star of David. I shall give you the money you'll need to purchase the evil thing to hang around your worthless neck, young fool.

"I want you to purchase the hatful medallion and chain to hang it from. When I send you out on your faithful mission, you'll understand the reason for this foolish request I make of you at this time, fool that you are." A wicked smile followed the stinging words Abdulaziz aimed at al-Awajy, as he held him in his angry stare for the moment.

"I shall do as you ordered without hesitation. I understand you have ideas in your mind I'm not aware of, to forward our attack aimed against the hateful lands of the lowly infidels and non-believers."Al-Awajy replied with a snap in his tone as he allowed a nasty sneer to cross his lips.

CHAPTER EIGHT

FRIDAY, MAY 7th, 2011, CAMP LEJEUNE, NORTH CAROLINA
ZERO THREE THIRTY HOURS

The specialized group of Tier One soldiers of the Multi-National Rapid Response Force were brought back to the massive military base stationed at Camp Lejeune in Jacksonville, North Carolina in the early morning hours, employing the cover of darkness to avoid any news reporters from discovering the sudden troop movement. The troops were sent to Jalaladad in Afghanistan as backup for the SEAL Team soldiers who went in and killed Usama bin Laden seven days ago. They were thoroughly exhausted and moving as such.

Captain Robert Walker was having a hard time getting the elite troops in gear now they were back on their main military base. Many of the exhausted soldiers had fallen asleep on the buses on their drive back to the base, and they did not want any part of waking up or moving. The young captain was being flanked by his usual soldiers from his group, the Mutt, Ramirez, Buckethead, and Neck. Walker turned to the Mutt and growled at the soldier, "Hey buddy will you give me a fucking hand getting a fire burning under some of these dead asses around here, man. We gotta get the plucked Eagles the fuck offa the damn bus before the fucking Colonel gets here, and he starts taking numbers and asses, dog man."

"Yeah, I'll get them moving easy enuf before the big growl starts bitching at us again, man. But I don't know why the hell I'm talking to you you're fucking dressed like a damn shrub." The Mutt fired at Walker, making a reference to his Gillie or bush blanket camouflage Unit he had draped over his shoulder, as he moved deeper in the idling bus. The Mutt started to shove some soldiers he saw sleeping, and then ordering them to get off the bus.

Slowly, the troops stumbled off the bus, dropping their equipment on the floor outside the barracks. Their orders were to leave the assault equipment outside, and it was scheduled to be picked up by the MPs, cleaned and stored from the soldier's future use. The Colonel was trying to get some responsibilities off his soldier's backs, so they could catch up on their rest.

Walker charged into his private quarters in the barracks, and the few soldiers always with him, followed their Commander in the room and the complaints started flying.

"Man, what the hell do you call that load of shit we just went through? Since when do we go on a fucking mission, and we end up sitting and spinning on our damn thumbs, while some uther stinking soldiers get all the fucking glory? I was trained to kill, not to take up space stacking pencils, dammit." The Mutt grumbled as he checked out Walker's icebox for a cold beer.

"You know what they say and get the fuck outta my damn icebox, will ya stupid." Walker snorted at his friend.

"No buddy, what do they say wiseguy?" The Mutt snapped as he closed the door to the chest.

"Some days you're the stinking pigeon, uther days you're the fucking statue. I warned you slobs we were gonna be backup for another Unit, so what's the stinking gripes about?"

"I'm still having problems being used as a fucking backup Unit for a group of uther puds. I feel like our Unit came in second on this last mission, man." The Mutt added to his complaint as he stared at his Commander.

"Coming in second place only means you're the first loser in the damn game, man. Look guys I know we got the short end of this stinking operation on this one. All I can tell you people is, wait for the next one, and then our Unit's gonna be the tip of the fucking spear again for the action. At least the king rat is where he belongs, soaking in the damn Ocean. I guess if you want to look at it this way, you can look at bin Laden's death as he received the largest water boarding action in the fucking world. Mutt, why don't you get out there and make certain our people are settled in, and they don't need anything. I know a few of them got some stinking nicks and cuts the medics hafta look afta. You gotta take some of this shit offa my damn shoulders, man. You're the only uther stinking Officer in the damn barracks I got to work with, buddy." Walker complained at the Mutt.

The extremely dangerous Ghost laughed at the Mutt as he left Walker's quarters, which caused him to grumble. "What's up your stinking ass, buddy? With all the crap facing our country, one would think you'd be working on what the fuck you're gonna do, once the Gov. puts your stinking ass out to pasture, man. The way the asses in Congress are screwing up our country, it makes me fear how long the United States is gonna continue to be the United States we know. I'm beginning to feel America is fast becoming the largest dwarf in the stinking room."

"Yeah Walker, one thing I gotta admit. Witnessing the way, the stinking Republicans and Democrats are constantly bickering over the fucking debt, is like watching two drunks arguing over their damn bar tab on the Titanic. One day the politicians are gonna screw up my mind by doing something useful for our country, instead of working against each uther and their stinking political parties. We're in this shit together, and the only way we're gonna get the fuck outta the mess is by working together." The Ghost smirked at Walker.

"Will you cut that out before I knock you on that damn knob you call a noggin, stupid." Ice, Sergeant Diane Morrison, growled angrily at Neck.

All eyes went to the two soldiers to see what was bugging Ice.

"What did the big slob do to you, baby?" Baby Tee, another female soldier from the group sort of dating the other huge trooper known as Buckethead, asked.

"He pinched my can, and he knows how much I hate it whenever he does that shit to me. I hate having to scream at the big sod. He's so stupid I wish I could make him understand he can't do whatever the hell he wants without making me angry at him all the time, dammit."

"Hey Ice, Neck has been screamed at by so many women in his wasted life that he's actually quite fluent in scream speech." The Hunter, Sergeant Frank Whitcomb, the other point man for the Unit fired at the large soldier, which caused the rest of the troops in the room to laugh over his comment.

"Hey man did you ever get the feeling the world was a tuxedo, and you were a pair of brown fucking shoes, I feel so outta place all the time." Neck replied, adding to the laughter.

"Ha big man, when the truth is ugly, only a lie can be beautiful, so here it comes. Buddy, you know what the fuck you're doing at all times." The Hunter remarked with a smile.

"You gotta understand something, no matter what the hell you do, you can't make Neck look good to the rest of us pukes, buddy." The Ghost, the second point man replied to his counterpart as he shot him a good smile.

"Yeah, I know, one day you're the stinking pigeon, and the next day you're the fucking statue, right people? I heard all that shit from Walker before when he was pissed off at me." Neck fired back at the other soldiers giving him a hard time.

"Okay you pack of twits, enuf clowning around huh. We gotta a shitload of crap to do and we betta get on it. I'm going under the assumption that once we check in and get all squared away and do our stinking act... Crap, listen up, while we were on this backup operation, the stinking Colonel clued me in on some uther crap he was getting concerned over, and he explained why we were stuck soaking up this new training program someone fucking dreamed up for our damn asses. Colonel Leadbetter informed me with the sorry ass shape the Intelligence Communities are in because of this new Administration being run by the Democrats, along with their desperate want to continue to dump on the damn Intel dudes.

"We're being forced to pick up some slack until the damn Intelligence people can get their fucking wheels back on track, now they're kinda dropping out of Congresses stinking sights. Colonel Leadbetter's concerned some Islamic terrorists are finding new ways of getting into the United States, and the lousy little pricks are planning attacks against us..."

"Did the Colonel offer how he thinks some of these terrorists might get in the States, Walker?" The Ghost asked as he stared at the captain.

"He was kinda vague about that part of his concerns, but I caught his drift okay. I believe he was getting concerned about the damn Mex border. Or the damn terrorists could come in by some commercial aircraft because the no-fly list is in shit shape. The Colonel was only concerned about a leader of some sort sneaking in and then that lousy prick organizing some home-grown assholes sucking up the benefits we offer anyone struggling in this fucked up economy we're mired in..."

"Hey Walker, the only reason we're in such sorry ass shape with the stinking economy, is because the people who work for a living are being vastly outnumbered by the ones who vote for a fucking living, man." The Hunter grumbled, and his words made everyone in the room grunt in agreement with his complaint.

"Yeah, whatever, I heard that shit already man. The stinking Colonel's certain we're gonna get hit, and soon and hard, and since he has a fucking itch in his damn jockies. That means we're gonna get stuck on the base learning his new tactics and uther crap, until we either get hit and we go afta the fucking lousy pricks. Or the Colonel's itch disappears somehow or the uther. If any of you guys wanna know how I feel about his concerns. I agree with them and his training crap. This new crap of an Administration has our Intel people screwed up into a stinking knot. This new guy picked the worst possible time to make a name offa our most important assets we have working for us to pit up against the radical terrorists and their damn threats." Walker offered and calmed down and looked at the facing staring at him.

The faces of the troops displayed the same concern Walker was. "What the fuck are you pukes staring at my ass for? The answers you're seeking isn't written on my damn puss."

"You'll be fucking surprised what I see written on your damn puss, buddy." The Neck smirked at Walker with a grin on his face.

"I could only imagine what your stinking mind is telling your ass, buddy." Walker fired back at his fellow trooper.

ABDULAZIZ AL-WAHHAD'S APARTMENT, NEW YORK CITY, A MERE SIX MILES AWAY FROM GROUND ZERO SATURDAY, MAY 8th, 2011

It was nine thirty a.m. when the first of the Islamic militants, started to show up at al-Wahhad's apartment. As always, al-Gasim, was followed into the apartment by Reemabdel.

The two youngsters entered the room looking over their shoulder. The three were waiting for Band Ibn Saud. He was the newly formed terrorist cell's bomb making expert. The fifth person to enter the apartment was the Iraqi, Awadh al-Awajy. He was the one picked to deliver the bomb to their first target in New York City they leveled their eyes on.

Al-Wahhad classified this man as the least needed asset to the group. So, he was picked to be the suicide bomber and Martyr for their opening war aimed against the United States. The terrorist leader let out his breath in a rush, he was that upset al-Awajy was late arriving, so they could begin their plans of attack. In a disgusted tone, he snarled at the group. "Where the devil is this fool of an arse? If he dares to keep me waiting a moment longer, I'll have his foolish eyes burned out by heated copper coins."

Just as al-Wahhad finished with his complaint, there was a knock on his door, and Reemabdel opened it and allowed al-Awajy entry.

"Pleased forgive my tardiness, but the traffic of the city was terrible out there. I think every worthless fool of an American was on the road on this foul day."

"Torturer of the truth, your lies are old, but you tell them very well. For the sake of Allah why do you not tell the truth you wanted to stay in bed with your bitch? Never mind, you're here and that's all that matters, fool. I ordered all of you here to share some news. Ibn Saud was successful making his explosive devices we'll use against the American fools. But I have better news to share with all gathered here on this day. I was able to contact a certain cursed Iranian Operative I worked with before. He's willing to make a certain weapon available for our attacks on the great Satan, and the worthless fools who live on his land. Our first attack will be aimed against the underground railway system on this evil city. The weapon I speak of is what I know as a shape charge, capable of cutting through the hardest of steel.

"The base of the weapon we shall use is constructed in much the same way as the weapons the foolish Americans call Improvised Explosive Device (IED) we employed against their cursed soldiers when they first invaded the land of my birth. The shape charge weapon explodes and super heats the copper lining of the device and propels it forward at supersonic speed. Then the molten copper wraps itself around the item it'll cut in half. In this attack, the molten copper will wrap itself around the axel of the lead train car, cutting the axle and causing the car to derail and tumble out of control within the narrow confines of the tunnel system. Huh fool, I see it written within your worthless eyes that you don't believe this attack on the lowly infidels, will be worth our efforts. That's the difference between you and me. You young fools I see with my mind, you see with your worthless eyes.

"Dog of an unbeliever, if we derail one cursed train car beneath the streets of Manhattan, that car will cause the trailing train cars to derail, and then tumble through the tunnel out of control. This tumbling will cause the cars to knock down many support beams holding up the road and foul buildings above ground. If the out-of-control train knocks out enough of these support columns, not only the street, but the buildings will crumble into the crater we shall cause. You see master of a thousand fleas, not only will we kill many infidels above the ground we shall also kill many of the lowly jackals on the train, and hordes of non-believers waiting for the cursed train to arrive at the station.

"If we play our cards just right and open our attack at the proper time of day and time and with Allah's will, all things that should be in place will be there. Our attack against the land of Satan and its lowly infidels could make the attack on the Twin Towers look like a minor attack on the fools. We'll pick the best train station to attack that has the highest value of destruction and death we could cause by such an attack on the infidels. Al-Awajy, you'll board the Hudson Line at the train station at Canal Street Six, and then you will ride that train to Grand Central Station. When the foul infidel Conductor calls out Grand Central Station that is when you'll go to the bathroom in the foul car which sits over the rear wheels of the wagon. You'll lock the door behind you and place your attaché case on the floor at your foul feet. Then you'll hit the detonation button and destroy the wheels of the lead train car…"

"Attaché case al-Wahhad?" Al-Awajy asked as he placed a puzzled look on his face.

"You dare much to interrupt me when I am speaking with you! Yes, fool who has feasted upon sour breast milk you shall carry an expensive attaché case with you. You'll be dressed in an equally expensive suit and tie, and your hair will be cut short and neat, you'll not dare to nick your foolish self while shaving. I want you to look more like our sworn enemy than they do, a Jew! In fact, you shall wear a Star of David around your worthless neck, and leave it exposed for all to see, as you enter the cursed train station. The lowly infidels will not be looking for a cursed Jew attacking one of their worthless train systems…"

Mohsen suddenly cleared his throat which caused al-Wahhad to stop speaking and turn to the young man, and then he growled at the young man. "Am I to take it that you have something you want to add to this foul conversation, al-Gasim? Speak while I wait your words of wisdom for my ears to hear, fool."

"I believe I have a suggestion and a much better attack area than the one you speak of, al-Wahhad. I want to do the most damage on our opening attack against the infidels." The younger man announced to the chosen leader of the group.

"Speak of this better attack area you dreamed up al-Gasim, who speaks to me as if I need your counseling and wisdom."

"Al-Wahhad, I suggest we level our eyes upon a true target out of the area where we're staying. We already discussed several other targets when we have a reason to attack the lowly infidels in their foul lands. I offer we go after an aircraft at maybe the John F. Kennedy International Airport. I have an old man waiting to die, and we can have him bring the explosive device on board the aircraft we wish to destroy. The way we plan to destroy the plane, this old man will be perfect." Mohsen offered to the leader of their terrorist group.

"Ahhh… suicide bombers are like the United States' cruise missiles, only cheaper to employ. I must say that was a good suggestion my foolish brother from the lands of sand. I believe we shall stay with my original plan until we carried it out to its conclusion. We'll hit the train station first, and then we shall see what damage we can cause to the station. We'll make the hit on the aircraft terminal in the same week as you suggested. That way we'll have the evil Intelligence fools of the great Satan, chasing unseen shadows where we were once working our craft against the foul fools.

"I thank the wisdom of Allah for this hated and so weak American Administration. The fool in command of this country is a gutless leader and caused the weakness we needed with his intelligence personnel. The foolish leader has opened the door to carry out our war against the evil land of Satan and his jackals. We must take advantage of this weakness from the United States' Commander if we want to be successful with our attacks against this hatful country. We shall hit the foul aircraft terminal second, and once we have destroyed so much of New York City. We will then make our way down to Washington and start our attacks there, while the lowly fools still look for us in this great city of sin. That is all I have to say."

Al-Awajy remained standing before his leader looking scared to death, and this forced al-Wahhad to address him further. "Fool of fools, why do you stand before me trembling like wash on the line? Your fears make you foolish, young one. Awadh, a golden thrown awaits you in Paradise, if you carry out Allah's wish faithfully on the earth. Here is what you will do. You shall have Farima Ebadi shave you every morning until you head out for your mission. You'll go to the cursed store called Macy's and buy a perfect fitting dark navy-blue silk suit, new leather shoes, black you fool!

"You shall buy an expensive attaché case, black, and a gold chain and Star of David with a red tie, silk. Today is Saturday, May 8th. I want to begin our attack against this evil land on Thursday, May 13th, that is the fool's payday for their worthless week's work. Few fools of this loathsome country would not dare miss their cursed payday, because they will have no money to waste on their sinful days of their weekend. So, there will be many more civilian deaths we can cause during our attack against their train system.

"Awadh while you're taking care of the chores, I have just ordered you to carry out. I'll have a meeting with the worthless Persian fool and acquire the shape charges that we shall need to attach to the bottom of your new cursed attaché case. Saud, I want you to make the weapon we will employ during our second attack against the hated airport. I demand you have that weapon ready for our use on the same day we attack the train station. If we can, I decided I want to carry out both attacks at the same exact moment on the same day. In this way, we can split the emergency responders, and cause great stress to their investigation teams at the same time. It'll also force the great fools to fear where we shall strike them next.

"I intend to cause the greatest amount of death and fear to the lowly infidels who infest this land of Satan. I want to hit the lowly jackals hard; I'll teach the lowly fools killing our leader will come back to haunt them in the worse ways. I shall never stop my attacks against this evil country until I feel enough non-believers have died, to make up for the death of Usama bin Laden. You fools have your orders. Saud, work on the weapon for the attack against the aircraft station. Awadh, acquire the items I have ordered you to purchase. I shall leave and make contact with the filth of the Persian and get the items I need from his evil hands.

"Mohsen, you and your girlfriend will report to the others of our group of faithful Muslim followers. You shall inform the fools of our plans to attack the lowly infidels how and where, and you'll have them remain ready, in case something goes wrong with our attacks against the hated jackals of this cursed nation. Mohsen, you'll also contact the old man you have made mention of and make certain that he'll carry our weapon onto the hated aircraft. If he's willing to do this for us, he'll become the second Martyr for our just cause against the non-believers of this land. With his death it'll stop us from losing one of our freedom warriors during this attack. I want to save as many warriors as possible I can, with our war we'll wage against the land of Satan. Leave my apartment, first Awadh then ten minutes later, Saud shall leave the apartment. Mohsen and Reemabdel will leave after waiting ten minutes, and I'll then leave on my mission.

"We'll meet at my room tomorrow morning at exactly seven a.m., and each of you fools will have carried out my orders faithfully, or don't allow me to rest my eyes upon your caresses ever again. Because if you fail to carry out my orders, I'll have your faces tied to bags of hot ashes until the pain drives you insane. The future of our war with the lowly infidels of this evil country depends on everyone carrying out my orders faithfully. Start to leave now Awadh!" Al-Wahhad placed a glare in his eyes as he waited for the young man to leave his room. Once Awadh left, he checked his watch and ten minutes later, he looked at Saud who left the room without waiting to be ordered to move out.

When Mohsen and his girlfriend left the apartment, al-Wahhad followed last. He was that anxious to linkup with the Iranian Operative who lived barely a mile from his apartment. Before he left for the meeting with the Persian, he stopped by the Imam or spiritual leader of the Lion's Den Mosque. The elderly Imam was in full agreement with his ambitions he wanted to carry out against the United States. The Imam was backing him with the cash he needed to carry out his plans of attack. Al-Wahhad left him all smiles, along with a fist full of cash.

It took the leader of the small terrorist cell fifteen minutes to make it to the Persian's room. Once there he knocked on the door in the series of knocked, he was instructed to employ, if he wanted to meet with him. He waited for the door to open, and a young but extremely dangerous looking well-tanned man stepped aside and allowed him to enter the apartment. Then the Persian slammed the door behind him. The noise startled him, but the move allowed the Persian Agent to get the drop on him. In a flash, he expertly padded the terrorist down, checking for a hidden weapon or taping machine.

Once the Persian was satisfied the Iraqi was free of any weapons or listening devices. He relaxed his stance, and then asked the first question of the Iraqi terrorist. "Ahhh… my brother from the troubled land of Iraq, you are twice welcomed to my arms in the name of Allah. It has been too long since the last time you have taken time to share a tent, or dried dates with me. What brings a faithful Arab man to my lowly door?"

Al-Wahhad politely nodded to the Persian Operative as he offered the man. "I expect your hospitality as is my right to request from you, my faithful Persian brother."

"And you shall receive it with my greatest of pleasure, because it is twice given to you my brother of the land of sand. I must repeat I fear, what brings you to my home so early on this day?" Kadhim Muslawi offered in a commanding tone.

"Kadhim, I come to your door to see if what we spoke of is within your possession, and I can acquire the items I need to forward my war against the lowly infidels of this cursed land?" Al-Wahhad offered calmly as he stared into the eyes of the Persian operative.

"It's good you get right to the point of your concerns with me, because I hate to waste time with any idle talk or exchanging worthless niceties, my Arab brother. Allah has sent you to me on this day, so I can assist you in your sacred war you wage against the foul infidels of the United States. To kill a cursed infidel is not thought of as murder, it's the true path to Paradise for all faithful followers of the Holy Qur'an, and the scared words of Allah. Your qualities will be known among your enemy. Yes, what you have requested of my government is here, and it has been waiting your presence." Muslawi remarked as he stopped speaking and turned and walked to his closet. He took a narrow packing tube and removed the top as he spoke to al-Wahhad.

"Here is what you have requested from my government, my Arab brother from the great land of sand. But I must explain the proper way for you to install the items, so they work properly for your attack." With that said, Muslawi allowed three thick, heavy strips of highly polished copper rails to slide out of the cardboard tube container. He released the tube and separated the rails in his hand, and then continued with his words of explanation.

"There are three copper rails and two of them are different from the third. Here, see these rails, they're constructed on a slight angle, they're the outside rails. They're angled inward while the third rail is constructed straight. The reason for this is because when the weapons are detonated, the straight rail will go down, and the two side rails will angle inward and connect with the molten copper of the center rail. Then the molten three rails now one will circle around the axle of the train wheel and cut through the metal as easily as the weapons we developed for use in Iraq when your soldier's waged war against the cursed Crusaders who had invaded your land.

"I'm certain you witnessed how easily our deadly IED's penetrated the worthless armor of the cursed invading infidel's foul war machine. Al-Wahhad, once these rails are fired off, the molten copper will cut through the axle of the train, thus causing the crash that shall mark your war." Muslawi, secretly a member of Iran's QODs, the Special Forces of Iran who trained others in terrorist tactics, offered. He was informed in advance by the Iraqi of their intended target, and how the terrorist cell was going to attack the train in the New York City Subway system.

"I see what you're offering to aid my war against this evil nation, my Persian brother. I understand how to install the copper detonation rails under Awadh's briefcase for the attack…"

"Ahhh… I see Awadh is going to be the first Martyr to your just cause waged against the hated infidels of the United States, al-Wahhad." Muslawi offered as he interrupted the Iraqi in mid-sentence, and then he waited for his response.

"Yes, he's the least useful fool to our just cause for Allah's sake and our revenge. I intend to eliminate him first." Al-Wahhad boasted proudly to the Iranian Operative.

"Very good al-Wahhad, a good Commander knows it's wise to get rid of the weakest link in the chain of your Command as soon as possible. Here is the detonation box and switch you shall install in the worthless fool's briefcase. This item is the trigger device, and you must have your bomb maker hide the thin wire lead inside the leather of the handle of the carrying case. So, no one can see it easily, and then all Awadh must do is simply put pressure on this button, and the charges will fire where he has placed the briefcase on the train floor as instructed. The great fool doesn't have to even think about it any further, all he must do is place the briefcase on the floor, place pressure on the handle with the button, and the weapon will do the rest for the great fool. I tried to make the operation as simple as possible for the one you picked to be the first Martyr." Muslawi looked al-Wahhad in the eyes and allowed a smile.

"I thank you my most cautious Iranian brother for all your concerns you offer me. Because the cursed worthless fool Awadh, doesn't possess much intelligence, I fear. I believe his mother must have mated with a filthy scorpion, and he's the son of a bothersome sand flea who has feasting upon foul camel dung in the vast sea of sands of our desert." Al-Wahhad's last words made the Iranian chuckle slightly.

When the Iranian stopped laughing, al-Wahhad went on with his words. He did not want to waste more time than necessary with the Persian, because he did not trust or even like the man as he added. "Muslawi, I thank you and your honorable government for all the help you have offered my cell. When our war on the West and their allies has run its course, and we're successful and have destroyed the great Satan and all its evil followers. I shall inform the world of your kind help. My Persian ally, I believe I'll take what you offered and be on my way. I have many troublesome fools I must keep a close eye upon, before they make a mistake and bring the eye of the law down upon my shoulders…"

"Don't be in such haste to leave my presence my friend; because there's another form of help, I'm free to offer you and your growing terrorist cell. The item I shall give you will make the attack you shall employ the item against will cause most devastating damage and death to our common enemy of all Arab nations of the world who follow Ali and Allah." Muslawi offered in his attempt to delay al-Wahhad's departure. He wanted to use the Iraqi and his terrorist cell to cause vast damage and death to the United States.

The terrorist placed a strained look on his face, informing the wise Persian Operative that he did not know what he was speaking about. This action from al-Wahhad caused Muslawi to add to the confusion he offered to the Iraq leader of the entrepreneurial and young terrorist cell rapidly shaping up to commit their first terrorist attack against the United States. "Al-Wahhad, please allow me to offer you a second weapon that'll lay the very heart of the land of Satan open and bleeding. I must ask you, because if you remember the incident, it'll make my story much easier for you to follow and understand, my Arab brother."

"Ask your question of me then, Muslawi." Al-Wahhad fired back at the Persian.

"Do you happen to remember the devastating earthquake that struck and destroyed much of the worthless nation of Chile on February 26th, of 2010?" Muslawi asked with concern.

"Yes of course I do. Why do you ask me such a foolish question, Muslawi? What does that incident have to do with what we were speaking about? You're confusing me further."

"Ahhh yes…my foolish and unlearned Arab brother, you must learn the important virtue Ali teaches us, fool. Patience my most unwise brother, and all will be explained to your troubled mind in good time, before you leave my side, I assure you. Al-Wahhad, what you and most of the others of the world don't know, the foolish United States has assembled a special National Nuclear Security Administration, or the NNSA Organization.

"These evil jackals working under the NNSA banner have one order and one order only to carry out in their wasted lives. They're responsible for the collection of HEU or Highly Enriched Uranium. Please, before you interrupt and ask me what I'm about to explain for your ears, al-Wahhad. For the past sixteen years, the American teams have been in a race against terrorist cells of the world. To collect the global supply of HEU, in their foolish attempt to keep such powerful threats of mass destruction out of the hands of al-Qaeda, and any of their terrorist followers. The reason I bring Chile and the earthquake to your attention, is because my brother.

"When the powerful earthquake struck Chile, that loathsome nation of lowly infidels was in control of thirty-five kilograms of highly enriched Uranium, given to that worthless nation by the fools of the United States, and the equally as foolish nation of Russia. Ahhhh… I see by the strained expression clouding over in your face that you don't understand why these nations, would dare give such a backwards nation as Chile, the ability to make ten nuclear weapons with the supply of HEU the cursed nations of non-believers gave to that foul nation. Al-Wahhad, the reason for the deadly gift was, at a meeting held between the seven nuclear nations of the world of that time. It was decided to give any nation who wanted such a threat their own supply of HEU. Even Viet Nam received twenty kilograms of HEU.

"The seven nuclear nations were of the foolish belief that if they supplied the worthless nations of the world with Highly Enriched Uranium. Those foul nations would not engage in trying to produce their own supply of HEU. Thus, the nuclear nations wanted to believe no other nation would dare to try and develop their own weapons of mass destruction in the possession of these seven nations. Those seven evil nations were the United States, Russia, France and United Kingdom, China, Pakistan, and India. That exclusive family has been extended by North Korea, the filthy nation of Israel and South Africa, and now even Iran.

"Again, I see the puzzled look written upon your foolish face, al-Wahhad. I speak the truth that the nation of Iran is now in possession of three complete nuclear warheads, and by this time next year, my nation will have ten more nuclear warheads at hand. We shall also be in possession of missiles developed and needed to get the nuclear warheads to target. These words are for your ears only, because the wise leaders of my country want the world, especially the worthless Zionist nation of Israel. To believe we're still involved with efforts to make enough HUE to construct the nuclear weapons we shall employ to destroy the cursed nation of Jews.

"Back to my story for your enlightment al-Wahhad, these unwise nations gave a total of forty-five thousand kilograms of HEU, to fifty lower class nations of the world, under the Atoms for Peace system. That's enough nuclear material for the construction of eight hundred nuclear weapons, and here is where Iran comes into the mix during this rapidly unfolding drama. Al-Wahhad, this nuclear material was supposed to be used in civilian reactors that are often poorly guarded and protected. That belief makes many civilian reactors vulnerable to theft from the worthless workers. Or open to Operatives working for other nations that want the same thing Iran and Iraq want, the end of the Western domination of the world.

"Al-Wahhad, the attention of my nation to this find was in November of 2007. That's when two terrorist teams hit Pelindaba. A thought to be well secured nuclear facility housing many kilograms of highly enriched weapons grade Uranium constructed in South Africa. The attack was successful to the point where the foolish terrorists were able to gain complete access to the control room of the nuclear facility. The worthless fools then fled the facility without removing any of the Enriched Uranium.

"That's all the history I'm going to lay out at your feet, al-Wahhad. The reason I give you this much information, is so you understand what has occurred in this unending drama. We had several deep Operatives working in Chile for many years. Al-Wahhad we were successful with acquiring eleven kilograms of Chile's Highly Enriched Uranium, long before the earthquake hit that cursed country of worthless jackals. The earthquake caused the situation that followed and made it easy to cover the missing nuclear material from America's workers who invaded Chile. That enabled us to remove the dangerous Uranium from Chile.

"The missing nuclear material was discovered by the American workers, but because of the situation and the need to remove the remaining Uranium from that devastated nation. Forced the Americans to overlook the missing material and the worthless fools had never revisited the situation, to try and discover what might have happened to the missing product. Highly enriched Uranium is an extremely important concern to the fools in command of the West, because of the easy in which this clean product can be turned into a mushroom cloud against the fools. Employing little effort and cost, and the effect if exploded in a city such as New York or Washington, could easily kill hundreds of thousands non-believing infidels.

"Thanks to the activities of terrorist groups such as al-Qaeda, Boko Haram, and al-Shabab that the Western world is so concerned with getting their hands on any nuclear material and making a successful dirty bomb to be employed against their interests and country. This United States Administration held a nuclear security summit in Washington. The fool's goal was met at this foul meeting, where the United States program was accepted by forty different heads of state. It was further determined the HRU produced by any nuclear reactors was to be sent to the United States and Russia. Where the deadly HRU will be processed down to where the once weapons grade Uranium would be turned into a form of Uranium that cannot be engineered into the construction of any nuclear weapons.

"At great cost to my nation, we were successful with transferring the missing product out of Chile. We imported the material to the border of the United States by using the Libyan Diplomatic Pouch protection for safe transfer of the material. I had a few very trusted Operatives working in the United States turning this product into a working nuclear item, and when you abandon New York City for your next target in Washington. I shall make much of this clean product available for your use in the attack on the heart of Satan. So, al-Wahhad, the whites of my eyes should be the last you investigate before leaving New York City for your next target.

"The reason why my nation targeted the worthless nation of Chile to acquire their Uranium supply was so this pure product couldn't possibly be traced back to my nation as its origin. Because as you can plainly see for yourself al-Wahhad, anyone involved in this acquirement and transfer of the missing Uranium, have met with sudden and deadly accidents. Those accidents removed any eyes from being aimed at Iran as the nation in question, when the weapon you'll detonate between the White House and Capitol Building occurs.

"Yes, al-Wahhad, since I offer you this pure nuclear product, I'm informing you of the target you shall destroy with our great gift to your terrorist cell. If this order goes against your desires, you're free to go on your way and attack any worthless target you already have in mind. But you'll not be able to employ this great gift from Allah of this product and kill hundreds of thousands of lowly infidels from this evil nation of Satan. If Allah didn't mean for the fools of the United States to be sheered, He would not have made them a nation of cursed sheep. So, what is it to be my brother? Will you attack where I suggest, or will you attack another worthless target in this country without the death and destruction I offer you, al-Wahhad? It's your choice to make, and I pray to Allah you make the right decision."

While the Persian Operative held the Iraqi terrorist locked up in his angry glare, Al-Wahhad quickly milled over the offer just made from the Iranian Operative. After drawing in air to settle his nerves, he finally replied. "By the wise Ten Prophets of Islam Muslawi, it'll be my sacred duty to attack the heart of Satan where you have suggested, while employing the product you offered to me. I thank the Almighty Allah for placing you within my faithful foot path, and the help you and your country offered my cell."

The terrorist leader continued to stare back at the Persian Operative while he responded to his question. The Iraqi was aware Muslawi was brought over to the United States through the new Libyan government politicians. They made the deal with the Iranian government once Iran promised the struggling new Libyan government vast amounts of cash and weapons, to maintain their grip of power over the fractured country. He knew this was the only way for an Iranian to get into the United States, because America and Iran had no diplomatic ties with each nation.

"Then so be it al-Wahhad, here is the weapon you shall employ on your opening attack against the nation of Satan. Please, take the weapon I offer you and quickly be gone from my side. Because I have much work to accomplish on this unending day, and I must begin that work now I fear." Muslawi offered al-Wahhad the three long copper rails, after he returned them to the protective cardboard tube for safe transportation.

Al-Wahhad bowed politely to the Persian Agent as he took possession of the narrow tube, and then he quickly left the Iranian Operative. He was pleased for the gift of the explosive rails. He was happy, because he understood he now had the power to hit the United States with catastrophic attacks. Al-Wahhad's attention was glued on the next part of his planned operation. That was to get back to his apartment and find the time and train to place al-Awajy on. So, he could do the most damage to the City of New York and her people.

Al-Wahhad also wanted to see if al-Awajy had followed his orders faithfully to buy the silk suit, the Star of David, and the expensive briefcase to carry the explosive charge in. He had a second part of his plan to place in motion as soon as possible. That was to attack the huge airport terminal stationed at the Kennedy International Airport in Queens New York, on the same day of his first attack aimed against the United States. He wanted this to stretch the emergency responders to their absolute limits, and to have more American civilians die in their twin terrorist attacks from lack of assistance and medical care.

These deaths will happen because of the lack of emergency care offered to the massive amount of wounded of the twin attacks. On his way back to his apartment, he stopped by a newspaper stand and brought a copy of the Wall Street Journal newspaper for al-Awajy's use. To help him avoid the ever-watching eye of the security people he understood would be watching everyone riding the train system.

Abdulaziz al-Wahhad further understood if he was successful with his dual attacks against the City of New York. Many civilians would die, and the emergency responders would be quickly overwhelmed with the mounting death and injured, so their treatment of the dead and wounded would suffer severely. This lack of treatment would cause the intended death rate to climb more than if he only carried out one attack against the city on that day. He increased his pace because he wanted to return to his apartment, so he could get the others of his terrorist cell moving with this planned attack against the United States and her civilians.

CHAPTER NINE

AL-WAHHAD'S APARTMENT, SATURDAY,
MAY 8th, 2011

The ex-Iraqi General Abdulaziz al-Wahhad was up early, and he was rather excited. This was because late last night before he went to sleep; he called Awadh al-Awajy, Mohsen al-Gasim, and Reemabdel Aziz al-Rowaili, and he ordered the three to arrive at his apartment at eight a.m. sharp on Saturday morning. He also ordered al-Awajy to bring the new suit and Star of David with the attaché case with him, because he wanted to make certain al-Awajy brought the right items for this attack.

Al-Gasim and Reemabdel were the first ones to arrive at his apartment which pleased al-Wahhad. Because he enjoyed looking at the very captivating and beautiful young Arab woman, who always wore the most reveling clothes whenever they met. The three were getting settled in when al-Awajy entered the room looking like he was afraid of the world. His expression made the terrorist leader bark savagely at the scared looking young Arab man. "Fool born from a jackal's arse, what makes you shake like you're standing with your foul feet resting in cold water? Never mind my question fool, did you remember to bring the cursed suit with the other items I have ordered you to bring with you today?"

With a shaking hand, al-Awajy held up the package and offered it to the leader of the terrorist group, again angering al-Wahhad as he snapped at the Arab man a second time. "Your fears, they make you foolish! I don't want the cursed items, put on the foul suit. I want to see how it fits your foolish body along with the other items you purchased…"

"Here! Now!" Al-Awajy offered with surprise as he cried further. "Al-Wahhad, there is a worthless woman in our presence, and I don't prefer to be naked before her worthless eyes."

"Believe me lowly dog who has feasted upon filthy camel dung. Reemabdel is not the least bit interested in seeing such a foul and so out of shape Arab as you are naked. I ordered you to dress in the foul suit you purchased and that is what you shall do before I lose my patience with you, fool. If you're so concerned with Reemabdel seeing your manhood, I order her to turn her back so she cannot see what she is not interested in seeing. Further complaints from your worthless lips and the whites of my eyes will be the last you'll see before you kiss the feet of Allah." Al-Wahhad growled as he turned away from al-Awajy. Then he laid eyes on the others in the room as he spoke to al-Gasim.

"Mohsen, I have a number of other items I must share with you, my friend. Here, look at what I have acquired from the Persian fool who acts like he was my brother. Yet I see in his worthless eyes he desired my death, as much as he desired the deaths, we shall soon offer to Allah of the hordes of lowly infidels who infest the earth." He offered as he removed the three explosive copper tracks from the round cardboard tube. He then handed the tracks to al-Gasim as he explained what they meant to them.

By the time al-Awajy was dressed in the suit, al-Wahhad finished explaining how the brass tracks were used. Al-Awajy moved to the center of the room and stood before the leader. Al-Wahhad and Reemabdel slowly circled the scared Arab as if they were sharks stalking their pray.

"Ahhh… I must say you clean up very well for a young fool. With the way you cut your foul hair and the closeness of your shave with no nicks. You look more like a lowly Zionist than the foolish Zionists do. Farima has done very well with shaving your cursed face for you. I must remember to commend her good efforts. Al-Awajy that cursed Star and attaché case finishes what I desired you to look like. Looking like you do I cannot believe any foul watchers would pay any attention of you or raise any concern against them as you get on the subway train. Get out of the suit and protect it from wrinkles as you store it for our future operation."

Al-Wahhad looked like his watch and then he added to his words to the others. "Yes, Thursday is the day Allah will blow His mighty breath out and take His revenge against the non-believers of this world. Tomorrow is

Sunday and al-Gasim, I wish to speak to the old man you offered would be pleased to assist us. I will order Saud to attend this meeting between the old man, yourself, and me also, and he'll bring his weapon with him. I want the old man to become accustom with the weapon he'll use in his part of this dual attack. I feel we have met long enough for this day, I don't wish to tempt fate for us to be seen together for long periods of time, until the day we attack the infidels. Be gone so I can attend to other problems I face in this operation. Remember al-Gasim to bring the old man at noon tomorrow because it's believed that time is when the watchers of this cursed land relax their attention the most."

Al-Gasim went to offer but was instantly cut off by al-Wahhad, as he nearly snarled at him. "No, you must leave your girlfriend behind for this meeting, fool. The fewer attending the meeting, the least eyes will be drawn to our actions. Remember this warning because I don't want any of our cell to communicate by phones, computers or any other forms of communications but face to face contact. You are ordered to communicate with direct contact and word of mouth only I want your foul mouths covered by your hand or other items, whenever you speak to one another out in public. One never knows when the cursed watchers are on duty and might be looking at you."

The terrorist leader said nothing more to the three other members of his budding terrorist cell, as he waited for them to leave his apartment. When they were gone, the first thing he did was place a call to the store where Saud worked, and he ordered a pizza to be delivered to his apartment tomorrow at twelve noon, to be enjoyed with the afternoon baseball game. This was to warn Saud he wanted to meet with him in code tomorrow at noon. When he added to his order, he wanted hot peppers on the pie. It further informed Saud he wanted him to bring the weapon with him to the meeting.

When Saud took the order, he knew he was going to complain he was feeling ill to his boss. But he would deliver the pizza as a favor and then go home for the rest of the day, so he could meet with the leader of the terrorist cell. It was always slow on Sundays, and he knew his boss would not mind his leaving for the day.

SUNDAY, MAY 9th, 2011, EXATLY TWELVE NOON

There was a light tap on his apartment door, and al-Wahhad cautiously opened it to discover Saud standing before him, wearing a smile, and holding a hot pizza in his hands. 4/85 No sooner did he allow the young Arab man to enter the apartment than did al-Gasim come strolling down the hallway along with an elder man in tow. He waited with the door held open for them, and when they entered his room, he closed the door behind them. The leader of the terrorist cell was not too concerned with anyone living or visiting the building, taking notice of the comings and goings of his room. Because mostly everyone on this floor, were either Arab or young people only interested in getting high and having sex.

The moment al-Wahhad closed the door, al-Gasim offered. "Shabbah," Al-Gasim took to calling al-Wahhad the Iraqi name of Ghost, and the leader took to the name immediately. He though it quite fitted the way he wanted to be known, as al-Gasim went on with his words. "This gentleman with me is Ali Abbas Hamad, and he's a well trusted Algerian, he has lived peacefully in the United States for thirty years now. In fact, he has two sons who are police officers of this hated city. He's highly respected and beyond reproach because of the work he has done for the community. He came to this country when the eyes were not aimed at the Arab peoples..."

"If this old man is so well-respected living in this cursed city of non-believers, why is he so willing to help us destroy this foul city? I hope you have not brought a fool working for the people we hate, al-Gasim?" Abdulaziz al-Wahhad growled at the young Arab man.

"No, Shabbah that is not the situation at all. The reason Ali is so willing to assist us in our time of need, is because he is found to be slowly dying from cancer and speaking with him, I was able to draw him back to the ways of the faithful Arabs of Allah. Besides Shabbah, I promised him we shall take good care of the rest of his family after he is gone, that satisfied and made Ali want to help our cause." Al-Gasim offered.

The leader of the terrorist cell turned from al-Gasim, and he aimed his eyes directly at the old man as if they were weapons as he grumbled at the old man, still not trusting him completely. "Ali, I understand and feel your pain, and if you're a true believer of the sacred words written in the Holy Qur'an. Your surviving family will have nothing to worry about for the rest of their lives I assure you, if you carry out my orders faithfully." Lying was becoming so easy for the terrorist Shabbah, he no longer believed he was lying with anything he said.

The old man nodded slowly and then he replied in a strained voice. "Thank you for your kind offer to protect my family for the rest of their lives, after I have gone to be with Allah in Paradise. Yes, that was my only worry when I received the death sentence from the lowly jackals who call themselves Doctors in this country. Mohsen al-Gasim has informed me of what is expected, and he has further warned me you are a Shagawah, an Iraqi man to be well feared. I shall not hesitate to do what you order done, al-Wahhad. I stand at your command."

"That is good Ali, that was all I had to hear from your lips to believe you stand by my and Allah's side, in this war ongoing against the cursed infidels of this evil country. It's time to show you why I ordered you to appear before me on this day, Ali. Saud." The terrorist leader said as he turned and looked at him, and then asked him with concern in his voice. "I trust you have brought the weapon with you, fool?"

"Yes al-Wahhad and I'll explain to you and Ali what has to be done to the weapon, to destroy the plane while in flight." Saud went through lengths to explain the workings of the weapon. Al-Gasim was not so interested in this part of the attack, because it did not concern him.

When Saud finished explaining the working of the weapon to the old man, and how to fire it off while he was on board the aircraft, al-Wahhad took over and he spoke to the ones gathered in his apartment. He asked Saud to explain how he was going to get the weapon on board the airliner with the security the airports currently employ to foil a terrorist attack against the aircraft. He wanted his bases covered now they had the old man willing to work with them.

"I want you and Ali to pay close attention to this part of the attack we have planned against the airport, and what I have to offer, and what Ali will do to complete his part of this mission. When Ali ordered the flight ticket for California and back to New York, I was with him, and I ordered the old man to request a wheelchair for his handicap needs. I met Ali through al-Gasim when he brought the old man up to my attention, al-Wahhad. The reason I ordered Ali to request a handicap situation, is because when you use an airport wheelchair. The fools who run the security don't send you through the metal detector, nor do they send you through the system that'll usually detect any explosive residue on your person or hidden within your luggage or anything you carry on board the aircraft.

"Al-Wahhad, they won't even send the cursed cane Ali has to use to walk properly with, through any detection device. So, for the future we can use this way to get weapons on board any aircraft we intend to destroy. Err…al-Wahhad I seem to be getting a little off the track here, once Ali has passed through the security of the airport, he'll sit peacefully in the wheelchair until it's time for him to board the foul aircraft. When he's on board and the plane is in flight, he'll suddenly run out of oxygen in his small portable air tank, and the aircraft will be forced to drop an emergency air line down for the old man to continue to breathe properly. Then the pilot will be forced to turn his aircraft and return to Kennedy Airport under an emergency. At the exact moment when the wheels of the aircraft are back on the ground, that is when Ali will detonate the foul weapon resting by his side.

"Once the explosion occurs on board the civilian airliner, because the foul aircraft will be still loaded with most of its fuel it needed to get the aircraft out to California. The airliner and explosion will do the rest of what we want accomplished for this action aimed against the lowly infidels of this evil nation.

"The cursed airliner will be allowed to land with the extra fuel still stored on board the aircraft, because it'll be designated as a medical emergency, and the aircraft will be given top priority to land without being forced to burn off their fuel supply, before their landing is accomplished. Or the pilot is allowed to dump the fuel because the aircraft will be so loaded with fuel. I have carefully studied every aspect of this attack by the time the airliner crashes, and the explosion takes place, and everything is over. I predict deaths of from five to seven thousand god cursed infidels who'll meet their fate in this attack on the airport." Band Ibn Saud offered to the leader of the terrorist group and his elderly ward.

The leader of the group turned to Ali and then he asked the elderly man with concern lacing his voice, as he stared the old man dead in the eyes. "Ali, do you understand what you have to do to make this attack a success for our just cause, my brother? What will become of your earthly body and you going to meet Allah in Paradise?"

Looking from Saud to al-Wahhad because he was the one asking a question, Ali nodded yes to the concerned leader of the terrorist cell.

"This is very good for me to see and hear, my elderly brother. From this point forward though, you'll not be allowed out of the sight of either Saud or al-Gasim for one moment until your part of this attack has been completed by you, old man. Today was the last time you shall see anyone from your honorable family I warn you. You have to understand that your family is our responsibility from this point forward, and I shall look after my responsibilities faithfully I assure you, my friend." Abdulaziz al-Wahhad offered the concerned looking old man as he turned and looked at al-Gasim before he offered him.

"Shabbah, I'd deem it an honor and a privilege if I'm allowed to look after Ali, until it's time for him to make his trip to Paradise and be with Allah. There he'll live like a King in the land of wonderment and glory, with many maidens to look after all his needs and desires."

"I'll bestow that honor on you. Al-Gasim, I demand you contact me every morning, until we attack the lowly infidels. I want to make certain Ali does not change his mind…"

"Al-Wahhad! I will not change my mind for any reason, because I have been given a death sentence of slowly wasting away until there will not be much left of me to bury here on earth, and the only way I can rest in peace. Is to understand that my honorable family is well looked after in my stead." Ali growled at the terrorist leader.

"Enough of this cursed long winded foolishness, I said what I had to say, and you'll follow my instructions as issued if you want to reach Paradise and stand at the side of Allah. Today is Sunday, counting the rest of this day means we have five days we must wait, until we can finally take our revenge against the cursed infidels of this evil land for the death of bin Laden. Saud, al-Gasim, Ali I am greatly pleased at what we have accomplished here today.

"We are done with this meeting for the time being then, and we shall meet again on Wednesday, and setup for our attacks against this evil land. You must leave and al-Gasim, you shall remember to contact me on each day, and if anything happens that might change our plans on us. You must throw all caution to the wind and contact me directly, so I can judge the situation and continue or cancel our planned attack against this land of lowly jackals. Be gone with the three of you now." Al-Wahhad aimed a sharp eye at the others until Saud was the first one to leave his small apartment that was just a room. Ten minutes later al-Gasim and Ali left, and Abdulaziz al-Wahhad busied himself for the rest of the day looking after what he believed was important to their plans to destroy the subway train.

Monday morning al-Wahhad was busy making coffee for himself when he was startled by a soft knock on his door. He cautiously opened it to find Mohsen al-Gasim on the other side, and he growled at the young man. "You have turned my blood to ice knocking on my cursed door like this, you fool. What is your problem and where the devil is that old man I assigned to your care yesterday, fool?"

"Forgive me for startling you so, Shabbah. But I'm only following your orders of contacting you every day, al-Wahhad. The old man is being well entertained by my girlfriend Reemabdel, who spent the night with us to help the old fool…"

"Yes, yes Mohsen I remember now, and I can only imagine how Reemabdel must be looking after you while she's supposed to be helping with the old man, Mista. You have left the old man in very capable hands I believe, al-Gasim. I'm pleased you remember my orders so well." The terrorist leader remarked as he allowed the fear the young man caused to leave.

Al-Wahhad went deep in thought for a moment and then he offered. "After rethinking my orders to you fool, I believe it'll not be necessary for you to come to my apartment every day to check in with me. You may make a call and if all is well, you'll merely say. 'I shall see you on Wednesday morning, and then you'll hang up with no further words."

"I understand your new orders and I'll do as instruct, al-Wahhad." With that said the young Mohsen left his apartment.

Tuesday morning at exactly nine thirty a.m., Mohsen al-Gasim placed a call to Abdulaziz al-Wahhad after he checked on Ali, to make certain the old man was still willing to do what he had agreed for the terrorist cell. Al-Wahhad answered the call on the third ring and listened to al-Gasim's words as he offered him. "Shabbah, I shall meet you on Wednesday morning as instructed." Then he hung up, but his call shook al-Wahhad to his bones when he called him Ghost in Iraqi, and added he was going to meet him on Wednesday as instructed. He could only hope the listening ears of the Intelligence Communities of the United States, did not pick up the less than three-minute phone call in their constant monitoring net.

MORNINGSIDE MARYLAND, NINE-THIRTY-ONE A.M. TUESDAY MAY 11th, 2011

In a secret and well secluded and highly secured government building less than ten thousand square feet, a bank of large main computers was running twenty-four hours a day, every day. The assignment for these computers was to monitor millions of E'mails, cell phone calls, land lines calls, along with any other form of signal communications employed throughout the world. When one of the ever on guard computers suddenly picked up a certain buzz word, the call was instantly rerouted to a side computer, and then saved in a special file for closer examination by the technicians when the call ended up in the hands of a human operative.

Al-Gasim's call to al-Wahhad was made and the Iraqi word for Ghost bumped the call up to the security computer. An exhausted human monitor noticed the red light and he grumbled more to himself than anyone else as he picked up the earpiece and then listened as the call was recorded. The exhaustion instantly left his body as he rose and then excitedly signaled the supervisor who immediately rushed to his side, and he hit the repeat button on the computer, and then he listened to the call as it replayed. When the Arabic buzz word for 'Ghost' was heard, the supervisor hit the button that instantly sent this message over to the CIA Command Center.

CIA COMMAND CENTER

Tuesday morning at nine thirty-seven a.m. CIA Director John Raincloud was resting in his office as he set his mind for the day's toils. He was enjoying a cup of coffee and a cheese Danish, when the light on his computer glowed, and he realized he was receiving a secured communication. With a groan of dissatisfaction, he sat forward while resting his cup and half eaten Danish on his computer table. The powerful CIA Director flipped on his computer and the notification printed out on the monitor screen. It was the entire print out of the phone call from al-Gasim to al-Wahhad, and when the Director picked up the Arabic word for 'Ghost', he quickly reread the alerted message.

The Director's hands then flew over the keyboard as he searched the FBI Security list of suspects considered a serious threat to any public officials, or that person was deemed a national security threat. He checked the list for anyone registered as the Ghost in Arabic. No name came to light, so the highly concerned Director switched over to the Pentagon JIPT, or Joint Integrated Prioritized Target List/watch list, and no name was attached to the Ghost on these files either. The Director then checked the watch list accumulated by his specialized branch of Intelligence. For the third time no name came up attached to the Ghost request.

A second possible terrorist warning alert was suddenly flashed on the Director's computer screen, lifting the first alert up to a Priority One, or the highest alert warning. Meaning it was being classified as a terrorist threat and imminent danger aimed at the United States.

"Shit, shit, shit." The angry Director growled as he hit the intercom, and then ordered his secretary to get the Chairman of the Joint Chiefs of Staff on the line for him. He released the button and checked the known watch and warning lists from all over the world, for the possible identification of the man called 'Ghost' in the intercepted call. Wherever he went in the intelligence world the results were the same, no identification was discovered for anyone called the Ghost in Arabic.

General John White was sort of dragging his feet, because he held a late-night meeting with certain members of his staff, over the ongoing green on blue attacks occurring by Afghanistan soldiers and police officers against American and NATO soldiers operating in that country. He just flipped his legs off the bed when his phone rang, and he grumbled into it. "Yeah, John here."

"Good morning General White, this is Cat from the Director's office, sir. John has just requested to speak with you immediately sir. I'll connect you with the Director, General."

"Thank you, sweetheart." No sooner did John get the words out then the excited Director's voice fill the line. "Good morning, John, sorry for the early call, I know you worked late last night. John, I just received a priority terrorist alert for an impending possible terrorist attack on our soil, sir. Before you ask, confidence is high, the highest possible. It's coming John."

"Where? When? How? And who the fuck is the brains behind this possible attack?"

"I don't quite know at this point John. All I know is some scumbag named "Ghost" is the ringleader of this possible terrorist cell. The call originated in New York City. The only thing I can deduct from the warning so far is the terrorist attack if it comes, will take place in New York City within the next few days, sir."

"God dammit, I knew with this President in command of the country, it'd be only a matter of time before we were hit again by some pack of fucking terrorist assholes. What about you? Did you check the watch lists to see if you can get a make on this lousy sonofabitch called Ghost, sir?" General White growled as he struggled to dress while holding the phone to his ear.

"Of course, I did General that was the first thing I did before calling you." Raincloud snapped, pissed the General would have the nerve to ask him such a question as he added to his words. "John, you have to remember with the problems this Administration gave the Intel Communities when he first took over command of the Presidency. Caused many of my people to duck and cover their damn asses, sir. That caused the Intel Communities to sort of neglect the terrorist watch lists, John. I'm quite certain that's why this jackass is not identified now. But I have confidence we'll pull up his identity before he and anyone working with his ass, gets a chance to hurt us, sir. I already alerted all my Operatives working in New York, as I sent an alert to Homeland Defense, and other security and law officials in the northeast region."

"Dammit, I should be leaving within the next ten minutes, Director. Where do you want to linkup?" The Chairman offered as he finished dressing.

"John, I'll meet you at your office, you have the same communications set up there as I do here, sir. I think I'd like to hold this meeting in the Gold Room of the Joint Chiefs of Staff of the Pentagon, General. I'd like to have the Director of PCIS (Pentagon Criminal Investigation Services) attend the meeting also. I want as much brain thrust as I can possibly muster for this meeting, if we have a possible active terrorist threat aimed at us in New York City, General White. I should be arriving at your office in half an hour at the latest, sir. Do you want to include the President in on this meeting, or go over what I have first before we report to the Boss, General White?" The concerned Director asked the powerful military officer.

"I want to know the exact extent of the possible terrorist threat being aimed at New York City first, before we go and bother the President. You know how the man is, if we see something coming down the damn chute, he wants to see something happen before he can deny it happened. Get over to my office as soon as possible, sir. I'll have the Director of PCIS stand in on the meeting to get his input, John."

THE GOLD ROOM OF THE PENTAGON, TUESDAY, MAY 11th, 2011 AT ZERO TEN TWENTY HUNDRED HOURS

General John White was seated and speaking with Edward Falcone, the Director of PCIS when the CIA Director John Raincloud was led to the room. Both men stopped speaking until the Director was seated and comfortable, and then the Chairman asked the full-blooded Sioux Native American. "Well John, you have me and Edward here, what do you have for us, sir?"

"Not very much more than I have already informed you of now I'm afraid, General White. I told you most of what I was able to assemble over this sudden terrorist threat alert, sir. Because the call originated so near Ground Zero in New York City, I immediately hit the panic button, sir. General, this is what I have accumulate as of this time. General White, you know we've been expecting and preparing for an Islamic terrorist attack against us, because we have successfully killed Usama bin Laden. That's the reason I'm placing the highest confidence on this call as being an extremely serious threat against our security and nation, sir.

"The damn call was placed to this prick the caller branded 'Ghost' over the communication, more threat was picked up because the name was said in Iraqi, made to this Ghost fellow. John, a few years back when we went after the madman of Iraq the second time. I seem to remember a powerful Iraqi General who was nicknamed Ghost.

"I immediately checked through my numerous sources and true as it was, there was an Iraqi General who was branded the Ghost, but the lousy sonofabitch disappeared from the face of the earth a number of years back on us, sir. Something I was able to discover about this man chilled me to my very soul though, John. I discovered maybe this missing Iraqi General somehow was picked up by another intelligence source, and he was invited to enter the United States for a certain reason. Because the man became a valuable cog with helping us settle down a certain area of Iraq after we secured Baghdad. Now don't get excited before you heard all the facts I assembled first, General! Although it'll take me time, I'll locate the other services that might have allowed this Iraqi General to come to the United States, if he's here that is sir."

"How the hell long do you think it'll take you to locate this fucking Iraqi General, John? Here's a better question, Director. Where and when do you think this attack will take place?" General White growled at the Director before he was able to get his temper under control.

"I'm afraid it'll take me a few days to get the answer to that question if this Iraqi is the man, they branded the Ghost. If this General was invited to the United States because of some help he offered our government and troops, and to answer your second question, General White. I believe the pending attack is only in the talking stage at this point, because this was the first contact, we were able to pick up on this possible terrorist obviously operating in New York City, sir. I immediately ordered an increase in monitoring all signal communications, because I had a gut feeling something was going to happen because of the killing of their king fucking rat bin Laden, General White."

"Get on it and I'm going to pull in a number of favors from other nations we work with, and see if they have anything on a fucking Iraqi General known as Ghost…"

"I'll do the same thing from my side and see if any other Intelligence Communities have something on an Iraqi General branded Ghost during the second invasion of that damn country, General White." Director Raincloud offered as he rose and turned to leave the General's office, but he was stopped by the Chairman when he said.

"Director Raincloud, I don't want any of this shit to be brought up to the President, not until we have a damn handle on this lousy Iraqi bastard, and if he did make his way to the United States and what the lousy bastard might be up to here, sir. At the next terrorist briefing with the President, I'll feel the boss out first. If I feel we can have a productive conversation over this possible terrorist situation developing with the Boss. I'll be the one who'll bring it up to his attention. Dealing with this guy is harder than trying to get the underwear off a damn virgin. He doesn't want to hear a damn thing about a possible terrorist action occurring in the United States. He still believes al-Qaeda is a beaten terrorist organization, and we know damn well any Operative for al-Qaeda, is working his butt off trying to get at us." General White went silent, and he watched the Director leave, but not before he added.

"John, you do understand that I want to be informed the moment, and I mean the exact fucking moment you get some concrete information about this sonofabitching Ghost fella, and what he might be up to here in the States, sir!"

The Director did not reply, all he did was give the Chairman the thumbs up signal, and then he quickly left the General's office.

WEDNESDAY, MAY 12th, 2011, TWELVE THIRTY IN THE AFTERNOON, NEW YORK CITY

Mohsen al-Gasim knocked softly on Abdulaziz al-Wahhad's apartment door with Ali Abbas Hamad standing to his right. He was following his orders to bring the old man to his apartment so he could be supplied with the explosive device needed to destroy the American airliner. Band Ibn Saud and Awadh al-Awajy were already at the apartment, and Saud was in the process of wiring al-Awajy's attaché case with the explosive charge that would destroy the subway train tomorrow morning inside the train tunnel system. Al-Awajy was attentively watching Saud's every move with the explosive device. So, he could understand how he was to set off the charge after being briefed on where he was to place his briefcase down where it would do what was expected of the explosive device in the subway train car.

Al-Wahhad watched as al-Gasim carefully worked the explosive device Ali was to use to destroy the aircraft into the cut in half small oxygen tank. Then he worked the detonation wires through the top of the tank and hid the button at the underneath of the pressure gage. All Ali had to do was press the button when the plane returned to Kennedy Airport, and it would instantly explode. The terrorist leader smiled, pleased at how well his attacks was shaping up as he watched al-Gasim put the two ends of the tank back together. The cut seem was covered with the warning of oxygen being used in the narrow metal air supply tank.

Abdulaziz's attention was torn between Saud, who was busy working with al-Awajy, and the explosive tracks he was securing to the bottom of the expensive briefcase. He was rather impressed because the copper tracks made the attaché case look even more expensive than it was. His attention was diverted by what the old man and al-Gasim was doing with the oxygen tank. Only when Saud completed his work on the briefcase, and al-Gasim finished with the wires on the oxygen tank, did al-Wahhad finally start to breathe normally again. He looked at his watch and allowed a smile as he offered proudly.

"Al-Gasim, would you send Reemabdel out to get us something to eat. I warn everyone in this room that no one will leave this cursed apartment until it's time to go into action against this land of sin and Satan's helpers. What time is Ali's flight tomorrow morning, were you able to get a flight near the time I want the explosion to take place inside the cursed train tunnel?"

Mohsen replied proudly as he flashed a quick smile at the leader of the terrorist cell. "Yes, al-Wahhad, I was quite successful in acquiring a flight for Ali to depart Kennedy Airport at eight thirty-nine a.m. That means Ali will destroy the aircraft around nine ten a.m. as the aircraft returns to the foul airport to get him his believe to needed emergency treatment. It was the best I was able to line up to the time al-Awajy will destroy the cursed train."

"That'll have to do because it's far too late now to try and change the flight now, you fool you. I wanted the explosions to take place at the same exact moment. That wish was to stretch the cursed emergency responders to their absolute limits during our attacks aimed against the fools of this worthless nation. I want the others of our cell to begin leaving this foul city tonight. They are to head for our location in Washington where our next attacks will take place. I thank Allah, to allow the cursed infidels to elect such a weak fool to lead their country. He has made it so easy for us to destroy so many of his worthless people and escape this foul city before the intelligence fools are able to pick up our trail." Al-Wahhad boasted as he allowed another smile.

His smile allowed al-Gasim to offer. "I shall be forced to leave the apartment at five a.m. tomorrow morning, al-Wahhad. This time will allow me to get Ali over to the airport in time, so the security people don't look at him with cautious eyes and suspicion. It should take us no more than an hour to get to the airport by cab, and that'll get him there by six a.m. Allowing Ali two and a half hours at the terminal before his scheduled flight, Ali has orders and enough cash to eat breakfast and buy the newspaper for his flight…"

"Al-Gasim, I want you to leave for the cursed airport terminal at four thirty tomorrow morning with Ali. Allow him three hours to arrive just in case the worthless traffic of this city is heavier than you might believe. I can't afford to have the old gentleman arrive late for his flight." Al-Wahhad gave a look as if it was more a command than suggestion.

Mohsen al-Gasim nodded as his girlfriend left the apartment to get some food for the small group of terrorists. After the nod, everyone in the apartment settled down and they began to wait for their food to arrive, and then they were all going to turn in for the night so they could wake early to begin their attacks against the city.

The alarm went off at exactly two thirty a.m., but the alarm was not necessary because everyone in the apartment was already up. Reemabdel was busy shaving al-Awajy and then she helped him dress. Her lover was helping Ali get dressed then get ready to leave for the airport terminal. Al-Gasim reserved a cab for their drive over to Kennedy Airport yesterday. It was a one-way ride, because al-Gasim ordered al-Mutairi to meet him at the airport, so he could take him back to the apartment. He did not want to chance taking a cab for his return trip for fear after the aircraft explosion, the security people might put two and two together, and they think to check the cabs to see who left the airport.

With Reemabdel's help, al-Awajy was dressed and Abdulaziz al-Wahhad carefully looked him over. His suit, shave and haircut were perfect, the gold Star of David and chain hanging outside his shirt over his red tie, finished the picture off perfectly. When al-Awajy picked up the briefcase and Wall Street Journal and he tucked it under his arm. It made him look like a man working on Wall Street, even his shoes were polished just right.

Al-Wahhad smiled over the handiwork on al-Awajy's body. His attention was shifted to Ali who was dressed and ready to leave the apartment. Just like al-Awajy, Ali was a perfect picture of an American citizen enjoying the country and what she had to offer.

No one was going to accompany al-Awajy to the train station, and like Ali, he was going to take a cab to the Canal Street Six Train Station where he would then board the Hudson Line train heading for Grand Central Station. Al-Wahhad wanted the explosion to take place at as near to eight thirty as possible, because he figured that would be the heaviest traffic time for the subway system to have the most civilians on board the train, and waiting at the train station.

Everyone was seated watching the clock and when they heard the beep from the cab outside. Al-Gasim and Ali rose and headed out the apartment without anyone saying anything to them.

There was a sigh as the two left and much of the tension left them. Now, all that was left was for the terrorists to watch the clock until it was al-Awajy's time to leave the apartment.

With each tick of the clock, it seemed like a lifetime passed. The stress in al-Wahhad's mind was overwhelming, and he was having a frightful time trying not to explode at anyone who dared to move around in the room. He cast a quick look at al-Awajy and was surprised to see him so calm and comfortable, as he sat on the edge of his bed, and waited for his time to leave the apartment. He was barely sitting for fear of wrinkling his new suit. The terrorist leader had to shake his head, because he was looking at al-Awajy's fingernails, they were manicured to perfection. The reason he shook his head was because he never gave a thought to his fingernails, and someone from his group picked up his failure to attention and cared for al-Awajy's fingers. Abdulaziz l-Wahhad suddenly snapped his fingers and announced.

"Al-Awajy, I must caution while you're standing on the cursed platform of the train station. You must remember never to look at a woman with distain clouding over your foolish expression, even if the woman near you is exposed, and her fat breasts are in your vision, fool. You must remember while waiting for the worthless train to arrive, there will be many eyes of security constantly scanning the platform, looking for anything or one out of place. A mean scowl from you will surely draw their attention, and security might take the time to question you, which you can ill afford to allow happen for any reason, fool. You must remove everything you were first taught about how to treat a woman in the Arab world. You must remember that you're in the land of sin and lust and you must act as the foul fools of this country always do. Keep your mind active and make certain of your actions on the train station.

"Bah, there is so much you must be aware of and understand while you wait for the cursed train to arrive at the station. Also, while you're riding on the train and seated, you must act properly and is a cursed woman is standing, you'll rise and give her your seat to keep security from resting their eyes upon your person. If you're captured, I shall have your eyes burned with hot copper coins. If you are successful, you'll kiss the feet of Allah and share life with seventy-two virgins looking after your every desire and want, my Arab br..."

There was a sudden noise that caused al-Wahhad to stop speaking and look in the direction of the noise. It was Reemabdel and she purposely made the noise to get his attention, and when he looked at her, she looked at her watch to draw his attention to the time. He turned to the clock and noticed it was seven thirty and nearing the time for al-Awajy to leave for his mission.

The terrorist leader smiled then spoke to al-Awajy in a very calm tone of voice this time. "You must remember to speak English and keep your Arab accent out of your speech. A better idea, pick up some hard candies and always keep one in your foul mouth while you're waiting for and are on the train. The candy will mask your accent from the lowly infidels. Al-Awajy, prepare your mind to carry out your mission faithfully for Allah. A golden thrown awaits you in Paradise. May the wombs of their mother's cry out for the infidel's pending death, our enemy will fall like leaves of the winter. Soon, the poisonous breath of the United States and its presence in the Middle East and Persian Gulf will be no more. Be silent and speak with Allah until it's time to be on your quest."

Abdulaziz al-Wahhad turned his back on al-Awajy as if angry with him, and that gave him a little privacy. The leader of the terrorist cell wanted the soon to be dead Muslim man to make his final peace with Allah. He did not care a grain of sand for al-Awajy, or his wife and family. In fact, when al-Awajy was dead, his last act while still in New York City, he was going to kill al-Awajy's wife and two children. This was so she could not possibly betray him to the local authorities. He busied himself speaking in a low voice with Reemabdel and Saud, while the three waited for al-Awajy to leave the apartment.

Al-Wahhad noticed the time was eight a.m. and he spoke calmly to al-Awajy. "The time has arrived for you to leave on your sacred mission for Allah's sake, and the ongoing war we wage against the non-believers and jackals of this evil nation. When you leave, you'll go with Allah's hand resting tenderly upon your shoulder, and it shall remain there until He takes you to Paradise, to be with Him and the other Martyrs of the Arab world. Pick up your suitcase and newspaper, and then leave and find a cab and head for your destination and fate."

The Commanding terrorist waited not so patiently for al-Awajy to leave his small apartment. The moment he did, the terrorist leader rushed for the window, and he watched until al-Awajy slowly walked out of the building. He continued to watch the man until he waved a passing cab down. Al-Awajy quickly climbed into the waiting vehicle, and it drove off while being honked at by the car the cab cut off, to get back in the flow of traffic. When he was gone, al-Wahhad turned away from the window and then announced to the others who were still inside his apartment. "Finally, the cursed fool is on his foul way for his mission. Now we wait for the results of our operations against the lowly infidels of this foul city."

CHAPTER TEN

JOHN F. KENNEDY INTERNATIONAL AIRPORT, SIX TEN A.M.
THURSDAY, MAY 13th, 2011

Mohsen al-Gasim and Ali Abbas Hamad arrived at Kennedy International Airport at the time ordered, that gave him access to the secured passenger gate side of the massive terminal. Al-Gasim decided to remain with Ali until he was placed in the wheelchair al-Gasim requested for his needs. He smiled and watched as Ali was carefully wheeled by an airport attendant to the main security gate. One TSA security guard ran his hand down the sides of Ali's body without making him stand, so he could search him properly. The guard did not even glance at the mid-size oxygen tank resting on the foot stand of the wheelchair, nor did the unconcerned inspector look at the metal cane resting on Ali's lap, as he quickly finished his search of the old man.

Al-Gasim remained hanging around the security passenger gate until Ali was pushed through the gate the inspector opened for him and his wheelchair. He remained standing in the area until Ali was completely out of view on the secured side of the waiting area of the air terminal. He let out his breath in a rush as he realized the old man safely made it through the usually rough security of the terminal with no problems. Then he rushed out of the airport and looked for al-Mutairi. Finding him he jumped in his car then they roared onto Belt Parkway. They were heading for downtown Manhattan as fast as the rush hour traffic would allow.

When the young and pretty female airport attendant left Ali seated in the only restaurant opened this early in the morning at the airport and the old man ordered eggs, white toast, and coffee. While waiting for his order to arrive, he dared to take a quick glance at the oxygen tank explosive device resting on his wheelchair. He breathed a deep sigh when he noticed the gauge was still reading the tank was full of oxygen.

It was uncomfortable to enjoy his last meal with the air hose and extremely annoying nose clip wrapped around his face, as if the tank was truly giving him oxygen. When his breakfast arrived, Ali forgot about the air gauge and annoying clamp as he quickly ate his last meal.

INSIDE A NEW YORK CITY CAB

Awadh al-Awajy sat in the cab as it weaved its way in and out of the heavy downtown Manhattan traffic. He checked his watch and noticed it was eight ten a.m. then he looked out the window and realized he was about two minutes from the train station. In less than a heartbeat, he found himself standing outside the banged up idling yellow cab fishing for fifteen dollars and twenty-five cents the driver demanded for the fare. He gave the driver an extra five dollars that pleased the driver as he bid his first fare good day, and then the driver shot his cab in the flow of traffic. Again al-Awajy checked his watch, it was eight fourteen a.m.

Al-Awajy smiled because he made it to the train station in plenty of time to catch the scheduled train needed to get him where he was going to attack the great city. The unshaken young Arab man headed for the stairs leading to the underground Canal Street Six Train Station. As he walked down the stairs, three New York City police officers hiding behind a filthy one-way looking glass in an offside small room, watching every one entering the train station. They easily picked al-Awajy up and one officer mentioned to his comrade.

"Gees will you look at this fucking pussy ass guy, I bet this guy doesn't even get his damn hair mussed when he screws his hen. Yep, he's a Jew alright as I thought, see his Star of David. Man, I bet he paid half a thousand dollars for his suit and look. The little prick must work on Wall Street, because he's got the propaganda sheet tucked under his damn arm. I got a good mind to stop this little prick and mess up his day for him, along with his suit and hair just for the hell of it. It'll teach the prick to look so perfect while I'm stuck in this filthy room sweating my damn ass off, looking for some terrorist and mess up my fucking day for the love…"

"C'mon Billy I see the man and he don't fit the profile of anyone we're instructed to keep our eyes open for, man. I know how you feel about the dude, but we can't bust some dude's ass just because you don't like him because he's a damn Jew and looks like he shits dollar bills from his asshole when he craps. We're doing an important job here, and we must act like professionals. Let him go unmolested and get back to what we're assigned to do, man. A second officer bitched at his partner, as he watched al-Awajy walk to the turn style.

The second officer kept watching al-Awajy until he stopped before the turn style. The officer watched until he paid five tokens then al-Awajy walked onto the overcrowded station platform and quickly disappeared in the maddening crowd. The air was stale, and the crowd was shoving and overwhelming and al-Awajy settled down to wait for his train, as a second train left the station heading south.

The concerned young Arab terrorist carefully scanned the length of the long and overcrowded train platform, and thought the crowd numbered nearly a hundred people waiting for the next train to arrive At eight twenty-eight a.m. the train pulled into the station. The massive crowd of humanity instantly surged forward and forced their way into the six waiting train cars. As was instructed, he made his way for the lead car and to his surprise this car was not as full as the other five were. Al-Awajy was able to find a seat right next to the small bathroom he was to use for his attack on the subway train. Sitting for a minute, he instantly realized why this seat was open, because any time someone used the bathroom, the terrible smell floated right in his face.

Nevertheless, he stayed glued in the seat and the train harshly jerked forward and left the station and quickly increased speed, causing many people standing to bump into others standing next to them. He found it interesting how they did not pay much attention to the person standing next to them, as they and the train rumbled down the tracks. The sound of the train's wheels clacking over the steel rails was mesmerizing and enjoyable. A person coughed, another sneezed and someone offered, "God bless ya" as another person moved to get more comfortable standing. The train slowed and stopped as the conductor announced the station the train was pulling into.

This was interesting to observe for al-Awajy at how so many people left the train, as another surge of humanity pushed on the train. Almost instantly, the shoving and pushing and grumbling stopped, as the new ones prepared for the train leaving the station. This scene was repeated seven times before the conductor announced the next station was Grand Central Station and was five minutes away. He rose and opened the door to the bathroom that smelt as bad as it looked.

He almost gagged on the terrible smell instantly engulfing him as he placed his attaché case down in the exact position he was instructed by al-Wahhad to put it. He sat on the filthy toilet seat and waited until the train made the hard turn that aimed it directly for the world famous Grand Central Station. Al-Awajy was planning to suppress the button on the explosive charge the moment the train came out of the hard turn, and then straightened and picked up speed again. This was the time the terrorist leader informed him would do the most possible damage to the underground train station, and the buildings and roads above the train tunnel.

As he sat on the filthy toilet seat, al-Awajy felt the forward motion of the train as it slowed, so the train could navigate the sharp turn of the tracks safely. Then as quickly, the train increased its speed again. In his mind he heard al-Wahhad scream the word 'now' as the young Arab terrorist rose and suddenly screamed out, "Allahu Akhbar" at exactly eight fifty-five a.m. He then pressed the button on the briefcase, and in a flash his world instantly turned upside down in a blinding glow of harsh light, and the roar of an explosion.

The instant the briefcase exploded, a large hole ripped open in the metal floor of the train, and the three copper strips of molten metal shot through the hole at blinding speed. The white-hot liquid copper wrapped around the axle of the train wheels, and easily cut through the harden three- and one-half inch chrome steel shaft like it was a soft stick of butter.

The narrow and small bathroom erupted into splintering steel, tin and ceramic from the toilet bowl and exploding attaché case. The shrapnel from the train became missiles as the torn metal ripped into al-Awajy's unprotected body, as it did to anyone standing or seated within ten feet of the powerful but small explosion. Bodies of straphangers standing near the bathroom were picked up and sent crashing into the other side of the metal car. Some bodies were thrown through windows with their bodies shattering the glass that cut into them.

The instant the axle was cut by the powerful explosion and melted copper, the train derailed. The lead train car jackknifed in the tunnel with three support beams causing the car to turn sideways in the narrow tunnel. Forcing the tumbling train to mow down any support beams it crashed into. Al-Awajy's torn and battered body was lifted and then pitched towards the ceiling of the car, as it began its tumbling death roll. His body was suddenly pitched out of a shattered window, and he came to rest lying on the tracks. The rolling train crushed all life remaining in his body, as the car rolled over him and other passengers thrown out windows and shredding wagon.

When the lead car derailed underground and tumbled along the tracks. This pulled the second train car from the tracks, and the lead car crashed into the second car, causing this one to jump into the next tunnel. This crashing into the car starts its own tumbling and ripping down more support beams for the street and buildings constructed above the subway tunnel. When the second car left the tracks, it pulled the third train car from the tracks, and this one crashed down the other support beams the first two tumbling train cars missed. A fourth train car was likewise pulled from the tracks as if it weighed nothing, and then it started to tumble and dump its human cargo out along the tracks and narrow tunnel system, with some of the injured and dead passengers being deposited right on top of the third rail. Their bodies instantly burned to death by the electricity tearing into their bodies.

The remaining train cars were derailed, and those two cars were mercifully pitched to the side of the tunnel. But those cars never tumbled, so many passengers on board these cars received minor bumps and bruises, but these straphangers remained alive. Many passengers from the first four train cars crushed and injured bodies covered the interior of the destroyed tunnel and tracks, as the cries for help called out from the injured and dying. Some bodies resting on the third rail smoked and erupted in flames, causing fires and terrible smells of burning flesh filling the air.

The lead train car derailed seventy-five yards away from the mouth of Grand Central Terminal. The countless number of support beams holding up the road and buildings above the tunnel in midtown Manhattan, were ripped and crushed out of position, or knocked down completely. The subway car continued to tumble towards the station platform, sending broken beams and ripped apart metal from the train car out before the tumbling car like spears. The metal ripped into the horde of civilians standing on the platform waiting for this train to arrive. Many stunned civilians stared in awe and disbelief as the car ripped apart before their eyes, and the debris crashed into the platform. This car crushed tens of civilians trapped on the train platform.

Panic took over the civilians as people began to run away from the destroyed train station. This scared mob crashed into the people waiting for their trains to arrive or was still moving into the underground system to catch their rides. Without knowing why, they turned and ran along with the others who witnessed the terrible carnage. Smoke and flames broke out, adding to the mounting panic of the fleeing civilians.

The train car crash literally destroyed the center of 42nd Street East because the train came into the terminal at a speed of more than thirty-five mph, and the tumbling cars mowed down many steel support beams holding the street in place above the station. The crash happened below the Chrysler Building area, and it collapsed the Chrysler East building, the crash damaging and collapsed a large section of the Chrysler Building at the same time. As the tumbling cars came to a rest wedged here and there in the confines of the narrow tunnel. The cries of the injured and dying replaced the sounds of the crash and crushing steel of the train car and steel beams, as the cries filled the air. Then another noise started to drown out the mournful cries of the living and badly injured civilians scattered about along the subway tunnel system tracks.

This sound first started as a low growl that rapidly turned into a grinding and loud screeching ear shattering cry of metal, concrete, and steel, as a massive void formed above the subway station in the middle of 42nd Street, directly in front of the Chrysler Building let go. The noise of collapsing road, sidewalks, and some buildings were deafening. The road of 42nd Street collapsed without hesitation into the rapidly growing void. This collapsing carried with it several civilian cars, trucks, cabs, along with two mass transit buses into the expanding crater carved out in the very heart of the midtown Manhattan by the subway train crash below the street. A civilian car was going fast enough as the road fell into the vast opening that it drove right onto the train station platform below, and the car crashed into several civilians still trapped on the crumbling train platform.

Scared straphangers turned and crashed into other people still trying to enter the destroyed underground train platform. Many civilians were knocked to the ground and then trampled under the feet of people running away from the carnage below for their lives, as they were showered by crumbling steel, concrete, and exploding lights and sheets of sparks and shattered glass.

A large part of 42nd Street's main road crashed into the void opened as the tumbling train cars ripped out tens of main support beams once holding up the road above the station. The road and buildings above the subway system, collapsed as support beams were taken out from under them. The 150 East 42nd Street Building collapsed in the street, killing hundreds of workers trapped inside the crumbling building, and other people walking on the street as they reported for their day's work. The Chaning Building opposite the 150 East Building was damaged by the train crash in the tunnel. The building was left in extreme danger of collapsing in on itself from the structural wounds it received in the train crash under the building.

People walking in the area were showered by falling glass smashed out of the structures, as buildings shifted on their foundations, and support beams ripped out from under the road and buildings. Parts of concrete and metal from the buildings began to crack and fall from the structures. This added to the shower of death assaulting the bodies of a horde of civilians who were trapped while walking around midtown Manhattan, as they window shopped and waited for their day's work to begin.

Hundreds of large plate glass windows shattered in the old Blue Cross Blue Shield Building constructed directly behind the damaged 150 Building, because the building moved on its foundation. Other buildings suffered some form of structural damage, as the ground under the buildings continued to tremble from the destruction growing below in the tunnel system. One of the tumbling train cars continued to roll side over side until it came to a rest sitting right on top of the Grand Central train platform, rolling over tens of trapped civilians.

A few civilian cars, trucks, buses, and taxies riding in the street above the damaged tunnel, continued to tumble into the void rapidly opening under their vehicles. The void gave way to a sixty-foot deep, and a thousand-foot-wide cavity created by the train crash, and the damage the tumbling train cars caused in the crippled tunnel. The death toll from the crumbling buildings above ground surpassed the deaths suffered at the Twin Towers terrorist attack. Because many people had no warning before their buildings collapsed on their bodies.

Four-foot-wide water mains snapped as if they were made of cardboard, as the ground around them suddenly gave way, along with three-foot-wide gas mains cracked. Thick stacks of electrical lines were ripped apart by the shifting ground once supporting the wires. Sending curtains of sparks flying in all directions, and sparking the shattered gas lines into roaring blowtorches, shooting walls of flames some seventy-five feet into the air under tremendous pressure. The trapped gases in the sewers built up from tons of human waste, followed and added to the number of explosions taking place in the city streets.

Sending one hundred- and twenty-five-pound cast iron sewer covers flying fifty feet in the air. These fires added to the flames from the destroyed gas main, and the sewer plate flying in the air, returning to earth crashing into buildings and landing on parked or crashed vehicles in the street. Electrical lines underground sparked and burned out of control, until the lines shorted out and snapped off circuit breakers charging the fractured electrical lines.

Countless fender benders were the rule of the day above the destroyed train station and in the surrounding streets. Drivers trying to avoid crashing into the massive crater jammed on their breaks, and they were crashed into by cars following too close and too fast to stop safely in time. Some drivers tried to drive on the sidewalks that did not fall into the hole, to avoid a collision. These cars hit any pedestrians still using the sidewalks or leaning against the buildings as the ground under their feet crumbled and, in some instances, gave way.

Several cars and trucks along with mass transit vehicles slammed into sides of buildings, some crashed through windows and ended up parked inside damaged buildings. These drivers tried to get out of the carnage taking place before them. Smothering smoke filled the streets surrounding the crash site, as fires continued to grow and burn out of control.

Emergency calls taxing the wireless communications systems, were placed to police and fire stations spread throughout Manhattan, and tens of police and fire trucks headed for the damaged midtown Manhattan area. The mournful sound of a flood of sirens soon filled the air, as the first emergency responders arrived on the scene of destruction. The responders were appalled at what they discovered at the scene of the tragedy. Entire buildings and large sections of other building collapsing as the first responders deployed to assist the injured and dying.

A horde of firefighters did a superhuman effort bringing some of the numerous fires under control, and then they began to assist the injured and dying as well. Requests for additional support from the five boroughs were broadcasted over the emergency police and firefighter frequencies. Reality struck home when the first 'Ten Forty-Five Code One' call came in over the squad radio from the firefighters. Reporting the first responders discovered many dead bodies mixed in with the rubble of destruction taking place in the center of midtown Manhattan.

Immediately, replies came in from firehouses spread throughout the five boroughs with fire company's, reporting they were responding with equipment to help with the fires and countless injured in concern. Firehouses from the Tri-state area responded by sending their firefighting and medical equipment, to support the firehouses responding to the disaster of midtown Manhattan, to make certain their areas of responsibility were covered.

The shortage of hospital beds, doctors, and nurses, along with much needed medical supplies and equipment were quickly discovered, as the first of the countless injured were transported to the surrounding local hospitals. This shortage forced the lesser injured to be transported to hospitals in Brooklyn, and as far away from the site as Connecticut and even Upstate New York.

THE PENTAGON, NINE TEN A.M. ON THURSDAY, MAY 13th, 2011

General John White, the current Chairman of the Joint Chiefs of Staff, was just getting comfortable in his office while preparing for the beginning of his day's work, sipping his coffee, and enjoying a cheese Danish and a little private time, when Director Raincloud excitedly charged into his office. The Chairman tried to look around the full blooded Native American to see where his secretary was, and why John was in his office unannounced.

The powerful military officer was rather concerned because the CIA Director was able to get in his office. He was wondering where his secretary was that allowed John to get this far in his office without his knowledge. Before he could raise a fuss over the concern, the excited Director began speaking. "John, evidently I was a little off base as to the readiness of the damn terrorist future attack against us, sir. Shit General, New York City just suffered a devastating train crash in their underground subway system I can't help but think this latest mess is the cause of this Iraqi bastard we branded the Ghost. From the first reports of the damn disaster site, place many civilian deaths and badly injured. Maybe numbering in the thousands, as the first responders arrived on site and began reporting on the situation, General White..."

"What the fuck are you talking about for the love of the Christ Child, Director Raincloud? I didn't get any fucking reports coming in about some kind of major tragedy currently taking place in New York City, my friend." The Chairman growled at the Director and was interrupted by his secretary who tried to enter the office and speak with him.

"Mary, where the hell were you hiding at for Pete's sake, and do you know anything about some kind of crap going down in New York City killing hundreds of civilians?" The General barked angrily at his secretary.

"Yes, General White Sir, that's why I was out of position when the Director arrived at your office, and I was unable to welcome him here sir. One of the secretaries reported there was serious accident that just took place in New York City, with some streets and building collapsing and numerous fires and explosions taking place, sir. I was trying to find out what was going down before I reported to you sir. My computer's out so I went to Helen's computer so I could pick up any real time information on the accident as it was taking place, General." Mary flashed one of her best smiles at her boss.

"Never mind that crap. Can you get John a coffee and then get in here and take notes while we speak? I'll heat up my computer and find out what the fuck's going down in New York City myself, Mary. John, relax until

I see what the hell's happening up there dammit." General White flipped his computer on, and his monitor flashed into life.

"Okay John if you think this was a damn terrorist attack in New York, forget what I told you before and get a Flash out to the President A-SAP. He needs to know what the hell's going down in New York, and what we think this latest situation might be, Director." General White growled at the powerful CIA Agent.

"General, the moment I received the first report about the situation going down in midtown Manhattan. I sent out an emergency flash message to the President, informing him that I believed we were just hit by an Islamic terrorist attack carried out in New York City..."

"Is zat so, did you get a reply from the Boss, Director Raincloud?"

"I certainly did, but I'm afraid you're not going to like the reply I received for the President one bit and believe me General. My flash warning went out to everyone from the White House, down to Secretary of State, to any and everyone else in the immediate need to know loop, sir. If we're coming under another god damn terrorist attack as is my duty to carry out, General. I take care of my duties faithfully, General White..."

"Don't make me repeat myself to you again, Chief. How the fuck did the President respond to your damn alert, sir. I know who gets informed when you send out one of those damn flash messages of yours every time, Director. Hey, I'm surprised I didn't receive one of those damn alerts from your ass, Director Raincloud."

"You got one General, and if your computer was on, you would've received it the moment I transmitted my flash, sir. As you can see, the red box blinking in the upper right-hand corner of your monitor, that's the alert I sent out to you, my friend." Raincloud gave the General a smirk.

"General White, the reply from the President informed me he didn't want any possible terrorist attack notification transmitted out to him under any circumstances, sir. He ordered me to sit on my report until I was able to send him a positive report this was truly a terrorist attack in the States. The guy doesn't want to hear anything about a possible Muslim attack carried out against us, sir. All he's concerned with is trying to make it seem like the damn terrorist like us and are not an ongoing threat against us, sir. Remember when we warned him not to taunt the remaining parts of the al-Qaeda Terrorist Organization when we killed bin Laden? General,

I believe this attack was a response to that killing and inform us al-Qaeda is still alive and well.

"General White, if we in the Intel Communities get things right then the damn politicians want to take the credit for it, as they did with the death of Usama bin Laden. If we get it right and the politicians don't like the outcome of the situation, and by them, I mean the White House. The bastards throw us under the fucking bus, and we always get it right, General. It makes me feel we in the Intel Communities are damned to hell if we do, and damned if we don't, sir." Director Raincloud took a second so he could calm down a bit.

"Okay Director Raincloud Sir, you made your point with me. Errr… one question I hafta ask you though John, how the hell come the FBI Director isn't making this fucking report to me and the President? Where the hell is he hiding at, and what the hell is he up to for Pete's sake." General White grumbled at the Director.

"I'm quite certain the FBI Director is presently reporting his findings to the President as I have, General White. I'm just as certain he received the same kind of reply as I received from our Commander in Chief, sir. I bet the damn bank on it if you were to go a little deeper into your computer, you'd discover an alert was already sent out from the FBI Director as well, General. White." Director Raincloud offered.

"Okay Director Raincloud you got me there I see sir. What say you get back to your people and see if you can find out if this new fucking mess was truly a terrorist attack against us sir? Or if it was just a damn natural disaster of some kind as is being reported by the local news services of the city, Director."

"Will do General White, I'll be back to you the moment I'm certain what I'm talking about is correct, and not working off a gut hunch over this latest situation, sir."

JOHN F. KENNEDY INTERNATIONAL
AIRPORT, QUEENS NEW YORK.
THURSDAY MAY 13th, 2011, SEVEN TEN A.M.

Ali Abbas Hamad was amazed at how easily he was able to get through the usually tight security precautions most airports were employing, ever since the Nine, One, One terrorist attack. The elderly Arab man could not believe his luck the security personnel did not bother to make him stand, so they could properly search his body. Or check out the medical equipment more carefully resting in his lap and on the wheelchair. The airport assistant even stayed with him, and she pushed his wheelchair through the security gate. Then she moved him over to the open food service counter in the secured section of the terminal. There was a TV at the counter and the channel was on Fox News, with Fox and Friends on. The female broadcaster spoke about the stagnated economy. Hamad let his breath out, because nothing was happening, and it was not scheduled to happen until he was safely on board the aircraft and in flight.

Ali remained seated at the food counter as other food service stations began to open for the day, and this section of the secured area of the airport terminal began to get crowded. Hamad drank his third cup of coffee and though he was nervous, he refused to order another cup for fear of drawing attention to himself. As innocently as possible, Hamad checked his watch for the umpteenth time, and this caused him to curse under his breath, because the time was moving so slowly. His attention was drawn to two people as the woman nodded politely to him as she ordered a coffee. She smiled at the old man, and spoke with the man she was with, as they enjoyed a conversation. As old as he was and how bad his health was, his mind was as sharp as ever, and he remained seated near the two young people in hopes any floating security personnel would think he was with his daughter and husband, giving him the appearance of normality.

The concerned acting Arab was staying so near the two young kids that soon they began to speak with him, they even included him in on their conversation. Laughs and jokes followed, with the young man telling Hamad he was taking his girlfriend to Chicago to enjoy a Cubs ballgame. He told Hamad this was going to be the first game his girlfriend will see in person.

Speaking pleasantly with the two young strangers made the time go by much quicker for Ali, and finally only because the young man made an announcement that they had to go to their boarding gate. Ali realized what time it was, and he began to push his wheelchair to Boarding Gate Twelve. From out of nowhere, a young female airport attendant appeared, and she took over and pushed the wheelchair for him. The old man had to look over his shoulder and smiled when he noticed the woman smiling as she announced.

"Oh no you don't sir you don't go pushing yourself around in my terminal as long as I'm on duty, sir. Please, allow me to help you with the wheelchair, sir. I'll get you over to the Boarding Gate in plenty of time for your flight, sir. Sit back and relax and enjoy, and allow me to handle everything for you, sir." The attendant offered to Hamad in an extremely polite tone of voice, as she took command of the wheelchair, and she glanced at the ticket stub locked in Hamad's hand, and she realized his flight was with Jet Blue Airlines. Within five minutes, the pretty attendant had Hamad waiting by the Gate for Air Flight One, One, Seven. The attendant left him sitting in the wheelchair by the door leading to the aircraft, as she spoke to the ticket attendant, and then they both glanced at him.

Hamad looked at his watch and noticed it was eight oh five a.m., and the ticket attendant spoke to Ali in a polite voice for the first time. She informed him they were boarding the aircraft, and he was scheduled to be the first person to be brought onto the airliner. He remained seated acting like he was trying to mind his own business, when a second airline attendant walked out of the boarding door, and she instantly took command of his wheelchair, and she rushed him on board the waiting plane. A second young female flight attendant help the first one gets Ali in his chair against the bulkhead supporting the landing gear of the aircraft, it gave him a little extra leg room. It was the widest area on the aircraft, so Hamad was able to relax with room as the flight attendant moved the narrow air tank from the wheelchair and placed it carefully by his foot.

As he got comfortable, a flood of passengers suddenly poured into the aircraft. Hamad smiled when he noticed the small TV built into the bulkhead. Using the selector in the handle of the chair, he changed it to the Fox News channel. Again, he smiled when he noticed Fox and Friends were still being broadcasted. A second passenger sat in the seat right next to Hamal and nodded after he placed his carryon bag in the overhead compartment above his seat.

It seemed like it took a short lifetime for the other passengers to finally settle down and get comfortable on board the aircraft, and then everyone waited for the aircraft to take off. Then the pretty female flight attendant went into her boring spiel about how to hook the seat belt, and what to do in case of an emergency on board the aircraft. Once she was done with her instructions, the small group of flight attendants prepared for the flight as the aircraft was carefully backed out of the berthing terminal. The airliner slowly moved down a flight path and aligned itself directly behind a second aircraft trailing another aircraft on the tarmac.

The confident sounding Flight Captain's voice came over the intercom of the aircraft as he announced they were the third aircraft scheduled for takeoff. The captain continued speaking while giving the passengers a rather detailed weather conditions and current temperature of California's, Los Angeles area. He gave the estimated flight time with one landing scheduled at Chicago's O'Hare's Airport, where some passengers will depart, and they were scheduled to pick up other passengers to fill the plane again. Just as the Captain stopped speaking did the aircraft move up and set itself for liftoff.

Hamad looked at his watch as he heard the aircraft's engines building up for full takeoff power. It was eight thirty-six a.m. which meant the airliner was leaving two minutes ahead of schedule. Ali cast an eye at the small air gauge on the tank, as he adjusted the terribly annoying airline hose under his nose. The gauge still read full even though there was no oxygen inside the tank, only explosives. He went over his orders and knew all he had to do was kick the side of the tank with his foot, and the gauge would drop to reading no oxygen in the cylinder. Then he could go into his act that would force the aircraft to return to the Kennedy terminal.

The aircraft finally took off and reached altitude and quickly leveled off in flight at its assigned altitude and a young female flight attendant came over to Hamad's side. She asked him with concern in her voice if everything was alright and if he was comfortable, and if he wanted something to drink or nibble on. The elderly man replied everything was good and he was not thirsty as he looked at the news channel. It was important for him to pay attention to the news broadcast because it was going to give him the exact time, he was to start his act to force the aircraft to return to the Kennedy Airport.

Hamad stared at the news station, not really listening to the commentator's words as he droned on about something bothering him. Ali took a second to look at his watch, and his eyebrow arched as he registered the time as two minutes after nine. He found himself wondering if something went wrong with their attack against the subway system of New York. He cocked his head to the side, because no one from the group explained what he was supposed to do, if the attack on the train station did not go off as scheduled.

The old man was extremely concerned as what to do next, when a news alert suddenly flashed across the small TV screen. Then the program went to an onsite news broadcast stationed directly in the heart of midtown New York City. The newsperson was reporting of a terrible situation taking place over his shoulder, as he turned slightly. Allowing the camera to slowly scan in and show the bellowing smoke curling high into the air, and the start of the crater rapidly eating up 42nd Street, just before the Grand Central Train Station. As the reporter was informing the listeners what was currently taking place in midtown Manhattan. The picture went to an overhead shot, showing the huge crater formed by the tumbling train cars trapped in the tunnels of the subway under the destroyed street. A news helicopter flew around the disaster area, showing all the carnage still taking place on this terrible morning.

A camera from the helicopter showed a flood of emergency vehicles as they piled up in the streets surrounding the affected area. Hordes of firemen, police officers and civilian first responders poured into the multi patient incident site, to lend medical assistance and aid to the countless injured and dying from the major disaster. They began to figure out what caused the accident as it was being classified by the emergency responders at this time. This was the time for Hamad to go into his act, as he suddenly kicked the side of his oxygen tank hard with his foot. He then started to display he was having a problem with his breathing equipment. A flight attendant noticed the slight commotion the old man was causing, and she rushed to his side to see what the problem was, and if she could correct it for him. Hamad's hand went from the air hose clipped to his nose, to a full mouth and nose mask, as he tried to draw in huge gulps of oxygen from the obviously empty air supply tank.

The attentive flight attendant noticed the unusual actions by the elderly man, and she rushed to his side and asked Hamad if he was having a problem as the old man held the plastic mouth mask over his face with one hand, and he pointed to the TV with his other, and then made like he was struggling to breathe. Hamad was trying to make the attendant believe what happened on the TV had caused the problems with his breathing. The flight attendant looked at the set and noticed the billowing smoke, and thought it was part of a movie. She leaned over Ali and looked at the gauge of the air tank and cried. "Oh God, you're out of oxygen, sir. I'll get help for you sir. Please, you must try and stay calm, sir."

The young and pretty attendant moved away from Ali's side, and she grabbed the in-plane phone to the cockpit and hit the talk button. The co-pilot answered the call for the captain, and the slightly excited attendant reported a medical situation with the elderly passenger in obvious medical distress. The co-pilot asked what she wanted him to do about the situation, and she replied she did not know what to do about the emergency.

The pilot took over the conversation and he replied to the concerned flight attendant. "Pat, use your key and open the overhead emergency oxygen system. Get the old man back on oxygen while I contact our people back at the terminal and see what they want me to do about this... Hold on Pat, I'm picking up an emergency from New York.

"Gees Pat, there was a situation where a main street collapsed in the heart of midtown Manhattan from what I'm picking up over the communications. It's a real mess..."

"Oh God, you don't think it was a terrorist attack, do you Captain?"

"No, not from what I'm picking up about the damn situation in New York City, honey. The reports are questioning if it might have been a small earthquake to cause the kind of damage they're reporting about the situation. Okay Pat, that's a secondary problem for the time being, our immediate problem is what we're going to do with the elderly passenger having trouble breathing. You do what you were told young lady. Yeah, I know, releasing the emergency air supply is going to set off all sorts of bells and whistles back at the Flight Tower at Kennedy. But I'll be speaking to them before they can overreact to our on-board medical situation, honey. Take care of that old man while I get instructions on what to do."

"Yes, Sir Captain, I'm opening the emergency plate now sir. I got one of the oxygen masks in hand and am placing it over his mouth, sir. I'm afraid he's in quite a panic from the lack of oxygen, and he's having a serious problem with his breathing, Captain."

"Okay you stay with him he's your only responsibility from this moment on, until we're back on the ground, young lady." The captain ended his conversation with the flight attendant and then he switched radio frequency and snapped into the radio. "Err...this is Captain Richards Flight One, One, Seven, I'm reporting an on board medical emergency. Over."

CHAPTER ELEVEN

The captain knew his report was going to cause tension at the flight tower. Especially with what was obviously currently taking place at midtown Manhattan. But he had to know what to do for the old man before he clocked out on him, and that would cause him a whole bushel basket of delays and problems, and it would also make the airline look bad to the public if the old man happened to die on his flight.

"Yes, Flight One, One, Seven this is Air Traffic Controller Two Seven, Captain Richards. What's the nature of your on-board emergency being registered on our threat board, sir? Over." The concerned Air Traffic Controlled grumbled at the pilot of the aircraft.

"Yes, Controller Two Seven, this is One, One, Seven. I have a man reported to be terminal on board my aircraft. He has no oxygen left in his personal carried on air supply, and the elderly man is having serious problems breathing. Over."

"Yes, Flight One, One, Seven, I understand your medical situation, and your first responsibility is to get a secondary oxygen supply flowing to that man in distress, before it turns into a life-threatening situation, Captain Richards." The Air Traffic Controller reported, but he was cut off by a second voice over the communication system of the Control Tower.

"Yes, Flight One, One, Seven this is Senior Flight Controller Ray Washington, sir. I'm taking Command of this medical emergency on board your aircraft, Captain. The first thing you have to do is get that elderly man stabilized and breathing normally again, sir. Once he's stable, you're instructed to turn your aircraft and go to an emergency heading of Three, Three, Niner, and drop down to Angels Twenty-Five Thousand Feet, sir.

"That Altitude will keep you well out of the way of all normal commercial flight paths for your emergency return flight to Kennedy Airport, sir. I'll clear all civilian flights out of your area of emergency flight as you commence your turn to this new heading, Captain Richards. You're instructed to return to Kennedy Airport and use runway One, Three for your emergency landing. Captain, under the circumstances you'll not dump or burn off your on-board fuel. You're instructed to land heavy. I repeat Captain Richards, permission to land heavy is granted, because you have too much fuel on board to either dump, or try burning off before landing, sir. I'll have emergency responders standing by for your return flight to the Airport, Captain. Captain has anyone thought to check the other passengers on board your flight to see if there's a doctor on board your aircraft, sir. If you have a doctor, allow him to take over responsibility of the endangered man in distress, until I get your aircraft back on the ground. Over Captain Richards."

The captain of the aircraft did not take the time to respond to the Controller last instructions as he changed frequency, and then he spoke directly to his flight attendant again. "Pat, this is Richards, how the hell's he is doing honey?"

"He's calming down quite a bit Captain, but he's still having serious problems with his breathing though, sir."

"Pat did you notice if any Doctors were on the flight manifest when you checked them in?"

"No sir and following latest orders Captain, we automatically check the manifest to note if any Doctors are onboard our flights, sir." The attendant reported calmly.

"Dammit to hell, okay Pat you do whatever you can to make him comfortable as possible. We have orders to return to Kennedy so they can remove him from our aircraft, honey. I must go I gotta inform the other passengers of our sudden medical situation and our latest orders to return to Kennedy. I'm quite certain most of the passengers are aware of what's going down in New York by now. I don't want them thinking this is going to be another Nine, One, One nightmare." The captain replied as he reached over his head and went from secured internal aircraft communications to cabin communications and announced.

"Ladies and gentlemen this is your Captain. The first thing I must report is some form of emergency has taken place in New York City. Please remain calm because there are no reports this is a possible terrorist situation. From what I'm picking up, there might have been a minor earthquake, or some other natural disaster that occurred in the city. I also must take this time to inform you all that we're having a slight medical emergency on board the aircraft with one of our passengers. We were just instructed to return to Kennedy for emergency services to take care of the on-board emergency. I'm sorry for this disturbance, but the life of one of our passengers takes precedence over any issues involved with this flight. We should be on the background within the next ten minutes. I thank you for your time and patience over this matter."

The captain ended the communication with his passengers, and then he went back to the Senior Air Flight Controller and reported. "This is Flight One, One Seven to Senior Flight Controller Washington. I'm reporting my medical emergency is stable at this point, and there are no Doctors on board my flight, sir. I'm reporting I have my aircraft on a heading of Three, Three, Niner, and am three minutes from touchdown at Kennedy. Over."

"Very good Captain Richards, I'm tracking your incoming flight every second of your flight, and will correct, if necessary, sir. Over."

"Thank you, Controller, by the way, do you have any further information on what the hell's going down in the damn City with this incident reported to us, sir? I find it kinda hard to believe the city was just hit by a possible earthquake, sir. Over." The captain was fishing for any new information of what was going on below him.

"I don't have much new to report to you at this time Captain, but what I do know is the city is in one helluva a mess. If this thing ends up as a possible terrorist attack, it's going to overshadow Nine, One, One times two over, sir."

"Shit, don't tell me you think this damn mess might be a terrorist incident, sir? Over." The suddenly concerned Flight Captain remarked in his mike.

"I have no information pointing to that type of situation at this time I assure you, Captain Richards. From everything I was able to pick up about the current situation taking place in Manhattan, sir. There are no reports referring to any possible terrorist situation taking pla…Ummm, hang on for a second will ya, Captain. I'm getting a fresh report about that situation right now as we speak, sir. Captain Richards, I just picked it up as reporting the situation was reported as a train accident with the subway cars taking out many streets support beams and causing a collapse of the street. Captain Richards, I'm not picking up any alerts or increase to our security orders, so that means the people in Command of this nightmare are not classifying this situation as a possible terrorist action, sir. Over."

"Thank God for that much Senior Air Flight Traffic Controller." The Captain of Air Flight One, One, Seven, replied as he began to bring his aircraft down to the ordered flight altitude of ten thousand feet. He turned on to his final approach heading for Runway One, Three at Kennedy International Airport. The captain did not like coming in heavily laden down with fuel. Between dumping and trying to burn off the extra fuel, would have taken over three hours to complete. So, he could land with the accepted amount of fuel left on board for commercial flight landings. In that time his passenger might have died.

"SATC (Senior Air Traffic Controller) to Flight One, One, Seven you're cleared to come down to one thousand feet and continue your descent in altitude, until you reach the first set of landing lights. From that point on you are cleared for immediate landing. Good luck Captain. Over."

"Thank you for permission to land SATC, and am dropping down to five hundred feet, sir. I'm one-half mile out from touchdown. Over."

"Roger that last Air Flight One, One, Seven, continue on your final approach, sir. Over."

"Touchdown, feet are on the ground. Landing successful SATC. Over."

"Roger that Air Flight One, One Seven. Captain Richards, you're instructed to continue down Runway One, Three to break off point Three, Seven. Then you're instructed to turn on Runway Six and move your aircraft over to the emergency responder zone, help's waiting in that area for your aircraft and your on-board Mae West (Person in distress) to arrive, sir. So, the emergency workers can take over and look after him. Glad to have you safely back on the ground, Captain Richards. Over."

"Glad to have a successful landing. Am heading for Runway Six, SATC. Over."

As the One One Seven aircraft glided down the long Runway One, Three. The airliner began to pass the huge terminal with other aircraft loading passengers for flight.

Hamad glanced out the window, and when he noticed the aircraft was about seventy yards away from the main terminal building. He suddenly roughly shoved the young female flight attendant away from his side with surprising strength. Then he reached out and grabbed the head of the gauge of the narrow oxygen tank. His sweating fingers searched desperately for the hidden button and when they found it, he pressed it.

The confused flight attendant shook her head and struggled back to her feet, as she wondered why the elderly man in distress suddenly struck out at her like he did. Her confusion turned to shock and horror, as she listened to the words the old man was saying to her.

"Please forgive me for this terrible insult, but what I do I do for the love of Allah."

There was a blinding explosion a foot away from the female flight attendant. Her body was instantly picked up and pitched hard against the bulkhead wall of the aircraft, snapping her neck and killing her instantly as she slowly crumbled to the floor.

The explosion as small as it was, dislodged three sets of seats and killing four civilians seated directly behind him on board the aircraft. The man sharing the seat with Hamad died instantly in the hellish explosion and flying shrapnel from the oxygen tank ripping apart. Ali's right leg was blown off his body just above the knee as chunks of metal from the tank ripped into his body, killing him almost instantly. Hamad never lived long enough to see the last of the destruction his terrorist attack had caused the terminal and civilians trapped inside the structure and aircraft. That was not why the explosion was set off, the results of the detonation inside the aircraft at this crucial position reacted just as al-Wahhad planned.

Most of the detonation of the explosive device was deflected down towards the bottom of the aircraft from the way the device was packed inside the narrow oxygen tank. The result of the explosion was it completely sheared off the landing gear of the left side of the still moving aircraft. Dropping the belly of the aircraft to the ground on one side and causing the aircraft to turn by the pull of the body of the airliner being dragged on the ground. To the disbelief of the pilot and co-pilot, they witnessed the nose of the plane being forced to turn right at three aircraft stationed at the terminal loading passengers for flight or unloading other passengers from their aircraft. The captain took to standing on his breaks, desperately trying to slow the aircraft, and he also pulled hard on the rudder with all his might, trying to turn the aircraft away from the terminal building it was now aimed at.

Everything the Captain of the aircraft tried with the damaged plane was for naught because the crippled plane continued heading directly for the overcrowded main terminal of the airport. As the disabled airliner continued to slide on its belly directly towards the other aircraft, the airliner suddenly erupted into a ball of boiling flames caused by friction created by the plane dragging along the tarmac. This caused the fuel on board the crumbling aircraft stored inside the main fuel and two wing tanks to explode, as flames reached the center fuel tank. The wreckage of the burning airliner continued sliding towards the terminal, all passengers on board the destroyed aircraft died almost instantly. Killed by breathing in bellowing smoke and flames or burned to death in the flaming aircraft. The nose of the airliner slammed into the first aircraft in the process of loading passengers for flight.

The flaming wreckage of the aircraft Flight One, One, Seven, continued and slammed into the second aircraft stationed at the terminal also boarding passengers. The collision caused that plane to erupt into a second fireball because of the fuel stored in this aircraft for its long flight out to the West Coast. The wing of Flight One, One, Seven, slammed into the third aircraft, and this one also erupted into a massive fireball. The fourth aircraft struck by wreckage of Flight One, One, Seven, was nearly cut in half by the separated tail section of the crumbling aircraft. This plane received severe damage but for some reason did not explode, because the tail section was not burning wreckage. That was not the extent of the damage caused by the destroyed Air Flight One, One, Seven aircraft though.

When the flaming remains of the aircraft slammed into the three other planes loading passengers at the terminal, the explosions from those heavily fuel laden planes sent flaming chunks of aircraft ripping through the huge plate glass windows of the main section of the Kennedy Terminal. This wall of shattered glass and flaming structure and debris from the four destroyed planes, turned into deadly missiles, as the debris ripped into thousands of civilians waiting for their flights. Or the horde of civilians gathered at the terminal to pick up their friends and family coming in for visits or returning home from vacation or work.

Hundreds, and then a thousand of unsuspecting civilians fell victim to the wall of death ripping into the terminal, with sheets of flames following the wall of shattered glass and flying metal and other debris, burning to death, and crushing the injured survivors of the wall of destruction assaulting the terminal. The oxygen inside the building was sucked out of the terminal, because of the massive fireballs churning into the interior of the terminal structure. Elderly safe from the churning flames, had serious trouble breathing because of the sudden lack of oxygen inside the terminal, as the flames consumed the oxygen. Anyone suffering from asthma fell ill, adding to the many problems facing the first emergency responders to enter the destroyed and still burning area of the terminal.

Instantly, the control tower personnel broadcasted an emergency alert for all inbound aircraft flights. As the airport firefighting equipment and other emergency responders left their protective hangers and headed for the burning center of the terminal structure. A horde of half crazed civilians trying desperately to escape the death and destruction inside the terminal ran out on the tarmac, causing sheer havoc for any incoming aircraft, airport personnel and emergency responders and their vehicles.

The Air Traffic Controllers broadcasted an emergency landing alert to all inbound aircraft tracking to land at the Kennedy Terminal. Informing in flight aircraft the entire Kennedy Airport was now closed to all incoming and outgoing flights until further notice. Aircraft scheduled to use the damaged airport were diverted to the surrounding airports of the Tri-state area, as far away from Queens as Steward Airforce Base Airport stationed in Upstate New York, and Inter-borough Airport in New Jersey.

Any civilian aircraft parked on the tarmac and near the terminal, were dragged away from the flaming structure by tow carts and terminal personnel braving the roaring flames to move the smaller aircraft away from the terminal. The airliners and other aircraft were deposited on runways, so no damage happened to them until the current emergency was over.

When the first emergency alert was transmitted from the control tower of the stricken Kennedy International Airport, many emergency responders were stopped responding towards the emergency currently taking place in midtown Manhattan. Some first stage responders were instantly diverted towards the emergency suddenly taking place at Kennedy Airport. Fire stations as far away from the two multi patient incident events, even some fire stations across the Hudson River in Staten Island, were requesting permission to assist with the twin disasters ripping apart the City of New York.

The pulling of these emergency responders heading for midtown Manhattan immediately placed added pressures and workload on the shoulders of the responders already working at the site of the first disaster to hit New York City. Many fire and police departments from Brooklyn sent their personnel and firefighting equipment into Manhattan, to assist those assets already at the site of the destruction. Special buses equipped to draw blood turn on the roads, and they headed for the incident site. EMTs (Emergency Medical Technicians) as far away as Putnam and Dutchess County in Upstate New York, jumped into their private vehicles and headed for the city, to aid the massive amounts of injured and dying.

Army personnel stationed at the massive Army Base Camp Smith in Peekskill, New York, loaded spooling Blackhawk helicopters. Then the rotor aircraft began to ferry medical and other supplies and medical personnel to the site of the first disaster in Manhattan. Both the Mayor and Governor of New York immediately activated extra emergency assistance, and then aimed it at the heart of midtown Manhattan, and to the second disaster site at Kennedy Airport. The Governor took the bull by the horns and did not hesitate in the least, and he immediately activated the Nation Guard, and ordered all emergency assets from the Guard to head for the twin sites of the disasters. Other National Guard Units were ordered to activate, so the soldiers could take over the security of both incidents to free up police officers and firefighters. So, they could assist the injured and dying of the crippled City.

Once the crumbling buildings and collapsing of the street started to stabilize, the emergency responders began to get a handle on the terrible situation. Structural engineers moved into the site by the carload, to see what was needed to check any possible further damage happening to the weakened street, and buildings. They were also checking the damaged subway system. The engineers mingled in with the firefighters, along with other workers and police officers flooding the site to assist the injured and dying.

National Guard Units showed up and lent a hand to the emergency workers, as the troops began to dig through the massive pile of rubble with their bare hands, while desperately searching for buried and injured civilians. The death toll began to mount and rapidly topped two thousand dead men, women, and children in the first few hours of searching for victims of the still referred to train accident. FBI Officers were the next to show up at the twin incident sites, as they began to search the area to find out what caused the accident, and if it was a possible terrorist attack.

An army of construction workers with heavy earth moving equipment from nearby construction areas spread throughout the city were the next group of helpers to show up at the site of the carnage. Cranes were quickly setup, and large backhoes began to dig through the mountain of rubble and drag destroyed cars, trucks and other vehicles caught up in the accident, out of the way of the emergency workers. A horde of large dump trucks were loaded with debris and hauled out of the area, making room for the workers to support the injured and dying.

The mob of FBI Agents went to work in the subway, because the agents knew right where to aim their main efforts of investigation. As the emergency responders and agents worked in the tunnel, firefighters did outstanding work putting out the many fires burning freely in the area. The third rail system was shutdown to eliminate the possibility of electrocution of the emergency workers toiling in the subway system. In no time flat did the FBI zero in on the set of wheels of the derailed subway cars. One agent found the cut axle and wheel still attached to the axle and brought his find up to the attention of his SAC or Special Agent in Command.

The train wheel and cut axle was left right where they were discovered, and countless pictures of it and also the ripped-up train tracks were taken, and then out shipped to their main headquarters for further evaluation. Along with the pictures, the FBI reports were sent to headquarters with the suggestion this incident was not an accident by any means. SAC added in no uncertain terms that he was leaning towards believing this accident was in fact, a terrorist attack directed at the subway system of New York City.

The FBI findings of the train axle and damaged tracks at what was believed to be the start of the crash were not only sent to their main headquarters. A separate and more detailed report along with a great number of pictures of the cut axle and ripped up track, was sent directly to CIA Headquarters stationed at Langley. This was so the Special Agents and their assets at the Virginia Headquarters, could lend their expertise and equipment in searching for the true cause and effect of the now believed to be terrorist attack carried out by any unidentified terrorist cell obviously operating in New York City.

CIA HEADQUARTERS, LANGLEY VIRGINIA, THURSDAY. MAY 13, 2011, ZERO TEN OH FIVE HOURS

The exhausted CIA Director John Raincloud was seated in his office when he received the first report came in from the gaggle of FBI Special Agents working at the first multi patient incident site at the train terminal. Director Raincloud smiled as he opened the report on his computer, and then he began to read it. Instantly, the half-smile left his lips as he realized the lead agent was suddenly classifying the once believed to be accident, as a terrorist attack against the New York City Subway System.

Even as the powerful CIA Director read the rest of the findings of the agents working at the incident site in Manhattan, his hands were already working over the keys of the computer with blinding speed. He wanted to be the first person to inform the Chairman of the Joint Chiefs of Staff General White, of the findings of the FBI Agents working out in the field. The deeply concerned Director was including the other accident at Kennedy Airport, as a confidence high terrorist action because of the report filed by the FBI Agents in the field at the Manhattan site.

Once Director Raincloud finished reading over the report and sending a copy out to General White at his Pentagon office, he opened communications with the FBI sub-station stationed at the Kennedy International Airport. The worried Director wanted to know if any of his agents there were able to get in the field at this second incident site. He was speaking with a local agent who informed him there was too many fires still raging out of control at the second incident site, for the agents to get inside the damaged terminal to begin their investigation.

CIA Director Raincloud did not mince words in the least with the agent in the field, as he informed him the agents at the first incident at the subway station in Manhattan, filed their report stating they were tagging the incident as a terrorist attack. This news did not come as a surprise to the agents in the field, because FBI Director Hidemann already informed his agents they were hit by terrorists in the New York City incident.

The Director's call was interrupted by General John White, as he used his power to cut in on the conversation, and he waited for the Director to break off his communication with the agents investigating the incident at the airport. The moment they were alone in their conversation, General White growled at Director Raincloud.

"Look John, what the fuck's this suitcase full of god damn bullshit you just sent over to my fricking ass, John? How the hell did the damn agents in the field come to the damn conclusion that this incident was a fucking terrorist attack on the damn subway so quickly? Jesus Christ and Miracles hold on to your reply, even though this is a secured line. I don't want to carry this conversation out on the fucking horn like this. Not with all the damn whiz kids who seem to be able to hack into anything we transmit lately. Director, can you get over to my office, or would you rather me getting my ass over to you, sir? I'm opened either way you want to handle this fucking mess, John."

"General White, I believe it'd serve me better if you come over to my office. That way I can keep a handle on the shit going down at both incident sites. Both incident sites are classified as MPI, Multi Patient Incidents sir. General, I believe we're in for an extremely long and trying day, sir." Director Raincloud warned the military officer as he shook his head in disbelief.

"Yeah, right, okay, I hear that, John. I'll head for your office after I activate my troops currently being stationed at Camp Lejeune. You know we labeled the Rapid Response Units by the code name of 'Dragon Fire', so we don't get the damn reporters jumping all over our stinking bases, trying to see who we're activating for a terrorist reaction within the borders of the United States."

"Damn General White, I don't believe you were able to wrangle Command over a terrorist attack within the borders of the United States from the FBI Command Units, sir." The surprised CIA Director replied to the powerful military officer.

"I thank God for the past Republican Administration. That President realized the need for these specialized units I constructed, to be able to operate within the borders of the United States with the authority to close any damn section of the State or country these specialized soldiers are working in. Also, John, these elite troops can arrest and interrogate any terrorist capture, before turning them over to Command for further processing. Enough of this bullshit, I'll get over to your office within the hour, after I speak with my Colonel." General White then broke off the communication with the Director, and he dialed the Colonel's number.

"Colonel Bruce Leadbetter's office, desk Sergeant John Kirkpatrick on duty. How many I direct your call please?" The Colonel's secretary snapped pleasantly into the phone receiver.

"Yes Sergeant, General White here son, it's a pleasure to speak with you again. Is the Colonel in? I need to speak with him toot sweet. We have an emergency, and it seems like we might need those crazy ass kids the Colonel's training down there, Sergeant."

"Thank you General White and how are you today, sir?" The Sergeant did not wait for a reply as he added. "The Colonel's in, I'll transfer your call immediately, General White."

"I'm fine, transfer my call, Sergeant." The General growled.

In less than a heartbeat, the Colonel's voice came over the phone as he offered. "Yes, General White, Colonel Leadbetter, sir. Why the call, sir?" The Colonel did not deceive himself in the least, because he understood if the Chairman was calling, it meant only one thing to his and his specialized troops. His units were needed somewhere in the world, and the General was activating his people for immediate action.

"I'm certain you're expecting this damn call if you're watching any of the fucking news station, Colonel Leadbetter. If you weren't watching the damn TV then listen up close, sir. We just received a terrorist attack in the subway system of New York City, with numerous dead being recorded, maybe in the fucking thousands, Colonel. We also suffered a second believed to be terrorist attack at the Kennedy International Airport, sir.

Colonel, even though the second situation isn't being classified as a terrorist attack yet take my damn word for it, it was sir. The reason for this call is to see if you have the specialized troops classified as Dragon Fire Units still stationed on the base, Colonel?" The General asked his lesser officer hotly.

"General White, I have the full complement of Dragon Fire troops stationed on base at this time, sir." The Colonel replied without responding to the situations in New York.

"That's fucking great Colonel Leadbetter, at least we fucking caught a break here and we don't have to wait for the damn troops to be called up and arrive back on base. Colonel, arm the soldiers and get them shipped up to the New York City area as soon as you possibly can get them on the move, sir. Errr… have the soldiers report to the Baker Armory stationed a mere three blocks away from the Grand Central Train Station in Manhattan, sir. I'll order the Armory opened so your pack of screaming squirrels will have a place to operate out of covertly. As far as I can tell at this point, we have little if any damn Intel on this possible terrorist cell who might be responsible for this latest attack against our country, sir.

"Especially with Director Raincloud, all he does is bitch about how this damn Democratic Administration has degraded his ability to track and kill known terrorists. The Director blames the restrictions this Administration has loaded down on the shoulders of the Intel Community for this shortage and situation. I can't tell you how many times the Director warned me we're heading for another Nine, One, One attack, and I guess it has arrived dammit.

"Arrr… Never mind, that crap's my fucking problem to deal with, not yours to concern yourself with Colonel Leadbetter. All you have to worry about is deploying your specialized troops in New York City and get them searching for this fucking terrorist cell that has just blackened our fucking eye but good today, sir. I want this damn terrorist cell Colonel I mean I really want this damn cell bad, sir. You have complete autonomy over this situation to do whatever the hell's necessary to stop the next attack from happening, and capture these lousy scumbags, Colonel. Pull in any Units from the Marines, Army, or any civilian support such as the local police, FBI, any one or thing you might need, you have the power to draft these assets, sir. If you need, direct any complaints to my office, I'll handle the fucking problems that crop up. Try to keep the collateral damage down to an absolute minimum and get this mess done."

"Will do as ordered General White, we'll get the miserable bastards, sir." The Marine Colonel responded proudly to his Commanding Officer over the phone.

"Good to hear, Colonel Leadbetter I have to go, I'm due at Director Raincloud's office ten minutes ago, sir. Get it done for me Colonel." General White replied as he broke the communication and rushed out of his office.

CAMP LEJEUNE, NORTH CAROLINA.
ZERO, TEN, TWENTY, TWO HOURS.
THURSDAY, MAY 13th, 2011

Colonel Bruce Leadbetter looked up from his desk as he hung up the phone with the General, and he made direct eye contact with Sergeant Kirkpatrick, and then remarked with a snap in his voice. "Well, my friend, it looks like we got ourselves another bloody nose in New York fucking City. You better hit the damn panic button and assemble our troops, we have some stinking work to do, and the General wants it done yesterday, Sergeant."

"I understand Colonel Leadbetter Sir, when the General called, I knew it wasn't good news for us, sir. I turned to the news and found there was two different what the reporters were reporting as accidents to hit New York City, sir. Anyone with a fucking eye could tell it was a fucking terrorist hit, sir. Just by the sheer numbers of civilians who died in the twin attacks, sir. The numbers are high, I'll send out assembly orders for the grinder."

"Do that and I'll contact Fort Brag and have them schedule a troop pick up for our troops, Sergeant. I'll have the soldiers land in New York City at errr..." The Colonel looked at his wall map and he quickly located the nearest airfield to the twin incidents and added to his orders. "Land at LaGuardia Airport. It's the largest airport in the fucking area capable of accepting our C-17 Globemaster aircraft. Dumping the troops there will get them over to the damn Baker Armory in mid-town Manhattan as quickly as possible. That's where we'll deploy and start searching for these scumbags who just attacked us, mister. Get a move on it double quick, Sergeant!"

As the Sergeant turned and quickly left his office, Colonel Leadbetter dialed the number for Fort Bragg, and ordered four Globemaster aircraft for immediate takeoff. He informed the flight controller to clear the way for LaGuardia Airport stationed in Queens, New York. Once he completed this call, he next dialed the base armory, and ordered his troops tactics gear and weapons to be loaded and transported over to Bragg's Green Monster, the base airstrip that was part of Pope Airforce base that was shared with Fort Bragg.

The Colonel next called the motor pool and ordered up enough humvees to transport his troops out to Bragg. When this was accomplished, he rose, took his cover, and plopped it on his head, and then he walked out the front door of his office.

A smile the Colonel tried to suppress when he noticed his Tier One troops pouring onto the large training area with a purpose in their movements. Some of the troops were in various stages of dressed in uniforms. Colonel Leadbetter spotted Captain Robert Walker standing at the head of the rapidly shaping formation of elite and specialized soldiers, and he headed directly for his young officer. He did not bother to salute the captain as he growled at him.

"Okay mister, we have a fucking terrorist situation going down in New York on our damn hands, sir. It seems New York City and Kennedy Airport was just hit by a batch of fucking scumbag terrorists. From the reports I gleamed up to this point, it looks like the lousy little bastards hit us hard and gave us a shitload of civilian deaths. We're heading for LaGuardia Airport, and then we're scheduled to be transported over to the Baker Armory, that's stationed three blocks away from the Grand Central Train Terminal in mid-town Manhattan. Before you ask, that's where the bastards hit us.

"Captain Walker, I have our gear and weapons being out shipping for Fort Bragg as we speak, sir. Have your horde of stinking pissants check their damn gear and weapons out, when they catch up to the crap. Anything missing or damaged equipment is to be reported and you'll order it replaced before we head out for New York fucking City. Talk to your troops and inform them where we're heading, and the fucking reason why we're heading there. Then get the troops on the fucking move, mister. Ahhh…here the shits come now, Walker." Colonel Leadbetter drew Walker's attention towards the convoy of humvee troop transport vehicles heading for them.

The line of fifteen humvees pulled up to the head of the grinder, and then parked while the drivers waited for the elite group of troops to board the large transports out to Fort Bragg as the machines continued to idle. The lead humvee was equipped with flashing lights and siren to help move the local civilian traffic on I-95 out of the military vehicle's way, as they made their way to the other military base.

"Captain Walker, get your controllers on the fucking move so they can help with this load of rift raft we call stinking soldiers around here, mister. We might get stuck interrogating any captured terrorists, so be prepared and ready to have your damn EODT (Explosive Ordnance Disposal Team) ready to disarm anything from a damn pipe bomb, all the way up to a fucking RDD." (Radiological Dispersal Device)

"Hold on a minute Colonel Leadbetter Sir, what the hell's a fucking RRD, sir? That's a new one on me, sir." Walker remarked as he shot a half a smile at his Commanding Officer.

"Yeah, I forgot to inform you of the politically correct word for a fucking dirty nuclear bomb. It's now being classified as a Radiological Dispersal Device, Walker."

"Jesus H. Christ, who the hell dreams up all this crap anyway, sir? Dammit Colonel, why the hell can't we just call it what it really is, a fucking dirty nuclear bomb. I hate when we have to act like we're so fucking political correct all the stinking time, sir." Walker bitched as he gave a couple of quick hand signals, and his troops started to board the idling humvees.

"Why the fuck are you bitching at my stinking ass for, Walker? You know the damn bleeding hearts would change the word for murder to accidental end of life, if they got half the fucking chance to, mister. With politically correct words for any crimes and the likes, I need a fucking list of the new names to know what the hell we're talking about lately. Enough of this shit, catch up with your fucking people, and get them heading for Bragg. I'll be out there before you board the trash haulers, (C-17 transport aircraft) yeah, that's right Walker. I'm coming with your pack of flaming assholes on this one, sir. I want to see you people in action firsthand and pick up where we might be able to sharpen up our stinking act a little better, and correct any possible errors I might detect, Captain." Colonel Leadbetter offered as he suddenly stopped speaking and then he glared until Walker headed off for the waiting military machines.

Colonel Leadbetter waited until Walker disappeared in the lead machine, and the convoy then pulled out. Then he turned to Sergeant Kirkpatrick and bitched at him in an angry snarl. "Get our fucking gear loaded up in the damn staff car, so we can get over to Bragg before these assholes cause a problem with the base."

CHAPTER TWELVE

AL-WAHHAD'S APARTMENT ROOM IN
DOWNTOWN MANHATTAN THURSDAY,
MAY 13th, 2011. TEN FORTY-FIVE A.M.

Abdulaziz al-Wahhad, Mohsen al-Gasim, Reemabdel Aziz al-Rowaili and Band Ibn Saud were gathered and hiding out in the terrorist leader's apartment. The small terrorist cell was glued to the Fox News Station displaying the massive amount of damaged caused by al-Awajy's assault on the New York subway system, along with the second attack that took place at the Kennedy International Airport in Queens, by Ali Abbas Hamad. Al-Wahhad's chest swelled with pride as he watched another large section of a midtown Manhattan building suddenly give way and slowly cave into the huge pit carved out right in the middle of 42nd Street. When the news station shifted it coverage over to what was taking place at the airport. He issued orders to the others in the room with him.

"That is enough viewing of what we have successfully accomplished on this glorious day. There'll be plenty of time later to gloat over our great success over the lowly jackals in the coming days, when the exact extent and scope of our attack on the cursed infidels is displayed for all the world to witness and enjoy. Al-Gasim, order our faithful followers to leave this evil City immediately. I want everyone out of this filthy city by no later than nine o'clock tonight. Every follower must be in Washington, so we can prepare for our next attacks aimed against the very heart of the land of Satan. Saud, you must disassemble your bomb making capabilities, and take them out to your new location in Washington. You'll destroy everything you're forced to leave behind, you young fool. I want nothing left that might be useful for the police authorities to discover who we are that have attacked them on this day.

"The same goes for you al-Gasim. You must also destroy everything you leave behind when you and your girlfriend leave your foul apartment in this cursed city of infidels. I demand nothing be left behind that might assist the local police to discover who has attacked the lowly jackals. Until the day I decided to claim responsibility for our great success, once we're safely out of this foul country. The fools will have to work overtime to find anything out about us. Now be gone with you, even though we have enjoyed great success against the land of the loathsome infidels today, our campaign has not been completed yet. We have our sacred duty to Allah to perform, so we can purge all the worthless non-believers from the face of the earth.

"Once everyone has left my apartment, I'll pack my belongings and prepare to follow the rest of you down to Washington. But not before I make certain I left nothing behind to help aid the hated police authorities of this evil country to discover who we are. Saud, you're one of the most important members of our terrorist cell. Do you think you need any help with wrapping up everything we need to take with us, for our upcoming attacks in Washington? If you feel you might need some help, you're free to order any fool from our group to assist you, before they leave this cursed city for Washington. You are needed for our plans, Saud." Al-Wahhad stopped speaking and looked Saud in the eyes.

Saud replied confidently to the leader of their terrorist cell. "No Shabbah (Ghost) I believe I need no assistance with wrapping up everything I must move to our next location. Shabbah, I'd be most pleased to work by myself, in that way no one might mistakenly destroy or forget to take something vital to my needs and efforts. I shall make certain everything I leave behind is destroyed, because I'll even booby trap my cursed apartment, and if the local police authorities discover where I was working from. When the filthy dogs dare to try and enter my apartment, they'll find themselves meeting Satan in a powerful explosion that'll greet them."

The terrorist commander continued to stare at the Saudi bomb maker, until he finally allowed an ugly sneer to slowly cross his lips as he replied proudly. "That's a good idea, because if the hated police authorities discover your presence here in New York City, and the lowly fools go to your apartment, many will die for daring to enter your room. That'll make the foolish jackals more cautious to try and discover who else was working with you, my Arab brother from the land of sand. Now we have settled that, you must carry out my orders faithfully. That way I can handle everything I must attend to, so I can leave this foul city of sin. Let us leave."

Abdulaziz al-Wahhad grumbled as he loudly clapped his hands together, and then looked from one face to the other of his terrorist cell, until they quickly filed out of his room. There was little caution by the group, because they knew every police officer on duty or off, were busy working at the twin disasters sites.

When al-Gasim was the last one to leave al-Wahhad's small apartment, the chosen leader of the terrorist cell went right into action. The first thing he did was to secure and prepare his belongings for his move down to Washington. He looked at the clock and noticed it was eleven ten a.m., and he picked up his phone and quickly dialed it. He held his breath until the phone was answered by a gruff sounding voice on the other end of it. "Yes, good morning, this is Abdulaziz al-Wahhad and I wish to speak to Kadhim Muslawi, if he's available. It's most imperative that I speak with him immediately."

"Huh, I know who the devil you are fool, and I'll see if Muslawi wishes to waste his valuable time with speaking to you on this day. Hold the line and if Muslawi does not wish to speak with you, the line will go dead, and you'll know not to bother him again unless he returns your call. It is that simple, Abdulaziz al-Wahhad." With that said the phone went to Arab music and al-Wahhad settled in and waited for the outcome of his call.

In what seemed like a shot lifetime, Muslawi's voice answered. "Ahhh… as I live and breathe, it's so good to hear your voice again, my Arab brother from the lands of endless sand dunes. What can I do for my faithful follower of your religion of the Arab world?"

"My Persian brother, I was wondering if it'd be possible for me to visit with you, before I leave this city to see even more of this great land of the United States." Al-Wahhad was playing the game again.

"Oh yes of course, I see no reason for you not to come by and visit with me before you venture out into the vastness of this great country, my fellow brother of the Middle East. There is so much to see of this vast country. But I fear I am committed for the entire day with scheduled meetings I set up in advance. But looking I see my calendar is opened from ten until eleven fifteen tomorrow morning. It would be my pleasure to visit with you between these times I have just stated to you, al-Wahhad." Muslawi replied as he smiled, he so enjoyed playing the game of deceit with the Arab fool.

"Between ten and eleven you offer me my Persian brother. I was really hoping to visit with you today, so I could begin my exploration of this great land as early as this afternoon."

"I'm sorry but as I have just stated to you, I'm already engaged for the entire of this foul day, and I cannot possibly put off any of my scheduled meetings for the day, just to accommodate your desire to speak with me al-Wahhad. Tomorrow at the time I suggested is the only time I can spare for your visit. If this is not good for your needs, then I fear you'll have to start your journey without our visiting." Muslawi snapped his words to show al-Wahhad he was getting upset with this conversation between the two of them.

"Please forgive me because I fear I might have insulted you, by daring to place pressure on you to allow me to visit with me on this day, my Persian brother. I shall meet with you tomorrow morning at ten a.m. as you suggested, and this will be fine with me, Muslawi. I shall pray Allah to keep you safe and bless your tent with many healthy and fine sons." Al-Wahhad replied while trying to keep the anger assaulting his body, out of his tone of voice for fear of insulting the Persian dog eater any further in this boring conversation.

"I thank you for your kind remarks for my family, and I shall count the hours until our visit tomorrow morning comes to past. Al-Wahhad, I must end this conversation, because I have another call coming in, I must attend to immediately, until tomorrow then." The young Persian Operative smirked over the fact he was bending this terrorist will to his by refusing to visit with him on this day. He enjoyed it when he had the power over anyone he was working with.

"Until tomorrow then my wise Persian brother." Al-Wahhad offered to an annoying dial tone.

For the rest of the day, he took time packing to use up the hours before his meeting with the disliked Persian Operative. He kept the TV on and stopped now and then, to see what was going on with the two targets he destroyed earlier in the day in New York. Everything what he saw on the attacks brought him pleasure over the death and destruction he caused to the City of New York. He had no idea several Special Forces troops were an hour from landing in New York, to hunt him and his terrorist cell down. He continued to pack his prized stuff, as he cursed the hours left until his time to meet Muslawi and take control of the Uranium. So, he could construct a dirty nuclear bomb capable of destroying miles of downtown Washington D.C.

THE BAKER ARMORY STATIONED IN THE BASEMENT OF THE U.S. POST OFFICE, EAST FORTH-FIFTH STREET ONE BLOCK UP FROM GRAND CENTRAL STATION, THURSDAY MAY 13th, 2011, TWELVE FIFTY-FIVE A.M.

Captain Robert Walker was the first of the Special Forces soldiers who climbed out of the commandeered buses that brought his elite group of troops from LaGuardia Airport to the attacked zone and the Armory the soldiers were going to use as their temporary headquarters in mid-town Manhattan. As he rapidly exited the bus, Walker looked south of the Post Office and he immediately picked up the thick black, billowing column of smoke still rising high in the air from the incident area. He shook his head angrily because another terrorist cell was able to kill more innocent American civilians in his country. He looked over his shoulder and growled at the soldiers bunching up behind him and looking at what he was staring at.

"Okay, you guys took your stinking little look down the fucking street and saw what I saw, and now your puds know what the fuck we're going up against here, dammit. Remember Colonel Leadbetter's orders for us to keep a low key as possible while we're working in the stinking City. Hustle out of the damn buses and get your fricking asses inside the damn Post Office and out of sight and move into the basement. You people betta remember no one knows there's a fucking Armory in the basement of this stinking dump of a Post Office, and you hafta keep it that way. We got a shitload of weapons stored in there, and we don't need any damn terrorists putting a hit on the dump and arming them with the shit. Get a stinking move on it, people!"

Walker kept a harsh glare aimed at his troops as they rushed out of the buses, and then they ran to the back of the Armory. Two reinforced metal doors were flung open, and five of New York's finest were stationed at the doors. The police officers waved the soldiers in the dark opening. Once the troops disappeared beneath the Post Office, the police officers closed the doors behind the troops, and then they sat in with the soldiers, so they knew what was going on and what the soldier's orders were.

Colonel Leadbetter jumped up on the table as the lights in the Armory were turned on, and when he could see his soldiers, he started right in on them. "Okay you bunch of fucking gun bunnies, we got fucking hit and hit hard today, and I for one don't like the fucking feeling one god damn bit. The lousy sonofbitches who attacked the city are laughing their fucking asses off at us for the moment and you damn Squids were brought here to remove the fucking smiles from their damn pusses, toot sweet.

"Captain Walker, I want you, Sergeant Ramirez, hmmmm let me see. Yeah, the Mutt of course, and you too Buckethead, and you might as well go along with them for ballast as well Neck. Ice, since you like that dopey big bastard, you better go with him and try and keep him out of fucking trouble, you too Baby Tee. You people I just mentioned are ordered to dress in your civvies, and then get out there and reconnoiter the fucking incident zone. See if you can pick up any information of use to us. I'm setting up communications with the Pentagon, CIA, and FBI HQs from this place we'll classify as our temporary headquarters for the time being and see if any of them pricks might've picked up something we could use.

"Get a fucking move Walker, and the rest of you shitbirds who were ordered to go along with him. I want live Intel on what the fuck those bastards pulled off against us. Carry your military ID's with ya. I'll place a call and clear the way for you Squids to go anywhere you want or need within the damn incident zone. Err…you better get a move on it while I clear you at the damn site." He glared at the few soldiers he barked orders at until they changed into civilian clothes transported with them.

Walker looked uncomfortable as hell dressed in his civilian clothes as he led the way for the rest of the soldiers, ordered to accompany him as the soldiers rushed towards the disaster area on foot. The young Captain was immediately challenged by three police officers when he reached the heart of the incident, and he flashed his military ID. The officer in command took Walker's ID and stepped away from the group and he spoke into his small handheld radio. Once he finished speaking to his Commander, the officer called out to the other police officers working with him. "Sam, Ed, they have clearance to go anywhere they want in the attack zone. Their clearance comes directly from the President. Let them pass, no need to assign anyone to escort them in the terrorist attack area."

Walker smirked when he heard the police officer call the hit, a terrorist attack. He cautiously walked over to the edge of the massive crater, and he instantly caught the attention of a few other police officers assisting with the emergency. But none of them bothered to challenge the new group, because they felt they were either CIA or FBI Agents, and the officers gave them a wide berth.

Sergeant Dorothy Ramirez caught up to her soldier, and then she looked over Walker's shoulder at the damaged the terrorists created with their sneak attack. Then she mumbled barely over whisper to him. "Jesus Christ Walker."

"Jesus Christ had nothing to do with this shit, sister. It was another fucking group of damn Muslim radicals who did this crap, and it's our duty to catch up to the lousy motherfuckers and teach them not to harm any American civilians wherever they might be hanging around, dammit." The Mutt growled angrily as he stared into the huge crater and picked up a few bodies crushed in the rubble below.

"Yeah, gun bunnies, let's get down there and see if we can pick out any shit that might help us identify the lousy bastards. I want you people to keep your fucking eyes and ears opened. We hafta pick out something these bastards done, before that can help us betta ID the lousy pricks." The captain grumbled as they headed for the subway staircase cleared on 42nd, Street that led to the station below what was left of the street.

WASHINGTON D.C. THURSDAY, MAY 13th, 2001
ZERO, ELEVEN FIFTY HOURS

The stunned looking President of the United States sent out an emergency order for his complete Security Council to make their presence in the Situation Room, as quickly as they could arrive at the White House. The President was already waiting in the secured room as the ordered people arrived. The Vice President was busy speaking with the Secretary of State, and FBI Director Richard Hidlemann, was listening in on their conversation.

The head of the NSA (National security Advisor) was seated in the room going over several latest reports he received of the terrorist attack that took place in New York City, when CIA Director John Raincloud entered the room along with General John White following him. When the CIA Director and General were seated, the President loudly cleared his throat, and all conversations came to an immediate end, as their eyes went towards the young American Leader to hear what he had to offer.

"Err… Ladies and gentlemen, by now I'm quite certain that everyone here is aware that we have suffered a pair of massive disasters, both occurred in New York City. There are many deaths reported, far more than we suffered at the Nine, One, One, Twin Tower terrorist attack. Anyway, I have called you all here to discuss the present situation still taking shape at these two incident sites, and see what we're going to…"

FBI and CIA Directors both interrupted the President at the same exact moment, which caused him to look from the FBI Director, and the President ended up staring at the CIA Director, to find out why they interrupted him.

"Yes, Director Raincloud, you have something important to share with the rest of us in this conversation that you dared to interrupted me, sir. Director you may speak."

The Director stood and started right in speaking. "With all due respect Mr. President, it has been reported by a team of Special Agents from the FBI and my office in the field, that clear evidence was uncovered indicating this was a definite terrorist attack leveled against us today, sir. We have also been able to determine…"

The President interrupted Director Raincloud, he was upset, and it clearly showed in his tone and mannerism, as he nearly growled at the powerful CIA Director. "Mr. Raincloud, I knew you were going to jump the gun and brand this damn incident a terrorist attack against us, sir. I just knew you people thrive on raising fear. How can you be so positive that these two tragedies were the work of any terrorists so early into the investigation?"

"I can answer that question a lot clearer for you if I'm allowed to speak, Mr. President." Director Raincloud offered and then he went on with his words for the American Leader while he tried to give face back to the FBI Director. "However, I do believe Director Hidemann should be doing the briefing for us at this meeting, Mr. President. Although we're quite accustom with the countless reports being filed by his Special Agents working out in the field, sir. It's Director Hidemann's place to make a terrorist attack within the borders of the United States report to the President, and the rest of this council sir."

The fuming President ripped his eyes away from Director Raincloud's face, and he aimed them as if they were weapons, right at Director Hidemann as he growled at the man. "Director Hidemann, are you of the same mind set as Director Raincloud is, to believe these two disasters was caused by a terrorist cell operating within the United States, Sir? If you are, what is the evidence your Special Agents discovered at the scene of these two accidents that leads them and you to believe this as fact, sir? Yes Director, I'm still referring to this incident as an accident until proven otherwise it was a terrorist attack, sir."

"Excuse me Mr. President Sir, but one of my Agents working at the site has discovered a set of train wheels that the axle was obviously cleanly cut through by what is commonly believed to be some form of a shape charge explosive device, sir. The explosive cut right through the axle and caused the train to derail inside the confines of the narrow tunnel system, sir. Mr. President with all due respect sir, it's a clear incident of terrorism, sir."

The President's eyes sharpened as he held his FBI Director in his harsh glare, and quickly milled over his words in his mind. The President wanted to believe the incidents were accidents and not the acts of terrorism, as he snapped at the concerned looking FBI Director. "Okay Director Hidemann, if you want to believe this was a terrorist act, you believe it sir. I'll tell you what I'll do though. I'll give your investigators Carte Blanche to carry out their investigation by any means necessary, to make certain this was truly an act of terrorism aimed at us. But I'll simply refuse to allow any word of this possible terrorist attack to leak out, until we're one hundred and fifty percent positive this was a well-planned terrorist attack aimed against us."

"By your leave Mr. President." Director Raincloud offered to the American Leader.

The President turned to the CIA Director and growled at him. "Yes!"

"Mr. President, you made mention this terrorist attack was an open…"

"Dammit, possible terrorist attack I said for God's sake, Director Raincloud!" The President growled at the Lead CIA Agent.

"Excuse me Mr. President. This possible terrorist attack was a well thought out and planned attack aimed against us, sir. Mr. President, with the amount of damage we caused to the terrorist organization of al-Qaeda recently, has forced their operatives to carry out what we have branded as microterrorism attacks, sir. It seems the terrorist organization has resorted to these so-called micro attacks, and these actions happened to net the possible…" Raincloud was making certain he stayed well within the guidelines the President set forth for this meeting.

"This terrorist attack happened to have made a large kill score, sir. It seems the new leaders of the al-Qaeda terrorist organization, have gone to the belief their further attacks do not have to be big against the West. The terrorists just want to keep hitting us any chance they get, sir. I read several reports over the past days since we killed their leader, stating the terrorist organization is working under the assumption of successfully attacking the enemy, is to slowly bleed the enemy meaning us, to death. The new leader of the radical Islamic organization has referred to this change in strategy as to allow your enemy to die by the death of a thousand cuts.

"In the past Mr. President, the al-Qaeda terrorist organization has operated under the belief if their organization was to be taken with a grain of salt in the world pulse again, sir. They had to plan and carry out several large-scale terrorist operations aimed against those they deemed their enemy, mainly the United States. With elaborate planning and thousands of dollars invested in their operations, Mr. President Sir. These large-scale terrorist attacks concluded in 2001 with the attack on the Twin Towers and Pentagon building, sir. Then the terrorist organization turned their intention on symbolic attacks carried out against other government buildings, business centers, and organizations, and even against American military headquarters on bases here in the States and aboard, Mr. President.

"The al-Qaeda terrorist organization's ambitions were staggering at worst, but since those attacks and our reactions against their terrorist organization. The terrorists now find they're being battered in their once safe havens in both Afghanistan and Pakistan, their once dominate control over these two nations weakening at every twist and turn in any other nation, they have established themselves in. Their money supplies are being tracked and taken from the damn terrorist organization. Their leader Usama bin Laden killed and their leadership under constant drone attacks and continuing harassment where we're scoring high rates of kill shots on their leaders as soon as they name them.

"Mr. President, we do have the al-Qaeda terrorist organization under the gun, and that's why the damn organization has now resorted to what we have branded microterrorism, and that's what I believe these attacks were all about, sir. This latest attack on the New York City Subway System was a quick, cheap, and easy operation for the terrorists to carry out, which netted the damn terrorist huge tolls in civilian deaths and destruction, sir. This was a quick thought out and well put together plan, employing the minimum of expense and preparation, with one and maybe a second terrorist attacker employed in the operation against the subway system, sir.

"The same thing goes for the attack that was carried out against the Kennedy International Airport, Mr. President. We know damn well it was a lone elderly suicide attacker that got on board Flight One, One, Seven, sir. Who detonated a small explosive charge we're trying to figure out how the sonofabitch was able to get the damn thing past our security systems, and on board the damn aircraft...".?

"You make this attack seem so easy for the terrorists to have carried out against us, sir. Mind you Director Raincloud if this was truly a terrorist attack as you believe." The President remarked hotly as he again stared at the Director.

"Mr. President! We must go under the assumption this was a terrorist attack, sir. With the reports coming in, the evidence assembled by the Agents working in the field, clearly point to this being a terrorist attack aimed against these two targets, sir." Director Raincloud nearly growled because he was beginning to lose his patience with the American Leader.

"God dammit Director Raincloud!" The President suddenly roared as he jumped to his feet, and then he began to pace behind his desk. The American Leader stopped and set both hands flat down on the surface of the desk, as he snapped angrily at the CIA Director. "I heard enough of this damn report of yours, mister! I'll not stand for any speculation as to what this tragedy was, an act of terrorism, or merely a disaster created by a simple accident, or failure by man. I'll not listen to any further words about this situation until you can say beyond, and I mean beyond a shadow of a doubt this incident was truly a terrorist attack, or just an innocent accident Director Raincloud. Gentlemen, I believe you have work to do, and I have other meetings scheduled I must attend to. Err… Director Raincloud, Director Hidemann, I expect to hear from you two constantly, until this present situation has run its course, and all is right again, sirs."

The President then stormed out of the room, leaving the others at the meeting staring at his back as he left.

ABDULAZIZ AL-WAHHAD'S APARTMENT

Abdulaziz al-Wahhad rushed around his apartment like a crazy man while packing his belongings, because he knew he was never going to return to New York City under any circumstances in the future. In his mind, he was telling himself he had to stop by the al-Masada, or the Lion's Den Mosque to gather the rest of his belongings stored in that building. He wanted to remove all possible evident that he was ever near or behind what had taken place in New York City and Queens. Once he was packed, he headed for the Mosque.

He had his own key for the building, because he was holding many private meetings with a few young members of the gathering. As he entered the building, he was greeted by an elder, and the Saudi man tried to brush past the old man. But the elder took al-Wahhad by the arm and he snapped at the angry acting Arab man.

"Al-Wahhad! Do not dare turn your foul back on me, because I know who and what you truly are, and what you have been preaching and poisoning the minds of our youth with." The old man looked in his eyes, searching for a spark of mercy or kindness in them.

Al-Wahhad's eyes narrowed to mere slits, and he forcibly ripped his arm from the grasp of the other man as he hissed savagely at him. "I don't need the council of an old fool who has outlived his reason for being on the earth. I have things I…"

"Al-Wahhad!" The old man interrupted and then went on with his angry words aimed at the terrorist leader. "We shall feel the full embrace of Allah's infinite mercy, because we have raised our hand against no man at this Mosque and its following. But you my foolish and wayward son, you're doomed to feel His Mighty wrath, because you are guilty of shedding the blood of the innocent of this earth."

"I told you I don't need the unwise council of an old and useless man who wastes my time needless with his worthless babble and stupid beliefs. Be still before I send you off to greet Allah, and he can tell you I and my followers are doing his work."

"Al-Wahhad listen, you must stop this evil cause you have set out on, before it's too late to seek redemption for your terrible sins committed against the innocent in the name of Allah."

"I told you to be still and you refused to obey my warning, fool of an old man. Since you refused to be silent, I shall silence your constant babble, and then I'll be on my way so I can continue with Allah's desires, old one." Al-Wahhad raised his hand and then brought his fist crashing hard down above the right eye of the old man, shattering the eye socket, and sending bone fragments into his brain, killing him instantly.

As the old man slowly fell to the ground, al-Wahhad left him lying on the ground and headed for the room he used for the private meetings with the kids of the Mosque, he quickly gathered the rest of his belongings and then left the Mosque as fast as he could leave the building. He had one more stop to make before he could finally leave New York City for Washington. His last mission in New York was to meet with the Persian Operative for the last time, to gather the eleven pounds of Highly Enriched Uranium. So, he could prepare to carry out his upcoming attacks against the government of the United States.

He did not notice the other elderly man standing in the shadows of the hallway when he attacked the other man, and when he moved off, this man moved out and checked and was stunned to find his old friend was dead. He rushed to his room and immediately placed a call to the police. Although the second man was deathly afraid of the terrorist leader, he did know Band Ibn Saud was working with him, and he was going to report Saud to the authorities. In his mind he understood if the police investigated

Saud, they would surely discover al-Wahhad, and they would arrest and stop him from doing further damage to the country he was living in.

When the call from the Arab came in, the police Desk Sergeant listened to his concerns. The officer then informed the old man to hold the line and he transferred the call over to the FBI office stationed in New York City. The agent manning the phone listened to the old man's complaint, and then he transferred the call over to a field operative. The operative was standing near Captain Walker at the incident that took place at the train station, and when the call came in, the agent allowed the young Marine soldier to listen in. The agent was warned that the specialized soldiers were the lead for the investigation, and the agents were to do everything in their power to assist the soldiers walking all over the crime scene.

When Walker heard what the old man was saying to the agent, he immediately wrote down the address he was turning in. He stepped away from the agent and then he contacted Colonel Leadbetter manning the Armory.

"Captain Walker to Colonel Leadbetter. Come in Colonel. Over."

"Yeah Captain, what do you have for my ass so soon, mister? Over."

"Colonel, we have an address of one of the possible Muslim radical attackers, sir. From the sounds of what an old man who turned this scumbag in. This lousy dude might be the little prick that made the devices employed that destroyed the train and aircraft, Colonel. What are my orders if any change, sir? Over."

"I'll tell you what your fucking orders are, Captain. You're to get your ass back here on the double quick. Then you'll gather the rest of these screaming squirrels of yours and make for this asshole's dump and see if you can locate and arrest the bastard. Captain, I want this prick brought in alive so we can interrogate his fucking ass and see who he's working with, and why the fuck they done this damn thing. We'll interrogate the man, and we'll get the correct answers we want the bastard, and fuck what the damn bleeding hearts think or say about how we got the damn info from this little prick."

Walker placed the radio back in his pocket, and then he turned to the other soldiers with him and snapped at them. "C'mon people, we're the fuck outta this dumps toot sweet. The Colonel just ordered our asses back to the damn Post Office."

THE SECURITY OF MUSLAWI'S APARTMENT

Al-Wahhad was put through the same rigmarole he was the first time he met with the Persian Operative Muslawi. It took over an hour before the Persian allowed al-Wahhad to finally enter his office. With all the usual niceties over, they got down to business as Muslawi offered in a commanding tone of voice to the Iraqi. "I have what you come for my faithful Arab brother from the lands of endless sand and scorpions. I offer you a word of caution though, al-Wahhad. At all times you must handle this item with the greatest of respect and care. For the first moment you allow your guard to fall, will be the time this item will kill you in a heartbeat. Even while you're transporting this extremely dangerous item, if you're foolish enough to disrespect it, it'll destroy you. Or it'll alert the authorities as to what you're transporting, fool."

"My Persian friend, I'm well versed on how to transport and employ this item you are about to bless me with. Fear not for my ability to handle this Muslawi, because this item will be the weapon that'll bring down the brain thrust, and command of this god cursed lowly land of the evil Satan. With the attack I plan against this worthless country, it'll kill the President, and worthless Senators who sit in that monument built to honor Satan. With one simple cast of the fable sword of justice, the leadership of this foul land will be on their way to hell." Al-Wahhad boasted proudly to the equally grinning Persian.

"I pray Allah all you have proudly boasted will come to past, my brother. I'm sorry to offer al-Wahhad, I fear I'm rather hard pressed for time today, and we must finish our dealing as quickly as possible. So, I might attend to the other matters I must look after, as is my duty that allows me to work at the Libyan Embassy. Follow me and take possession of what you come for, so we can conclude our dealing, and then you can carry out Allah's biddings faithfully." Muslawi offered as he led the way for the terrorist he could not wait to be rid of.

Muslawi lead al-Wahhad down a long hallway and stopped before a door and he cautiously opened it. Behind the door was a heavy safe that filled the entire doorway. Once the safe was opened, Muslawi disappeared inside and in seconds he carried a heavy metal case out. The Persian

Operative struggled under the heavy weight of the case, and then he placed it down at the feet of al-Wahhad and complained at the Iraqi Operative.

"By the cursed Nomad's filthy hide who wander the foul desert on their never-ending quest to rob the faithful followers of Allah. I don't remember the cursed evil case being so heavy, al-Wahhad. Take possession of the foul item and then be off with you, so I can get on with my scheduled work for the day. My Arab brother, I shall wait to hear of the great success your attack will net the people of the Middle East." Muslawi stepped away from the case and asked with concern lacing his tone of voice. "Al-Wahhad, you have transportation for this evil thing?"

"Yes, my Persian brother, I have my car that I shall use to travel down to Washington with, so I can prepare properly to eliminate the brain thrust of this foul country of evil." Al-Wahhad picked up the case, even though he was fifteen years younger and in much better shape than Muslawi was, he nevertheless struggled under the heavy weight of the lead lined case.

Muslawi smiled as he observed the terrorist leader struggling with the case as he slowly walked him towards the elevator. Once the Iraqi was out of sight, Muslawi allowed himself to breathe normally and a smile to cross his lips.

Outside the Libyan Embassy building on the front porch, al-Wahhad was forced to wait a few moments until his car was brought before him by one of the security guards, who parked the vehicle when he first arrived at the Embassy. While he waited for his car to be brought before him, he held his head down in fear someone from the intelligence authority of the United States, might be taking pictures of everyone visiting the Libyan building under observation. He let his breath out in a rush when his car was brought before him, and the Libyan guard held the door opened for the Iraqi terrorist commander. The guard nodded politely as he closed the door, and al-Wahhad gunned the engine and was off. He followed the street signs that brought him close to the George Washington Bridge and route I-95.

CHAPTER THIRTEEN

THE UNITED STATES POST OFFICE ON FORTHY
FIFTH STREET IN MID-TOWN MANHATTAN.
TWO TWENTY-FIVE P.M. THURSDAY, MAY 13th, 2011

Captain Robert Walker and the rest of his specialized group of elite soldiers arrived back at the Post Office as ordered by his Commanding Officer. The line of humvees that brought the soldiers to mid-town Manhattan when they first arrived in New York City, was parked in the rear Post Office lot. Walker informed the Colonel what he found at the incident site, and the Colonel let down his guard and ordered Walker.

"That's great work to find this amount of information out so quickly, Captain. Walker, you take who you want with you, and get out there and arrest this lousy little prick, and then you'll bring his ass back here for interrogation. We'll use this dump as HQ (Headquarters) until we rounded up the rest of the damn PoS's (Pieces of Shits) who carried out these two attacks, and we have their nuts roasting over an open fire. Err… Walker, you better take the EODT (Explosive Ordnance Disposal Team) along with you, just in case this damn sand flea isn't home, and you must make a hot entry into his fucking dump he's staying at, sir. Never know if the scumbag placed any booby traps inside his damn dump, sir." The Colonel warned his lesser officer.

"That's a good idea sir, what are my orders with taking this stinking prick in custody, Colonel Leadbetter?"

"Walker, you do whatever the hell you have to do to take this little prick in custody, sir! You can bend him up a little, bust him up is fine with my ass. You can even bring him in dying for all I fucking care if you have to, Captain. Just make damn certain we can still question and get information we need from what you left of the lousy prick before he checks out on us, mister."

"You got it Colonel Leadbetter Sir we'll bring him in still breathing one way or the uther, sir." Walker replied with a snap in his voice, and then he gave orders to the concerned soldiers gathered around them. "Okay people we have a fucking purpose, and you guys know who's with me. So, pack up your gear and get ready to move out. We have a stinking little scumbag we hafta take into custody. You puke from the EODT are with us, so pack up your crap and get ready, we move out in ten! Anyone not read to move out will be shot. Move it people."

Walker and the rest of his troops that accompanied him to the incident area followed him, and they quickly changed into their military uniforms. When the troops were ready to move out, Walker headed for the double doors leading out of the Armory. He never bothered to look over his shoulder, because he did not think any of his people would not be ready to follow him to the gates of hell if he so ordered them.

Captain Walker, along with six others military humvees following his lead machine, tore through the streets of mid-town Manhattan. Colonel Leadbetter was smart enough to order a police escort to lead the way wherever Walker and his group of Tier One troopers traveled in the city that never sleeps. The elite soldiers headed for a known three-story apartment building in the Chinese section of downtown Manhattan. The convoy of military vehicles dropped down to Forth Avenue while still heading downtown. The two police squad cars clearing the way and having the military machines going through red lights they were caught by. It took the machines forty-five minutes to get below the Manhattan Bridge area, and once the heavy military machines entered the extremely narrow Canal Street area. They were forced to drop down to a crawl speed while rubbing several parked cars along the way with their heavy military machines.

"Man McNip, I don't know how the fuck any of these fucking cars can drive through these narrow ass stinking streets, let alone any damn UPS or uther delivery trucks for crap's sake. Crap, hey stupid you just knocked off the stinking mirror from that parked car, man." The Mutt called out to McNip, the designated driver of their vehicle, anytime Walker and his troops had to get someplace in a fast hurry.

"What the fuck can I do about it man? These fucking streets are so damn narrow I can barely get the fricking point of the damn machine down the fucking street. Besides dog man, I don't give a flying shit about any of them stinking civilian junk cars parked all over the damn place, brother. I'm not in the shit giving businessman. Say Walker where the hell do I gotta turn next in this crazy ass maze zone of narrow ass streets, man?"

"Turn right at the next fucking light, McNip." Walker picked up his mike and barked into it, informing the trailing machines of what was their next move. "Okay assholes, listen up, we have two blocks to the right and we're there. Keep your stinking eyes open and your heads on a fricking swivel. We stop anyone who even looks like a fucking A-rab from this point on in our responsibility, people. We don't need no damn reason to drag anyone's ass in for questioning over this latest mess."

Walker stopped speaking and looked at the Mutt for a few seconds, before adding a warning to this one soldier. "Look buddy, I don't want you stopping some hot looking chick just because she's damn good looking, and you wanna strip search her stinking ass, buddy. This is a serious situation, and you have to act like the professional you were trained to be, soldier."

The Mutt shook his head yes as he gave Walker a thumb up signal and a wide grin.

Ramirez smiled as she watched the Mutt reply. But she never passed up a chance to get on the Mutt's backside as she added with a snap in her voice at her Commanding Officer and lover. "Walker, you know the Mutt's pick-up line usually ends up with the chick filing a restraining order against his sagging ass." Then she aimed a great smile at the Mutt.

"That's its little sister, get on my stinking ass again. Don't you got something else betta you gotta do uther than busting my fricking horns like this, baby sister?" The Mutt grumbled as he returned the smile from Sergeant Ramirez.

"Hey Raz, the Mutt's still upset over God's promise to man." Ice, Sergeant Diane Morrison offered as she got in on getting on Mutt's backside along with Ramirez.

"What promise was that? I gotta hear this one." Walker asked as he looked back at the pretty female soldier as dangerous as any of the male soldiers from his unit.

"You didn't know this one Walker, well God promised man he'd find a loving and most obedient woman in every corner of the earth he searched. Then God made the earth round and laughed ever since." The pretty soldier smiled as she looked at the Mutt to see if he was going to react against the slug, she just fired at him.

Every soldier riding in the lead humvee laughed, but the jokes ended quickly when McNip announced to the group of elite soldiers in the slow-moving machine. "Hey Walker, this is the stinking street you fucking wanted, man."

The soldiers did what they did best. They immediately took on the role of an extremely attentive and on the alert soldiers, as they took in the surrounding landscape of the area, they were interested in.

"Stop the fucking machine right here then, McNip. I don't want you pulling right up to the front of the fucking building, and possibly alerting the fricking shithead who might be hiding inside the stinking dump that we're out here, man. Ghost, I want you and the Hunter out and hunting the fucking area, now! I don't want anyone charging up to the stinking apartment in question, without you two birds getting to them before they get in our stinking way. If this lousy fuck's supposed to be the explosive expert of these fucks who attacked us, he mighta booby trapped the stinking door to his dump.

"EOD team, I want you people to check out the fucking front door to their stinking apartment and whatever else you can see of the damn apartment first, and if you clear it for us. Then we'll make a hot entry into the fucking dump toot sweet and get this lousy spudhead. Okay, everyone knows what they're supposed to do with this damn mess. So, look a fucking live and be ready for anything coming at our sagging asses on this shit filled mission." Walker warned the group of gathered Tier One soldiers.

Walker and the rest of his specialized troops quickly took up a security position on the two doorways leading onto the third-floor landing of the dilapidated and badly neglected apartment building. He allowed the EOD soldiers to cautiously work their way towards the apartment door. Walker carefully watched as one of the EOD members stopped right in front of the door, and then he placed his ear up against it and listened. A second EOD (Explosive Ordinance Disposal) soldier moved in and used a medical listening device on the apartment door. Then that soldier shook his head to the soldier with his ear against the door. That soldier instantly dropped down to a knee, and he silently removed something Walker did not recognize right off from a pocket on his leg, and he carefully slid it under the door of the apartment.

The EOD soldier slid the telescoping mirror under the door as he bent his head low to the floor so he could see the mirror, along with what he could see of the interior of the room. Instantly he removed the mirror and announced barely over a whisper to the second EOD member. "God dammit, I picked up a number of wires hooked to the doorknob, sir. I also noticed other wires set on the hinges of the damn door, sir. It looks like the bastard has his room wired to explode, if anyone tries to enter the damn thing."

"Crap, shit, dammit, okay. I must report these findings to Captain Walker and see what the fuck he wants to do about this shit. Keep this doorway secured and everyone well away from the damn thing." Gun Powder, Colonel Frank Brettel ordered the other members of his team as he headed back for the young Marine Officer. Walking up to Walker, Brettel grumbled at him.

"Captain Walker, Mocher, Sergeant Bradford has detected a number of wires hooked to the doorknob and hinges of the damn door leading into the fucking apartment, sir."

"God dammit! That's gonna really screw up the stinking cocktail dip a might on us, Colonel. What the fuck are we gonna do about its sir? You know more about this shit than I do. All I know is we hafta get our asses inside that fucking apartment ten minutes ago, sir. Time is of the essence on this one Colonel Brettel. We hafta look for any possible evidence and names of the other damn terrorists working with this cocksucker we're out here searching for, sir. Did Mocher pick up anyone moving round inside the damn apartment when he checked the place out, sir?" Walker growled as he removed a cigarette and lit it. He did not bat an eye when the Colonel grabbed the cigarette from his mouth and began smoking it as he added for the captain.

"Mocher didn't offer detecting anyone moving around inside the damn room, Captain. If he didn't say so then you can bank on it, there was no one inside the fucking room he detected, sir. Captain Walker, it's going to make it damn difficult for us to make a hot entry into the fucking room, if the place is wired to explode against us, sir. No telling what the lousy little prick might have setup inside the damn room against us, sir. If only we weren't on the third floor of the damn building, we could check out the apartment from a window, and if he didn't have that setup to explode. We could've used the window to make an entry into the room easier, Captain." Brettel offered as he flipped the half-smoked cigarette to the floor, and then he grounded it dead with the heel of his boot like he was angry at it.

"Hey Walker, I got a fucking idea. If we use it, it gotta work out well for our asses, man." Buckethead offered in an excited tone, as he broke ranks and moved up to Walker's side.

"What the fuck are you looking at my damn ass for, stupid? What's your stinking idea, big fella? I'm opened to any possible suggestions to get us safely inside that damn room in one fucking piece." Walker growled at the massive soldier as he waited for him to reply.

"This hasta be good, the last time Buckethead had an idea. It stopped the rotation of the earth." The Mutt grumbled as he stared at the huge soldier. His words drew an angry glare from the captain as he waited for Buckethead to go on with what he had on his mind.

"Walker, when we first turned up the stinking road leading to this fucking dump. We passed by a parked Con-Ed electrical truck, and the three workers had a small man lift setup on the backend of the damn truck, sir. If the trucks still parked out their sir, all we hafta do is commandeer the fucking machine on the stinking pukes. Then we can use the damn man lift to get the EOD team up to the damn window of the stinking apartment, and then they can enter the room that way and avoid the booby-trapped door to the stinking place, sir."

Captain Walker stared at the large soldier, surprised the big man came up with such a good solution to their present dilemma. Shaking his head to get his tongue moving, Walker ordered the soldiers bunched up with him in the hallway of the building. "Someone get the fuck outside and see if that damn truck is still parked out there, dammit."

"Walker, I think that's what Raz is up to. She took off like a shot the moment Buckethead said something about the truck, sir." Ice, Sergeant Diane Morrison offered with a smile.

"I'm damn glad someone's using my stinking head to think with around here, dammit. Everyone, get outside and form up a strong security perimeter surrounding the entire building. No one and I mean absolutely no one get within five hundred yards of this fucking dump, and lives to tell bout it. Ice, I want you, Baby Tee (Sergeant Teri Dorland) and Three Martines (Sergeant Cheryl Grantham) to bang on the fucking doors to the apartments in this stinking building. You're to order anyone you find inside this stinking dump the hell outta the damn place for their own fucking safety.

"I want the chicks to do the evacuating of the damn civilians, because they aren't as threatening as the rest of you slobs are. Anyone gives you girls any kinda stinking trouble, back off and allow the males to move in and straighten out their way of thinking. They'll explain any errors in the way anyone's fucking thinking round here but quick. Okay people, move it out and follow your orders so we can place a period to the end of this stinking situation."

Walker watched as his group of elite troops rapidly moved as one to carry out his latest orders. Colonel Brettel waved his hand at his team, and those soldiers rushed down the hall towards the Captain and their Colonel's side. When his team gathered around them, the EOD Commander instantly informed them. "Okay we're not going to make a hot entry into the damn apartment using the front door of the place. One of Walker's people noticed a man lift truck parked outside the building, and we're going to employ that machine to get us up to the outside apartment window. I doubt the damn terrorist wired the window like the door. At least we'll be able to see a helluva lot more of the room from the window, to make certain we're not walking into a fucking trap in there. Outside people."

Walker led the way for the remaining soldiers on the landing. As Walker exited the building he smiled as he picked up Sergeant Ramirez. She was busy directing the driver of the beat-up Con Edison truck where she wanted him to park the machine for their use.

Walker charged up to Ramirez and remarked, "Hey baby I'm damn pleased you're working on my stinking side, sister. Thanks for getting on this damn thing as quickly as you did."

"I always have your back mister." Ramirez replied as she flashed a beautiful smile at him, and then she ripped her attention away from Walker and barked at the truck driver. "There, stop the truck and setup in that spot, sir. That's where I need you setup. I have to be able to get up at that window there, sir." The Sergeant pointed to the center window of the three windows facing this side of the building on the third floor. She stepped back as the first support leg of the truck came to rest on the cement of the service driveway for the building.

Captain Walker looked over his shoulder and quickly picked up the rest of his specialized troops moving out to secure the perimeter surrounding the building in question. He was proud over the way his soldiers rapidly carried out his orders, as the EOD team members gathered and watched the man life being setup.

The young Marine Captain knew he did not have to order the female soldiers from his team out to secure the interior of the building, once they moved the civilians out of the structure. There was a slight commotion taking place to Walker's right, and the two soldiers Snatch and Caviar, (Russian Sergeant Lana Dostoyevsky) rushed forward while dragging a scared looking young man by the back of his neck. The two soldiers dragged him up to Walker's side, with Snatch offering in an excited voice to his Commanding Officer, "Hey Walker, I put the grab on this little fucking dude here, because he looks like a stinking A-rab to my stinking ass, man. I'm willing to bet the fricking bank on it that he's the lousy prick who owns the fucking apartment we wanna get into, sir. Did I do right grab the little fuck, sir?"

Walker glared threateningly at the young kid as he pulled the man free of Snatch's grasp, and he yanked him to his face and snarled at him as he ignored Snatch's last question. "Look you little mutherfucka, if you're the stinking rat fuck who owns the fucking apartment we're interested in, speak up before I rip your stinking lungs outta your fricking nose! I need to know what kinda fucking explosive charges you setup in there, buster."

"Who are you sir? What do you want from me? I have no idea what you're talking about, mister. I was just walking home from school and saw all the excitement and wanted to know what it was about, that's all. Let me go mister, I want to go home sir." Band Ibn Saud cried as he tried his best to look and sound as innocent as he could possibly act.

"You ain't the lousy little fucker who lives in that fucking building, buster!" Walker growled hotly at the young and scared man again.

"No sir. I live five blocks south of here, sir. I just want to go home, please sir."

Walker placed a disgusted look on his face, almost believing the kid's weak story. But he still wanted to hold him in custody, just in case he was the one they were after, as he roughly shoved the kid back at Snatch, and then he ordered the soldier in no uncertain terms. "Snatch, you found the little fuck so you keep security on his stinking ass until we're done here, buddy. I'm not that convinced he's not the little prick we want, and until I know for certain, I want his ass secured."

"You got it Walker, C'mere buster I wanna keep my damn hands on your skinny stinking ass, man." Snatch growled angrily as he wrapped his hand tightly around the kid's neck and pulled him close to his body, and then he watched what was going down with the EOD team.

The Russian soldier branded Caviar, Sergeant Lana Dostoyevsky, moved up to Snatch's side and she pulled the kid's arms roughly behind his back. Then she cuffed his hands behind his back using a set of flex cuffs she had looped over her utility belt. Then she kneed him in the back of his leg and forced the kid into a kneeling position at her and Snatch's feet. Then they watched the action taking place by the other soldiers of the unit.

Walker turned to what the EOD people were doing with the commandeered man lift truck. Colonel Brettel and Major Abraham Robinowitz were riding in the metal basket slowly being lifted to the third-floor window of the apartment building in question. Once the lift basket had the two soldiers hanging just outside the window of the apartment, the Colonel went to work on the glass. He attached a large round suction cup to the window, and then he carefully cut around the eight-inch cup with a glass cutter. Once this was accomplished, the EOD Colonel lightly tapped on the suction cup with his fingers, and Walker noticed the cup move. Then he removed it and the circle of glass from the window.

As he placed the suction cup and circle of glass still stuck to the cup in the life basket, Major Robinowitz moved and went to work next. The Major known as Shadow, removed a small hovering remote-controlled vehicle, and he turned it on. As the motor lifted the small machine from the Major's hand, he carefully guided it through the circle the Colonel just cut in the window. The Colonel was already monitoring the four-inch screen of the camera of the ROV, as it began to scan the entire interior of the room. The Colonel moved the machine towards the apartment door and picked up the plastic explosive charge attached to the entry door. Then he turned the machine around and had the camera scan the frame of the window they were working from. It was free of any explosives, and he let out his breath.

Colonel Brettel continued moving the tiny ROV around the interior of the apartment, looking for any more possible explosives or booby traps setup by the terrorist, or anyone hiding inside the room. Once he and the Major were certain the only explosives setup inside the apartment, were the ones setup against the entry door, and no one was hiding in the room waiting to ambush them as they entered the large room. Brettel landed the ROV on the floor of the apartment in the center if the kitchen area, and then he put the control on the deck of the basket of the man lift, and he raised his foot and kicked in the window. The moment the glass was shattered, the Major immediately jumped inside the room, and he went right to work quickly dismantling the explosive device setup on the door to protect the apartment.

The rest of the EOD team members instantly charged into the building and quickly gathered around the doorway leading into the apartment, and then they waited for the Major to open the door for them. He expertly disconnected the wires from the detonator and removed the blasting cap from the Sytex plastic explosive charge. Once the cap was out of the explosive, the Major took the four pounds of plastic and bounced it in his hand as he opened the door, and the other soldiers charged into the room. The Colonel jumped in the room from the lift basket and took the plastic explosive from the Major and he tossed it to the soldier who caught and then secured the explosive inside a metal box he carried on his hip.

Colonel Brettel took command of his EOD team and issued orders to the members. "Okay people you know what I want in here. Swab every inch of the fucking place down, I want to know everything that was being done in here. Secure all explosives or devices you discover in here. Check the place out for possible biologics, chemicals, or radiation, or any other threats of mass destruction they might have been working on in this dump." Then he stepped back and watched as his people went in action, and the soldiers explored every inch of the two-room apartment.

Captain Walker entered the room and headed right for the EOD Colonel, and he offered him a cigarette as he lit one, and then watched the Colonel's people do their act.

Ramirez walked into the apartment next and stood by Walker's side. She began to scan the interior of the room and noticed a small stack of pictures of several young Arab looking people resting on the table. She began thumbing through the stack. She stopped the instant she discovered a picture of the man Snatch was guarding outside the building, and she instantly brought the picture to Walker's attention.

"Sonofa fucking bitch! That lousy little bastard coulda saved us a helluva lot of fucking time and trouble if he woulda owned up to being the stinking little prick we wanted, and he got us in this stinking room safely, dammit. I'm gonna get my hands around the fuck's stinking neck, and I'm gonna squeeze it until his fucking eyeballs pop outta his stinking skull. Then I'm gonna fuck the shit outta his damn eye sockets, Raz. Get outside and order Snatch to drag that little fuck's ass up here on the double quick, so I can question the lousy bastard. What the hell is this uther shit you got going here, Raz?" Captain Walker asked as he took the rest of the pictures from Ramirez's hand, and he rapidly flipped through the stack.

"Walker, I'm willing to bet if the kid outside is in that stack of pictures. Then the rest of his damn terrorist cell is also depicted in those pictures we have." Ramirez sexily wiggled her hips at Walker and then gave him a quick wink of the eye.

"Geees baby I just had a stinking epiphany here. I bet you're fucking right sister. What a fucking stroke of luck for us for a stinking change. If we know what the lousy fucks look like, that's half the damn battle. Great work Raz, you earned your pay for the week, sister." Walker replied as he began to thumb through the stack of snapshots a second time a little slower while carefully studying the faces of the people. As he went through the pictures, he found two depicting an older man. Most pictures were of kids, males and females ranging between the ages of twenty through twenty-five. But this one guy in the pictures looked like he was in his mid-thirties or older. He put these two pictures aside, hoping he just got the face of the leader of the terrorist cell. The captain was interrupted when one of the EODT members came over to the Colonel's side and reported to his Commander in a dead pan tone of voice.

"Colonel Brettel, we completed our first scan of the interior of the two rooms, sir."

"Very good Colonel Tauvy, report sir. What were you able to discover in here sir?" Colonel Brettel demanded from the soldier from the Canadian 22nd Royal Mounted Regiment.

"Colonel Brettel, on our first run of the interior of the apartment, we clearly picked up some strong traces of up to three percent of pure hydrogen peroxide commonly sold in pharmacies and other stores, sir. We also found in strong concentrations built up to a strength of at least thirty five percent, by employing common acids usually found on hand in most homes, sir. Between the acids and the hydrogen peroxide along with the strong traces of Acetone we picked up, we also found several empty bottles of nail polish remover discarded inside the apartment, sir. The terrorists were obviously cooking away the Acetone they needed for the basic construction of the weapon they were after, sir.

"We were able to pick up strong traces of Acetone on the chrome ring on the fan vent over the stove, which shows me the terrorists were also cooking up the compound commonly known as Triacetone Triperoxide or TATP, sir. The explosive TATP is a notoriously unstable chemical compound explosive usually employed by most Middle Eastern terrorist cells, sir. Most Middle East suicide bombers favor this powdery but highly unstable weapon, because of its helically energetic explosive characteristics, and the many deaths it could cause if exploded properly.

"Colonel Brettel, the risks of employing TATP is clearly outweighed by the numerous advantages of employing the so dangerous an explosive, sir. The Middle Eastern terrorists like working with the sugar like crap because of its lightweight, and nearly odorless characteristics that severely hampers and helps evade most of our bomb sniffing dog's abilities to detect this crap possibly hidden on the body or in any luggage, sir. Colonel, the TATP compound contains no nitrogen, which foils the ability of our scanners deployed to detect Nitrogenous bombs, sir. That's why the terrorists continue to work with this highly dangerous crap, sir."

"That was a detailed report, Colonel Tauvy. Was that all you detect inside this fucking apartment, sir?" The Commander of the EOD team asked his fellow officer.

"Well not exactly Colonel Brettel Sir and it gets kinda real scary from this point on in my report, sir. Colonel, Brettel, on an extremely detailed scan for possible radioactive contamination inside the apartment sir, I was able to pick up some strong traces along with positive evidence of what the terrorist was trying to construct a possible Radiological Dispersal Device commonly referred to as a RDD, sir..."

"Yes Colonel, I'd like to give someone the politically correct reaction for them damn bleeding hearts always trying to take the sting outta the fucking crime, by labeling it with a new and kind of romantic, or much less threatening word than what it truly is, a killing fucking item sir." Walker bitched angrily because it always angered him to no end, whenever someone changed what a weapon was or could do to the human body.

"I hear you there, Captain Walker Sir. Anyway sirs, I was able to detect many still active ingredients needed to construct a RDD inside the two rooms on several different surfaces I swabbed down just for the search of these items, sir. I found several small racks the terrorist employed for the drying of radioactive beryllium that the bomb maker was trying to extract thorium from the commercially accessible tungsten electrodes, by soaking them in a peroxide bath for a few days, sir. I also discovered several pamphlets on how to acquire Uranium online over the damn internet in a few different strengths, sir, medium, high, super high, and even ultra-high radioactive blends, sir.

"I further found a number of papers showing the bomb maker was on the hunt to locate Cobalt-10, Cesium-1 and even Strontium-90, sir. Colonel Brettel, on my swabbing down of the stove and surrounding area of the entire kitchen, I further detected trace amounts of aluminum powder. Thermite, thermite igniter to cause the explosion and a few samples of cooking thorium and Uranium traces on the surface of the stove top, sir. This sonofabitch had his hand in everything that'd kill people, sir..."

"And here is the little sonofabitch who was the fucking brains behind the stinking bomb making abilities of this damn terrorist cell who hit the subway system, and the stinking airport we're afta, Colonel." Walker growled as Snatch dragged the worried looking young Arab man into his apartment.

The two Colonels looked at the man being dragged into the room by the soldier.

Captain Walker did not wait for Snatch to bring the prisoner over to him, and he charged after the young man. Ripping the Arab from Snatch's hands, he dragged Saud over to a chair and literally threw the young man at it, almost knocking him and the chair over. The fuming Military Captain then reached out and stabilized the man and chair, and then he got right in Saud's face as he snarled directly at. "Look mutherfucka, I ain't got the fucking time or the stinking patience to dance or be danced around by your stinking little ass, buster.

"I'm gonna ask you a number of fucking questions, and if you don't give me the stinking information I need and demand from your ass. You're gonna rule the fucking day you papa ever fucked your mama. Now mutherfucka, I wanna know the names of the rest of the lousy little scumbags working with your stinking ass. I want the addresses of where these bastards live, and I want everything ten minutes ago from your lousy ass, fucker!" Walker glared at the frightened man, leaving no doubt he would kill Saud in a heartbeat.

Saud was so scared by the seething presence of Walker so near his face, he turned away from him to try and avoid his foul-smelling breath and threatening eyes.

"Oh no you don't mutherfucka! Whatsumatter scumbag, you don't like looking at your friggin death standing right in front of your pansy ass puss? You ain't turning your stinking puss away from my ass for nuthin, buddy." Walker growled angrily as he pulled Saud's head around until the man was looking directly at him again, as he added to his threatening words aimed at him. "Now buster, I asked you for fucking information and you failed to reply to my damn request. I asked you once and I won't ask you for a second fucking time, buster. I know you understand me, so I'm waiting for you to stinking reply, pal."

This time Saud maintained direct eye contact with the dangerous looking soldier. Slowly, Saud allowed a small smile that turned more into a sneer as he continued smiling at Walker and now staring him right in the eyes.

"That's it mutherfucka, I'm done screwing round with your stinking little ass. Mutt, get this prick back on his fricking feet and No Neck depants the fucka. We'll see how he likes having his fucking balls cut from his damn body."

The Mutt immediately moved in and roughly grabbed Saud by his arms, and he pulled him up to his feet as he complained to Walker. "C'mon Walker, you know this fuck is gonna Code Brown (Military slang for shitting one's pants) himself if you do what we did to the uther stinking guy we grabbed a few days ago, man. I hate this shit, the last dude we did this to, shitted on my fucking boots man." The Mutt winked to Walker.

Walker nodded at the Mutt because he knew the captain was not going to really harm the scared kid. Neck moved in and ripped the pants from the kid's body. The moment the kid was naked from the waist down, Walker removed his deadly Marine K-bar knife, and he slowly walked up to Saud while removing a cigarette from his pack. He slowly twirled the cigarette between his fingers as he moved the razor-sharp knife up to the cigarette. He slowly dragged the edge of the knife against the side of the cigarette, and the razor shape knife easily peeled the super thin paper from the smoke, while leaving the tobacco intact.

Walker looked for any change in the eyes of the still grinning young kid. There was no reaction, so he knew he was going to be forced to go to the next step with his interrogation of the Arab man. "Okay mutherfucka, you remember you asked for this shit so here it comes, buster." In a blinding flash of speed, Walker roughly grabbed Saud by the sack and whipped his blade under his balls, and then applied slight pressure against them with the back edge of the blade.

"Captain Walker you can't do this..." Colonel Brettel began to complain at the captain.

"Shut the fuck up! I don't have the time to dance around with this little fuck. They're trying to make a dirty nuclear bomb, and I won't allow the sonofabitches to use the damn thing against the civilian population of this country. Okay pal you know where I have this fucking knife, and if you keep your stinking mouth shut until I cut your nuts off. We'll see how fucking brave you are when I split your dick in half the long way, before I cut the damn thing off on ya ass, stupid.

"Now I asked you for the stinking names of the rest of your fucking friends, and where the hell they live or where they might be hiding around here, and I'm not going to ask ya again. Talk buddy if you want to save these here little babies of yours, buddy!" Walker snarled in Saud's face as he applied even more pressure with the dull end of the knife, and then he added to his warning aimed at the young kid. "Hey, pal you can only get up so far up on your damn toes before you run outta fucking world, asshole. You got anything you wanna tell my stinking ass? If not say good fucking bye to these little pearls…"

"Captain Walker…" The EOD Colonel went to offer but was again cut off by Walker.

"Colonel, I told you once to shut the fuck up, shut the fuck up! Talk mutherfucka talk!" Walker snarled as he turned his attention back to the young Arab terrorist.

"Okay! Don't hurt me mister, I'll tell you what you want to know. Oh, please don't hurt me that way." Saud suddenly cried out as he tried to get even higher up on his toes.

"You betta talk like you never talked before in your stinking life, fucker." Walker warned Saud as he moved the blade away from his dick and allowed him to regain his composure.

Sergeant Ramirez moved up to Walker's side, and she handed him the pictures of all the Arab people. Then she took out her pad and pen and prepared to write down the names and addresses of the ones Walker wanted identified by Saud, when the kid started to name the people in the snap shots.

"Okay mutherfucka, look at these fucking pictures and tell me who the fuck these stinking people are, and what the fuck they did, and what they intend to fucking do, and where the hell they're hiding in the stinking area. I'm warning you pal; you stop speaking for one stinking second, and I'll cut ya fucking ass up good and proper so much that even your own mother wouldn't recognize what I'll leave behind of your stinking body, sucker. And this time I won't stop until you're a fucking Unick, and you'll never enjoy the virgins they promised you!" Walker warned Saud as he held out the first picture of the kids for him to ID.

"The man in that picture is Mohsen al-Gasim, and he was the once leader of us before we turned into terrorists and until Shabbah took over command of all my friends and formed us into a good operating terrorist cell. The woman in the picture is Reemabdel Aziz al-Rowaili, she is the girlfriend of Mohsen al-Gasim…"

Walker knew Shabbah meant Ghost in Arabic, so he barked at the kid savagely. "Skip that stinking bullshit Mac, and tell me who the hell is the guy you just called the fucking Ghost in the snapshot, buddy?"

"Mr. Soldier, the Ghost came to your country invited by your foolish military officials. He came from the nation of Iraq after he helped your cursed soldiers hunt down several important insurgents, operating in my country against your occupational forces. The Ghost turned out to be an important cog to..."

"Give me his fucking name before I rip the fucking information outta your friggin head with my bare hands, sucka! Betta yet pal, point his ass out in these fucking pictures!"

Saud looked at each picture as fast as Walker flashed them before his eyes. The few pictures of the Ghost were not in the stack, and he could not understand that. He knew he had a number of pictures of his friends together, as he cried to Walker in his defense. "I am sorry, but I don't see the Ghost in any of the pictures you are showing me, Mr. Soldier."

"Is that because you don't wanna identify the lousy sonofabitch for me, scumbag? I'm warning you if you're lying to my fucking ass, I'll do a helluva lot more than just cut off your stinking balls, buddy. I'll skin your damn ass a fucking live and then I'll stick your body inside a pig skin, pal." Walker warned the young Arab terrorist.

Saud realized the warning the extremely dangerous acting American soldier just aimed at him and what would happen to his soul, if his body was stuffed inside a pig skin as he offered in an excited voice. "I'm not lying to you because you are not showing me all the pictures I had in my room, Mr. Soldier. A few of them are missing from the stack of pictures you have shown to me, and they are the ones with the Ghost in them. Please, I'm not lying to you show me all the pictures and I'll pick him out for you!"

"God dammit!" Walker growled barely over a whisper, as he remembered removing two pictures of the older Arab looking man from the other snapshots. He grabbed the two pictures from the table, and then held them before Saud's face, and he roared at the young man at the same time. "Okay pal you got me there pissant, is this stinking guy the scumbag you're calling the fucking Ghost on this snapshot?"

"Yes, that is he. The man in that picture is the Ghost, and he is the leader of our terrorist cell. He came to our Mosque, and he successfully turned my friends into a threatening terrorist cell capable of carrying out attacks against your people where they hide within your own country, Mr. Soldier." Saud began to boast at Walker as he regained his strength and then dared to grin at Walker, which was his worst mistake.

"Boy you got a fucking pair of mighty large fricking balls to dare grin at my stinking ass like that mutherfucka." Walker snapped so angrily at Saud as he suddenly swung his fist without thinking. He punched the terrorist square in the face with enough power to shatter his jaw, and punch out three of his teeth and knock his slumping body out of the grasp of the Mutt. Who merely let him go and allowed Saud's body to drop to the floor with a thud?

"Hey man killer, you really laid one out on that lousy little mutherfucker's stinking ass, Walker. It's gonna take the rest of the fucking week for the stinking little pissant to return to the real world from lala land, Homes. Whatdaya want me to do with the little fucker now Walker? We can't just leave him lying on the stinking ground like he is, man. We gotta turn him over to someone else to look afta while we catch up to the rest of his damn friends, man." The Mutt asked as he looked at the prone body of the kid crumpled up on the kitchen floor.

"Throw the lousy little sonofabitch outta the fucking window, what do I care what you do with the fuck's ass now? I got all of what I wanted from the asshole, so he's of no further worth to my ass or our orders, man."

"You really want me to pitch him outta the damn window, Walker? You know the Colonel Leadbetter's gonna want to interrogate his sagging ass. I'm sure General White's gonna want his to show up alive so he can talk to the little bastard to, man. I say we keep him alive until we catch the rest of the bastards working with this one, Walker. We can't just kill the little prick, man." The Mutt asked and complained, and all he received from the fuming Marine Captain was a dirty look and a slight nod.

"Captain Walker…" Colonel Brettel snapped at the officer again as he moved forward and got his body in front of the Mutt who was speaking to the captain.

CHAPTER FOURTEEN

INSIDE THE TERRORIST'S APARTMENT,
FIFTEEN FIFTY-FIVE HOURS MAY 13th, 2011

Captain Robert Walker turned so quickly that he caused Colonel Frank Brettel to take a step back, as he snarled at the other officer's face. "Colonel Brettel, you betta learn real fucking fast when to keep your fucking mouth shut around here, sir! With you constantly interrupting my stinking interrogation of that lousy fuck, you almost cause the motherfucker to shut down and not answer my fucking questions on me, man."

"Captain Walker, you couldn't expect me to just stand by in silence, while you were torturing that poor kid right in front of my fucking eyes, sir?"

"That's exactly what I expected you to do, Colonel. Look sir, I don't have the stinking time or luxury to try that water boarding, or any of the uther fancy shit on this damn kid, to get the damn information I needed from his stinking ass, sir. The damn terrorists have changed the way we're forced to deal with the sonofabitches to get the real time intelligence we need from the lousy bastards. They wanna slaughter the innocent then they want and expect us to treat them with kid fucking gloves and respect while we're at it, sir.

"Not on my stinking watch is that gonna ever happen, sir. Shit Colonel, if Command turned me loose for one stinking day with those damn sacks of shit we're still holding down at Gitmo. I'd have the lot of them singing like fucking canaries and begging to go surfing on a fucking water board, Colonel. If these fuckers wanna act like damn animals then I'm gonna treat them like fricking animals, sir. You know what these lousy scumbags we're hunting here are working on, a dirty bomb that could kill millions of our civilians. And you didn't want me to put a little push on this stinking kid's slimy ass, Colonel? How the fuck else was I gonna get the damn information I needed from him, without putting a push on his ass?"

"Captain Walker, you know there are certain restrictions that we have to deal with, any time we're questioning a possible suspect no matter what he or she might have done, sir. I'm afraid I'm going to be forced to make…"

"You can end you stinking gripe right there and now, Colonel. Because I know damn well where the fuck you're going with the damn thing. Maybe in your part of the service you have your stinking hands tied behind your friggin back when you're forced to deal with any stinking terrorists, sir. My Unit has no such stupid ass restrictions hampering their asses with questioning any fricking terrorists, sir. When we need any intelligence from a sap, we arrest for suspicion of being a stinking terrorist, we'll get the fucking information by any means necessary.

"Colonel Brettel, I'd rather face a stinking court martial, and allow the bleeding hearts take my damn birthday from my ass, because I was guilty of bending up a damn terrorist a might, than be forced to bury a shitload of stinking civilians by the truck load. Colonel North said it betta than I can ever say it, 'what the hell did ya do, come here to have a conversation with a gentleman, or a fucking soldier?' I'm a damn good soldier Colonel, and my job is to kill any possible threat aimed against God, my country, or the people of my country, and that Colonel Brettel is what I intend to do no matter how I get there, and who I hafta step on to get it done, sir."

"You're right Captain Walker, and we better let this crap go for the time being, sir. We have more pressing matters to look after, than to get involved in an argument neither of us is going to win. Captain, why did you knock the kid out before he told us where this Ghost fella is staying, sir?" Brettel looked at the terrorist lying on the floor, drawing Walker's attention to him.

"Yeah Colonel, I hit the dopey fuck because he was grinning at my lousy ass. Besides Colonel, a call from me to Colonel Leadbetter and before you can light a smoke. I'll have the little prick's address…"

"You'll have it sooner than that, Walker." Sergeant Ramirez offered sexily as she interrupted the two officers speaking, as she handed Walker a slip of paper with an address printed on it, as she added to her words to her Commanding Officer. "I already made contact with Colonel Leadbetter the moment this one," she said as she made a motion towards the terrorist lying on the floor as she continues with her words. "Our government invited this Ghost character to enter our country because of the help he gave our troops in Iraq. It took the Colonel just two minutes to find out who this supposed Ghost person was, Walker."

"You did real well get this information for me, Raz." Walker replied as he took the paper and read the address. Then he checked his GPS system and found the Ghost was living a mere seven blocks away from where he and his troops were presently positioned. The captain turned to the Colonel and informed him.

"Colonel Brettel you see what I mean, I want you to leave a few of your people behind to finish checking out this stinking dump. You and the rest of your people are with me, sir. We know where this fucking Ghost prick is staying, and if he's still there, we can end this damn nightmare right here and now, sir. Sweat Stain!" Walker turned to Sergeant Michael Nettestad and added. "I want you and Gang Green (Sergeant Jack Jorgensen) to remain behind and take charge of our fucking prisoner here, until we can have his rotten ass transferred down to the Post Office, and then turn him over to Colonel Leadbetter to have a little fun with. Standby and be ready to lend a hand to the EOD people we're leaving behind with you guys. The rest are with me and the EOD people. Let's get a move on it, double quick people."

As one every soldier Walker ordered to follow him moved out. Each soldier was dying to get payback for the terrorist attacks against the civilians. They were amped up because they felt they were going to place a quick end to any further threats coming from this batch of terrorists.

The excited soldiers rushed out of the dilapidated apartment building and quickly piled into the waiting humvees. In less than an instant they were charging for the Ghost's apartment, along with their police escorts leading the way for the military convoy. As usual, Walker led the way for the rest of his troops, as they rushed up the stairs leading to the apartment in question. Without hesitation, Walker lowered his shoulder and crashed his body's full weight into the closed door, shattering it and ripping the door from its hinges. He instantly dropped to the floor and took a defensive stance as the Mutt followed him into the apartment and remained standing by the broken door, while aiming his weapon into the darkness of the obviously empty room.

Both specialized soldiers quickly scanned the interior of the large room, and once they were certain no one was hiding inside the darken apartment. Walker struggled to his feet while breathing heavy. The Mutt grinned as he offered. "Well, I really liked the way you knocked on this sucka's fucking door there, fella. If the little dude was here, he woulda gone fucking Code Brown on our asses over the way you crashed into his room. All I know is it's a good thing this shit didn't booby trap his stinking apartment like the uther sack of shit did against us, or we'd be traveling towards the damn moon by now, man. Are you okay Captain?"

"Enuf with the wiseass shit will ya, man. Start searching this stinking dump and see if we can find out where this lousy scumbag's hiding." Walker did a quick look around the fair size room and grumbled as the soldiers still flooding into the apartment. Many of the soldiers were forced to remain hanging around out in the hallway, because there was not enough room inside the room for them to enter it.

"Man, from what I can see of this lousy dump, it's been picked cleaner than a bird's nest in winter, which informs me the stinking fuck's long gone on us. Check the dump out anyway, maybe we can pick up something that'll help inform us where this stinking jerk's heading. Colonel Brettel, have your people do a full sweep of the interior of this place, and see if they can pick up anything that might help us out some."

As Colonel Brettel's people started to carefully work over every inch of the one room apartment. Walker stepped outside to give the searchers a little more room to work with and to enjoy a cigarette. In the hallway, a few concerned residents came out of their rooms to see what all the commotion was about. When Walker noticed the nosy bodies, he was hit with an idea, and he started to question some of them.

Most of the scared acting civilians were Arab in nature, and they outright refused to speak with him, and when Walker approached them, they merely rushed back into their apartments and refused to answer the knock on their doors. All but one man that was, who seemed to be waiting for the young soldier to walk over to him and speak with him, and when the Marine captain noticed the man seemly waiting to speak with him, he put out his hand and the old man shook it as Walker announced in a clam tone of voice.

"Sir, my name is Captain Robert Walker, sir. I'm looking for the man who was renting this room here. It's vitally important I find and speak with him as soon as possible, sir. I believe he had information that'll assist me in my investigation, sir."

"Then you are obviously looking for Abdulaziz al-Wahhad, Captain Walker. I must warn you young soldier that he is Shagawah. In your language that means a man to be in fear of. Ever since that one moved in this building, all sorts of dangerous acting young men and women were constantly visiting and hanging around his room every day and even at night. I knew it would be just a matter of time before someone searched for that young fool, because of what I feared he was up to. What has the worthless fool done against you, Captain?"

"He hasn't done anything wrong and I wanna keep it that way, sir. I'm just looking for the man to see if he might be willing to assist my government like he has done in the past, that's all, sir." Walker lied to the old Arab man to not cause him any further alarm and keep him talking.

The old man laughed and then he offered to the staring Walker. "Please, don't speak the untruth to my old ears young soldier. I see in your eyes you are desperate to find al-Wahhad. Son, I have listened to the radio all day, and I heard the reports of the death and destruction that has taken place in the city, and at the airport. If you are looking for al-Wahhad then I'm forced to believe he's the worthless fool is somehow behind these terrible attacks against the land I have adopted as my home. I curse al-Wahhad and all who follow him to the fires of hell for the terrible deaths of the innocent he has caused. I'm sorry my son, because I told you all I know of this foul man and his evil deeds. I feared him ever since he rented a room here, so I tried to avoid him and his young friends when I was out, American soldier."

"You have no idea where al-Wahhad might be at, sir? Please, it's imperative I speak with this man as soon as possible, sir." Walker offered to the old man, anyway, hoping against hope he might know where this terrorist was heading.

"Not at all young American soldier, because it is as I already told you, sir. I tried to avoid him any chance I had, because I was able to see the danger and death growing within his evil heart and eyes day after day, sir. He's one I would never allow the pleasure of sharing my tent with, because his presence meant the death for anyone, he leveled his foul eyes upon." The elderly Arab man replied to the concerned looking Captain Walker as he quieted down and waited for the soldiers to respond to what he just offered him.

Walker noticed Ramirez walking out of al-Wahhad's apartment from the corner of his eye, and she seemed like she wanted to speak with him. He cut his conversation with the old man short by replying to him. "I thank you for your time and patience in this matter and thank you for taking the time to speak with me, sir."

The old Arab man nodded as the young soldier turned away from him and went over to a female soldier and began speaking in private with her in a rush of words.

"What's up Raz, you seem like you have something on your mind, baby?"

"Robert, we just searched the interior of the apartment from top to bottom, and all we found was a slip of paper with a roadmap of downtown Washington printed on it. Bobby, I think the one we want has moved his effing (fucking) operation down to Washington for the next part of his attack against our country. God Walker, I hope the sonofabitch isn't going to hit our nation's leaders in his next attack against us."

"Bet the stinking bank on it that's what the lousy bastard's gonna do. I gotta contact Colonel Leadbetter and inform him of what we just discovered here. If I know the stinking Colonel, he's probably checking our security and Intel people, to get a handle on this missing fuck, and what he might be up to." Walker looked around and picked up Neck and noticed he was carrying the Prick 25 secured radio system on his back. He motioned the man over to his side. When Neck went down to a knee, Walker took the mike and keyed it.

"Captain Walker to Colonel Leadbetter. How copy? Over."

"Copy all it's about fucking time you checked in with my damn ass, mister. I was just about ready to send the rest of our people out and order them to put a damn cap in your lousy ass for not communicating with me before this time, Captain. What the hell do you have for my ass, mister? Over."

The captain ignored the way the Colonel was getting on him as he reported. "Colonel Leadbetter Sir, we're presently stationed at Abdulaziz al-Wahhad's stinking apartment, sir. The thing was empty sir. Sergeant Ramirez found a slip of paper in the dump, and it displays a sort of detailed roadmap of downtown Washington, sir. I believe our missing little fuck's new target is somewhere in Washington, and the rest of his shitbags have obviously shifted his operation at the brain thrust of our country, sir. We picked up a young punk running by the name of Band Ibn Saud, Colonel. We conclude he was the terrorist cell stinking bomb maker, or at least one of the lousy fucks…" It was at this point the Colonel cut Walker's report off in mid-sentence as he barked at his officer.

"Yeah Captain, and I have Intel on this kid you obviously have in custody. When I was informed of his name from Sergeant Ramirez, I immediately ran a background check on his fucking ass, soldier. I found out in Oh Eight the fuck went to Pakistan, and the lousy turd was trained in making various bomb making abilities by an important al-Qaeda operative there. One thing I must warn you about Walker. This little prick could make a dirty bomb. Walker, from this point forward this operation has a new code name. You people are now being classified as Dragon Fire, and I'm Dragon's Lair. Okay mister, your orders are to return to the damn Post Office. Once here I'll prepare with getting everyone shipped down to Washington, and we'll start looking for this terrorist cell…"

"Colonel Leadbetter, were you able to gather any Intel on this damn terrorist cell, sir? How many of the fucks make up the damn cell?"

"You got brass balls to dare interrupt my ass while I'm speaking to you, Captain. But it was a damn good question that needed to be asked. Walker, when you closed in on our targets, I went to work checking with Interpol's Red Alert, along with the JWICS (Joint Worldwide Intelligence Communications System), and their systems were beaten to death like our Intel was attacked by our government. This new Administration set our Intel capabilities back eight to ten years, and the overseas Intel Communities are in just as bad a shape as ours are in, Captain. Nevertheless, I checked with our Intel starting with SIPRNT. (Secure Internet Protocol Router Network)

"It's the Pentagon network created in Ninety-Five and is available to all Pentagon top Officers to the troops out in the field, helping to track intelligence for units in operation. I also checked with the NCDD (Net-Centric Diplomacy Database). This department stores all classified information on their database up to the top-secret level. All agencies across the government had direct access to all state information through their secured networks. I even checked with the FBISL, (FBI Security List) of dangerous people considered to be serious threats to public officials, or our national security, Captain.

"Hell Captain, I even checked in with NCTC, (National Counterterrorism Center) that connects all the fucking dots and dashes on any possible terrorism intelligence gathered by Intelligence Agencies spread throughout the rest of the world. The last office I checked in with was the Pentagon's JIPTWL, (Joint Integrated Prioritized Target and Watch List) shit I missed one of the damn offices I checked in with, dammit. I also checked in with FBISIL (FBI Security Index List). I found nothing about this new terrorist cell other than it being classified as a home-grown cell recently organized that went in action at the train station and airport, sir.

"So, it looks for the time being that we're going to be on our own for this entire operation, mister. Captain, I have every possible Intel asset working on finding out any damn information on this new terrorist cell they can discover both day and night. Shit, yeah, alright Walker, that shits for another day and time to bitch about. You have orders, so you carry them out as received, sir. It's late and I expect you and the rest of your gun jugglers back here toot sweet, Captain. I'm ordering you to leave one member of your group behind at both locations, to secure them until we can get back to the places and really rip them apart, sir. Get the rest of your people back here to the damn Post Office, so I can get them heading for Washington. Crap, if these fucks are after our politicians, we have to get them before they get at our President, and anyone else they want to kill, Captain."

"Yes sir." Was all Walker responded as he broke off the communication with the Colonel.

ABDULAZIZ AL-WAHHAD'S PLIGHT; FIVE FORTY-FIVE P.M. THURSDAY, MAY 13th, 2011

After Abdulaziz al-Wahhad left the Persian Operative's office, he loaded the Uranium stored in the heavy lead container in the back of his car, and then he quickly left the site. He drove his car to a secluded parking lot within sight of the George Washington Bridge. When he turned into the parking lot, he pulled up to a car he planted in the lot two days before. He rapidly unloaded his cargo into the second car. He understood it would not take the American government long to discover his identity and place a nationwide search out for his vehicle. The parked car was one he borrowed from a trusted female friend and lover, and he sworn her to silence if he had her car. The last thing he moved into the second car was the container securing the Uranium. He slammed the trunk closed, opened the door lock, and placed the key in the ignition, revved the motor twice, and then he pulled out of the parking lot.

After ten minutes of driving, al-Wahhad started over the George Washington Bridge. The traffic was light at this time of the day, and he attributed this to the civilians wanting to stay off the roads, because of his twin attacks in New York City. The traffic bottlenecked at the line of toll booths on the New Jersey side of the Hudson River. Al-Wahhad shook his head as he fished out eleven dollars for the toll and handed it to the woman smiling at him from her booth. All the while driving through New Jersey; he kept looking in his rear-view mirror, while keeping a close eye on his speed at the same time. He did not want to do anything that would cause one of the police departments to stop and check his vehicle.

As the sun slowly started setting, the terrorist leader was already driving through Delaware, and he spotted the first sign declaring he was rapidly closing in on the Washington D.C. area. Automatically, he checked his speed and smiled when he noticed he was traveling at sixty-eight miles an hour, and the limit was seventy. He looked at the clock on the radio and discovered it was seven ten p.m. He opened the window more and breathed in a huge gulp of the cool air.

Traffic was getting lighter, and it was almost a pleasure to drive on the highway with the sun setting, and people getting off the road. Several times al-Wahhad found himself yelling because he absentmindedly increased his speed. For the first time he put the radio on and turned it to the news channel. He listened to the many countless reports on his terrorist attack against the New York Subway System. He was surprised the announcer was remarking the search and rescue operation on the subway system had shifted to a recovery operation. There was no report on his attack on Kennedy Airport, and he found this strange.

Suddenly his blood ran cold when he listened to a new report stating the police authorities were looking for him, and were announcing his plate number, and giving a good description of his car and person. The terrorist leader was pleased for taking his girlfriend's car. The report stated the authorities believed al-Wahhad was driving alone and heading for Washington. The report also stated all local police and highway officers were on a heightened state of alert and armed with orders to stop and search any vehicle answering the description of his car.

Al-Wahhad instinctively lowered the dashboard lights lighting up his face inside the vehicle while he was driving. He even slowed his vehicle down to sixty-five mph and traveled in the slower lane. Bile built up in his mouth when he noticed the flashing lights of what he took to be a police vehicle rapidly speeding up on him. He did not breathe normally again until the ambulance pulled out in the second lane and then sped by his slower moving vehicle. Suddenly he was picking up police vehicles passing him just as fast, and he looked off in the distance and noticed the traffic was building up in front of his vehicle.

He started to look at the traffic signs and noticed an exit coming up. He put his blinker on and pulled off the highway and took the service road running along the highway. He slowed his vehicle down to a crawl when he noticed the police had setup roadblocks on the main highway, and the officers were checking out the drivers of every car they were allowing past by the roadblock. Again, he began to breathe easy as he passed the roadblock on Route I-95. Once he was passed the roadblock, he drove to the next entry to I-95 and got back on the highway, finding out he was only five miles out of Washington.

THE UNITED STATES POST OFFICE ON EAST FORTY FIFTH STREET MID-TOWN MANHATTAN; SIX TEN P.M.

By the time Captain Robert Walker assembled his specialized troops and secured the two rooms, it was well after six p.m. Thursday, May 13th, 2011. The humvees pulled up to the closed Post Office and another soldier quickly opened the security gate for the humvees to park in the rear of the lot, and then that soldier secured the gate again. Colonel Leadbetter stood in the lot with his arms folded over his chest while glaring at the vehicles as they slowly pulled into the lot.

Walker was the first soldier out of the war machines, and he proudly walked up to the Colonel and gave him a half ass salute that the angry Colonel did not bother to return, as he immediately got on his Captain's backside. "Jesus Christ and miracles, you people certainly took your ever-loving fucking time with getting your asses back here."

Walker smiled at his Commanding Officer, and then instantly started his report. "Colonel Leadbetter Sir, it took me a bit longer than I figured to secure the two apartments the stinking criminals used, and then getting our people heading back to the damn Post Office, sir. Colonel Leadbetter, I won't begin to tell you about the horrors of the crazy ass traffic of this damn City we hadta drive through, and what we had to do to get here, sir."

"Yeah, I read you loud and clear over that bitch, mister. Walker, so far it seems everything but catching the damn leader of this fucking terrorist cell, is working out rather well in our favor. I feel with our fast reaction to the twin attacks on the city, forced these damn scumbags to get the hell out of town faster than they planned to move their operations down to Washington. Now, all we have to do is figure out where the fuck their targets in Washington might be and stop the lousy bastards from accomplishing their next damn act, sir. It seems like the once lagging intelligence information is rapidly starting to catch up with this damn situation. That's why it was easy for me to find the info we needed about you prisoner, and these other fucks we want."

"With our fucking help Colonel." The Mutt offered while getting into the conversation.

"With your help huh stupid? Let me tell you something hot shot soldier, you couldn't run a fucking red light without someone else's help, buster. On the annoyance scale you fit right in between fucking rap music and a crying baby, you damn ball sack you. Keep out of any conversation that's not directed at your stinking ass, mister." Colonel Leadbetter growled at the young soldier as he stared him down for a few seconds.

The Mutt bobbled his head on his shoulders as he crossed his eyes at his Commander.

"The only reason you're still alive is because it's illegal to put a cap in your stinking ass, mister. Now shut the hell up and pay close attention to this conversation, because we're in one helluva mess here, soldier." The Colonel turned his attention back to Walker and bitched at him. "Captain, you better tie a half knot in the Mutt's ass and yank up on it, mister. Maybe that'll keep his damn mouth shut for a change, buster."

"Hey Colonel, you betta listen to me once in a while. I really know what the hell I'm talking 'bout sir, I once dated a chick from L.A. Law, and she taught me…" The Mutt offered while trying to ride his Commanding Officer's ass. But before the Colonel could respond to the Mutt, another soldier got in on the conversation and bitched at his Commanding Officer.

"Colonel Leadbetter, one of these days you're going to say something nice about one of us soldiers, and you'll never forgive yourself, sir." Ice purred as she smiled at the Colonel.

"That'll be the fucking day little Miss Wiseass. Crap, it looks like I just woke up the sleeping dead. Sister, I wouldn't speak further with you even if we were alone in the Garden of Eden, and apples were selling for five cents a fucking pound. Walker!" Colonel Leadbetter snarled as turned back to his officer and then went on with is words. "Do you mind if your trained seals flap their fucking fins the hell out of my damn sight, so we can speak in peace?"

Walker laughed and then he snapped at the rest of his soldiers gathered around him. "Okay, enuf fucking clowning round people. Evidently the Colonel has something important on his mind, and we betta listen up if we know what's good for us." Walker looked at his Commander and smirked, and then waited for him to continue with his new orders for his troops.

"Walker I have transportation already setup for our teams to get you and the rest of your people down to Washington, sir. We're going to convoy over to LaGuardia Airport where I have two trash haulers waiting to pick up our Units, and get our asses down there, mister. When we land at Reagan Airport, we'll linkup with our road transportation, and then head for another secured location where we'll setup our next headquarters. Walker, from the little bit of evidence we discovered at that punk's apartment, we know this damn terrorist cell is working on a radiological dispersal device that could kill millions of our civilians, and make Washington a useless ghost town for many years to come… Err… hold on for a second I have some crap coming in over the communication's radio, Captain."

Colonel Leadbetter removed his radio and barked into it. "Yeah, this is Dragon Leader, identify yourself and tell me what the hell you have for my ass. Over."

"Dragon Leader now huh Colonel?" Walker smiled to his Commander over his mistake.

Leadbetter glanced at Walker and then gave him the finger as he went back to his conversation over his radio.

"Hey Colonel, is that you're IQ or the number of white parents you got?" The Mutt grumbled.

The Colonel's glare was so severe that it caused the Mutt to take a step back.

"Yes, Dragon Leader, this is Sergeant Williams from the New York police department, sir. I received your APB (All Points Bulletin) to be on the lookout for a Two Zero Ten, Blue Chevy Malibu vehicle with the plate number One, Seven, Niner, Charlie, Lincoln, Ida, sir. Dragon Leader, I located the missing vehicle in the alert, it's parked in an out of the way parking lot near Interstate Two Eight Five, sir. Colonel, I believe the one driving the vehicle has parked this car here and he must have jumped into a stashed vehicle, and he's now heading directly for the target area we were alerted about in the new vehicle, sir."

"You did really well with locating that damn thing for us, sir. Okay Sergeant Williams, this is what I want you to do. Secure the area around that damn parking lot and vehicle at least a block in all directions from the center of that damn lot. I'm heading your location in a few moments with a few of my people, and we're going to go over that damn vehicle with a fine-tooth comb, sir. Maybe, we can discover where this missing scumbag is heading for, Sergeant. Stay on guard and secure the area as instructed, Sergeant. I'm on my way to you as soon as I get my people on the move here. Over." The moment the Colonel was off the radio he turned to Walker.

"Captain Walker, get your people on the move for LaGuardia Airport as fast as you can get them moving, sir. The trash haulers (transport aircraft) are already waiting on the tarmac for your troopers to show up. The captains of the aircraft were informed where they're to get you people too. I'm going to hold back two of your troops, and they'll accompany me and help check out the fucking terrorist's vehicle the damn police Sergeant just found, sir. Get your people on the move as fast as you can get them moving, Captain." The Colonel repeated and then he called out two troop's names and ordered them to accompany him. He walked over to a box and removed a handheld Geiger counter, and he and the two soldiers walked to one of the parked humvees, and the other soldier started it and they quickly headed off for the reported parking lot.

Walker ordered his people into the other humvees, all the while the Colonel and Walker spoke. The other soldiers were busy packing up their equipment and stowed it inside the humvees, so they would be ready when Walker wanted to move out.

ABDULAZIZ AL-WAHHAD'S VEHICLE DRIVING ON I-95. FRIDAY, MAY 14th, 2011, ZERO, TWO, THIRTY, ONE A.M.

Abdulaziz Al-Wahhad drove perfectly to Washington. He stayed five miles an hour under the posted speed limit of the highway and kept the dashboard lights low, so they gave no glow to the interior of the car or on his face. He carefully turned off the Interstate and got on the side roads of downtown Washington. Again, he drove slowly to draw no attention towards his vehicle or himself. The terrorist leader was searching for a road where he knew his safe home was on, along with the others of his group who left New York City before he did the day before.

Easily finding Salem Drive, he smiled as he looked for the cross street of Ash. Finding Ash Street, he cautiously turned down that road and drove to the home of Nine, Twenty-One. The neighborhood was quiet, and he turned in the driveway of the five-bedroom building owned by the Arab Relations Group. The home was opened to any person of Arab decent needing a safe home to work from or hide in. Al-Wahhad set it up with the Emir to reserve the building for him and the rest of his attackers.

The terrorist leader parked the car in the driveway then got out and closed the door quietly, not to disturb the neighbors mostly Arab in nature. He walked over to the front door and cautiously entered and found the others of his group already waiting inside the building, aiming their weapons at his body. The terrorist Commander smiled and then announced sharply. "Alhamdulilah (Praise be to God), I thank the Almighty Allah to make it possible for all you young fools to arrive here safely. I trust no one is missing from our group?" Al-Wahhad asked as he looked at his second in command, al-Gasim who stood with his young and pretty girlfriend Reemabdel Aziz al-Rawaili, while she still aimed her weapon directly at al-Wahhad's chest.

Mohsen Al-Gasim drew in his breath and then spoke to his leader in an extremely clam tone of voice. "Shabbah, all members of our terrorist cell are here, all except for Band Iba Saud that is. I don't understand this because he left the same time, I left to remove our belonging, and then head for this safe house in Washington. Maybe Saud is trapped in the cursed traffic of this foul country that drives us crazy?"

"Don't be such a fool. If Saud has not arrived yet, then it's a good bet he has been taken prisoner by the great fools who search for us constantly. This is a problem for us to deal with if Saud was arrested by the police authorities. Then the fool has crippled our plans to make the nuclear weapon to destroy the heart of Satan's foul land…"

"That's not correct Shabbah, we have Abdullah al-Mutairi. Shabbah, he's well trained with the abilities in making bombs and other weapons we need to crush the non-believers who dwell within this god forsaken land of Satan." Al-Gasim offered in haste to the leader.

Al-Wahhad searched the many young faces staring at him, as the other terrorists relaxed and lowered their weapons. The Ghost continued to search until his eyes locked upon the face of al-Mutairi. He was a young Iraqi man who served in Saddam Hussien's well feared Republican Army, and he was known to be trained in the various ways of making a working bomb, or other destructive devices needed by the Arab soldiers at war. Al-Wahhad allowed a slight smile to slowly cross his lips as he grumbled at this young man. "Is it as al-Gasim has just offered to my worthless ears, fool? You have been trained in the construction of the nuclear weapon we'll employ to destroy the god cursed lair of Satan? Don't speak words of assurance unless you're able to do what you offer to me, young fool."

Al-Mutairi replied confidently to al-Wahhad's last question. "Yes, I'm skilled to assemble the weapon we'll employ to destroy the hated heart of the non-believers."

Al-Wahhad was greatly relieved this young Arab man would be able to carry on with Saud's work, and finish constructing the nuclear weapon needed to finish their attack against the lowly infidels of Washington. Although he did not let on, his mind was deeply troubled over Saud, and what must have happened to him. He was concerned if the authorities had arrested Saud, was he going to be able to stand up to the interrogation and hold his tongue. Or was he going to fold and give up his terrorist cell to the hated authorities and end his dream to destroy the leadership of the United States. He decided and addressed the others of his terrorist cell.

"I shall speak with all of you fools because I'm changing our original plans for our attack. Yes, this is a safe house, but if Saud was arrested by the police authorities as I fear he was, they might be able to loosen his worthless tongue, and Saud might give up this house to them fools. If you remember correctly, I spoke about a second house, but I kept the location of this other haven from all of you. I order you to pack your equipment because we're going to move. I have a bad feeling and I shall react to that feeling. Follow my orders and once you have your belongings stored in our vehicles. I'll lead the way to our next house ten miles from this foul location. Pack quickly my Arab brother and sisters, because Allah is waiting for us to carry out His revenge against the lowly jackals of this cursed country."

The terrorist Commander placed his hands on his hips and then glared at the other terrorists. He waited not so pleased for the others of his group to pack, and once they hauled their belongings out to their vehicles. He ran a last check of the interior of the safe house, to make certain nothing needed by them was accidently left behind that might identify them to the police authorities. Once he was certain everything was secured, he left the structure. He entered his car and pulled onto the road and hesitated for a moment until the other vehicles were on the road directly behind his vehicle.

THE SECLUDED PARKING LOT IN THE
SHADOW OF THE GEORGE WASHINGTON BRIDGE

Colonel Bruce Leadbetter, along with the soldiers branded Sleeper, Sergeant Carl Youngblood and Mule, Sergeant Steve Steingold, pulled into the parking lot offering a place for commuters to park and carpool to work. Leadbetter immediately picked up the two police squad cars parked near a third car, and he drove his vehicle to the car. He jumped out of the war machine and walked over to a police Lieutenant who had a clipboard in hand, and he introduced himself to the young police officer.

"Yes, Lieutenant I'm Colonel Leadbetter, sir. Is this the vehicle you called in on sir?"

"Glad to meet you Colonel Leadbetter Sir, I'm Lieutenant Frank Buttler, sir. Yes sir, this is the vehicle the alert was sent out on, sir. I was stunned to find it parked here like it is sir."

"Did you guys search the damn vehicle, Lieutenant?"

"No sir, we didn't go anywhere near the damn thing as ordered by you when we first contacted you, sir. We were just ordered to secure the vehicle and keep the civilians or other vehicles far away from parking in the lot until you people arrived on site, and you took over command of the parked vehicle in question, Colonel." The Lieutenant reported to the military officer as he sort of smiled at him.

"Outstanding work Lieutenant, I'm please you followed your orders as instructed, here's what I want from you guys now. You did well with securing the damn parking lot and keeping it free of any nosy civilian pain in the asses getting in our fucking way. I want you to run security for the parking lot while we check out the interior of this damn vehicle. I'm hoping the lousy asshole left something inside the damn thing that might help us identify where he and the rest of his rat pack are hold-up in Washington, sir."

"Yes sir, I'll follow your last orders to the Tee, Colonel Leadbetter Sir. Is that all you want from us, Colonel?" Lieutenant Buttler replied proudly then issued orders to Sergeant Williams and the officers who helped secure the vehicle and lot. Buttler settled in and watched the soldiers cautiously approach the parked car like it might explode on them.

"That's it, Lieutenant." Colonel Leadbetter replied over his shoulder as he led the way, and he carefully tried the driver's door of the vehicle. It was locked and he cursed under his breath and shook his head. Sergeant Steingold rushed to the other side of the car, and he tried the passenger door, it was also locked, and he reported so to the Colonel.

"Dammit, okay I'm not going to play any fucking games with this damn thing, stand aside mister. From what I can see the damn vehicle isn't booby trapped." Not waiting a second longer, the angry Colonel reared up and kicked the side window of the car with his foot, it shattered under his heavy assault, and he growled at the Mule. "Now that's how you open a fucking locked car door, mister. Search the damn thing thoroughly. If you find anything I want to know about it immediately, buster." The military officer stepped aside and took a cigarette, lit it as he offered the concerned police Lieutenant one.

The police Lieutenant moved a little closer to the terrorist's vehicle, and he asked with concern lacing his voice. "Colonel Leadbetter Sir, are you quite certain that the people you're searching for, are the ones who are responsible for the explosions that took place in the city recently, sir? I sure hope we're on the heels of the bastards who attacked us, sir."

"Damn right I am Lieutenant, and with this vehicle and the bird we have in custody. It's only a matter of time before we find out where the hell the rest of these lousy popinjays are hiding at, and we can get them wrapped up before they do any further damage to our country, Lieutenant." The Colonel snorted as he went back to enjoying his cigarette.

"You have one of the terrorists in custody, Colonel Leadbetter? I wasn't informed we got one of the bastards already, sir." Lieutenant Buttler replied, pleased over the new information.

"That's correct Lieutenant, but that information's locked up under the Zip Lip order, sir. If it gets out to damn news people, we got one of the bastards, you'll be walking a beat under the fucking Brooklyn Bridge, sir."

"I got it sir and it dies with me, Colonel Leadbetter."

"Good." Leadbetter's conversation was interrupted by Sergeant Youngblood, who moved to the Colonel's side and waited to speak with his Commanding Officer. When the Colonel noticed him, he barked. "What do you have for me soldier?"

"Colonel Leadbetter, we went from one end of the damn vehicle to the uther, and we searched it but good, sir. We found nuthin sir, not a fucking thing was left inside the damn thing."

"Dammit, okay, err did you happen to run the interior of the damn vehicle with the Geiger counter, Marine?"

"No sir, I wasn't ordered to do so, and I wasn't about to do anything I wasn't ordered to do, sir." The suddenly concerned Sergeant replied, and then he barked at the other soldier who was assisting him. "Hey Mule, run the clicker over the interior of the damn thing and let me know if it's hot, man."

Leadbetter, Buttler and Youngblood watched as Steingold rushed over to the humvee and removed the small handheld Geiger counter and rush back to the parked car. The Sergeant turned the counter on and then reached the head of the counter inside the car and it immediately registered a high count of radiation. The stunned soldier cried out in an excited tone of voice. "Holy shit Colonel, the fucking counters pegged out to the top of the damn gauge, sir. It's hot as hell in this damn thing."

"Then get it and your stinking ass the hell out of the damn thing, stupid. What's the range you're registering the count in?" The concerned Marine Colonel asked the scared soldier.

"Colonel, the gauge is registering in the zone of Highly Enriched Uranium, sir. It's registering at near the damn top of that zone, sir. It's hot as hell inside the interior of the fucking thing with radiological contamination, sir." Sergeant Steingold replied as he pulled his body out of the car, and then he stared at his Commander.

"Will you get the fuck away from that damn thing, you just told me it was hot as hell and you're still standing there like a damn jerk absorbing Rads from that damn contamination for no fucking reason at all, stupid." Colonel Leadbetter turned to Lieutenant Buttler and offered him. "Lieutenant you heard my trooper's report. The car's contaminated, which means the terrorists have a certain amount of Highly Enriched Uranium with them, sir. That confirms this terrorist cell's attempting to put together a radiological dispersal device…"

"A what Colonel Leadbetter?" The Lieutenant interrupted the military officer.

"Arr… shit, I forgot you people might not have been informed of the new term we're employing for a dirty bomb. We call that damn weapon a radiological dispersal device now, sir. Evidently the assholes have somehow got their grubby little hands on some of the damn crap, and they plan to deploy the device somewhere in Washington."

"Then we have to stop them before they can accomplish their plans, Colonel Leadbetter." The police Lieutenant replied with concern lacing his tone of voice.

"That's exactly what we're going to do, stop the sonsofabitches before they can deploy that damn device and destroy parts of Washington, Lieutenant. Okay, the vehicle's the police problem from this point forward. Pack it up, we must get our asses down to Washington and find these damn puds and ruin their fucking day. Lieutenant, get in contact with Hasmat and have them take command of this vehicle, and get it moved over to a safe place, so they can decontaminate the damn thing. Good luck and remember anything you witnessed with this damn mess, remains locked in your head until further notice sir."

"You got it Colonel Leadbetter Sir. I'll have the vehicle removed to the police impound unit, good luck Colonel and get them bastards, sir."

The fuming Marine Colonel Leadbetter looked over his shoulder and gave the police officer a half assed salute, as he quickly climbed into the still idling humvee, and then he ordered Sergeant Steingold to head for the nearest airport, whether it was a private or commercial one. The Colonel was going to get down to Washington one way or the other, even if he had to highjack an aircraft and force the pilot to fly him there.

CHAPTER FIFTEEN

CAPTAIN WALKER'S CARAVAN OF MILITARY VEHICLES
HEADING FOR DOWNTOWN WASHINGTON D.C.
SATURDAY MORNING, MAY 15th, 2011

Zero Nine Fifty-Five Hours Saturday morning, and Captain Robert Walker's convoy of military vehicles was just pulling onto the military sub-station, constructed about midway between the White House and the Capitol Building. Walker's vehicles were forced to fuel up seven times while traveling from New York City down to Washington. He had his military credit card that enabled him to pay for the fuel his machines needed while on the move. The specialized soldiers were ordered to drive down to Washington, rather than employ the trash haulers, because they needed their vehicles with them when they started their searching for the group of terrorists who just moved down to the Washington area from New York City.

As the fifteen heavy war machines pulled onto the military sub-station installation, the moment the humvees stopped, the soldiers poured out of the heavy machines. The elite group of soldiers were stretching and complaining with the Mutt leading the bitching. "Man Walker, you'd think with all the fucking good we're doing for the country, they'd move us people around in fucking stretch limos for the love of Christ."

"Stop your damn bitching and get our stinking gear secured while I locate the resident penis of this stinking dump and see if anything new has taken place while we were fucking traveling down here to Washington. The rest of you pukes help the dog man with his fucking orders, once the gear is stowed away, you people are free to catch up on your stinking rest and take in some food while you're at it. I suggest you people get some sleeping in, because once we deploy in the field, there's no telling when and if we'll sleep or eat again before these damn operations completed. Move it." Walker glared angrily at the concerned looking group of his specialized soldiers as they slowly dragged their asses and moved out as ordered.

Once he was certain his troops were working, he headed for the main office of the structure as a soldier stationed on the military sub-base helped his people. The base soldier had the humvees moved inside the building, to keep the machines out of vision of any reporters hanging around the capital and military bases, in search of a story.

Walker plowed into the small private office nearly making the young Lieutenant on duty jump out of his skin, as he instantly snapped to attention and saluted the strange officer who just crashed through the door to his office.

Walker ignored the salute as he growled at the soldier nastily. "Lieutenant whatever the hell your damn name is, I'm Captain Walker, and I am damn certain you were informed in advance to be expecting me and my troops, sir?"

"Yes, Sir Captain Walker, I was ordered in advance to make my base your temporary headquarters for the duration of this operation you're in command of before you arrived here Captain. I'm having your machines moved into the secured parking inside the structure, to keep them out of the limelight, sir. We don't need to wake up any sleeping pain in the ass news reporters, by leaving your vehicles parked out in the open, sir. I'm afraid the sleeping quarters are a little under par for your soldiers use though, sir..."

"Don't go fucking worrying 'bout our sleeping arrangements any Lieutenant. My people will sleep anywhere they hafta, even under their machines, if necessary, sir. Lieutenant, I have a command communications humvee in my convoy, and I'll order it setup so I can have constant secured communications with my Commander, and all Intelligence Departments I might need to communicate with. I'm gonna need this office to work outta though, so you betta move anything you want the hell outta here, before I move in on ya ass, sir. Because once I take over your office, your ass won't be allowed to enter the room again until I completed my assignment as instructed. Errr... you and your people are responsible for getting some food and anything else we may need for my troops."

"Captain Walker Sir, all that has already been taken care of in advance of you and your troop's arrival at this military sub-base, sir. A flood of food and other needs are heading for the sub-base as we speak, Captain Walker Sir. It has all been ordered by a General White, who is the Chairman of the Joint Chiefs of Staff. Boy Captain, he's been on the horn so much since he had ordered this sub-station to be opened to your troops needs that I feel I know the Officer already, sir." The Lieutenant smiled pleasantly at Walker.

THE SECOND TERRORIST CELL SAFE HOUSE, WASHINGTON D.C.

It was a little after eight a.m. on Saturday morning, May 15th, by the time the terrorist leader Abdulaziz al-Wahhad, lead the rest of his people over to the second safe house in Washington. He ordered some of his cell to stall while he and a few others of his group went to the safe house first, to check it out and make certain the building was not compromised. The Ghost did not want all his vehicles to pull up to the second home at the same time either. He understood if they did that, it would more than likely draw the attention of everyone living on the block to what they were doing, and he surely did not want that. Al-Wahhad wanted five members of his cell in his vehicle and had Mohsen al-Gasim place his girlfriend and three others in his car.

As they pulled up to the second secured building, the Ghost was the first one out of his vehicle and he rushed towards the front door of the safe house and opened it as the other terrorists quickly filed out of both vehicles, and then cautiously and slowly followed him towards the building. Before the leader of the terrorist cell entered, he took a moment and looked over the area outside the building. This house was constructed on a large grass covered lot, and there were many plantings that sort of shielded most of the building from view of either house on the two sides of his safe building. The structure he was to make use of was covered by plants from the street side also.

Once inside the second house, al-Wahhad made a call and ordered the rest of his cell to approach the building and get inside the house and out of sight. When he completed this order, he then checked out the rest of the building. He was surprised there was food and the electric and cable were turned on for them. He even had internet service, and he picked out the largest bedroom for him use and comfort. He did not care a lick on how the others of his group were going to sleep cramped up in the rest of the house, he was only concerned for his comfort.

When every member of the terrorist cell was safely inside the second safe house, the terrorist leader relaxed, and then ordered Abdullah al-Mutairi to check out the garage area, where he would assemble the weapon, he needed for this latest attack on the United States. He wanted to see if it was proper for him to construct the bomb he planned to plant between the White House and the Capitol Building. He had no idea he was planning to set the device three blocks away from where Walker and the rest of his elite troops were currently stationed and preparing to start searching for this terrorist cell.

Al-Mutairi followed his orders and rushed out to the garage, and he was pleased with the space he had to work in. He reported back to al-Wahhad that the garage was perfect for his needs. The lead terrorist stared at the young man, and then reached in his pocket and removed a set of keys to his vehicle and barked at him. "Here are the keys to my cursed vehicle. Behind the driver's seat you'll find a heavy lead lined box. Remove the cursed filthy box and move it through the house and out to the garage. Inside the box you'll find eleven kilograms of Highly Enriched Uranium in which you'll use to construct the weapon that'll eliminate the ruling government of the hated land of Satan. Think of it my young Arab brother from the land of clean sand with this one device we shall kill all the cursed leaders of this worthless country.

"I order you to get right to work with assembling the nuclear device that'll complete our revenge we wage against the lowly infidels of the United States. I'll get the other fools from our cell to start work on the weapons that we'll use for our third attack aimed against the land of Satan, and all who dwell within the foul borders of this evil place. I don't want the children out there to become complacent and forget why they have come to this foul area and what our mission is all about. Al-Mutairi, I cannot wait until we have completed our sacred mission for Allah, and we can finally return to the pure sands of our homeland and honored ancestors and enjoy the great success we shall share in destroying the hated leaders of this land of non-believers and lowly jackals."

"Yes Shabbah, I'll get right to work on the device, once I have retrieved the Uranium from your vehicle to construct the device with." With that said, al-Mutairi grabbed the keys and rushed out of the safe house.

The proud terrorist leader smiled as he watched the young Iraqi terrorist and bomb maker, rush out of the building and then he walked into the living room where the rest of his terrorist cell was gathered and waiting further orders. Glaring at each of the young faces staring at him, al-Wahhad snarled at the group angrily. "Young fools, although I understand you must be thoroughly exhausted by our endless drive down here to Washington. We have come down here to accomplish a sacred mission for Allah and our Arab lands, and that is exactly what we shall do. I plan to make our next attack aimed against this land of lowly infidels in three days' time. I don't want to give the hated searchers time to try and locate, and then stop us from accomplishing Allah's sacred work. Bassam!"

Iraqi born Bassam Abu Fallabi straightened his stance as the angry al-Wahhad locked his face in his glare, and then he growled at him.

"Bassam, Allah has decreed at nine thirty on this foul morning, I want you to leave this place of safety and walk this foul neighborhood in search of the nearest store, where you can buy a newspaper of this foul state of cursed infidels and worthless jackals. I know my intended target, but I need the local newspaper to help me discover the exact time and date of our next attack against these fools. It is nine twenty and you have ten minutes before you must leave on your ordered mission. I warn you and the other fools from our cell. I order all of you if you meet any of the worthless jackals that pollute this filthy state, you'll smile and be very pleasant and friendly with them. I don't want any trouble with the local population or the police authorities of this seat of Satan. We'll show these non-believing worthless jackals how we truly feel about them, when we completed our attacks against them.

DELTA THIRTY-ONE SUB-STATION; WASHINGTON D.C. SATURDAY, MAY 15th, 2011. ZERO ELEVEN FIFTY HOURS

Captain Robert Walker was able to get his troops organized. He setup the communication's vehicle for his rapid response force when a call came in from his Commanding Officer.

"Dragon Lair to Dragon Fire. Come in. Over."

"Dragon Fire to Dragon's Lair. I see we went back to Dragon's Lair, Colonel."

"Keep it up wiseass and I'm going to take a giant shit on your damn puss, mister. You'll respond no matter how the fuck I sign in for your ass, Captain. The reason for this communication is to bring you up to date on what the hell's happening around your damn head, fella. The twin incidents in New York have gone from a search and rescue to a recovery operation at both the subway and airport sites. That bit of information wasn't why I called your ass though, Captain. Walker, the terrorist Shabbah had parked his damn vehicle we ID at an out of the way parking lot in the shadow of the G.W. Bridge. We ran a counter over the interior of the damn thing, and it registered a reading indicating the bastards got their hands on an unknown amount of Highly Enriched Uranium with their cell. This informs me the fucking terrorists are more than likely in the middle of developing a damn radiological dispersal device.

"Walker, we have to take it as fact the reason this fucking terrorist cell has moved its operation down to Washington, is because they plan to place this RDD where it'll do the most damage to the damn leadership of this nation. I'm going to contact General White and have him order the President and the rest of his staff, along with the two Houses of the Senate and Congress the fuck out of Washington, until we caught up to these lousy assholes, and we sent the batch of the bastards on their way to Paradise. Captain, your orders are to deploy and find this terrorist cell and stop them, period. No matter what you must do to accomplish this order I just aimed at your ass, mister. Over."

"I read ya loud and clear sir. Over."

"I have further orders for you to carry out, Dragon Fire Leader. You have carte blanche for this entire operation, sir. You're going to be operating in a free fire zone, Captain. I want you to always keep in mind though that you're operating within the borders of the United States. Almost everyone you're going to encounter during the full duration of this mission is going to be a horde of innocent American civilians. You're to keep a damn leash on your pack of crazy ass gun jugglers and keep the collateral damage down to an absolute minimum. Dammit, I might have to order you to leave that trooper you branded the Mutt behind. He follows orders like my damn sons do for Christ's sake. I fear that jackass running around the stinking streets of Washington with a loaded weapon and armed with orders to kill anyone who even looks at his ass the wrong fricking way. Who the hell knows how that one's going to react when you finally catch up to these Islamic scumbags?"

"Dragon's Lair, Colonel Leadbetter, the Mutt's my problem sir, and I'll control his ass, or I'll cap his ass and take him outta the damn picture, sir."

"Yeah, right, okay Dragon Fire Leader, if you want to place your dick in a fucking blender for that dumb fuck, it's your life to deal with, sir. Captain, you know what I want from you people, so carry out your fucking orders as received mister. When I'm done with my bullshit up here in New York, I'll be heading your location to run operations down there, sir. I'm activating the NEST (Nuclear Emergency Search Team) headed by that pain in the ass Doctor Joel Russbinder. Even though the Doc's in command of that unit, they'll be working under our banner that clears you to employ nuclear detection equipment at our disposal. That's about it, Captain. Out."

"Roger that last as received Dragon Lair. Out." Walker broke off the communication with the Colonel, and then he addressed the rest of his troops. "Okay people, listen up, we're hot and ready to trot as of this moment, and we're working with that Doctor Russbinder dude and his crew of stuff shirts again! We have a terrorist cell operating in Washington, and it's our job to find the lousy sonofabitches before they can pop off a radiological dispersal nuclear device aimed primarily against the leadership of our country. For you asses who have been asleep for the past few months, a radiological dispersal device means these lousy pricks are working on a dirty nuclear bomb in Washington."

COLONEL LEADBETTER'S HEADQUARTERS IN NEW YORK CITY

When Walker broke off his communications, the Colonel immediately dialed General White, the Chairman of the Joint Chiefs of Staff, to inform him of what he was able to discover on the terrorist cell that attacked New York City. He had to report to his Commanding Officer he discovered who was the leader of the terrorist cell was, and the prisoner they also caught and who was giving them all the information they were operating on.

"General White's office, how may I direct this call for you please?"

"Morning Mary this is Colonel Leadbetter, Ma'am. I need to speak with the General A-SAP. Is the General available, please?" The Colonel offered to the General's secretary.

"Good morning, Colonel Leadbetter, it's a pleasure to be speaking with you again sir, and yes the General's in. I'll transfer your call immediately to him sir. It was a pleasure to speak with you this morning, sir. Colonel Leadbetter if we're disconnected for any reason, you must call back instantly, sir. Hold the line please, sir." Mary did not wait for the Colonel to reply as she instantly transferred the call to her General.

General John White was conducting a private meeting with CIA Director John Raincloud, and when the phone buzzed, he excused himself and picked up the receiver and barked into it. "Yeah, General White! Who the hell is this and what's on your mind? I'm busy."

"Morning General White, this is Colonel Leadbetter, sir. I'm still in New York Ci…"

"You must have a sixth sense about you, Colonel Leadbetter. I was just discussing your ass with Director Raincloud here, Colonel. What the hell's going on in New York?" The Colonel's Commanding Officer demanded of him.

"General White Sir, I want to report we have successfully captured one of the bomb makers from this damn new terrorist cell, sir. I further want to report the cell has moved their operations down to Washington D.C, sir. General White, we have accumulated strong evidence the terrorist cell members were able to get their lousy hands on an undetermined amount of Highly Enriched Uranium, sir. We believe the scumbags are working on a radiological dispersal device aimed at the leadership of our country, sir. General, I diverted Captain Walker and the rest of his elite troops to the downtown area of Washington, and the soldiers are currently setting up operations to begin their search for the rest of the missing terrorist, sir." The Marine Colonel reported to his Commanding Officer.

"Dammit, how the hell did these lousy scumbags get out from under your damn troops up there in New York City, Colonel? I thought your troops were better than that. Why the hell do you think I sent your pack of gun bunnies up there in the first place for, Colonel? For Christ's sake, I can't believe we're forced to expand our damn search for these pricks. I was laboring under the illusion your elite troops were going to put the period at the end of this sentence by capturing these bastards in New York, sir. Now you tell me we must expand our search, and these terrorists are now threatening the damn leadership of our country with shitty nukes. Okay Colonel, what do you suggest we do next to protect them, sir?"

"General White, therefore, I placed this call to you sir. General, I activated the NEST team and got them moving on this operation. Also, sir, I suggest you order the President, along with his entire staff and all Senators and Representatives the hell out of Washington, until this present situation is over with, and we have successfully captured or killed all the damn terrorists involved with this latest threat, sir." The Colonel offered without missing a beat.

"Holy Shit Colonel, let me get this shit straight in my mind, mister. You're suggesting to me I order the President, along with all Congressmen and women and Senators the hell out of Washington until you successfully captured all these damn terrorists, sir? In case you don't understand the ramifications of this suggestion, Colonel. Allow me to explain it a bit clearer for you, sir. Never since our battle with the Brits has the leadership of our country ever been ordered out of Washington. Not even during the two World Wars, sir..."

"I understand what I'm suggesting to you General White, and we did order all our leaders out of Washington during the Nine, One, One attacks, sir. Besides sir, I fully comprehend the situation currently facing us, sir." The Colonel replied with confidence, as he dared to interrupt his Commanding Officer, and then he went on with his comments. "General White Sir, if these damn popinjays are working on constructing a dirty nuclear weapon, and planning to detonate that damn thing off near the center of Washington D.C.? I believe it'd be most prudent a move to get the leadership of our country the hell out of the danger zone, sir. Until we know for certain what these damn people are up to, or we have destroyed them and their damn plans, sir."

"Colonel Leadbetter, it does my heart good to see you have the bravos you were born with sir, to dare interrupt my ass. I hate like hell to be forced to agree with what you're suggesting to my ass though, Colonel. We do have to protect the damn leaders of our country at all costs, Colonel. Dammit to hell and back again, sir!" The General suddenly growled as he went deep in thought for a few seconds, and then added for the Colonel. "I'll tell you what I'm going to do, Colonel Leadbetter. Since I have the CIA Director sitting in my office, I'm going to have him order Directive, One, Seven, Niner. With this order issued by his office, all Congress and Senate men and women and the President and whoever else he wants to drag along with his ass, will be forced out of Washington until this present national emergency has been handled either way, sir."

"I'm not very familiar with that Directive, sir. I take it this Directive is a National Emergency Evacuation order, General White?" The Colonel asked his Commanding Officer.

"Again, with the fucking interruptions I see mister, you don't give a flying fuck how you're living, and breathing do you Colonel? I allowed the first interruption to go by unchallenged sir, and this one I'll overlook as well, mister. Colonel, if you dare to interrupt my ass for a third time, you'll find yourself stationed at the North Pole counting polar bears for the rest of your damn hitch in the service, sir. Arrr…Colonel, what the hell are you doing while we get this Directive transmitted out, and shake up the pain in the asses down here?" General White asked as he cast a glance at the CIA Director to see if he was paying attention to this conversation.

"Sorry about the interruptions sir, I assure you they won't happen again in this conversation, General White Sir. I'm waiting for a hookup flight to get my ass down to Washington, sir. So, I can get back in Command of my troops and get my ass involved with the search for the terrorist cell along with the rest of my troops, sir." Colonel Leadbetter replied as he let out his breath in a deep sigh as he looked at one of the other two soldiers with him.

"That sounds like a plan to me Colonel Leadbetter. Don't wait for a damn flight, I'm giving you permission and the power to take a charter flight, or just commandeer a military or civilian flight, and order it down here, sir. Colonel, I need your ass down here keeping tight control on your damn troops currently stationed here in Washington, sir. I can ill afford to have you wasting your damn time hanging around some airport up north while this crap is going down here. Colonel, I'm done speaking with you. I don't want to hear from you again, until your ass is here in Washington, and you're in proper Command of your troops, sir." The General snapped as he nastily broke off his communication with the other military officer.

The moment the General hung up on the Colonel, he turned to the CIA Director and grumbled at the man. "Well Chief, you heard everything that just went down with my damn Colonel still stuck up there in New York City. Director, Colonel Leadbetter was correct requesting we evacuate the leadership from Washington, until we get these damn scumbags. Do you agree with my assessment, Director?"

"General White, I happen to agree with you and if you'll give me a few moments sir, I'll contact my switchboard, and have them transmit the Directive out to the President and members of Congress and Senate. General, we have no idea where the hell the damn terrorists are operating from here in Washington, so the longer we wait to order everyone to get the hell out of Washington. The better the chance these damn fools might fire off that bomb they're working on, and really fuck up our day but good on us, General."

General White stopped the Director before he got up and left his office and asked the CIA Operative. "Wait a second Director, what the hell are we going to do with the damn civilians of this city? Are you planning to get them moving out of town along with the President and his people? We must remember the civilians. By the way director, you know damn well that both you and I are going to stay in Washington, no matter the outcome. We have to remain in command, especially if the rest of the brain thrust of our country is running for the hills, sir."

"I understand that, and I don't know what the hell I'm going to do with the civilians, General. What do you suggest I do with them, sir? I believe we can't possibly order all of them out of town as you put it, sir. If I sent out an alert and order to evacuate the entire city of Washington, the mayhem that order would cause is frightening to even think about, let alone witness, sir. Besides General, we'll tip our hand to the damn terrorists that we know what they're up to and that might make them move against us quicker than they plan. I believe if we sent out a mass evacuation order, it'll cause more problems than what we're trying to prevent. I have faith in your troops, and believe they'll get the entire terrorist cell before they can detonate that dirty bomb against us. General White, I believe we're going to get hit once more with a conventional weapon attack, before the terrorists try and hit us with that nuclear device no matter how primitive it might be, sir."

"Why do you believe that shit, Chief? Are you reading the damn smoke signals again, sir?" The General smirked as he stared at the power full blooded Native American.

Director Raincloud gave a quick laugh over the General's smart remark as he replied. "Not really sir, I have no connections or knowledge to any advance events, sir. I wish to hell I did, General. It'd make my job a helluva lot easier to accomplish. But it's my belief the terrorists don't know what they're doing with constructing that damn bomb quite yet, sir. Therefore, I'm of the nature to believe this ass running the terrorist cell, will order his group out to hit us again, before they try an attack with a nuclear device against us.

"General White I have no real clue where the damn terrorists might try to hit us though, but I have a gut punch feeling they're going to hit us again, kind of just to drive their damn point home against us, sir. I wish we weren't so damn hampered by this present Democratic Administration tying up the hands of the Intel Community though sir. The damage done already will take years to repair and reorganize and get back on track again sir.

"Although we were set back a bit by having the threat of my Agents being dragged before Congress in open session, the fear and concern that caused the Intelligence Community having their Agents identified to the public, or any Secret Service Organization from other countries by visiting the hearings of Congress. We're starting to close the gap and getting the arms of the security systems working together again. We're getting back to marking the damn terrorists floating around the United States, or anyone we're considering a threat to our security, duck for a change, sir.

"General White Sir, I'm stuck fighting a damn gut feeling that the damn terrorists didn't come down to Washington just to explode a nuclear device against us, sir. It's not going to be that easy for the damn terrorists to accomplish, sir. I'm quite certain the damn terrorists haven't finished with their desire to inflict the pain they want to hit our civilians with. The damn asses want to bleed us more before they deliver the final knockout punch against our country.

"Yes, General White, I'm certain this terrorist cell's going to hit us once more. Maybe twice and use up some of their time, so they can better perfect the nightmare of a dirty nuclear device exploded in the heart of downtown Washington D.C. General White, I better contact my switchboard, so they can broadcast that damn Directive out, so the leadership of our country can get out of harm's way until this present emergency has run its course, sir." Director Raincloud stopped speaking and looked at the General while waiting his reply.

General White allowed a slight smile as he sat back and let out his breath in a rush, and then replied. "John, I think you should broadcast that warning out to the President. You're the only man who has the power to you know, sir."

Director Raincloud placed the call to his headquarters from the General's office instead of leaving the office, and after giving the order to transmit the evacuation directive for the leadership of the country. He broke off the call and looked back at the General.

"Well Chief, how long do you think it's going to take? I'm taking seven minutes." The General smirked as he looked at his watch.

"I think it's going to take ten minutes to go into effect, General." The Director replied.

"I have twenty bucks riding on my seven minutes." General White offered.

"I got you covered I'm sticking with the ten minutes, sir." The CIA Director remarked as he checked his watch.

The buzzer went off by the General's hand, and Mary announced General White had an incoming call from the President.

"I'll take that call." The General replied as he looked at his watch and noticed it took six minutes for the call to come in. He covered the mouthpiece and announced to the Director. "I'm closer than you are with the time, so I take the bet my friend."

The Director nodded in the positive as the General answered the call from the President.

"General White, you know damn well who the hell this is, mister! I was just informed that pain in the ass CIA Director Raincloud was visiting your office, sir. General White, what the hell was this Directive I just received transmitted from CIA headquarters about? What the hell's going on with you two for the love of God? General White, do you realize the countless problems this damn Directive is causing me and the members of Congress and the Senators? Gees, this order is going to upset everyone who keeps the government running for who knows how long for the love of God. Damn, why am I wasting my time speaking with you? You didn't send this damn Directive order out. General White, I want, no correct that, I demand to speak to Director Raincloud!" The angry President went quiet as he calmed down a little.

"Yes Sir Mr. President, Director Raincloud's in my office, sir. I'm giving him the phone this minute for you sir. Please, you must calm down a bit sir. I don't want you hurting yourself, Mr. President." The General did not wait to hear the President's reply as he quickly handed the receiver over to the Director, and then he placed a wide grin on his lips.

Director Raincloud smiled back and flipped the bird at the powerful General as he took the receiver and placed it against his ear. He immediately moved it a few inches from his ear as he offered over the President's yelling in the receiver. "Never mind telling me to calm the fuck down mister! Where the hell is that damn CIA Director at, dammit? I want to speak to that man immediately General White, and that's what I'm going to…"

"With all due respect Mr. President, I'm waiting to speak with you, sir." Raincloud replied as he could not remove the smirk on his lips over the President being so excited.

"Never mind with that all due respect bullshit from you mister, I see you two wiseasses are screwing around with me and my Administration. One of you piss me off and then you pass me to the other. I'm warning you Director Raincloud, I'm going to remember this little game you two gentlemen are playing with me, and if this alert is not a true national emergency. I'm going to have four nuts roasting over an open fire, before I fire the both of you two. Director Raincloud, what the hell is this national emergency alert about, and is it necessary for me and the rest of my staff to abandon Washington? Just how long is this damn alert going to remain in effect? I demand answers from you mister, and I demand them right this moment!"

"Mr. President, we have strong evidence the terrorist cell that hit New York…"

"Dammit Director Raincloud, how many damn times do I have to remind you and your damn partner in crime in that office, not to refer to anything that's happening within the borders of the United States as a terrorist incident? Hell, Director Raincloud, we don't know for certain this was a terrorist attack in New York City." The fuming President roared in the phone as he cut the Director off in mid-sentence.

"Mr. President, I was under the impression FBI Director Hidemann has sent you a memo stating the two incidents in New York City, were definitely being classified as a terrorist action, sir. If you correctly remember Mr. President, I also sent a memo to your office, stating this was a terrorist attack. Sir, you must look at the evidence we have amassed over the two incidents and act accordingly with this information. Mr. President, the evidence assembled shows beyond a shadow of doubt, this terrorist cell's working on constructing a dirty bomb, and they're planning to set it off in the heart Washington. Sir, that knowledge makes it absolutely imperative that you, your family and your staff leave Washington as soon as possible…"

"Director Raincloud, I'm sick and tired of anything happening here in the United States, is constantly being branded by your intelligence people as a terrorist attack aimed against us." The President interrupted the Director, and then he went on with his angry words. "Director Raincloud, I'm trying to assure the public they're safe in their homes, and you're trying to shake that confidence I'm trying to build. All I know is I should've had all the prior Administration's people let go when I first took over command of the country, dammit.

"That way I could have a better control over what you want to put up to me, or get the public up in arms against me, mister. Director Raincloud, this is what I intend to do. I'm going to refrain from classifying these two incidents in New York City as a terrorist attack against us, until I'm a hundred percent certain it was a terrorist attack. I don't want to alarm the citizens with any clouded facts. On the other hand, Director Raincloud, I'm going to take your advice and follow the Directive ordering me, and all members of Congress and the Senate out of Washington, until this present emergency has ended and…"

This time Raincloud interrupted, as he nearly growled at the American Leader, before getting a handle on his emotions. "With all due respect

Mr. President, you have no other choice in the matter, sir. It's the law if I transmit the Directive you're bound to conform to that order, sir."

"How dare you take that tone of voice with me, your Commander in Chief, Mister? How dare you sir. I know I'm bound by law to follow this damn order of yours, and I don't need you informing me of my duties of office. Dammit, okay Director Raincloud, you won this round, I guess. But I'll remember this insult you and your partner have leveled against me, and I'll react accordingly after this emergency has run its course. Now, how are we going to run the evacuation of myself and my family and staff and the Senators and Congressmen and women from Washington, Director Raincloud?" The President asked with concern.

Director Raincloud noticed the President showed little if any interest in the safety of the civilians of the city, as he replied to his Commander in Chief. "Mr. President, I suggest you have one of your press secretaries announce you're taking a quick vacation at Camp David. Have the press secretary add this is going to be a working vacation, with all members of Congress and the Senate attending these special meetings at the Camp, sir. In this way we can kill two birds with one stone and get everyone the hell out of the city at the same time, sir.

"This announcement will surely get you and both Houses of Congress and the Senate out of Washington as quickly as possible, until we can get a handle on this terrorist cell and stop them in their tracks before they construct this dirty bomb and set it off in the heart of downtown Washington, Mr. President. I'll arrange the transportation for the Senators and Representatives, along with the few people you want and need to go to Camp David with you Mr. President. I'll have those other members driven out to the Camp, sir. The other Senators will be dropped off to their families, and they can get the hell out of Washington on their own I guess, Sir.

"Mr. President, under the present circumstances and situation, I don't think we'll have many problems with getting the Congress and Senate men and women and their families moving out of town, sir. Your personal staff will be your problem to deal with though, sir. One thing you must impress upon the people you're taking along with you to Camp David, sir. This must be a Zip Lip Operation Mr. President, if any of your people speak to a news reporter and tells that reporter what the hell's truly going on and word gets out on us, sir. There'll be mass confusion, mayhem and panic ripping through the civilians and streets of Washington. I understand this is going to be one helluva damn mess for everyone involved with the situation to deal with, sir. But we must do our best with this damn situation, sir." Raincloud announced.

"I understand what you are telling me, and I'll take care of my family and staff myself, sir. Director Raincloud, not one of my people will speak to a news reporter under any circumstances I assure you sir. I'm going to get the gears turning in the White House. I'll be in constant communications with you and the General's office, until and even after my family and I have successfully reached Camp David safely, Director Raincloud.

"One question I must ask you though Director. Is Camp David out of any danger zone if the terrorists release a nuclear device in downtown Washington? I don't want to move my family out of Washington, only to keep them under the threat of a dirty bomb, and the horrible effects such a nuclear blast could cause our health? I don't want to be out of the frying pan and placed into the damn fire, Director Raincloud. By the way Director, I want to know the truth about this damn weapon, and the possible effects a release like the one we're speaking about, will cause the city of Washington, sir?" The President asked with concern in his voice.

"Mr. President, the amount of radiological mass this terrorist cell has in its possession that we're guessing at, sir. We believe the blast zone if the terrorists detonate the device in Washington, will not cover more than ten square miles of Washington, under the best of conditions for the blast release, sir. That makes Camp David well out of the threat zone, if Washington comes under attack by these terrorists, sir. Mr. President, we have classified this nuclear weapon as a sort of gun point bomb, which means the damn weapon can be loaded in the back of a truck, or even in the rear of a mid to large size SUV.

"Then merely driven to a point of detonation position, and then detonated where the terrorist feel it would do the most possible damage to not only the leadership of our country. But they also want to create the most damage to the structures and monuments of Washington, sir. I suggest you get your family and staff on the move, Mr. President." Director Raincloud offered while trying to sound confident on what he was offering the American Leader.

The stunned President let out a quiet "Jesus" over the phone as he sank deep in his chair, and then he put a look as if his cat had just died, as he moaned to the Director just above a whisper over the phone. "Director Raincloud, do you have any idea what you have just stated to me, sir? Maybe ten square miles of downtown Washington might be erased from the face of the earth, if this possible terrorist cell detonates a nuclear device in the city. Director, do you have any idea how many people living in that ten-mile square block of death, are going to die?"

Director Raincloud raised an eyebrow in surprise over the President's sudden concern for the safety of the civilians of the city, as he replied. "Yes Mr. President, I know how many people, civilians, might die in that ten square mile block of death, if this damn weapon's detonated in the suggested area I mentioned, sir. I believe we might be looking at well over one million deaths, depending on the position and size of the epicenter of the damn blast, Mr. President. We're positive at the minimum amount of death if the size of the weapon we believe is correct, will be in and around one hundred thousand people, sir. But if the weapon is larger than the one, we suspect the terrorists are working on. Then the number will surely go up to the one million or more-mark, sir. I'm terribly sorry for the bad news I'm hitting you with sir."

"Bad news you say to me Director Raincloud, it's far worse than just bad news you're dumping on my shoulders. Dammit, I won't stand for this shit not for one second will I. No, I won't allow this to happen on my watch, no way no how. Director Raincloud this goes for you also General White. I know you're listening in on this conversation, General. I'm giving both of you the power and assets, both military and civilian you need to stop this possible terrorist attack. Whatever you want or need, order it and make it happen. Neither of you need my permission to react against this possible terrorist cell. I want this attack stopped before it happens, gentlemen.

"Director Raincloud, if you capture any of the terrorists alive, you have my permission in advance, to employ any means of interrogation necessary against that terrorist. For you to gather up to date intelligence information on where the other extremists might deploy this damn weapon in the heart of Washington. Order the General's high-priced soldiers out on the damn streets of Washington! Declare Marshall Law, if need be, Director

Raincloud, and you too General White. Do whatever the hell you have to do but save Washington from this pending attack and disaster." The President went quite as he tried to gather his thoughts.

"Mr. President, we have one terrorist already in our custody sir, and he's being interrogated by Colonel Leadbetter at this very moment, sir. We also have our Rapid Response soldiers already deployed in the streets of Washington, and the elite troops are setting up their communications and command structure as we speak, sir. I believe we're covering all bases, and we're going to stop this damn terrorist cell before they have a chance to pop off that damn weapon against us, sir." Raincloud offered while trying to keep the air of confidence in his tone.

"That's outstanding news for me to hear Director Raincloud, and maybe we can still stop this possible terrorist nuclear attack against Washington, before it happens after all, sir. I want to end this conversation if I'm to get my family and staff the hell out of Washington immediately, Director Raincloud. I also need to get the Senators and Representatives on the move as well, so please allow me to go so I can accomplish what I need to accomplish, sir." The President remarked as he began to look for the papers, he needed with the names of the people he wanted to take to Camp David with him.

"You do that Mr. President and that way it'll free me up to do what I have to do to protect the civilians of Washington, and to also find the damn terrorists before they can hit us again at the same damn time, sir. I'll keep you well informed on what's happening in Washington, and what we're doing in our efforts to capture the other members of this terrorist cell as soon as anything crops up, and I have something to inform you over, Mr. President." Director Raincloud offered in an exhausted sounding tone of voice in hopes of getting the President to end this conversation, so he could get on with his other duties.

"I'm ordering you to remain in constant contact with me during this entire emergency, Director Raincloud. I want to know everything that's always going on during this present emergency, and with this attack aimed against Washington and our country's leadership. At all times I tell you, Director Raincloud, you too General White. I want to be kept well informed over this situation; in case I have to address the public over this situation." The fuming President snarled at the powerful CIA Director and at General White.

"Mr. President, it'll be as you ordered, sir." Director Raincloud replied while letting his breath out in a sigh. He was beginning to lose his temper over the way the President was trying to keep him on the phone and stopping him from looking after the search for the terrorists.

"Very good Director Raincloud, that's all I have to say to you and to General White as well, sir. Allow me to get my family and staff out to Camp David, so I can start to run my office from that facility, Director. I think it was a good idea to order my family and members of the leadership of our country out of harm's way, in case the terrorists were successful in detonating that damn weapon in the heart of Washington, sir. I'll contact you when we're firmly established at the other facility, and we're unpacked and ready to get back involved in this present emergency, Director. Is that it for us at this time, Director Raincloud?" The President asked with concern lacing his tone.

"Mr. President, I believe that's about all I have for you until you're safe at Camp David, and you're ready to help with the search for the missing terrorists, sir. I have my Agents in charge of the facility jumping, and they're opening and airing the place out for you and your family, sir. There's plenty of food and drinks stored at the facility at all times sir, and anything you don't have, will be brought out to you upon request or need, sir." Director Raincloud offered the President while still trying to end this conversation.

"Then please allow me to get on my way so I can have my family pack to leave Washington, Director Raincloud." The President snapped at Raincloud, this time because he felt the Director was keeping him on the line needlessly now.

"Mr. President, I'll be in constant contact with you at your temporary Command Center stationed at Camp David at all times over this present terrorist matter, sir." Director Raincloud replied, surprised the angry sounding President was the one now referring to this situation as a terrorist action, and then he ended the conversation with the American Leader. Before the President was able to add anything else and forced him to remain on the phone a while longer. The moment the Director hung up with the President. He turned to the Chairman and complained to him.

"Man John, when that guy wants to tell you can't shut him up for a damn second, sir. You heard the conversation I just suffered through with the President. What did you think and the orders he just issued us, sir? Were you able to pick up something in the conversation that I might have overlooked, John?"

"To be quite honest with you John, the President kind of surprised me when he displayed some concern for the citizens of Washington, sir. I'm also surprised he's finally starting to refer to this latest terrorist situation as exactly what it is, a terrorist fucking attack, dammit. The man also took the Directive much better than I first expected, and that's another surprise to me. John, I know where my Tier One troops are stationed here in Washington. I been thinking I just might go and get my ass over there and take command of the soldiers myself, until Colonel Leadbetter's here and then he can takeover Command of the soldiers. Are you interested in taking a little ride with me to my troops, Director?"

"Yes, I believe I'd really enjoy seeing your troops in action out in the field, General White. I can run my operations easy enough from my car, or wherever the hell I end up with you and the troops, John. Shall we get a move on it General? I was wondering what the troops were doing since they made it to Washington, General White."

CHAPTER SIXTEEN

DELTA THIRTY-ONE MILITARY SUB-STATION;
WASHINGTON D.C. SUNDAY, MAY 15th, 2011.
FOURTEEN TWENTY HOURS EST.

Captain Robert Walker was able to get his headquarters pretty much up and operating when the food and other provisions arrived at the military sub-station. His people attacked the food as if it was the only keg of beer in the world. Walker smiled as he watched his troops chow down on the food and kept his ear open for any new radio traffic.

The young Captain was informed by Command that Colonel Leadbetter was finally able to locate a private aircraft to get him down to Washington. The Colonel was expected to land and get over to his position at the sub-station by Sixteen Ten Hours, and then he was going to take command of the troops and get them out on the streets of Washington, searching for the terrorist group and the weapon they were believed to be working on.

The captain just reached for one of the sandwiches when General White and Director Raincloud, walked into the overcrowded cramp troop quarters, as if they owned the world. The two powerful men were grinning from ear to ear at the Tier One soldiers, as they entered the small section of the military sub-base.

Blood Clot, the Unit's medic, Sergeant Richard Burmbach was the first soldier to recognize the powerful General enter the area, and he stood and snapped to attention while saluting the General and barking out loud to the other soldiers in the room with him at the same time. "Attention on Deck!"

The soldiers crammed in the building stopped what they were doing, many dropped their food and jumped to their feet and snapped to attention and saluted the two men.

"At easy!" General White fired as his eyes locked on Walker's face, and he walked through the milling about group of soldiers for him. The General lightly rested his hand on his shoulder as he asked the captain.

"How the hell are you and your troops making out with this damn situation, son? Do you have everything you need to track the terrorists down, Captain?" The General was not really interested if the soldiers had enough to eat all he was concerned with was the military end of this operation.

"Yeah, General White, we got everything we need and what we didn't have, this here little Army puke filled my needs, sir. General, my troops are foaming at the damn mouth to get started on the fucking search for the stinking terrorists, sir. What the hell are we doing getting crammed into this lousy building and spinning on our damn thumbs, sir? General…"

"Can the damn bitch soldier and pay close attention to what I'm about to tell you, mister. By now you must understand we'll never allow your troops to go out on the streets of any city armed to the fucking teeth like you people are, without a normal Officer to keep you loose cannons under tight control, Captain. You might as well get fucking used to it Captain Walker, because you're not going to step one fucking foot outside this damn building, until your Commanding Officer is in complete command of your pack of ball sacks. I can't possibly have any of you pukes marching around the streets of Washington, while looking like you soldiers are ready to kill anyone you people look at…"

"Errr… excuse me General White, I don't have one of those ugly things hanging between my legs, sir. So, does that mean me and the other ladies from the Unit must remain inside this building along with these ugly animals, sir? All they do is fart and are damn happy about it, and they even brag while one tries to out due the other with their damn farts, General."

General White turned to face the female soldier busting his horns, and with just the look was enough of a warning for Baby Tee, Sergeant Teri Dorland. She immediately lowered her head in submission and took a few steps away from the General. He turned back to Walker, pleased with the reaction from the female soldier. He understood he just put her in her place with just a look. Looking at Walker he offered. "I understand your bitch soldier, and hope you understand where I'm coming from?"

"Yes, Sir General White, your response makes perfect sense to my ass sir. Errr…General before you ask, I had a communication from Colonel Leadbetter a few moments ago, and he informed me he got his hands on an aircraft, and he's heading our position now, sir."

"That's good Captain, I was going to ask if you heard from your Commander. The rest of you soldiers, eat or do whatever the hell you people were doing before I arrived. Captain Walker, the mess in New York City's bad, real bad sir. We're looking at casualties ranging over ten thousand possible dead at just the damn train station, and about the same number of possible dead at the airport. They hit us hard, real hard with this one, sir. Walker, when you're finally let loose in Washington, I want these fucking bastards. Do you understand what I'm saying mister? I want every one of the sonofabitches, and I don't give a fuck how they come. I don't want you to have any misunderstanding soldier. I don't care if what remains of each of the bastards fits into a fucking shoe box. I want them brought down. Do you read me loud and clear son?" General White stared Walker dead in the eyes.

"General White, I read you loud and clear, Sir."

"Good, Captain you better get used to seeing my puss hanging around your people for the duration of this damn situation, sir. I'm going to be here until Colonel Leadbetter takes over command of you people, but I'm still not leaving. I want to be part of this operation, and that's what I'm going to be. I'll make certain you people have everything, and I mean everything you'll need to capture and or kill the damn terrorists. Captain, I'm certain you recognize Director Raincloud here, and if you don't, that's who this man is." General White offered.

Walker stretched his neck looking over the General's shoulder and nodded at the CIA Agent. Director Raincloud nodded back at Walker in response to his recognizing the soldier.

"Good, I see you two have met before. Captain, Director Raincloud is with us. He's going to be running his batch of Special Agents from here, so get used to seeing his puss hanging around you as well, soldier. Arrr… you might as well make use of the damn down time stalling you until your Commander arrives to take over command of this operation. Eat, soup up (drink water) and check and recheck your equipment. I don't want any malfunctions plaguing you people when you're operating out in the field. The scumbags you're hunting are constructing a bomb. Yeah, a dirty nuclear bomb, fuck that bullshit name we tagged this weapon with, Captain.

"The reason why I'm telling you about the damn terrorists having, or they're most likely working on constructing a damn dirty nuclear device. Is because I want you to understand no one is going to leave this area until we get all the fucks involved in this shit, Walker. That means if the terrorists pop that damn thing off. You, I and a good number of Washingtonians are going to die from sucking up the damn Rads (Radiation) from this weapon. So, you see Captain why it's absolutely imperative that you find and stop by any means necessary, the fucking terrorists before they can pop that damn thing off." The General looked at Walker, to make certain the soldier understood the warning he was leveling at him and his troops.

"I feel ya General, we'll find every stinking terrorist before they can pop that damn thing off, or we'll die trying sir. This isn't the first mission we were sent out on that there was more of a chance our asses wouldn't make it through the stinking mission alive, sir. General White most of us made it through the operations and lived to brag about them, sir."

"I understand, and that's exactly why we have trained you people for this very reason, Captain. I guess you better eat something, because you might not be able to eat again until you have completed your orders, sir. Walker, if you're out in the field too long, you're at liberty to send some of your soldiers out to buy or commandeer food and drinks for your Units. By drinks I mean soft drinks, I don't need your damn soldiers armed and walking the streets of Washington drunk as skunks, mister. Damn, I think I'm going to grab one of those damn sandwiches for myself. I didn't realize how hungry I was, until I saw you people munching down on this crap. You want a sandwich also, Director Raincloud?" General White turned to the CIA Director and smiled. The military officer was trying to bring the Director in on the conversation with the young Marine Captain.

COLONEL BRUCE LEADBETTER

Colonel Bruce Leadbetter was fit to be tied, as he waited not so patiently for the small aircraft to finally lift off, so he could get down to

Washington to be with his specialized troops before they went out after the terrorists. He could not believe he was away from his elite troops on such an important mission as the one they were currently facing. The two troopers with the Colonel were staying well out of eyeshot of the obviously fuming officer.

The Colonel figured by this time; he would have had his elite troops out in the field searching for the terrorist cell. Twice his radio went off, and when he realized it was not Walker contacting him, he ignored the calls. Anything happening in New York City was of no further interest to him. His main concerns now were for the terrorists, and what they were preparing to unleash against the brain thrust of his country. The commandeered plane finally took off once it received permission to takeoff from the control tower.

DELTA THIRTY-ONE MILITARY SUB-STATION. WASHINGTON D.C.

Captain Robert Walker noticed it was getting near the time for his Commander to touch down in Washington. He decided to dispatch a humvee out to pick up the Colonel, and the other two soldiers with him. It was a blast for the soldiers to be hobnobbing with one of the highest-ranking soldiers in the armed forces. The jokes were flying, some pot was passed around, and some ladies from the unit began to flash not only the foot soldiers, but the General and Director.

General White was having himself a real blast as well because he forgot how close the ground troops always were with each other. It was really refreshing to be around this group of young and extremely dangerous soldiers, who he knew and protected each other's back. Being around the elite soldiers made him realize just how shallow the politicians in Washington truly were. The only time any politician acted like they had your back, was when it would serve the politician more than the soldier. The General enjoyed the jokes and constant bantering, and laughed when the female soldier busting his horns, suddenly flashed her breasts at a huge soldier she obviously had a romantic interest in.

The Chairman of the Joint Chiefs of Staff noticed Walker leave the group and pull two other soldiers away with him. He did not miss a trick and got up and trailed the three soldiers. The captain led the two to the other building that housed the vehicles, and they entered the structure.

General White entered the second building right behind the three soldiers, and they listened to the orders Walker was giving them. "Okay you two clowns, Colonel Leadbetter's scheduled to land in fifteen fucking minutes, and that gives you two more than enuf time to get your asses over to the damn airport and pick his ass up. I think it's a betta idea if we pick the fuck up rather than allow him to look for his own transportation here. You know if the Colonel hasta wait for transportation to pick his ass up, he's gonna take his anger out on our fucking asses."

"We hear that Walker. Which vehicle do you want us to take to pick up the Colonel?"

"Take the One, Five. For some reason she eats the least fuel. You ball sacks will pull up to the main doors, and tell the first security person you meet, you're working under the code word 'Red Dot Three, Three' order. That'll give you the clearance to get through all the damn security blocks, so you can get to the Colonel right off. I want him to know you're waiting for his ass, so he's at least civil when he takes over Command. Move out…"

"Hold on for a second there, Captain Walker. I can collect the Colonel much easier than your people can. In fact, I have a number of my people stationed at the airport. They have security clearance, and don't have to compromise their position like your troops will." Director Raincloud offered while standing behind General White. The suddenness of the Director speaking so close made the General complain.

"Gees man, I'm going to tie a fucking bell around your damn neck so you can't sneak up on my ass like this. I see you didn't lose the soft feet you Indians had, my friend." The General grumbled as he smirked at the Director because he was unaware, he followed him into the second building of the Sub-base.

"You'll do that, Director Raincloud?" Walker asked the powerful CIA Agent while ignoring the General bitch at the Director.

"Consider it's done as we speak Captain Walker, give me a second. Command to Niner, Five, Five. Come in." The Director spoke in a phone unit he removed from his breast pocket.

"Yes, this is Niner, Five, Five, sir. Go with your traffic Command. Over." A strong voice on the other end of the call responded.

"Niner, Five, Five. I have a Marine Colonel arriving in a few minutes your position. You're ordered to pick this Colonel up and get him through security blocks, and then pour him in one of our vehicles. You'll bring him to…" Raincloud stopped speaking and looked at Walker.

"It's a secured position Director, but you are being who you are, you gotta know where this place is. It's the Army Delta Sub-station east of the White House, and west of the Capitol Building."

"Got it kid, Niner, Five, Five. You're instructed to bring your subject to Sub-station Delta, Thirty-One. This is a security Red Blanket order so act accordingly. Out."

"Have received your orders and understand and will comply same. Code Red Blanket. Out Command."

"And that settles that nice and simple, Captain Walker." Director Raincloud offered as he put his phone away and smiled at the captain.

"Dammit, I knew there was a reason for my keeping hanging around with you." General White offered with a smirk as he looped his arm over the back of the Director. Then they walked out of the storage structure, leaving Walker and the soldiers watching them go.

"Hey Walker, you know something man?" Danko, (Sergeant Christopher Danko) remarked.

"Naw, I know enuf, stow your bitch." Walker replied as he walked out of the building.

"Nevertheless man, I think I like having that big bird Director's ass hanging round us like this man. Someone with that much pull in fucking Washington, is needed by us dumb shits I tell ya. Think of all the trouble that stinking bird can get our asses' outta, man. Didja see how easy it was for him to order his damn people to pick up old hot shit and get his stinking ass over here, Captain? I like that kinda shit and power, Walker. It's good to see that power working for our asses for a stinking change, Walker."

"Like I said, stow it and let's get back to our people, before one of them gets in some trouble in the uther stinking building."

COLONEL BRUCE LEADBETTER

The Colonel charged off the small plane as if he was mad at the world, with his two soldiers following close behind him. No sooner did he take the first step on the tarmac, than he was quickly approached by two men dressed in civilian clothes. Leadbetter looked at them and knew right off they were spooks as one of them asked. "Are you Colonel Bruce Leadbetter, sir?"

"Yeah, I'm Leadbetter, what can I do for you fucking Spooks?"

"I take it you realized we work for the CIA, Colonel Leadbetter? That's correct sir." The lead agent replied to the Colonel's remark.

"Are you shitting my fucking ass, buster? Even Stevie fucking Wonder would've been able to see you two asses are stinking Spooks. I asked what I can do for you two shitbirds once." Leadbetter snarled at the two agents, he hated all so-called spooks with a passion.

"Colonel Leadbetter Sir, we've been ordered to pick you up and bring you over to a specified location here in Washington, sir. Care to get in the vehicle we supplied for your transportation to this destination, sir? I'm sorry Colonel Leadbetter, but we were ordered to pick you up sir. We were not informed you were traveling with two other soldiers, sir." The lead agent informed the military officer as he ignored Leadbetter and the way he was speaking to him.

Colonel Leadbetter looked over his shoulder and noticed the two young soldiers standing behind him and he snorted at the agents. "I don't give a flying fuck what you two ball sacks were ordered to do, mister. These two shitbirds are with me, and if you expect me to get in that fucking machine of yours. Then those two birds are coming with my ass, period. Yes, and don't bother to ask, they're armed, and they'll not turn over their fucking weapons to you or anyone else under any circumstances. By the way, there are three boxes in that aircraft that goes with us."

The agents straightened and stepped aside and allowed the angry Colonel to walk by them. The soldiers with the Colonel carried two of the boxes. The second agent went in the aircraft and in less than a heartbeat he walked out of the plane carrying the third box. The lead agent opened the door for the Colonel and left the officer to close it as he rushed to the driver's seat. He climbed in the vehicle and waited for the other three to get in. It took the vehicle seventeen minutes to arrive at the location where the agents deposited the military officer where they were to deliver him and the two soldiers with him.

DELTA THIRTY-ONE MILITARY SUB-STATION; WASHINGTON D.C.
SUNDAY, MAY 15th, 2011; SIXTEEN FORTY HOURS EST

Because of the heavy rush hour traffic, it took the vehicle longer than expected to arrive at the destination. The agent's unmarked black vehicle with heavily tinted windows, pulled to the front of the non-descriptive building in the center of Washington. The agent stopped it by the loading door, and he remained in the vehicle while Colonel Leadbetter and the two other soldiers climbed out. All three soldiers carried the boxes they brought with them. The moment the three troopers walked to the door of the building, the car pulled out and left the soldiers entering the structure.

Captain Robert Walker, General John White and Director John Raincloud met the upset Colonel by the door, and three other soldiers took command of the boxes, while Colonel Leadbetter saluted his Commander sharply and offered in an exhausted tone of voice. "General White, I got here as soon as possible, sir. New York City and the tri-state region are in one helluva fucking mess from the twin terrorist attacks, sir. As I was ordered before I left New York, General. I commandeered the three boxes of the RAI's (Radiation Alert Inspectors) and brought them here with me, sir." Leadbetter stopped speaking and made a quick head movement towards the three boxes stacked one on top of the other at his feet.

The General cast a quick glance at the boxes and then responded. "I knew you were going to have a problem acquiring transportation to get down here, Colonel Leadbetter Sir. No matter, the only thing that really mattered is you got here, sir. I'm pleased you remembered the damn RAI's. I want the troops assigned in the field, to always have one of the items in their groups during this emergency. If the fucking terrorists are working on a radiological dispersal device, these here babies will alert the troops before they stumble into something unaware." General White remarked as he flipped the lid of the box and removed a radiation inspector and examined it.

Every soldier watching the officers speaking closed in. They looked at the small handheld device the General was rolling around in his hand. It was no larger than one of their regular handheld radios, but this one had a three by two-inch monitor screen mounted on the face of the item.

There were two knobs on the front, one for volume, the other to turn the device on and off. There was a symbol of a horn blowing on the bottom of the screen. Each soldier knew that symbol meant if the alarm went off, the device was registering a radiation source. General White looked at the concerned faces staring at him, and he spotted Walker and tossed the device to the captain for his inspection.

Walker easily caught the detector and examined it and then mumbled. "Damn, there's not much to the damn thing is there, General White?"

"I guess the technicians went by the slogan of keeping it simple, stupid. No matter how it looks, the damn thing works just fine, and that's all you need to know about the damn thing, mister. It'll save your life, always keep this in mind Captain. Even though we'll be successful with stopping these fucking scumbags, there'll always be the next batch of assholes ready to try the same damn thing against us. The more they keep coming, sooner or later one group will succeed, and that group will detonate a dirty bomb inside the borders of the United States, sir. I'm telling you Captain Walker; I'm dreading that fucking day I understand is coming sure as shit. The lousy pukes are going to keep coming at us, until we deal with them the way we must deal with the bastards. We must hit them harder than they're hitting us.

"We have to force the damn terrorists to be scared to raise their fucking heads above their asses for fear of having it shot off on them. Captain Walker, we must go after any nation offering a terrorist group a haven to work their evil craft from, sir. We must make these rebel nations understand if a terrorist cell originating from their country, detonates a bomb or an attack against our country. We'll return the favor and bomb their damn nation off the face of the fucking earth. We must organize the rest of the civilized nations to stand united against all terrorist groups and rebel nations. Captain, if a peace-loving nation is hit by a terrorist group, every nation of the world must condemn their action. Those nations must work with the attacked nation to seek revenge against the damn terrorists, along with the nation the terrorists are working from. It's that easy if we can make them see what we're seeing.

"Captain Walker, if any nation thinks they can peacefully exist with a terrorist group working from their damn country. That nation is living in a fool's paradise. If a nation offers a terrorist group a safe haven to operate from, thinking that move will stop them from turning their hatred against them in the future. It'll be only a matter of a time before the fucking terrorists will expand their influence, and then they will turn their eyes against the safe haven nation's leaders. The terrorists will make the moves necessary to overthrow that government like they did in Afghanistan. So, they can completely takeover that country, and then export their rotten hatred to the rest of the world from a stronger seat of power.

"I keep hoping that the dumb nations turning a blind eye to the terrorist groups operating within their nations. Will wake up sometime soon and realize they must join the other civilized nations of the world and stop fostering this terrorism. That Captain Walker is the only way to place a fucking end to their dirty work.

"There's another way to stop fostering terrorism throughout the rest of the world, but it'll require the other nations to stick together and stay to this decision. If a radical nation's allowing an Islamic radical terrorist group or any other terrorist group to fester in their country. That country must be shunned by the rest of the civilized world, and by shunned, I mean. Every nation of the world must stop all monetary, agricultural and commodity exchanges with that nation allowing a terrorist group to operate in their country. We have to offer a nation infested with terrorists, military assistance that nation requires, when that country decides to erase the terrorists from their lands.

"Mind you Captain Walker my ideas are pure fucking pipedreams. Somewhere in the damn future, I hope every nation allowing terrorists to exist within their borders, will come to the same conclusion it's not in their best interests to allow this lousy situation to continue unchecked within their damn nations, sir." General White mumbled the last of his words while shaking his head slowly. He understood he was dreaming of the perfect scenario, and not allowing himself to believe it might ever happen in his lifetime. In his heart he understood no matter what the circumstances and terrorist attacks. The other nations for one reason or another, would never band together to jointly fight the hatred of the terrorist groups. It was not the nature of the nations to work closely together for any reason.

Colonel Leadbetter allowed the powerful Chairman of the Joint Chiefs of Staff to vent his complaints, but when he saw his chance to cut in, he offered while interrupting the military officer. "Errr…General White Sir, I'd like to start gathering any intelligence information we can pick up on this stinking terrorist cell we know have entered the Washington area, sir. I don't particularly like standing and spinning on my damn thumb, while a group of Muslim radicals plan their next attack against our country and our innocent civilians, sir. At the risk of sounding like a fucking commercial sir, it's time we make the lousy terrorists duck. I hate wasting time sir I want to have my troops out in the field hunting the lousy bastards down, before they accomplish what they came to Washington to accomplish, sir."

"Yes, I as well would like to be out there hunting the bastards down myself, Colonel Leadbetter. You're in Command of these troops, so get them operating like they have a purpose in mind and get these damn terrorists before they hurt us again, sir." General White allowed a smile to cross his lips, and then waited for the Colonel to react.

Colonel Leadbetter snapped to attention and ripped off a sharp salute to his Commanding Officer, and then he turned and barked at Walker standing directly behind him. "Captain, I want to speak with you! We have some work to complete, and we're burning daylight sucking air and not doing what we were brought to Washington for, mister."

Captain Walker easily caught up to Colonel Leadbetter as he pulled a map from the container, and quickly spread it out on one of the boxes he just brought with him from the New York Armory. It was a roadmap of downtown Washington, and the Colonel started studying the map.

"Hummmm…we're deployed at the District Building just off Pennsylvania Avenue and Thirteenth Street, Captain. We're so close to the damn White House, we'll be able to hear the President fart if he cuts one off. I'm pleased this building is in a direct line of sight with the damn Capitol Building. Captain Walker, the people who think these things through. Believe the damn terrorists if successful constructing a Radioactive Device, would likely want to detonate the damn thing off near as they possibly could to the center between the White House and the Capitol Building.

"That belief has narrowed our search area down quite a bit for us, sir. When we deploy in the field, I want you to set up three different search groups. Captain, you'll be in command of the first group and your AOR

(Area of Responsibility) will start from this position we're presently at, and it will extend all the way to the damn Capitol Building. It'll go beyond Second Avenue and Pennsylvania Avenue and Independence Avenue. The second group will be under the Command of, may God forgive me for this order, Lieutenant Hall. You hear that, dog man?" Colonel Leadbetter barked over his shoulder at the Mutt.

"Yo Colonel Leadbetter, sir."

"Yo your mother, you fucking idiot! You better command your people properly working this damn operation, mister. Or you'll have my ass to contend with, if you screw up anything on this suck ass mission, buster." Colonel Leadbetter snarled at the Mutt a second time.

The attacks on the soldier instantly began by the other soldiers from the group.

"Danger Colonel Leadbetter, the dog has a weapon, and he refuses to take his medications properly, sir." Baby Tee called out, not missing the chance to get on Mutt's case.

"We just heard from the Dutchess of Knockers." The Mutt retorted at the female soldier, as he turned and grinned at her.

"Colonel Leadbetter Sir, you have to be a little more patient with the Mutt, sir. Even a toilet can only handle one asshole at a time, sir." Ice, Sergeant Diane Morrison chimed in and attacked Mutt.

The Colonel looked at pretty but dangerous soldier branded Ice and barked at her. "Watch it there, young lady, you're starting to tread on some dangerously thin ice there. I could take that comment two ways little sister."

"Ice, the secret of being happy is having a damn good sense of humor and very dirty mind, baby." Neck said as he smiled at the beautiful female soldier.

"Yeah, tree trunk, and we know where your stinking mind is all the time, buster. That comment came from a dude who's trying to figure out where his damn lap goes every time he stands up. He's the one man I know who invested money into a pig farm in Israel, people." The Mutt fired back at the Neck.

"Colonel Leadbetter, the Mutt's been so damn angry all day, he's even getting on his own nerves, sir." Buckethead aimed hid attack at the well-liked Mutt.

"Colonel Leadbetter, why are you putting the Mutt in Command of second group of soldiers, sir? Hell Colonel, the Mutt can't run a red light without needing help, sir. He's gonna get us all in trouble if he's in Command of a group, sir."

"You're a pal, not mine but you're a real pal there sucka. Huh, three hundred million sperm are fired off in one splat, and you're the fucking one that got through." The Mutt snapped at the grinning Blood Clot, who took the last shot at him.

"Hey Mutt, be honest with me man. Are you qualified to lead soldiers in effing combat? Or are you only good for your ugly looks and dirty mind." Ice called out as she got on Mutt's ass.

"I don't know girl, you kinda handcuffed me there with that be honest bullshit with this gripe, baby girl." The Mutt smirked at Ice.

"The Mutt's at war with normal, Colonel Leadbetter."

"You Squids are rather short on stinking ears and long on fucking mouths I see. Okay you ball sacks and bouncing tits, enough, this shits serious so pay attention, dammit. I'm not going to repeat myself so if any of you misfits don't hear what I'm saying the first time around. Then you people better be able to read my mind because I won't repeat myself a second time. Now where the hell was I, before you shitbirds interrupted my ass?"

"I see you weren't paying attention to yourself as well as the rest of us, Colonel." Baby Tee remarked as she flashed one of her best smiles at her Commander. But the look she received was enough to shut her down.

"That's better peanut gallery, as I was saying. Mutt, you'll be in Command of the second group of these screaming squirrels, and your AOR (Area of Responsibility) is the section of downtown Washington extending from Pennsylvania Avenue up to Massachusetts Avenue, and from Sixteenth Street all the way to Second Street. The third group of soldiers is going to be Commanded by Sergeant Ramirez, and her AOR will be the lower section of downtown Washington, extending from Pennsylvania Avenue to Southwest Parkway or Three Ninety-Five, from Sixteenth Street to Sixth Street. All Group Commanders will refer to their funny papers (Maps) to get directions to your Area of Responsibilities during this situation.

"We have to blanket the entire area of central and downtown Washington, in hopes of cutting off this terrorist cell, before the little bastards can hit this District of Colombia. I want these fuckers, all of them, and I want the sonofabitches in any condition you soldiers leave them in. I want a few of them left alive for interrogation purposes only. Yes, they can be bent up some, but still breathing and able to get around on their own power."

"Colonel Leadbetter, putting the Mutt in Command of second group of soldiers sounds like fun, in a way I really don't mean, sir." Baby Tee offered, still wanting to stay on Mutt's back.

"Look little sister in the training bra, if you interrupt me again before I'm done speaking with you pack of crazy ass misfits, you're going to be really sorry, girl. As I was saying to you gun jugglers, since I brought the thirty-six Radiation Alert Inspectors. Each group will take ten units apiece with them. The remaining detection units will be split up between command of operations personnel. Namely I, General White, Director Raincloud here, and any other person who'll need one of the damn things. The units will be left operating every second of the day and shut down only when recharging is required.

"Colonel Leadbetter, I don't wear a bra, sir." Baby Tea replied to her Commanding Officer.

The Colonel ignored Baby Tee's last remark as he added to his troops. "A hot or fully charged battery lasts twenty hours, before needing charging in the damn things. So split up the charge times of the detection units, so each group will have at least half the damn units always working during this present situation. The call names for this operation will be I'm Dragon Lair. Captain Walker's group will maintain their original name Dragon Fire tag. The Mutt's unit is Dragon Claw and Ramirez Dragon Breath…"

The soldiers broke up over Ramirez's call name. The laughing stopped when Leadbetter looked up and glared at the group as he snapped at them. "Did I say something you ball sacks took as funny? Yeah, I didn't think so." He growled at the soldiers then he went on with his instructions for his troops to deploy. "That's better you pack of twits, once you people are deployed to your AORs, you'll keep a low key about yourselves at all times. You'll keep your eyes open, and anything that strikes you as a concern, you'll act against that concern immediately. I'm not going to allow you wingnuts out in the streets of Washington dressed in military uniforms. Civvies will be the order of the day, each of you gun bunnies will have backpacks where you'll carry your MP-5 nine-millimeter automatic pistols, along with the ammunition for the weapon, and anything else you want or might need in the damn field.

"I thank God these damn radiation alert things look so much like a civilian radio. So, the systems won't cause the civilians you come across any undue concern, if they happen to spot one of you asses carrying the damn things on your person. People, this operation might be the most important single mission we have ever been sent out on. You were trained like no other soldiers in any armed services were ever trained before. This mission is exactly what you people were trained for, so I expect a positive outcome over this situation, or heads will roll I assure each one of you Squids. I'm warning you shitbirds if we don't stop these followers of Islam dead in their tracks, and they're succeed with detonating that damn nuclear device off right in the backyard of our nation's capital. Not only the brain thrust will be killed, but each of you people will suffer the same fate.

"That's because we're not going anywhere until we have successfully located, and then destroyed the entire terrorist cell screwing around with our asses. I know you people were told this before, but I'm going to refresh your memories for you asses. There are hunters and there are victims in every walk of life. By your discipline, your cunning, your obedience to your duty and alertness, your actions will decide if you people are the fucking hunters, or if you people are the damn victims in this ongoing drama. Remember people, the most important six inches of any operation is found right between your fucking ears.

"Those last lines of wisdom came from one of our greatest Generals to ever call himself a Marine, General James Mattis. Well, I believe that's about all I can tell you people at this time. The rest will be up to you once you're let loose out in the field, and our intelligence people are working on finding this terrorist cell, and then alerting us to their presence.

"Mind you people, I'm not only relying on our damn Intel Communities to help us locate these scumbags for us. I'm also counting on our civilians noticing one of the lousy cocksuckers acting like a damn terrorist, and that civilian puke turns the bastard in for us. There are too many eyes out there for someone not to notice any of these bastards we're looking for.

But before I finally release you troops to your Commanders for action, I remembered another bit of wisdom the General once offered, and this present Administration should play close attention to might I add.

"'No war we're involved with is ever over until the fucking enemy say it's over. Yeah, we may think it's over, we might even declare it over, but the fact is the stinking enemy has a vote in the matter on whether the war is over or not'. That means if any stinking popinjay out there tries to tell you the damn war on terrorism is over with. That stupid person is only trying to spoon feed you a line of pure bullshit, people. Only believe it when the enemy declares the fucking war is over." With that said, Colonel Leadbetter stopped speaking and then he took a step back away from the table. Then he allowed Captain Walker to step before him and issue his orders to the elite group of soldiers.

"Okay killers, you heard what Colonel Leadbetter had to said about this stinking operation, and he made sense to my ass. Sergeant Ramirez, you have the first pick of soldiers you want in your Unit. The Mutt will pick the troops he wants next, and I'll be left with the cream of the crap I guess on this fucking mission."

The group of close-knit soldiers shared a quick laugh over Walker's last remark, and then they settled down to see who they were going to be under the command of. Once the picking was over, Walker added to his orders for the troops. "It's rather late and I don't particularly like deploying troops in the field in the stinking dark. We'll deploy to the field at exactly Zero, Six Hundred Hours tomorrow morning. You all know your areas of responsibility, so deploy accordingly to cover those areas properly. Once we start on this mission, we're gonna stay out in the field until this damn thing is over with, so all Commanders will appoint one member of your group to acquire food and drinks for the rest of your group as needed.

"Mutt, Ramirez, you have military credit cards on your person, so use the damn things to pay for whatever extra you may need out in the field. We'll remain active until we find the damn terrorists, or they hit us again and we're forced to react against their new attack. I want everyone ready to deploy the first thing in the morning." Walker went quiet and stared at the soldiers for several moments, before going on with his orders to see if anyone of them had something they wanted to add or ask of him.

"I don't hafta tell you people I have no intention of waiting to find the scumbags until they hit us again. I want their stinking asses hanging on a friggin fence post before they hit us for a third time. On this mission I intend to be proactive, meaning I'm gonna get the lousy fucks before they get us again. Okay Squad Leaders, when you're deployed in the field, if you come across a terrorist group, you'll observe the pricks until we can gather and work them over together. I don't want any one group engaging the bastards, unless it's necessary. We're gonna hit them as one group, and we're gonna hit them as hard as they hit us. That's about all I have for you people for the time being, so eat, drink, and rest up, because once we deploy. Who knows when we might enjoy any of these luxuries again before this operation has run its course and we successfully stopped the lousy bastards?"

CHAPTER SEVENTEEN

ABDULAZIZ AL-WAHHAD'S NEW SAFE HOUSE ON TENTH STREET AND MARTIN LUTHER KING JR DRIVE; WASHINGTON D.C.

Monday, May 16th, 2011, at the second safe house in central Washington, with the leader of this terrorist group, Shabbah, who was busy was waking the others of his group of young Arab terrorists. It was four thirty a.m., and he wanted his attackers up and aware, as he planned their next attack. Once he was certain he had the attention of everyone from his group, Abdulaziz al-Wahhad began to lay out his further plan of attack for his group.

"Yes, young fools, Allah has decreed by His command that I assembled you here in this filthy city of Washington, to carry out His sacred will. We need more time to assemble the great weapon that'll destroy the will of Satan's worthless followers of this land of non-believers and lowly jackals. Since we're not prepared yet to attack the foul jackals with our nuclear weapon, I decided to go with another attack against the worthless fools of this cursed land. I have the local Washington newspaper Bassam Abu Fallahi retrieved for us. Fools, today is Monday, and I checked the newspaper, and I located our next target within the foul pages." The Ghost waited for his words to sink in the mind of the rest of his terrorist group. When he was certain they were following his every word, he began anew.

"Fools, the foul newspapers will tell us everything we need to know, to better formulate our plans for the next attack against the loathsome infidels. It states Wednesday, May 18th, the baseball team called the New York Mets, will face the Washington Nationals here in Washington at their evil stadium. What better target can we possibly level our faithful eyes against, than two of the United States' worthless baseball teams branded with the names we hate the most in the land of Satan, Washington, and New York? Think of it my fellow Arab brothers and sisters, with just one attack against these the cursed infidels. We shall be attacking both New York and Washington at the same moment. What a glorious target Allah has delivered into our faithful hands to destroy in His name. With this attack on the two worthless baseball teams, we shall place at the feet of Allah, the enemy from both cities of this sinful land.

"With this attack on the foul baseball teams, we shall harm two of the United States' most powerful cities. We'll harm the trash from hell on the side of Satan from New York and Washington in the same breath of death we'll unleash upon all the enemy of Allah. With this one attack, Washington and New York will feel the pain, because they have allowed their foolish children to honor a false God. We'll show all the non-believers that the world of Islam is the one true religion of the world, and anyone who refuses to respect Allah and his wise Prophet, will continue to suffer the wrath of the followers of the one great religion. Allahu Akhbar my Arab brothers and sisters." Al-Wahhad bellowed as he lifted his hand towards the Heavens.

"Allahu Akhbar." Was repeated by the rest of the group of terrorists.

"Now I realize each of you fools are backing my plans to attack this foul country. I'll continue laying out my plan for you young fools. Since Bassam was the one who retrieved the newspaper for us, today I shall give him American cash. He will go to the Ticket Master Station I heard about, and the master of a thousand fleas will order four seats for the foul ballgame for Wednesday late afternoon. Bassam!" The terrorist leader had to turn to see Bassam as he bellowed out his name. Once he held him in his angry glare, he added to his words.

"Young fool of little account, you'll buy seats at the stadium referred to as the nosebleed seats I have read of. These seats are the highest from the foul baseball field. I have knowledge there are four stairwells leading up to the bleacher seats we'll attack the hated jackals from. I want one of our attackers' seats by each entry to this certain area of the structure, so one of our people can be stationed by each of the foul exits. Once our attack begins, it'll be completed as quickly as it had started. Don't dare look at me as if I might have lost my foul mind. I'm in full command of all my brain cells and wits at all times I assure you fools." Al-Wahhad smiled and then he went on with his harsh words for the group.

"My faithful followers of Islam, our attack we shall aim against the lowly infidels of this worthless country, will be one of a minor attack that should last no longer than two minutes in its full duration. Our attack against the loathsome non-believers of this hated land will net us no more than a mere hundred to one hundred and fifty dead infidels. But this is only the beginning of the death we shall level against the cursed people watching this sports event. By the time the attack has run its full course.

"The countless number of death and crippled we shall create, should reach well into the thousands, and I'm counting on the death toll from our attack to be in the tens of thousands, my faithful followers of Islam. Therefore, I'm figuring the death toll and the maimed of these jackals so high. I'm counting on the evil self-preservation mode of the foul mind set of the lowly cowards of this evil country, who shall think nothing of trampling to death the weak of their worthless lands without thought or mercy under their foul feet. Just to save their sinful hides from the justice of Allah's all reaching Might.

"Soldiers for Allah, my warriors, all the worthless ones of this cursed land should have their eyes burned out by heated copper coins. Their uncaring way of sinful life shall raise the death toll against their neighbors by being who they truly are in life. The worthless fools have been raised from the start of their shallow lives to worry about only themselves, and to hell with their neighbors and the weak and defenseless ones of their foul lands. This evil way of life will lend itself perfectly to our just cause for Allah and our own needs for revenge.

"The foul ones from this evil land will kill their own, by their cursed and unworthy actions aimed against the wounded and the weak and helpless. These foul fools have not come to realize what the Holy Qur'an has taught the faithful followers of Islam throughout life that their neighbor's life is more important to the true follower than their own worthless beings. That one belief is the contributing factor that glues the faithful Arab people together and makes us stronger than any other race of people walking on the face of this earth.

"My soldiers, we have to be strong and positive about our actions and ourselves to carry out what Allah has placed before us. It has been entrusted to our hands to deliver the fatal blow aimed against all the enemy of Allah. We'll start our next attack with the foul baseball teams and their hated stadium. But first I'll send Bassam out to buy the tickets to begin our attack against the loathsome infidels. Bassam." For the second time, al-Wahhad turned to see the man, and when his eyes rested on his face, he offered in an angry tone of voice at him.

"Bassam, young fool who should be pleased to know that golden thrones await us in Paradise. I shall give you five hundred filthy American dollars to acquire the tickets to get our attackers into the ballpark arena, so they can carry out Allah's commands faithfully. Take the cursed money of this country, the American cash soils my pocket with its foul presence." Al-Wahhad stuffed his hand into his pocket and took out a wad of cash. He quickly counted five one hundred American dollar bills out and handed it over to the younger Arab man. Then he stuffed the rest of the cash back in his pocket before finishing with his orders to the young terrorist.

"Bassam you must buy four tickets for this area in the stadium I demand, even if you have to go to four different Ticket Master places to not draw any attention to you buying these filthy tickets. I understand each location will display the seating arrangements for the foul stadium, and that'll allow you to purchase the correct seats we need. Each Ticket Master location will inform you where the next location is in the stadium. Yes Bassam, I believe it's the correct course of action for you to visit four different ticket locations. Buy one of the foul tickets at each place, that way no one will pay any special attention to your purchases, until you have acquired the four tickets we need. Since you'll not be a part of this upcoming attack, when you leave, I'll inform the attackers who are how and when they'll open their attack on the infidels.

"Yes Bassam, I know it's early for you to begin your mission for our cause, fool. Leave now and be the first one to arrive at this foul ticket location. When you leave my presence, kill time by enjoying breakfast; eat slowly fool to use up more of your wasted time. Window shop, look as if you're enjoying what this cursed city of sin has to offer its evil civilians. By no means look suspicious in any of your worthless actions and mannerisms.

"Don't shave today either, because it seems like the in thing is to have a few days' growth on one's face in this hated country of jackals. If you come across a policeman, you will smile and nod politely at the infidel, and always look pleasant, fool. Be gone with you now and with Allah's guidance, your mission will be fruitful. My heart pounds in my chest, because soon we shall stop the poisonous breath of the United States, and end America's military presence in all the Middle East and Persian Gulf region. For the first time in countless years, there will be no American jackals in Arab lands."

Everyone connected with this terrorist group went silent, and they watched Bassam as he cautiously walked out the rear door of the safe house. The instant the young Iraqi man left the building al-Wahhad spoke to the others of his group. "I decided who'll work this next attack against the lowly infidels of the United States. I'll send two men and two females for this attack at the cursed ballfield. Once the ones I picked for this operation entered the sports arena, you'll meet at a concession stand and once there you'll divide the explosives you'll use in this attack. Each of you will be given two explosives each in the form of hand grenades for your use.

"Everyone from our terrorist cell has been well educated on the use of hand grenades in your training times. So, there's no need for me to refresh your worthless memories on how to employ this simple weapon. Once you have taken your seats, you'll wait patiently for what the jackals of this country call the seventh inning stretch at the foul ballpark. It's at this time that each of you fools will pull the pins from your hand grenades, and then you shall pitch one hand grenade in opposite directions in the seated infidels. With the eight grenades going off at nearly the same instant at the baseball stadium, should kill at least one hundred seated fools so close together.

"Sending one grenade in the opposite direction around each of the exit stairwells, will surely cause mass panic and confusion, and turn the fleeing fools into each other, thus causing even more infidels to be trampled underfoot of the strong who want to save their own worthless lives. I have finished my plan of attack, so if you fools have any questions. Now is the proper time to ask them of me. Because once you're on our just cause for Allah, all the talking will have been concluded and only actions will be the course of your actions after that time." Al-Wahhad waited for the questions to start, the first hand went up.

"Yes, al-Gasim, you have a question for me I, see? Ask it of me and I shall do my best to try and answer it for you, so you might understand what I want and need from our future attackers at the cursed baseball stadium."

"Shabbah, you made mentioned that four of us will be involved in this next attack against the infidels of Washington. But you failed to mention the names of the chosen ones to hand out Allah's wishes and revenge against the lowly jackals of Satan's domain."

With a slight laugh the Ghost offered in a calm tone of voice this time to his second in command. "Ahhhh... yes, you see you fools are not the only ones who lose their way occasionally. Of course, the four warriors I picked for this cause are. I chose the Iraqi, Farideh Karbaschi as the leader of the four attackers. I do this because he has the fire of a leader burning within his body, born from the lowly infidels invading his country not once, but twice in one lifetime. That fire in his heart will ensure Farideh will make his attacking cell successful on this mission. I chose another Iraqi as Farideh's second in command. He's Mohammed Taborzadi, I chose Mohammed because he has the smarts to take command of the lowly females in case anything happens to Farideh.

"The two females I chose for this mission are Maha Ajwad al-Fassi. She is Saudi Arabian, and she comes with the knowledge even though Arabia makes kind talk of being the United States' friend. Arabia is far from a true friend to the lowly infidels of this evil country. Al-Fassi's actions for this just cause will honor her country, and it shall cement that nation of Saudi Arabia as a true friend of all Arab peoples of the Middle East. The second female I chose for this mission is another Iraqi, she is Farima Ebadi. Although Farima is not the smartest of our group, she'll do as order faithfully and without hesitation. Even if that action will cause her to become a Martyr for our sacred cause, and that makes her an important cog to our mission. I hope these followers of Allah are approved by the rest of our group?" The leader of the terrorist cell looked from one staring young face to the other. Seeing no one disputed his picks, the Ghost allowed his body to relax a little.

Al-Wahhad abandoned his order for his Islamic terrorist cell to go by the names the United States customs bestowed on them when they first applied for citizenship to this country. In his mind, he could not come to grips with calling the faithful followers of Muhammad's sacred word, by the cursed American names.

Another hand from the group of terrorists raised, the movement instantly caught the attention of the Ghost, and he snapped angrily at Nizar Hamdoon. "Yes, I should have known there would be more than just one simple question from you fools. Nizar, you have something troubling your worthless mind I see, now is the time to get what is troubling you out in the open before the other members of our cell. What is it you wish to bring up to my attention, my brother from the sands of Iraq? Speak, for time is wasting and we have a lot to accomplish on this foul of days."

"Al-Wahhad, I don't want to be the cause of any unrest in your mind, but I feel I must bring this concern of mine up to your attention to see what you feel about this problem, my Arab brother. You told us of the explosives we'll incorporate during this next attack against the lowly infidels of this foul nation, yet you failed to inform us on how you intend to smuggle the hand grenades into the hated ballpark. Al-Wahhad, I'm quite certain you're aware of the strong security protections the cursed ballparks employ lately against anyone guilty of trying to smuggle any form of weapons or explosives into their foul ballparks. How do you intend to smuggle eight hand grenades into the arena under the very noses of their security workers, and have them not discover the weapons on our person?

"I know the guards will think nothing of strip-searching male or female, if they think that person is trying to smuggle something dangerous in the place. The guards are prepared to rip the clothes from a body at the very gate, right before the others waiting to enter the foul ballpark. The worthless fools will think nothing of exposing the searched one's body to the gaze of the other infidels waiting to enter the cursed ballpark."

"Ahhh… it's good to see you're paying attention to the many problems we face while carrying out Allah's sacred bidding, Nizar. Yes, the part of smuggling the hand grenades into the foul park did pose a slight problem to us. But I decided to go with what has worked in the past for us. I ordered another emergency oxygen tank to be cut and then fitted with a sleeve, so the two ends of the cylinder can be joined back together, after the eight hand grenades are placed inside the narrow cylinder. I went one step further this time, by dressing up the hand grenades to look like baseballs, by having them painted white and the print of stitching painted on the sides of the foul things. Since we're using the American made M-62 fragmentation grenades. They helped us by the fools designing them to look much like their worthless baseballs. Handing them out will look like the other three attackers are buying trinkets to bring home to their children.

"Yes, before anyone of the group asks the question that needs to be answered. This is going to be how we shall transfer the hand grenades inside the ballpark. The transfer will take place in a male bathroom, where Farideh will open his breathing cylinder in the privacy of the stall of the bathroom commonly used by the handicapped of this evil land. He'll hand two hand grenades to Mohammed who'll follow him into the bathroom. Mohammed will then take the hand grenades and linkup with al-Fassi who'll be standing outside and slightly away from the male bathrooms and give her two of the hand grenades. Once this has been accomplished, Mohammed will return to the bathroom where Farideh shall be waiting his return.

"Once Mohammed returned to the bathroom, Farideh will hand him another set of hand grenades, and Mohammed will deliver them to Farima, who'll meet him secretly outside the bathroom just as al-Fassi was. While Mohammed is giving Farima the two hand grenades, Farideh will be busy with removing the last four hand grenades from the foul cylinder, and he'll carry them loose in his pocket. When Farideh links back up with Mohammed for the last time, he'll hand Mohammed his two hand grenades he will employ in the attack, and then they'll head for their positions by their assigned stairwells.

"Once armed with their two hand grenades a piece, the four attackers will wait as instructed for what the fools of this cursed country call the seventh inning to arrive. While the foolish Americans are enjoying the song to honor their vile country, death will be unleashed against the loathsome fools in the form of Allah's great breath. The slaughter of the lowly infidels will begin once the hand grenades have been tossed, and then the attackers will merely sit back down in their seats and watch all the carnage they have created. Then you shall witness the width and breathe of how the hated infidels will trample underfoot without thought, their helpless women and children while trying to save their own foul necks from the fate Allah has decreed for their demise and suffering."

The terrorist leader stopped speaking as he reached for a bottle of water. He opened it and took a pull then worked the water around his mouth, when he was refreshed, he asked the gathered Arabs. "Are there any more questions that has to be asked and answered by me?"

Mustafa Saleh, the only Afghan member of the terrorist cell, began to shift his weight in his chair. This movement instantly drew al-Wahhad's attention, and he barked angrily at the man. "Yes Mustafa, you have something you want to add to this unending conversation. I suggest if you have a question troubling your mind. Ask your question of me, so I could set your mind to peace. Mustafa, what is troubling you?"

"I do have a question that needs answering form you, al-Wahhad. I want to know if this is a suicide mission, you're sending the four attackers out on. I feel it must be, because I heard no one mention of how our four attackers will get out of the foul stadium alive, once they have attacked the lowly infidels with their hand grenades. I understand most Arabs have no problem with blowing themselves apart for their beliefs in Allah's word. But we Afghan's believed to remain alive so we can attack our enemy a second and even a third time, will serve Allah more wisely than merely attacking his enemy once, and then forfeiting his foolish life in that effort. Enlighten me on how our attackers will get out of the stadium alive." Mustafa became quiet and stared at the Ghost while waiting his reply.

"You're correct to be so concerned about this part of the mission, Mustafa. No, this is not a suicide mission I'm sending our faithful brothers and sisters on at all. The reason I haven't mentioned an escape plan until now. Is because I believed the attackers would be smart enough to decide on their own how they would escape the carnage they have created inside the hated ballpark. It's a simple matter for our four attackers to leave the foul stadium. All they have to do is once they have tossed the two hand grenades in the infidel's laps. They'll merely sit in their chairs and wait until the mayhem had died down, and once the coast is clear.

"The four warriors for Allah will then stand and merely walk over the bodies of the fallen non-believers, and then quickly make their way to the exits and then leave the area as if nothing had happened. Once the attackers are out of the stadium, they'll get to their vehicle. Start it up and drive to one of the monuments of this sinful city, and waste five hours looking at the marble placards. As the other fools who visited these wastes of vast money seem to want to do when they are visiting the sinful city of Washington.

"I don't want the four attackers to return to this safe house, until we know how the foul searchers sent to find them, are going to react to their attack. When we discover how the searchers are reacting, I'll contact Farideh with one of the uses and throw away cell phones given to the poor of this evil country by their foolish President. I'll give him orders to have the attackers come back to our safe house when the coast is clear. Or I'll order them to stay away, if I feel the cursed searchers are on their path to discovery. I'll order the four to leave Washington, and then they'll make their way to the South of this worthless country where they'll blend in with the locals and disappear until it's safe for them to return to us.

"If I feel the searchers are on to our four attackers, I'll order them to stay away and take their chances making their way down to Mexico. Then the four fools will work out on their own how they'll get out of the United States alive and get back to our land. I know if the American searchers detect who it was that attacked them, they'll make every effort to try and capture or kill our attackers. The searchers will hound them to the ends of the earth, and our warriors will make up their minds if they want to be captured by the searchers, or if they want to become Martyrs and take a few of the loathsome searchers with them to Paradise. I warn all members of our terrorist cell, our only thought, our only purpose in life should be to inflict damage to the enemy of Allah, even if it costs us our worthless lives.

"We have to destroy all infidels, all the non-believers of this world before they weaken our faith by keeping their false religions alive. The infidels steal the true believers and turn them into infidels and non-believers as they are." Al-Wahhad allowed a trace of anger to enter his tone and he lifted his fist to the heavens, as he stared at the Arab faces looking at him as if he was Allah.

After a few moments of trying to get his temper under control, al-Wahhad finally asked. "I believe I have answered all your concerns to satisfaction. Now if there are no more questions for me to answer, I believe your time will be better used if you turn your attention to the weapons and explosives, we need to carry out Allah's wishes. Since Mustafa and Nizar were so concerned about our action, I order you to look after the weapons and ammunition if the American searchers discover where we're staying, and we're forced to shoot it out with the worthless infidels. Ali Abdullah Tlas and Abdel al-Ahmar, you'll apply your time checking on the explosives. Al-Mutairi, you know what you must look after, finish the construction of the freedom weapon we shall employ against the leadership of Satan.

"Al-Mutairi, I order you to understand as long as you're a member of my terrorist cell, if you need any help constructing your weapon of mass destruction. You can demand help from any of the others of our group. Because you are the most important person to our entire mission in this cursed land of non-believers and lowly infidels. You're more important to our cause than even I. I'm here only to order and guide the attacks for our terrorist cell and see to it the attacks are carried out as ordered, successfully. You're making the weapon of unlimited death and destruction that'll open the eyes of the foul world to our sacred plight.

"The freedom weapon you shall construct will teach the hated non-believers and jackals of this world that the Islamic world is to finally be taken seriously, from the glorious day we have detonated the nuclear weapon right in the very heart of Washington and seat of Satan. I just issued orders for the others to carry out my orders were issued in a calm way. But if I don't see everyone carrying out those orders, I'll be anything but calm the next time I speak with them. The fools I did not assign any duties are to remain free to lend a hand to anyone who needs a hand working on this next attack."

Al-Wahhad's stomach suddenly growled loud enough to be heard by some from his young terrorist cell. The noise caused the few to laugh and the Ghost to add to his words with a smirk. "I see by the sound of my stomach that it's time for the females to prepare breakfast for the rest of us fools. I understand it's hard to work when your mind is concerned on your hunger than the work you need to accomplish. Yes, let me see, Hatoon al-Muneef, and Leila Alibabic, you'll prepare the food for us to enjoy.

"You women make eggs, toast, and cook meat for the men, we have beef cook it at once. Make certain you make enough for all the men to eat our fill. If you need more provisions to complete this foul meal, go out and buy it without my having to tell you. We men must keep our strength up for the future attacks planned against the lowly infidels of this Allah forsaken country. You women have orders so get busy making food. Bah, I am done speaking, I'm tired and it seems like I have worked for two days' worth of time on this morning. If none of you young fools have anything to do with your foul time, let me know now and I'll surely find something for you to do, I promise that."

Again, the angry Ghost stopped speaking and glared harshly at his followers until they moved to carry out his last orders. When the young ones were out of the room, al-Wahhad allowed himself to relax and enjoyed a quick smile over the way he was able to control the children he had working under his foot and control. The Ghost looked at the table by his feet and noticed a large yellow envelope resting on it. He picked it up and discovered it was sealed and belonged to the one who setup the safe house for their use.

He allowed wrinkles of concern to slowly cross over his forehead, as he carefully studied the large envelope. He shrugged and then slid his finger in the side of the envelope and ripped it open almost as if he was angry with the envelope. He found a detailed map, along with a key with instructions on how to follow the map. Reading them, he discovered the writer was informing him there was a large warehouse built like a concrete bunker. The writer further stated the warehouse was large enough to construct anything the builder wanted in secret, and it was secluded and hard to locate. A thought instantly hit the Ghost and he called over his shoulder at his young bomb maker. "Al-Mutairi!"

In a flash, the Iraqi terrorist was standing by al-Wahhad's side looking at the leader as if he committed an infraction, and the Ghost was upset with him.

Seeing his face, a masked with concern, al-Wahhad smiled and then offered to the young man. "No, you are in no trouble with me, young fool. Al-Mutairi, it has come to my attention we have at our command, a warehouse large enough for you to work very comfortable in. This warehouse is reported secluded and constructed like a bomb bunker. I believe I'm going to order you to move your lab there, you and two others who shall help you working on your freedom weapon. In this way in case the cursed American searchers discover this safe house, there are so many watching eyes in this land of Satan. They'll not end our faithful mission against the hated infidels of this country. Al-Mutairi, pick the fools you need to help you, and take them and everything you need and move to this second location."

He laid out the map and pointed to the location of the warehouse. He carefully dragged his finger over the roads al-Mutairi would follow, so he could arrive at this other location. Once he pointed the structure out, he growled at the concerned looking bomb maker. "I want you to move your operation to this location. I no longer believe it's a wise decision to keep all our faithful fighters bunched up together like we have them, where if the hated police authorities discover one, they'll not discover all of us. Al-Mutairi I have a fear of being discovered by the authorities, and this fear is why I want you to move your operation to this other building.

"Huh, if we're discovered by the local authorities, I'll leave the other fighters to stop them from blocking my escape. Once free, I'll make my way to this new position and conduct our last attack against the evil infidels from this warehouse. Al-Mutairi, take those you want and need and go to this location."

"I hear and I shall obey your new orders faithfully, Shabbah. I understand your concerns of discovery by the hated authorities of this country. Because lately I to have been fighting my spirit with troubling thoughts of the American searchers discovering us, before I'm able to complete my work on the weapon. Working with the extremely dangerous Uranium is not an easy item to work with. I fear this weapon as I do the authorities. I shall do as ordered and move my operations to this location, and Talal bin al-Ahmady and Hussein Ali Soruch will accompany me there. These two displayed interest in what I'm preparing to attack the lowly infidels with. They'll be all the help I need to construct my weapon properly." Al-Mutairi offered as he bowed to the leader of the terrorists proudly.

"This is good for me to understand, because I have need of every member of our small terrorist cell. Some fools I shall assign to work with the attackers I shall send out in the next few days, and the others I need for defensive purposes. Yes, al-Mutairi, take the two you requested and the white vehicle and components for the weapon. Then you shall move everything to the new location. Be gone with you now al-Mutairi, while I make certain the worthless fools I'm forced to rely on, are doing as I ordered." Al-Wahhad placed a smile on because he truly liked al-Mutairi and wanted him to survive the mission as much as he wanted to survive it.

The young bomb maker walked into the next room and called out the names of the other two terrorists he wanted to assist him with finishing the construction of the nuclear weapon. Once he collected the two, they went to the garage and quickly disassembled what al-Mutairi had already assembled of the weapon. The men wrapped up the other items he needed to finish assembling the weapon of mass destruction. They then carefully packed the equipment and weapon into the Chevy sedan, and when the car was packed carefully, al-Mutairi ordered the others to wait in the car, and he went to inform the leader what was going on. He walked into the living room and found al-Wahhad studying the map of Washington. The monuments and streets and side streets were clearly marked out on the map. Al-Mutairi loudly cleared his throat to get the attention of the Ghost as he waited to speak with him.

He heard the harsh sound and looked up from the map, and when their eyes met. Al-Mutairi offered in a rush of words. "Al-Wahhad, I have everything I need for the construction of my weapon packed up and stored inside the car. My helpers are waiting for me, and I wanted to inform you I was ready to leave for the new location before I left your presence."

"Yes, al-Mutairi, it was wise you have thought to inform me before you left my presence for the second safe location at the warehouse, my faithful brother. You should take this cash in case you need to buy anything needed to complete my orders. You have to eat and buy other items for your comfort and needs. I don't need you to want for anything, and not have the means to acquire what you might want. I'm going to give you five thousand American dollars for your needs. I feel that should be more than enough cash to hold you until your time to attack the lowly infidels had arrived." Al-Wahhad handed al-Mutairi the cash, and then added to his instructions.

"You have made my plans of attack against the non-believers and lowly jackals of this world much easier to accomplish. Al-Mutairi, without your much needed help and intelligence, I would never have been able to accomplish Allah's will aimed at the evil infidels of this worthless country. I thank you for your help and loyalty to the cause in my heart. I want to inform you after we have detonated your weapon against the enemy of Allah. I and you will be the only ones I'll care to get out of this land of sin alive. The others are expendable to our cause, and not worthy of concern nor want to save their worthless lives.

"I feel it better if the other fools met their foul fate at the hands of the American searchers. That way I would not have to worry about them being captured and betraying us, because they couldn't control their worthless tongues. When we commit the last attack against the non-believers, I'll make certain we're together. I'll take you through my planned escape to Mexico. Once we're in that filthy land of fools, we'll make our way to Cuba. Once in Cuba, we'll meet a plane sent from Saudi Arabia. This aircraft will bring us back to the sacred sands of Mecca. There we'll wait orders on who to attack next for Allah's sake.

"Al-Mutairi, I long to see the vast deserts of our homeland, and again breathe the pure sweet air of our faithful ancestors. Soon, we shall return to the land of our birth and be treated as true heroes for Allah's sacred cause. You must remember the area you're ordered to head for, it lies between the streets of Massachusetts Avenue between First and Ninth Street of that section of this forsaken city of filthy liars and lowly thieves. This area of Washington is right in the center of the industrial area, and any activity in this area should not arouse any undue suspicions by the workers in this region of the city. I believe the loathsome workers of this area would only be interested in their foul work and going home to their fat wives after work.

"Bah, no matter what I believe, when you safely reach the warehouse, you must keep the lowest profile possible while you're toiling in this area. Don't allow the worthless fools with you to walk around outside the building unnecessarily, with nothing to do. Try not to draw any attention to your actions. Remember the countless eyes of the cursed infidels are constantly searching for our Arab brothers. If the hated police authorities find us, the lowly infidels will destroy us before we can carry out Allah's will against this foul land.

"If you're forced to leave the foul building for any reason whatsoever, you'll make it look like you have a real purpose for being on the property and in the area, and what you are doing on that property. Remember al-Mutairi, you must always keep those two foul fools with you inside the building. They're not smart and without knowing it, they could possibly cause you to be discovered. If one infidel sees either of the two fools walking about like they might be doing something wrong, or they should not be on that property, they'll more than likely call the local police authorities for no reasons other than the way they look and act." They shared a laugh over al-Wahhad's attack on their fellow terrorist.

His remarked back to the leader of the terrorist cell. "Abdulaziz al-Wahhad, I believe it's time to leave and construct my new lab at this other location. Be safe, and remember that Allah will love you, and He shall welcome you to Paradise for carrying out His sacred bidding."

"Yes, my Arab brother al-Mutairi, you're correct, go with Allah's hand resting protectively upon your shoulder to keep you safe, and He will give you the power to carry out His will successfully. Allahu Akhbar." He offered to his fellow terrorist, and then he put out his hand and waited for the man to shake it.

"Allahu Akhbar al-Wahhad, our mission shall be successful to please Allah's will." With that said, al-Mutairi quickly walked out of the building. Al-Wahhad did not breathe properly again until he heard the Chevy sedan starting up, and then pull off the safe house property.

Under his breath, the commander of the terrorist cell mumbled just above a whisper. "Now it starts the final path of war to be waged against the lowly infidels and jackals of this world. Soon, there'll be no other religion on this earth but the only one true religion for all to believe, Islam. I cannot wait until Allah's grace will be felt by all who we shall allow to live. Because only the true believers of Islam will be allowed to enjoy the earth and all it has to offer, once we have eliminated all who don't believe in Allah's sacred words written in the Holy Qur'an. Our war with the evil infidels shall not end until the Western world ends. Because these lands give birth to the non-believers who are the serious threat against Islam and pollute the world. I pray Allah He gives me the strength to carry out His will, until the Western world no longer exists."

Without realizing what he was doing, al-Wahhad absentmindedly looked out the window and stared at the branches moving by the light breeze.

In his mind he was witnessing the death of all who did not believe as he did. His being was taken over with the belief that he was truly doing Allah's work on the earth. He was placed on the earth to kill in the name of Allah, not realizing if his belief was true and when he finally met Allah, God would destroy his soul for killing in his Holy Name.

CHAPTER EIGHTEEN

DELTA THIRTY-ONE MILITARY SUB-STATION,
WASHINGTON D.C. EXACTLY ZERO SIX
HUNDRED HOURS, MONDAY, MAY 16th, 2011

Captain Robert Walker was heavily riding the backs of the group of elite soldiers he was preparing to send out in the field, to try and locate where the missing terrorist cell was hiding in downtown Washington D.C. Walker was still fuming because of the recent attack by these terrorists carried out against New York City, and he wanted them bad.

Standing on either side of him was Sergeant Dorothy Ramirez and Lieutenant Frank Hall, known as the Mutt, and they were the other Squad Leaders of the other two groups of soldiers. The soldiers of the MNRRF (Multi-National Rapid Response Force) operating under the code name 'Dragon Fire' were gathered in the storage building of the military sub-station where the vehicles were parked. The vehicles did not have the usual camouflage paint on the machines, they were painted flat black. Overnight, Walker ordered the Marine markings and armament removed from the vehicles. He was trying to make the machines look more like they were owned by civilians, and they turned them into their civilian vehicles.

Walker issued orders to the Squad Leaders. "Okay Raz, Mutt, you guys have your AOR, (Area of Responsibility) and I want you two to deploy our people in the best place possible to cover every stinking inch they can in the streets of Washington. Once we're out there, we won't come back until we successfully destroyed every one of these stinking cocksuckers. Get your people loaded up and get on the roads. We know the damn terrorists are gonna hit us, and I wanna be out there trying to find them before they do us again. I want these bastards…"

"And you shall have them if I have anything to do about it, Robert." Ramirez replied.

Walker gave her a quick smile and nod then placed the look 'get a move on it' on his face as he stared at her. Ramirez understood the look and barked orders at her team.

"Okay, anyone assigned to Red Team mount up, we have our orders."

Instantly, the twenty-five soldiers assigned to Ramirez's team moved towards the vehicles. They mounted up, closed the doors and the machines started. Ramirez turned to Walker and offered. "I'll see you out in the field, lover. Good luck Robert, I hope we get the sonofabitches before they hit us again. Here's something to take with you for luck, and for later Bobby." Ramirez planted a kiss that warned him of things to come.

Walker returned the kiss then he pulled away and replied. "We'll get the lousy cocksuckers before they get us, or we'll die trying. Move out!"

Ramirez climbed into the lead machine, and it immediately pulled out the overhead doors and in the streets of Washington. Walker watched as his lover disappeared in the morning flow of traffic. When the machine disappeared, he found the Mutt grinning and snapped at him.

"What the fuck's your major malfunction now, shithead? Didn't I just order your ass to get out there with the rest of the pukes under your command, stupid? Look Mutt, this ain't a game we got going on here, man. The mutherfuckers got some serious crap that could destroy half this stinking dump, and kill thousands, and maybe even millions of our people. You gotta be on top of your fucking game on this one man, or we're gonna be picking up stinking civilians from their attack with sticks and spoons. What the hell are you grinning about anyway, asshole?" Walker barked at his lifelong friend.

"Man Walker, I thought Raz was gonna suck your stinking whole puss in her mouth with that kiss. How far down your throat was her stinking tongue, man? I bet she was tickling your balls from the inside with that one, buddy. Man, you two turds really know how to start off a fucking mission." The Mutt complained at his Commanding Officer.

"Never mind that crap, dog man. We got orders and we're gonna carry them out accordingly, man. Again stupid, get your asses in gear will ya." Walker fired back at the Mutt.

"I'm going, I'm going man. Hey Walker before I leave, I gotta ask ya man, you know the stinking Mets are coming to Washington for a four-game series with the damn Nationals starting tomorrow? You know how I follow them. Do you think it might be possible for me to catch one of the games while I'm stuck here in Washington, man?"

"That's what you're worried about here, huh stupid? The fucking Mets, why the hell do you follow them for anyway man? They always end up in last or next to last place every stinking year they play, buddy. This year ain't gonna be any different either man, hell stupid they're already in last place or we're young into the damn season as it is. Fuck the damn Mets will ya and get your ass in gear and get the hell out there and find this lousy sonofa fucking bitches." Walker snapped at his friend.

"I know but keep it in the back of your stinking mind that I wanna see the Mets play while we're hanging round this stinking city. I wanna go to a damn ballgame, Walker. Well, I'm outta here fella. Okay, anyone linked up with the Blue Team, mount up. We gotta get out there and find these stinking slugs." The Mutt bellowed out over his shoulder.

"I'll see what I can do for ya my friend I'll talk it over with the Colonel. If he gives me the okay, its yes and you can go."

"Thanks, I wanna see the stinking Mets in action if I can, man." The Mutt replied to Walker a second time as he quickly left his side.

"I wanna see your ass in action, so shove off and get the fuck out there and find these lousy little pricks." Walker said and then he watched as the second search team mounted the waiting machines. Then they pulled out in traffic starting to get heavy as the rush hour was starting to get going in the heart of Washington.

When the Mutt's team pulled out and started searching, Walker looked at the rest of the soldiers remaining inside the military sub-station and barked at them. "Okay pukes, everyone hooked up to the Gold Team, mount up. We're moving out."

Before Walker could get into his humvee, Colonel Leadbetter said in a raised voice. "Captain Walker, I'll hold the rest of the troops in reserve, and engage them when the call comes in one of our search team's discovered where the terrorists are hiding. Good luck Walker, we have the best soldiers in the world searching for these fucks, and we're going to get them."

Captain Walker when to attention and he proudly saluted his Commanding Officer. He was pleased over Colonel Leadbetter's thinking these troops were the best the world had to offer. When the Colonel returned the salute, Walker jumped into the last humvee. His Commanding Officer watched as Walker's machine skillfully maneuvered to the lead of the other vehicles. The traffic was getting heavy because rush hour was in full swing now, and his convoy caused many horns to blare at them as their slow-moving vehicles moved out.

The young pretty soldier branded Fire, (Sergeant Ashely Reeks, moved over to Colonel Leadbetter's side and she offered him. "Colonel Leadbetter Sir, I'm concerned about this damn terrorist cell we're looking for, sir."

"How is that Fire?" The concerned Colonel asked as he faced the female soldier.

"Colonel Leadbetter, usually when a terrorist cell goes on the hunt, they release a video announcing why they're harming the innocent of any nation. So far sir, no one has claimed responsibility for the two attacks in New York City, sir. There has been plenty of time for the perps to brag why they hit us. I'm getting really concerned over the fact no one is taking responsibility for the attack, and that makes me believe this group is home grown or might be a pack of copycat attackers trying to make a name for themselves, sir."

"Sorry Fire, but we already came to the same conclusion that this group of assholes is a pack of home-grown shits. I didn't get the chance to share this information with the rest of our people. We're one up on the sonofa fucking bitches though. Because we know who their damn leader is, and we also have pictures of the lousy fuck's puss. I like you're putting your mind to work trying to figure out who, and what the hell the damn terrorists are up to though, soldier. You keep your mind working like it is, and I'm quite certain you'll be one of the most important cogs in this entire fucking operation. Now allow me to put my mind to work. Don't you have something to do, Sergeant?" The Colonel asked his fellow soldier.

"Yes, Sir Colonel Leadbetter, I'm working on setting up the communication links between the teams operating out in the field and our command center here at the sub-base, Colonel." Sergeant Diane Morrison offered.

"Good, get back to work and allow me attend to my work, Sergeant."

CAPTAIN ROBERT WALKER'S SEARCH TEAMS

Walker's six vehicles split up the moment his column of humvees entered his AOR. The first vehicle broke off on Pennsylvania Avenue and Eleventh Street. Walker smile when he noticed Buckethead's vehicle pull over to the curb and five of the six soldiers inside, poured out of the war machine. They took off in different directions and started to hunt for the terrorists on foot. The captain did not notice the other vehicles drop off their troops, and the humvees start to drive the streets to lend their eyes to the search teams. The soldiers on foot had orders to remain in constant contact with Walker. Each soldier had a civilian fieldpack loaded with their gear, food, weapons and radios.

The first day of searching for the terrorists was uneventful. Walker got on the radio and ordered the Red Team to break off their hunt for the terrorists and report back to Delta Thirty-One Base for a quick rest and food stopover. He gave the Red Team four hours down time, and when Sergeant Dorothy Ramirez reported her troops rejoined the search. The captain ordered the Mutt's team to take their four-hour rest period. When the Blue Team reported to Walker that they were back in the search, he informed Squad Leaders Ramirez and the Mutt, he was going to take his team in for a quick break. For the rest of the time, the captain kept the teams working for twelve hours with a four-hour break, and then back on duty for another twelve.

By the end of the second full day of searching for any signs of the missing terrorist cell, Captain Walker was beginning to believe he was looking for a needle in a haystack. Colonel Leadbetter and the other backup troops were not just hanging around the sub-station doing nothing. He dispatched his group out to the subway system and had the soldiers checking out anyone using the underground rail system of downtown Washington.

WEDNESDAY, MAY 18th, 2011. WASHINGTON D.C.

Captain Walker's search team was resting at the military sub-station at Zero, Seven, Thirty-Five Hours, and he was just preparing to reenter the search for the terrorists. The troops from the teams were suffering from total exhaustion, and he was considering allowing each team to break off the search for a twelve-hour rest period. He discussed this thought over with the Colonel, who would not hear of it, and he told him he was out of his mind if he thought he was going to allow the soldiers to break off for a twelve-hour rest period.

The young Marine Captain was angry as hell as he led the way for his team. He was dragging his feet and could only imagine how tired the rest of his troops were. The other teams were out and when he looked at his time sheet, he realized the Red Team was the next Team scheduled to break off for a four-hour rest period. He picked up his mike and growled. "Dragon Fire Leader to Dragon Breath. Over."

"Dragon Breath Leader to Dragon Fire, send your traffic. Over." Sergeant Ramirez replied.

"Dragon Breath, I'm ordering you to break off your damn search for some needed down time. Get some rest and food in your troops, I need everyone on their damn toes, I got a stinking gut feeling shit's gonna go down today. It's just a fucking feeling nagging my ass, but I can't shake the shitty feeling I got eating away at my guts. I had it all day and it's really bugging the stinking shit outta my damn ass. Dragon Breath, I'm giving you permission to stretch out your break to five hours and make certain you eat and soup up on your down time. I believe this is gonna be one helluva fucking day for our asses. I really feel it in the air, and I know they are going to attack us again, today soldier. Over."

"Roger that last Dragon Fire, and thanks for the extra sixty. Heaven knows my people are working on pure instinct I'm afraid. They're breathing out of memory, Dragon Fire. Talk about walking Zombies, I have a mess of them on my hands, Captain. Over."

"Dragon Breath, talking about Zombies walking round ya, you should get a gander at my stinking people, I've been shinning a light in their eyes and getting no kind of reaction from halfa them. Walker, I'm beginning to believe searching for the stinking terrorists is harder that trying to find an honest politician in Washington, man. Over." The Mutt offered as he stuck his two cents into the other soldier's conversation.

"Dragon Claw, stay offa the net unless you have something important to report in, asshole. Besides stupid, you have nuthin to worry about, Zombies only eat stinking brains. Dragon Fire. Over." Walker fired back at his friend. He was angry the Mutt used the communications to goof off.

He knew the Colonel was going to eat the Mutt alive for the joke when he relieved the Mutt's team for their down time.

THE PENTAGON; ZERO EIGHT THIRTY HOURS

General John White, the Chairman of the Joint Chiefs of Staff was at his office for an hour, he was also fighting the same feeling that something bad was hanging over his head since he woke. Giving into his troubling thoughts, he picked up the phone and dialed.

"Yes John, what do you want so early in the morning? I just walked in my office, and I didn't have a chance to check my computer yet, to see if anything has happened last night sir."

"Sorry for the early call Director Raincloud, I'm battling a real shitty feeling today, and I guess I needed someone to hold my damn hand. You up for breakfast, I'm starving, John?" The General offered the CIA Director.

"If you need someone to hold your hand, why didn't you stay home and play patty cake with your lovely wife, General? Yes, I guess I could stand for something to eat at that, sir. Do you want to come to me, or do you want me to stop by the Pentagon?"

"I'd like you to come here I don't want to leave the building with this feeling I'm suffering from. Like I told you, I have a shit feeling something's going down today, John." General White added as he let out his breath in a hiss.

"What's got you standing on the edge of a knife, General?"

"I don't know what I'm feeling nor were the threats of intercepted communications to feed my concerns. I just have this bug up my ass today, and I'm having a real problem with relaxing, that's all John."

"Got ya General, give me a few minutes to check my threat board, and if nothings coming down the chute. I'll warn my secretary to have my calls shifted over to your office, and I'll be at the Pentagon before you know it, sir. Do you want me to bring anything with me sir? I can do a run of the Middle East to see if anyone's going nuts there, I know nothing's going on here in Washington. John, a few of my Agents ran across some of your young soldiers in the streets. I got a good report on your guys, I like the way you have them dressed as civilians. If my people didn't know who to look for, they would've never known who your people were, sir. This damn terrorist threat is the only problem I know of that's still active on the threat board, sir. If the terrorists were successful making it to Washington, they're keeping a low key for now, sir. I got nothing new on them, nothing." The powerful CIA Director offered.

"I hear ya there John, I spoke to Colonel Leadbetter earlier this morning, and he was fuming he was unable to get anything new on the damn terrorists. I asked him if he felt the lousy bastards were in Washington, he replied he was certain they're here, Director. I hate to have my troops roaming the streets of Washington armed to the teeth, and out there hunting bear. Some of these damn kids want to kill anything breathing that look at them the wrong way. Dammit, I wish this President would give us the backing the past Republican Administration did.

"This President's having a hard time allowing my troops to walk the streets of Washington armed as they are. He wants this entire operation done with, and he's starting to threaten ordering my people out of Washington, and only allowing them in if, and when the terrorists hit somewhere in Washington. That statement has me going over the falls, how the hell could the leader of our country think of forcing my people out of Washington, and bring them back only if there's a terrorist action against the capital? John, I like the man as a person, but as for him running our country, he leaves a helluva lot to be desired."

"I feel ya there General, and I feel this President has a lot to learn in dealing with terrorist, or security threats aimed against our country, sir. I wonder if he realizes how many people, I have searching Washington for the terrorist cell. FBI Director Hidemann knows, and he's having fits over allowing my Special Agents to work the streets and overlapping his Agents. Anything that goes down within the borders of the United States, are usually the FBI's domain and problem to deal with, sir. Frank's letting me have it anytime one of his Agents comes across one of mine out in the field, sir. I have bitches from the FBI Director stacked up to the damn ceiling I must answer. I've been putting off responding to his countless bitches, mainly because I'm not in the damn mood to get involved in any of his grief at this time. I've got enough problems I'm dealing with as it is already, General." Director Raincloud complained.

"Yes, these twin terrorist attacks in New York City couldn't have come at a worse time for us, Director. Not with the damn problems this Administration's been hitting us with lately. Damn Democrats, I miss the old Administration, at least I knew exactly where I stood with that President. John, I had enough jaw jacking on the damn phone, get your backside over to my office so we can speak face to face." General White said.

"Give me time to check my threat board. If nothing's happening, I'll be to your office as soon as I can, sir." Director Raincloud offered as he broke off the communication.

THE SAFE HOUSE ON EIGHTH STREET OFF PENNSYLVANIA AVENUE WASHINGTION D.C. EIGHT THIRTY A.M. WEDNEDAY, MAY 18th, 2011

Abdulaziz al-Wahhad was geared up, today was the opening series scheduled to begin between the New York Mets and the Washington Nationals. That meant he was going to send his terrorists to attack the civilians enjoying the ballgame at the stadium. The game was supposed to begin at six p.m. and the terrorist leader wanted his people at and in the ballpark by four. So, they could settle in and get the feel of the stadium and crowd. The Ghost felt if his attackers were at the ballpark early, the longer the terrorists were there, the less attention they would bring to their mission and themselves. He wanted his small group of attackers to be well set in place early, so Farideh could hand out the hand grenades to the others of the group, so they could begin the attack against the civilians at the stadium to enjoy the ballgame. The day was beautiful, warm and clear, and it was supposed to be seventy-five degrees at game time.

Al-Wahhad was up since five twenty this morning, and he was full of energy. He was mind set on checking out every detail before his terrorist attackers headed out on their next mission. The first one he searched for was Farideh Karbaschi. He found him working on the modified oxygen tank. Seeing him in the outer room, he offered. "Allahu Akhbar, good morning, I should have known I'd find you checking your equipment, Brother Karbaschi."

"Allahu Akhbar al-Wahhad, it's good to see you this morning my brother. I placed the eight hand grenades inside the oxygen tank, and I'm about to slip the two ends back together. Do you care to watch, so you can see how well the tank will look once it has been placed together again?" Farideh offered as he moved so the Ghost had a good and clear view of what he was doing with the narrow oxygen tank.

The terrorist leader moved a little to his left so he could see Farideh's hands easier, as he picked up the other end of the tank, and he carefully guided the free end over the opening of the cylinder. Farideh had to wiggle and struggle slightly with the other side of tight-fitting end of the tank, as he worked the loose end close to sealing the tank. Once the two ends set flawlessly in place, the Ghost cautiously inspected Farideh's handiwork with the item. The two ends fitted perfectly together, and all one was able to see was a slight cut line going completely around the cylinder. After inspecting the tank, he asked Farideh with concern in his voice.

"How do you intend to hide the obvious cut in the foul tank, Brother Karbaschi?"

"That's easy to accomplish Shabbah, please observe what I assembled to hide the cut in the foul tank." Farideh reached behind him and picked up a three-inch wide, fifteen-inch-long strip of colorful paper, and pulled it across his lap so al-Wahhad could see it.

Al-Wahhad moved a little more so he could see what Farideh was showing him. Seeing the strip covered with the Mets logo, and information on how to contact the team and follow them on the internet. Al-Wahhad looked Farideh, and he announced with a smile on his lips, because he knew how the logo strip was going to conceal the cut in the tank.

"I see by the expression lacing your eyes that you're unfamiliar with what the lowly infidels labeled as a bumper sticker, al-Wahhad. There are many items the cursed infidels have that offers their souls pleasure. That's why I chose this item to use during my attacked against the non-believes." Farideh offered with a smile, trying to calm al-Wahhad's concerns.

"I have not seen such an ugly piece of paper as the one you hold in your hands, fool. What's the purpose to what you called a 'bumper sticker', my brother?"

"Observe and enjoy and you'll understand the principle to this evil looking thing, Shabbah." Farideh replied and then he pulled the backing from the sticker. He then carefully worked the sticky paper around the tank and then cut off the excess from the sticker. When Farideh finished working the sticker in place, it covered the cut in the tank perfectly. With a smile of victory, Farideh looked at al-Wahhad and nodded.

The terrorist leader lightly touched the tank, as he traced the cut covered by the sticker with his finger then grumbled. "By the sacred gray beard of the great Prophet, I cannot believe I'm unable to see the cut, let alone feel the slight depression with my fingers. The cursed infidels from the land of Satan offer us everything we need to carry out Allah's will against the lowly jackals. Bah, no wonder the future of the worthless infidels is numbered."

Al-Wahhad reached out and shook the tank. His thought was what if the security guards checking everyone entering the ballpark, decided to inspect the tank closely and they suddenly shook it by mistake or on purpose. Would they hear the hidden grenades inside the narrow tank rattle? He cocked his head to the side, trying to hear rattling from the grenades. Not a sound was made by them, and this forced the Ghost to ask Farideh with concern in his voice.

"Farudeh, how is it possible the cursed hand grenades trapped inside this metal cylinder make no noise when I shake the foul tank? How were you able to accomplish the great feat of silence from the two metal objects? I'm not surprised though that you thought to silence this in the matter you have accomplished, my Arab brother from the land of sand. I'm interested in how you were able to command this feat."

"Al-Wahhad, I was in fear the grenades would make alarming sounds when I was moving the tank around at the ballpark. That is why I chose to wrap each hand grenade with bubble wrap I found stored in the foul garage, when I first searched this worthless house. I also filled the tank with the bubble wrap, so the filth would lock the grenades in place and not rattle around. I keep my eyes open in search of anything that would help me survive, and items I find will serve my mission, Shabbah. If the worthless security people shake my tank, all they'll hear is nothing in return. I had the foresight to lock the air gauge in full range, and that'll make the guards believe the extra weight was due to the tank being full. It's rather easy to fool the cursed infidels who pollute the land of Satan.

"Shabbah, I looked at the countless problems of fooling the lowly infidels of this foul nation. So, I can prove to the arrogant Americans that they are not as smart and alert as they believe they are. It's almost a game with me to easily confuse the non-believers of this evil land. Al-Wahhad, though I mentioned this as a game, I take it as everything but. I take my work against the evil infidels extremely seriously, and any mission I'm sent on against the lowly infidels, I'll be successful with. I strive to destroy all the faithless non-believers of the world." Farideh offered as he placed a look of confidence on his face.

"You speak in words of confidence, and that's exactly what's needed to assure the success of our next attack aimed against the non-believers of this evil country, my brother. Farideh, we have to be extremely confident and diligent to our work when we're attacking the fools in their worthless country. Allah how I hate the evil non-believers of the world, I want to prove to the cursed jackal American murderers who killed Usama bin Laden. With his death it did not stop what our leader had in mind when he opened his holy war aimed against the non-believers of the Western world.

"Although the cursed leader of this worthless land has boasted on many different occasions, at his countless press conferences that their foul war against terrorism has been won by the evil fools with bin Laden's death. The great fool forgot to check with the ones they war with. Because the lowly infidel in command of Satan's land says the war is over, it does not make it so with the Muslim world. We are many followers who fight for Allah's will, and each of us had to declare the war over before it is truly over. We'll never utter those words of defeat until all the cursed infidels from the West are destroyed. The few fools we'll allow to live will have to convert to Islam to save their loathsome lives." Al-Wahhad offered as he straightened his back.

"All you stated will come to past I assure you my faithful Arab brother. Soon all the foul infidels from the West world will be an ugly memory to endure, until their once heavy influence in the Middle East has completely evaporated, and everything about the great fools has been erased from history and mind and the earth. Shabbah, with the plans we have in mind, we're the instrument that shall destroy the influence of the hated West, once al-Mutairi completed his part of this operation. With the detonation of that nuclear weapon in the heart of Satan's land, we'll bring down the entire leadership of this foul land.

"Have no fear my faithful Arab brother, because Allah will show us the proper way to destroy all the lowly infidels of the earth." Farideh replied confidently as he went back to work checking his handiwork on the narrow oxygen tank. He wanted to make certain he did not overlook anything that might give away his mission to the security of the baseball stadium. Turning his back on al-Wahhad, informed the terrorist leader he was done speaking.

With a mere shrug, al-Wahhad announced he was going to check on the others of his terrorist group. The Ghost was surprised no other members of his cell were hanging around them and watching what they were doing with assuring the success of their mission. This angered al-Wahhad to all ends and he stormed out of the living room in search of the others of the terrorist cell, to see what they were up to.

Al-Wahhad charged up to the second floor of the safe house used as the sleeping quarters for the rest of his terrorists, he burst into the room three members of the stadium attack were sleeping in. He was instantly embarrassed when he found them and four others kneeling on prayer rugs and praying towards Mecca for their morning prayers. Silently, he slowly backed out of the room, in the hallway he leaned against the wall and took a deep breath. The Ghost was angry for not joining the morning prayers.

Leila Alibabic walked out of the bathroom with just a towel wrapped around her exquisite body, and her hair still wet. Seeing al-Wahhad standing in the hallway, she smiled and when she turned sideways in the hall to get around him. She opened the towel and flashed him with a full-frontal view of her body. In her mind's eye, she did not flash him for sexual pleasure. She only flashed him in hopes of relieving some of the exhaustion he displayed on his face and body.

The full body flash from the stunningly beautiful Iraqi woman served its purpose for the terrorist leader. Al-Wahhad pushed his painful body off the wall with just the strength in his shoulders. Then he returned Leila's smile as she continued down the hall. He made no bones about staring at her outstanding body, until she disappeared in her room. But before she disappeared completely in the room, with one hand she held the towel out in the hallway and she shook it a few times like a flag, and then she sexily allowed it fall from her hand before she closed the door to her room.

She then pointed her index finger out and waved her hand in an Egyptian way and continued waving as she pulled it slowly into the room, and then she finally closed the door. From the hall, he heard the women laughing at his expense over what Leila did in the room.

With a quick shake of his head and a smile, the terrorist leader headed downstairs. His anger left as he remembered his wife waiting his return to Iraq. Although he convinced himself he no longer loved or even cared for her, he still suffered a pang of wanting her. He killed that feeling by talking himself into thinking about Leila. A fellow Iraqi who had the best shape out of the seven women in his terrorist cell, in his mind he was planning to make certain she was one of the few survivors, once they completed the mission in the United States. Again, he smiled as he thought of the problems, he was causing himself. Here he was, making plans to kill thousands of American civilians, and his driving concerned was about his love life.

Although Abdulaziz al-Wahhad was enjoying the pleasant thought for a moment, he minds suddenly snapped at him that he had to get back to the pressing matters at hand. The matters of the heart will come later when his attacks had successfully been carried out by his followers against the hated infidels of this country. He checked his watch and instantly, all good thought left his body as his anger grew anew. It was ten after nine and the others of the group were still upstairs. Losing his patience, he walked over to the head of the stairs and then he barked angrily for the remaining members of his terrorist cell.

"By the grace of Allah, you young fools might find Him merciful, but you'll find the exact opposite of me. This day is extremely important with our plans to defeat the lowly infidels of the West. Time is passing and you fools are hiding in your foul room's doing who knows what with each other. If you want to live to see tomorrow's sunrise then get your lazy bodies down here quickly and lend hand to those who shall do Allah's work on this foul day. I give each of you fools one minute to stand before me, so I can give you further orders to follow. Anyone not standing before me will be eliminated from our group, and you'll never be allowed to walk in

Allah's grace in Paradise. Get down here before I come up and throw you down the foul steps! I'm waiting to get everyone in motion."

The terrorist commander stepped away from the stairway and then waited. Instantly he heard noises created by men and women rushing around to complete what they were involved with. The three members of today's attack rushed down the stairs so quickly that they almost tumbled over each other. Mohammed Taborzadi, Maha Ajwad and Farima Ebadi stood before al-Wahhad as the others followed his orders and quickly assembled behind the three attackers. The fuming Ghost looked at the clothes the three chose to dress in for the attack. The leader smiled when he noticed the women, Maha and Farima were both dressed in blue jeans, and wearing a shirt brandishing the New York Mets logo.

He was surprised with the women's choice of clothing, and he offered with concern to them. "You women have made me pleased to have the smarts to wear clothes in this manner. I'm quick certain the cursed infidels of this country will never believe you were out to harm the fools." The Ghost turned to Mohammed and complained at him.

"Huh, what is this foolishness I see standing before my foul eyes? Don't make me believe the women are smarter than my second in command of this cursed attack against these jackals, fool from the land of hot sands of the vast deserts of the Middle East. Mohammed your poor choice in clothes is not fit to wear to the worthless ballfield. For the love of Allah, you're going to the cursed infidel's sporting event you're not going to a cold place. Master of a thousand fleas, what you have on will make you sweat to death while baking in the glare of the mighty sun. Go back upstairs and put clothes on lighters and cooler to wear. Huh, I cannot believe I'm forced to think after everything that you worthless fools must do. Get out of my sight and return when you're dressed properly for your foul quest, fool."

Mohammed rushed back upstairs under the harsh glare of the Ghost. When Mohammed was out of sight, al-Wahhad turned to the others and barked savagely at the gathered. "Young fools who only obey my will. I'm ordering each fool to spend this day assisting our attackers, until they're carrying out Allah's commands. If I see any of you not assisting the others, you'll regret the day your mothers mated with a scorpion in the desert and gave you birth. Our only concerns on this foul day are to make certain all preparations for our attack against the lowly infidels are completed, and our Arab brothers have everything they'll require for a successful operation..."

The Ghost's stinging words were interrupted by Mohammed, who returned to the group of terrorists. This time he was dressed in the light over shirt with the logo of the Washington Nationals' team printed boldly on the front of the shirt, and the number seventeen on the back. Mohammed was also supporting a baseball cap with the same logo, and that completed his outfit.

Al-Wahhad smiled because he noticed the two-day old growth of beard on Mohammed's face. He was surprised it made him look as well as he did. Gone from Mohammed's face were all traces of his good Arab looks and full beard, and the slight beard made him look so much like the American males he was going to destroy, and young also. The baseball cap made Mohammed look imprudent and dumb in al-Wahhad's eyes though. It also made the Ghost hate the Americans more than he did.

The terrorist commander ripped his angry eyes from Mohammed body, and then he looked at the others of the group while he quickly collected his thoughts for a quick moment. He wanted everything perfect for this upcoming attack on the ballfield. Especially because it was going to be his first attack in Washington, what he believed was the heart of Satan. He searched his mind, praying to Allah that he had all his bases covered, before he turned his group loose on the unsuspecting civilians of Washington. He continued staring at the other terrorists and then a thought suddenly hit him, and he turned to Farideh Karbaschi. The leader of the attack group and snapped angrily at the man.

"Fool making me think again about placing you in command of this attack cell! Have you had the smarts to make certain the cursed vehicle you're employing to get your attack team to the baseball stadium, has enough foul fuel to make the trip there and back here? Or is it necessary for me to think of everything for you, fool?"

Farideh's face turned ashen, because he knew he failed to make certain the vehicle was properly fueled up. He did not want to tell al-Wahhad he did not think to check the fuel level.

"Huh fool of fools, I know what makes you tremble like wash on the line. So, I'll not force you to lie to me, torturer of the truth. Beggar of no importance, you need many nightmares spent on the rack to teach you correctly how to prepare for any mission you are sent out on, fool. How many times do I have to tell you and the other fools of our terrorist cell, our mission aimed at the lowly infidels of this foul country should be the only thoughts, the only goals held in your hearts and minds? You fools must think there are no limits to the time and patience I wasted upon you. By the grace of Allah, I'm trying to make our terrorist cell the most notable weapon ever aimed at the enemy of Allah, and you pack of worthless fools are fighting me every step of the way. If I must tell another one of you what to do, the whites of my eyes will be the last thing you shall witness, before you kiss the feet of Allah."

The Ghost turned to Farideh and snapped at him in a hot voice. "Dog of a non-believer, our mouths have been shut by the sands of a thousand years, but upon your soul rests our salvation. My eyes stand witness to the fact we have to destroy all the faithless of the earth. In your hands rest the beginning of our sacred battle against this trash from hell standing on the side of Satan. We have time so I want you to take Mohammed and fuel the foul vehicle before I have you skinned alive for your failures to our mission. Be gone with you, young fool!"

Abdulaziz al-Wahhad continued to glare at the two young terrorists until they were out of sight. Then he turned his angry glare on the others still standing before him and staring at him and instantly, everyone scattered to get out of the sight of their leader.

Farideh and Mohammed rushed out of the safe house and jumped into the SUV. They laughed over how angry their leader was. They enjoyed the quick drive to the gas station. Farideh pulled up to the pump and then rushed into the Circle K station and ordered forty dollars of gas to pump four by the attendant. But when he stuck his hand in his pocket, he realized he did not have any American cash on his person. He begged the attendant to wait a second and he rushed back to the car and cried to Mohammed. "I pray Allah's mercy you have some American cash on your person. I failed to take money for this unscheduled trip, Mohammed."

"Fear not my scared young Arab brother from the land of sand, I always have some American cash on my person. How much do you need, fool?"

"I ordered forty dollars' worth of fuel for the vehicle. The fool is waiting my return so I can pay for the brew for this worthless machine."

Farideh put out his hand and Mohammed counted out forty American dollars. In a flash he disappeared back in the store.

Wiping the sweat from his brow with the back of his hand, Farideh handed the angry looking attendant the forty dollars, and received a harsh glare from the other man, because he was forced to hold his register open until he returned. Three other customers looked at Farideh with anger over being forced to wait for his return, before they could be waited on and be on their way. The attendant placed the money in the registered and did something Farideh did not to see. He then snapped at him. "The pump's waiting and make sure you replace the nozzle before driving off sir. Come again and have a nice day, sir."

"Thank you and I'm sorry for making you wait like I caused. I left my cash in my vehicle. It will never happen again when I return for more fuel, sir." Farideh replied, trying to make the attendant feel a little better for his delay in paying him. No matter what he offered the man, he could not erase the trembling his body was displaying before the clerk.

The attendant gave Farideh a hard look and a smirk because he detected the nervous actions, and then he shrugged and smiled at the young man. He gave Farideh a slight nod, clearly dismissing him as he returned to work with helping the next person standing in the line of customers before him.

Farideh rushed to the pump, put the gas in his vehicle and replaced the nozzle. Then he drove off and returned to the safe house, only to find al-Wahhad waiting their return. He was looking out the window and when he picked up the SUV return, he stepped away from the window and waited for the two to enter. Upon seeing them, the leader growled angrily at them. "I trust you two young fools had no problems fueling your cursed vehicle. I cannot believe if I don't look after everything, this mission would fall apart around my worthless ears."

CHAPTER NINETEEN

"No Father of Kindness and Understanding." Farideh offered, hoping the homage he paid to the leader of the terrorist would soften his stance against him. It did not work.

"You have the cursed tongue of a true liar, Farideh! Is there anything else you might have failed to look after before you leave on your mission for the sake of Allah's will?"

After a slight hesitation, Farideh responded to the leader of his group with a sharp snap in his voice. "Sami, (The Rock in Iraq) I believe I have looked after everything necessary for our mission's complete success. I have the hand grenades placed securely inside the oxygen tank as you have witnessed yourself. I also went over where we're scheduled to meet inside the baseball stadium, so I can disperse the hand grenades to the others of my assault team. I made certain using the seating arrangement we received with the tickets, each attacker knows exactly where our seats are in the huge baseball stadium. Abo Haru, (Father of Terror) I when over with the others when we're supposed to open our attack against the lowly infidels of this foul country, during the seventh inning stretch, I believe I have looked after everything I was supposed to look after for the attack."

Farideh was being extra kind when speaking with al-Wahhad, trying to make the leader of the group ease up a little on him and the other members of his attack team.

"Huh, butter would not melt in your worthless mouth, Farideh. You trouble me like a woman, son of a flea feeding upon camel dung. You assured me and I see you have clearly failed to paid attention to your duties, by overlooking the fuel problem with the cursed vehicle. If Allah does not love you, how could you possibly have accomplished all you have for His great will? You're Father's Kingdom was in his heart and mind, and that

Kingdom cannot be surrendered to the infidels. With your attack against the hated infidels of this evil country, their dead will mount like the leaves of winter on the worthless ground. When you go into battle, I pray you remember the lines from the Surah, known as al-Anfal, or the spoils of war. 'Against them make ready your strength to the utmost of your power, including your great steeds of war to strike terror into the foul enemy of Allah, and your enemy'.

"We shall fight all the foolish non-believers of the earth, until the scales of justice are once again perfectly balanced, and all is as it should be with the world. We'll eliminate the regurgitated filth of the Vultures, until there's not one worthless non-believer left alive. We are the true Thar Allah, the true Vengeance of God. Alas, it's time to go forth and carry out Allah's sacred will, for Paradise awaits her heroes. Farideh, collect your other assault members and head for your assigned mission. Time grows short, and I want you four to be at the cursed baseball stadium well before the foul ballgame starts.

"The longer your assault teams are at this evil stadium, the less your attendance will arouse any suspicion from the lowly animals of this evil country. If you're successful with this operation, I shall fill your mouth with pearls, if you fail me, fear me. Remember these words, 'to kill a lowly infidel or non-believer is not murder, it's the true path to Paradise'. Collect the others and leave on your faithful mission, Farideh."

Abdulaziz al-Wahhad stepped aside, and he allowed Farideh to speak to the rest of his attack team members before they started off for their terrorist action aimed at the ballgame. He looked at Mohammed Taborazadi and ordered him. "All is as it should be, order the worthless women to come to my side. Once they're with us, we shall leave on our mission for Allah. In a few hours Mohammed, we shall deal a lethal blow to the evil non-believers of this filthy land. A blow the lowly infidels will not be able to get up from the floor. I shall wait for your return, go Mohammed, we have to leave immediately."

The leader of the terrorist cell smiled because he was proud of Mohammed, and the way he took over command of the other attackers from the group as he, and Farideh watched Taborzadi called for the women of the assault team to come downstairs, so they could leave for their attack.

The two women rushed downstairs, and the Ghost was easily able to tell they were still working on their appearance. Their hair was combed to perfection, and their face makeup was correct and flawless. The women immediately fell in step with the men, and they quickly marched out of the house. Al-Wahhad rushed to the window and pulled the curtain aside so he could watch this assault team piled into the vehicle.

He remained standing by the window until the SUV pulled out of the driveway, and then the vehicle rapidly drove out of sight. With a release of his breath, he did not know he was holding, al-Wahhad turned away from the window and walked across the room and flipped the TV on, and he placed it on the channel scheduled to display the ballgame later on tonight. He wanted to watch for two reasons, he wanted to see if he could detect his attackers before they opened the assault against the gathered infidels, and two; the Ghost wanted to watch as the attack unfolded live on TV.

The traffic of downtown Washington was heavy as always. Even though the stadium was no more than eight miles away from where the terrorists were hold up, it took Farideh just over forty-five minutes to arrive at the parking lot in the shadow of the stadium. He drove to an empty spot, parked the SUV and then the four terrorists piled out of the vehicle. It took Farideh a minute to set the breathing tube perfectly under his nose, after he removed the narrow oxygen tank from the SUV. Mohammed and Farima went into their act and made like they were young lovers, as they held hands and bumped hips and laughed together. Maha held back a little and she looked after Farideh as he struggled with the small air tank. Because they did not have a handicap sticker, they had to park further away from the stadium's main entrance.

The four young Arab attackers walked over to one entry gate that had growing lines of people waiting to enter the massive stadium. Farideh looked over his shoulder and noticed a good number of cooking pots, and men handing out hot dogs, hamburgers and sausage sandwiches to friends, or anyone who wanted to buy one of the delights from them. He knew this was called 'tailgating parties' and smiled over the way the hated Americans enjoyed life with such passion.

Mohammed and Farima walked in front of Farideh and Maha, and when they moved up in the line to the man who took their tickets. The angry sounding stadium attendant growled for Mohammed to put his arms out away from his sides, and then he quickly ran a small metal detector wand over his entire body from top to toe. The guard looked as if he was angry at the world, as he barked orders at the four young Arabs who looked nothing like they just came from the Middle East region. Mohammed stepped aside when he was cleared by the angry acting security guard so he could check Farima.

Mohammed watched Farima step up and the guard growled for her to put her arms out, he did the same to her. The guard dragged the wand over Farima's breasts, across her shapely rearend and up her thigh between her legs. Anger filled Mohammed's heart over the way he insultingly ran the wand slowly over Farima's body. The guard seemed like he was enjoying the way it was gliding over her beautiful body. With a quick nod, the guard indicated Farima had passed his inspection, and he wanted her to move on. When she walked between the two metal rails, Mohammed stepped up and took her hand and walked her through the rest of the rails. Then they waited as the guard waved Farideh and Maha over to him.

Maha led the way for Farideh and she acted as if she was helping him with the troublesome tank, and the quarter inch oxygen hose that seemed like it wanted to get tangled up on everything Farideh passed. The guard seemed to relax a little, and he even reached out and helped Maha with the hose that got caught under the wheel of the small tank dolly. Maha smiled at the guard helping her with Farideh, and he returned her smile kindly.

When they were where the guard wanted them to stand, he barely checked Farideh with the wand. He kept the wand away from the oxygen tank because he knew the metal would set off his wand alarm. Maha had to step aside when the guard motioned, he was done with Farideh, and he was allowed to continue to enter the stadium.

Remembering what the guard demanded from Mohammed and Farima moments before, she instantly stepped forward and moved her arms away from her body. She waited for the security guard to run his wand over her body, but to her surprise. The guard simply smiled at her and made the same head movement for her to go on passed him. Maha smiled beautifully at the young guard as she walked past him and then she took charge of Farideh as if he truly needed her assistance before, he would move on into the huge complex.

The guard barely smiled at Maha as he turned back to his job, and he waved the next person over to him. The guard went to work checking everyone else who wanted to enjoy the ballgame. The line of people wanting to enter the stadium was growing rapidly.

Maha walked by Farideh's side as they headed for the second-floor commissary area by the bathrooms, according to her map of the stadium given to Bassam, when he brought the tickets. Mohammed and Farima walked ahead of Maha and Farideh as if they did not know the other pair, and they reached the commissary first and ordered frankfurters and sodas to enjoy. Maha led Farideh over to the bathroom and allowed him to struggle into the room by himself. When Farideh reached an empty handicap stall, he entered the booth and instantly locked the door behind him. Then he set to work with the sticker from the tank, so he could separate the two ends and get at the hand grenades stored inside the narrow metal cylinder out.

The moment Farideh disappeared into the bathroom, Mohammed wolfed down the rest of his frankfurter and then went in the bathrooms carrying his soda. All the bathroom stalls were taken so he made like he was waiting for a stall to become empty. The bathroom was overflowing with a horde of excited men using the facility or combing their hair or otherwise looking after their appearance.

Mohammed had to fight to keep a smile of distain off his lips, as he watched some of the fussing men messing with their hair or clothes like the women usually do. He laughed because he thought the women fussed and wasted so much of their time over their appearance but seeing the men doing the same thing in this bathroom, made him shake his head in disgust. When a man came out of a stall, another man instantly ran in. It was almost mayhem in the bathroom, with men leaving while others rushed in, so the bathroom never cleared out enough for a man to have enough room to breathe properly.

Farideh came out of the large handicap stall and Mohammed walked like he was going to rush into the suddenly empty stall. Instead of entering, he made like he was worried about the handicapped man, and he carefully helped him get through the overcrowded bathroom. Most men gave way so the man dragging the narrow oxygen tank behind him was able to get by them. It was so overcrowded it made it easy for Farideh to pass the hand grenades over to Mohammed unobserved. He cautiously slid the four hand grenades in his shoulder bag as he slowly walked Farideh over to the long line of sinks. The moment he was standing by the sink, Mohammed left and quickly walked out of the bathroom.

Farideh washed his hands, and then he headed back to the larger handicapped stall still empty. This was so he could remove two more of the hidden grenades in private from the narrow oxygen tank. There were four of the larger handicapped stalls in the huge restroom area, and these stalls were usually open because there were not that many handicapped men waiting to watch the ballgame alive. Farideh went back in the stall he used moments before, and he repeated separating the cylinder and removed the next four hand grenades.

WEDNESDAY, MAY 18th, 2011, WASHINGTON D.C., SIXTEEN TWENTY HOURS. THE SEARCH TEAMS

Captain Robert Walker was riding down a side street in his altered heavy military humvee vehicle from Pennsylvania Avenue, when his radio suddenly went off. He had his small handheld radio stored in his breast pocket and had the speaker wire woven through the inside of his shirt, and the mike came out his right arm and rested in his hand. He raised his hand to his mouth as if he was biting a hanging string from the sleeve and barked in a whisper into the receiver. "Yeah, this is Dragon Fire Leader here, go with your fucking traffic, talker. Who's reporting in, dammit. Over."

"Dragon Fire Leader, this is Dragon Claw reporting in, sir. Man Walker, this is pure bullshit and bad manners out here if you were to ask me, Homes. We might as well be looking for a fucking needle in a damn cornfield for all the good it's doing us looking for these lousy little scumbags out here like this. I've been bumped into by so many of these damn civilian slobs around here that I'm gonna start knocking some of them the fuck outta my way with my foot. I'm telling ya Walker, I'm getting really sick and tired of..."

Walker cut the angry Mutt's complaint off in mid-sentence as he snapped at the other soldier. "Dragon Fire to Dragon Claw, stow your stinking bitch and you'll do no such thing against the damn civilians, dog man. I don't want ya to engage them under any circumstances, man.

Mutt, I understand this detail sucks shit outta a dead dog's ass. But this is the only thing we can do to try and find these little bastards before they hit us again…"

It was the Mutt's turn to interrupt Walker as he grumbled back at his Commanding Officer in a hot tone of voice. "Dragon Fire Leader, do you really think we're gonna happen to stumble over these lousy little fucks before they hit us again, by just walking round like we're a pack of stinking civilian pukes gawking at these marble shitting things around here? We gotta do something more than just walking around like this, man."

"I'm hoping the fucks kept going and by now, they're probably heading for the stinking Mexican border. So, they can get the hell outta our country before we nab their stinking asses, and level our revenge on their damn asses, man. But I'm gonna repeat my orders for the last time to you, dog man. I'm battling with the gut feeling something bad is gonna go down today, and since I feel that way. Every mother's son and daughter from our Units are gonna stay out in the stinking field until this fucking day's over with, man. No one is going back to our sub-station to get offa their feet for a minute, so get used to it man. Keep alert and stop your damn jaw jacking my ass will ya." Walker snapped at his friend.

"Well pardon my ass for stating my opinion to you, my friend." The Mutt replied angrily as he got upset with Walker.

"Dragon Claw, clear the net and keep your damn eyes opened for any signs of trouble, wiseass." Walker fired at the Mutt as he checked out a kid, he spotted fooling around by a garbage can. One look from Walker and the kid took off in a dead run from fear of the look.

A second buzz came in over Walker's radio, and he replied in a hiss as he rolled his eyes. "Dragon Fire Leader, go with your traffic Dragon Breath. Whatdaya got for me?" Walker was wondering why Sergeant Ramirez was trying to communicate. His first thought was she spotted something that aroused her interest.

"Dragon Breath to Dragon Fire Leader. Captain, I hate to agree with the Mutt on anything that comes out of his filthy mouth. But I must tell you, I feel the same way he does about what we're doing out here, sir. I think we're wasting our time trying to find the damn terrorists by just dumb chance in this maddening crowd of people, Bobby. What makes Command believe for one moment we might just happen across the effing people we're out here looking for, by just walking around on the streets of Washington? I think we'd have a better chance of getting hit by lightning than finding these lousy bastards this way, Walker."

"Thanks for backing my ass up like this, Raz. It's good to know you agree with me occasionally, baby sister. We are walking sandbags gotta stick together you know. We're the backbone of these specialized Units you know." The Mutt offered as he cut in on the conversation going on between Walker and Ramirez.

"Dragon Claw don't do me any favors keeping me trapped in that dirty thing you call your mind, buster. I don't want to be caught hanging around in your filthy mind for one second, mister. No telling what I might catch roaming around in there. Besides dog man, I thought Walker gave you orders, so why the hell are you still talking to me for…"

"You guys' betta knocks off the stinking fun and games and pay attention to what the fuck you're doing out here in the field. C'mon guys, things are starting to breakdown in drips and drabs around us, and I won't stand for it for a stinking second. You pukes have call names to ID yourselves with over the damn net, and to our uther Units. I'm warning everyone connected to this stinking operation, if anyone's caught not using the correct protocol, will be pulling extra duty when we break off surveillance in the streets of this fucking dump. Dragon Claw, break off and get back to work! Dragon Breath, I feel ya complaint but until our orders are changed, we're gonna follow them as if we have a stinking purpose for being out here, dammit. Do you have anything else to add to this damn conversation? Over."

"Dragon Breath to Dragon Fire, I have nothing to add to this conversation. I understand my orders and will carry them are as received. Out." Ramirez replied with a snap in her voice.

The young Marine Captain smiled as he shook his head, because he picked up the trace of anger lacing his girlfriend's tone, as she signed off on the communication. He continued to smile because he knew he was going to make it up to her when they were alone, and they could finally have a little private time together. He was as bored as the rest of his troops were, but he was going to carry out his orders until they were either changed for him, or they stumbled over the terrorists and eliminated them. His attention was brought back to his assignment when a car suddenly slammed on its brakes directly in front of his heavy humvee jeep and made awful sounds as the driver barely avoided an accident ahead of him by the skin on his teeth. The curses from both drivers replaced the screeching brakes, as the second driver drove away flipping off the other driver.

The captain checked his watch for the umpteenth time on this day. It was only half passed five and his stomach growled because he was so hungry. Sticking to his orders, he had no intention of breaking off his search for the terrorists, to get something to eat and some rest for him or the other members of his search teams. As ordered, the other soldiers of his teams checked in. Each soldier had orders to check in with their squad leaders every fifteen minutes, to make certain they were on full alert and following orders. This order was to be followed to inform Walker and his command his people were prepared and alert.

Walker listened as the others checked in with their squad leaders. He was please his people were staying on the top of their orders, even though he realized each trooper was suffering from sheer boredom and pure exhaustion, and their need for food and rest. There was not a worse detail for them than to pull surveillance. Time crawled by at a snail's pace, and the detail seemed to never end for the troops use to going into a hard-hitting operation with weapons blazing.

After breaking off his communication with Sergeant Ramirez, and listening to his other units checking in, Walker grumbled at his driver. "Dammit, how I hate this shit filled missions we always seem to get stuck with. Not only do I have to force my ass to remain alert. I also must make certain my troops are on the alert. Man, I'd take some punk ass puke shooting at my ass all day long, rather than pulling this shit filled boring ass duty one time. They couldn't train my stinking ass good enuf to like this kinda shit detail, dammit."

He drew in a breath then let it out in a sigh as he motioned his driver to pull onto a side street. Here, his attention was drawn to a small group of young black kids gathered around a park car. Two girls were busy speaking to the driver, while the passenger was speaking to another woman out his side window. He knew the boys were trying to pick up the girls. As his humvee passed the car, the driver mad dogged him and Walker smiled at the young kid, and then moved on.

Their humvee drove up to an intersection and the driver looked to Walker to see where he wanted to go next. He was as stiff as a board because he was sitting in the same seat since he first left the sub-station hours before. Shaking his head in disgust, he motioned the driver to turn left at the next intersection and continue the patrol down that road for a few blocks. He looked at the sky and noticed the first signs of night rapidly closing in. The sun was getting low, and the heat of the day was lessening. The traffic was picking up because the rush hour was starting to pick up in downtown Washington.

"Man Walker, I'd rather have my balls beaten flat with a wooden hammer than pull this surveillance crap again." Nintendo, (Sergeant Nakamura) the driver complained.

"I feel ya, sometimes life sucks the jelly outta your damn donut." Walker replied as he looked out the side window. He was searching for someone walking around a threat.

"Walker, can't we pull over and get out and stretch our legs a bit, man? I haven't heard jack shit from my feet in over a stinking hour now, man. What the hell's it gonna hurt if we take a few minutes for ourselves, who's to know?"

"You're starting to get on my stinking dick nerve buster, keep driving and keep your mouth shut…" Walker was pissed he was cut off by his driver but listened to his bitch anyway.

"C'mon Captain, I'm starving and I wanna get out and get my circulation going in my legs again, man. This detail sucks the big one man." Nentendo continued to complain.

"I'm warning you for the last time, buster! You're about to exceed the limits of my stinking medications, and you know how I get when that shit happens. Shut the fuck up and keep driving this damn thing, I can't shake the stinking feeling something heavy's gonna go down today, and until this stinking day ends. We're gonna stay on the damn hunt, and make sure nuthin goes down on our watch, fella." Walker warned his soldier and then he ripped his eyes from the driver of his humvee and looked out the side window of the machine again.

SIX O'CLOCK IN THE EARLY EVENING AT
THE BASEBALL TEAM STADIUM

Six o'clock was an odd start for a baseball game, but that was the starting time. The four young Arab attackers were bored to death waiting their time for the game to start. By the time the grenades were handed out to the other members of the Arab assault team, the attackers were in the stadium for three hours. Farideh used his time by trying to spot the other members of his team, but the stadium was a madhouse with waves of civilians moving and climbing over seats and trying to get comfortable for the start of the game. He gave up trying to locate the other members of his attack team, and he settled in and rose as everyone else in the stadium did, as the National Anthem started.

At the end there was a loud roar from the massive audience as four F-16 Falcons flew over the center of the stadium in tight formation. Then everyone sat as the players from the teams charged onto the field and took their positions. The umpires spoke to two players then he placed an iron mask on his face, bent down and sweep off homeplate and bellowed. "Play Ball!"

The umpire's words caused a second roar from the huge audience, as the pitcher threw the first ball to homeplate. The player from the Mets missed the ball, and that caused another roar from the crowd. By the end of the third inning, Farideh had to admit he was beginning to enjoy the game. This was the first one he ever witnessed, either on TV or in person. He was starting to figure out the game and the more he understood of it, the more he enjoyed it. He realized when he should stand and yell when a player from the Washington team did something good.

A man suddenly yelled in the isle next to him, and Farideh jumped over his voice. He did not understand what the man wanted, and when the vender offered a frankfurter on a bun, he took it and started to eat it. He stopped when the man put out his hand and wanted something from him. He looked at the angry man, and when he barked, he owed him seven dollars and fifty cents. He understood what he wanted and smiled as he fished in his pocket for the requested money. His moving almost caused one of the grenades to roll out of his pocket, but he was quick to secure it while handing the money over to the vender. When the man was paid off, he moved away calling out franks, and loudly barking like a dog. That was the only thing he did not understand, was why he barked like a dog as he walked off trying to sell more of his frankfurters.

Farideh enjoyed the frankfurter and started to look for the man, so he could order a second one. But the vender was so far away from him now and it was impossible to get his attention. Now his attention was split between watching the game and looking for the vender. It was not until the fifth inning the vender was near enough for him to get his attention, and he ordered a second and even a third frankfurter. The sixth inning went by quickly and the seventh started.

When the beginning of the seventh inning started, Farideh's attention was glued to the game and what was happening on the ballfield. Again, he tried to locate one of the other attackers from his team, but it was completely impossible to pick out any other member of his group. Now, with his attention glued on the ballgame, it seemed like the Mets players would not strike out, all they did was foul off balls and standing at the plate. The Mets scored three runs this inning and tied the game, and the first half of the seventh inning was taking fifteen minutes to play, and there was still only one out.

When another Met player slowly walked to first base Farideh grew angry, almost enough to begin his attack on the unsuspecting civilians enjoying the ballgame, and not wait for the break in the game as ordered. He had to restrain himself from starting the attack early, because he knew the other members of his assault team would follow their orders and wait until the end of the song 'America' the stadium always played at half time of the seventh inning. He reasoned he could not possibly start the attack early, because if he started and the others did not attack with him, by the time the others joined, many of their targets would be already out of the area. He understood he had to be patient and wait for the start of the second half of the seventh inning, if he wanted his attack to go off as planned, and all involved attacked at the same time.

Farideh looked at the clock it was eight thirty and quite dark. He could tell because it was an opened stadium and he knew once his attack started, the darkness would help conceal him and his other attackers when they made their escape from the stadium. He saw no problem with getting the attackers out of the arena after his attack was completed. Everything was working out in his favor, everything but for how long it was taking for the Mets to finally end their part of the seventh inning of the ballgame.

Finally, the Mets centerfielder made the last out of their part of the inning, and many of the people enjoying the game suddenly rose and stood, obviously waiting for the song to begin. The horde of venders was pushing their food and trinkets in hopes of making that last minute sale before the game ended. Many of the crowd rushed for the bathroom and other places in the stadium, while others spoke on cell phones, or they watched a replay of the last out of the long inning. Even Farideh rose while trying to locate one of his other attackers. It was still totally impossible for him to find at least one of the other attackers in the colossal crowd shoving anyone who came near the others standing.

The song started and even though Farideh did not know the words to the song, he remained standing on his feet and merely mouthed the words like he was singing along with the rest of the crowd. All the while he was faking singing, he continued searching the crowd in a hunt for any of his fellow attackers. The terrorist was so intent on locating another attacker that he did not realize the song ended. When the cheer from the crowd started, he was drawn back to reality and shook his head, trying to clear the troubling thoughts. Almost instinctively his mind willed his body to react, and he reached in his pocket and removed one of his grenades. He looked to his left as he pulled the pin and allowed it to fly in the direction he was looking. Instantly, there was a blinding hot flash and loud explosion, and chairs, people and body parts were tossed in the air from the force of the powerful little explosion.

Without hesitation Farideh turned right and removed the second grenade from his pocket. Like a robot going through the motions, he pulled the pin and tossed the second grenade twenty-five feet away from where he stood with the same results. There was a large explosion, followed by a blinding flash of heat and light, and then all hell broke out. He remained standing because he did not know what else to do, and then he scanned the interior of the stadium. He noticed more explosions in three other locations in the so-called nosebleed section of the massive stadium taking place. To his surprise, he noticed two explosions below the upper section, causing mass confusion and panic in the crowds in the lower seat section.

A series of deafening screams quickly filled the huge stadium, and because of the circular configuration of the arena, it kind of amplified the screams of the masses. The announcer was yelling over the mike as he questioned what was taking place. The ball players stood motionless on the field and in the dugouts, as they stared at the mayhem taking place with the civilians who moments ago were singing 'God Bless America'. The announcer watched in horror as thousands of men, women, and children charged for the down exits in a wild surge to try and escape the death taking place from the explosions. People fell or were pushed to the floor and then trampled on by the hordes of people scared and trying to flee the stadium and death.

It was impossible to tell what was happening in the bleacher seats as the eight explosions did what they were intended to accomplish during their attack. Killing many innocent civilians in the opening attack and then causing mass panic in the crowd who would react as al-Wahhad hoped they would to his terrorist attack against them.

AT THE SAFE HOUSE OF ABDULAZIZ AL-WAHHAD

The Arab terrorist leader called Shabbah, was glued to his TV as the first grenade exploded on the live feed. A huge grin of victory instantly crossed his lips, because as the first explosions took place. The field cameras turned to cover the attack area instead of the ballgame, and he was seeing in living color how his attack was being carried out by his people. His smile grew as he noticed a horde of civilians shoved, knocked, or jumping from the bleacher seats. The bodies crashing down on other civilians staring dumbly up at what was taking place above them, before reacting in mass confusion. The terrorist commander watched with great pleasure as the lower seating area civilians charged wildly for the already overcrowded exits of the stadium.

Hundreds, then thousands of civilians rapidly bunched up at the four main exits to the stadium. The mad rush to escape the death stalking them, started to crush people blocking the main exits, because the exits could not possibly handle the massive amounts of people trying to use them so quickly. Hundreds of mostly women and children were pushed by the hordes against concrete support walls, their chests crushed by the sheer weight pressed against their bodies. The sixteen elevators were impossible to get anywhere near with the mass mobs bunching up, all trying to get into the elevators for a fast exit from the arena. Sections of the hallways leading towards the exits became death traps that started when the first person fell in the walkway, causing many others to trip over his body, adding to the death rapidly mounting in the middle of the hallway.

Anywhere displayed on the live feed showed hundreds of civilians tripping over each other, and stomping the weak under foot, as the massive wave of humanity tried to flee the stadium. The announcer once happy to describe the play by play of the ballgame, was mortified over what was taking place in the arena with the fleeing masses. He searched his mind to do something to try and save some of the masses running wildly for the crammed-up exits. The announcer noticed a man wearing a Marine tee shirt displaying the devil dog emblem and missing his right arm, was trying to divert several the crazed civilians out of the death zone.

The announcer realized what the obviously ex-soldier was trying to do, and he picked up his mike and opened it to the speaker system surrounding the building. He screamed in the mike. "People, people, people, don't try to get out of any exits, they are all blocked. Turn around and run for the opened ballfield. Gather on the field and wait there until this emergency is over. Please, run for the open field and safety. If you run for the exits, you're going to trample each other to death. Go to the field and wait for further instructions."

The disabled soldier turned to where the announcers were stationed in the press box, and he gave the thumbs up signal to them as he pressed his attempt to turn many of the civilians towards the ballfield. Slowly, some then more civilians began to listen to the soldier and announcer, and they ran for the open field. Quickly, the infield was overflowing with civilians gathering with men taking up protective positions around the women and children and prepared to attack anyone who attacked them.

As is the case in times of emergencies, men and women stopped worrying about their own wellbeing, and they started to look after the dead, dying, and injured. As the smoke from the explosions started to settle down, order began to return and the injured started getting help. Outside the stadium it was still sheer mayhem, with the injured collapsing in the parking lot, and speeding cars doing their best to try and avoid running over the downed civilians, as the drivers tried to get safely out of the area.

DELTA MILITARY SUB-STATION

Colonel Bruce Leadbetter had a small TV on, and he was trying to watch some of the ballgame as he continued to keep his troops working in the field on the ball and moving. A second soldier was the one who sounded the alarm when he called out to the rest of the soldiers in the sub-station. "Holy shit, I think there was some kinda fucking explosion inside the fucking ballpark."

The Colonel turned to see what the other soldier was crying about and happened to glance at the TV at the same time, and he instantly froze in his tracks, as he watched the wild mayhem taking place on the set. He picked up people falling out of the bleacher area and other hordes of civilians running wildly in all directions in the stadium. He focused on the TV and reached for his mike and keyed it at the same time, and then he growled into the radio to his search teams doing their duty out in the field.

"Dragon Lair to all search teams in the field. Dragon Lair to Dragon Fire Leader, come in this shit is important. Over!"

"Dragon Fire to Dragon Lair, go with your traffic. To all Dragon Fire Units, pay attention, we obviously have a flash message coming in from Command. Go Dragon Lair."

"You're correct Dragon Fire Leader, you and the other search Units are instructed to head for the damn baseball stadium. From the look of it, it seems our party has just sent us another message. I want your Units at this damn ballfield to see what the fuck you people can do about finding the senders of this message. I want to talk to them."

"Dragon Fire to Dragon Lair, I copy all, and am sending all search teams to the ballfield immediately, sir. Over!" Walker replied to his Commander in an angry voice.

"I'm not done with you yet Dragon Fire Leader. Captain Walker, this one look bad, real bad sir, far worse than the twin hits up there in New York City earlier this week. From what I was able to pick up live on the fucking TV, I spotted many dead, many injured in this latest attack. The lousy bastards knew how to hit us with this one, and they hit us hard,

Captain. They had the damn civilians trapped inside the damn stadium, and when they popped off their damn explosives, the civilians weren't able to get out of the area without causing more death and injuries than the explosives caused, sir..."

"Dragon Fire to Dragon Lair, do you have any idea what type of explosives were employed against the civilians at the ballgame, sir?" Walker asked, starved for information.

"You're damn lucky I have more important things on my mind than getting heated over you are interrupting my ass like this, mister. No, there has been no determination as to what kind of explosives the lousy pricks used in their attack this time around yet. However, since I was able to witness some of it on the TV live feed. I have the mind to believe the explosives were definitely grenades, or a form of explosive made to resemble a damn grenade, and the death that type of explosive would cause packed together bunch of damn civilians." Colonel Leadbetter offered as he kept his eyes glued to the TV, so he could keep up to date on what was happening on the live feed while still speaking with Walker. As the Colonel continued to watch the TV, he picked up something that caused him concern, and he growled at Walker. "Hang on a moment Dragon Fire Leader."

"Roger that last Dragon Lair." Walker replied as he backed off some on the Colonel.

Colonel Leadbetter concentrated his full attention on the TV, and what he picked up made him feel a little better over the present situation. On the set he spotted the skull with the extended top jaw that was the adopted patch of SEAL Team One. Now he understood the powers in command, decided it was wise to have the elite assault team working at this baseball stadium, in case of a terrorist attack. He understood if the SEAL Team One was at this event, then there was a good bet the other members of the Specialized Units were also being employed at sporting or other gathering events throughout the United States.

He was just about to go back to Walker when he picked up another member of one of these Units moving around in the crowd. His patch was the skull and long top jaw, but this soldier's patch was in a green field. The Colonel realized not only members from SEAL Team One were there. The green field meant members from SEAL Team Five were also assigned to protect the civilians at the ballfield.

CHAPTER TWENTY

"Errr…Dragon Fire, evidently members from SEAL Team One and Five were assigned to the protection of the civilians at the ball gam…"

"Jesus Christ Almighty Colonel, if that's a fact sir, then how the hell did the rotten bastards get their stinking attack off the damn ground against us, sir?" Walker growled, venting his anger as he went on with his complaint to his Commanding Officer. "Dragon Lair, if those soldiers were there, the terrorists shoulda been spotted and killed, long before they were able to begin their attack against the stadium, sir. Those damn troops shoulda been on the terrorists like flies on a stinking turd. Dammit…"

Colonel Leadbetter interrupted his angry Captain as he offered the young military officer. "Dragon Fire Leader, you know as well as I do that those elite soldiers were there to protect the civilians from a frontal all out wild assault from a possible terrorist action aimed at the masses. Those soldiers were assigned to the inside of the damn stadium as backup units, and they're armed with probably MP-5s, and they were ready to hit any terrorist attacking the crowd with live weapon's fire, mister."

"Yeah, right, okay Dragon Lair, you're correct Colonel. I was kinda grasping at straws I guess, sir." Walker replied as he let his breath out in a rush of angry air.

"I understand your frustration Dragon Fire Leader. I feel the same way, dammit. Enough of this bullshitting Captain get your damn people over to the stadium A-SAP, sir. Dragon Fire, you better display your shields so you'll be afforded easy access to the damn arena, and that shield will give you access to every location, even the attacked areas. Get going mister!" Colonel Leadbetter ordered as he broke off his communication with is angry Captain, and then he turned back to what was still going on at the stadium on the TV.

"Dragon Fire Leader to Dragon Lair, I have a question before I break off communications with you sir." Walker grumbled into the radio.

"Go with your question Dragon Fire Leader." Colonel Leadbetter replied.

"Dragon Lair, do you have a number on the civilians in the stadium at the time of attack?"

Colonel Leadbetter turned to CoCo-G, (Sergeant Milton Pettibone) and waited for a reply from this soldier before he reported to his Captain.

The soldier grabbed a paper, and he quickly ran his finger down the long list, and then he offered to his Commander. "Colonel Leadbetter Sir, it states here that the stinking stadium can accommodate a crowd of up to sixty-five thousand civilian pukes sir, and that number doesn't include the damn stadium staff, personnel, and people who hawk their damn wares in the stadium, or their security people working there either, sir. Nor does that number consider the TV and broadcasting and their support people, nor does it consider any illegal's that might have snuck into the damn stadium, sir."

"Shit, okay, Dragon Lair to Dragon Fire Leader. Mark the number down as a helluva lot of civilians and let it go at that. Over." The Colonel reported to Walker.

"Dragon Fire to Dragon Lair. Understood last, am heading for the ball stadium. Out."

As Walker signed off with his Commanding Officer, Colonel Leadbetter leaned a little closer to the TV and watched as a flood of Washington Police Officers started to pour onto the field, and then the officers circled the civilians gathering on it. It was obvious the officers were taking a protective stance around the civilians, as they tried to comfort each other. The officers were watching the stands and pushing civilians running onto the field passed them. This was so the officers could continue watching the stands to make certain whoever attacked them, did not hurt the civilians on the ballfield under their protection. Suddenly, the feed went dead, and the fuming Colonel found himself staring at a black screen, and he roared in anger.

"God dammit, the jerks dropped the damn feed, the flaming idiots. Okay mount up people because we're all heading for the stadium pronto. Arm and make certain you people have your damn ID shields on your person, or you'll not be allowed into the damn park. Get a move on it, before I start to take names and numbers on you pack of screaming squirrels." Colonel Leadbetter gave the TV one last look and a color pattern now displayed with stand by printed on it. The colonel had to restrain from kicking the set as he ran after his troops.

CAPTAIN WALKER'S COMMAND
VEHICLE, WASHINGTON D.C.
WEDNESDAY, MAY 18th, 2011, TWENTY-
ONE TEN HUNDRED HOURS

Captain Robert Walker glanced at his watch, it was nine ten p.m., and the Washington traffic was light. He just ended the communication with Colonel Leadbetter, and he keyed his GPS to find the fastest route to the ballfield. Locating it he barked in his mike. "Dragon Fire Leader to Dragon Claw and Dragon Breath, all Units connected to your search teams are instructed to head for GPS coordinates R, One, Three, Three by W, Niner, Niner, Eight. We have a terrorist situation going down at the ballfield, and we're instructed to lend a hand. Our Units are in Command of this situation and all rescue investigations and capture of said terrorists is up to us, people. We'll coordinate efforts with the Washington Police Departments, FBI, CIA, or any other Intelligence Agencies at work at the new incident area.

"I want all responding Units to remember this order at all times while we're assisting in investigating this latest terrorist incident. We're in this mess together, and by working together we're gonna find the lousy scumbags who attacked us and bring them to justice. I don't want any bickering between emergency responders and our Units. Any infractions to this order will be dealt with by me, and I'm warning you pack of puds. If I receive any complaints about you gun bunnies, I'll handle that complaint personally, and I promise. You guys won't enjoy what I'll do to you if I receive any gripes about your reactions. Read me guys?"

"Loud and clear." Was replied by the two squad leaders over their radio units.

"Good then let's get a stinking move it people, we have a friggin terrorist situation on our hands we have to attend to but quick." Captain

Walker replied and then he slapped Nentendo on his back and snapped at his driver. "Get my ass over to this damn ballfield so we can see what the fuck's happening there. You know the damn Colonel's on his way there already, and I wanna beat his stinking ass there, or there's gonna be hell to pay."

Walker leaned back as Nentendo picked up the soldiers assigned to his vehicle. When he had them in his machine, Nentendo headed for the field as fast as the heavy military vehicle could travel and the traffic would allow.

As Walker's vehicle rapidly closed in on the ballfield, the civilian traffic leading away from the field was heavier and heavier. Quickly, about everywhere he looked, he noticed several car accidents, some serious but mostly just fender benders. Mixed in with the traffic were a horde of emergency responding vehicles, police cars, and firefighting equipment. The traffic coming from the ballfield was seriously interfering with the emergency responders trying to get to the stadium. A line of military vehicles suddenly appeared behind Walker's humvees. The trucks quickly linked up with his machines because the captain had emergency lights and sirens to move the civilian traffic out of his way. Nentendo noticed the trailing vehicles were Army, and he quickly informed Walker of that fact.

Seeing the height of the stadium in the distance, Walker braced himself for the mayhem he was certain was surrounding the area. He was not disappointed, because the parking lot of the stadium was a mass of confusion. There were hundreds of injured people sitting, or lying on the ground, and they were being looked after by the flood of emergency workers rapidly descending on the incident area from all directions. Hundreds of civilians were piled in one section of the massive parking lot. Those were the ones who died of injuries when they were taken out of the stadium, many of the dead were displaying terrible signs of being crushed to death.

Nentendo weaved his Humvee between a few parked vehicles and the people helping the injured on the ground. Walker ordered his driver to head for the main entrance to the arena. This section was guarded by a heavy police presence, and they did not look friendly. As Walker's vehicles pulled up in front of a group of fifteen police officers, they immediately surrounded his vehicle and a Commander ordered Walker to have his vehicles move out of the way.

Walker jumped out of the machine and flashed his military shield, informing the police officer challenging him he was there under direct orders from the Pentagon. Seeing the shield and recognizing what it meant, the Commander stepped aside and began to fill Walker in on everything he knew of the terrorist attack.

The police commander led the way for Walker and the rest of his Tier One troops, as he cleared them to enter the stadium with the other police officers who assumed security of the arena. By the time Walker's people arrived at the incident site, most of the civilians who could move under their own power, were kind of just milling about outside the huge structure. His troops carried weapons hidden in their backpacks, and the soldiers were ready to protect them, or anyone else who might be placed in their charge.

Everywhere Walker looked, he noticed a civilian either sitting or lying on the ground. Many were bleeding from injuries. A few people badly hurt and still inside the stadium were not being looked after for their injuries by emergency responders.

Walker looked up at the massive structure and could still see a thick cloud of smoke still hovering over it. Then he turned to his snipers, the Ghost and Hunter, and ordered Sergeant Casper. "Ghost, I want you and Hunter to work your way into this dump. Get up to the best perch possible to report a good AA (Area Assessment) so I know what the fuck's going on, and what we might be facing, and if any attackers are still trapped inside this stinking place. Roach!" Walker growled as he turned to Sergeant David Burgwald.

"I want you to take errr…Three Martines (Sergeant Cheryl Grantham) and get over to the damn security station of this dump and scan the tapes of the fucking ballgame. Watch them carefully and try and pick out any of the lousy pricks that might have pulled this damn attack off against us. With all the damn cameras working the stinking ballgame, one of the damn things hadta have picked up a few of the damn terrorists. Errr… Shot Gun, (Sergeant Dennis Sassano) take Small Change (Sergeant Edward London) with you and get your asses over to any stadium TV broadcasting areas and have them play back their damn tapes for ya. See if you two birds can pick out any of the terrorists. You have orders so move it…"

"Wait a minute, who the hell are you people, and what the hell makes you people think for one second that I'm going to allow any of you guys to step on the toes of my police officers, already working this damn situation, mister? In case you're unaware of its buddy. My department is in Command of this present situation until the FBI comes along, and they take Command of the damn investigation from us, fella." A second Police Commander moved forward, and he growled as he puffed up his chest to make himself look larger than he was. He placed his hands on his hips and glared angrily at Walker.

"Look pal I'm not gonna get in a pissing contest with your stinking ass over who you think is in Command of this fucking mess, buddy. I have orders and they come directly from the Pentagon Command Center, mister. This is my shield, and it comes from Homeland Defense, and in case you're unaware of it yet, my friend. This stinking shield gives me Command over you and your entire damn police department, buddy. We even have Command over the stinking FBI, if we have to override their friggin orders or actions. Now if you wanna continue standing in my way then you and your friend's betta be prepared to be walked over. Commander, I understand this is a terrible terrorist incident, and the number of dead will be staggering from their attack as far as I can see from here. But we're on the same side here sir, and we all hafta work together if we wanna get to the bottom of this damn incident.

"Commander, why don't you do what you guys do best and take care of the injured and crowd control and work with my troops. From what I can see where I'm standing, we have a shitload of stinking civilians walking around in a stupor, and they can be tramping over crucial evidence we need to help ID the lousy bastards who pulled this attack off against us, sir. Your guys hafta take control over them and get the damn civilians the hell away from the damn stadium. Commander, we might have some of the stinking attackers still trapped inside the dump, and if my people come across any of them and we get involved in a firefight. The civilians still walking around this dump could be caught up in the crossfire, and I don't wanna add to the dead and injured civilians, sir." Walker stopped speaking and stared at the officer while waiting for his reply.

The still rather angry and excited Police Commander took a long look at the shield Walker shoved in his face, and understood this young soldier had Command of the incident as he let out his breath in a rush, and then he replied to the young and angry looking soldier. "Yes, sir I see what you mean Captain, but the next time you want to take Command of my police officers. I suggest you wear your damn military uniforms with your rank pinned on your arm, so I know who the hell I'm speaking with, sir…"

"Sorry Commander and allow me to introduce myself to you sir. I'm Captain Robert Walker, and I'm in Command of the Dragon Fire troops, sir…"

"I've already been briefed in advance about your specialized Unit, Captain. I'm aware Dragon Fire Units have carte blanche to deal with any possible terrorist situation we encounter, sir. I wished to hell your Command took the damn time to inform my people your Units were working over this damn area, sir. Captain Walker, with the knowledge your Units are on this attack, makes me feel a helluva lot better about this damn situation, sir." The Commander offered in a calm voice as he interrupted Walker.

"Commander, I'd like to continue to jaw jack with your stinking ass all day long sir, but I hafta get my troops moving in there immediately sir. Are my people gonna have any further problems with the rest of your guys you have operating inside there, sir? As you already stated to me ass sir, you're aware of my RRU (Rapid Response Units) and our orders, sir. I can't have your people interfering with my actions once I disperse my troops inside the damn stadium, and we start to check out what happened in there, sir."

"Captain Walker, I'll clear it with my fellow Officers to give your troops with these shields top clearance to go anywhere in the damn stadium, sir. I'll cut orders to my Officers they're to lend any assistance to your troops they may need, right down to working with your soldiers during this investigation if needed, sir."

"That's good to hear Commander, now can I get my damn Vipers inside the stinking stadium, sir. So, they can start searching for any possible terrorists still hiding inside the structure, sir?"

"Vipers, Captain?" The Commander asked with concern.

"Sorry Commander, by Vipers I mean my Unit's Snipers, sir. Before you allow your shit to get hot on ya, yes, they're Snipers but they're going inside the damn arena, sir. The soldiers will employ their Sniper training to try and locate any possible terrorists still alive and hiding in there, sir.

My Vipers aren't going in there to use weapons to kill anyone inside the arena, sir. Unless Commander, the ones they pick up become a threat to my troops, or the civilians or emergency responders working inside the damn structure, sir." Walker offered as he made a quick head movement, and his Vipers immediately moved out.

Walker watched out of the corner of his eye as the Ghost and the Hunter walked up to the police officers protecting the entrance to the stadium. He allowed himself to relax when the officers moved aside, and they allowed his advance soldiers to enter the mayhem still raging inside the building.

"Captain Walker, are your troops going to be moving around with their weapons exposed inside the arena, sir? I'd have to caution you to have your troops conceal their weapons while they are working inside the stadium, sir." The Commander asked with concern.

"C'mon Commander, none of my stinking troops will be carrying their damn weapons out in the open exposed, sir. I don't need them scaring the shit outta the injured or the damn civilians still trying to get the fuck outta the damn structure, or even any of the emergency workers in there, Sir. The troops won't carry any weapons in the open for another reason, sir. I don't need the lousy reporters detecting and identifying any of my guys, because they were picked up by their damn cameras as they scan the incident area, sir. My soldiers have the weapons they need hidden in their backpacks, to end any possible predicament they might stumble into, Commander. Now if you'll excuse my ass Commander, I have several troops I hafta get in motion, sir. I issued orders, and I hafta make certain they're being carried out properly as ordered, sir. By your leave Commander!" Walker remarked and then looked at the officer.

The Police Commander nodded as he stepped aside and allowed Walker and his soldiers to charge past him. He watched with anger as Walker and his troops rushed through the rail system. He kept watching until the elite group of soldiers rapidly disappeared inside the structure.

Walker and his troops had to shove several stunned civilians out of their way, as the specialized soldiers quickly worked their way deeper into the craziness still taking place inside the stadium. He was concerned there were still many civilians walking around, and they were already getting in his soldier's way, and it was going to be only a matter of time before an incident took place because of the masses and his troops.

When Walker's group reached the concession stand on the second floor of the stadium, he made certain the soldiers he ordered to check out the security room, along with the troops he wanted to check out the TV stations, to see if their cameras might have picked up any of the terrorists, were carrying out their orders. As he and several his troops loosely gathered around the concession area, a man and woman rapidly walked past them. The concerned and alert Marine Captain made eye contact with the man, as the two people rushed by him. He continued to stare at them, because the man did not seem to upset by what just took place inside the stadium. For a fleeting second, he almost stopped the man.

Farideh looked into the eyes of the stranger staring so intensely at him, and it caused him immediate alarm. Not wanting to get stopped by this stranger who he felt had something to do with the security of the stadium just by the way he stood in the mist of the others obviously with him. Fear suddenly filled his mind, and he did the only thing he could think of doing. He gave the man a weak smile and a quick nod.

The intensity in Walker's stare left him the moment the other man nodded at him, and he returned the slight nod with one of his own.

Farideh then increased his pace out of the stadium, mainly because of the look he had received from the stranger. Once outside the stadium, the two young Arab attackers headed for their car. He was stunned by the lack of civilian vehicles still parked in the massive lot. Fighting the want to leave the area immediately, Farideh leaned against the side of his SUV for a moment, and he tapped out a cigarette, lit it and took a drag.

He did not bother to see if Maha wanted to enjoy one with him, as they settled in and waited for Mohammed and Farima to link back up with them.

It was due to the agreement on where Maha was instructed by Farideh to wait for him that he was able to locate her in all the confusion still taking place inside the massive baseball stadium. The reason Captain Walker did not challenge Farideh, was because the man was walking with a woman. That made him quickly lose interest in the guy, because he never believed any Arab terrorists would be in the presence of a female on an attack, nor did he believe a woman would be part of the terrorist cell either.

Farideh flipped the cigarette at the ground and stepped it out as he fought to get control over his rampaging emotions, as he stared at the main entrance to the structure. He shook his head in disgust, because there was still a heavy flow of people still rushing out of the arena. There were so many civilians hanging around and still pouring out of the building, it was impossible to detect the other members of his group, when they came out of the damaged structure. Farideh continued to stare at the entrance as he allowed a smile to cross his lips, because he witnessed the police moving the civilians away from the building.

Detecting his concern, Maha moved a little closer to her ally and she whispered low to him. "It will not be long before we enjoy the beautiful gardens of Allah again, my Arab brother. The vastness of the desert is where we'll lose ourselves, as the cursed world searches for us. Take faith in His sacred word Farideh, Mohammed and Farima will be along shortly, and then we can finally leave this foul heartbeat of Satan."

Still trying to make Farideh feel better, Maha rubbed her breast against his arm. This made the Arab break off his trance of staring at the stadium, and he looked Maha in her beautiful eyes.

In the confusion still taking place inside the damaged stadium, Taborzadi finally rose to his feet as this section of the bleachers rapidly emptied out, and only a few injured and helping civilians were left in the area. As Mohammed stood, the brazing terrorist took time to straighten out his shirt and pants, before heading for the bathroom on this level. The restroom was between where he was seated and where Farima was placed. He left instructions for her to meet him there as soon as she was able to arrive there.

As Mohammed walked to this section he was hit with a flash of anger, because Farima was nowhere to be seen. Here, there were many civilians still milling about and getting in his way and shoving each other. Fighting to maintain control over his anger and ordering his feet to remain still. He waited for his fellow attacker to arrive, so they could leave the arena together. Then link back up with the other Islamic terrorists waiting for them by their vehicle.

Mohammed was trying to act as cool as a cucumber while waiting for Farima to arrive at his side. He stood near a crowd of overly excited people, many women were crying, and some were protecting their children. A few other women were trying to hide behind their husbands or boyfriends, as they waited for someone to tell them what to do next. From where he stood, Mohammed was able to see the ballfield and he smirked. He noticed hundreds and maybe even thousands of civilians standing, sitting, or lying down on the grass field.

More anger filled him, because seeing so many civilians he wanted to kill on the grass, made him feel his attack had failed. He cursed because he only had two grenades, if he had more, he would have surely killed many more fools enjoying the game.

Someone accidently bumped into him, and this broke his concentration, and he looked angrily at the young woman. The terrible look on his face and burning eyes, made the young lady take a step back in cold fear of this man glaring so angrily at her. Then she placed distance between her and the stranger.

Walker waited for the soldiers to carry out his orders. He had no idea where the Ghost and Hunter took up their positions inside the stadium. But he was confident the two usual point men, were carrying out his orders. The Mutt moved over to Walker's side and bitched at Ramirez.

"Hey man its Malice in Wonderland. Whatdaya wanna fucking do oh fearless leader of mine?" The Mutt added as he turned his attention to his Commander.

"Huh, here comes the King of Slim Square. What do you want from the two of us, mister? You have troops under your Command that you have to look after, Frankie." Ramirez fired back at the Mutt.

"No screwing round Walker, whatdaya wanna do now, man? We got one helluva stinking mess on our hands in here. Say Walker not for nuthin man, but I got a strong gut friggin feeling the damn terrorists are still inside this dump."

"I'm fighting the same feeling, buddy." Captain Walker offered as he drew in some air, and then added to his words to his fellow soldier. "If I was one of the lousy bastards, I'd wait until more civilians got outta the damn stadium, and it was safer for them to move around. We gotta keep our damn eyes peels and look for anyone outta place, or not as scared as they should look afta an attack like this one, man. I don't know how so many stinking civilians got the hell out on the damn field, but if someone directed them there then that one saved a helluva lotta lives. Did anyone pick up what kinda explosives were involved in this attack?"

"Walker, didn't old what's his puss, the stinking Colonel say he thought the explosives were grenades? I believe you told me you thought they were grenades the terrorists used during this attack, Captain." Blood Clot, Sergeant Richard Burnbach, offered as he moved closer to Walker.

"Yeah, that's right so knowing that isn't gonna help us out much, I guess. Shit even my kid could find grenades for sale in this country. Well, I know we hafta get up to where the damn explosions took place and start our search from that area. That's as gooda place as any to start our hunt for any stinking evidence and possible terrorists still hiding in this stinking dump. I believe most of the damn explosions took place in the nosebleed section of the damn stadium. So, we might as well work our way up there. Raz, I want you to keep in contact with both search teams I sent to gather information on the possible identity of the damn attackers. If the soldiers discover something, I wanna know 'bout it toots sweet." Walker smiled at his girlfriend.

"You got it Captain. If something turns up, you'll know about it that quick." Sergeant Ramirez replied as she returned Walker's smile.

Walker took the lead and started to work his way deeper into the arena. As they moved, it was easy to see the soldiers were getting upset by the heavy number of dead and injured civilians they saw lying on the floor or leaning against the walls waiting for help. Men, women, and children were down and dying. The first area Walker headed for was the elevators, but there were so many downed civilians in that area, he changed direction and headed for the up stairway. He was hit with the same situation with one difference. There were countless civilians suffering, slowly dying, or dead they had to step over to make it up to the next level of the stadium.

The Mutt was furious, there were so many civilians suffering that he was having a serious problem keeping his temper under control. He was slowly moving behind Walker as he struggled and watched where he placed his feet on the steps, so he did not step on some of the injured. Sergeant Ramirez was moving right behind the Mutt, and she detected his anger and moved past him and got up to Walker's side and warned her lover.

"Walker, when was the last time you checked on the pain in the ass Mutt?"

"Now why the hell do I hafta check on his ass for? I'm having enuf trouble trying not to step on any these downed people, for the love of the good Christ Child." Walker grumbled as he watched where he was walking, as he headed for the second level of the stadium.

"Walker, I think when we get up to the next landing, you better call for a quick break and check on the Mutt for a minute. I just looked at his face, and the way he's hunch up and so red in the face, scared the hell out of me, Robert. I noticed anger in his motions I never saw before, Bobby. I'm getting really concerned over his condition and what he might do if he finally pops off on us. I must admit Walker, seeing so many downed civilians are turning my stomach sick, and making me as angry as hell over the damn situation, and I can only imagine what it's doing to the dog man. He's such a passionate man to deal with and his need to protect the innocent all the time, Robert." Sergeant Ramirez warned the captain with concern lacing her voice as they reached the second landing.

Walker looked back at the Mutt's face as he quickly caught up to him. He easily read what was troubling Ramirez, and he snapped at the Mutt as that soldier drew in some air, and then he rapidly shook his hands to try and get his circulation going again. "Are you okay my friend? You look like shit warmed over, buddy."

"Thanks for the friggin condition report on my stinking ass, fucker. How the fuck do you think I'm fricking doing over seeing all this crap I'm walking over, man? It seems everywhere I look I see a horde of downed civilians, people from my damn country, man. People I might know or even went to friggin school wit, dead or dying at my stinking feet, man. I want fucking blood! Someone is gonna pay big time for this shit I'm seeing I tell ya man." The Mutt growled savagely at Walker as he looked at the body of a young woman on the floor.

Walker rested his hand lightly on his friend's back as he offered calmly to him. "I feel ya and I'm with ya man. It's like you said man, someone's gonna pay big time for this stinking attack, buddy. You wanna take a little break, or you wanna get to where the attack started, so we can see what we discover up there, buddy? I wanna see if we might be able to trap one or more damn terrorists, I believe are still hiding their asses inside this stinking dump. The best way to leave an attack area is to wait until the dust settled, and the emergency responders are doing their act and not looking for the scumbags who carried out this attack."

"Fuck the damn break Walker I wanna get my stinking hands on one of these sonofa fucking bitches. I'm telling ya buddy, by the time I finish interrogating the lousy little creeps. I won't leave enuf behind for the stinking bleeding hearts to try and protect. There won't be any complaint of water boarding or harsh interrogations; just a pile of raw red meat left for the uthers to pick over." The Mutt snorted nastily as he looked at a second woman's body crumpled on the ground, and he could tell she was trampled to death.

"Yeah, I wanna continue for the fucking bleachers without a stinking break. I wanna see what the fuck went on up there, and what we might find out about the damn terrorists and how they attacked us. I want the bastards so much they're actually leaving a bad fricking taste in my stinking mouth." Walker complained bitterly.

"Look, there are too many of us to get up the same stinking stairwell safely. I want half you guys to split off and head for the other exit and work your way up those stinking stairwells for the bleacher area. We know from the reports that the stinking terrorists carried out this fricking attack from the bleacher area. So that'll be our best bet of finding any evidence on who the lousy cocksuckers might be. Raz, I want you to control the second group of our people, get them up to the stinking bleachers. I'll take the rest of the troops with my ass." Walker smiled and it was right because the smile sparked Ramirez in action.

"Okay, you know who's assigned to my group, gather round and follow my lead." Sergeant Ramirez offered then she waited for her group to surround her.

Walker watched Ramirez and the other soldiers fall in line behind her, they followed her without hesitation. When she was out of his sight, he continued working his way up to the second stairwell leading to the bleachers. The closer they got to the bleacher area, the more downed civilians they came across. No matter how hard his heart grew over the death and destruction he came across during his many years in the service. The death of a child always got to him, and there were quite a few dead and severely injured children he was coming across.

The closer to the bleachers the troops got, the more bodies Walker found bunched up on the stairwells and entrance sections to the stairwells. The soft moans coming from several injured were getting to his mind. Each time he heard a moan, he looked in that direction and what he saw turned his stomach, and that increased the anger and hatred he was fighting, for the people who caused the death in the arena. Being the soldier he was, he refused to allow the carnage to stop him from carrying out his orders to find and stop the terrorists before they hit again. At last, he was able to finally see the sky above his head through the stairwell, and knew he was about to come out in the bleachers.

Even though there was a wide roof structure covering half the bleacher area. The way the stairwell came out in this section of the stadium, showed the open air overhead as Walker was the first one to break out into the bleacher area. Scanning the area, he immediately picked up the section that had a good number of seats dislodged and ripped away by the force of the grenades exploding. He realized where the grenade exploded, and he headed right for that spot. The rest of the soldiers with him followed his lead, and they headed for the same place.

Walker was fuming over what he found when he reached the spot where the grenades exploded. Blood, body parts and dead scattered about twenty feet of the area. Further out were more civilians lying on the floor and spewed over the back of the chairs, suffering ripped open wounds. One lady he figured was about nineteen had her stomach split open, and she was sitting on the floor holding her intestines and looking at him with pleading eyes for help.

"Blood Clot, get your stinking ass over here on the double quick and start helping out this poor kid will ya, dammit!" Walker swallowed hard and then bellowed angrily for his medic to work on the injured lady. But there were a lot more than this one person hurt in the multi patient incident area, and Blood Clot was unable to help all the injured in this section.

Siberia, Sergeant Taras Zarugnaya, one of the three female Russian soldiers on loan to the Rapid Response Force. Moved up and they gave Blood Clot a hand working on some of the injured, two other soldiers who had some medical experience, moved in, and helped also. The rest of the other soldiers quickly fanned out as if they had a purpose, and they started to search for evidence on the terrorists.

Sergeant Dorothy Ramirez and her group moved as quickly as they could amidst the countless injured and dying semi-blocking her way while heading for the second staircase. She was trying her best to keep her eyes peeled for any sign of someone looking suspicious. The stairway she was aiming for was so crowded with civilian injured and dead from the wild stamped, it was almost impossible for her and the other troops with her to get up this stairwell safely. Knowing her way around most stadiums, the female Sergeant led her troops to the far end of the arena, and there they started to work up this less crowded stairwell.

It was a good break for the female Sergeant, because as she got to the landing of the bleacher area. She immediately noticed a man who seemed more angry than scared, and she aimed her attention on him, as she slowed her pace and watched every move he made. As she kept her attention glued to him, she felt he was hanging around waiting for someone to meet him, and she started to think that might be the reason for his anger more than fear. The more she looked at this man, the more she felt there was something bugging her about him.

When Mohammed Taborzadi turned sideways and Sergeant Ramirez got a strong look at his profile, she instantly realized what was drawing her attention to him. Seeing the size of his nose and other features of his handsome face, she immediately recognized this man had to be from the Middle East. Putting the hubbub about the racial profiling thing over the Arab nationality aside, she decided she was going to keep this man under her constant surveillance. She held up and waved her hand the other troops behind her past her, as calmly as she could move them away from her position.

Once the troops moved away from her without question, Ramirez took up a position by a wide concrete support column. There she rested her back against it like she was spent and looked at the man out of the corner of her eye. She wanted to see who he was waiting for, so she could speak to them both at the same time.

The other soldiers kept moving until they were out of the way. Then they held up and waited for their Sergeant to link back up with them. The large soldier branded No Neck took command of the rest of Ramirez's troops, and when they were out of the way. He held them up and moved them to a position where he could keep Ramirez in his field of vision. They were so well trained and used to each other's actions that the troopers knew Ramirez spotted something or one that drew her attention. Without being ordered, they took a backup stance, in case their Sergeant got into a firefight with whoever had drawn her attention to them. The troops did not want the Sergeant going against someone without their backup for support of her actions.

Neck was joined by the other massive soldier branded Buckethead, who got behind Neck's back and whispered at him. "What the fuck you got going down man?"

"Beats the fuck outta my stinking ass man, alls I know is Ramirez went in fucking hunt mode man, and that's enuf to know she's on to someone or thing, buddy. Man, look at that stinking chick work out there will ya. I got it man she's eyeing that stinking little puke standing over there by the sign of some crap soda. I can read her eyes from here. She's hot and glued to that fucking dude's ass like a tick to a hound dog's backside, man." Neck warned as he kept Ramirez locked up in his gaze.

"What's so special about that stinking little turd, he looks normal enuf to my ass, Neck?" Buckethead replied as he stretched his neck out to get a better look at the man causing Ramirez all the concern.

"You betta take a second look at that stinking little cocksucker big man. I can see why Ramirez locked onto his stinking ass easy enuf. He looks like he just walked outta the fucking desert, man. Look at his fricking legs, they're still fucking bent from riding his damn camel." Neck complained at the other soldier.

"He looks like anyone else running around like a stinking chicken with their heads cut off in this dump, man. I say Ramirez is picking on the little prick because he got a damn good tan and a big snot (nose)." Buckethead replied as he looked at the man in question again.

"That's why no one's asking your fat ass about anything in case you haven't noticed it yet, big man. Shit, okay arm up people, I think we mighta just discovered a stinking terrorist dickhead trapped in this here fricking mess. Be careful guys, I don't wanna scared any stinking civilian pukes by waving our weapons at them. Try to keep your weapons hidden as best you can until we see what Ramirez is gonna do about this lousy little scumbag she picked up on." Neck offered as he pulled his head back until the wall hid his body from Ramirez and her target's view.

Once he was behind the wall, Neck ripped his backpack from his shoulders and unzipped it and removed his MP-5 nine-millimeter automatic weapon. He checked the chamber to make certain he was cocked, locked and ready to rock. Then he hoisted his weapon to his shoulder and allowed the weapon to rest against his body in a position that gave him immediate action with the weapon. The sheer size of the soldier made the weapon look like a kid's toy in his mitt size hands. Every action Neck displayed, show everyone around him he was all business.

Once he was ready to get down and dirty with anyone Ramirez wanted neutralized. Neck leaned against the wall again and he carefully slid his huge body along it until he was able to look around the edge of the wall without being seen by Ramirez's target, and then he locked the man up in his glare and weapon sights. The other troops bunched up behind Neck, took up their positions that offered them the best possible way to assist their fellow soldier eyeing her target and waiting for some reason for not jumping off on the guy.

Ramirez did not have to look to see where the rest of her troops were setting up. She understood her actions alarmed and alerted them, and the troops would automatically take up positions to back her actions against the one she classified as a possible terrorist. She made it look like she was not interested in the man who kept shifting his eyes from one stairwell to the other that led down or up to this area. She turned her head now and then away from this stranger, as she made like she was waiting for someone to linkup with her as well. Even though she turned, she never fully took her eyes off her target.

Mohammed could not keep the mounting anger out of his eyes, and he continually shifted his weight on his feet while waiting for Farima to finally meet up with him, so they could escape from the arena area. The longer it was taking Farima to link back up with him, the more his anger grew, adding to the problem of his trying to control his temper.

CHAPTER TWENTY-ONE

Farima was having a serious problem leaving the position where she threw her grenades from, mainly because so many civilians were still milling about the area and trying to assist some of the injured and dying. Finally, she was able to shove her way past two men who removed their shirts, and they ripped the garments into long strips. They were tying the rags on a woman's legs that had massive injuries from the grenade exploding so near her body. When Farima pushed one man out of her way, he growled angrily at her.

"Hey what the hell's wrong with you anyway, bitch? Can't you see we're trying to help this poor lady who is badly injured here? Instead of trying to leave the fucking area, why don't you pitch in and help with looking after some of these injured people for Pete's sake. We can use all the help we can get with these injured people."

Farima totally ignored the man growling at her as she quickly made her way from the bleacher seats to the landing where she was supposed to hook up with her fellow terrorist Mohammed. When she got on the stairwell, she immediately picked up twenty-armed people bunched up on the stairs. Her blood froze in her veins because she knew they must have picked up Mohammed as he waited for her to arrive. She instantly went in her act, and made it look like she was having a serious problem with getting by all the bodies of the injured littering the stairs.

Always on the make for a woman, Buckethead offered to assist the young and pretty woman, and he put out his hand and helped her get over a body of a man obviously stomped to death. He helped the woman until she had her feet on the lower landing. Then Buckethead placed his finger to his lips and pointed in the direction he wanted her to leave in.

Then he gave her a slight shove forward to get her moving away from the other soldiers.

Farima looked in the direction the large man lightly shoved her in, and realized the way she would have to move, would completely hide her from Mohammed's view. She made up her mind Mohammed was on his own, and she was going to escape and save herself. She knew he would be unable to see her leaving, and this would assure her she would get away safely from the area. Farima gave the man a last quick look, and then she allowed him to shove her again, and she started to walk in the direction he was guiding her in.

Moving as quickly as the conditions would allow her, while trying not to draw Mohammed's attention to her movements. Farima moved until she reached a stairwell leading to the next down level of the stadium. When she reached the second level still heading down, there were fewer bodies and injured in this area. When she reached this level, she realized why there were so few bodies on the upper level. Many of the injured and dead were moved down to this floor, and the emergency responders were working on the ones they might be able to save. She barely looked where she was walking and stepping, as she reached the stairwell leading to the first floor and then outside the structure.

When she reached the first level of the stadium, Farima noticed a horde of police officers gathered, and one of the officers helped her to the main exit. Once she was outside the structure, she looked for their parked SUV, spotting the vehicle and seeing both Farideh and Maha standing by it, she rushed down the ramp, and hurried through the rails and out to the large parking lot. She was amazed how these hundreds of caregivers were working on the injured and dying in the extremely unfavorable and unsanitary conditions. She found herself starting to respect the Americans for the care they offered to one another at times of trouble. She shook her head as she ordered herself to run.

Farima went into a dead run as she headed directly for the parked SUV. Farideh was the first one to see her running towards them, and he growled angrily at Maha. "Here comes the lazy and worthless Farima, and she's alone. There must be trouble and the foolish Mohammed is not coming back with us, woman. I hope the foul fool does not allow himself to be taken prisoner by these cursed police and other authorities I see running into this foul structure. They have many ways to make even the strongest of hearts, speak. Take the keys and start the foul machine while I wait for the foolish woman to reach us, Maha. Once we're out of this foul parking lot, we're going to ignore al-Wahhad's orders, and we're going to head right back to the safe house and inform him of Mohammed being taken in custody by the local authorities of this evil city."

Farima rushed up to Farideh out of breath, and she immediately warned him. "Farideh, I fear Mohammed is about to be killed by the ones I saw with weapons held at the ready, and they had him blanketed in. There's no possible escape for our brother but Paradise, Farideh."

"Huh, the worthless fool must have done something that drew the attention of the cursed infidels towards him. His fate was pre-ordained, and Allah's mercy with care for him when he enters Paradise. He served his purpose for our just cause. Come worthless woman, we must leave before our actions draw the attention of the security and police authorities of this cursed institution. We have to return to Shabbah and report to him." Farideh moved aside and allowed Farima to get in the back seat of the SUV, and then he rushed around the vehicle and jumped into the passenger seat and ordered his driver. "Get us out of this foul parking lot and take great care with your driving and obey all the foul traffic rules. I don't want to draw any attention to us from the evil authorities protecting these fools we slaughtered. We have to report to al-Wahhad and inform him of how our attack against the lowly infidels went, and inform him the foolish Mohammed is either dead, or he was taken prisoner by the hated authorities." Farideh decided to allow Maha to drive, in his mind he thought the police would not be looking for a woman driving a car with terrorists inside.

INSIDE THE BASEBALL STADIUM

Sergeant Dorothy Ramirez was caught in the open while she stood near the person, she felt might be a possible terrorist, or someone of interest. She was unable to get into her backpack and remove her weapon, so she was forced to remain unarmed while she kept this man under her surveillance. Occasionally, she glanced to where the rest of her troops headed, and she caught a slight movement and realized her troops had her back. For the umpteenth time, she looked at the man who aroused her interest, and noticed he was looking for someone to meet up with him. She was unable to tell if this man was armed, so she was going to be forced to act accordingly, if she had to go up against this one. She hoped her backup would come to her aide before this stranger could get the drop on her, and maybe even killed her before the other soldiers opened fire and killed him.

Sweat dripped in her eye as she tried to concentrate her full attention on the man and his angry looking movement, while trying to look as inconspicuous as possible as she continued her observation of her target. Suddenly, he moved away from the crowd towards the stairwell blocked by the injured and dead civilians. Ramirez took this move as her chance to separate her target from the rest of the crowd using the commissary as their haven, until the authorities told them where to go. She drew in her breath and moved out behind her target, all the while she fought wanting to arm herself. Taking a quick glance to her left, she picked up the other troops as they cautiously came out of the stairwell and started to trail her and her target.

Ramirez rapidly closed the gap separating her from her intended target. When the man stopped by the foot of the stairwell, he glanced up the stairs leading to the bleacher area of the stadium, she cleared her throat loudly. The noise caused Mohammed to stop and turn to see who was near him.

"Excuse me sir, but you seem to be a little confused sir. Why are you walking towards the stairwell leading to where the attack happened?" Ramirez asked with concern in her voice.

"Why are you bothering me, I have committed no crime, young woman?" Mohammed replied hotly as his eyes narrowed, and then he stared right at her face.

"Why would you say you have committed no crime to me, sir? I didn't ask you if you committed a crime, sir. I just said that you looked a little confused that's all, and I didn't want you to go wandering in the way of any of the emergency responders helping with the injured and dying, sir. That's all I said and is my only concern, sir." Ramirez added as she continued to challenge the stranger now glaring so angrily at her.

"And I asked you why are you bothering me, woman? Are you part of the security of this establishment? If you must know what I am doing nosy woman, I have lost my girlfriend in the rush to escape the explosions that killed so many of these people, and I'm trying to locate her so we can leave this place together and return to our home safely. I want to make sure she is all right if it's any of your business to know, woman. I beg you to allow me to look for my missing girlfriend in peace and leave me alone."

By the way this man spoke and the words he chose replying to her questions reinforced her concern that this man was an Arab. Drawing in her breath a second time, she spoke further with the angry acting young stranger. "Sir, your actions are causing me some concerns, sir. I believe I want you to come along with me sir, so I can ask you a few more questions in private, sir. If everything is as you say, my people will assist you in your search for your missing girlfriend, sir. Now if you wouldn't mind sir, please turn around and place your hands behind your back, sir. I want to search your person to make certain you have no weapons hidden on your body, sir." Ramirez offered in a calm voice as she squared her body, so she faced this man properly, and waited for him to carry out her orders.

"I will do no such thing for you, woman. What kind of devil are you anyway woman? I see no identification marking you as someone from the security or police with authority to command anything of me. That thing you have hanging on your chest is no police shield I have ever saw. Why do you not leave me alone and allow me to search for my missing girlfriend in peace. She might be injured, and I want to help her if you don't mind, woman!"

"Sir, I understand the way you must feel, and the concerns you're suffering for your missing girlfriend, and as I stated already sir. If you answer the questions, I want to ask you, and you're found to be no threat to anyone. My people will be more than pleased to come to your aide and assist in your search for your missing girlfriend, sir." Ramirez replied with a little anger creeping into her tone of voice this time, as she removed a pair of flex cuffs from her hip pocket, and then she waited for the stranger to turn so she could secure him, and then lead the man to security room inside the stadium.

"What are those foul looking things you have in your hands? Oh no you don't, you're not going to place those evil looking things on my hands, woman. No, I will not allow you to make me helpless to defend myself in case anything happens where I have to protect myself against those who attacked this stadium." Mohammed stopped arguing and shifted his eyes around in search of a quick escape route away from this woman challenging him.

Picking up his actions and his sudden want to flee, Ramirez stiffened her body and prepared to stop this man from running as she added in a commanding tone this time. "Please sir, I suggest you don't try anything foolish that I might take as a threat to my person, sir. All I want to do is ask you a few questions, and if everything checks out sir. You'll be on your way, and I'll help you find your missing girlfriend, sir."

Mohammed looked over Ramirez's head because he had six inches on her. When he noticed two men with weapons held in their hands coming directly at them, he decided to save his life by reacting in the manner he was trained. Throwing caution to the wind, he suddenly reached out and caught Ramirez by surprise, and armed with strength she was ill prepared to defend against. He roughly grabbed her by the shirt and flung her body hard up against the wall. The shock of the move dropped her down to one knee, but she quickly shook off the shock and pain from the assault and was back on her feet and charged after the stranger.

Neck was so close to Sergeant Ramirez that he easily picked up the attack from the stranger against her, and he instantly reacted in the manner he was trained. Without the slightest bit of hesitation, the large and overly excited soldier raised his weapon up to a firing position and bellowed out at the attacker. "Hey stupid, stop resisting and drop your ass down to the fucking floor, and place your fricking hands behind your damn back, buddy. Stop resisting or I'll shoot ya fricking dead mutherfucka!"

Ramirez moved her hand out before her body as she called out at the excited soldiers the exact instant Neck fired at the fleeing suspect. "No Robert don't shoot him; we need him alive so we can ask him some questions and see who he's working with. It's impossible he can't possible escape the damn area, every exit's blocked by the police and we need him alive if… Arrr… shit, dammit." She watched as the stranger was pitched forward as three rounds ripped into his chest, killing him instantly.

The moment Neck fired at the fleeing suspect, the crowd gathered around the concession stand, or hanging around on the landing. Dropped down to the floor and covered their heads with their hands. Screams filled the air, as women started to cry for fear they were going to be killed by this wild man with the weapon firing it. Police stationed on this floor immediately charged to the area, and they moved in front of the mass of scared civilians and aimed their weapons at the one shooting on the floor.

A new problem was immediately confronting the Sergeant, and she realized she had to act fast before the amped up Neck turned his weapon against the threat coming from the excited police officers. She called out in a commanding voice for everyone involved in the drama taking place before her eyes. "Hold on Officers, we're Special Forces connected to the Dragon Fire Force. No one shoot! Officers, hold your damn fire. Neck! Lower your damn weapon so the Officers know you're not a threat against them, stupid. You heard me, I just issued you a direct order, and I expect it to be carried immediately, mister. Did you hear me soldier?"

Ramirez's heart was pounding wildly in her chest, as she witnessed the soldiers from her unit bunching up and taking up a supportive position alongside, and directly behind the soldier under threat from the gaggle of police officers aiming their weapons at him. Taking command of the situation, Ramirez bellowed a second time at everyone involved in the drama. "You people from my Squad heard the orders I just issued Neck. The same goes for the rest of you people. Lower your damn weapons and stand down! Those Police Officers are on our side, so stop your threat against them, dammit! I ordered you people to stand down and that's what you will do! Or I'll put lead in your asses myself. Officers, stand down, I told you to stand down, dammit."

Sergeant Ramirez glared angrily at the soldiers and police officers, as she waited for both sides to obey her orders and back down. She only allowed herself to breathe normally again when she picked up two concerned police officers cautiously lowering their weapons, and that move made her troops do the same. In a matter of second, both sides were calmed down and moved towards the suspect lying on the floor.

Ramirez was the first one to reach the downed suspect, and she was quickly joined by Buckethead, Neck and Ice. She checked the condition of the man and hissed out her breath in anger when she realized he was dead. Three police officers joined her, and one of them asked the upset female Sergeant.

"Do you have any idea who this purp was, and what he was up to, Ma'am?"

"I have no idea who the man was or what he was up to sir." Ramirez replied, not taking her eyes off the dead man.

"If you had no idea who the person was and what he was doing. Why did you challenge him, and almost cause World War Three to break out between my Officers and your damn crazy ass troops, Ma'am?" The stunned police officer asked as he glared at her while waiting for her reply.

"Look Lieutenant who ever the hell you are, I don't need you questioning any of my damn moves, mister. I picked up this man acting rather strangely and decided to challenge his ass, solely because of the way he was acting. I noticed the man was obviously from the Middle East from his looks and skin color and he…"

"So, you reacted against this poor soul because you racially profiled the man, is that what you're trying to tell me Sergeant?" The Police Lieutenant asked as he continued to glare at the female soldier.

"You better take the effing vinegar out of your damn stare when looking down your stinking nose at me, buster. Yes, sir I certainly did racially profiled the sonofabitch, and I'd do it every damn time if it'd save just one civilian life here, Pal. Neck, search his body and see if the bastard has any identification on him. Everyone else…" Ramirez's words were cut off when Walker and his troops charged down the stairwell almost covered with bodies and injured. He was not being very careful where he stepped as he headed for the sound of weapon's fire.

Walker looked at the downed man and barked angrily at his female Sergeant. "What the fuck's going down here, dammit! We almost killed ourselves getting here, Sergeant."

The Police Lieutenant started to speak but was stopped by Walker as he growled at the officer. "Who the fuck are you, and why the hell are you addressing my ass for, buddy? My fucking question was aimed at my stinking Sergeant here, not your ass mister. Ramirez, what the fuck happened here, and who the hell is this sonofabitch you people just wasted? Dammit, didn't I warn you guys I wanted suspects breathing, if we came across them inside this damn dump when we first entered this dump? I told you people I didn't mind if the suspects were bent up a little if they were still able to communicate when you guys got control of the lousy bastards. The Colonel's gonna be fit to be fucking tied when he hears we just iced one of the possible terrorists in here, dammit. Arrr… fuck it, begin your damn report Sergeant." Walker glared at his girlfriend as he waited for her to tell him what when down here.

Ramirez stiffened to an attention stance as she began the report to her Commanding Officer, and Neck continued to search the body of the downed suspect on the ground. "Captain Walker Sir, I picked up actions that caused me some concern from this dead suspect here, sir. When I challenged him over his strange actions, he suddenly grabbed my person and slammed me against the wall, and then he tried to escape from my custody. I recovered my wits and began to chase after him, but Neck saw what happened and he…"

"You placed the suspect in custody as you started to question the lousy little scumbag, Sergeant?" Walker was taking Ramirez's side and looking at the dead man as a terrorist.

"Yes sir, I brandished the flex cuffs and ordered him to place his hands behind his back, but he failed to obey my orders. Instead, he attacked my person and then he fled…"

"That's placing his stinking ass in custody alright once you flashed the damn flex cuffs at his dead ass, Sergeant. Continue with your report, Sergeant. I wanna know everything that went down here dammit." Walker growled at her after interrupting her report.

"Captain Walker Sir, when the suspect attacked me and then he tried to flee the area, sir. He ran right in front of our other soldiers who were acting as my backup of this suspect, and they took him to be a serious threat against the civilian population and myself, sir. The troops acted accordingly in my opinion sir. They immediately opened fire and met his threat with deadly response, Captain."

"Dammit, I guess you guys couldn't just wound, arrr…what the fuck am I saying. You did right to kill a threat against our people. You!" Walker turned to Neck searching the suspect.

Neck looked up at Walker and waited for a response from his Commander.

"I take it you're the flaming asshole who shot up this turd lousy ass, right buster?" Walker growled at the large soldier.

"The one and only and you got that right Captain Walker and I'd do it again just as fucking quickly to any stinking bastard who threatens one of my fellow soldiers in front of me, Captain." Neck replied in an angry response.

"And that's the way you betta respond if one of our troops come under threat from any turds, soldier! Does the rotten sonofabitch have any fucking identification on his body?" Walker asked the huge soldier as he looked over his shoulder while he checked out the body.

Neck threw a driver's license at Walker's feet and then pulled other papers out of the dead man's pocket, and he checked them for help.

"What the fuck do you call that last bit of shit, mister? Since when do you just throw something at my fucking feet like that, buster? Hand me that stinking driver's license before I rip your throat out from under that thing you call a stinking noggin, and then piss down your throat for that shit filled move." Walker growled at the soldier.

"Sorry sir, I'll get it for you sir, here you go Captain." Neck replied as he picked up the license and then handed it to his Commander. As Walker looked at the license Neck offered. "Captain not for nuthin sir, but I think you'd be a helluva lot more interested in this here slip of paper I just found on this little prick than you are in that stinking license, sir."

"Whatdaya got there stupid?" Walker asked the soldier then took the paper from him.

"Stupid huh Captain?" Neck snapped, insulted over the captain's statement as he handed him the paper, and then he let his breath out in a rush to calm down.

Captain Walker quickly unfolded the small slip of paper, and then he allowed a smile to slide across his lips. Then he looked at the other soldiers bunched up behind him, and he barked at them. "Okay people, we have a good lead on this fucking sucka's stinking hideout, and we're gonna act on it toot sweet I tell ya. If the lousy fuckers are still hanging around the damn area, I wanna get their stinking asses before they decide to move on us again. Saddle up, we're heading for a new location."

The Police Lieutenant asked with concern lacing his tone of voice. "Captain Walker, do you mind if I take a look at that paper, you have there, sir. If it's a lead on the whereabouts of the attackers who pulled this thing off, I and my Officers want to be part of the team who captured the damn terrorists, sir."

"Not on your life, Lieutenant whoever the hell you are? That stinking paper along with its information belongs to my stinking ass and that's that, buddy. But I'll give you this much Lieutenant, I don't know how many people you have under your stinking command sir, but if you wanna. You guys can tag along with my troops in case we need any extra personnel and support, sir." Captain Walker offered, and then smirked at the officer.

"I have fifteen police officers under my command, and they're foaming at the mouth to be a part of this operation as it's shaping up, Captain Walker." The Police Lieutenant offered to Walker as he shot him a smile.

"Fine then you pukes can tag along with our asses, Lieutenant. No telling if we might have need of some crowd control once we get to this uther destination. I'd rather employ your officers to handle that shitty detail than wasting my troops with keeping stinking nosy ass civilian pukes at fucking bay, Lieutenant." Walker snapped at his soldiers.

"Okay you pack of screaming squirrels we gotta get the fuck outta this here stinking dump and back to our vehicles ten minutes ago. We have a hot lead on the whereabouts of these rotten ass friggin scumbags might be held up, or at least in the general vicinity of where they might be hiding and…" Walker's words were cut off in mid-sentence when the speaker systems of the stadium suddenly announced.

"Captain Walker. Captain Robert Walker, please report to the first-floor security room by Stairwell Seven at R section of the structure. Repeating…"

Walker did not bother to hear the message repeat itself for a second time as he snarled at the rest of his concerned troops gathered around him. "Okay people you heard the order. We gotta get down to the first floor where we were heading anyway. Either one of our people found something on the damn tapes of the stinking ballgame. Or the stinking Colonel finally got his lazy ass here, and he wants to bug our cans before he allows us to get on our way after the rest of these lousy scumbags. Let's get a fucking move on it people."

Captain Walker was reacting without a doubt in his mind that this attack was committed by the same Islam terrorist group who attacked the train station and airport in New York City a few days back. He was fuming for not seeing this attack coming before it happened. He cursed, growling at himself, thinking he was beginning to slip a little and not paying better attention to the warning signs being flashing before his mind.

FARIDEH KARBASCHI'S SUV

Farideh was keeping a close eye on how Maha drove the large vehicle. He was also trying to keep an eye out for any law enforcement officers, so he could warn his driver to be extra careful if they happened across any police along their route. The only thought he had was to get back to the terrorist Commander al-Wahhad, and report on how the operation went, and to inform him Taborzadi was thought to be dead or worse, captured by the police authorities.

Farideh was dreading informing the Ghost that Mohammed was discovered by the police while still inside the baseball stadium. He realized their operation was compromised, either by the death of Mohammed, and the police finding something that might help them identify their position. Or if he was taken alive and they were questioning him, and he knew the longer the police questioned Mohammed, the better chance of his giving them up to the police.

"Drive careful foolish woman, you nearly drove right through that last red light, fool. That would have been all we needed, for you to go through that god cursed red light and bring us to the attention of the hated police authorities of this city of sin." Farideh looked over his shoulder at his passenger and grumbled at the other woman.

"You lazy woman, you did not think to remain behind and witness the fate that had befallen our Arab brother trapped by the authorities inside that cursed structure of sports? Not knowing if Mohammed followed his faithful orders not to allow himself to be taken alive by the hated police authorities is causing me much concern. All I know is we must move our operation to only the Ghost knows where. Al-Wahhad is not going to be a very calm person to deal with, once he's informed that the foolish Mohammed was discovered by the police authorities, and we have no knowledge if he was taken prisoner or if he's dead or not. Woman, you should have remained behind and if necessary, you should have made certain he did not survive to be taken prisoner by the police."

Farideh shook his head in disgust over the way the last part of his operation had fallen apart on him. He knew al-Wahhad was going to be furious he was going to be forced to move his operation to another safe house in the area. He realized the Ghost was going to place the blame for this failure upon his shoulders, because he was in command of this assault team.

The extremely worried terrorist kept his eyes glued to the outside of his vehicle. He was counting off the blocks before they successfully returned to their safe house. Farideh was keeping an eye out for any possible police enforcement vehicles trailing them. That would be the last thing he wanted, bringing the authorities right to their front doorstep, and they are capturing the entire terrorist cell in one action.

CAPTAIN ROBERT WALKER AND HIS TROOPERS

Walker headed for the Security Seven Stairwell R Section of the damaged stadium. Once he was in the room, he linked up with the two soldiers the Roach and Three Martines, who he ordered to go over the video tapes from the ballgame. Seeing Roach in the room, he snarled at the soldier. "Whatdaya have for my stinking ass, buddy?"

"Damn, I'm glad you got here so quickly Captain Walker Sir. We found a goldmine of info in here sir. I got one of the fucking scumbags dead to right on the stinking tape we discovered here, sir. I got a real great shot of his fricking puss, clear, and easy to see his whole stinking face as clear as a fucking bell, Captain."

"Great, you just won yourself a fucking beer, lemme see what you found for me, Sergeant." Walker leaned forward while locking his eyes on the small screen and waited for the Roach to pull up the shots he had of the suspected terrorist. It took a few moments for the Roach to get to the section of tape he wanted, and when he did, he announced proudly.

"Here you go Captain, look closely and you'll see a man stand when everyone else is seated at the stinking stadium, sir. Here you go Captain Walker Sir, this is the fucking guy I wanted you to see, sir." The Roach stopped the tape from running and pointed out the man with his finger. Then he moved the tape forward slowly frame by frame and added to his explanation.

"Here you go Captain, look, he's starting to move, and the camera closed in tight on his damn puss for a few seconds for some reason sir. Here you can clearly see him doing something with his stinking hands sir, and then he turned to his left and he's obviously throwing something in that same direction, sir. There, see that sharp, blinding light, that's the first grenade going off, sir. I'm sorry Captain, but once the camera picked up the fucking flash, the damn thing turned away from him and towards the explosion and we lost the lousy dude's stinking puss, sir. So that's all we got on this mutherfucka, Captain."

"God, damn you did good, real fucking good Roach. You earned your stinking pay for the friggin day man. Is there any way we can get a clear picture of that bastard's lousy puss, so we can take it with us?" Walker asked one of the security guards as he turned and looked at the guy.

"Already done that for ya Captain Walker, after I placed the stinking call out to you to come over to this security closet, I had security do a printout on the bastard's face. Hell Captain, I gotten copies of his stinking puss in living fucking color, sir." The Roach announced as he handed the copies of Farideh's face to his Commanding Officer.

"Out fucking standing, you did real well Sergeant. Okay, wrap it up in here and then you and Three Martines are to link back up with us outside. Armed with this sonofbitches' picture along with the damn gas receipt we found on the dead dude. We're gonna catch these lousy little pricks in a fast hurry it up but quick. Let's get go people." Walker growled as he headed out of the small security room.

Walker was having some problems getting his people out of the stadium, between the dead, dying and countless injured, and the hordes of police, firefighters, and emergency responders still working on the injured and dead. It was nearly impossible for a person, let alone a Commander and his troops to move around freely inside the damaged arena.

Fighting his way through all the mayhem, Walker and his troops headed for the main entrance of the stadium. He stopped moving forward when he noticed a second group of soldiers fighting their way into the structure and going against the flow of people trying to get out of the structure. He tried to fix an eye on the group pushing and shoving their way into the stadium, when the Mutt caught up to him and offered in an angry voice.

"Hey Walker, I don't wanna bust your fucking bubble on your ass, man. But that uther group of slugs trying to force their way into this stinking dump, is the fricking Colonel and the rest of our people working with him. Whatdaya wanna do now man? Do you wanna take the stinking time to explain to the hot shot Colonel what we're up to? Or do ya wanna just pass by the big shit and ignore his stinking ass and keep going? According to you, we got a hot lead on where these little fuckers are hiding in Washington. If we don't get to the fucks in a hurry, it up, the lousy scumbags are gonna pull out to another location on us man. Then we're never gonna find the sonofbitches again in Washington until they hit us again."

"I know that shit Mutt, but the Colonel's armed and if we just ignore him, he's gonna put a cap in our asses. We gotta inform the stinking Colonel of what we discovered about the terrorists, and what we got going down, man. We're gonna hafta take our chances the damn terrorists will hold up until we can catch up to, and then ream their damn asses but good. Drop back and warn the uthers we're gonna hafta jaw jack with the stinking Colonel for a little while and see how he wants to handle this mess. Mutt, I got a good MOE (Mark One Eyeball) on him. I'm gonna talk to the dickface, you control our guys and keep them moving outta this dump. I don't wanna have to steam them up again to get their asses on the move once I finish up with the Colonel." Walker warned his friend as he slowed down his pace and got the Colonel's attention.

Colonel Bruce Leadbetter easily picked up Walker moving in the crowd coming directly at him, and he raised his hand and stopped the forward progress of the rest of his troops into the building. When his group stopped, Leadbetter left them and walked up to Walker and after slapping him on his back, he growled at the captain, yelling over the noise from the civilians still trapped inside the stadium.

"Jesus H Christ Walker, what a fucking mess. In all my years, I've never saw so many stinking injured and dead civilians in one place. What the hell are you and the rest of your stinking slugs up to, mister? You should be up in the damn bleachers searching the area for any damn terrorists still hiding in here. Did you get up to the bleachers yet Captain?"

"Yes, Sir Colonel Leadbetter Sir, we made it up to the damn bleacher where the attack took place and it's a helluva lot worse up there than down here, sir. We're trying to get out of the stinking building sir. We got a gas receipt from a station we found on the body of a dead terrorist, sir. We were on our way to find out if the station attendant could possibly identify the scumbag, we have a picture of. The receipt gives us a location where the pricks might be hold up, Colonel." Walker offered as he removed the paper and gave it to him.

Colonel Leadbetter quickly read the cash bill for forty dollars, and the name and address of the gas station and quick stop printed on the receipt. Then he took a hard look at the picture of the terrorist they picked up throwing one of the grenades at the bleachers. Then he handed both items back to Walker as he asked the young Marine Officer with concern lacing his tone of voice this time. "You have told me you got this fucking gas receipt off the body of a dead terrorist, mister? Explain this shit to my ass why he's fucking dead and not a fucking prisoner and still breathing so we can interrogate the rotten bastard, Captain."

"Colonel, Ramirez picked up the dumb shit acting suspicious when she and half our people used a secondary stairwell for the bleachers, sir. She challenged the sucker and questioned what he was up to hanging around on the landing, rather than trying to get outta the structure and he attacked her. Then the sonofabitch tried to escape when he knocked her to the ground. Neck witnessed the attack on her by the purp and he ordered the suspect to stop. When the suspect didn't comply with his order, he shot his ass dead as ordered." Walker reported.

The Colonel cast a quick and warning glare at the huge soldier as he griped at Walker. "I guess the piece of shit couldn't just wound the sonofabitch, could he?"

"Colonel, the Neck didn't have the time or space to aim to wound the damn suspect, sir. All he witnessed was this slob attacking Sergeant Ramirez, and then try to get away from the Sergeant, sir. The soldier was concerned with the suspect possibly grabbing a damn hostage and allowing the situation to get outta hand on us if that happened, sir." Walker was trying to find a way not to get the Colonel to dump on his fellow soldiers.

"Yeah, sure Walker, I'm certain that big slob had the damn smarts to think that far ahead of himself. That fuck can't wipe his damn nose without help, mister. Arrr… it's too late to worry about that part of this mess now, Captain. The suspect is dead, and we must deal with that the way it went down. What are you doing about this information, and who are those police officers gathered up behind you, and what the hell do they want?" The Colonel growled at his officer.

"Colonel, those cops are gonna be our backup and crowd control units when we hafta go hot against the terrorists, once we discover where they're hiding, sir. I'm planning to head for this gas station once I'm finished with you and question the dopey attendant. Show him the picture of the slob we got the snapshot of Colonel. I wanna see if he could identify the prick in the picture, sir. We have a good shot of a guy known for certain part of the terrorist attack team, sir. We got him pitching a grenade in the crowd to his left side, sir. The picture is so clear if any attendant saw this guy in the past few days. The pukes will recognize his ass from the shot of the bastard. That's what I'm betting my stinking wad on."

CHAPTER TWENTY-TWO

Colonel Bruce Leadbetter went deep in thought for a few moments as he slowly rubbed his chin, and then grumbled at Walker. "Captain, let me see the snapshot of that prick again."

Walker handed the picture over to the Colonel then stood by.

"Yeah, God it's a clear picture of the sonofabitch. I'm taking your word for it you have this lousy prick tossing the grenade in the crowd. That and that reason alone is the only reason I'm allowing you to go after what you believe is the damn terrorist, Captain. Snatch!" Leadbetter shouted over his shoulder as he called for Sergeant Weaver to move up to him. Once the soldier was near him, the angry Colonel added. "Get a copy of the address of that damn gas station from the captain, and then take a hard look at the picture Walker has in his hand, and commit his puss to memory, mister. It's going to be up to your ass to recognize the prick when we link back up with the captain. Once I see the damage the terrorists committed in this damn building."

"Colonel, I have a copy of this man I can leave with you sir." Walker offered.

"Outstanding Captain, hell, I must say Walker. You're beginning to surprise my ass with your leadership abilities, mister. It's good to see you had the smarts to make a few copies of this terrorist's face. I believe Command made the right decision when they decided to make an Officer and a Gentleman out of your ass, Captain." The Colonel offered as he rubbed his chin a second time and then added to his words.

"Okay Captain Walker, this is what we're going to do from this point forward. Walker, I want you to take the three Units under your Command, and then you people will head for the damn gas station and question that attendant's ass. See if he knows where these lousy pricks might be held up in the area. I'm going to take the soldiers assigned to my ass, and we're going up to the bleacher area of this place and see what went down. Once I finished my part of this damn investigation here, I'll communicate with you and see how you're making out with trying to be locating the Islamic radicals little rat nest. If you're successful finding the fucking cocksuckers, I'll move to your location and my units will act as backup squads for yours. The way this thing's shaping up, it seems like we might be able to wrap this mess up by tomorrow sometime. Walker, it's time for you to head out to that damn gas station, sir." Leadbetter gave his Captain the look, informing him it was time to go in action.

He took a step back then snapped to attention and saluted his Commanding Officer as he replied. "Yes, Sir Colonel Leadbetter."

The Colonel returned the captain's salute and remarked. "Very good Captain, get a move on it and remember to maintain a constant communication link with my operator. I want to know where you are every second you Squids are out in the fucking field, mister. Err…I want to know the instant and I mean the exact god damn second, if and when you locate where the damn terrorists are hiding for crap's sake."

"Yes, Sir Colonel Leadbetter." Captain Walker replied with confidence as he made a quick head movement, and every soldier watching the two officers speaking together, immediately went in action. The captain looked at the Police Lieutenant and then barked at the man. "Hey, Lieutenant, whatever the hell your name is."

"My name's Lieutenant Haylan Johnson, Captain Walker." The officer replied as he allowed a huge smile to cross his lips as he waited for the captain to finish with his words.

"Yeah, whatever Lieutenant Johnson, you betta get organized with the rest of your people if you wanna tag alone with our asses, sir. You guys have your own transportation setup I take it? We ain't got the stinking room to take you people along with us in our Humvees, Lieutenant." Walker snapped at the police officer.

"Captain, we have our squad cars parked in the lot, sir. This is going to work well, because we can clear the way for your vehicles with our squad cars. We can use our lights and sirens for…"

"Lieutenant, our stinking machines come equipped with their own emergency lights and sirens, sir. But thinking 'bout it a little further sir, I believe it might be betta for your squad cars to clear the way for us, until we get close to our damn target area, sir. Once we get near the damn target, we wanna enter the zone completely blacked out. We don't wanna warn the damn terrorists we're on to their assess and coming for them." He fired back at the police officer to make him realized how he wanted to enter the danger zone.

"I understand what you're saying Captain Walker, all you have to do is cut in over the radio and warn me we reached your target area. Once you inform me of this fact sir, we'll immediately shut down our lights and sirens, so your troops can enter the zone undercover as you have subjected, sir. This action won't be the first one we came to the site cold, sir." The Police Officer Lieutenant reported to the military officer.

"Good then your orders are to get us over to Pennsylvania Avenue A-SAP. Once we get on that road, shut down your damn lights and sirens, and only flash your lights if some civilian vehicle gets in our fucking way, Lieutenant." He replied with a snap to the police officer.

"Got 'cha Captain." The Lieutenant smiled at Walker who ignored it.

"Good, let's get the fuck outta this stinking dump so we can get afta these lousy little pukes, Lieutenant. Well, stop looking at my ass and get your cans in fucking gear." Walker growled at the police officer to get him moving.

The Mutt and Sergeant Ramirez stood on either side of Walker and the Mutt grumbled at the young Marine Captain. "You know something Walker, if we were able to get that lousy puke the Neck iced off in there. I woulda loved to have had a chance to interrogate the sonofa fucking bitch. If hooking one rag head terrorist's balls to a damn car battery to get the friggin truth outta his camel shagging ass. I have three fucking things to say to your ass, Captain. One, red is positive, B, black is negative, and Three's make certain his balls are soaking wet before putting the damn juice to his fricking ass."

"I feel ya Mutt and I feel the same way about these lousy shits. One, B, three huh, I see we still hafta work on your counting abilities, mister." Walker offered with a smile.

"Hey Walker, I didn't stay in the fifth grade for three years to learn my A, B, D's for nuthin, man." The Mutt came back with his own joke.

"Huh dog man, the only reason you got out of the fifth grade, was because your ass no longer fit in the damn desk." Ramirez added as she looked around Walker so she could see Mutt's face.

"Man, you chicks never miss a stinking chance to ride my ass into the stinking ground." The Mutt bitched at the pretty female Sergeant.

"That's because you give us so much ammunition to use on your ass, mister."

"Keep the stinking flap jack on the fucking grill a little bit longer Raz. I got something I can use on your ass swinging right here between my stinking legs, baby." The Mutt shot back at the Sergeant as he grabbed his member and shook it through his pants.

"Yeah, sure dog man, if you came at me with that damn thing swinging between your legs. You'll be arrested for assault with a dead weapon, buster." Ramirez returned Mutt's slug.

"Whoa, ouch, man that one really hurt there, little sister." The Mutt offered as he tried to look around Walker to see Ramirez's face.

Mutt's joking was cut off by Walker who blocked his way and he snarled at the other soldier. "Hey stupid, are you about fucking finished joking around for crap's sake? Can't you take something serious for once in your wasted life, dog man? Shut up, you know damn well you'll never win a battle of wits with the Raz. So, knock the shit off so we can get down to brass tacks."

"Hey, he's stupid too huh Captain? Now I don't feel so stinking bad with that slug you fired off at my ass before, man." Neck offered as he got in on busting Mutt's horns along with the rest of the soldiers.

"Am I gonna start having some stinking trouble with your ass now too, buster?" The captain mumbled as he looked at the other soldier.

"Hey Bobby, when it comes down to the Mutt getting involved in a battle of the wits with anyone. The fool comes to the war totally unarmed." Sergeant Ramirez added as she stayed on Mutt's ass.

Walker turned and bellowed at his Sergeant. "Enuf fucking round already, you know the more you egg the damn Mutt on, the longer he's gonna come back at ya. The Mutt will stay on ya longer than a blackhead, baby sister."

"You're damn right I will Walker. Hey man, was that statement a racist remark, pal?"

"Let me tell you something right here and now stupid. If I ever fired off a stinking racist remark at your half ass black backside, you'll know it right off the fucking bat, buster. You can call me a lot of things in life, but a stinking racist. Naw that shit won't float on my fucking pond. Besides Mutt, I'm an equal opportunity bigot I hate everyone equally, man. Now, if you don't mind shitbirds, don't your assholes think its bout time we linkup with the rest of our people, and the cops bunching up outside this damn dump? We gotta get over to that damn gas station and see if anyone there can identify this prick in the picture."

The elite group of soldiers started to make their way out of the damaged stadium. Once outside, Walker was amazed at what he was seeing. There was a constant flow of ambulances coming on to and quickly leaving the massive stadium parking lot. He watched with concern as one ambulance was quickly loaded with more than one injured inside, and it took off and another one immediately replaced it. He was pleased to see the emergency responders getting two and sometimes even three injured persons inside the ambulances.

This made him feel there was still some hope for humans after all, over the way so many people come out of the woodwork to try and help someone injured in a car accident, fire, and injured from a terrorist attack. He wondered where these people came from, and how they would help the injured at the cost of getting injured or killed themselves in the process. As he looked at the horde of emergency responders and ambulances moving around the injured, his humvee was pulled up to where he was standing and the driver, the soldier branded Nentendo opened the passenger door from inside and called out to him. "Hey Captain, you need a lift sir?"

"Funny, ha, ha you friggin twit you. Okay you pain in the asses, get in the damn Humvee. Nentendo, when the cops get in front of our caravan, follow them over to Pennsylvania Avenue. That's where we're gonna go covert and sneak up on the sonofbitches. Once we had a chance to speak with the pissant gas station attendant and see if he can shed some stinking light on where the damn scumbags we want are hiding in the area. Arrr… shit, try and stay up with the damn cops and don't lose the little pricks in traffic. We got a shitload of cars going down the wrong way on many of the streets trying to get outta the incident area."

"You got it Captain the stinking cops won't be able to lose my ass in this mess."

"If you wanna impress me, do as you're ordered and be quick 'bout it. If you lose the cops, I'm gonna pitch your ass outta this damn thing, and you can run behind us while we catch up with the damn cops." Walker warned his driver and then settled in to watch the road, as Nentendo navigated his way through the streets of central Washington.

"Hey Walker, when the hell are you gonna allow me to drive this damn thing, huh?" The Mutt griped as he looked at the captain as he got comfortable in the humvee.

"You drive this fucking thing huh? You gotta be shitting my ass, dog man. You can't even drive a fucking nail with a hammer. Hell, you can't even drive a stick up a dog's ass, man. So, there is no way in hell I'm gonna allow you to drive this damn thing until you get a little serious about yourself." Walker fired at the Mutt.

ABDULAZIZ AL-WAHHAD'S SAFE HOUSE

The Chevy SUV carrying the surviving three terrorist attackers from the stadium, Farideh Karbaschi, Maha Ajwad and Farima Ebadi pulled into the driveway of their safe house. Maha was driving so cautiously that al-Wahhad barely heard the vehicle pull on the property from inside the building. The moment the lights of the vehicle flashed across the interior wall of the safe house, al-Wahhad immediately rushed for the front window. He cautiously pulled the curtains back just enough for him to see outside and watched the three attackers climbed out of the SUV and approach the house.

Al-Wahhad's eyes narrowed to mere slits of anger, the moment he realized the assault team was a person light. His eyes searched the faces of the three approaching the house, and when he noticed Mohammed Taborzadi was the one missing from the group, his anger grew. The middle-aged Muslim terrorist was fuming over the fact one member of the attack team was left behind for some reason. His mind went into overdrive as he thought of the reasons for the attacker missing. All this made the short hairs on the back of his neck stand on end.

When the three exhausted and filthy terrorists walked to the front door, al-Wahhad abandoned the window and he rushed for the door. Five other terrorists of his cell came up behind him and waited for the other team to enter the house.

Farideh lead the way for the two women, and he was the first to try the door. Even before he could turn the doorknob, al-Wahhad beat him to it, and he savagely yanked the door open. The suddenness of the movement startled the three exhausted attackers, and it forced the two women to step back away from the door a bit. Farideh was momentarily stunned, and it forced him to take a defensive stance, because he had no idea if it was the police authorities ripping the front door open, and they were going to kill him.

The instant Farideh realized it was the Ghost who pulled the door open. He relaxed and allowed a quick smile. But the smile disappeared when al-Wahhad snarled at him.

"By the great gray beard of the Prophet Muhammad, what the devil has happened to the other fool who I had the misfortune to send out on such a special mission for Allah and our cause? Farideh, you better not dare try and tell me that the great fool Mohammed was taken alive as a prisoner by the police authorities of this foul city? I warn you fool, if you allowed the foolish one to be taken alive by the local authorities. I'll have your foul face tied to a bag of hot ash, until the flesh of your face has been burned away from your worthless skull, fool.

"I ordered you before you left this safe house, not to allow any of your attack team to be taken alive by the police authorities. You had orders for none of you to return to this safe house if one fool was captured during your attack. Tell me what happened to the fool Mohammed?" The Ghost snarled so savagely and held him in his glare while waiting his reply.

Farideh moved deeper in the home as he allowed the two women to sneak behind him, and they quickly rush to the kitchen. Once the women were out of the way, the fuming Ghost waited for Farideh to make his report about what happened to Mohammed.

Drawing in air, Farideh explained what happened to the leader of the terrorist cell in a rush of excited words. "Al-Wahhad, the mission went off like clockwork as you had suggested. The hand grenades killed many of the worthless civilians at the stadium, but their deaths were far less than the way the fools had trampled over their weak, their children, and their women. Our attackers carried out their orders properly, and we created the death and fear our attack was meant to cause the lowly infidels of the land of Satan. Al-Wahhad, as I was leaving the cursed stadium, I was unable to count the death we caused the jackal fools. It was like you predicted; the dead will mount as does the leaves of fall on the ground. We killed and injured far more lowly infidels than was killed and injured with the attack against the Twin Towers in New York City. Al-Wahhad, I'd offer we killed three times the death we caused in New York.

"Al-Wahhad, we have accomplished all of what we had set out to do to the lowly infidels for this evil land. It was glorious to witness all the carnage we caused the filthy jackals of this foul nation. The lowly beings thought nothing of trampling over their children, wives, and their elderly. All the young and middle age of this evil land thought of was saving their own god cursed worthless lives, and to the fate of Satan goes their weak, their women, and their children. Shabbah, I swear on the pages of the Holy..."

"By the ten Prophets of Islam, fool who is empowered by a breath that is endless for me to endure. I care not one worthless grain of sand for the outcome of our attack against the non-believers of this foul nation. Their fate was preordained by Allah's will. Farideh, I witnessed the destruction this attack caused the foul ones as it was played out live on the TV. So, save your foul breath bragging at what you fools have accomplished. What I'm concerned with, is the fate of the worthless Mohammed. I trust now that he's no longer a member of my terrorist cell, and he no longer breathes the air upon the face of this earth?" Al-Wahhad hissed.

Farideh cocked his head to the side as he tried to absorb the terrible insult just delivered against him from the leader of the terrorists. Winning the battle of controlling his temper, he replied almost in a pleading tone of voice to the Ghost. "Al-Wahhad, I fear Mohammed's fate is unknown to me. The last time I had laid eyes upon his foul face, was when I handed him his two hand grenades. I was unable to locate him in the maddening crowd of jackals once he moved to his seat and waited to attack the lowly infidels. I worry the one who might be able to inform you of Mohammed's fate, is Farima, because she was assigned to be his backup during the attack. The woman was ordered to wait until Mohammed came to her, before they were to leave the area and linkup with us waiting to leave the arena."

Al-Wahhad ripped his eyes from Farideh face and looked to the kitchen and roared at the two young women from the attack group. "Farima, get your worthless being out here before me at once I tell you. I demand to speak with you, and I warn you worthless woman. If I don't like what you must tell me, I'll order the flesh of your back peeled away by the bite of the lash. I'm waiting for you to obey my order, worthless woman!"

Farima was trembling and looked at Maha before daring to move an inch.

Maha picked up the fear in the other woman's face, and she offered her in a calming tone of voice. "My sister, you have to speak with Shabbah. Yes, he shall scream loudly at you, but he would never order your back to be visited by the tongue of the lash. I'm quite certain you must understand Shabbah only yells at you, but he never carries out his threats against us. Go my faithful sister because he's waiting your presence."

"Yes, my sister who offers me great words of wisdom and understanding. I understand that Shabbah only barks, but rarely does he bite one, I thank Allah for that. But I fear the terrible day when he decides to be bitten." Farima allowed a slight laugh to escape her lips, and she was joined by Maha. Then she stopped moving and looked into Farima's eyes, trying to order her to speak with the angry and waiting al-Wahhad.

"I know he's waiting. Please say a prayer of protection for me to Allah before I speak with Shabbah." Farima replied and then she left the kitchen as if she was about to meet her fate. She stopped when she was standing in front of the leader of the terrorist group, and he instantly snarled at her.

"Well worthless woman, you took your god cursed time getting out here to speak with me. Bitch from the sacred sands of Mecca, I trust to Allah that you have carried out your orders faithfully, and that you made certain the foolish Mohammed was dead before the hated police authorities got their foul hands on his loathsome body. Am I correct to believe the way I am thinking about this situation, woman?" Al-Wahhad snapped at the frightened young Arab woman as he stared hotly at her.

"Al-Wahhad, I fear you're in error with the thoughts you're entertaining. Shabbah, when I was able to leave my place of attack after the confusion created by our assault on the worthless fools, we were sent out to attack had calmed down enough for me to move safely. I went to where I was ordered by Mohammed to meet up with him again. Once with him we were to leave the stadium together as safely as possible. When I came down the stairwell, I passed fifteen to twenty men and women dressed in civilian clothes. What separated them from the other civilians running around inside the stadium was the fact these evil looking ones were armed with automatic weapons, and it seemed they were hunting someone.

"Fearing to give my part in this attack away to these armed people who had Mohammed covered, I cautiously walked by the group of strangers as if I was one of the people enjoying the ballgame of no worth. As I moved by this armed group, I noticed a young woman speaking with Mohammed. This woman was supporting the same type of backpack as was the fifteen or so other strangers. I quickly realized he was compromised by what I believe to be a group of undercover police officers. I weighed my situation and concluded with Mohammed being so compromised. There was no reason for me to compromise myself, so I didn't try and gain his release or kill him. The reason I didn't kill him was, when we had to go through the security system of the stadium, I was ordered not to carry any weapons on my…"

"What cursed fool was stupid enough to order you attackers to be unarmed when you fools entered the foul baseball stadium?" Al-Wahhad snapped at the shaking young female terrorist.

"I fear my response will only anger you further Shabbah, because it was you who issued the order to be unarmed when we entered the evil structure, al-Wahhad. Being I was unarmed, there was no logical way for me to try and kill Mohammed, because the police authorities had him well surrounded. If I dared to attack to free or kill him, my attack would have drawn a respond by the police. I would've been killed or taken prisoner myself, and my attack would have surely failed. So, I carried out what I felt was the most logical response, and I quickly left the area and made my way outside the arena. In this way I'd be able to join Farideh and Maha and report the fate of Mohammed to them. Then we three could return to your side and inform you of what happened in the foul baseball stadium." Farima replied to the Ghost's demand.

Fighting not to smile over the way Farima had described who it was who ordered the assault team to be unarmed. Al-Wahhad went in thought for a few seconds, collecting his wits he growled at the young female terrorist again. "By the sacred sands of Mecca, Mohammed's fate is his to suffer. We can no longer be concern with what the hated police authorities will do to him, in their attempt to force him to betray us. Our concern now is to protect our mission against the lowly infidels to our faith. Farima, since you left Mohammed's side, I order you to remain at this house with the Iranian fool, Adelah al-Faiz, and the fearless Afghan fighter, Mustafa Saleh. Huh, I shall leave to defend our house, the Jordanian, Nazira Zayn Abbus, she is well trained with the use of weapons. I shall also leave the Saudi, what was her name…yes, Hatoon al-Muneef.

"I should leave another male fighter to help better protect this foul place from the hated police authorities, so I'll leave Morteza Mohammed behind as well. Lazy woman, I'll order the Afghan fighter to be in command of the ones I shall leave behind, because the great fool is a weapon expert. He has spent many years fighting, first against the ugly Russians, and then the malicious infidels from this foul land who had dared to invade his worthless country. I'll take the rest of our freedom warriors and move them to where al-Mutairi is constructing the weapon that'll certainly break the backs of the lowly infidels of this nation.

"The faithful warriors that I shall take with me will protect the second structure with their worthless lives, while the other fighters I leave behind to protect this foul place will assume the responsibility of it. There is nothing more sacred for any Arab to do than to die proudly for his beliefs in Allah, and the sacred words of the Holy Qur'an. Golden thrones await the faithful in Paradise." Al-Wahhad stopped speaking and he looked at his female terrorist, to see if she had any questions for him. She responded instantly.

"Shabbah, I feel you're leaving us behind to defend this safe house as a suicide mission. I believe we should all stay together; I feel together we have a much better chance of carrying out our next operation against the non-believers of this foul nation. I further believe…"

"I care not one cursed worthless grain of sand from the vast deserts of our great homeland in what you might or don't believe evil woman who speaks to me as if you're my equal, and I seek your guidance. No woman born to this foul earth is an equal to any male Arab, bitch born from camel dung who speaks to me as if I need your worthless counseling. But since you are part of my terrorist cell, I shall take the time to explain the reasons for my decisions to you. Yes woman, you might be left behind on a suicide mission, the fighters with me are on the same mission as the one you fear so much. We'll be at the same risk to be discovered by the police authorities. If we're discovered first, it shall be your team who might make it home safely to the lands of our ancient ancestors. I remind you lazy woman, a fact because you're a woman you're overlooking, and you have failed to understand.

"Lowly woman, you're taking it for granted that Mohammed will surely inform the police authorities of our whereabouts in this foul city of sin and lies, because they ask him to betray us. Woman, you must have faith in the spine of a true Arab male warrior. Because your fears make you weak, those fears are not known to an Arab male fighter. I fear not of his betraying our safe house to the hated police authorities because he knows we need a week before we'll be ready to attack this cursed land with hatred Allah has endowed within us. Mohammed will hold out no matter what the evil non-believers do to his body or mind. Until we can commit to the final attack, I shall do everything in my power to unleash the revenge this weapon of freedom we constructed by the middle of next week. If by chance the police authorities discover this safe house, you must engage the lowly infidels to the death, and fight them if you can.

"You see worthless woman if we become aware you come under attack by the authorities. That'll give us the time we need to move our operation out of the new area, so we can finish constructing the sacred weapon to destroy this entire evil city. That's the only thing causing you concern, our ability to complete our sacred mission. I'll confess if we're discovered, and your group is not. We'll fight the lowly cursed infidels long enough to know your team will have time to successfully escape this evil land." Al-Wahhad aimed a harsh stare at the young Arab woman, as a final warning he finished speaking.

Farima lowered her head in her attempt to get out from under the Ghost's ugly and threatening glare. When she did this, al-Wahhad snapped angrily at her. "Foolish woman, I must move the others over to the next safe house. You and the few I leave behind will fight to your death if discovered by the hated police authorities of this evil city. I have no further words to offer you but these few. Organize your defenders and have them arm themselves. I shall gather my fighters and take what we need from this foul building, and then we'll go to the second safe house and continue our work there. May Allah keep you safe, woman."

"Allahu Akhbar al-Wahhad, and we shall do our best to delay the police from discovering where you have moved your operations to." Farima offered.

The Ghost understood what he was doing. He was taking the few terrorists already aware of the second buildings located and leaving the other fighters who did not know where it was. This way he was assuring if the radical Arab fighters were taken alive, there was no way they could possibly betray them to the police authorities, especially if they did not know where the second location was within the boundaries of Washington.

The moment Farima broke off her challenge of his control over of his terrorist cell. Al-Wahhad charged through the interior of the overcrowded house almost in a blind rage. He issued several fast orders to every terrorist he was taking with his to the next safe place to work from. Telling them what to take, and what to be prepared for, when they were challenged by anyone from this country, he issued further orders to the Muslim fighters he was leaving to protect this safe house. What he was trying to accomplish was to keep both places protected in case one became compromised by the authorities. He wanted to make certain he had one place to run for protection if he was discovered by an American defender.

Every Islamic terrorist sharing the safe house instantly went in action. Al-Wahhad did not fool himself in the least that he wanted to get out of this area quickly. In case Mohammed did break under the harsh interrogation he was certain he was enduring at the hands of the hated local authorities of Washington. And he finally gave in and informed the inquisitors where this safe house and the other Islamic warriors were located and hiding. He knew Mohammed did not know of the other location he was soon to be heading for, so it was impossible for him to betray the ones with him to the Washington police.

Al-Wahhad was rushing around the building, as the other terrorists gathered on the ground floor. One by one, the small group of terrorists piled up and waited for the leader to collect what he wanted from this location and then they would move out to the next location. The terrorist's weapons were broken down, so they fitted in the travel suitcases they were stored in.

As al-Wahhad collected what he needed for the new location, he ordered the others. "What in the name of Allah's grace do you foul fools call what you are doing, by just standing here wasting your foul time like this? Why are you fools standing like you have nothing else to do but stare at me and what I am doing? Do I have to think of everything for you worthless fools and order you to do everything you must do, to assure our safety and the success of our sacred mission? Can not one of you worthless fools think for yourselves, and get some of this pressure off my broken back? Bashir al-Beidh, you above the others, I expected more from you, fool. You're the most intelligent one of a lot of these jackals. Bashir, you're to take command of them, and have them store what they're taking, and what I want, out to our vehicles.

"By the time I retrieve what I need from this foul place, have these other items placed in our vehicles. Fools, time is rapidly running out on us, because I believe the police authorities are closing on us. It's only a matter of time before the evil ones discover our location, and we're forced to engage them to the fight to the death. Get the items I need out to the vehicles, and then make certain your weapons are hidden from the prying eyes of our worthless neighbors. Bashir, you must make certain our weapons are always in easy reach of our fighters, in case the authorities reach us before we can leave. I have but a few more items I must take. By the time I finish collecting everything, these items better be stored in our vehicles, or you'll kiss the feel of Allah before it's time for you to do so."

Al-Wahhad stopped speaking and he gave Bashir a savage look, and then he reacted as if he was just slapped across the face. Instantly, Bashir issued orders and the terrorists were carrying everything out to their vehicles. All were acting like they had a purpose to their being, and when al-Wahhad carried the last items into the living room. Everything else was moved to the vehicles by the other terrorists.

Dropping what he carried in his arms on the floor, the terrorist leader turned to the few terrorists he was leaving behind to defend this safe house. Another reason he was leaving them was he hoped if the police authorities located this house and they attacked. Killing these few defenders might be enough to fill their lust for revenge, and in their minds maybe they might believe they killed all the members of the terrorist cell that attacked New York City and now Washington. He was no fool, and he realized believing in this thought was just a wish. He understood how tenacious the police authorities of this country were, and they would not rest until they were assured, they killed or captured all the terrorists who attacked them.

Looking into the eyes of the defending warriors, al-Wahhad searched for the man he wanted to speak with the most. Spotting Mustafa Saleh standing just behind Farima, he offered the well respected and feared Afghan fighter. "Mustafa, my faithful brother from another land, I trust that you're the best fighter I shall leave behind to protect this safe house and wait our return once we have detonated the great weapon of revenge against the lowly infidels of this evil country. You are the smartest fighter when it comes to the use of weapons, and how to deploy the defenders properly, if you come under attack by the police authorities of this evil land. So, it's right I appoint you as my replacement to command this foul cell.

"Mustafa, you must control the worthless fools I shall leave behind with you, so they don't draw any attention to themselves, and the worthless ones are discovered by the hated police authorities of this evil country, before we're ready to engage the fools in combat. You must command your fighters faithfully Mustafa, if you do come under attack before we come back to you. You must defend this position to the last of your fighters if you possibly can, fight the cursed authorities to the death.

"I fool you not one second my brother Mustafa, there's a strong chance you'll be discovered and attacked as is the same for the group I shall continue to command with me. I swear by the mantel of Allah's sacred word that we'll fight until the death, to give you time to escape, and you must offer us the same respect. The worthless news reporters will broadcast over the cursed TV and radio, if the police authorities had engaged either of our two groups of freedom fighters. The ones not under attack must use the battle the second group offers, to escape to the country of Mexico, and the safety that country offers us.

"Mustafa, by no means am I leaving your group behind for a suicide mission. I warn you of this possibility, because the foolish Mohammed was captured, and we have no idea if he was taken alive. We must assume he was, and the inquisitors are applying their evil methods to break his foul will and force him to betray us to the police. We pray Allah that Mohammed's heart explodes in his foul chest before he has a chance to betray us. Remember after I leave if your warriors are engaged by the lowly infidels searching for us, you must fight with all the hatred your heart can possibly muster against the evil non-believers. We'll need all the time you can afford if you come under attack by the fools, because for us to move our operation to a better and stronger secured location. Our, my future attack must be protected.

"Mustafa, it's by my hand once I set off the device of revenge, to kill the hated command of the land of Satan with the blinding light I shall release against the lowly infidels. That light will cleanse this foul land and make it pure and clean for us Arabs to inhabit and replace the non-believers who have paid homage to the hated Devil. Mustafa, I'm relying on you and the other fighters I leave in your charge if you come under attack, to fight the lowly infidels with the heart and strength offered you through Allah's grace."

Al-Wahhad took a second, and this silence allowed Mustafa the break he needed, so he could respond to his leader's words. Coming out from behind Farima, Mustafa offered cautiously. "Shabbah, rest your mind at ease, if my group comes under attack. The worthless fools will think us a thousand strong hiding within these foul walls. We shall unleash a wall of death to kill anyone who dares to challenge our sacred cause. We'll fight until not one breathes is shared by any of my faithful warriors. We'll fight the lowly dogs of non-believers for a week, and their dead will mount so they'll be forced to break off their attack against us. All I want you to concern your mind with, is constructing the weapon that'll silence the worthless heart of Washington. Once that weapon cleanses the evil of this foul city, the rest of this land will be cleansed once we removed the yoke of suppression the minds of this evil city hold their civilians under."

"My ears are pleased to hear the sacred words of comfort you offer to me, Mustafa. If you're true to your proud boastful words, we'll be successful in this upcoming attack against the filthy jackals of the United States. We shall destroy all the lowly leadership of this evil country with one blinding light of justice. Soon there'll be not one evil soldier from this foul and sinful land still walking on the sacred sands of any Arab country of the world. The Arab lands will be pure and free of the evil that the

United States binds their foul people with." Al-Wahhad allowed a quick smile to cross his lips, as he reached out then took Mustafa's arms in his hands and he hugged the fearless Afghan fighter as he added.

"Mustafa, my faithful brother from the endless world of sand of our great ancestors, I only wish that I could remain behind and join you in this holy war with the hated infidels of the world. But alas, I have a much more important mission to accomplish for Allah's sake and our cause. I leave you with a heavy heart, because my mind will be with you in your faithful struggle against the hated jackals of Washington. Go in Allah's light and be successful and safe." With that said, the terrorist commander released his grasp of the Afghan fighter, and he picked up the remaining items he needed then he rushed out the door.

The leader of the small Islamic radical group of terrorists left the house and moved to the lead vehicle parked in the driveway. He checked to make certain everyone he was taking with him, was inside the three vehicles vehicle. Then he started it and carefully backed the car onto the road and took the lead for the other cars. Turning on Ninth Street, he drove until he came to First Street East. He turned on the road taking him to the next location in the heart of the central, commercial section of Washington.

Upon locating the large commercial structure, the Ghost allowed himself a quick smile. Because he understood he, and the rest of his group of terrorists made it safely to this new location, and the defenders he left behind at the other safe house, was going to give him the cover needed to complete his task. The only thought still clouding his mind, was the want to complete the construction of the nuclear device, and then exploding it between the White House and the Capitol Building, and thus ending the reign of the United States in the world's pulse.

Slowing down a little so he could control his vehicle easier, al-Wahhad cautiously turned into the gated area of the large parking lot of the commercial site. Instantly, he was fuming because the ones he sent to this location with al-Mutairi a few days before he arrived at the site had foolishly allowed the security gate to remain open. Thus, allowing anyone who wanted to see what the activity going on inside the building was about, and they could enjoy the ability to see everything his terrorists were doing with constructing the bomb.

Al-Wahhad continued to drive through the parking lot completely carefully and slowly around the long building with the other vehicles following him. Then he parked next to the vehicle that al-Mutairi used to get his terrorists to the location. He picked up Mohsen al-Gasim and Reemabdel Aziz al-Rowaili, the two were obviously doing security for the building. He was pleased for sending these two young terrorists as support for al-Mutairi's much needed work.

CHAPTER TWENTY-THREE

CAPTAIN ROBERT WALKER'S CARAVAN

Captain Walker allowed the Lieutenant's Capitol police squad car to lead the way for his vehicles and Tier One soldiers. When his caravan turned off Pennsylvania Avenue and onto Seventh Street where the gas station was located, the police cars immediately went silent, and they turned off their lights and allowed Walker's machines to pass by them.

The young Marine Captain grabbed his mike and growled. "Okay, you police officers make like fucking ghosts and disappear up the damn side streets, and then stand by in case we need you guys. If you hear any weapon's fire popping off, keep everyone outta the friggin area until we clear the site. All vehicles under my command, I want your machines to park anywhere you can park the damn things away from the damn gas station. You guys are to stop all civilian traffic coming up and down this damn road. Squad Leaders, you have a copy of the little puke's stinking puss, so keep your eyes peeled for the crud's ass out there maybe just walking round. My vehicle's the only one that's gonna approach this fricking gas station, and I'm gonna flash this rotten prick's face around, and see if anyone recognized the little cocksucker. Take up support and security positions as ordered and stand by. Over."

The Marine Captain concentrated his attention out the windshield of his vehicle. He stared at the Mobile Circle K gas station as it came in view. With his jaw set and read for any situation to come at him, he glared at the station as his humvee slowly pulled into the lot, and he ordered his driver. "Nentendo, fuel this damn thing up. We'll never know when the next time we a chance might have to fuel up, take advantage of this break to do it." Even before he climbed out of the humvee, his radio came to life. It was Colonel Leadbetter contacting him.

"Errr… Dragon Lair to Dragon Fire Leader. Come in. Over."

"Jesus Christ, what fucking now dammit?" Captain Walker complained as he grabbed the mike and growled. "Dragon Fire Leader to Dragon Lair. Go with your fucking traffic. Over."

"Dragon Fire, I want to know what the fuck you people are doing out there for crap's sake? What's your present position on your vengeance patrol, Captain?" Colonel Leadbetter snarled and then he waited for Walker's reply.

"Dragon Lair, I just entered the stinking gas station where our terrorist obviously fueled up his stinking vehicle, and I'm gonna see if anyone here knows this little prick. My position is East, Three, Five, Niner by West, Six, Six, Eight. Over."

"It's about time you got your ass over to that damn gas station, Dragon Fire…"

"Dragon Lair, how is it going back there, sir? When we left the incident area, it was still a helluva a stinking mess, sir." Walker asked his Commanding Officer.

"It's still a helluva mess here, Captain." Colonel Leadbetter replied with a snort.

"I guess so, has anyone been able to place an estimate on the number of dead and injured, Dragon Lair? Over." The captain asked with concern while stalling because the station was crowded, and he wanted to wait until some of the people left the gas station before he entered it.

"Dragon Fire, the police are throwing the number of dead at around twenty-two hundred souls. Many deaths were caused by possible heart attacks, Asthma attacks, disabled men, women, and children being trampled to death underfoot with about ten thousand more injured to various degrees ranging from extremely critical, to walking injured. It was estimated there were over sixty-five thousand asses in the seats watching this damn ballgame. So, this shit could've been far fucking worse than it's shaping up to be, Captain.

"Arrr… this is all bullshit and bad manners if you were to ask my ass, Dragon Fire Leader. Walker don't concern yourself with the dead and injured back here, mister. Your assignment is to find the scumbags who attacked us and make certain the death toll and injured doesn't climb any higher on us. Listen up you have orders so carry them out as received. I'm about done at this latest incident area, and once I am I'll join your search squads in the field. Out Dragon Fire!" The fuming Colonel ended their conversation abruptly.

"Out." Was all Walker replied into the receiver, and then he left the machine and walked for the store part of the busy gas station as if he owned the world. He entered the establishment and quickly surveyed the interior of the structure to pick out his intended targets. There were three women and one man inside the establishment, and four other people were busy fueling up their vehicles outside. The lone guy was obviously paying for gas, while the three women walked the isles picking several items off the shelves. Walker's eyes instantly leveled on a young man unpacking a box, and knew this guy had to work for the station, so he approached him as if he was about to attack the young man and grumbled at him.

"Hey buddy, I wanna speak to your ass for a few seconds, man. It's important I do so, pal." Walker almost snarled at the kid.

The kid looked up and offered politely. "Yeah sure, what can I help you with sir?"

"I hope you can help my sagging ass, pal. Look at this stinking prick's puss and see if you recognize his ass for me, buddy." Captain Walker flashed the picture of Farideh at the worker.

"Yeah, I recognize the dude okay, sir. He's been in and out of the store quite a few times in the past few weeks, sir. But Johnny working the counter can tell you more about the dude, because he had a slight run in with the guy just yesterday in fact I believe, sir. I think the problem was over gas or something like that sir. Why do you want this guy for, did he stiff you outta money or something, sir?" The kid asked while keeping the conversation going in his search for information from the threatening stranger.

"Nuthin like that kid, the dopey guy was interested in a set of rims for his car I have for sale, and I got the damn things with me. But I never got the guy's stinking address when we talked 'bout the friggin deal. When I first met the dude, it was at this gas station a few days ago. Errr…you said the guy behind the counter was named Johnny?"

"Yeah, John's a cool dude, and probably knows where the guy lives, sir."

"Thanks, a shitload for your help, kid." Walker offered as he walked briskly for the counter. He ended up standing behind one of the women in the store, and when the other women came up behind him. He knew he was going to be forced to speak to this guy in private. When the lady in front of him paid for her soda and stuff, she moved away from the counter. Walker stepped up and he grumbled at the man as he flashed his badge at the guy.

"Hey, look bud it's time for you to take a stinking smoke break, pal. I gotta speak to your ass pronto, buddy." The captain stared into the man's eyes until he reacted.

The counter man looked at the strange, shaped badge. By the way Walker was acting, he was certain this man was a cop, as he called out to his helper. "Hey Richie, you got the counter for a few minutes. I'm going to step out and grab a quick smoke."

"Oh please, can't you wait until you checked me out first to have your smoke, mister? I have other things to do with my life rather than waiting for you to have a damn smoke." The older woman growled angrily at the counter man.

"It's no problem, Ma'am, Richie knows what he's doing behind the counter and besides, he's quicker than I am with the cash register, Ma'am." John flashed a smile at the elderly woman.

"Well, if he's better with the register. Maybe you should be stocking shelves, and allow him to wait on the customers, so we can get out of here quicker." The elderly lady snapped at him.

"Sorry Ma'am, Richie will be right with you." John stepped away from the counter and when Richie stepped in front of him, he offered to Walker. "Come on sir, I'll have that smoke now."

Walker followed him to the side of the structure where the bathrooms were, and he lit up a smoke and then leaned up against the building. John took a breath and blew the smoke out over his head as he offered to Walker. "Look sir, I told the other cop bugging me yesterday that I didn't know the damn radio was stolen. The damn thing was only worth a hundred bucks anyhow. I paid twenty for the damn thing when I brought it off the guy selling it. So why the hell are you still riding my ass over the damn..."

"Look pal, I ain't here over some damn radio crap, fella. Look friend, if you help me out here, I'll get the cops offa your ass, and I'll buy any radio you fucking want, man. All you gotta do is look at the puss in this fucking picture then tell me if you recognize the little cocksucker. Maybe you can even tell me where the scumbag lives round here, pal." Walker flashed the picture of Farideh's face at the man and then added.

"Take all the time you need to study the fucking picture and make certain you know the little prick before you answer, but you betta answer in five seconds or less. If you know what's good for your stinking ass that is, buddy." Walker warned the young man hotly.

The kid glanced at the picture and then moaned at Walker. "Oh, that guy huh, yeah I recognize him okay, sir. He's a real pain in the ass lately if you were to ask me, sir."

"Look pal, I don't give a friggin rat's ass what you might think of this lousy scumbag. All I asked you was if you recognized his damn ass, that's all I wanna know from ya. Now friend, one more question and then I'm done with your ass. Do you know where this little scumbag lives, and is it anywhere around here?"

The counter man stared at Walker for a second and then replied. "Yeah, sure sir, the guy gotta live somewhere around here. I've even saw him walking to the station a few times in the past few days. So, he must live well within walking distance of the store, mister. But I don't know exactly where it is though. That's the best I can offer you, sir. Mister, are you going to get the cops off my ass for buying that damn radio like you said?"

"Well, you're a lotta help to my ass, buddy. Can you at least point me in the fucking direction you last saw this prick walking?" Walker asked, still fishing around for added information.

Neither Walker nor John noticed the elderly black lady from the store who followed them around the side of the building. She wanted to bum a cigarette from the young counter man. When Walker flashed the picture, she looked at it from behind John's back. She immediately offered to Walker. "Errr…excuse me young man, but I know where that man lives. He gave me a ride home from the station a few times. In fact, he lives on the same block I do. But it's going to cost you a cigarette or two, if you want me to tell you where he lives, sir." She put out her hand and wiggled her fingers, and then she waited for either man to offer her a smoke.

Walker pulled out his pack of Marlboros and handed the full pack to the lady and barked at her at the same time. "Look lady if you can take me to where this little prick lives. I'll buy you a stinking case of god damn cigarettes, Ma'am."

"Why aren't you the nice young man? I'll be pleased to take you to his home, sir." The elderly lady replied as she made the pack of cigarettes quickly disappear as she added. "Since you gave me your cigarettes, I'd be happy to take you to that house, sir. I must warn you though that he doesn't live alone. Since he and his friends moved on the block a few days ago, sir. I saw a few young men and women moving around on the property or coming and going from the place to do who knows what. There are quite a few people living with this man, sir."

"You said that there were other people sharing this stinking dump with the guy I want, how many other people would you say are sharing this fucking guy's place with him, Ma'am?" Walker asked as he completely ignored the man who worked in the gas station now.

"Oh, let me see, yes young man. I noticed at least ten men and women staying in the home with this man, sir. Maybe a few more than ten could be sharing the home as far as I'd know for certain. Gees, maybe there could be up to fifteen to twenty men and women sharing the home, sir. Oh, by the way, there is one much older man in the home also, and he seems to be the one controlling the kids. I witnessed this man giving the kids money and tell more like an order what to do. The more I think about it, yes, every time I was allowed near the home, sir. It seemed when this older man came near the kids, they seemed to change their dispositions…"

"Whatdaya mean the kids changed their dispositions? Whatdaya mean, how did they change?" Walker asked with concern lacing his tone of voice.

"Well sir, whenever the older man was near, the kids stopped talking freely. Yes, and they also stopped smiling and being so pleasant also, sir. There were a few times when this older man came out, the moment the kids saw that one coming at them. I was rushed out of the home not so politely might I tell you, sir. Very abruptly might I add even, sir." The elderly lady offered while staring into Walker's eyes.

"Look lady, my name's Robert. Honey, I need you to search your mind and try and give me a more accurate count on the number of people you saw inside this damn home, Ma'am. Please, this is extremely important I know exactly how many stinking people I might be going up against inside that dump, Ma'am." Walker was trying not to curse as much and possibly scare the old lady as he fished around for more information from her.

"Well Robert, are you a police officer? The police are always bothering my people you know."

"No Ma'am I'm not a stinking cop, I'm a soldier, a special ops soldier, Ma'am."

"A special kind of soldier you say huh Robert. Why is a special soldier so interested in what these young kids are doing in their home…? Oh, excuse me, with you being interested in what the kids are doing there, sir. Could it have anything to do with what happened in New York City a number of days ago, Robert?" Melba asked with a smile.

"That's exactly why I wanna speak to this stinking little puke in the picture, Ma'am. To make certain he's not one of the bastards involved in that mess in New York City. Mind you though Ma'am, there's no real evidence pointing to this kid as doing anything wrong yet, Ma'am. I just wanna speak to him and see if he could possibly help me like you're doing, Ma'am."

Walker slipped by admitting this kid might have something to do with the terrorist attacks in New York City. He feared if this woman felt she might be betraying this young kid. She might get hit with a severe case of the forgets and clam up tighter than a clam and decided not to help him any further with this mess. So, he tried to change the reason why he wanted to speak to the kid, to not scare the lady from helping him any further. So far, he was lucky no one was linking the explosions at the ballfield to a terrorist attack. So, he wanted to get to the guy before the kid had a chance to disappear on him.

"After thinking about it a little younger man, I believe there were a few more than fifteen kids sharing the house with the older man. A few of them are most unfriendly though, but for the most part they seemed to be on the friendly side, Robert." The lady replied cheerfully.

"Okay Ma'am you said you had no problems with taking me to where this kid lives?" Walker asked as he flashed the old lady a smile and then he waited for her reply.

"Mr. Robert, my name's Melba Watkins, and as I said before sir. Because you gave me your smokes, I'd be more than happy to take you to where this child lives. If I correctly remember Mr. Robert, the boy in the picture said his name was Farra, Faridman, Farideh, or something like that, sir. I'm terribly sorry, but I simply cannot remember how he pronounced his name properly to me, Mr. Robert."

"His name doesn't concern me in the least, Ma'am. I'm more interested in where this guy lives, and who the hell he lives with, Melba. Are you ready to lead the way for me, Ma'am?"

THE SHABBAH (THE GHOST)

Abdulaziz al-Wahhad slammed his vehicle in park and jumped out of the SUV, leaving the others of his group to get out of the machine as the other vehicles parked behind his car. He walked up to Mohsen al-Gasim and his girlfriend and offered them. "Ahhh... it does my heart good to see someone I chose to work with, have the ability to take orders seriously, al-Gasim."

Al-Gasim could not remove the astonished look covering his face, as he shook hands with the Ghost. Al-Wahhad then scanned the exterior and discovered most of the building was like it was explained in the letter he read. The work area was made of thick concrete and cement block, but the front of the building had many windows, and the frame was constructed of a thin metal skin. This will certainly open his forces to attack from the local authorities if they discovered where he moved his fighters to. The terrorist leader turned to al-Gasim and smiled pleasantly at him.

Seeing the look of concern on Mohsen's face, al-Wahhad remarked. "Yes, follower of the one true religion, I brought the other fighters with me because our safe house might have been compromised by the worthless fool, Taborazadi. The woman I assigned as his partner during the attack on the cursed baseball ballfield allowed the great fool to be captured by the hated police authorities. That is the reason why I removed these few faithful fighters and left a backup group of fools as a defending force with Farima at our old safe house. Those I left behind have orders to fight to the death, and I have no want or desire to save the worthless lives of those foul fools. They earned their foul fate because of their foolish actions."

"The ones you have with you, you chose to live for another action in our future, al-Wahhad?" The confused young terrorist asked his leader.

"Yes, and they'll be well prepared to defend our escape if this place becomes compromised by the foul police authorities There are but a few from our cell who I'm concerned saving their lives, yours, your girlfriend, Leila Alibabic and Abdullah al-Mutairi. Those few I have further plans for, while the rest of them other fools will be the defenders for our escape from the loathsome land of Satan." Al-Wahhad shrugged.

Al-Gasim looked over the shoulder of the Ghost at the others he brought with him. The group remained well out of ear shot, and that freed al-Wahhad to speak freely of the ones he planned to save from his small group of terrorists. The terrorist leader did not have to look over his shoulder to understand what al-Gasim was concerned with as he remarked. "Al-Gasim, have the extra vehicles removed from view and then get the fighters…Never mind what I said, I'll take command of the foolish fighters. You look after the vehicles and get them out of sight for me." The Ghost stopped speaking and faced the others and then barked at them.

"Why in the name of the great Prophet, are you cursed fools standing out in the open like this? Do you fools not have the God given smarts to disappear like a desert mirage? Must I take you fools by the worthless hand, and then lead you like old women and young children to your proper place, to be of assistance to our sacred cause? By the great gray beard of the Prophet Muhammad himself, get inside the foul building and get out of the sight of any enemy stalking our every move in this hated land of Satan! Dealing with your foolish ones is like dancing on the heads of snakes." Al-Wahhad remained standing with al-Gasim and Reemabdel. The three of them watched as the other terrorists quickly disappeared inside the commercial building. Once the radical fighters were out of sight, al-Wahhad added to his words. "I trust you shall look after the foul vehicles I brought here as I instructed al-Gasim?"

"Please allow your mind to rest at easy al-Wahhad. I shall look after the vehicles and get them out of sight of any watching eyes. Shabbah, why do you not go inside the building and see how well al-Mutairi and the others, have progressed with our great weapon of justice? You'll be pleasantly surprised at what they have accomplished with the weapon in so short a time." Al-Gasim offered as he left al-Wahhad standing with his girlfriend, and he went to the three vehicles. Al-Gasim and Reemabdel who followed her lover, crawled into a vehicle apiece, and they started and moved them to the back of the commercial building.

With that said the still rather angry Ghost turned away from the two and headed for the large building. The interior of the structure was like what he noticed from the outside. The vast work area was constructed like a concrete bunker. The front of the building was the weak spot he was certain would be the area the police authorities would surely attack from if they discovered where his cell was working on their next attack plans.

The Ghost rushed through the building, heading for where al-Mutairi was busy constructing the weapon. He walked up behind al-Mutairi and waited to be acknowledged by him. Al-Wahhad knew al-Mutairi was aware he was standing behind him, but the bomb maker was in a crucial point of his labor, and he had no intentions of stopping his work to speak with the leader of the terrorists. When al-Mutairi screwed the last bolt giving him trouble with the weapon, the bomb maker gave a deep sigh of relief, and then allowed his shoulders to sag a bit as he finally acknowledged the presence of the Ghost. "Ahhh yes…al-Wahhad, I'm pleased to see you."

"Al-Mutairi it does my heart good to lay eyes upon your kind face again, my faithful Arab brother from the lands of our great ancestors and endless sand. How does your work go with our great weapon of revenge? I fear we're fast running out of time to deploy the weapon of our revenge against the hated enemy of Allah." The Ghost replied as he looked over al-Mutairi's shoulder, and he studied the weapon.

"I report work on the weapon goes very well for us. Al-Wahhad, I completed the main structure that'll house the heart of the weapon, so we can set it out against the enemy of our religion. I have the basic component of the weapon completed, and all I have left to do, is to construct the firing mechanism. Then it'll be good to be deployed."

"This is good for me to hear from your faithful lips, al-Mutairi. You must work diligently with the task I have set out before your skilled hands and eyes, to finish the work on the weapon of justice for our just cause. Things are taking place that I don't wish to burden your mind down with, my Arab brother. But I warn you that you must be prepared to move your entire operation out of this miserable structure at a moment's notice I council you. Time is of the essence for our operation to be successful against the lowly jackals of this evil land. We must complete the weapon as quickly as possible."

"Al-Wahhad, your words make me fear that the police authorities are rapidly closing in on our mission. Shabbah, is there time left for me to complete the weapon before we're discovered by the hated ones? Or is my work all for naught?" Al-Mutairi asked with concern.

"As I have just stated to you al-Mutairi, I don't want you to worry your mind about anything else but completing the work I have assigned to you, my faithful Arab brother. Whatever is happening otherwise is of my concern and my concern to deal with only, and I'll handle the any problems we might face on my terms. You just worry about completing the weapon and that is all." The Ghost glared at the young bomb maker.

Reading the angry look in the eyes of his dangerous leader, left no doubt in his mind that trouble was fast coming at them. He let his breath out in a rush and then put his head down and went back to work on the sloppily constructed nuclear weapon.

When al-Wahhad saw al-Mutairi had went back to work on the weapon again, he relieved the concern he was suffering, and walked away from the bomb maker and his project. He was more concern with what the others of his cell were doing. He wanted every man and women working with one thought in their minds. That thought was to protect al-Mutairi and the weapon at all costs to them, and the others were to be prepared to defend this building from the local police authorities when they attacked them.

CAPTAIN ROBERT WALKER

Captain Walker escorted the elderly black lady over to his waiting vehicle, and she had a hard time climbing into the high machine. She complained all the way as she struggled into the heavy military vehicle. "My dear Lord in Heaven, how am I ever supposed to get inside a vehicle this high up from the ground, young man? My word, why on earth do you need this vehicle to be so tall and hard to get into Mr. Robert? My old legs are..."

Walker stopped her complaining by picking her up and carefully deposited her inside the front passenger seat of the vehicle. Once Melba was comfortable inside the Humvee, he climbed in the rear seat and ordered the driver. "Nentendo, this young lady here is Melba, and she is gonna direct you on where to drive this damn thing. You're to follow her directions as if they were coming from my ass, mister."

"I read ya loud and clear, sir." Nentendo replied to his Commanding Officer.

"Good, give me that stinking mike and move this damn thing out to where this young lady directs you go, man. Melba, you tell my driver where to go, so we can locate this damn kid and his stinking friends, thank you honey." Walker offered and then he keyed the mike.

"Dragon Fire Leader to all Dragon Fire followers on personnel. Listen up people. My vehicle is gonna be the only one that'll turn down the block in question. All uther units are instructed to stop at the beginning of the road and wait for further orders. Once we're certain where we're heading, I want half our units to split up and deploy to the uther side of the road, and then use your machines to block off all fucking civilian traffic from entering the danger zone. Once we have properly secured the entire block and area in question, I want the women from our units to make for the civilian houses surrounding the target building. I want you chicks to get the damn civilian shits the hell outta the danger zone before we let loose and go hot against the lousy pricks we want. Squad Leaders how copy orders? Over."

Both the Mutt and Ramirez replied simply to Walker's orders. "Copy all."

"Good, carry them out as received then. Out." Walker replied and then he looked over Melba's shoulder as she instructed Nentendo where to drive. It took the caravan of military vehicles ten minutes driving, before Melba announced in an excited voice. "Err... Mr. Robert, this is the road where the kids live on, sir."

Nentendo stopped the vehicle at the head of the road. Then he automatically handed Walker the mike and settled down and waited further instructions from his Commander.

Walker took the offered mike and gave Nentendo a nasty look as he barked in it. "Dragon Fire Leader to all Dragon Fire personnel. We're parked at the head of the stinking road leading to the structure in question. Dragon Breath, I want you to take your Units and deploy said personnel down the uther blocks. So, you can cut off all civilian traffic leading onto this damn street, and the surrounding roads to this area of responsibility.

"Dragon Claw, I want you to take your Units and close down all friggin roads leading into the danger area from this side of the area. Squad Leaders, deploy your chicks for clearing the damn civilians from the surrounding blocks of the target structure. Then have the troops move on the block our targets are deployed on and get the damn civilians the hell offa the block as silently as possible, and undercover at the same time. Do it this way once you cleared the damn civilians from their homes. Hop the fences and get into the backyards of the homes surrounding the target structure and terrorists, and then you are ordered to hunker down. You people are well trained, and you'll know when to react to any actions taking place against the structure.

"You women warriors working with the damn civilian's outta the area, are instructed to get the pukes the fuck outta their damn homes. I don't give a rat's ass if you must use strong arm tactics against the damn Alfa Hotels (Ass Holes) to accomplish this order. You chicks hafta move the stinking civilian's outta the danger zone before we go hot against the fucking targets. Get me right the first time on the instruction. I don't give a shit if you guys hafta knock any damn Alfa Hotels out, and then carry their limp asses to the fences and pitch their asses over them to get them outta harm's way. We hafta get the civilian's outta the incident zone before we can go to work on the lousy scumbags. We have orders to keep the collateral damage down to an absolute minimum, and that's exactly what I intend to do, dammit.

"Okay people, we're gonna move out and turn down the stinking block of the building, and when our helper identifies the target structure. I'll ID the structure to all Squad Leaders, and then you people can commence getting the stinking civilian pukes the hell outta the damn area. Look like you people have a fucking purpose here, we're closing in on the lousy bastards who hit us today. We're ready to start our vengeance patrol against the cocksuckers. Over."

Walker held on the mike as he hit Nentendo on his shoulder. The instant he was tapped, Nentendo started down the block as he listened to Melba's instructions. About halfway down the street, Melba announced.

"Mr. Robert this is the house where the child you want lives. I live three more houses down the block on the other side of the road."

"Which house you looking at sweetheart? You gotta point the damn thing out to me a helluva lot clearer please. I'm not a mind reader you know, honey." Captain Walker grumbled while not giving a care where the old lady lived on the block, as he looked in the direction Melba was pointing in. There were three homes in his line of vision.

"My word Mr. Robert, I'm pointing to the green house with the white picture window on the first floor, and the wraparound porch in the front of the home. This is the home I'm pointing to, which house are you looking at? If you follow my finger, you'll know which home I'm pointing at, young man."

"I got the dump pegged you're pointing to in sight, honey. Gees lady will ya give me a stinking break here?" Walker grumbled and then he growled in the mike again. "Dragon Fire to all Dragon Fire personnel. Target is the seventh structure down on the right side of the street heading south to north. I repeat the target structure is the seventh house on the street from south going north on my right side. To all personnel you have fucking instructions, so carry out orders accordingly people.

"Be advised people, I'll setup our temporary CHQ (Command Headquarters) at the north end of the stinking block. All personnel are instructed to check in with my ass when you secured your areas of responsibility for this operation. Once you secured your area, then you people will hunker down at position, and be ready to lend a hand if the operation is forced to go hot against the suspected terrorists hiding inside this stinking building. All personnel, once the damn civilians are cleared from area, remember only personnel left in the incident area will be our people, and our fucking targets.

"I'm warning all you shitbirds to pick out your targets correctly, people. We'll not have our body armor on, so be alert and damn careful out there. Also remember this order I demand no enemy targets will be allowed to escape this operation alive. Our first responsibility is to clear the civilian personnel the fuck outta the target area, and then we can go to work on the lousy bastards. Squad Leaders are ordered to report to our temporary HQ, so we can go over our plan and coordinate our attack. Then we wait for the female elements to clear the stinking civilian assholes from the Red Zone, so we can go to work on the lousy fucks. Over."

Captain Walker signed off and barked at his driver again. "Nentendo, get this damn thing down the end of the stinking block, and then pull the machine onto the connecting side street, so the damn thing's outta sight of the stinking terrorists. That's where we're gonna set up our CHQ. I wanna get everyone the hell outta sight until we've coordinated our attack against this rat shit in that damn structure." Walker turned and looked Melba, and then informed her of what he was going to do, once they were off the block.

"Well love you done everything I asked of you and more, sweetheart. I'm gonna remember your help and when this thing's over with. I'm gonna look you up and I'm gonna take you out for one helluva dinner, and a crazy ass night out on the stinking town you'll never forget if you live, honey. Melba, without your help, we woulda spent who knows how many stinking days and time looking for these damn people you lead us right to here. In that time, the stinking terrorists woulda attacked more innocent people of our country and killed who knows how many more of our people in their terrorist attacks.

"Honey, I'm gonna give you three hundred bucks, that's all the stinking cash I have on my ass, but when I look you up. I'm gonna make certain you receive a well-earned reward of ten thousand bucks, sweetheart. I gotta get you the hell outta the line of fire when we go afta the lousy turds, Ma'am. Only Heaven knows what the scumbags might pitch at us, and I don't want you getting hurt afta helping us out so much, Melba. When my second squad leader gets here, I'm gonna have him take you over to a safe place until the shooting is over, and you civilians will be allowed back in your homes…"

"You really think it'll come down to an all-out firefight with those poor kids in their home, Mr. Robert?" Melba asked the young warrior with concern.

"Afta seeing what these stinking slugs done to the damn ballgame earlier today, coupled with the two attacks they successfully carried out against us in New York City a few days ago, Ma'am. Yes sweetheart, it's a good bet it's gonna come down to one helluva stinking firefight, and that's why I wanna get you over to a safer place to wait it out, honey."

Walker replied with surprise in his voice. He was impressed she'd know the military term of 'firefight'.

"Mr. Robert I'd be more than pleased to speak to the kids over the phone. Maybe I can talk them into surrendering, so no one must lose their lives in this confrontation. Really, I wouldn't mind in the least with trying to talk to the children so they can live. They're so young and it'd go against God's will and be a real shame to kill so young a bunch of children." Melba offered while looking Walker in the eyes. She was that concerned for the welfare of the kids.

Captain Walker returned the stare while milling over her offer to try and talk the kids out of the building. He wanted to capture a few of them alive, if possible, to make certain there was not a splinter group of terrorists he did not know about, operating somewhere else in the Washington area. After thinking about Melba's offer, a while longer, he remarked calmly to her. "You know something Melba, I just might keep you hanging around a while longer, sweetheart. In case there might be a slight chance of you talking these lousy popinjays outta that damn rathole of theirs. Looking at you, I see in your eyes you're definitely the right person who'd be able to get the job done, young lady."

"You're damn right I'm the lady to do that job for you, Mr. Robert." Melba replied while supporting a grin at the good-looking American soldier.

"Okay sweetheart you just brought yourself a job and I'll surely use your services if the need arises over this situation, Ma'am. Until that time, here's what I want you to do for me sweetheart. You see that large oak tree across the street there? I want you to stand, sit or do anything you want if you keep that tree between you and what's going down on the stinking block, Ma'am. If I need your help, I don't want you getting hurt before I use your services, sweetheart." Walker warned the elderly woman, and then he waited until Melba left his side. He stared at her until she disappeared completely behind the wide tree. Only then did he allow himself to breathe again and get back to the matters at hand.

Sergeant Dorothy Ramirez's Humvee was the first to report to the temporary HQ. She opened the door to the machine and climbed out of before it completely stopped. Once outside she headed for her Commander. Still trying to keep the cover on the operation, she failed to salute Walker on the street. No soldiers were acting like soldiers, only the troops in command of moving the civilians out of their homes were acting like soldiers.

Ramirez asked her Commanding Officer with concern lacing her voice. "Just say it, Robert. What do you think about this operation as it's turning out for us so far? Do you think the terrorists are really stacked up inside this place? Or do you think some of them might've moved to a second location in the area we don't know about in case we located this one on them? I'll tell you what I think about this crap, Bobby. I believe we have only half of the damn terrorists trapped inside that building. If there are any of the terrorists still hiding in the place as it is? Robert, if I were them after the attack on the baseball stadium, I would've surely moved a few my cell over to a second secured location. Because I believe they must understand we're rapidly closing in on their cell and the place they're hiding in, Walker."

"I dunno what to fucking think about this stinking operation any longer, Raz. All I know is if this damn Administration didn't go so hot and heavy against our stinking Intel Communities. We woulda known a helluva lot more about where the lousy cocksuckers are hiding. I believe we have some of the stinking terrorists trapped inside that damn dump, and I promise there ain't any of the lousy scumbags gonna get outta there a fucking live, unless they give up to my ass real peaceful like. And the shitbirds come crawling outta there on their stinking bellies and the fucks are telling me what I wanna know from their sagging asses.

"Raz, we're gonna setup as if we have the entire god damn terrorist cell trapped in this stinking structure, and if it's like you think, and some of the lousy bastards are hold up at a second secured location in the area. I wanna get a few of them damn pissants the fuck outta there still breathing. So, we can question their assess and find out about any other possible Muslim radicals from their cell operating outta a second location against us. I wanna make damn sure we got all the stinking slugs before we let down our defenses. Okay Sergeant, this is how we're gonna go down with our attack…" Walker's conversation was interrupted when the third vehicle carrying the Mutt and his troops pulled up to the Humvees, and he climbed out of the machine.

Walker turned and came face to face with his two point and sniper soldiers, the Ghost and Hunter. They were the ones he wanted to speak with the most, and he started right in with them. "Good, I want you two fucks to dress in your tree tux and deploy, I want you hunters to pick out your damn perches to operate from. Perches that'll allow you to keep all four points of the stinking building from north, south, east, and west in your constant view, until we go hot against the lousy pricks in there. I want you two birds to keep this building under tight surveillance, and if you detect anyone moving around. You're free to waste the targets the moment we go active against the scumbags.

"You two Vipers (Slang for his snipers) heard my fucking orders, so get in your camouflage outfits and pick out your damn perches and then hunker down and wait further orders. One uther thing, at the first crack of weapon fire, you'll need no further orders from my stinking ass. It'll be a free fire zone involving a terrorist situation, and you'll take out all damn targets of opportunity detected inside the friggin structure. You got your orders so get dress and head out, while I get the rest of our troops in action. Good hunting Ghost, Hunter. Move out." Walker watched as the two Vipers quickly pulled out their gear and started to dress in the outfits that made them look more like trees than soldiers. Walker's thoughts were interrupted a second time by Sergeant Ramirez.

"Oh, good here comes the King of Slime Square. Mutt, your brain has to go in gear before your mouth starts to operate, mister." Sergeant Ramirez moaned as she stared at the Mutt.

"Shit, you must be part of my stinking hangover, baby. Let me call you sweetheart cause I'm in love with you. I can't see your face dear, but your legs will do." The Mutt sang at the female Sergeant, and then he turned to his Captain and asked. "What's up Walker? Do you think we're that lucky to get all the stinking militants in one fucking building this easy, man? I'll bet my dick half the stinking cocksuckers aren't inside that damn dump we got covered. I believe finding all of them in there, is as hard as finding an honest politician in Washington."

CHAPTER TWENTY-FOUR

"Funny man, Ramirez is of the same mind as you are, buster. She thinks there might be a second location someplace nearby where the rest of the stinking fucks are hold up on us, man. No matter, I believe we have some of the stinking bastards trapped in there, and we're gonna act accordingly, Mutt. Phew, is that your fucking feet or your stinking breath? You gotta clean up or I'm gonna bathe ya ass myself, mister."

Neck moved up and announced to his Commanding Officer. "Hey Walker, me and the Mutt wanna pull up to the back of the da…"

"You and the Mutt huh? You and Mutt nuthin! Between the two of your assholes, you couldn't peel a fucking banana if you took all fucking day to try, buddy. You stand there and listen to my fucking orders, and then you two pissants will carry them out as received. As for you," Walker growled as he turned to the Mutt and hissed at his long-time friend and fellow soldier. "I want your stinking troops to protect the uther side of the stinking block for this damn operation. I don't want any civilians going down this fucking block until we have completed our operation against the assholes trapped inside that structure. No matter how many terrorists might be held up in there, we're gonna get them all or else. Move out and get command over your troops and set them up where they'll be of the most use, buster."

"Another day another dollar, another wall another tower, they're all gonna come tumbling down when we go hot against these suckas. Walker, I'm gonna stick with the stinking Mutt and his Units. I wanna protect his ass." Neck offered.

"You're still at it I see, and what the hell are you speaking?" Walker asked the huge soldier.

"English man!" Neck responded with a snap in his voice as he smiled at Walker.

"Is that what you call that gibberish coming outta your stinking mouth, buddy? I woulda never took it for English, asshole." Walker snapped at the large soldier while grinning at him.

"Yeah, and you don't gotta press one to fucking hear it either, man." The large soldier fired right back at his Commanding Officer.

Walker laughed and then added with a snort at the huge soldier. "You know you couldn't be a stinking seeing eye man for a fucking blind dog, buster. Mutt, do you want this slug hanging round in your damn Unit, buddy?"

"Yeah, why the hell not Walker, I'll take him with me for a fricking anchor. He ain't doing you any good standing here like a stinking tree trunk growing in the ground. So, I might as well give him something to do." The Mutt replied with a smirk.

"Good then get him the hell outta my stinking hair. Okay the rest of you screaming squirrels, recess is over so takeoff and setup for an attack against these stinking asses trapped inside that stinking dump. We move out against the lousy pricks in ten minutes. Dammit, didn't I just tell you two assholes not to leave your area of responsibility, and you asses did anyway? Okay, which one of you two jerks changed my stinking mind?" Walker snarled angrily at the two soldiers still standing by him staring at their Commander.

Neither soldier responded to Walker's question, as the Mutt and Neck took off and climbed into the idling military machine. Then they headed for the other side of the road with the terrorist's house on it.

"Those two are really something to work with Walker. Okay Bobby, what do you want me to do until we're ready to hit the radicals?" Ramirez asked as she stared at her soldier.

Walker ignored Ramirez's question as he responded to his female Sergeant. "I know I told you to have your stinking troops secure this side of the fucking road. Since I'm making this area our temporary CHQ, there's no need for you to carry out that order any longer, baby. Here's what I want you to do now Raz, take command of the troops moving the damn civilians outta the danger area. Yeah Raz, that's what I want you to do alright. I want you to have the female soldiers speak to the civilians and move them outta the damn area. The chicks aren't as intimidating as our male soldiers are to the dopey ass civilians. I told the Mutt and his tree trunk partner we're jumping off in ten minutes. I have no intention of attacking the shitheads, until I know for certain all the damn civilians in the area are outta harm's way, so we can operate without the fear of hitting any civilians when we go red on these fucks, Raz.

"Then all bets are off for the stinking terrorists, and we'll go hot and heavy against the lousy assholes, Raz." Walker understood he changed his orders to Ramirez, but since he was playing this operation close to his vest and making his attack plans as they came to him. He was going to keep changing his orders until he felt every soldier was well prepared for any opportunities, as they exposed themselves to him, and there was going to be little if any civilian causalities, once the operation when active and hot.

Walker's radio went off and the talker reported to the commander of the operation. "Hey Walker, I just got a coupla heavy armored vehicles pulling up to my position, man. I guess the Colonel's gonna setup a number of stinking Toll Booths for this fucking operation."

"What kinda stinking machines did whatshis fucking puss send up to us? I gotta know this shit, so I know how to betta respond and organize these new troops properly, stupid."

"Stupid huh? Walker the stinking Colonel sent up two BFMs (Bradley Fighting Machines) and the damn things took up positions blocking the entire road leading into the area in question here, man. Also, oh fearless leader, the soldiers riding the fricking machines look like they're just itching at the trigger to do some bad intentions against anyone they come across, man. The damn machines are setup for fucking bear, Walker." The Mutt reported after taking a shot at Walker for calling him stupid.

"Dragon Fire Leader, Dragon Breath. Respond, over."

"It's 'bout fucking time someone used the proper protocol around here when they wanna speak to my stinking ass over the damn radio for this damn operation, for crap's sake." Captain Walker growled more to himself than anyone standing near him as he replied to Sergeant Ramirez's call in. "Dragon Breath, Dragon Fire Leader. Go with your stinking traffic. Over."

"Dragon Fire Leader, reporting I have two same type vehicles arriving my position as well, sir. It looks like Colonel Leadbetter's planning not to take any shit from the damn terrorists. Captain, I ordered the Toll Booths (military slang for heavy armored vehicle roadblocks) to deploy about a block and a half away from my position, sir. The Commander informed me they have orders to stop all intended targets from escaping their nest under any circumstances encountered, as they lend support to our operation, sir. I'm comfortable with the extra help Walker. Over."

"Roger that last Dragon Breath, I'm gonna get in contact with the stinking…"

A second call came in and it over road his communication with Sergeant Ramirez as the speaker barked at him. "Dragon Fire Leader, this is Dragon Lair. Captain, I just sent in four pieces of armor for added protection and support of your operation, sir. You're ordered to place this armor where it'll support your damn operation the best, sir. The Commanders of said machines have their orders, and they're instructed to take any change in orders from you, until I'm able to deploy your location and takeover command of the entire operation, Captain. I should be arriving your location in fifteen, I repeat, fifteen minutes sir. I'll bring the rest of our Units as backup support; in case your Units get involved in a firefight with the scumbags. Over."

"Roger all as stated and received Dragon Lair, armor's set-in place for support for action by the extra Units, Commander. Over." Walker reported to his Commanding Officer.

"Dragon Lair, roger that last response Dragon Fire Leader, I'm on my way your location as we speak. Captain, I want the damn Kill Chain (Military slang for the time of locating enemy targets and destroying said targets) made as short as fucking possible for the duration of this damn operation, mister. Out!"

Buckethead hovered over Walker's shoulder while listening to his conversation with their Commanding Officer. When Walker was done the concerned soldier asked him. "Are we gonna jump off against the stinking terrorists before old hot shot gets his ass up here, man? Or are we gonna wait for the stinking Colonel to takeover command of this operation from our asses?"

"Let me tell you something buddy, by the time the fricking Colonel gets his stinking ass up here, this damn mess will be over with I promise ya. Besides Buckethead, the stinking Colonel does much better when he's commanding operations from the cheap seats, where his pussy ass will be safe and sound, and he's a hard target to get at by the enemy, man." Walker fired back at the soldier, and then he gave him a wink of the eye.

"Now you're fucking talking my stinking language, man. I'm gonna dip back and take up position with the rest of the guys for this attack, Walker. I wanna get some payback from the lousy turds for what they did at the damn ballfield today, man. I had money on that damn game."

Walker watched Sergeant Lombardo move off, and then he turned his attention to the building. The only thing stopping him from ordering his soldiers to go hot against the terrorists was he was waiting for a final report. One informing him the civilians living in his area of responsibility were moved out of the danger zone by the soldiers assigned to that task. The first call came in.

"Dragon Fire, Ice, (Sergeant Diane Morrison) here sir. I'm reporting all civilian personnel from right and directly behind target structure are out of the danger zone, sir. The civilians are secured at a church free of terrorist attack well away from the building in question, sir. Over."

"Roger that Ice, outstanding. As soon as I hear from Baby Tee, we go hot on target. Over."

"Roger last, Dragon Fire Leader, I'm ready to go hot against the bastards, sir. Over."

A second communication came in the instant the captain broke off speaking with Ice. "Dragon Fire, Baby Tee, I heard that transmission and am reporting all civilian personnel living or operating in the danger zone from the front of and left side of target structure, have been safely removed from the area, sir. Over."

"Fantastic Baby Tee, now we'll give the stinking trapped Muslim extremist some payback for what they had done to our civilians in both New York City, and Washington, sister. Okay, people listen up. All Squad Leaders check your watches and set them to my time for the opening of this attack. It's now Twenty-Three Forty-One and Three Second Hours. Set your watches accordingly now, now, now people. We go hot at exactly Twenty-Three Fifty-Five Hours. Be alert and all Units prepare to lend a hand to any Unit who might come under fire from the trapped subjects. This order is for the Vipers, (Snipers) Ghost, Hunter deploy and find perches that'll give you two birds the best possible advantage over the subjects in question here. I want you two working out there, people."

"Ghost to Dragon Fire Leader, reporting that Hunter and myself are already deployed in the field as prior instructed, sir. We have the entire area blanketed from both sides of the fucking building with the terrorists held up in, sir. We cover the dump from the front and back of said structure we're assigned to cover, sir. If the bastards show themselves, they're gonna be history that fucking quick Walker. I want some heavy ass payback for what these lousy little cocksuckers did to our people in New York and here in Washington, Captain. Over."

Captain Walker blushed because he forgot about already deploying his two extremely dangerous snipers out in the field, when his Units first entered the area in question. He hoped none of his other troops picked up his slight blunder, or he was going to get stuck buying his troops supper on their next leave for the entire group. That was the deal the elite soldiers made, whenever you screwed up on an operation then you owed the entire outfit supper and a night of drinking on your tab. It was just another way the soldiers had of staying tight with each other, and to also be able to carry out any operation they were sent out on, while holding each soldier together with the rest of the group of elite soldiers.

When Captain Walker regained his composure over his slight blunder with his two snipers, he shook his head and grabbed in the mike and snapped in it and grumbled. "Dragon Fire to Dragon Breath and Dragon Claw Squad Leaders, report readiness for operation immediately. I need this report, so I know when to jump off against our targets. Over."

"Dragon Fire Leader, this is Dragon Breath Squad Leader. All elements under my command are set in place and ready for immediate action against this terrorist cell, sir. Over." Sergeant Ramirez replied to her Commander.

Even before Walker could reply, their communication was interrupted by a second report. "Dragon Fire Leader, Dragon Claw Squad Leader reporting. My people are ready for immediate action." The Mutt informed his Commander.

"Roger that last, Dragon Fire Leader to Dragon Breath and Dragon Claw Squad Leaders. We jump off in exactly two minutes. I repeat, jump off time two minutes. I want this thing to go off like fucking clockwork people."

"Negative, negative, negative on that last order, Dragon Fire Leader! This is Dragon Lair Commander and I'm ordering your troops to stand the fuck down until I reach your position and take command of the damn operation. Dragon Fire Leader, I'm going to reach your position in ten minutes, sir. The fucking traffic on the streets is horrendous, and with your Units cutting off so many downtown roads to civilian traffic. Your actions have flooded the local streets with extra vehicles and traffic jams and fender benders. I repeat Dragon Fire Leader, I'm ordering your Units to stand down until I reach your location and take command of situation. Do you copy Dragon Fire Leader?" Colonel Leadbetter snarled into his radio then waited for his reply.

Walker rolled his eyes and moved his hand as if he was masturbating in response to his Commander's last order. He wanted to jump off against the trapped Arab terrorists before the Colonel could reach his position, because he knew his troops would respond to his orders better than to the Colonel's orders. Besides, with the effort he placed in this operation so far, he had no intention of turning over his mission to the Colonel now that it was setup and ready to go active. With his back against the wall, he decided to respond to his Commander's orders.

"Errr… Dragon Lair… this is Drag…Fir… I am hav… troub… rea… your Traff… Please repeat all after Drag… Fir…" Walker let go of the mike after using it to interfere with his communication with the Colonel.

Colonel Bruce Leadbetter was fuming as he turned to the driver of his Humvee, and he screamed at him while holding the mike opened, enabling Walker to hear every word he growled at his driver. "What the fuck's going on with this damn thing for fuck sake, mister? I can't fucking communicate with my damn Officer in the field for the love of Christ, and I need to carry out my communication with my Captain!"

The Colonel's driver knew what Walker was doing, and how he was screwing around on the Commander. But the soldier was not going to be the one to burn the captain down to the ground over it as he replied to Leadbetter's bitch at him. "Colonel Sir, I don't believe there's anything wrong with the system, unless it's being fucked up by some sunspots or something like that, Colonel Leadbetter Sir."

Colonel Leadbetter's glare sharpened as he held his driver locked up in his angry stare, as he growled savagely at his driver. "Sun fucking spots you say to my stinking ass, huh Wiseass. I'll give you fucking sunspots when we get back to damn base, mister. I know what that little sonofabitch is doing with the fucking radio, and I'm going to cook Walker's fricking backside for fucking around like this with my ass when this thing is over with, and we're back on base." Colonel Leadbetter placed his attention on the mike and snarled at his young officer.

"Dragon Lair Commander to Dragon Fire Leader, I don't know for certain if you're having real problems with your fucking radio or not, mister. I further don't know how much of this damn communication you're receiving. If you're screwing around with my ass, you'll rule the day you decided to fuck around with me, buster. Dragon Fire Leader, I'll repeat this for the last time, because by the time I repeat my damn orders, I'll be standing on your fucking throat. I order your Units to stand down until I reach your present position and assumed command of the operation. That is what you'll do if you know what's good for your ass, Captain!"

The Mutt was monitoring the communication going down between the two officers, and he was laughing his ass off over the way Walker was screwing around with the fuming Colonel. Now he knew they were going to jump off against the terrorists before he was able to get to their position and take over command from Walker. He was angry as hell over the thought of the Colonel taking over command of the operation from Walker.

Captain Walker was certain he'd be able to hear the Colonel screaming if he ended the communication, the officer was screaming so loud over the radio. He shrugged and then screwed with the Colonel for the last time over the radio. "Drag… Fir… to Drago… Lair… Evidently we are sti… hav… proble… with commun…" It was at this point he ended the communication and then jumped the frequency up a point and ordered his troops in the field. "Dragon Fire Leader to all Units. The color is Green, I repeat Green, were opening operations against the terrorists. I'm gonna drive down the road from north to south. Dragon Claw you'll come down from south to north, and we'll meet in the middle directly in front of the stinking structure.

"I'm gonna cut that pain in the ass off but good from bugging my stinking ass like he's doing for crap's sake. Dragon Fire Leader to One Charlie. Report." Walker barked in his radio as he went after another soldier from his Unit, because the Colonel was still trying to communicate with him, and he was interfering with his orders to the troops.

"Dragon Fire Leader, One Charlie here sir. Go with your traffic sir. Over." Roach, (Sergeant David Burgwald) replied. He was the satellite communications soldier for the elite Units.

"One Charlie, I want you to drop an electronic fucking haze over our asses for ten blocks out in all directions, man. I don't want any of the scumbags in there making a cell phone call, computer or any uther stinking communications outta the target structure. So, they can't possibly alert their brother scumbags if we don't have all the lousy bastards trapped in this one basket. I also want it done to stop any surviving terrorists from using a cell phone to detonate a possible explosive device they mighta left behind. A third reason is the electronic haze will get the stinking Colonel offa my stinking ass, so I can carry out this damn operation without him still bugging my fricking ass. Get it done for me soldier."

"You got it Walker but I gotta warn ya sir, the stinking Colonel has the means to bypass my electronic haze, so he'll still be able to be a pain in your ass over this operation, sir." The Roach reported to the captain.

"Shit, yeah, right, okay, I want you to drop the fucking haze wall down anyway. I'll deal with the stinking Colonel when the time arises. Okay, listen up the rest of you people, this is how we're gonna attack this fucking situation. Dragon Breath, you and your troops will come in at the structure by cutting through the backyard from the next street over, coming out right in front of the subject building from the west. I want six personnel riding in each of your attacking Humvees, so we have eighteen Units at the attack location when we go hot against the subjects. To all other personnel, you're instructed to be on the alert to stop any possible Squirters (enemy insurgents) from escaping our setup and be ready to lend a hand to any attacking Units if we run into heavy resistance from the lousy turds. We go active in twenty-seven seconds. Over."

Colonel Leadbetter was desperately trying to control his raging temper, and when Walker's radio went dead on him all together, he snapped as he stared at the mike he was trying to crush in his hand. "I know what that sneaky sonofabitch is doing with this damn radio, and when I get my hands around his throat. I'm going to squeeze until his fucking eyeballs come popping out of his damn skull. Then I'm gonna skull fuck the little shit to death before I finally release my death grip on his damn neck. What the hell's going on with this damn thing, it went completely dead on my ass now, dammit?"

"Colonel Leadbetter Sir, Captain Walker's Unit just dropped an electronic haze down around the entire area in question to stop any possible communications from the terrorists getting out, sir. Also, Colonel, you know the captain's radio didn't die on him sir. Standing orders are, if one freq is having jamming problems, sir. We're instructed to jump up to the next freq and listen for any further orders, sir. I'm certain Walker's operating on the next freq up, Colonel."

Colonel Leadbetter glared angrily at his driver as he responded to his words with a snarl. "Look buster I know damn well what the fuck the orders are, dammit. I was the one who issued the fucking things to you damn Squids in the first place, asshole. You get my ass up to Walker's position pronto, even if you have to drive over any civilian parked vehicles. Or driving this fucking thing through some backyards or through homes, get my ass up to Walker's position before I put a cap in your ass on general principles!"

While the Colonel was riding his driver, he was setting the radio up to the next frequency and managed to pick up the end of Walker's last orders to his troops. Colonel Leadbetter then keyed the mike and hissed in his radio. "Walker I know what you're doing with this damn thing, and I'll settle your hash after this fucking thing has run its course, mister. I heard your last orders to go active in twenty-seven seconds. Yes, time is of the essence, and I can't possibly be at your position in that short a time, mister. So, you'll have to go active without my ass being there. You go active and when I get up there, the troops under my command will take up supportive roles and assume backup operations for this action. Good luck Captain. OUT!"

Captain Walker ignored the Colonel's words, as he stared at his watch and at the exact moment ordered, he tapped his driver on his shoulder. Nentendo immediately punched the engine, and the large military vehicle lunged forward, and he carefully guided the machine down the block while scraping two civilian vehicles parked on the side of the road. The driver was moving the machine without lights, but he was able to see the Mutt's vehicle coming at him from the other end of the block. The two Humvees met right in front of the suspected terrorist's structure, and the soldiers immediately piled out of the machines and took up defensive positions.

When the Tier One no fail soldiers took up their defensive positions behind the parked vehicles, Sergeant Ramirez's Humvee rumbled out of the driveway of a home, that structure was directly across the street from the building the terrorists were believed hiding in. The overanxious troops out for revenge riding in her vehicle, immediately jumped out of the machine and instantly took up positions supporting Walker and the Mutt's troops who were already deployed for attack, as they prepared to go active against the trapped terrorists.

The moment the troops were set in place, the captain gave orders to the drivers who remained inside the idling vehicles in case they had to move them in a hurry. "Okay assholes, light 'em up and we'll see what the fuck the sonofabitches are gonna do in there. The rest of you guys stand ready against the fucks. Ghost, Hunter, we're active, are you two birds ready to pick off any targets you get a clear shot at? I'm gonna try and talk the fucks outta the nest first. If that don't work, then we'll go out for bear."

With a loud click the powerful floodlights mounted on the top of the heavy Humvees burned to life, and the operators turned them on the structure and lit up the place brighter than natural sunlight. Walker ripped the megaphone out of the machine and bellowed in it. "Okay you people hiding in the stinking house with address One, Five, Three, Four, Four. This is the Commanding Officer of the troops gathered outside the damn structure. You people hold up in there are instructed to come the fuck outta the stinking home with your damn hands held over your friggin heads. Then you'll follow all further orders issued to your asses without hesitation, or you pricks will be shot dead that simple. I will not repeat these orders a second time." As Walker warned the trapped terrorists, he heard his soldiers' chambering rounds and relaxed, as he waited for a reply from one of the terrorists.

INSIDE THE STRUCTURE WITH THE ADDRESS
OF ONE, FIVE, THREE, FOUR, FOUR

The young Islamic defenders hold up inside the dwelling, jumped from their chairs and beds when the interior of the building was suddenly bathed by the harsh glare coming from the heavy floodlights mounted on the Humvees. They had no idea the Special Forces soldiers were gathering outside their building, because they failed to post any of their people to watch for out trouble. The four males and two female Islamic defenders scrambled for their weapons. Once they had them in hand, they checked them then rushed for the windows of the structure to defend themselves and the safe house. No one inside the building turned on any lights, but the soldiers outside were supplied with special and powerful vision equipment that allowed them to see-through materials that constructed the building walls. At least four of the six terrorists were detected taking up defensive positions by the windows of the structure.

Captain Walker was immediately informed of the actions adopted by the terrorists inside the building. Again, he raised the megaphone to his lips and roared in it. "Look at you assholes, we know what you're doing in there. I'm warning you people if you wanna live then throw your damn weapons out the stinking windows. Then you are instructed to come outta the damn building one at a time with your fricking hands on the back of your noggins. That's if you wanna life for another fucking day." Walker had to wait as Ice repeated everything, he said to Arabic for the terrorists understanding in case they did not understand English.

Mustafa Saleh, the Afghan leader of the Arab defenders, looked over his shoulder to make certain no searchers were inside the structure with them. He had no idea how the soldier with the big mouth, knew they were taking defensive positions in the darkened home, as Walker's words were repeated in Arabic by a woman's voice.

The only Jordanian of the terrorist group, Nazira Zayn Abbus, took up a position by a window and he hefted the RPG (Rocket Propelled Grenade) to his shoulder, and smashed out the window with the tip of the powerful grenade. He then aimed the weapon directly at a Humvee parked no more than thirty-five feet from where he was setup, and he prepared to fire the weapon at the vehicle. He placed the machine dead center of his sight and held his fire for the moment.

Snatch, (Sergeant George Weaver) attached to the Mutt's Unit, instantly picked up the shape of the weapon aimed at them from inside the home. He roared out for the other troopers. "RPG, Holy shit man, the sonofabitches have a fucking RPG and the damn shooter's gonna fire the damn thing at us. Take cover."

The soldiers using the heavy Humvees for cover, immediately leaped away from the parked machines, and they laid down flat on the ground, as they covered their heads with their arms and prepared for the explosion. They did not have to wait long, with a telltale white streak from the launched grenade, the explosive device slammed into the side of Walker's Humvee. Because of the heavy armor the machine employed, the complete destruction of the machine did not happen, and the damage to it was not as severe as it would have been if the Humvee did not have the heavy armor plating on the machine.

Nevertheless, there was a good amount of damage done to the side of the vehicle. The machine was rendered totally disabled from the powerful blast, and the exploding vehicle showered the soldiers with shards of burning hot shrapnel and ripped apart metal parts. The blast was deafening, and it left several Walker's troops having some trouble with ringing ears, and slightly stunned from possible concussions.

Even before Captain Walker could grab his mike and get on his snipers to fire at the shooter of the RPG. He heard a few rounds being fired at the building, and he knew his Vipers were on the target. Six rounds, three each from the Ghost and the Hunter's weapons, ripped into the head of the RPG shooter as he struggled to rearm the deadly weapon.

The report came into their Commander. "Dragon Fire. Viper One, (code name for Sergeant Walter Casper) reporting we took out A-rab RPG shooter, sir. Over."

Walker's ears were still ringing from the force of the explosion that he had to shake his head a couple of times, to try and get rid of the cobwebs clouding his mind. He was fuming for not realizing the terrorists might be armed with an RPG. He dusted the dirt from his face and chest and then checked the rest of his body to make certain he was not hit by any shrapnel. When he was sure he was alright, he checked on the rest of his troops. He noticed the Mutt was still lying on the ground and a soldier was doing something to his body. He slid over to the Mutt's side and the Roach reported to him.

"Walker, the Mutt's tagged. We have Blood Clot coming up to look afta his ass, sir."

"Dammit, how bad is the dumb shit hit, let me see for my fucking self, Roach?" Walker growled and roughly shoved the soldier out of his way, and then he checked his friend's condition. There was a good size blood stain spreading on the Mutt's right leg and rearend, and when he checked it, he was able to tell a shard of shrapnel entered the Mutt's thigh, and it came out on his ass. With a good look at his wound, he bitched at the wounded Mutt. "You're shot in the ass, stupid. Don't worry about it too much, asshole. The wound's too far from your stinking heart to kill ya ass."

"Man, I can see you have a shitload of stinking sympathy just pouring outta your friggin mouth for my wounded ass, man. I thank you for all the fucking concern you're showing for my ass, Walker. You wait till I tell Raz about this shit, buddy. She's gonna get on your ass for it, pal. She'll teach you how to properly care for your friend who's wounded, you, lousy prick!" The Mutt complained at the grinning Walker.

"You know where to find the word sympathy in the fucking dictionary, don't'cha, pal?" Walker offered the Mutt as he closed his pants and prepared to engage the trapped terrorists.

"No fucker, where do you find the fucking word 'sympathy' in the stinking dictionary, Wiseass?"

"You find it between shit and syphilis, stupid. Get your stinking pants on so we can get afta these lousy scumbags and end this shit once and for all. So, I can go home and tie one on, man."

"I don't get a lollypop for my stinking injury. The Mutt complained at Walker.

"I'll give you a fucking lollypop, asshole." Walker fired back at the Mutt.

"So much for our President bragging 'bout having the al-Qaeda terrorist organization on the fucking run, with all his bragging 'bout bin Laden's death, and the demise of his terrorist organization. Our President has the stinking A-rabs flocking to terrorist organizations to get their revenge against us, man. All the new wannabe terrorists wanting to get a stinking piece of our asses, like the fucks held up inside this dump. I wish he'd keep his damn mouth shut and get off trying to take the stinking credit for what our Navy brothers did killing UBL.

"Hell man, I can still remember the stinking President crying the SEAL Team Six Troops were our government's hired killers, when the uther President was in command of the country, and how he wanted to try them elite soldiers for breaking some terrorist nose when we had a Republican President. How things changed when this guy took over the damn Presidency. I'll tell ya Walker with the constant debating we're doing on the way we're trying to protect ourselves against another possible terrorist attack in the United States. It's tantamount to rearranging the fucking deck chairs on the stinking Titanic and I for…"

"Are you 'bout done with your stinking bitching, shithead? Now is not the time to get involved in this type of stinking conversation." Walker grumbled while getting on the Mutt's ass again. A sudden barrage of rounds was let loose from the interior of the building the terrorists were held up in, from every window facing the street from the front of the home. Someone inside the building was shooting at the Rapid Response forces gathered against them outside the structure.

Buckethead, who was armed with a heavy M-60 machine gun, immediately began to return the terrorist's fire. He racked over every window on the first floor of the building with rounds pouring out of his weapon.

The Mutt stopped what he was doing and looked from the building to Walker, and then he remarked. "Hey man, I think we should call in some serious backup for this shit."

"Yeah, whatdaya wanna fucking do asshole? Call in a stinking air strike right in the heart of downtown fucking Washington D. C, pudhead? Get your ass dressed so we can get involved defeating the rat fuck terrorists trapped inside that damn building, buddy." Walker snapped angrily at the other soldier.

Over the Captain's shoulder, more weapons fire was being directed at the terrorist structure from many of his troops, as they got involved in the fight. Tens and then hundreds of rounds were being fired from both sides. Windows shattered not only inside the target building, but the over shooting was hitting several the homes directly behind the soldiers, as they tried to get at the trapped terrorists. The Rapid Response soldiers were pounding clip after clip of rounds at the building and enjoying it.

There were so many rounds being fired at them that the trapped terrorists were forced to duck down and move away from the windows to save their lives. Even though the heavy barrage of rounds continued unchecked from the American troops gathered outside the structure, the only fatality so far was the RPG shooter, Nazira Zayn Abbus. For the moment, the incoming rounds were being aimed more at the windows of the structure. Slowly, the rounds started to hit and penetrate the lower section of the civilian structure, moving the terrorists even further away from the windows and the front of the building.

Anything made of glass, wood or plasterboard was being shattered by the hail of rounds being fired at the building. Holes were ripped into the plaster walls and two plumbing pipes were cut by the rounds and were spraying water all around the interior of the building. Light fixtures exploded, sending glass shards flying and the air inside the building was suddenly clouded over with a thick layer of dust and spent gun powder.

Walker was keeping an eye on the fire from his troops. He wanted to make certain the rounds fired, were hitting the building with little over shooting as possible. Even though the civilians were moved out of the zone, the captain did not want their homes eaten up by over shots.

When he realized no rounds were coming out of the structure, he raised his hand and barked aloud. "Cease fire! Hold your god damn fire! Christ's sake, hold your damn fire will you people, dammit! The sonofabitches are no longer firing back at our stinking asses. The terrorists might all be dead in there for all we know. Cease fire, I told you fucking people to stop firing at the damn structure, dammit!"

When the heavy weapon fire ended from both sides, Walker looked for his megaphone, finding it he picked it up and raised it and bellowed in it. "Okay you kiddieidiots hold up inside that damn building, fun times over with. If any of you, dumb shits are still alive in there, I suggest you dudes come the fuck outta there with your hands held high over your heads. I'm gonna give you dopey twerps to the count of ten to come outta there real peaceful like. After that your time is up, and we'll come in there and drag your dead asses outside and leave ya naked and lying on the friggin sidewalk for all to see. So, what is it gonna be assholes, you jerk coming outta there real peaceful like, or do you wanna die in place? It doesn't mean jack shit to my ass either way you jerks come outta that damn building, dead or alive. But take my word for it, one way or the uther you'll come out of there. Your time's running and you're fast running outta fucking time in this world."

Walker stopped speaking and watched the time click away, and when the ten seconds were up, he bellowed again at the trapped terrorists. "You people are outta fucking time so what's it gonna be? Are any of you survivors inside the damn building gonna come the hell outta there real peaceful like and live or what? I won't ask you fucking people a second time, once I'm done talking, we're coming afta your lousy asses."

Walker barely lowered the megaphone when he received his answer when a new round of weapon fire erupted from inside the badly damaged building. Many rounds landed against and all-around Walker's destroyed Humvee. Not needing to issue the order, Walker's people immediately began to return fire. There were so many rounds being fired at the building again, that he was concerned the structure was being so badly weakened by the countless rounds ripping into it, that it was in danger of collapsing in on itself.

The heavy weapon fire was deafening and when the post supporting the wrap-a-round porch suddenly snapped and half the porch collapsed. The captain raised his hand and ordered his troops to stop firing again. This time the fire from the soldiers found their mark. The Iranian terrorist Adelah al-Faiz, the Iraqi Morteza and the female stadium attacker, Farima Ebadi, were killed in the attack against the terrorists. The female Saudi, Hatoon al-Muneef along with the Afghan terrorist, Mustafa Saleh were wounded, with Hatoon receiving the worst of the injuries.

She was hit twice, once in the shoulder, and the second round hit her dead in the stomach. Mustafa was wounded in the hand and his thumb was blown off his hand. He was in a lot of pain but still operating and ready to continue defending his position, until he realized he was the last man standing from his terrorist group.

Realizing Hatoon and he were the only ones still alive, his resolve left and suddenly he wanted nothing more in life than to live. He carefully crawled over to Hatoon who was unable to get up under her own power, and he checked her condition and knew she was of no further use to him physically. He smiled at the badly wounded young and pretty female terrorist, and then he rolled away from her and cautiously worked his way over to one of the shattered windows. He raised his hand in the opening and then waved as he called out to who he believed were police attacking him from outside.

"American authorities outside, everyone inside this cursed structure is dead but me and one badly wounded woman fighter. Are you so in want of blood on your foul hands that you're willing to kill a helpless injured woman, and wounded male fighter for Allah? Here, I am throwing my weapon out the window because there is no more fight left within my battered and wounded body. All I ask of you authorities are for me and the female fighter to live and be well treated by you. I give up and the woman fighter is no longer able to fight, so she is out of the equation. Do you hear my offer to surrender to you people, American policemen?"

Walker barked without the use of the megaphone this time. "Yeah, I hear ya okay buddy. I'm no stinking police officer, so I don't have my friggin hands tied behind my back like they do fella. I'm a stinking soldier which means I can skin your sagging ass alive, fuck your wife and kill your damn dog, and no one is gonna care in the fucking least 'bout it, pal. So, you betta listen up good to my damn orders, and carry them out to the fucking tee, buster. This is what you're gonna do. You're gonna stand up in that window with your hands in the air. Your ass will remain standing in the open until my people get to your ass, and they take charge of you. If you make any foolish moves, you're gonna be blown offa the face of the stinking earth. Do you understand my fucking orders, pal?"

"Yes, American soldier with the large mouth, I understand your foul orders and I shall do as you commanded me to do. Please, when I stand do not shoot me, because I'm giving up to you peacefully as you have ordered, sir." Mustafa Saleh replied as he rose slowly in the open in the window with his hands held high.

CHAPTER TWENTY-FIVE

"That's it mutherfucker, you stand that way until my people get to your slimy little ass and take you in custody, buddy. I'm warning you mutherfucker, if you're bringing my people into a stinking trap in there, you'll die before they do, buster. You won't like the way I'll kill your ass either I assure you, mister. No one else betta be alive in there except for you and your bitch fighter you say can no longer fight because she's severely wounded, got me fucker?" Walker warned the terrorist as he aimed his weapon right at his face.

The upset Marine Captain looked out of the side of his eye and spotted the Mutt, and he hissed at the soldier. "Hey Mutt, take four troopers and get your stinking asses in there and take command of our prisoner."

"Not for nuthin Walker, I must be suddenly suffering from a serious case of anal blindness here, man. Because I just don't see my ass frigging going in there, before we know for certain all the uther stinking terrorists are fucking dead in there, Homes. I'm not walking into any stinking ambush for nobody. Let's send in a stinking drone first and check out the place, before anyone goes in there, man."

"A drone, and where the fuck are we gonna find a stinking drone on so short an order, asshole? Look, do as I ordered or that terrorist is gonna be the least of your stinking problems, you'll hafta worry 'bout around here, fucker. Take five soldiers with ya and get in there and clear the stinking building for us, man. What the fuck are you worried about anyhow, Mutt? I got the dopey bastard covered, so he's no longer any threat against your stinking ass, buster."

"Cute, real cute buddy, that little fuck there isn't the one I'm concerned with man. We can see his stinking ass easy enuf. I'm more worried about the slugs in there he's trying to make us believe are fucking dead. Arrr…

it's a good day to die anyway I guess man. Bucket, Neck, Wacko, CoCo and Roach, you guys are with my ass. We just pulled the shit duty, so we're gonna be first to get revenge against the fucks…"

"Hold on a second there, Mutt, your ass isn't going in there to get fricking revenge against the lousy fucks. I'm sending you in there to take this guy and his stinking bitch girlfriend in custody, so we can question the lousy fucks and see if this terrorist cell is all the members of the damn thing. We need Intel, and this fuck's gonna give us it if he knows what good for his slimy ass. I want you to go in there with the intent to take this lousy prick in custody, ALIVE. You guys are not going in there to kill the fucks. Don't get me wrong if you guys receive any kinda threat entering the stinking building. All stinking bets are off, and you guys will protect your asses by any means necessary. That means even if you hafta kill every stinking soul inside that damn building, you will do it." Walker warned the Mutt and the other soldiers he picked to help him. All the while Walker was speaking to the Mutt, he was still holding the terrorist locked in his sights, and he was ready to drop him if he breathed wrong.

"I'm bout fucking done talking to your stinking ass here, Mutt. Since when do you question any of my fucking orders, asshole? Mutt, I have this fucker under control, so get your ass in there and take this fuck in custody and hold his ass until I can get in there and take charge of him." Walker bitched as he let his breath out in a hissed.

The Mutt shook his head, and then he hefted his weapon to a better firing position, and he and the other soldiers broke and rushed for the building.

Walker split his vision and watched the Mutt's group cautiously approach the building in the standard two by two formations while keeping the injured terrorist still locked up in his sights. The Mutt's crew carefully entered the building with the Mutt leading the way. Each soldier rested their hand on the shoulder of the soldier before him, as they cautiously moved deeper into the interior of the nearly destroyed building and kept moving their weapons before them left and right. Making the laser dot light dance all over the main room and come to rest on each downed terrorist they picked up lying on the ground. The smoke-filled room and dancing laser lights and darkness made it an eerie entry. The Mutt kept moving forward until he picked up Mustafa standing with his hands in the air. He broke ranks and charged him.

Walker let out his breath when the Mutt's group finally entered the building. He heard the slight commotion from inside the building and smiled when he witnessed the Mutt roughly get a strangling headlock on the wounded terrorist standing in front of the shattered window. He ripped the wounded terrorist down to the ground with the throat lock. The instant the terrorist was taken down Walker put up his weapon and made a mad dash for the building. He along with every other soldier still on guard outside the building protecting the soldiers who entered the structure, changed in to lend support for the other soldiers who made the insertion into the severely damaged civilian structure.

The young Marine Captain charged the building and noticed the soldiers with the Mutt were busy checking the bodies of the downed terrorists. They were stripping the bodies to make certain they did not hide any explosive devices or traps on their bodies. Walker laughed when he noticed the Mutt still holding on the injured terrorist in a throat lock for dear life. He even had his legs wrapped around the terrorist he was controlling.

"Okay Mutt you can let the little fucker go, man. I got his ass covered, buddy."

"Let him go, not on your fucking life man. I'm gonna have the little fuck stuffed, and then I'm gonna have his slimy ass gift wrapped real pretty like, buddy. So, I can give his damn ass to the fucking Colonel for a stinking Christmas present, so he gets offa my stinking back for a little while, my friend." The Mutt fired back at Walker.

"That was good. You made me laugh, but it's over now so gotten offa the fuck so we can start questioning his lousy ass. We hafta know if this was all the stinking terrorists involved it the attacks in New York City and here in Washington, or if there's another fraction of their cell out there somewhere still working against our stinking asses, man. Get the fuck offa the damn floor and sit his stinking ass in a fucking chair, I'm gonna question the little fuck right here and now. Where the hell's his damn girlfriend at he said was the uther shit still alive in here, dammit?" Captain Walker snorted angrily as he quickly surveyed the interior of the severely damaged building. He found himself wondering how the structure was still standing because of so many bullet holes shot in the structure.

"I got the bitch on the floor over here Walker she's in real bad shape man. The fuck in the Mutt's arms was right, the uther fucks in here are all dead, sir. Four in all and we're still checking out the rest of the stinking building, to make certain no uther fucks are setup in an ambush against us." Neck offered his Commander.

Walker looked down at the wounded female and shook his head slowly. One look at her condition and he knew immediately she was not going to make it. Nevertheless, he ordered the Neck in a commanding voice. "Drag her damn ass over by her stinking boyfriend and sit her ass in the chair across from the uther stinking breather, buddy. I'm gonna start to work on her ass first. Then I'll move to her boyfriend when she craps out on my friggin ass. Move it while I get a swallow of stinking water."

Captain Walker grabbed a water bottle from Buckethead and downed it completely, before coming up for air. Then looked at what Lieutenant Frank Hall was doing with the male terrorist.

The Mutt had the terrorist secured in a chair across from him and the injured female slumping in a chair. He did not bother to secure the wounded woman because she was barely alive. When he was satisfied how he had the male terrorists waiting for their interrogation to begin, he gave a look at Walker, and his Commander gave a nod. Walker moved to the two and knelt in front of the female and looked her dead in the eyes. The look made her shiver it was so threatening.

Seeing his female prisoner flinch a bit from his mere presence, the wise Captain instantly realized he had her right where he wanted her, as he growled at her square in her face. "That's it bitch, you see in my stinking eyes how much your fucking life means to my damn ass, sister? I'm gonna ask you some questions and if you don't understand my fucking lingo, my soldier here will translate my stinking words to your lingo for your lousy ass, bitch." He stopped speaking and waited for the soldier branded Ice, to translate his words to Arabic. To his surprise the wounded Arab terrorist acknowledged she understood English. She also warned the captain she was not going to tell him anything, no matter what he did to her body. As weak as she was and slowly dying, she was going to defy her young inquisitor for as long as she still had some strength left to fight him.

"Oh, you think you're that fucking good and strong you can hold up to what I intend to do to your body, to force you to tell me everything I wanna know from your slimy little ass, huh bitch? We'll see just how good you think you are here. It's gonna be a damn shame what you intend to endure for the sake of protecting your uther stinking friends who left your purdy little ass behind to die like this, bitch. It's been a mighty long time since the last time I had the pleasure of destroying a stinking bitch, because she was stupid enuf to try and withhold information from my ass, darling. I assure you you'll live just long enuf to tell me everything I need to know from ya. Shall we begin our little fun and games bitch, times wasting and I wanna have some stinking fun with your damn ass before you die on me, honey?" Walker moved his face so close to Hatoon that she was forced to turn her head to avoid his terrible breath as she hissed at him.

"Foul evil American pig, you'll be wasting your time, if you think for one second, you'll get any information from me, lowly jackal. Get your filthy face and terrible breath away from a true follower of the sacred words written in the Holy Qur'an, you are lowly non-believer to the sacred words of Allah. You do your best to my temple of Allah, remember to bury me in the garden of Allah (the desert) facing East."

"I just fucking love it when someone thinks they can outlast me in anything I do, bitch. You think you're that good you can hold up against my stinking ass huh baby? Let's see just how fricking good you think you really are, bitch." With that said, Walker slowly stretched out his pointer finger and then he moved it towards the gaping wound ripped in her stomach, as he warned the terrorist in a terribly threatening tone of voice.

"Baby, I don't have the fucking time or the patience to make this interrogation a long and drawn-out thing. I need answers and I need them quick, and you're one of two stinking slugs still alive in here who can give me that information. Are you gonna talk to me or do you want me to dig out the damn round that opened you up like an overripe friggin watermelon with my damn fingers, baby? I give you this one stinking chance to talk to my ass sweetheart, and then I'll begin to rip your ass apart with my bare hands." Walker hissed nastily at her.

"I expect nothing less from a foul mouth evil god cursed lowly infidel than what you have just displayed before a true and faithful follower of Allah's laws. American pig born from the very armpit of Satan; you would not dare do what you have just threatened to do against my body. Foolish American jackal, you have laws that govern how you must act against and treat your prisoners, fool. That is the curse of you so called civilized soldiers from the land of the non-believers to the sacred words of Allah. You fool's honor life and we Arab's honor death. You fear death and we welcome it, so save your wasted breath on me because it is wasted upon my ears, you loathsome thing you. I am not in fear of dying for what I believe in. And I believe every cursed infidel should be erased from the face of the earth." Hatoon al-Muneef snarled in the sneering face of Walker, and then she glared defiantly at him.

"Wow, are you a stinking female or a fucking male, because you brag just like a man, bitch? So, let's see if I can separate the two from your stinking little ass, darling." Walker snapped as he suddenly savagely ripped the front of Hatoon's blouse open, and then he tore the bra from her body in the same motion. He knew what he was doing he was trying to thoroughly embarrass the young and badly injured female Arab, by exposing her body to all the soldiers inside the building. He knew once he weakened her resolve, he would own her mind and she would tell him everything he needed to know from her. He went further by crudely grabbing her breasts and rolling them in his dirt covered hands, as he continued to sneer right in her face.

Hatoon tried her best to pull her breasts free of Walker's hands. But he did not let go until he felt he embarrassed her long enough. Then he threatened her wound with his finger for a second time, as he aimed it at her exposed stomach wound. Even Mustafa Saleh started to squirm over the terrible insult the American soldier was offering to the rapidly dying young female Arab fighter sitting in the chair directly across from him.

He slowly moved his finger towards the terrible wound on Hatoon's stomach. When his finger lightly touched the bloody and extremely painful wound, she immediately let out with a terrible scream, and she stiffened her entire body against his assault. The female soldiers of Walker's Units stiffened over what he was doing to the female prisoner. Sergeant Ramirez went to speak, but she was immediately silenced by the captain who fired a nasty look to silence her gripe.

When he started to work his finger into the wound, he offered the female terrorist as angrily as he could say his words. "Look bitch, I know this shit must hurt like fucking hell, and it's a damn shame you wanna endure this kinda pain I'm about to unleash on your stinking body. All for the sake of the lousy pricks that left you behind to defend them."

The captain was taking it for granted there were more members from this terrorist cell than the few they already killed in this home, and he wanted to know where they were hiding. He spoke like he knew of the other terrorists in hopes of breaking Hatoon's resistance down, by making her believe he truly knew of the other terrorists. Feeling like this woman was not going to speak, he suddenly buried his finger to his knuckle in Hatoon's wound. All the while he probed the wound with his finger, he continued to sneer in her face as she cried out in pain, and desperately tried to wiggle away from his hand. When he felt she had enough, he yanked his finger out of the wound to cause the most pain to her. So, she could think about it when he went after her again, and he snarled at her face.

"Shut the fuck up bitch, that little bit of shit didn't hurt that much. C'mon bitch, a few moments ago you were acting so tough and confident. I only stuck my stinking finger a mere inch into your lousy wound and you pissed yourself, wait until I stick my damn dick in there and belly fuck ya ass for fun, bitch. That'll give you really something to cry about, but who knows you might even enjoy it a little. Well, your time's bout up to talk to my stinking ass sweetheart. You wanna talk, or shall we see how many fingers I can stuff in your stinking wound before you shit yourself.

"If you're that good baby, you should be able to hold out until I had my hand buried in the wound up to my damn elbow, sister. That way I can play with your damn tits from the fucking inside. What say, you wanna talk to my ass, or do you wanna see how much pain you can endure, before your fucking heart bursts in your stinking chest, bitch? Ahh… you still wanna keep your damn mouth shut I see. That's just fine with my ass, because I wanna see how your tits feel from the inside. Here we go baby."

The angry Marine Captain again pointed his finger out straight as he slowly approached the injured terrorist fighter's wound for a second time. He moved in on the terrified woman pressing her body so hard against the chair she was seated in. This time Hatoon screamed in anticipation of the pain he was about to unleash on her body. She was screaming so loud and eerily and long, that her cried gave the rest of the soldiers inside the structure the heebee jeebies.

The upset Sergeant Dorothy Ramirez was so angry over what he was doing to the poor and defenseless woman prisoner, that she had to turn her back and move to the outside of the building, because she realized Walker had to get the information from the slowly dying woman. But she did not want to witness the damage he was inflicting on her. Three other Tier One women warriors followed Ramirez out of the building and drew in gulps of cool fresh night air.

The Hunter entered the building while leaving the Ghost outside with the woman warriors for a quick smoke. He walked up behind the Mutt as he tapped out a smoke and stuck it in his mouth. Then he grumbled at the Mutt as he lit up his smoke. "Fucking radical man, I wouldn't want Walker interrogating my stinking ass for nuthin, man."

The Mutt turned to see who was speaking to him and replied. "You got that straight pal."

"When is he gonna start on the fucking dude prisoner? He looks like he's one pain away from speaking to anyone." The Hunter remarked as he stared at the wounded terrorist male this time.

"Will ya huh for crap's sake! I don't know why I'm wasting my stinking time talking to some jerk dressed like a fucking tree. Isn't, you got someone you gotta go kill hanging round someplace out there, man?" The Mutt snorted at the dangerous sniper for stopping him from watching what Walker was doing to their prisoners.

"Yeah, I got me someone to kill alright stupid. When you are coming outside, fucker?" The Hunter grumbled as he dropped the cigarette on the floor, and then he grounded the butt into the rubble covered wood floor of the building with the heel of his boot.

The Mutt straightened his back but did not reply to the Hunter's threat, because he knew he did not want to tangle with the soldier branded the Hunter. He went back to watching Walker working on the female terrorist.

The captain ignored the troops moving around and speaking behind him as he continued working on the wounded terrorist. He kept his eyes glued to the distorted face of the once female terrorist, as she continued to scream out in pain, to hopefully stop what Walker was about to do to her body. Hatoon's face was glowing red, and she was barely stopping screaming long enough to draw in another life-giving breath, as she screamed a continuous and soul shattering wail. Her scream made Walker hesitate for a brief second, before he continued his threat against her. He moved his hand forward and when his finger lightly touched the wound. Hatoon stop screaming and drew in a huge breath and held it.

The female terrorist let her breath out in a rush of air, but it was not a breath of air she released. It was the death rattle as her heart burst within her chest, and she immediately hemorrhaged to death on her own blood. Hatoon's head slumped down on her chest as blood still seeped from the terrible wound in her stomach.

"You killed her you cursed lowly son of the hated jackal! You killed an unarmed and defenseless woman. What has happened to all the cursed merciful American soldiers who pride themselves on wanting to help their prisoners once they have secured them, you evil thing you? Hatoon was correct when she called you a hated and lowly infidel, capable of committing any terrible atrocity on a defenseless female. I will lodge a complaint with the foul leaders of your hated government, and I'll not be satisfied until I see them hang you from your evil neck for what you have just committed against my sister Hatoon, and…"

Walker reached out and slapped Mustafa hard across the face as he growled at him at the same time. "Shut the fuck up scumbag. If it pissed your ass off over what I had done to your stinking bitch girlfriend here. Just wait till I start work on your stinking ass, and we'll see how you fair under my interrogation of your ass, buster. I didn't even really start on your stinking girlfriend, and she already fucking crapped out on me. I wonder how good you are gonna hold up before you crap out on my ass as well, or you break down and tell me what I wanna know from you, pissant."

Captain Robert Walker allowed a wicked sneer to slowly cross over his lips, as he continued to stare into the eyes of Mustafa, as he again hissed at him. "Look mutherfucker, I'd be a lot more concerned 'bout what I'm about to do to your slimy little ass body, than what just happened to your bitch partner here, pal. I can't waste my fucking time trying to force you to tell me all I need to know 'bout the rest of your damn terrorist cell, and its uther fucking members not dead inside this stinking building with the rest of this shit in here, buster. What say, you gonna talk, or are you gonna give me a little fucking sport like your damn girlfriend did, before you tell me everything ask of you, scumbag?"

"Evil jackal born from the fires of hell, you might have been able to scare a worthless female who believed in your cursed lies and worthless threats. Your wasted threats have no credence in my mind. I don't fear your threats in the least because I am prepared to absorb all the pain you think you can deliver against me. American, my body has experienced all the pain you think you can cause. I am a warrior in the Army of Allah, and I fear nothing you think you can cause to…"

The Mutt smirked and then asked Walker with laughter in his voice. "Hey man you're not gonna kill the lousy little mutherfucker in cold blood, are ya buddy?"

"Naw, I'm gonna allow the little prick to warm up a little first, and then I'm gonna kill the lousy bastard, if he doesn't tell me everything I wanna know." Walker replied as he continued to hold the terrorist in his angry glare.

Mustafa's boast ended when the captain suddenly grabbed the chair the dead female prisoner was in, and he roughly slung it around. He pushed the dead women and her chair out of the way with his other hand and continued to pull the chair around until it was aligned directly across from Mustafa's chair. The stunned male terrorist looked to Hatoon whose body was now lying in a heap on the floor under the overturned chair, her face and upper body pushed down on the floor, as the chair rested on her back and neck.

Walker did not speak again until he had the chair where he wanted it. He sat and smiled nastily at Mustafa; it was more a warning than a smile. A warning that informed the unlucky receiver he was about to have a very bad and long and painful day.

Captain Walker sat in the chair speaking calmly to the terrorist, as he slowly removed his razor-sharp K-bar knife from its sheath. He began to drag it slowly back and forth over his pant leg, as if sharpening the weapon on a leather strap, as he watched what he was doing with the deadly blade. The seven-inch-long cutting-edge blade was an extremely threatening weapon. He was making the best of displaying the knife before the scared terrorist. Not bothering to look at Mustafa, he offered as if he was talking to himself more than to the terrorist.

"Hey scumbag, did you ever see a man have his stinking skin slowly cut away from his slimy ass. So, he can remain alive until he looked like a stinking fish about to be stuffed on the damn cooker? I remember one stupid fucking dude we found in the jungle, who had every inch of his skin skillfully removed from his body, and he was hung upside down and left for the insects to have a fucking field day on. I can guarantee you the stinking dude was a raving lunatic long before he was finally allowed to die. It was one helluva sight to see, man." Walker looked up and stared Mustafa dead in the eyes, as he continued with his threatening words.

"Well, my fine feathered friend, you're about to receive the same fucking experience as that uther dude enjoyed. I'm gonna tell you the same thing I told your little stinking dead bitch girlfriend over there. I don't have the damn time or the stinking patience to draw out a lengthily interrogation of your fucking ass, pal. Nor do I wanna see how much pain you think can absorb from my hands, before you cry like a little girl, and you tell me everything I wanna know about your damn terrorist cell. So, I'm gonna jump to the things I know to do to your ass that'll give you the most stinking pain, pal. But you won't die until I kill your ass dead, or you talk.

"So, I'm gonna ask you one time and one time only, to tell me about your uther fucking friends I know are out there someplace, fucker. If you're stupid enough to try me on for size, your ass won't enjoy what I'll do to it, before you tell me everything, I want to know from you, buddy. I wanna know how many more creeps are in this stinking cell of yours, buster? Where the fuck are the rest of your rotten ass stinking friends hiding, fucker?

"I wanna know what the rest of your damn friends are up to, and what their next fucking targets might be? Are you gonna talk to me, or do you wanna do this shit the hard way, pal? So, you can see how quickly you'll talk when I really start to work on your fricking ass. I'm telling ya pal you'll talk to me long before I allow you to die, or if you're smart enough. You'll tell me what I wanna know nice and easy and quick like. You talk and you'll live, keep your trap shut and you'll die hard, real fucking hard, man." Walker looked at Mustafa as he continued to slowly drag the blade on his pant leg while waiting Mustafa's reply.

"Evil non-believe to the sacred words written in the Holy Qur'an. I shall not defile my religious beliefs for the sake of a lowly jackal that is not fit to... Ahhhhhhhhhhhh."

Without a blink of his eye, Walker suddenly stabbed Mustafa in the thigh, burying the blade the full depth in the fleshy area of the leg. He kept the weight of his hands resting on the hilt of his blade, and he slightly twisted it back and forth in the wound, to cause the terrorist the utmost pain. He was smart enough and had the medical knowledge to make certain his blade did not come anywhere near the Femoral Artery and Vein and miss the Great Saphonous Vein and Small Saphonous Vein of the leg. So, the terrorist would not bleed out in mere moments.

The angry Marine Captain turned the knife slightly in the wound to cause Mustafa more suffering. He gave a victorious smile when he felt his blade deflected in the wound when it scrapped the Femur bone, and the bone stayed to the inside of his blade. This warned him his blade was in no danger of coming near the major veins and arteries of the leg. When he stabbed the terrorist's leg, Mustafa tried to lean forward and arch his back, to try and absorb some of the terrible pain he was instantly suffering from Walker's attack on his leg. Walker shoved the terrorist back in the chair by both shoulders as he let go of the handle of the blade so he could control the terrorist.

Mustafa was forced back down on the chair, and he then threw his head back and lifted and then dropped his rearend back in the chair, in an effort to take the pain as he screamed out. "Allah, Allah, Allah, please help your faithful child in his time of need. I swear Allah this worthless fool will…"

"Man, your bitch girlfriend took the stinking pain a helluva lot betta than your fricking ass is doing, you big girl you." Walker grumbled at the terrorist and rested his finger down on the hilt of the blade stuck in Mustafa's leg again, and then he wiggled the blade slightly in the wound with the tip of his finger.

For a second time, Mustafa stiffened and pressed his back hard against the chair, almost knocking it over as he again begged Allah for help. He also tried to absorb the terrible pain the American soldier was causing him.

Walker allowed the terrorist to calm down a bit and get use to the pain, and when Mustafa was kind of taking the pain, he leaned forward again and growled in the Arab's face. "I hafta warn ya pal I'm getting kinda bored with this macho crap you're offering my ass. Again, I don't have the time or patience for this crap, buddy. Are you gonna talk to me, or do I hafta do something more drastic against your dumb ass, fella? I hafta tell ya pal, if you force me to cut your Femoral Artery, asshole. You'll have a minute before you bleed the fuck out. I don't have the medical personnel available to help your ass if I mistakenly cut that damn artery on ya, buddy. Are you feeling me? Do you hear what I intend to do to your stinking ass if you don't talk?"

Mustafa tried to get his breathing under control as he snarled at Walker's face. "I see you still don't understand the way of us Arabs, evil infidel born from the pits of hell. What you do to my body is of no consequence to my belief in Allah's sacred word, because my body is only the form Allah recognizes as His temple, jackal from the hot desert sands. If you must cause pain to make you happy and feel good about yourself and what you are doing to me then so be it. I shall suffer all that pain you can possibly offer me for the sake of Allah's mercy. Lowly dog of the desert breath, do your best against…Ahhhhhhhhhhhh."

"Oh, fuck this bullshit." Walker cut off Mustafa's proud boast off in mid word when he grabbed the hilt of his blade and dragged the knife through Mustafa's thigh. This time the Mutt had to reach out and steady the chair and Mustafa's body, or he and the chair would have turned over because of the way the Arab was struggling. Mustafa looked down in fear and watched in terror as his inquisitor pulled the knife through his leg until it broke free of his skin, and a large flap of skin, muscle and blood was cut from his leg.

Walker smirked as he moved the thick chunk of flesh a little with the tip of his blade, to show the prisoner the severe amount of damage to his leg. He looked Mustafa dead in the eyes and warned him in no uncertain words, employing a voice as cold as ice. "Well, my fucking stupid friend, that stinking leg's a fucking real mess on ya, all because you wouldn't tell me what I wanted to know from your dumb ass, pal. I guess I'll hafta start on your uther stinking leg and see if that'll make ya tell me what I need to know from ya ass, buster. I can keep this shit up all stinking day, and not allow your ass to die until there isn't enuf of your skin and muscle left to hold your fucking body together any longer, bub. You feel like talking or do you wanna see if you can withstand more of what I'll do to you, pissant. Until you tell me everything I wanna know from your dopey ass?"

Walker began to flip the blood-soaked blade from one hand to the other before Mustafa's face.

The terrorist again drew in a huge gulp of air, and then he hissed at his inquisitor at the same time. "Again, I warn you lowly American infidel, no matter what you might choose to do to my body, not one single word of information will ever cross my lips and help…"

Shaking his head slowly, Walker did not wait for more words to pour out of Mustafa's mouth, and he slammed his hand down on the terrorist's left leg. This time he was further from the Femur bone as he buried the blade deep in Mustafa's other leg. The concerned Mutt reacted and instantly wrapped Mustafa's mouth in his hand and stopped the man from crying out. The Mutt struggled with the desperately wiggling Islamic terrorist, as he tried to get away from the man causing him so much pain. The American Captain again asked the terrorist if he was going to talk, while the Mutt continued to cover his mouth and wrap his head in his arms and struggled with the man to try and hold him in place, seated before Walker.

Mustafa began rapidly shaking his head yes as he eyes nearly bulged in their sockets, and he now begged Walker not to cause him any further pain, while trying to speak through the Mutt's hand still covering his mouth. Gone was his once proud boast of not to talk to Walker. The Mutt seeing the terrorist was willing to talk now, released Mustafa's mouth and the Afghan began to beg Walker in a trembling voice.

"Please, no more pain American soldier. I shall tell you everything you want or need to know from me. I swear American soldier, you'll be extremely pleased with the information I shall shower your ears with. Please, no more pain American soldier, no more pain. I can't take any more of it, American soldier"

"Now you're using your stinking head for more than just a friggin hat rack, buster. Wisdom is beyond price, be grateful you have some to use, pal. Blood Clot, get your ass up here and look after this soldier's wounds, while he tells me where the rest of his fucking friends are hiding at around here." The concerned Captain waited and when the medic got up to him, and he began to look after Mustafa's terribly damaged thighs. He began his interrogation of the Afghan terrorist and pulled his blade out of Mustafa's left leg. The second wound was in no danger of killing the prisoner, so it was left to bleed until Blood Clot got to it and rendered first aide to the wound after he looked after the more serious injury.

"Okay pal, you offered to talk to my stinking ass, so start talk to me, man. Let's have all you know, how many uther fucking terrorists are in this damn terrorist cell of yours, pal? Where the fuck are your miserable friends hiding at? I wanna know what the next target they intend to hit? I wanna know how are the lousy fucks gonna hit us? What kinda weapons your friends are gonna use in their next attack? You betta talk if you know what's fucking good for ya lousy ass." Walker growled at his prisoner as glared at the restrained man.

Mustafa squirmed as Blood Clot rapidly worked on his terribly injured legs. The medic was amazed at the amount of damage the captain caused, as he did his best to close the injury with what he had available. Walker never tried to cut the man free of his bonds, as he waited for his prisoner to talk.

Drawing in his breath deeply, Mustafa let it out slowly and then spoke to his angry looking inquisitor in as calm but painful a voice as he could possibly muster under the circumstances. "American soldier, there are eighteen members of what you call my terrorist cell. I must clear something up, so you understand our reasons why we are doing what we're doing in your cursed country, American soldier. We don't call ourselves terrorists. No, that is not it in fact it's the furthest reasons for our existence and actions aimed at your country.

"We refer to ourselves as the Hydra of al-Qaeda. Because when you kill one of us, or as we like to refer to it, cutting off one head of the dreaded Hydra. Six others will appear and take its place, and they'll continue with their original orders of attack for Allah's sake, to rid the earth of all non-believers and lowly infidels to His sacred word. The Muslim religion is the one true religion of Allah and the world."

"Cute, real fucking cute buddy, stow the stinking commercial Charlie Brown, and get on with answering my uther fucking questions, pal. You're not fucking impressing my ass in the least with that kinda bullshit you're spitting outta your stinking mouth. I asked you questions, and I expect answers. Or I'm gonna cut your hide from your body, and then I'm gonna put a fucking cap in your bonnet to end your grant standing, before I bury your stinking body afta I stuffed you ass inside a pig skin, fucker." Walker growled at his prisoner.

"Yes, American soldier, I shall tell you everything you demand from me and more, but first you must promise me you'll never put my body inside a pig skin. You understand how we Muslims feel about that most filthy animal. This is a very serious threat against my person. Yes, yes, I shall go on with my words, the other members of my Hydra group are hiding in a commercial establishment located two miles north of this destroyed safe house. I don't know the exact location of this second safe place though I promise you. I was not privy to this vital information from the leader of our Unit. But after what I tell you, you should not have many problems detecting where my Muslim freedom fighters are at.

"Their next attack will consist of setting off an explosive device between the seat of your American Leader, and the seat of where your evil laws are born from." Mustafa cried while displaying he was in serious pain, and he stopped speaking for a moment, to allow his words to sink into the mind of the American soldier questioning him so threateningly. The prisoner looked at Walker and noticed he was thinking and remained quiet.

The captain did not pick up what his prisoner said, and he turned and looked at the female soldier called Ice, who was watching everything he was doing with the prisoner. When he looked at her, she replied immediately. "Walker, I guess the asshole means the White House and Capitol Building, sir. That's the only two structures he must be referring to, Captain."

"Yes, American soldier, your foul and lowly woman is correct, and those are the buildings I refer to." Mustafa replied as he was getting into informing Walker of their future of attack.

"Got it mutherfucka, what kinda fucking device are you referring to, that your stinking pals are gonna hit us with?" He asked and did not pick up the fact that Colonel Leadbetter had just entered the nearly destroyed home. The Colonel remained silent and standing in the background and listened as Walker gathered more information from the injured prisoner. He understood what he was doing, and he continued keeping the colorful words in his conversation with the Afghan terrorist. He was aware what the cuss words did to the Muslims, and the threat to bury him inside a pig skin. He was employing the cuss words to keep the Afghan off step.

"Abdullah al-Mutairi, is constructing the freedom weapon, a weapon your country refers to as a mass destruction device. One that'll employ the use of Enriched Uranium I was told. I believe in the land of Satan; this weapon of freedom is classified as a dirty bomb." Mustafa replied while allowing a slight smirk as he defiantly stared back at his angry inquisitor this time.

"Well at least we know why we were detecting such strong traces of stinking radiation at the uther locations we discovered on you fucking guys back in New York City, buster. Okay pal, you got one more fucking answer to give my ass, and then I'm done with ya and my medic can finish up repairing your stinking legs fur ya, pal. How the fuck are your stinking friends gonna deliver this damn weapon to point of detonation, and how the fuck are they gonna detonate the damn thing off?" Walker asked the prisoner with concern in his voice.

"Alas, I am not with the knowledge on how my Muslim brothers intend to detonate our great weapon of freedom against your foul leaders of this evil country. I do know they plan to load the weapon for Allah inside a vehicle from your country. Then they'll drive the weapon to a location of an equal distance between the two intended targets. This is so there is an equal amount of death and destruction melted out to both areas of this cursed city by the Almighty Hand of Allah, against the non-believers of this foul land. I have informed you of everything you demanded from my limited knowledge. I take this time to laugh in your worthless face because you demanded this information.

"My words shall be useless for you, and all who follow you against my fellow Arab brothers and sisters doing the sacred work of Allah. Because by the time you react against us and our attack against the lowly infidels of this country, it shall be far too late for you to stop our sacred quest to destroy the lands of Satan, and all who dwell within this country of evil. What shall give me the greatest of pleasure and peace of mind, is the knowledge not only you, but all the cursed soldiers under your worthless command. Shall perish in the same fate that shall befall all the evil dwellers of this sinful land you soldier proudly call Washington.

"You see foul American soldier; in my country we believe too much knowledge is fatal as you have found out for your evil self by my words. How does it feel to know you only have a few hours of life left in your worthless body, in which to continue to pollute this earth? I spit on your cursed memory with a smile, as I shall witness your life being burned to a cinder in the nuclear holocaust, we shall release upon…"

CHAPTER TWENTY-SIX

"Arrr… fuck you and the stinking horse you rode in on, mutherfucker! How does it friggin feel to know you're gonna die this fucking minute, scumbag?" Walker growled so angrily at his prisoner, and he flipped the blade over in his hand and then jammed it up under Mustafa's chin. He slammed the man so hard with his fist and knife, that it drove the blade all the way up to the hilt, and penetrated the brain, killing the Afghan terrorist instantly. Walker never pulled the knife out of Mustafa's face as he shoved his body and chair back with his foot as he straightened his body and kicked out, spilling both on the floor.

Blood Clot had to stop working on the prisoner's legs when Walker attacked the man again. He had to jump out of the way, or he might have been caught up in Walker's attack against the taunting and grinning prisoner.

"Walker, you had done really well with the way you interrogated that fucking POS (Piece of Shit). Captain, after hearing what that prick had to offer, this is what you're going to do. I'm ordering you to take charge of my command vehicle because it comes equipped with the full range scope radiation detection equipment on board. Take the damn Humvee and get your damn ass out there and find where this lousy prick's other fucking friends are hiding at. You can't possibly allow any of his scumbag friends of this bastard…"

Colonel Leadbetter stopped speaking just long enough to lightly kick the leg of the dead terrorist lying on the floor with his foot, as he went on with his orders to the captain. "To get their damn weapon to where the pricks intend to detonate the fucking thing off against us dammit, if the bastards pull this damn thing off, the deaths will be counted in the millions, in the fucking millions I tell you mister. So, get out there and make every second count."

Walker was a little caught off guard when the Colonel started to speak to him from behind him because he was unaware, he entered the building while he was working on the terrorist. But he recovered quickly, and he and his troops charged out the building to carry out his latest orders from his Commanding Officer.

Sergeant Ramirez moved forward, and she complained as she easily caught up to her soldier and lover. "Bobby, I have to tell you I didn't care very much for the way you treated those two prisoners in there. I can't believe we're allowing ourselves to get as bad as the effing (fucking) lowlifes we're trying to stop from bombing the Capitol and White House. We're better than the way you treated the prisoners, and I don't like…"

Captain Walker slowed his march then stopped all together. He turned and looked at his girlfriend and replied in a calm voice to her. "Look honey, the stinking terrorists have changed the way we have to defend ourselves against the lousy pricks and their friggin terrorist actions. We're in the battle of our lives to save not only our own asses. But the lives of millions of innocent civilians of Washington, if the damn terrorists detonate that dirty bomb off against us. That fear makes it imperative that there's no time to employ elegant technique or subtle countermoves, to try and get the information I just got from the two dead fucks so quickly.

"My fucking aim in this operation is to so completely demolish the enemy in a concerted effort to stop them from popping that damn thing off against us. Not dance around with the lousy bastards so they can have the time to hit us again. Do you, have it? Are we cool with the aims I'm setting for this damn operation? Are you still with me all the way?" The captain asked of his Sergeant as he stared her right in the eyes while waiting for her reply.

Ramirez let out her breath in a rush and then she replied. "Yes Robert, I know where you're coming from, and the aims of this operation. Yes, I'm with you as always Bobby. I had to tell you that I really hated the way these people are forcing us to react against them and their evil aims. I can't believe these people are so damn hell bent on killing innocent people who done absolutely nothing wrong against them or their religion. I can't wrap my mind around the way and effing lengths the Muslim radicals will go, to hurt people they never met before in their damn lives, and who are only guilty of trying to live their lives in peace."

"Sergeant Ramirez, I'm a fucking fraid no civilized person will ever be able to wrap their minds around what makes these damn gullible lunatics tick. You hafta let it go and act accordingly against them when dealing with these types of backasswards fruitcakes. Now is not the time to raise these devils and looking for sensible answers to the damn situations they're creating. We hafta find and stop the flaming assholes before they're able to do what they're planning." Walker remarked in a huff as he gave Ramirez a slight shove forward.

Walker gave a quick hand signal once he was outside the destroyed building, and every soldier assigned to his command immediately left their positions, and they rapidly gathered around him. Once his troops were in earshot, he growled at them as he issued the troops new orders. "Okay gun bunnies, we have information the fucking terrorists are within a two-mile distance north of this stinking position. We're commandeering the Colonel's vehicle because it's equipped with long range radiation detection capabilities. We're gonna pile in any damn Humvees not damaged by the uther scumbags during our slight battle with the cocksuckers.

"Once we're mobile and on the road again, we're gonna drive up and down every stinking block north of this lousy position, until we detect a radiation hit on our equipment. When we find that bounce, we'll know we found the location for the rest of these stinking bastards. Then we'll take out every one of them as we come across the dopey fucks. Mount up, each of you have the portable RAI's (Radiation Alert Inspectors) issued to you people when we first started this damn operation. I want the fucking things hanging outta every damn window of the Humvee you're in. Although we have use of the Colonel's command machine, the more powerful radiation detector in his vehicle can only do so much.

"I want all the help I can get from you guys. That's why I want your radiation detectors hanging outta the windows of your vehicles, until we find the lousy fucks. If anyone picks up the slightest bounce of radiation out there, I wanna know 'bout it the instant you get hit with one."

The Mutt walked up to Walker and smiled at Ramirez as he remarked. "Hey Walker, what's up with Malice in Wonderland over there? She looks kinda upset buddy. Didja hurt her itty-bitty feeling again man?"

"Arr... she's giving me a case of ass over the way I interrogated those two stinking slugs." Walker replied as he cast a quick look at Ramirez and noticed that she was still upset with him.

"I don't know why she might be upset man; I didn't see nuthin wrong with the way you handled those two scumbags. I have a first class hardon for all bleeding hearts who cried over the harsh interrogation methods we employed on the lousy pricks still being held down at Gitmo. Where were they when the stinking terrorists hacked off the heads of their hostages? You didn't hear jack shit coming from any of them stinking pricks. I wish some of these crybabies realize what we're facing when going up against any pack of these radical scumbags. When we deployed to Iraq, we were told not to be captured alive by the turds under any circumstances. You told us if we were captured, we'd be tortured by being forced to drink crude oil, and belted round by the little bastards and beheaded on the internet.

"Walker we had cash bounties placed on our asses by the damn insurgents operating in Iraq to any Arab prick that brought in an American serviceman or woman alive or injured to the radicals. If I remember right man, you told us every fucking fight we got in during our engagement of the terrorists, was a fight to the death. Surrender wasn't an option in our book, because of the way we knew we were going to be treated by the enemy. Yet we didn't hear jack shit from these bleeding hearts over our treatment if we were taken prisoner. But the same damn pack of stinking crybabies cried because we were giving some radical cocksuckers at Gitmo fucking baths and swimming lessons, and it wasn't a Saturday night we were doing it on.

"Those same lousy little bastards didn't give a lick if we were tortured, and had our damn heads chopped off in living color, if we were unlucky enuf to be taken prisoner by the Arab radicals, and we're their soldiers protecting their asses back here in the States. I wish for just once, every one of our countrymen and women would support us soldiers like they wanna make sure the damn animals that wanna kill our civilians, are supported by the dopey fucks. That shit doesn't make any stinking sense to my ass. What the fuck, are we worth less than the stinking pricks who wanna hunt us down and kill our asses like we don't mean shit?"

"Hey, pal I'm gonna tell you the same fucking thing I just told Raz. Now is not the time for these kinds of shit. We have uther work to fucking do, buddy. If you try to analyze what these dumb fucks are trying to accomplish with their warp logic, you're gonna end up drive yourself crazy, man. Even the fucking terrorists don't understand what the hell they're truly trying to accomplish, and the way they're trying to fucking do it. Okay huh, get in your damn Humvee, we got a pack of assholes we gotta track down and kill, to end this damn operation once and for all." Walker complained as he gave the Mutt a shove forward then glared at him.

"I hate this stinking crap Walker. Shit, this is the fucking reason why I hadta put clean underwear on for Pete's sake." The Mutt griped as he headed for his parked Humvee.

"Yeah, that's why, and don't go Code Brown (Shit in your pants) in that new underwear if crunch time comes a knocking against your ass, my friend." Walker fired back at his friend and watched the Mutt take off. When his Humvee was packed with soldiers, he plopped down in the passenger seat and growled at the driver.

"Nentendo get this damn thing moving will ya. Head to Ninth Street which is I-50 and take a left when you hit that stinking road. I'll give orders for our follow-on troops while you drive. Dragon Fire Leader to all followers listen up. Raz, you're following my machine, and the Mutt's group will follow yours. Here are the orders, the last two Humvees will cut off and make a right turn on the next corner coming up. Then the next last two Humvees will turn right at the upcoming corner. I want the rest of you to use your heads, and the next trailing vehicles will take the next block and turn right. All vehicles will travel for six blocks east bound on your assigned roads. Then assemble on the sixth block of each road, and we'll take the next six blocks and so forth. Until we finally find the lousy fucks and do them in good and proper.

"Be advised people, I plan to take the road marked down on your funny papers (Maps) as I Street. It's the height of the commercial district in this stinking section of Washington. I have a gut feeling this is where the lousy scumbags are hold up on us. If you gun juggler's pick up the slightest trace of radiation on your equipment. Call it out and all Units will immediately close in on your position as reported, and then we can…" Walker's orders were suddenly interrupted as Sergeant Ramirez cut in and offered.

"Dragon Fire Leader, Dragon Breath. Be advised there's a small park I took notice of when I was first deployed to my area of responsibility during my search for these bastards. It's located on I-50 just over the Pennsylvania Avenue line heading north. Dragon Fire Leader, if I was planning to take out the White House and Capitol Building from a centralized location, sir. I feel this location would be the perfect spot to setup my attack from. I think we should send some of our people over to this location in case I'm right."

Before Walker could reply to Ramirez's suggestion, their conversation was cut off by another voice as he broke in on the radio net.

"Dragon Lair to Dragon Fire Leader. Nagitory on that last suggestion, all Dragon Fire Units will continue their assigned orders as issued, Captain. I'll take my backup soldiers and deploy to the area Dragon Breath brought up to our attention. Good work Dragon Breath, that's what I'm looking for from the people under my command, using your fucking heads, ladies and gentlemen Continue with your present orders as issued, Dragon Fire. Out."

Captain Walker did not reply to Colonel Leadbetter's last orders, as he craned his neck and noticed the trailing Humvees make a right on the block as ordered. His Humvee was about a block and a half away from the road he planned to turn down, and he suddenly picked up two slight ticks from the radiation detecting equipment. At first, he did not think it was a true radiation detection pickup as he growled at the other soldiers inside his Humvee with him.

"What the fuck was that shit I just heard, dammit? Did any of you guys hear that shit? Did we just pick up a few clicks of radiation on this damn system? Are we picking up anymore fucking clicks? You people did hear the clicks, right? I wanna make damn certain it came from the stinking detection system, and not from someone's fucking cell phone, dammit." Walker growled at his fellow soldiers.

The other soldiers nodded in the affirmative, or replied they heard the two ticks, and they were coming from the radiation detection system.

Sergeant Ramirez's Humvee turned down H Street from Ninth Street and was about seventy-five yards further down the road than Walker's machine was. She was about halfway down the street when two handheld radiation detectors suddenly started to click off. Both detectors were hanging outside her vehicle on the left side of the machine, and she turned her eyes to that direction. She was on the first street of the commercial district, and all she could see was old warehouses and tractor trailer rigs and cargo storage containers parked and stacked up in large parking lots of several the commercial establishments. The Sergeant looked harder out the window and noticed more commercial warehouses on the next block up from where she was driving, and those buildings were on both sides of the road. Ramirez only had commercial buildings on the left side of her Humvee because she was just shirting the commercial district.

Knowing what she was picking up on her detector she immediately grabbed the mike and reported her findings to her Commanding Officer. "Dragon Breath to Dragon Fire Leader. How copy, this is important sir? Over."

Just as Walker reached to take his mike and respond to Sergeant Ramirez call in, his radiation detector suddenly erupted in a long and loud series of clicks. He held the mike as he read what was being printed out on the small computer screen mounted on the dashboard of the machine. The radiation detector registered the accepted way of measuring radiation levels of the earth. It takes one thousand Mille-Renkins to make a count of one extremely dangerous and deadly Renkin, and Captain Walker's detector was picking up a Mille-Renkin score of one hundred and fifty counts per hour.

This amount of radiation was well beyond the normal background radiation of the earth. A human could stay in this amount of radiation safely for no more than six hours, before starting to feel slight effects radiation has on the body and feel a little sick from the radiation, and damage attacking their bodies. Now, all he had to do was make certain none of the commercial establishments in the commercial area had anything to do with the radiation field of employment. The last thing he wanted to do had his troops invade a legitimate business, and scare the devil out of workers, as his troops wildly charged into the building that might be hiding the terrorists.

As he continued to stare at the computer screen and what it was registering. His trance was broken when Sergeant Ramirez who called him a second time. "Dragon Fire, Dragon Breath Leader. Come in, this is important I need to speak with you immediately, Captain. Over."

Walker had to shake the cobwebs clouding his head as he responded to his Squad Leader. "Dragon Fire here. Go with your traffic. Over."

"Dragon Fire, be advised I'm reporting I am picking up a weak radiation count of only sixty Millie-Renkins per hour sir, which is more than ten Millie-Renkins background radiations accepted as normal and harmless to the body. I peg the source of radiation coming from the left side of my machine towards the road you're currently driving down, sir. Are you picking up a raise in radiation levels sir? The reading I'm picking up is a constant and positive mark now Walker. I'm requesting further orders. Over sir."

"Dragon Fire Leader to Dragon Breath and Dragon Claw, I'm currently picking up a constant and strong count of one hundred and fifty Millie-Renkins per hour of radiation. To all units attached to this here crapshoot. You're ordered to close in on I Street between roads I-50 and Sixth Street. I'll continue down this stinking road until I feel I located the source of this increased radiation level. Then all Units will react accordingly once we established the location of the stinking weapon, and the damn terrorists working on the fucking thing. Squad Leaders will close in on my command, and we'll go on from there, people. Carry out your orders as received. One more thing before I break off this communication. Ghost, Hunter, I want you two birds out and hunting the first moment we locate this place where the damn terrorists are hiding at. I want you two pukes to stay on top of these lousy fucks and thin them out some for us. Out."

Both the Ghost and Hunter were riding in the fourth Humvee in Walker's column of vehicles, and the moment they heard Walker's orders, the Ghost asked Hunter. "You got the shit with ya, buddy? I wanna use it on these fucks this time man."

"Yeah, I got it with me alright, Walt." The Hunter replied as he held up a small vial of blood, and then he added. "Gimme your stinking ammo and I'll drip some of this fucking pig blood on it fur ya. Shit man, I'd like to see the faces of those fricking Islamic shitbirds, if they understood we're soaking our stinking ammunition in pig's blood, man. I'd bet the bank on it they'd shit themselves if they discovered what we're up to, man."

"I'm friggin willing to do anything to stop the fucks from attacking us. Right down to hitting the assholes with rounds soaked in pig's blood, to stop the fucks from believing they're gonna go to Paradise. The stupid fucks believe they can't get in Paradise if they eat pig." Casper replied.

The moment Walker broke off communication with the Squad Leaders of the other Units he decided to quickly go over some of their back training with the troops riding in his vehicle. He was upset no one in command dared to think the soldiers might be going up against a nuclear radiation contamination environment. If he was on the ball, he would have ordered the troops to make certain they carried their CBRN (Chemical, Biological, Radiological and Nuclear) gear with them, in case of this exact situation cropping up on the soldier.

"Okay, listen up slugs, because I wanna remind you people of your basic training you might have forgotten, and aren't employing this training now we're faced with this crap. You know your stinking training goes out the fucking window with the first crack of enemy rounds fired at your asses. From that point on its controlled by the seat of your pants survival that'll keep you alive now of engagement of enemy forces. Mixed in with what training you can remember and pull up during the stinking fog of war. In most times of stress and pressure on your mind, the usual thinking process, and normal ways you'd respond to any situations, are sorta cut off by your brain. Your brain doesn't allow for any reasonable contemplation to help you outta the stressful situation when you need your wits the fucking most.

"During the stress of the stinking fog of war, your brain will not allow the normal processing of vital information for survival your eyes are picking up, the way it normally does when you're in a much calmer state of mind. The fear factor is gonna be the hardest thing for you pack of criminals to keep under control during any enemy engagement. The advance parts of the brain that allows for all normal and clear decision-making capabilities, are gonna shut the fuck down on your stinking asses surer than shit hitting the friggin fan, when you'll need them the most on the damn battlefield. I understand this shit was explained to you pissants beforehand, but I wanna remind you shits what the crap happens to your fricking mind during any possible enemy engagements. Without your conscious knowledge, the first round fired at your asses will automatically send a warning signal to your brain stem. This alarm message will pass through the stinking Amygdale…"

"Amygdale, what the fuck is that shit, man? I got a fucking Amygdale hanging round in my stinking noggin, Walker? If I got one of the damn things in my head, how the hell do I get rid of the stinking thing, sir?" The Roach called out from the rear seat of the Humvee.

"It figures it'd be your stinking ass fucking up what I gotta tell the rest of you shitbirds, before we end up engaging the enemy on this damn crapshoot, Roach. Shut the fuck up for a few moments and listen up and yes, you got a stinking Amygdale planted in your damn noggin, stupid. That's the little almond shape thing that controls the fear factor of your body, and your response to that friggin fear that originates within the brain's temporal lobe of your damn noggin and …" Again, Walker's words were interrupted.

"Hey Walker how come suddenly you know so fucking much about the stinking brain, and how it works and what it's gonna do on me, and how it's gonna react in a life and death situation I'm trapped in, man? How the brain of mine will protect my ass out on the field of battle? Are you a stinking Doctor in disguise suddenly man? Or are you a stinking seer who can see in the future, and how we're gonna react in a fucking war, Captain." The Roach called out daring to interrupt Walker again.

"I know this shit because I fricking pay attention when someone takes the damn time to explain to me something that's fucking important to my survival on the damn battlefield, stupid. And, if you interrupt my stinking ass for a third time buddy, the damn terrorists are gonna be the least of the friggin problems you'll hafta deal with around here, asshole. I just told you once to shut your ass up and pay attention to what I'm trying to explain to you pack of screaming Eagles, man. I'm telling you for a second time, and I won't tell your damn ass for a third time, asshole. Now Squids, once the Amygdale receives this alarm and response life or death message, it triggers off a shitload of other changes raging throughout your bodies. Your blood vessels will restrict, this will be your body preparing to protect your ass if you get wounded, and you'll bleed a helluva lot less because of this order to your body.

"Your heart rate and blood pressure will climb dramatically under this stressful pressure, as further protection for your wounded body. Your body will be hit with a gush of raging hormones to help harden your body against the stinking pain you'll be experiencing. This flood of hormones will inject a rush of superhuman power and strength and adrenalin to your major muscle groups of the body. This rush of power and added strength will help to aid you if you find yourselves trapped in a situation where you'll hafta fight or flee. Or if you hafta drop back and aid a fellow soldier wounded and down hard.

"Now this isn't the only thing your body will go through at times of engagement and severe stress. Another thing you gotta remember is when your body prepares for battle. Along with the gifts your brain gives your body to help your ass survive. Your body will remove other vital thought reactions you'll need to survive. It's sorta like a tit for tat thing, and your brain will give you what it thinks you'll need the most to survive any engagement you enter.

"Your stinking brain will react in this manner, and it'll slow down on how it'll process certain thought messages and reactions like time itself. Like most people trapped in a life-or-death struggle in any pressing situation, your brain will manipulate your normal perception and concept of frigging time. Your brain will also slow it and your response time down dramatically. Places you're looking at will seem further away from your position than they really are, and if you hafta run towards or away from a deadly engagement or uther situation. You'll find yourself feeling like you're running in slow motion. Your objective will seem further away from you than first thought. It's gonna make you feel like you're running through mud with a stinking piano loaded down on your backs and you'll also…"

Walker's words were cut off when some of the soldiers inside the Humvee laughed over this last statement. Ignoring the laughter, he continued with his words of concern for his troops. "In some uther fucking instances during times of enemy engagement and heavy stress, you like everyone else usually feels during these times. You're gonna swear you're running faster than you thought possible. But your subconscious mind will be guiding you and your fucking reactions. It'll make you search for a safe place to drop your ass down behind and better protect yourself, without you even realizing you're doing this shit. It's your mind working on its own to work out the problems you're facing.

"The confusion and hormones and superhuman strength you'll be experiencing, and battling is called the FOW or the Fog of War. It's a real thing that we all must contend with, every stinking time we're facing a life of death struggle on the field of battle. I wanted to take this time to remind you people of our training when we get outta these damn metal cans on wheels, and we fight these stinking slugs. There's gonna be severe tradeoffs in your normal ways of thinking and reacting to whatever we'll face in a few minutes when we engage the dopey ass terrorists.

"So, stay alert and keep your damn heads loose and on a stinking swivel, and try to call up every bit of your training you can possibly pull up on your own. That's 'bout all I gotta tell you people. The rest of this shit you'll hafta battle with when we engage the Islamic radicals, we're about to give a bad fucking day to. Stay safe and alive people."

The moment Walker stopped speaking to the other soldiers riding in the Humvee with him his mind registered the clicking sound from the Geiger counter mounted in the Colonel's command vehicle. He listened to the series of loud clicks for a few seconds, and then grumbled at Neck. "Obviously we're picking up the fucking Rads while we go off looking for these lousy cruds. What's the count of the damn Radiation we're picking up, at soldier?"

Neck turned so he could see Walker's face better and he replied. "Hey Walker, the count went up some, and we're now picking up the count as two hundred and eighty Millie-renkins per hour and still climbing man."

"Shit!" Walker growled angrily as he shifted his weight so he could see the viewing plate of the radiation detector himself. He narrowed his eyes so he could read the numbers as the sun started to come up. As he stared at the small computer screen, he noticed the number tick passed three hundred Millie-Renkins per hour, and he started to grow deeply concerned over the now heavy amount of radiation he, and the other troops with him were picking up. At three hundred and sixty Millie-Renkins per hour, he quickly grew extremely concerned, and wondered how much radiation was being released by these terrorists.

The worried Captain rubbed his eyes so he could register the numbers a little clearer. Three hundred and forty Millie-Renkins was being registered. The number went down slightly, and he bellowed out at his driver. "Slow this fucking thing down a little, the number's dropping some on us. If it continues to go down, then that means we passed the stinking hot spot."

The captain stared at the radiation display, and when the number dropped down to three hundred and twenty Millie-Renkins per hour. He growled a second time at his driver. "Holy shit man, stop this damn thing Nentendo. We got the scumbags dead on! I'll bet the stinking bank on it the friggin pricks are working inside the fucking building just behind our machine." He then went on the radio net and warned the other soldiers under his command.

"Dragon Fire Leader to Dragon Breath and Dragon Claw Squad Leaders be advised. I determined the damn terrorists are held up in the massive green commercial building with the address of, One, Three, Three, Five, Niner, East on I Street. To all Squad Leaders and troops on his hunt with me, you're ordered to converge on my present location. We're gonna stage up here, and then we're gonna end this thing this morning, for fuck sake. If these terrorists are held up inside the building, I believe they're in, we got them dammit. Over!"

The moment Walker broke off his communication with the two Squad Leaders from the other Units he turned to Nentendo and ordered him. "Back this damn thing up until we're right in front of the damn target building. I wanna take up position in front of that dump before the rest of our vehicles converge on this location, and they screw up where I want this thing stopped."

Nentendo drew in air and then he announced to his Commanding Officer. "See Walker, I can't back this damn thing up, because our follow-on Humvees and troops are bunched up behind our machine. I need new orders."

"It's fucking simple then man, if you can't back this damn thing up then turn it around in the middle of the damn road, and then drive it back until we're positioned where I ordered you to be, asshole. I'll get on the net and order the other Humvees to stop where they are, and for our troops to dismount and deploy for immediate action. Dragon Fire Leader to all drivers, you're instructed to stop your machines where you are, and your troops are ordered to dismount and deploy. My vehicle is going to turn around, and we're gonna park right in front of the structure in question and begin the next part of this damn turkey shoot with the last of this terrorist cell.

"The rest of you people have your stinking orders, so carry them out properly." The captain looked out the windshield, as Nentendo had to back up twice to turn the cumbersome hard driving heavy machine around correctly. Then he slid his Humvee past the other vehicles stopped behind them, as they rapidly unloaded soldiers.

As his machine passed the bunched-up Humvees parked on the other side of the road, he glanced in the parking lot of the commercial establishment he had his eyes on, and he picked up two people kinds of just hanging around in the middle of the large parking lot. One youngster was obviously a male, the other one a female. They seemed to be speaking and smiling at each other, and the male was enjoying a cigarette and the lady's presence. But the moment they looked at Walker riding inside the military type of machine, the male immediately threw his cigarette to the ground, and he pulled the female to him. Then they both darted inside the building.

"God dammit, the fucking terrorists must have stationed a coupla stinking spotters in the damn parking lot of this stinking dump, and the two shitbirds just picked up my stinking ass." Then he complained to Nentendo, as he reached for his mike and barked into it. "Dragon Fire Leader to all Dragon Fire personnel, be advised, the rat fucks know we're out here and coming for their stinking asses, and they must be forming up a welcoming party for us. Take up your positions in that drainage ditch on the opposite side of the damn road as ordered. Stay low and be prepared for anything coming at your asses. I believe we got the bastards trapped in there."

Walker stopped speaking because Nentendo informed him their Humvee was directly in front of the building he wanted. He looked west and noticed a few other Humvees plowing down the road and stopping behind the other already parked machines. Then the troops rapidly climbed out of the machines, and they took positions in the drainage ditch running the full length of the long road. The drainage ditch was about four feet deep and about six foot wide. He looked east down the other side of the road and picked up the same thing happening there. Everywhere he looked, Humvees and soldiers were converging on his position.

He felt he had to repeat the warning to the other troops, and he suppressed the mike button again and offered the troops. "To all personnel attached to this damn operation. Dragon Fire Leader repeating, I was just eyeballed by two suspects hanging around in the damn parking lot. The two were obviously lookouts for the rat bastards hold up inside the damn building. Be advised, our operation has lost the element of surprised, and we're gonna hafta fight for everything we want from this lousy crapshoot. Since we lost the surprise element, I'm gonna park in front of the fucking place and start from there.

"Once my machine is parked, I'm gonna get back on the damn megaphone and give these stinking twerps in there five fucking minutes to come crawling outta their damn rathole, with their hands over their damn heads. If the dopey assholes refused to come outta there real peaceful like. We'll show them the errors in their ways of thinking in a fast fucking hurry it up, dammit. A word of warning to you people, if we hafta go active against the lousy slugs, don't fucking worry about taking any stinking prisoners outta there a friggin live. We're not here to dance around with any of these lousy assholes.

"We're here to destroy the mutherfuckers plain and simple, and that's exactly what we're gonna do, even if we hafta engage the flaming assholes in a fucking all out firefight. Huh? What? What the fuck's bugging your damn ass now, Nentendo? What the hell do you want from my stinking ass anyway, man? You just drive this damn thing and that's all, buster!" The upset Captain had to shake his head in an attempt to clear his thinking, and Nentendo's words finally registered in his mind, and he snarled at the other soldier. "What the hell do you want a stinking medal? It's about time you got me here."

"Man, you gotta go get a fucking personality for yourself, man. Because what you're displaying here really sucks the big one, Captain. You gotta remember Walker that I'm on your fucking side sir, so why the fuck are you biting my damn head off for, man?" Nentendo fired back at his Commanding Officer as he glared for a tense moment.

Captain Walker put on a face because he was disgusted with himself over the way he just addressed his fellow soldier, and then he smiled at his driver as he offered in a much calmer tone of voice this time. "I can't argue with you there, Dave. Look man, I allowed the stinking pressure of this fucking operation to get to my ass, man. Nentendo, I feel like the south end of a north bound horse for barking at ya like I did. Are we good man?"

He asked as he extended his arm out and Nentendo instantly did what the soldiers referred to as slapping sticks together, as they both bumped forearms together. This informed Walker that Nentendo was no longer upset with this childish like outburst, and everything was cool between the two elite soldiers.

"Thanks, a shitload soldier, I owe you a stinking beer when we finally complete this stinking mission, and we can get back of ourselves. Damn, I can't fricking believe the amount of stinking pressure these damn terrorists are placing on my fucking ass over this damn mess they started. Shit, I've been out on so many other stinking missions in my life covering just about anything one stinking human being could do to the uther, and none of them have ever affected me half as much as this one stinking mission is doing, man. I gotta get a damn hold of myself so I can command this stinking mission properly, or the rest of the stinking troops are gonna vote me outta the damn Unit all together, dammit. Hell, how I hate when some assholes start hitting us right in our own country for crap's sake."

CHAPTER TWENTY-SEVEN

The moment Nentendo stopped the Humvee, Captain Robert Walker popped opened the door as his hand searched for the megaphone. Finding it, he rolled his legs out of the machine, and when his feet were on the ground, he darted to the other side of the Humvee not facing the building obviously hiding the terrorists. He leaned up against the cool metal skin of the heavy war machine and noticed Nentendo was still sitting in the driver's seat of the vehicle. He shook his head and barked at the soldier, "Well what the fuck are you waiting for man, a special invitation to join the rest of us dealing with these mutherfuckers? Get your butt the hell outta that damn machine and take position with the uther troops."

"Man Walker, I thought that lame excuse for a stinking apology was too good to be fucking true a few moments ago from you, man. You must move your ass away from the damn door of the machine, so I can get the hell out of it and then join in on the fun, Captain. Or do you want me to climb over your stinking body to get outta this damn machine and take my position out there with the rest of the troops, sir?" Nentendo replied as he fired a disgusted look at his Commander as he waited for him to move away from the door.

The captain smirked and then slid his rearend over a little alongside the vehicle, to make some room for Nentendo to get out of the parked military machine. The other soldiers in his vehicle rapidly dismounted and they quickly took up positions in the deep drainage ditch along with the other soldiers from the Unit. Walker slapped Nentendo on his back and then he raised the megaphone and growled in it.

THE DESTROYED TERRORIST SAFE HOUSE

Colonel Bruce Leadbetter had enough of the destroyed building and the few dead terrorists, and he ordered the elite group of soldiers under his command to take control of the dead terrorists, and once that was completed, he gave the troops further orders. "Okay people, you heard the suggestion about that damn park from Sergeant Ramirez. Saddle up, we're heading for that damn position as soon as I contact our Toll Booth Commanders."

The Colonel watched his specialized troops snapped in action, and when they were doing as ordered, he keyed his mike and snapped in it. "Dragon Lair to Toll Booths One, Two, Three, and Foxtrot (Military slang for fucking) Four Commanders, I have a change in your current orders. You tracks are now ordered to abandon your present positions and Toll Booth One Commander, you're now ordered to take up your new position stationed at Mike, One, One, Three, West, on your funny pages (Maps). Toll Booth Two Commander, you'll take up your new position stationed at Romeo, Nine, Niner, One, East. Toll Booth Three Commander, you are ordered to take up your new position at Alfa, Two, Two, Niner, South. Toll Booth Four Commander, you'll take up your new position stationed at Charlie, Four, Four, Seven, North, and you are ordered to man these positions until further notice.

"These are the only corrections in your orders at this time. Your previous orders still stand for the duration of this damn operation. If you have a PID (Positive Identification) on any possible hostel targets, don't hesitate for a second. Destroy the fucking enemy targets as discovered in your area of responsibility with extreme prejudice. Period! These latest positions I just distributed will afford you the ability to blanket the entire commercial district area where our troops are currently operating. Be advised all Toll Booth Commanders, we have many friendlies working in your areas of responsibility at this time. I'll skin your hide alive if any of our troops fall victim to fratricide on this fucking mission. I demand none of our soldiers fall victim to friendly fire on this fucking operation under any circumstances, ladies and gentlemen. Reply to these orders! Out." Colonel Leadbetter broke off the communication.

"Dragon Lair, Commander Richardson Toll Booth One, sir. Have received corrections in orders and shall follow the changes to the letter. Guarantee no fratricide on mission. Out."

Colonel Leadbetter listened until the other three track roadblock Commanders confirmed their new orders. The moment they replied, he flew out of the building and jumped into a waiting Humvee. He ordered his driver to head for the park Sergeant Ramirez brought up to his attention.

When the Marine Colonel was certain the Commanders of the roadblocks detail understood their new orders, he took the next steps to forward his operation. He made direct contact with General White, the chairman of the Joint Chiefs of Staff and his commanding officer for this mission. He had a need from the General as he called in. "Dragon Lair to Charlie, Victor, One, One. Come in sir. Over."

THE PENTAGON

General John White was in his office speaking to the CIA Director John Raincloud, when his contact computer informed him, he had a call coming in. He read the call name and breathed out angrily more to himself as he grumbled at himself, "It's about time you made contact with me, mister." as he opened the communication with his Commander working in the field. "Charlie, Victor, One, One to Dragon Lair. Go with your traffic Colonel Leadbetter. Over."

"Dragon Lair, Charlie, Victor, One, One, I have a request for you sir. Over."

"Go with your request and I'll provide an answer immediately, Dragon Lair. Over." The General replied to his Commander in the field.

"Charlie, Victor, One, One. I need something to place the damn item in that'll maintain a safe environment for said item and my soldiers working in the field, once Dragon Fire Leader takes command of said item, sir. Over." Colonel Leadbetter was speaking in sort of a code. Even though the soldiers were communicating on a secured net, with the computers, the hackers and the news people, nothing was secured when it came to military operations going down.

General White was slightly confused over the Colonel's request, and when he cast a quick look at Director Raincloud. The Director immediately shook his head yes, to inform him he knew what the Colonel was requesting from him. Reading the nod from the Director, he replied to the Commander of the troops working in downtown Washington. "Dragon Lair, I shall take your request under advisement, and I'll inform you of my decision shortly, Colonel Leadbetter. Out." General White broke off the communication with the Colonel and looked at the Director as he waited to hear what he had on his mind.

"Errr... General White, I can't believe neither one of us smart asses had the smarts to think about what the Colonel's requesting from us for this operation, sir. We should've known the soldiers would need something safe to place the nuclear items into for safe transportation to a more control site where the damn weapon can be disassembled, and then properly destroyed once the troops have taken poss...."

"C'mon Director Raincloud and tell me what the hell you're talking about for Christ's sake. I haven't the slightest fucking idea what you're babbling about here, sir. If you know what my damn Colonel needs, inform me so I can get to work on it for him." General White growled.

"General White, all nuclear power plants have heavy lead lined canisters they're constantly transporting their nuclear parts or waste, safely through the streets of the cities the reactors are constructed in. I suggest you contact the nuclear power plant stationed in Maryland, which is the closest nuclear establishment to the incident zone. Request not only a transportation canister, but you have to request personnel trained to handle this kind of crap, sir." Director Raincloud spread his hands and shrugged as he looked at Military Commander.

"Shit! Right. Of course, we needed something to place that crap in for safe transport from the damn incident zone, Director. But I do have the personnel at my command needed to handle the nuclear item for my troops properly. So, I won't be forced to rely on some crazy ass civilians to accomplish what I have trained military personnel to do for us. Dammit to hell, I'm angry at myself, and if I could I'd boot myself in the fucking ass for missing this shit like..."

"I don't care whose personnel you employ to secure this nuclear item, General White. All I know is the damn item needs to be secured safely, sir. And the soldiers you dispatched to search for this crap are not the personnel trained to secure and decontaminate anything that might become contaminated by the terrorists playing around with this crap. We need a special Deacon Unit sent out to secure the item and treat any possible contaminated surfaces or crapped up soldiers, sir." The Director interrupted the General.

"Shit, I really screwed up again on this never-ending god damn operation I see, Director Raincloud. I never gave a second thought to the possible contaminated surfaces the terrorists might screw up, or any soldiers who might encounter any contaminated surfaces and need to be scrubbed down and decontaminated in a hurry, John. Excuse me for a moment I have a number of calls to make so I can get the correct personnel on the move to clean up the mess once this mission has been completed." General White offered as he reached for the phone and spoke with his secretary.

"Do you want me to leave so you can make these calls in private, sir?" The Director asked the powerful military officer.

General White looked up and shook his head no and waved his hand to keep the Director in his seat, as he announced to his secretary. "Mary, make a call over to the nuclear plant in Maryland for me please. I need to speak with the plant manager of operations at that installation immediately young lady. Also, once you connected me to the plant manager, make a second call out to Edwards Airforce Base, and find out the closest Unit of soldiers specially trained to deal with nuclear material and possible contaminated surfaces. Keep that damn Commander online for me while I speak to the nuclear plant manager. This is important and I need you to handle this crap for me immediately, young lady."

The moment the General was through speaking with his secretary, he turned to the CIA Director and bitched at him. "Now why the hell would I want you to leave this fucking office while I was handling this crap, Director? I need to have you hanging around in case I need some of your input when I get that nuclear plant manager on the line, Director."

Even before the CIA Director could reply to the General's question, Mary cut in on their conversation and offered to her boss. "General White Sir, I have a Mr. Robert Knowles on line three for you, sir. He's the plant manager for the Blue Crab Nuclear Power Plant in Maryland, sir. I was informed he was the man you wanted and needed to speak with, General."

"You're a real doll, patch him through to me please, Mary." General White barely had the time to put his thumb up to the Director, before a man's voice echoed in his ear on the phone. "Yes, this is Robert Knowles, I was informed I'd be speaking to a General White at the Pentagon..."

"That's correct Mr. Knowles, this is Chairman of the Chiefs of Staff, General John White, sir..."

"It's a pleasure to speak with you General White. I'm a big fan of yours and this is a real pleasure, sir. What can I do for you, sir? I'm afraid I'm a little pressed for time as always at the plant, General White."

The powerful General ignored the words from the plant manager as he started right off speaking to the man. "First off Mr. Knowles, were you ever in a branch of military service, sir?"

"Why yes is that General White Sir, I spent seven years in the Navy, sir. I was a nuclear sub mariner, General. That's how I received the training needed for my line of work in the nuclear field, sir. Please don't tell me you're thinking of drafting me, General White?" Knowles offered while trying to be funny.

General White offered a nervous laugh as he went on with his words to the plant manager and ignored his lame attempt at trying to be a wise guy. "No Mr. Knowles, this is nothing as drastic as that I assure you, sir. The reason I asked if you were ever in the service sir, is so I know you're aware of what a top-secret situation is all about, sir? Believe me Mr. Knowles, what I'm about to inform you of, falls under the top-secret label if anything surely does, sir. By the way Mr. Knowles, any personnel I might be forced to use your word, "draft" during this present emergency, will be likewise warned this operation is a zip lip situation, sir. Your workers will be sworn to secrecy under the penalty of being incarcerated, and if the breach is severe enough, the penalty of death will be leveled against the offender, sir. Mr. Knowles, the reason for this call to you is as follows, sir.

"Mr. Knowles, we and by we, I mean a specialized Unit of Special Forces soldiers, are in the process of tracking down and eliminating a terrorist cell operating in downtown Washington, sir. Here's the hard part of this present situation, sir. The same terrorist cell is thought to be in possession of an unknown amount of what we suspect is Highly Enriched Uranium…"

"My God in Heaven, sir. What is it you want from us here at the plant, General White?"

"Yes Mr. Knowles, I fear we'll all need a helluva lot of help from God in Heaven, before this damn thing is played out to its conclusion, sir. Since you asked, what I need from you is special container my troops will be able to place this Enriched Uranium crap safely in, once they're in possession of the crap after they have successfully eliminated the terrorist threat against our country, sir. So, the troops can secure the crap properly for safe transportation out of the area of downtown Washington. Do you have anything like that available for my troops use on your complex, sir?"

"Yes, indeed General White Sir, I certainly have the very thing your troops will need to safely secure, and then transport this nuclear material in, parked right on my plant site, sir. It's a twelve-inch-thick lead lined high impact cylinder we commonly employ to safely transport our nuclear materials and waste through the streets of the cities we have to move this waste through at any given time, sir. The cylinder weighs over thirty-one tons and is secured to the back of a flatbed truck, General White. One thing I must inform you of though General.

"The cautious handling and securing, and the decontamination of contaminated Enriched Uranium surfaces are not a small feat to accomplish, sir. The highly trained personnel you'll have to employ for that specialized type of situation, is going to be awful hard to keep as a national security situation, sir. A highly radioactive contaminated environment like the one we're speaking of here will employ hundreds of specialized personnel, vehicles, machinery, equipment, and the likes to contain the possible contaminated situation, sir. How will you possibly be able to keep that amount of personnel and equipment from telling the news reporters what they're doing in downtown Washington, sir?"

"Mr. Knowles, the security of this damn situation is my problem to deal with, sir. And I assure you sir. I'll handle that with my usual efficiency Mr. Knowles. Also, to make my job a little easier to contend with sir, I intend to employ only military personnel during this entire current emergency, sir. I'm dispatching two soldiers to your plant, and they'll drive the truck with this damn cylinder out to the incident site, sir. That'll be the extent of what I need from your plant personnel and you currently, Mr. Knowles. Once my soldiers leave your plant with this truck, your part of this situation will be complete. You'll swear anyone who helps these soldiers to secrecy, sir. I hope I'm making myself perfectly clear about this situation and your part of this operation, Mr. Knowles?"

"Yes, quite clear at that General White, and to make your part of the security a little easier for you to accomplish, sir. I'll drive the rig off the site myself and park it in the secluded loading field we have stationed just outside the security area of the plant site, sir. I'll have my security personnel clear the area of all plant personnel and themselves, General White Sir. That way no one from the plant will know any military personnel are on site, or what they're doing with our truck and the cylinder, sir."

"That's outstanding Mr. Knowles, I knew I could count on an ex-serviceman for help, sir. My troops should be arriving at your site within the next ten minutes or so, sir. Thank you for your assistance and understanding in this matter, sir." General White offered pleasantly as he ended the communication with the concerned plant manager. He was confident with the knowledge his secretary was monitoring his call, and by now she had already dispatched the soldiers he spoke about, out to the nuclear plant.

CAPTAIN ROBERT WALKER'S TROOPERS

"To the fucking people hold upside in the friggin commercial structure with the address of One, Three, Three, Five, Niner, East, on I Street. This is Captain Robert Walker, and I'm the Commander of the Rapid Response Force protecting the streets of Washington D.C. I'm a Captain enlisted in the service of the United States Marine Corps, and I've been endowed by the President of the United States with powers that cover what you people are illegally doing inside that damn building. I'm quite prepared to give you one full minute to come out of that structure with your fricking hands in the air real peaceful like.

"If at the end of those sixty seconds you people have ignored my fucking orders. Then I'm likewise prepared to level that entire commercial structure right to the damn ground with you people still hiding inside the damn thing. The clock is ticking on you guys! Do the right thing and come outta there in peace, or in pieces. It's up to you, assholes it doesn't fucking matter to my ass which way you come out of there, but you will come out of there I promise ya that."

INSIDE THE STRUCTURE ONE, THREE, THREE, FIVE, NINE, EAST I STREET

Mohsen al-Gasim and Reemabdel Aziz al-Rowaili charged into the structure the moment he noticed the odd painted military type machine, and several obvious soldiers riding in it slowly driving passed their building. Mohsen rushed over to al-Wahhad's side and cried. "Al-Wahhad, our safe house has been discovered, one from our group must have informed the police authorities, and they're massing outside the building preparing to attack us…"

"What in Allah's world are you talking about, you great fool you?" The sudden upset Ghost snapped at his second in command, as he held him in his harsh glare.

"Al-Wahhad, I saw a military truck with a threatening American soldier riding inside the thing. Shabbah (Ghost) I looked into the eyes of this evil looking soldier, and I saw our deaths written within his loathsome eyes. This American soldier displayed his desire to kill us and stop what we plan to do to the land of Satan. Al-Wahhad, we must prepare to defend this position until you make the final decision of what we intend to do with the weapon of freedom. Arrr… listen, the foul thing is trying to order us to come out of this building with our hands in the air." The second in command of the cell reported.

"What makes you tremble like wash on the line, fool? I hear the cursed lowly infidel's worthless threats he is aiming at us, and I shall not pay any attention to them. I order you to ignore the words of the great fool from outside as well, my foolish Arab brother. Because I know in my heart there is no God but Allah whom I believe in, and we have to answer to. Huh, the whites of my eyes will be the last thing this piece of trash from hell on the side of Satan will ever see before he kisses the sacred feet of Allah. Mohsen, take command of our freedom fighters, and have them prepare a harsh welcoming for the cursed infidels and jackals gathered outside this foul place. We must be prepared when the cursed jackals try to take over our building and destroy the dreams we have labored to accomplish.

"Yes, I shall be busy applying my attention to al-Mutairi and his work on the weapon, and I'll try and move him along with the construction of our great weapon that'll sterilize the hated infidels from this evil lowly nation. Al-Gasim, I must be standing at his side in case I'm able to lend any assistance to his project. If we are forced to detonate the great weapon from here, the blast will be powerful enough to destroy the most important targets we have vowed to Allah to destroy, when we first set out to attack the evil land of Satan. Be off with you now and carry out my orders faithfully my brother.

"But before you leave my side my Arab brother, I must remind you to keep me in your sight from this moment on, while we're being threatened by these gods cursed animal soldiers of Washington. Because if the evil forces gathered outside this building are too powerful for us to contend with, and they're able to stop our quest then you and your girlfriend must follow me. Because you two are the only ones I truly wish to save from this entire group of these worthless fighters. The failures we have suffered were created because the fools we have rested our trust in, did not do as they were ordered to accomplish. They have allowed themselves to be captured by the hated police authorities of this evil land, and obviously they have betrayed our whereabouts to these lowly dogs. I curse these fools to the very fires of hell for all eternity.

"Now do as I have instructed you my faithful Arab brother, take command of our small group of freedom fighters, and place them in a defense posture where they'll do their best good to defeat the evil forces that this foul country have mounted against us. I'll see how al-Mutairi is doing with completing our weapon. Use everyone from our warriors you need, and every weapon we have at our disposal to defend us from the lowly infidels stalking us from outside this foul building. You must hold off the advances of the cursed jackals for as long as you possibly can. I fear al-Mutairi needs more time to complete his work on our weapon to make it operational. Mohsen, we must complete the work of Allah if we wish to destroy the evil nest of Satan's head rest, Washington D.C.

"My faithful Arab Brother al-Gasim, if you see any lowly jackals lurking about outside this cursed building is on the verge of defeating our freedom fighters, after we have engaged their evil forces of Satan in the battle to the death for Allah's sake. You must be smart and swift to leave your position with your foolish girlfriend and search me out inside this worthless building. Wherever al-Mutairi is working, is where I shall be standing and offering him any help, I can give him to complete the weapon. Once you linked up with me and al-Mutairi if there is no longer any hope for us, and the four of us will leave this worthless building and make for the nearest highway where we'll hijack an infidel's vehicle.

"Then we shall leave this useless city of the United States and their worthless leaders for the last time and make our way to the Mexican border where we'll successfully escape and head for the safety of Central America. Once there we'll find a way to get back to our beloved land of Iraq and the pure sand of our deserts, and then disappear forever from view of the cursed infidels. I have to check with al-Mutairi while you get our fighters set in position."

With that said, the terrorist leader al-Wahhad turned, and he headed for where al-Mutairi was still working on the weapon. Mohsen drew in a gulp of air and then he headed for the rest of the Arab fighters of his terrorist cell who were trying to look busy for their leader, as to not upset al-Wahhad and suffer his feared wrath.

Al-Wahhad walked up behind al-Mutairi who was trying to set a piece of the weapon in place with a tube type thing in his hands. The terrorist leader branded the Ghost did not make a peep as he watched what his bomb maker was doing. Al-Wahhad could see the concentration al-Mutairi was laboring under, and he tried to keep out of his way.

The young Arab bomb maker was so intent on completing his work on the nuclear weapon that he did not pay any attention to the Ghost's presence standing behind him. For the past half an hour, he was desperately trying to set a double A battery case in place. This two-battery set was needed to carry the electrical impulse that would start the process of exploding the poor man's nuclear weapon. All the while he worked of the metal casing of the weapon, he cursed himself for completing the main structure of the casing without setting this battery in place first.

There was no way for him to back engineer the weapon down to where he would be able to set the battery case easier inside the weapon. When first constructing the weapon, he had to weld the three main pieces of metal together, and that was now stopping him from taking the bomb down to where he could easily set the battery properly. It was his mistake, and he was suffering the pains and anger of trying to set the battery now that it was impossible for him to set the batteries where they were supposed to be placed inside the weapon.

Al-Gasim rushed to where most of the rest of his warriors were assembled. The fighters were waiting further orders to follow from either of the two terrorist leader, Al-Gasim or al-Wahhad. The terrorists were all nervous because of the enemy troops gathered just outside the building, and one of those American soldiers were ordering them to come out of the building with their hands up. Seeing the Iraq ex-soldier and weapon's expert Nizar Hamdoon, the second in command of the terrorist group when he was busy, Mohsen offered to him. "Hamdoon, there are many cursed lowly infidels gathered at the gates of our sanctuary. We must prepare to defend our positions against the foul fools. You must deploy our faithful warriors in the areas to defend this structure against the attack planned at us by our enemy.

"Al-Mutairi needs more time to finish his faithful work on our weapon of revenge. I'll take a few of our fighters with me, and we'll setup our defenses at the rear of this foul building. The bulk of the lowly infidels have taken positions at the front of this foul structure. So, I'll take a few of our warriors to defend our rear position against them, if the fools try and attack us from our rear area. You have been trained in the Iraqi Army on how to defend a position of defense. So, I'll leave most of the setting up of our defenders to your abilities. Reemabdel and Leila will come with me to defend our rear."

Mohsen knew what he was doing with his picks of the fighters he wanted to take with him, because he was aware al-Wahhad had eyes on Leila as a mate, since they first become a terrorist organization, and that was why he wanted Leila part of his small group. When the American forces too powerful to be defeated by so few of his defenders began to overpower his warriors, he could take Reemabdel and Leila, and then linkup with al-Wahhad and al-Mutairi and escape the building. His thoughts of the brotherhood of Arabs were long gone from his mind, and he was having no problem with leaving the other fighters behind to fight to their death, while the few of them made their dash for life. Mohsen had no want to die inside the commercial building, because he had dreams of making a life with Reemabdel and living in the United States and having many male babies to enjoy.

Nizar Hamdoon looked at who spoke to him and replied to al-Gasim's chilling words. "I heard the loudmouth American fool bellowing his worthless words of threat at us from outside the building. I was wondering what we were going to do, and how we were going to reply to this lowly infidel's worthless threats aimed at us. Mohsen, I was right in the middle of handing out weapons we shall employ against the foul fools, when they start their attack against us. I thank Allah for His great wisdom that we looked after our weapons so carefully.

"All weapons are ready for immediate use, and each of our faithful followers carries ten extra loaded clips of ammunition on their person. All I needed was the order on how we were going to respond against the hated infidels threatening us from outside this foul building, since you gave the orders. I have no further need for orders from you or anyone else from our fighters. Mohsen, Paradise awaits her heroes to come to her waiting arms and give us rest from hatred." Nizar Hamdoon replied as he handed out the weapons for the last of his fighters.

"I'm pleased you're so well prepared to defend our positions with our few freedom fighters we still have against the loathsome invaders outside, Hamdoon. It seems to me you have everything under your control, so I shall leave you and your faithful warriors, and take the two worthless women with me to defend the rear position. Yes Hamdoon, you're correct when you stated Paradise awaits her heroes. May Allah keep you safe, and may you find peace sitting at the right hand of Allah for all eternity."

AT THE WEST SIDE TOLL BOOTH

As the civilian tractor trailer carrying the massive lead lined heavy containment cylinder on the flatbed truck, pulled in the area as instructed. The aged Army driver found his progress suddenly blocked by a parked Bradley Fighting Machine, and two other armored track vehicles. Immediately, the Bradley turned its two-man turret and aimed its 25 mm Chain Gun directly at the cab of the trailer. The 7.25 mm coaxial machine gun of the Bradley also zeroed in on the cab of the truck, but neither weapon opened fire on the machine.

The surprised Army Sergeant jumped out of the cab of the rig, and he immediately flashed his orders at the three soldiers standing guard outside the parked war machines. A second Sergeant from the roadblock walked up to the other Sergeant like he owned the world. While his partners kept the second Sergeant under his cross hairs, as he took hold of the orders and quickly read through them. Once the Bradley Sergeant was certain this Army Sergeant was a fellow soldier, and not a threat against him or his fellow soldiers. He waved his arm at the Bradley and the turret slowly turned away and resumed its surveillance of its area of responsibility.

The Sergeant from the roadblock crew next keyed his mike and then said as if he was bored with his life. "Dragon Fire Leader, this is Toll Booth Three, West, sir. Come in. I have an updated report for you, sir. Over."

"Yeah, Toll Booth West, this is Dragon Fire Leader. Go with your stinking traffic. Over." Captain Walker replied, peeved his concentration with the terrorists trapped inside the building was being interrupted by this radio call in. All the while he was responding to the call, he refused to remove his eyes away from the structure.

"Dragon Fire Leader, I have an obviously commandeered civilian tractor trailer truck stopped directly in front of my present position, sir. The machine's operator is reported he's moving under special Army's orders, sir. The soldiers are offering they're connected to the Dragon Fire Operation by order of the President of the United States, sir. The damn rig has a huge metal cylinder shaped thing resting on her tail end, sir.

"The Sergeant's orders state he and his nuclear response teams will be responsible for the safe removal of the Foxtrot item we're out here after sir. This Sergeant and his dopey team are further ordered to clean up any crud (Military jargon for radioactive contamination debris) from this Romeo Foxtrot (Rat Fuck) mission, once it has been completed by us, sir. Dragon Fire Leader, the Army Sergeant's orders further state no personnel involved in the Dragon Fire Operation is allowed to leave the immediate incident area under any circumstances. Until this Sergeant and the rest of his crew checks us out first for any possible radiation contamination sir, and they clear us for any pull out of the Foxtrot area. Over."

"Damn, that takes a shitload of stinking crap offa my fucking ass, I tell you man. I was wondering if we were gonna get stuck cleaning up any Foxtrot crud, once we leveled the lousy Romeo Foxtrots trapped inside this damn building. Sergeant, I'm ordering you to have that damn rig stay put at your present position until I order it released. The moment we end this damn crapshoot you'll be notified, and then you can send the damn rig and Sergeant's teams in, and they can take over command of this damn operation from that point forward with my Foxtrot blessings, Sergeant."

Captain Robert Walker decided to employ the code word for "fucking" over the net, because he was using a non-secured frequency while speaking with the Toll Booth Sergeant, and he did not want to cuss over the open radio. The grunts developed the code words whenever they used the radios, so they could dump on their Commanders without recourse, if they did not like the orders that they had received from their Commanders.

"Roger that last Dragon Fire Leader, we'll take command of the rig and Foxtrot Alfa Hotels (Fucking Ass Holes) attached to this damn thing, sir. Dragon Fire Leader, we'll standby until you finished your act with the Foxtrot Bravos (Fucking Bastards) you're about to deal with, sir. Then we'll allow the blocked Richard Craniums (Dick Heads) to pass our position and get their asses down to the incident site, so they can do their act and then they can take command of the situation for us, sir. Good luck with your operation, Dragon Fire Leader. Remember sir, if you need our fire power, all you must do is call for it, and we'll move in and level any problem facing you, sir. Out." The Toll Booth Sergeant responded confidently over his radio, and then he broke off the communication with the operation's Commander.

Both Walker and the Toll Booth Sergeant was aware the Army Sergeant in charge of the cleanup teams understood their code. But neither soldier cared a lick over the insults they aimed at these new units.

When the young Captain broke off his communication with the concerned Sergeant, he concentrated on the commercial structure he held under surveillance, waiting for the time limit to end. He had to admit he was looking forward to getting a quick end to this operation in any manner the terrorists wanted to end it at this point.

STRUCTURE ONE, THREE, THREE, FIVE, NINER, EAST I STREET

Inside the commercial building with the terrorist cell reacting to the threats from Walker, it was a beehive of activity as they Arab radicals rapidly took up positions of defense. All windows facing the American troops outside the factory were shattered, and then the radicals aimed their weapons at the American soldiers and prepared to open fire.

The concerned Mutt moved a little closer to Walker's side, and then bitched at him. "Hey man, what the fuck are we waiting for the love of Christ, before we start cracking some fucking heads around here, man? Look at them stinking popinjays moving around inside the damn building. The lousy fucks are setting up against our asses and forming up a pretty damn good defense against us, Walker."

"All I know is you betta remember who the devil you're talking to, dog man. And get the damn vinegar outta your tone when addressing our Commanding Officer out in the field, mister. In case you might have forgotten Lieutenant Hall, Robert's your Commander, and he should be respected during this operation." Sergeant Ramirez warned as she held Mutt under her gaze.

The Mutt turned from Walker to stare at Sergeant Ramirez for a moment, and then he grumbled at her. "What the hell's this Lieutenant Hall shit all about, Duchess of Knockers?"

"Somebody has to shut you down once in a while, Boozo the Clown. I believe you were overstepping your bounds speaking to our Commander that way." Ramirez offered in an angry voice.

"Hey baby unless you're a fucking hemorrhoid, stay offa my stinking ass…"

"Hey, hey boys and girls, what the fuck's going on between you two birds?" Walker growled and then he glared angrily at the two specialized soldiers. Then he added to his bitch at them. "Since when do we argue with each uther, especially before our uther troops from our ranks? Raz, the stinking Mutt has a pretty good bitch to pitch there, and I feel we mighta gave the damn pricks in there a little too much stinking time, before we went after them and placed an end to their damn aims. From the looks of it, the flaming assholes in there intend to duke it out with us, and that suits me just fucking fine. Okay Mutt."

Walker turned back to his friend and growled at him. "You're damn right I mighta waited too fucking long to go afta these stinking guys Mutt, and now we're gonna go afta the fucks hot and heavy and with evil intent. I'm bout done chasing the stinking assholes all over the damn States. I'm also done with trying to talk the asses into surrendering to our asses, Mutt. I'm finished answering this damn radio and allowing uther assholes to break up my damn thoughts, and then I hafta start over with my damn plans of attack against these lousy fucks. I don't believe the lousy fucks have any uther ideas than trying to kill our asses. So, there's no sense jaw jacking any sense in their damn noggins. It's time for action."

"Good, now we get rid of Moose and Squirrel. It's time we place the period at the end of the fucking sentence for the rotten bastards, man. I can't wait to send this pack of fucks to Alpha, Whiskey, Romeo (Allah's Waiting Room). Then I wanna get back to base and take a dump and enjoy an hour long hot as hell shower, and pig out on some stinking steaks cook raw as hell at the damn mess. Then I'm gonna put my crack in the sack and sleep for a fucking week or more, man. I'm beat up from the feet up and I want a break, Walker." The Mutt complained as he checked his weapon and then hoisted it up to his shoulder and aimed.

"You'll hold your fire until told to do utherwise, buster! You fire when I give the word to go hot and heavy on the lousy fucks and not before. I don't need you setting off World War Three in there just because you couldn't control your fucking self like always. Also, Mutt and this goes for the rest of you guys also, so pass this warning down the stinking line. Remember the fucks fired one RPG round at us already. So that shit means they have more than likely have more Rocket Propelled Grenades in their damn group of stinking misfits. Shit, I want you guys to be on your toes about that fucking weapon when we open up on the creeps." Walker warned the Mutt and the other troops, and then he aimed his eyes back at the commercial building.

"Obviously the dopey fucks in there are not gonna come outta there peaceful like, so we're going hot on their asses. Pick out your targets, and if you have a shot at any of the fucks, send them on their way to Paradise.

The order is Green, you have permission to engage all hostel targets of opportunity as they appear as of this time, and I want you to make…"

Walker's words were cut off by his radio call coming to life. "Dragon Fire Leader, Ghost here man, I have a good MOE (Mark One Eyeball) on one subject inside the place. Requesting permission to takeout the subject? Over."

"Dragon Fire Leader to Ghost, we're hot as of this moment. At your discretion shooter, you have clearance to take out your target. Over."

"Roger that last man and thanks for the green order." A single shot instantly rang out, and a window on the structure shattered.

Unseen by Walker, one of the Arab defenders was violently pitched back by the 308 round that just ripped into his forehead. But none of the American soldiers was prepared for what happened from inside the structure next.

A fusillade of heavy rounds was fired as the terrorist's response against the soldiers, when one of their people was killed inside the building. Round after round was fired from the collection of Kalashnikov Assault Rifles in the hands of the terrorists, ripping into the line of parked Humvee machines parked in the road in front of the building. The endless rain of rounds pounded the dirt and machines in front of the soldiers using the drainage ditch as protection from the rounds.

The second sniper did not have a clear shot at any Islamic shooters trapped inside the building from where he set up his firing perch from. Nevertheless, the Hunter drew a bead on a rifle stock he picked up sticking out of one of the windows, and he fired at the weapon. The weapon fired by the terrorists was ripped out of his hands and went tumbling out the window. The young American soldier felt good because he thought he took out a weapon firing at his fellow troops. Almost instantly, a second weapon was shoved out the same window, and it was firing wildly at his hunkered down troops. This angered the Hunter to no end, and he tried to pick up this second weapon in his sights. But the radical shooter was awful sloppy with his firing rate, and he was allowing the weapon to jump all over the place. This made it impossible for the Hunter to get a good bead on the dancing weapon.

The pounding enemy weapon fire was so heavy that Walker's troops chose to hunker down and allow the terrorists to waste their ammunition without taking them out. As always, the wild Mutt was by Walker's side, and he was bitching at him hot and heavy. "Holy shit man, how the fuck many of them crazy ass mutherfucka's are held up inside that stinking dump? I can't pop my ass up long enuf to get one round fired off at the lousy bastards, without losing my fucking noggin in the process. This shit sucks the big one man, I wanna kill me some lousy terrorists, and I can't get one round off at the lousy assholes, dammit."

Walker let out a grunt as he offered to the Mutt. "It looks like there is plenty of them fucks to go around for each of us, buddy. Stay low and let the assholes waste their stinking ammunition. At least we're able to mark out where and how many fucks are firing at us, my friend. I'm certain the stinking Ghost and Hunter are moving round out there, so they can pick off some of the fucks hiding inside that damn dump and…"

"Walker, request permission to pop off a few forties, I'm sure I can pop a few of them through one of them windows they knocked out." Buckethead offered as he cut in on Walker and Mutt.

"Christ's sake, why the fuck are you asking my permission to fire anything at the fucking terrorists, you asshole? Lay some heat on their stinking asses, stupid. I told you people before, this is a weapons free action, dammit. Fire away with the damn Two or Three, asshole, who is your backup and how many fucking grenades do you two birds have between you asses for that damn thing? I want some warheads on foreheads out there ten minutes ago."

"Walker, Siberia, (Sergeant Taras Zarugnaya) is my backup since we first started this damn op., and between the two of us we have at least fifteen rounds of forties, man. I know Danko (Sergeant Christopher Danko) has at least six more fucking rounds for my weapon with him. Here I go outta the fucking tube, boss." Buckethead announced in an excited voice as he sent the first grenade at one window in the factory.

Walker watched as Buckethead opened fire with his forty, and the first grenade flew perfectly through one of the shattered windows of the structure. The projectile exploded inside the building, and a large chunk of the thin metal skin was blown out by the explosion. One Islamic terrorist flew out of the fracture due to the explosion going off close behind him. The Arab's body was on fire as the defender crashed hard to the ground. But the terrorist did not stop moving until the Tier One soldiers outside stopped firing at it and allowed the terrorist's body to rest on the ground still burning.

Liking the effect of the grenade going off inside the building, Walker growled at the huge soldier angrily. "Hey stupid, keep pounding away at the fucking windows with that damn thing, try and hit each window any of the lousy little fucks are firing outta, Buckethead. I want you to drive them stinking asses deeper inside the damn building, so we can hit the structure hard with less rounds coming at our asses from the terrorists trapped inside the stinking dump. We gotta open up on the fucks so they understand we mean fucking business against them out here."

Buckethead ignored Walker calling him stupid as he tried to get a better bead on any of the windows of the structure. Because of the sharp angle he adopted when he first setup to fire on the structure. He already took out the only window he was able to get a good target on. The huge soldier shrugged and then fired at a second window, to see what kind of damage he could do to the building with another round. The grenade struck the side of the thin metal skin and bounced off before it exploded harmlessly outside the building.

Even though the grenade exploded outside the structure, it did some damage to the building, but most of the blast was wasted outside. The round did not stop many terrorists from firing at the American troops gathered against them outside. But the force of the explosion caused two terrorists to stop firing, and it forced them to duck down behind the walls, until they realized the explosion did not harm them. In a flash, the terrorists were back firing at his troops.

CHAPTER TWENTY-EIGHT

The slight interruption of enemy weapon fire gave Walker's troops the opportunity to fire a heavy volley of rounds of their own at the terrorists trapped inside the building. Hundreds of metals ripping full metal jacketed rounds easily tore through the windows and thin hide of the commercial building, as the fired rounds searched for their human targets. Now, it was the Islamic terrorists forced to hunker down, and then wait out the barrage of rounds fired at them.

During the heavy return weapon fire, Buckethead slid down the line of troops who took their positions in the long drainage ditch. He was searching for another position to fire a third grenade at the terrorists hiding inside the building that would do most damage inside the structure. The large trooper stopped behind Snatch, and then he got down on a knee and aimed the M-16-203 grenade launcher attachment at a second window of the structure. The grenade flew through the window, but the round did not explode immediately, instead the grenade slid on the polished concrete floor and exploded well behind the gathered terrorists deep inside the structure.

The way the grenade exploded, infuriated the Russian soldier assisting Buckethead, and she bitched angrily at the huge trooper. "Big stupid ass useless American soldier you. You no know how fire that dom inferior American made piece of shit properly. Give me worthless weapon you big clod and then get out of way and allow good Russian soldier show how proper use dom weapon against enemy inside that building, dopey." Siberia complained as she put out her gloved covered hand with the missing finger ends and wiggled them at Buckethead as she waited for him to turn over the weapon so she could use it against the terrorists.

"Pissoffsky bitch and stay behind my stinking ass and the fuck outta my way and watch how I waste these friggin assholes hiding in there. I don't need some foreign stinking Pambo bitch showing me nuthin but your damn tits and lovely little ass, baby." Buckethead fired back at the good looking but angry female Russian.

"You get another poor made American grenade through window of building and kill any terrorists, I do lot more show you my tits and ass, big American soldier asshole. I please you greatly than ever you pleased before in you wasted life, fool of an American soldier." Siberia replied as she sexily wiggled her hips at the huge soldier, who was busy trying to set himself up to fire another round at the terrorists through one of the shattered windows of the structure.

By this time most of the trapped Islamic terrorists had moved away from the windows and front of the thin metal sides of the building. The extremists moved deeper inside the structure as they dumped over heavy commercial metal tables and desks and other items of protection. The terrorists also started to hide behind anything they could find that would stop rounds fired from their enemy at them.

Buckethead fired a fourth grenade and the projectile hit the side of the building below one of the shattered window frame and exploded perfectly, ripping a large hole out of the thin metal skin.

The sniper branded the Hunter, acting as an observer at this time, reported to both Buckethead and Walker at the same time. "Oh man what a fucking hit that one was, big man! It was perfect on target, but the round was wasted, it didn't catch any of the damn terrorists with the blast, man. Walker, by what I can see from my perch, it seems like the stinking terrorists have all moved deeper inside the damn structure. I'm betting my dick on it the stinking shitheads have setup against our asses, and they're waiting for us to make our charge against the damn building, man.

"I read you loud and clear Hunter, and from where I'm setup, I concur with your assumption of that last round fired at these stinking fucks in there. I can't see one of the sonofabitchs in there though. That means they all musta moved deeper inside the stinking building." Walker drew in a breath and then added to his words aimed at his troops. "All troops listen up. We're gonna move forward and hit them hard and get against the sides of this fucking building. Then we're gonna do a hot entry into the stinking dump and place a quick end to the damn terrorists and their damn actions. Raz, you take the First Squad and move out, and you other pukes give the moving troops heavy cover fire as they move up."

The captain looked at Sergeant Ramirez as she took command of first squad, and as one the specialized troops moved out behind her lead. The cacophony of hundreds of rounds of machine weapon fire fired at the trapped radical Muslim terrorists, coupled with the heavy explosions going off from the 40 mm grenades, made it a hell of a nightmare for the elite troops stacked up outside the building. The armor piercing ammunition shredded the metal walls as the rounds followed the troop's movement forward, to force the terrorists to hunker down, so the advancing troops could move up on them.

The terrorists could not believe the number of rounds being fired at them, as they tried to hide behind the debris, they piled up to create a good defensive position for themselves against the attacking elite soldiers inside the building. Nizar Hamdoon, who was in command of the defending terrorists, and he bellowed at his Arab defenders in a loud and angry voice. "By the great gray beard of the Prophet Himself, how many cursed hated infidels do they have stationed outside this foul place stacked up against us?

"My faithful Arab brother and sisters, you must keep your heads low and allow the lowly Khawajis (Outsiders) waste their evil ammunition uselessly. Keep your eyes opened because I'm positive once the evil ones stop firing at us. The lowly beasts will commence their attack against us, and they'll try to penetrate the walls of this cursed building as sure as I draw in another breath allowed by Allah's grace. The defense and our sacred mission had been placed upon our worthless shoulders. We must carry out Allah's will to destroy all the non-believers wherever we find them hiding.

"Prepare yourselves because Paradise awaits our presence. The weapon fire coming from the non-believers is dropping off drastically now. That means the lowly jackals are about ready to test our resolve and attack us. Pick out your targets carefully and kill as many evil ones as you can possibly kill, before Allah calls us home to his protection. Our Holy Jihad aimed against the hated American soldiers is an obligation for us to observe." Hamdoon understood he did not have enough of his terrorist fighters nor weapons and ammunition at his disposal, committed to successfully fight off the attacking American troops he had mounted against them.

So, he planned to takeout as many of the enemy soldiers he was able to kill, before he and the rest of his defenders were killed during the attack by American soldiers.

Captain Walker's troops continued to pound away at the light metal skinned of the massive structure with rounds. Once he was certain he made his point and drove most of the terrorists away from the front of the building. He waved his hand over his head rapidly, and each soldier knew it was the warning to stop firing at the building. He stopped the fire because Sergeant Ramirez's squad moved up until they were positioned against the left from the west side of the structure.

The worried Walker stared as Sergeant Ramirez sent Boot Camp, (Sergeant Fred Moorehouse) out so he could get a better look inside the heavily damaged front section of the commercial building. The female Sergeant wanted Boot Camp to gather some live intelligence on where the Islamic defenders might have setup their defensive locations against them inside the structure.

Boot Camp cautiously slid his way along the ground as he headed for one of the blown-out section of the metal structure, so he could get a better look inside the nearly destroyed front of the building. What he was able to pick up was surprising; the interior of the building was a mess and dark as night. Countless ripped papers were scattered about across the floor, and some pieces were still floating in the air. Small shards of metal skin and ripped apart building insulation, covered the floor along with a sea of spend shells. A number of empty water bottles and wrappings from food the terrorists ate while defending the establishment against the American soldiers, were scattered about over the floor. Boot Camp continued to move his body to better see inside the place.

A quick look into the cavernous interior of the massive building, Boot Camp spotted a mess of what looked like heavy overturned metal tables, a number of desks, and four tier heavy commercial metal filing cabinets. Also, there was a ton of boxes, garbage cans and other stuff stacked up forming a good size wall of protection for the terrorists to defend against his troops, when they began their assault against the building and trapped terrorists inside. As Sergeant Moorehouse continued to peer into the factory, two shots were suddenly fired at his head. The Sergeant had to move so quickly to avoid being hit by the rounds that he rolled down the concrete driveway and ended up stopping by a concrete pillar and flowerbox. Some of the elite troops giving Ramirez's group cover fire, laughed at the way Moorehouse rolled out of the way. The laughter caused Moorehouse to fire the finger at the other soldiers.

Walker was angered over the way the troops were laughing at Moorehouse and he bellowed at his fellow soldiers. "Okay you bunch of fucking girls, knock the crap off, this shit's serious people." Then he keyed his mike and contacted Moorehouse directly. He had to know what was facing his troops when they assaulted the terrorists held up inside the building. He was positive Sergeant Ramirez was going to listen in on their conversation, so she knew what was going on as well. "Sergeant Moorehouse, what the fuck didja see in there, mister?"

Moorehouse responded to Walker's call by bitching at him over his squad radio unit. "Man Walker, the stinking creeps inside have the fucking Berlin wall constructed against us in there, man. I picked up several heavy overturned desks, metal tables and filing cabinets, along with a shitload of fucking boxes with who knows what else stacked inside the damn things. These creeps also stacked up a mess of garbage cans to hide their slimy asses behind. It's gonna be tough to root the mutherfuckers outta there, man. We gotta get some of our people in there from the backside of this fucking dump and have them come at the lousy little fucks from behind the damn wall. While we hit the asses from the front, or we're in for one helluva firefight in their Captain." Moorehouse reported sharply to his Commanding Officer.

"You hit the nail right on the fucking head Boot Camp, and that's exactly what I'm gonna do about this damn situation, buddy. Mutt, I want you to take Second Squad and make for the backside of this fucking dump. Use the stinking driveway of the next building to your left, to get your people back there safely. When you hear us open fire from the front on the scumbags, that's your signal to make your entry and attack the fucks from the rear of them. I'm gonna give you five stinking minutes from this second to get your ass back there, so check your watch and get set in position, buddy. Then we're gonna fire on the fucks as we make a frontal assault on their current position." Walker growled at the Mutt.

The Mutt, staring at Walker as he issued his orders, raised his hand and stuck up his thumb. In an instant he was gathering the squad and had the soldiers following him to the second building.

The captain received another call over the radio. "Errr...Dragon Fire Leader, this is Toll Booth East Commander, I'm reporting a gaggle of Foxtrot Alfa Hotel (Fucking Ass Hole) news reporters are currently showing up my position, requesting I allow them to pass so they can cover what you people are doing out there, sir. Before you go postal on my Foxtrot ass sir, the reporters are crying I'm obstructing their right to cover a Foxtrot news story, Captain Walker. Shall I allow the pain in the asses to pass my position, or do you want me to hold them back until further orders, sir?"

"November Foxtrot Whisky (No Fucking way) Sergeant. You'll not allow one of the lousy bastards to pass your present position under no circumstances, mister! Absolutely no one gets past your position until this stinking operation has run its course, and we finished dealings with this trapped pack of motherfucking pricks inside this commercial building, Commander. I don't give a shit if you hafta shoot some of the dopey Alfa Hotels on the spot, to stop them from trying to pass your position, period Commander."

"Let me get this order straight Dragon Fire Leader, you're telling me and my troops we're free to ice off some of these Foxtrot news reporters if they try to pass my position, sir? It that correct as repeated, Dragon Fire Leader, sir?" The Commander of the roadblock team asked not for Walker's benefit, it was asked because a number of the reporters were so close, they could easily hear what the Commander was asking of the leader of the operation over his radio.

"Jesus Christ and miracles Commander! Of course, I'm not giving you fricking permission to ice off some of the sonofa fucking nosy ass bitches. I only said that to stir your ass up that's all, Commander. Look sir err... just report there's an active investigation going on down here, and until it has been completed, no one's to get past your roadblock under any circumstances, Commander. Do you read my ass loud and clear, Commander?" Captain Walker roared in his radio at the other officer.

"I read you loud and clear Commander, if any of the fucking reporters try to pass my position, I'm cleared to use deadly force against them, sir?"

The Commander of the roadblock replied to Walker's last order, cursing in the open again.

Walker suddenly understood what the Commander was doing while he was confusing him. Obviously, some of the reporters were in ear shot of his communications, and he was using his communication with him to scare them off of his back.

INSIDE THE DAMAGED COMMERCIAL BUILDING

The leader of what was left of the terrorist cell, Abdulaziz al-Wahhad, along with Abdullah al-Mutairi, Iraqi Moshe al-Gasim and Reemabdel Aziz al-Rowaili, stopped what they were doing and listened as the American soldiers continued to fire on their fellow Arab defenders. Al-Wahhad could not believe the vast number of deadly rounds being fired at his Arab fighters by the American troops outside. After listening to the force of the attack being waged against him, he realized all was lost to him, and he decided to make good his escape from the compromised commercial building. With the few fellow terrorists, he wanted to save, he turned to al-Mutairi and barked savagely at him.

"The cursed hated lowly infidels have mounted a force of soldiers we're unable to successfully defeat with the minor forces we have left at our disposal, my faithful Arab brother. I fear all is lost to us, so I'm ordering you to pack up what you have constructed so far of the nuclear weapon. We'll make the best use of the sacred weapon of evil the way it's constructed as it is to kill the largest number of non-believers of this evil land. I have no doubt in my mind the cursed soldiers of the Devil, are about to assault us in force. I want the four of us to be well out of this loathsome structure before they attack us.

"We shall take the needed weapons and ammunition clips for the weapons with us. Then we shall leave this worthless place by the means of the back area, and stealthy make our way out to a highway of this evil land. Once we are outside, we'll simply commandeer a vehicle from one of the American fools after we killed the cursed driver and make way for where the evil leaders from the cursed state that makes up this evil land meet. We shall destroy that place and any worthless leaders trapped inside it.

"The vehicles we have used to arrive here are compromised by the evil forces stationed outside this foul building. We must abandon those worthless vehicles, and that's why we have to commandeer another foul vehicle from one of the fools who live in this evil city. When we have a new vehicle at our disposal, and after we have successfully set the sacred weapon in place where I intend to detonate it from. Then we shall get on the highway and head south to the worthless lands of Mexico. From there we'll make our way down to Central America. Once there we'll easily buy airline tickets for our homeland and the sands that warmed our ancestor's souls. When we're home, we'll forget about the successful attacks we committed against the lowly infidels of this foul country of jackals. We shall live out the rest of our lives in the light and peace of Allah's unending grace and love."

While Abdulaziz al-Wahhad spoke to the other terrorists he wanted to live, Leila Alibabic remained as silent as death as she listened to him making his plans to escape, along with the few people he mentioned. She was shaking and scared to death, because he never once mentioned her name. She did not want to be left behind only to die at the hands of the horde of American soldiers lurking outside the establishment.

Al-Wahhad noticed Leila standing near him shaking like a leaf, and noticed she was on the verge of crying. Seeing her condition he snapped angrily at the young woman, "Foolish woman, why are you shaking so? By Allah's good grace you'll come with me wherever I go. Pick up your cursed weapon and get several extra clips for the foul thing. Do you think I was going to leave you behind to die in this foul place at the hands of the hated American soldiers? Move quickly before I open your back with the sting of the lash for disobeying my orders."

The leader of the small terrorist group smiled as he watched the scared young woman rush to carry out his orders. He turned to the other terrorist he was speaking with before the interruption by Leila and noticed al-Mutairi had already gathered up the weapon and the other items he wanted to carry off with him, and he was now waiting to move out. The terrorist leader called the Ghost by the young terrorists, turned to Mohsen and his girlfriend, and saw they were holding weapons and were likewise waiting to go. Leila quickly returned with her weapon and a few extra clips stuffed in her pockets. Feeling they were ready to go he ordered.

"Ahhh…I thank the Almighty Allah for giving me such loyal warriors to carry out my sacred mission against the hated infidels of this foul country. There is no sense for us to remain in this cursed building for a moment longer. Because I know we're fast running out of time before the lowly jackals gathered outside, open their attack against our faithful fighters. Let us move swiftly while we still have the time to do so safely and then…" Al-Wahhad noticed Mohsen's sharp look and he grumbled at the younger man with a snap in his tone of voice. "Don't look back because there is nothing we're leaving behind of any worth to our cause. Our fighters knew what they signed on for when we left on our mission."

Without another word passed between the small group, the five terrorists with weapons and the half constructed nuclear device, quickly left the damaged commercial building by means of the back door. As the five Islamic terrorists ran through the large backyard, the Mutt's group happened to turn the corner and Just Bob, Sergeant Robert Bossily, called out to the Mutt in an excited voice as he pointed in the direction, he wanted to draw his attention to. "Hey Mutt, I think I just picked up a number of friggin pukes running outta the fucking building into the area where the trucks are parked, man."

The Mutt looked in the direction the excited Sergeant was pointing and did not pick up any movement as he called back to Sergeant Bossily. "I don't see nuthin moving in that fucking area buddy, besides we have our orders to attack these lousy fucks in there from their stinking rear. If you saw anything a moment ago then it musta been a few stinking civilians running for their damn asses, or a lousy dog or something like that, man. Either way man, our fucking attention has to be leveled on the fucks trapped inside this stinking dump. If any of the dopey bastards escaped our trap, our uther guys will easily pick them up and settle their hash good and proper. So shut up and follow my ass when we haft jump off against these fucks."

Captain Walker kept a close eye on his watch, as the minutes quickly clicked off to the five-minute mark. He suddenly stood and fired his weapon at the shattered windows of the heavily damaged front of the commercial building, and then he charged wildly at the structure. Every soldier under his command did the same thing, and they charged the factory while firing in a controlled but rapid manner. The moment he opened fire on the warehouse from the other side, the Mutt tried the backdoor and to his surprise, it was unlocked. He and his troops cautiously snuck into the interior of the vast building and when he realized how dark it was inside, he growled at the troops under his command, "It's dark as three feet down a fucking cow's throat in there, so we're going dark, go dark, go dark people!"

The Mutt reached in his leg pocket and removed his night vision equipment, and quickly hooked it to the bracket of his helmet. He waited a few seconds before moving forward again until he was able to see properly through the night vision system, and then he penetrated the building the moment his eyes became adjusted to the night vision apparatus. He was followed closely by the rest of his specialized troops after they set their night vision equipment on. "Sweep forward." The Mutt growled at them.

The six-man team quickly fanned out with three of the elite troopers rapidly moving to the east side of the massive building, and the other three troopers moving to the west side of the structure. The soldiers cautiously moved into the dark shadows of the interior. Slowly, they moved closer to the wall of furniture haphazardly stacked in the middle of the vast warehouse by the group of terrorist fighters.

Walker's troops still positioned outside the establishment, continued to pound away at the factory with their weapons, as they reached the metal walls of the building and flattened up against the side of the building. The soldiers were stacked up on either side of the blown-out windows and part of the front wall of the building.

When the weapon fire from Walker's attackers stopped, it gave time for the Mutt and the rest of his unit to get set in positions to open fire at the radical Arab extremists from their flanking position. Through a jumbo of silent hand signals and quick movements of his body, the Mutt set his people out in formation where they would do the best to kill the terrorists when they hit them.

When the Mutt's group was set in place and ready to attack, they hunkered down and waited for Walker's group to open fire again on the ensnared Arab terrorists trapped inside the vast structure under their attack. He lightly tapped his mike and blew in it, informing his Commanding Officer he was ready to begin his attack against the trapped terrorists. All weapons of the attacking troops were silenced, and each weapon had the laser guided green sighting systems attached to their weapons.

The interior of the structure was dark as night because the only windows in the structure were the ones in the front of the factory, and the terrorists had the interior lights turned off, and the wall of trash was blocking what light they would have received from the windows from the front of the building. The darkness was helping to hide most of the terrorists from view and making them much harder targets to locate for the Mutt and Walker's attacking troops to locate where they were hiding in the mess.

When Walker's crew was set in place, he waved Buckethead over to his side. Once near, he ordered Buckethead to get where he could lob a few 40-millimeter grenades into the structure easily. He wanted the grenades to confuse and blind the trapped terrorists before they went up against them. So, he could hit them while the defenders were in a sort of dazed confusion from the exploding grenades. He watched as Buckethead setup position behind a brick column that offered him good protection. Yet the column gave him a direct line of fire into the ripped open front of the factory. When he was set to fire, Walker ripped off a flash bang grenade from his Alice vest and held it out for the other soldiers to see.

The moment the other troops noticed their Captain's actions, the rest of the Tier One no fail troops followed suit, and they quickly removed a stun grenade from their vests. The soldiers understood Walker wanted to confuse the terrorists with the flashes and explosions and concussion from the special stun grenades, to cover their hot entry inside the structure behind the explosions and flash of showered sparks.

Captain Walker's mind was working on the six other soldiers from the Mutt's group. He did not want to end up firing at the terrorists and have some of his rounds hitting his fellow soldiers attacking the extremists from the rear area. That was the problem facing him, by attacking a position from two separate locations at the same time in a hard-hitting terrorist operation.

Walker was pleased he ordered the troops to shift from their civilian clothes back to their military uniforms and gear stowed inside the heavy Humvees once they narrowed down where the terrorists were held up against them. He had his troops carry their usual military equipment and weapons whenever they were sent out on any operation. The only thing bugging him was their lack of CBRN (Chemical, Biological, Radiological, and Nuclear) gear, if the terrorists let go with that weapon they were supposed to be working on, they'd be hurting.

The young Marine Captain prepared him and the rest of his troops to open their attack on the hidden terrorists. He knew how the Mutt thought, and he was confident he would have his soldiers hitting the radicals from the far sides of the interior of the massive building. If the Mutt carried out his attack that way, his troops would be well out of the line of fire from his attackers.

The time was now, and Walker pulled the pin, and then he tossed the stun grenade through the window. His grenade was followed by twenty more, and all seemed to explode at the same exact moment inside the building. His troops followed the grenades into the badly damaged commercial building, the blinding light and shock wave had the desired effect of the trapped militants as they hunkered down for the moment.

The terrorists never experienced the strong effects of a stun grenade before, and they dropped deeper into the thick wall of debris thinking the explosions were coming from regular hand grenades. The lack of fire from the terrorists made it easy for his troops to easily penetrate the building. His troops plowed in and instantly fanned out and dropped behind anything they could hide behind. The invading specialized soldiers got in good positions, and then they aimed their weapons at the wall of furniture and hunkered down and waited until they could find a target.

The exploding stun grenades had an opposite effect on the Mutt and the rest of his attackers. The blinding flash of light emitted from the grenades was severely amplified by the night vision equipment. It caused temporary blindness to his attacking troops already inside the building. He had to close his eyes for a few quick moments, and once his eyes were adjusted again to the poor light inside the factory. He dropped his night vision apparatus back in position and was again able to see pretty well in the pitch darkness of the interior of the structure. He setup where he was able to pick out two of the terrorists hiding in the wall of debris and aimed at his first mark and pulled on the target. A short three round burst fired off and the terrorist locked in his sights, slammed forward into the heavy metal desk he was hiding behind. The terrorist's body then slowly sank to the floor and stopped moving.

The Mutt's rounds caused a few the other terrorists to move around in the wall of debris, so they could see who was suddenly firing at them from their rear positions. The terrorist slight movements immediately drew Walker's troop's attention towards them. The second these troops picked up the subtle movement from the group of terrorist defenders, they instantly open fire on them. One, two, three enemy defenders dropped from the heavy rounds being fired at them, and then all hell broke out inside the massive structure, as the rest of the trapped terrorists opened fired at the soldiers attacking them from their rear and front positions.

Sharp lines of long green targeting lights crisscrossed the open area and walls and the wall of furniture stacked up as the terrorist's protection inside the structure, as the rapid response troop's weapons searched out the darkness for any possible targets. The constantly moving and narrow bright beams of light, were adding to the maddening confusion taking place inside the interior of the building, as calls from the troops filled the air.

"I got a fucking breather hunkered down by that red filing cabinet next to that stinking overturned desk at the bend in that shit wall these lousy pukes are hiding in." Neck called out in an excited voice as his laser light singled out the extremist Iraqi, Morteza Dastjerdi.

"Well take out the fucking breather if you got him pegged out in your damn sights you idiot! We don't wanna know where the fucks are hiding in that mess, we wanna kill the lousy little fucks, man." Shot Gun, (Sergeant Dennis Sassano) barked at the large soldier as he urged him on with their attack against the terrorists.

A shot instantly rang out and the target Neck aimed at, dropped to the floor with Neck reporting to the rest of his fellow troopers. "The fucking breather's been naturalized man."

Hussein Ali Soruch was relieved helping al-Mutairi finish constructing the weapon by al-Wahhad, when the rest of his terrorists started to engage the enemy troops who just entered the structure. He was ordered to help defend the building against the attacking American soldiers. He moved away from the wall of debris and was trying to work his way to the back of the building to escape the trap he was mired in.

Fire's (Sergeant Ashley Reeks) once partner of Ice, (Sergeant Diane Morrison) and now part of the Second Unit, picked up the terrorist moving away from the pile of overturned furniture, and she immediately reported to her acting Commander, the Mutt. "Lieutenant, I have a slow rover moving away from the wall of crap to our left, he's heading towards the far side of the building."

The Mutt looked in the direction Fire was drawing his attention to, and then he responded to the female soldier from his group. "I got your fucking rover located, Fire. He seems to be trying to get the fuck outta this stinking dump. I guess his balls have turned to water and he wants ta save his stinking life, little sister."

"What do you want to do with the sonofabitch, Lieutenant?" The female soldier branded Fire, asked with concern.

"You're free to corpse your friggin rover good and proper like Fire. We're operating under a termination order, so drop the stinking mutherfucker where you got him locked up, sister." The Mutt replied with a snarl.

Another spit of a shot rang out and the terrorist rover instantly dropped to the ground. The terrorist was dead before his body landed on the floor.

"Hey Walker, I got a shot on a fucking asshole in here man. Requesting permission to take out the stinking target toot sweet, sir. Over." The Hunter called out to Walker. The two snipers, the Hunter and Ghost, skillfully worked their way into the interior of the building, and the both began searching for their own targets to kill. They took up perches offering each clear shots at their hidden targets. Their weapons were never silenced, along with most of the other soldiers who already removed their silencers to make their weapons more accurate, prepared to take their shots at the terrorists.

Captain Robert Walker shook his head as he grabbed the mike and bitched at the extremely dangerous sniper. "What the fuck's wrong with you stinking guys anyway for fuck sake? I already told you guys this fucking operation is a free fire op. Each of you stinking puds are clear to take out any fucking targets you people come across in here, dammit. Without asking for my friggin permission to neutralize any stinking enemy targets. Dammit, I'm gonna say this shit one last time to you pack of flaming assholes so listen up and allow my words to sink in this time. Sniper! At your discretion, take out any fucking target you get locked up in your damn sights, period. Now don't ask for further permission to do so, or I'm gonna pop a cap in your ass myself, dammit to hell anyhow!"

The extremely dangerous Hunter did not take offense over the way Walker just snarled at him, as he pulled on his detected target. In a heartbeat, Bassam Abu Fallahi, was hit in the middle of his forehead by Hunter's round. His body was ripped away from the wall of furniture and tumbled to the ground in a heap. The sniper smirked over the knowledge he just injected pig's blood into the dead Arab's body, and if his beliefs were right. The Arab's soul could never enter Paradise because of the pig's blood, and that suited him just fine.

It was a maddening situation raging inside the thirty thousand square foot interior of the commercial factory where both sides were doing their best to kill each other. Walker and the Mutt's Units were firing nonstop at the wall of furniture, and the terrorists hiding in the mess was replying with their own wall of lead fired at the American soldiers trying to kill them.

Buckethead, had enough of the situation starting to get out of hand, and he popped off a 40 mm grenade at the wall of debris. The heavy explosive ripped a wide hole in the middle of the overturned furniture and other items of protection the terrorists were doing their best to hide behind. The powerful explosion launched two terrorists out of the mess. One terrorist, Abdel al-Amharic, the second explosive expert of the terrorist group, who was ordered to defend the wall and his fellow terrorists went down, stunned by the power of the blast from the grenade. He was rendered unconscious because of hitting his head hard on the concrete floor. The second dislodged extremist remained standing on his feet and mobile and was shoved ten feet away from the wall by the blast.

Esmatullah Basir, the other Iranian terrorist of the cell tried to rush back for the wall and its protection. But he was not quick enough to get back in the mess. Fifteen laser beams instantly lit up areas on his body, and then a barrage of bullets followed the lasers, and ripped into his body, killing the Persian instantly. The terrorist was hit by nearly fifteen rounds.

Walker realized the fire from the terrorists was starting to slacken off dramatically, so he decided he was going to try and talk some sense with the remaining terrorists still alive inside the building, by calling out to his troops. "To all Dragon Fire troops, cease fire! I repeat, cease fire, immediately. Stop fucking firing at the lousy scumbags for a minute will ya, guys!" Walker stopped screaming and then waited for his troops to respond to his last order, and when the weapon fire continued unabated. He bellowed out a second time over the roar of the mini war raging inside the huge structure. "This is the damn Commander of this fucking Dragon Fire Operation. I'm ordering all troops to cease fire immediately, dammit."

Some of the excited soldiers did not hear his command, or they might have even chosen to ignore the orders, as they continued to pour rounds into the overturned furniture, trying to pick off any terrorists by dumb luck. Several of his troopers wanted to end this situation at this point.

"Dammit you people! I just ordered a fucking cease fire command to you people, and you guys are ignoring my fucking orders. Get control of yourselves will ya. I repeat, all soldiers attached to this Dragon Fire Operation are to cease fire immediately, dammit. This is a direct fucking order, people!" Captain Walker let out his breath in a rush, and then he listened as his troops started to obey his command. Soon, the only fire was coming from the terrorists.

Slowly, the fire from the terrorist still alive also started to slacken down to near nothing as well. The battered and exhausted Marine Captain breathed out a deep sigh of relief because he felt the militants might want to hear what he had to offer, as he addressed any terrorists who might reply to his words.

"To the foreign soldiers (He addressed the terrorists as soldiers in hopes of having one reply to his words) inside this fucking building. I believe enough of our friends on both sides have died in this damn crap shoot." As far as he knew, none of his soldiers were even wounded by any enemy fire, as he continued with his words.

"No one else has to fucking die for anything they might believe in this dump. What say you use your stinking noggins for a change, and drop your damn weapons and come the hell outta that fucking crap so we can talk a little face to face? You jerks will be well treated and any wounds will be well looked after, if you guys give up that is. I'm only gonna give you guys a few moments to think this offer over. Then I'll place a stinking period to the end of this fucking nightmare we're dancing through, once and for all either way I hafta accomplish it. I give you guys ten seconds to make up your stinking minds, continue to fire at my troops and its fucking game on, and all you guys are gonna die for nuthin. Your time to live starts as of this moment. One second is already used up, so use your stinking heads."

Ali Abdullah Tlas was getting fed up with the way his people were being slaughtered so easily from the enemy soldiers positioned on two sides of him and the rest of his terrorist group. He checked his AK-47 Kalashnikov Assault rifle and noticed he had no more rounds or extra loaded clips for the weapon. So, he decided to try something with the angry sounding American soldier addressing him in such a booming and upsetting voice.

"American soldier with big mouth, what you say is wise to think and offer, because I don't wish to die in this filthy establishment like a lowly dog. Here is my weapon I toss it out before you so you can see I'm no longer armed and a further threat against you or the rest of your proud American soldiers with you." Tlas tossed his useless and out of rounds assault weapon out in the open, and then he went on with his words. As he began to speak again, the smug acting terrorist reached in his belt and removed the 9 mm pistol. He checked the chamber and saw he had a round lodged in the weapon ready for use, as he continued to speak further with Captain Walker. "American soldier, you see my weapon lying on the ground, please? I am now unarmed and helpless and I pose no further threat to you or your fellow soldiers."

The captain was surprised his words were working on what was left of this terrorist cell, as he replied. "Yeah, buddy I see your fucking weapon on the stinking ground alright. Now I wanna see your stinking ass crawl out from under that fricking mess, with your hands held over your damn head. If you do that, everything will be cool and you'll fucking live buddy. It's 'bout time we put an end to all the death and destruction we're causing each uther, pal."

Every soldier attached to Walker's command; knew why he was attempting to talk to the terrorists for. Each of the elite soldiers was all for putting a stop to the deadly rounds flying about them. But being so well trained, every one of the soldiers continued to aim their weapon at where they believed the terrorist talker was hiding.

Sergeant Dorothy Ramirez held her breath while biting her lower lip, as she tried her best to subconsciously connect with Walker's mind. So, she could beg him to remain hiding undercover while he continued speaking to this extremely dangerous terrorist. She was worried to death it might be a trap this evil man was attempting to do against her lover and soldier, to draw him out in the open. So, the terrorist could kill him before he himself died inside the building. She kept her eyes glued on what she could see of the terrorist, daring him to do something foolish so she could end his life before he could hurt her soldier. She was fighting a gut feeling this man was setting him up and he was somehow going to try and kill her soldier.

"I will come out from my protection when I'm positive I will not be shot dead by one of your proud American soldiers, the moment my body is exposed to you non-believers and enemy to Allah and his sacred word. I fear I do not trust you American soldiers, so I'm hesitant to leave my protection and expose my body to your weapons." Tlas snarled at Walker as he smiled to himself. He was confident he was going to be able to kill at least one of the attacking enemy soldiers who successfully killed so many of his fellow Arab warriors. Tlas was of the mind this one soldier had to be the Commander of the other American soldiers attacking his, what he felt were freedom fighters. The terrorist though of the honor he would receive once his fellow Arabs found out he killed the lead Commander of the enemy soldiers, if he was able to kill this one soldier before he was killed.

"Look buddy, I'm fucking telling ya you'll not be shot as long as you come the hell outta there with your stinking hands in the air, and unarmed and peaceful like, buster. As long as you're not a continuing threat against my ass, you'll be safe if you come outta there, buddy." Walker snapped at the terrorist.

"American soldier threatening me, I shall come out and then we can begin to discuss terms of surrender, and how my surviving warriors will be treated by your proud American soldiers." Tlas replied with anger etching his tone and saying the word 'American' as if it was a four-letter word as he straightened his body, and then cautiously started to follow his weapon to the opening in the vastness of the building interior.

When the terrorist straightened his body and stiffened his back, Walker was finally able to see much more of him, and he believed the terrorist was going to truly surrender to him as he called out to the rest of his troops. "Listen up people, this lousy little dude's gonna do the right fucking thing here and surrender to my ass. So that means no one shoots the dopey little mutherfucker unless he's up to something stupid, and he tries to take me out. If he is, take him out as fast as shit through a fucking goose. You people read my ass?"

A bunch of 'ayes' was replied to Walker's last orders to his troops. Nevertheless, Abdullah Tlas's partially exposed body was covered by at least thirty bouncing laser light dots from the numerous weapons trained on his body. The concerned Captain's troops were taking no chances with any of the trapped Islamic terrorists, and they covered him in case he tried something against Walker or the rest of his troops.

From the other side of overturned furniture and other debris, Lieutenant Frank Hall's group were aiming their laser assisted weapons at the body of the radical terrorist who just stepped out from behind the rubble wall.

The soldier branded Stainless, (Sergeant Alan Langworth) spotted something and he immediately scrambled up to the Mutt's side, and then he warned him in an excited voice. "Hey Mutt, I think that mutherfucker's holding something in his stinking left hand, and he's trying to stop Walker from seeing what it fucking is, man. Dammit Mutt, I think the rotten sonofabitch has a fucking pistol in his damn hand. Yeah Mutt, it's definitely a fucking pistol alright, I'm positive of it now man. The fuck's gonna ambush Walker's fucking ass and do him in man, I'm gonna take the stinking fish out, Mutt."

"Don't take any fucking chances and get that lousy bastard, dammit! I don't have a good bead on his stinking ass, or I'd take him out myself for crap's sake." The Mutt offered as he suddenly roared a warning out at his Commanding Officer. "Walker, get your fucking ass down, the stinking prick has a damn weapon in his left hand, and he's gonna try and do your ass in, dammit. He's not giving up, he fucking plans to kill your ass, man!"

The warning from the Mutt and Stainless opening firing on the terrorist came too late for Walker to react quick enough from the threat aimed against his life. When the terrorist stepped out from his protection and had a clear shot at Walker's body, he instantly raised his hand and aimed and took his shot at the young American soldier. He even moved a little to his right, so he had a better shot at the American Captain.

Sergeant Ramirez nearly jumped out of her skin when she heard the round go off, and saw Walker grab at himself, and then he went down hard to the ground. When Tlas fired at the captain, his round hit the M-16 he held in his hands, and it fragmented and a piece of it hit Walker in the hip and came out on his rearend.

Sergeant Dorothy Ramirez could not believe her eyes as she watched Walker hit the ground and stayed down, and then he rolls over on his side and he curled up. The nature of the soldier took over her body, and she roared in rage as she opened fire on the Arab extremist who just fire on her lover and soldier. The soldiers on both sides of the overturned furniture wall, fired on Tlas. His body seemed like it was being held locked in a standing position by so many rounds hitting it from both the front and back. Tlas's body suddenly flipped to the ground, and the Tier One soldiers did not know if his body fell from being killed or if it fell because so many rounds entered his body and weighted it down to the ground.

Sergeant Ramirez was fuming, and she was not done with her rage as she screamed at her heavies, ordering both soldiers to fire on what was left of the overturned furniture wall with their M-60 machine guns. The female Sergeant continued issuing further orders to the troops, and she was not bothering to watch her mouth either as she dished out those orders. "I want you fuckers to rip that effing crap wall down and continue firing until you people killed every damn terrorist hiding in that effing mess.

"Buckethead, the same order goes for your ass too, mister. You're ordered to keep lobbing the damn grenades at that shit wall until it's ripped apart, and no place is left intact for any of the fucking terrorists to hide behind. Mutt, Walker's down, have your people get undercover. Hell's coming your way, and I don't want any of our people getting hit by friendly fire from this side of that shit wall when we open fine on it again."

Both the Neck along with Mother Flanagan, (Sergeant Richard Flanagan), opened fire against the wall of furniture with their heavy M-60's, equipped with two hundred and fifty round belt feeds for the weapon. Both shooters kept pounding away and ripping the furniture wall to shreds. Neck was firing so fast he completely depleted his first belt of rounds for his weapon, and he had to stop and string a second strap of rounds in place, before he opened fire on the remaining wall and the rest of the hiding terrorists again.

Buckethead fired on the rapidly crumbling wall with every round he had for the 203-grenade launcher. He was so angry the terrorist giving up to Walker, used that ruse to shoot his Commanding Officer. His only thought was to kill every Islamic terrorist he was able to see hiding in the mess constructed twenty feet before him. The massive structure was quickly filling with a thick cloud of choking arid eye burning smoke coming from all the weapon fire going off inside the structure.

Siberia, the female Russian soldier on loan to the American group went around the rest of the group of elite soldiers, collecting every round for the 203, 40-millimeter grenade launcher from any soldier working against the trapped terrorists. She kept busy feeding the grenades to Buckethead as quickly as he fired one off, she handed him another. The spent rounds and grenades going off echoed terribly and were amplified loudly by the tunnel like massive structure. The amped up specialized soldiers continued to pound away at the rubble stacked up about midway of the long structure, as each soldier wanted to kill the terrorists for the sneak attack just played out on their Commanding Officer.

CHAPTER TWENTY-NINE

On the other side of the rapidly crumbling wall, the Mutt, Lieutenant Frank Hall's assault squad moved inside two twelve-inch-thick concrete support walls holding up a pair of super heavy duty electric motors that operated the overhead cable crane. The Mutt realized it was used to move heavy machinery and other equipment around inside the interior of the structure for the workers. Once his people were protected hiding behind the cement walls, and they were well out of the line of fire. He reported to Sergeant Dorothy Ramirez that her troops were free to fire at the terrorists without worry about hitting any of his people on the other side of the mess. No soldiers on either side of the wall wanted to be the one who wounded one of their own troopers during this present engagement.

While Neck, Buckethead and Mother Flanagan's weapon fire continued to rip apart what was left of the terrorist's protection. Sergeant Ramirez left her position and quickly worked her way over to the wounded Captain's side, she wanted to see how seriously he was wounded from the sneak attack from the Arab terrorist. Again, she growled in her mike, but this time she roared at the Unit's only medic. "Blood Clot get your fucking ass up here double quick and check on Walker's condition. The damn fool's hit and I don't know how bad he's wounded, dammit. He's still down on the damn ground and I don't see him moving either."

The soldier branded Roach, the Unit's One Charlie, or Sitcom (Satellite Communication) operator, got over to Walker's side first, and the first question he asked made Walker more upset than anything else.

"Hey Walker, you fucking hurt bad, man?"

Walker's eyes narrowed to mere slits as he glared angrily at his fellow soldier, as he growled at him. "You ever fucking see anyone hurt good, you fucking idiot you?"

The Roach laughed at Walker's angry reply as he asked him another question while trying to still be funny with the wounded soldier. "No man, I wanna know if you just experienced a sharp pain in the ass, sir?

"No stupid, I experienced a fucking blowjob you asshole! What the fuck do you think I experienced, fucker?" Walker snarled back at the Roach.

"Look I might be stupid, but I'm not the one with the extra hole in my fucking ass, Captain." The Roach came back with as he continued to bust his Commander's horns.

"You betta get the fuck away from my stinking ass before I commit a fucking homicide on your damn butt, asshole." Walker growled at the soldier trying to be funny, and then he held him in his angry glare until the joking soldier finally moved away from him.

The Mutt bellowed out to Sergeant Ramirez in an excited voice. "Hey Raz, how the fuck is Walker doing, little sister? I can't get over to you right now, and I wanna know how the hell he's doing and if he's still alive or not, dammit. I need info on his damn condition, little sister. I don't want anything to happen to that guy he's my favorite turd." His words were drowned out by the heavy weapon fire continuing from the other soldiers.

"Dammit! This shit sucks the big one!" The Mutt mumbled until he found his radio and snarled. "Hey Raz, what kinda condition is Walker in? Is he still fucking alive?"

Raz stopped moving for Walker's side as she took the time to reply to the Mutt's call. "I don't know yet Frankie, I'm not to him yet. I'll report his condition to you when I know how he's doing, Frank. He's still down."

"Fuck this stinking shit I'm coming to you for fuck sake. To all troops on the south side of this crap, keep your fucking eyes opened for my ass. I'm coming at you guys from the west side close to the east exterior wall. Don't shoot my stinking ass I gotta see what condition Walker's in." The Mutt called out as he moved out from the safety of the concrete wall, and quickly worked to the other side of the crumbling wall.

By the time Ramirez finally worked her way to Walker's side, the Mutt was limping his way for his friend. The young Marine Captain was already being looked after by the medic, Blood Clot. The Mutt and Ramirez got down on one knee and the both watched Blood Clot clean the exit wound of the fragmented round on Walker's rearend. Both soldiers smiled because Walker's pants were down to his knees, and he was lying on his stomach.

"Hey buddy, we're both fucking simpatico now, man. We're both hit in the fucking asses on this damn mission. Now I can say there are two men with two assholes in the Unit." The Mutt smirked with a grin, and it caused Ramirez to laugh because she was so relieved Walker was not badly wounded, and he was not in danger of dying.

"I'm so happy my fricking pain amuses you so damn much, asshole. I'm fucking dying here and you're making stinking jokes about my damn ass. Are you sure you want your cause of fucking death to be one too many bad jokes about my ass, my friend? Hey, will you take it fucking easy back there for Christ sake, Blood Clot! After all I was only put together with one fucking screw, buddy." Walker growled at the medic as he tried to turn around and look at the man working on his wound.

"Will you hold still for a fucking minute, you big baby. I gotta clean the wound before it goes septic on me." Blood Clot snapped back at Walker.

"Hey stupid what's that stinking mark on your ass, buddy?" The Mutt asked his friend as he decided to keep busting Walker's horn to try and take his mind off the pain.

"It's a fucking bullet hole you flaming asshole you. What the hell didja think it was, jackass?" Walker fired at the grinning the Mutt.

"Well stupid, I didn't think it was a fucking birth mark, buddy. Didja at least get the shooter who put that divot in your stinking ass, man? Look Walker, I won't force you to lie to me by answering that last question. We got the stinking slug who ambushed your fricking ass for ya, in case you're interested, buddy."

"Oh good, you're gonna nag my fucking ass now I see. You betta get the fuck offa my damn can before I put another cap in your ass, buster." Walker snapped at his friend.

"After all this time, I'd think you'd have the damn smarts to duck outta the way of a fucking incoming round, asshole." The Mutt again smirked at Walker.

"Hey man if I die, I want you to take my boat and charter business and keep it going for me. I put too much time and money in that damn boat and business." Walker offered Mutt over his shoulder as he continued to jump because of what Blood Clot was doing.

"No problem, does Raz come along with the stinking deal, buddy?" The Mutt asked his friend still being worked on by their medic.

"What? What the hell's this shit all about, fucker? You'd take my stinking boat and charter business, and my lady too without me, you lousy little fuck you?" Walker snarled at the Mutt and then he gave him the mad dog look.

"Yeah, and I'll take on Raz if you fucking clock out on my ass, man."

"Why you lousy sonofabitch you! Where the hell's my fucking weapon at, dammit? I'm gonna put a stinking cap in that half black ass of yours, buster. How the hell do you have the fucking balls to be so willing to take over my stinking life, if I clock out on your ass?" Walker complained at the Mutt.

"I thought so, you're fucking fine buster. The round went through your stinking hip and came out your damn butt and it's only a fat (Flesh) shot, asshole. There's no bone damage so stop being such a damn baby and get on your feet and get back in the stinking fight." The Mutt snorted back at Walker as he pulled up his pants.

"You sure it's a simple flesh wound? It still hurts like fucking hell, man." The captain complained at the Medic as he again turned to try and see his face and his injury.

"Oh, you poor baby, get on your damn feet and back in the game will you please. This thing is far from being over with, Robert." Ramirez offered; she was relieved Walker wasn't badly hurt.

"How does it feel Walker?" The Unit Medic asked with concern in his tone as he finished up working on the Commander's wound.

Walker stamped his foot on the ground and paid the price for the stupid move, by receiving a shooting pain going up his back as he replied to the Medic. "It's just fucking dandy Blood Clot. Thanks, a shitload for fixing it up so good for my ass, buddy."

"That's good but you gotta remember Walker, once this stinking mess is over with man. Both you and the stinking Mutt gotta check in with the base infirmary and allow the Doc's to really clean the wounds out properly and look after the wounds a helluva lot betta than I was able to do out here in the stinking field, you two. We don't want either wound to become septic." Blood Clot warned both Walker and the Mutt at the same time while the two of them were together and in ear shot of the medic.

"Yeah, yeah Blood Clot we hear ya. Right now, I have shit I gotta clean up so I can end this fucking little crap shoot sometime today, man." Walker grumbled as he walked around the staring Medic while the Mutt handed Walker his weapon back and offered to him while following his Commander. "Remember Walker, the stinking bullets come outta the barrel."

Walker stopped moving and looked at the Mutt as he hissed at him. "You got a pair of brass balls to hand me a loaded weapon, and then go and fuck around with my friggin fantasies."

"If you wanna shoot somebody, shoot one of the bad guys so we can end this damn thing, man." The Mutt remarked with a smirk.

"Yeah, friend let's end this stinking turkey shoot already." Walker replied with a snap, and then he turned to what was left of the protective wall the terrorists constructed in the center of the large warehouse. He was surprised at the amount of damage created by the M-60s, and Buckethead's grenade launcher. Most of the desks and metal file cabinets were chewed apart and offering little if any further protection for the surviving terrorists.

Captain Walker tried to focus his eyes on the darkness of the interior of the massive building to try and locate any surviving terrorists. He was trying to see if any terrorists were still alive and continuing to fire at his specialized soldiers. A shout rang out for all soldiers employing night vision equipment to remove the apparatus. After a moment, the interior of the cavernous structure was suddenly bathed in glaring harsh light, as long rows of overhead florescent lights still working, were turned on by one of the elite soldiers, as the three troops still pounding away at what was left of the wall of furniture protection, stopped firing on the debris without being ordered to do so.

Walker mumbled at the Mutt standing by his side. "Christ, I don't think a fucking cockroach coulda live through that stinking barrage. Okay, I think we got all the lousy bastards, get in there and do a body count. I want this thing done with."

The captain's troops cautiously came out of there cover, and they swiftly moved over to what was left of the wall. Each soldier held his or her weapon at the ready, prepared to kill any terrorists who possibly survived their deadly assault. One by one, the bodies of the terrorists were pulled from the wall of debris. Every one of them were dead, their bodies riddled with a horde of rounds that ripped through them.

Caviar, (Sergeant Lana Dostoyevsky), assumed a security stance over one of the bodies of a terrorist, and she called out to her fellow soldiers. "I have breather here! This fool alive still." She moved her foot and stepped on Abdel al-Amharic's AK-47 weapon, and then she put pressure on it. Then she slid the weapon across the floor well out of the reach of the injured terrorist with her foot, as she continued to cover the downed man with her weapon, as the other soldiers quickly rushed over to her side. The female Russian soldier keep the terrorist covered as the other troopers circled around them. None of the soldiers dared to touch the body, they were waiting for Walker to take charge of it.

Walker moved up to the group of gathered soldiers until he was standing over the downed body. He watched as al-Ahmair's chest rose and fell with a steady rhythm, and then he growled at Neck. Ordering him to grab the man and wake and get him up on his feet, so they could begin to interrogate the terrorist. The Arab radical had a knob on his head the size of a baseball, where it bounced off the concrete floor and knocked him out cold during the attack.

Neck roughly grabbed the terrorist by his shirt and pulled him up to his feet with little effort. Still supporting the terrorist's weight in his hands, Neck shook until al-Amharic's eyes fluttered open. The terrorist found himself staring at a huge and extremely angry looking American.

Captain Robert Walker still hurting from his flesh wound, ripped a bottle of water from McNip's hands, and he splashed some of it on the face of the groggy terrorist to bring him back to reality, and then he snarled at the man. "Okay mutherfucker here's the stinking story! I hope like hell you like the taste of fucking dick, fella. Because I'm gonna cut your stinking dick off and shove the damn thing down your fucking throat if you give me any further grief here for crap's sake. You and your fucking rotten ass friends here killed a number of my people, so your ass is working on borrowed fucking time here, man. I'm gonna ask you a series of fucking questions, the moment you hesitate, or I feel you're fricking lying to my ass. I'm gonna rip your body to pieces with my bare hands. Are you getting my fucking drift here, buster?" Walker had to wait while Ice quickly translated what he was saying to the terrorist to Arabic, in case the injured man did not understand English.

Abdel al-Ahmair's body was battered and bruised, and he was so exhausted and hungry that his will to deceive or stand tall before Walker left his aching body. He replied to Walker's question in a sluggish voice. "Mr. American Soldier, I understand and speak your language very well, sir. What is it you wish to know from me, sir? I am tired and I shall speak truthfully with you as long as you allow me to live."

"You betta be fucking truthful if you know what's friggin good for your dumb ass, buster. The first thing I wanna know from you is. How many of you fucks made up this stinking terrorist cell of yours, fucker? Then I wanna know if the rest of your fricking cell was killed inside this damn building! Did we get all you fucks or were some of your stinking bastards able to escape, before we got the rest of your fucking friends, and put a quick end to whatever the hell you lousy little pricks were trying to accomplish here in Washington, buster."

"The answer to your question was there were twenty-five faithful warriors for Allah who entered your country years ago legally. Nineteen of us were males and six worthless woman fighters who did more harm than good for our ambitions, came with us and we..." Al-Ahmair replied in an exhausted voice as he tried to glare at the angry military officer.

"Who the fuck was the damn leader of your fucking murder squad, pal?" Walker barked savagely at the terrorist as he interrupted the surviving Arab radical's words.

"The leader of our cell was Abdulaziz al-Wahhad. He was a Shagawah, a man to be well feared of. Mr. American Soldier, for me to be able to answer the next part of your question, I must view the bodies of my fellow soldiers slaughtered by your evil soldiers inside this cursed structure. Before I can tell you truthfully if you were successful in killing every one of our faithful warriors from my terrorist cell."

"In that case mutherfucker, walk around the stinking bodies and see how great a warrior your fucking friends were, pal. Get a move on it and check out the dead pricks and bitches and let me know if we got all the bastards that were hiding in here. I want you to point out the stinking leader of your pack of murderers while you're at it, pal." Walker snarled at the beat up and exhausted Arab terrorist. He was pleased he did not have to get involved working the terrorist over to get the information he needed, and this guy was giving up so easily to him.

Al-Ahmair slowly walked over to where the American soldiers laid out the dead of his once terrorist cell. He was thoroughly embarrassed to see the naked bodies of his male and female members, as he looked each one of them in the eyes, and then he began to mumble a silent pray for their souls. The soldiers stripped the bodies of the terrorists in search of any possible explosive belts, or any other booby traps or information hidden on their bodies. It was standard reactions when dealing with a bunch of dead terrorists who were well noted to hide explosive devices on their bodies.

When al-Ahmair finished viewing the bodies of his fellow terrorists, taking in consideration the others al-Wahhad left to protect the safe house, along with the few of their group they lost on the other attacks. Al-Ahmair looked at Walker and then he announced to the captain. "Mr. American Soldier, there are five warriors missing from the slaughtered you have laid out before my sad and weeping eyes!"

"That's it mutherfucker, try my stinking patience and see what the fuck it gets ya fucking ass, pal. You say five of your fucking friends are not in this pile of shit we got gathered here, fucker. Who the hell's missing from the stinking lot of this crap, buster?" Walker snapped angrily and looked at the terrorists' bodies.

Sergeant Fred Moorehouse who was branded Boot Camp because he had to repeat Boot Camp, moved over to Sergeant Ramirez's side, and he cautiously showed her the radiation level being registering on his handheld Geiger counter. The gauge was pegged at seventy-five Millie-Renkins per minute, which meant there was some form of nuclear materials, or there were once some nuclear items stored inside the nearly destroyed building.

Ramirez nodded at the concerned looking soldier, and then she whispered some orders to the extremely worried soldier. "Sergeant Moorehouse, take a five-man team and start searching the shit out of this damn building. See if the nuclear items were out here looking for is still stored in here. If you find the crap, immediately secure it and we'll call in the damn cleanup teams and allow them to secure the shit for transport to wherever the hell they plan to take the crap. Then we can concentrate on finding the few missing terrorists."

Sergeant Moorehouse moved out and he tapped four other soldiers, and the search team began to check out the interior of the massive structure. The soldiers were using their handheld Geiger counters to search the place for the missing Highly Enriched Uranium package.

Sergeant Ramirez watched Captain Walker's actions with the surviving terrorist while waiting her time to interrupt and inform him of Morehouse's find.

Abdel al-Ahmair thought for a second and then replied to Walker last question. "Mr. American Soldier, the five missing warriors consist of three male fighters and two worthless female fighters who must have escaped when your soldiers started to attack us and…"

"I'd like to give you worthless female fighters, you little prick you." Ramirez hissed barely over a whisper at the smug looking terrorist, and then she lowered her weapon and aimed it right at the terrorist's chest. The upset female Sergeant was fuming one of this man's friends shot and hit her lover, and here this guy was dumping on his female warriors. She was looking for any reason whatsoever to place a cap in this ugly man's head.

"I'm ordering you to back off some Raz, this stinking prick's talking, and I need him alive to continue talking to us, soldier." Walker snapped at Ramirez then he turned back to the extremist. "You were saying, prick?"

"Yes Mr. American Soldier, the five faithful warriors you have failed to slaughter, is the leader of our group, Abdulaziz al-Wahhad. We called him Shabbah, in your language, the word means the Ghost. The second warrior missing from this group is Abdullah al-Mutairi. He's the warrior constructing the weapon to employ that we came to Washington to destroy the cursed leaders of your foul country, Mr. American Soldier and he…"

"Keep it up mutherfucka, you're starting to get on my last dick nerve with the crap you keep aiming at my country and my fellow soldiers, fella. You do that and your fucking life isn't gonna be worth a pinch of fucking dog shit in a god damn rainstorm, pal. You hit on my country again, and I'm gonna cut your stinking balls off, and then I'm gonna shove the damn things down your miserable throat. Just tell me who the fuck the missing sacks of shit are, and skip the uther shit for fuck sake, if you wanna continue breathing in this damn world that is, buster." Walker warned the terrorist in no uncertain terms.

"Yes Mr. American Soldier, I shall do as you have instructed me. I'm sorry if I might have offended you with my words. The third male warrior who is not among the dead lying here is Mohsen al-Gasim. He was picked and being mentored by al-Wahhad to take command of our terrorist cell, and he was to split the cell in two operating and successful terrorist cells working inside your foul country. So, we could continue with our war against the West. Mr. American Soldier, one female who is missing is Leila Alibabic, she's the favorite of our faithful leader. She's a Saudi and a good fighter." Al-Ahmair cast a quick look at the female soldier still glaring so threateningly at him. He wanted to see if he might have just pleased her by saying this was a good female warrior missing from the group of dead.

The nasty look did not change in the least as Sergeant Ramirez continued to glare so angrily at him. Shrugging over the terrible look, al-Ahmair added to his words. "Mr. American Soldier, the last warrior who is not among the dead lying here is Reemabdel Aziz al-Rowaili, and she is the girlfriend of the second in command of our terrorist cell, Mohsen al-Gasim. I feel the fools will soon marry..."

"In a pig's fucking ear those two sacks of shit will marry. I got news for your fucking ass, Mac. Those two scumbags are soon to be dead if they don't surrender to my ass right off once we find the missing fucks. I got uther news for your ass to absorb as well, buster. We'll find all your damn friends, and we'll kill the missing cocksuckers plain and simple."

"Then I fear I have seen the faithful warriors for Allah in this world for the last time. Mr. American Soldier, these few missing warriors will never give up to the likes of you, without a fight to the death. They'll kill some of your evil soldiers before they allow you to kill them, I can assure you, Mr. American Soldier." The Arab terrorist al-Ahmair allowed a trace of anger in his eyes as he looked at Walker.

That was the straw that broke the back of the camel, as Walker instantly reacted against the nasty look coming from the suddenly defiant terrorist, by slugging his prisoner and knocking him out cold with one punch. Sending the terrorist flying back and he ended sprawled out on the floor. The Mutt moved up to Walker's side and offered him. "Man, you certainly have a helluva way with fucking words for that lousy little dude, man."

"Arrr…the lousy fuck got on my stinking nerves, and I had it with the scumbag and the way he was trying to make me feel he was…"

Sergeant Ramirez moved over and offered to both Walker and the Mutt at the same time. "If you two so called he-men are finished showing us girls just how tough you two really are. We have five other terrorist who are obviously armed with a dirty nuclear bomb we must find, before they can detonate the damn thing off somewhere here in Washington. So, I suggest we finish with our mission before we start to stretch our cocks and taking any bows over what we have not accomplished so far, guys. By the way you two fools, how are your wounds doing? I can't believe you two birds are both shot in the asses, taking about not using your smarts while out on an operation."

"She's right Walker, we hafta finish with our mission before we allow ourselves to relax any, man. Say Raz, my ass is doing just fine, it hardly hurts any longer." The Mutt replied as he aimed a quick smile at the Sergeant.

Walker never replied to Ramirez's question of how his wound was doing as he grumbled. "Yeah! Right! Okay, we hafta find these few missing little fucks and their damn weapon before they can possibly use it against us. We gotta search the interior of this stinking dump to make sure they didn't leave the damn thing here to detonate. First two Squads search this place, Third and Forth Squ…"

"Calm down a little Bobby, I have people already searching the interior of this building for the weapon. They should be about finished searching the place. Sergeant Moorehouse, were you able to find anything the terrorists might have hidden inside this structure?" Sergeant Ramirez called out to the soldier she ordered to take other troopers and search for the weapon.

"Sarge, we searched the shit outta this dumps from one end to the uther, and we found nuthin, Ma'am. It looks like the shitbirds musta took the damn thing along with their damn asses when they escaped from the fricking building, Sarge. We located three hot spots marked out in this dump that hasta be looked after by the cleanup crews when they get here though and start cleaning the place up." Sergeant Moorehouse called from about thirty feet away from Sergeant Ramirez and Captain Walker.

Walker growled at his SatCom soldier. "Hey Roach, get in contact with the damn Toll Booth people still blocking the way for the damn cleanup teams. Have them release the Richard Craniums that have orders to clean up any crud inside this damn building and have them move forward and start cleaning up this stinking dump. While we continue looking for the missing scumbags and that damn bomb of theirs."

"Will do Captain."

Sergeant Ramirez remained standing right by Walker's side, and she waited for him to reply to her if his wound was doing okay.

Reading her eyes, Walker understood what she wanted from him, and he replied. "Raz, my ass is doing just fine, and it'll be doing a helluva lot betta once we find these missing fucks and their damn bomb and place an end to this damn operation. Look at those uther fucks."

Walker turned away from his Sergeant and then he bellowed at the rest of his troopers. "What the fuck are you shitbirds looking at my fucking ass like I just took your damn crayons away from the lot of ya? Our targets have gone to ground, and that makes them a helluva lot harder to fucking locate and destroy. Dammit, you guys don't gotta wait for any further orders from my damn ass. Your professional soldiers and as such, you pack of shitbirds should know what the fuck to do next during this non-ending operation, without my having to tell your asses what to do. Find the missing pukes and their fucking weapon, move out."

As Walker was getting on his troops, a call from Toll Booth North went out, and it was intercepted by Colonel Bruce Leadbetter, who was constantly monitoring all communications from the soldiers working out in the field. "Dragon Fire Leader, Toll Booth North, am reporting I have a number of breathers moving fast on foot like they have a real purpose in life, and they're trying to make themselves as small as possible as they move at the same time, sir. The movers are attempting to be invisible as they make their birds from the area in question, but we have them on heat signal and a good MOE (Mark One Eyeball) on the Foxtrot slobs, sir. We have five targets on the move on hoof, sir. What orders Dragon Fire Leader? Over."

"Break! Break! This is Dragon Lair Commander! Toll Booth North! Commander, what the fuck are you calling in and requesting orders from my ass for, mister? You have your fucking orders and I'll repeat them for ya, so you understand them better, I guess. If you discovered any enemy combatants moving in your area of responsibility, you've been instructed not to wait until fired upon. Your orders are DID (Defeat In Detail). You're to destroy the enemy piece by piece. Your orders are to eradicate any possible located enemy targets, period! There are no fucking civilians moving in your area of responsibility, so if you detected any movers and they're not any of our troops, they're to be considered enemy fucking combatants, Commander. Kill them with evil intent and kill them fast, mister!" Colonel Leadbetter fired his angry words at the talker as if they were weapons.

"Toll Booth North responding Dragon Lair Commander. I Roger last and am firing on the movers. Out." The moment the Commander of the Bradley Fighting Machine finished speaking with Colonel Leadbetter, he issued orders to his machine crew. "Out of the fucking tube and keep 'em coming until all detected movers are naturalized."

The three-man crew went right to work and started to pour rounds out from the 25-millimeter cannon at the targets caught moving in tight formation on foot. When the first round exploded nearly right in front of the small group of movers, Mohsen al-Gasim and his girlfriend Reemabdel, were killed instantly. This was because of the red-hot shower of metal fragments from the exploding round ripping into their unprotected bodies.

Abdulaziz al-Wahhad reached out and grabbed the arm of Leila and he savagely pulled her back, and then forced her down close to the ground. The smaller group immediately changed direction, and the three headed away from the incoming cannon fire, after receiving several minor cuts and injuries from the exploding round.

Al-Mutairi followed the other terrorists from the rear, because he was being weighed down by the heavy nuclear device he was building. The eighty pounds strapped on his back, was causing the third terrorist to lag behind the two others. What al-Mutairi did not understand was his body was absorbing massive amounts of radiation being emitted from the Highly Enriched Uranium being exposed to the air. He was carrying the item in the open wrapped in just the cloth backpack looped over his back and resting across his shoulders. He was as good as dead already from his constant exposure to the radiation.

As the Bradley continued to fire rounds at the moving terrorists, some overshot rounds hit and exploded two parked cars, the rounds also exploded at or inside some of the civilian homes constructed so close together on the narrow street. Blowing holes, the size of basketballs into the civilian structures, as the cannon crew tried to kill the movers trying to escape their area of responsibility.

With secondary explosions and a thick column of smoke rising from fires the rounds from the light tank caused inside homes. The explosions and fires gave the three moving terrorists the cover they needed to change direction again and get away from the area safely. The remaining three terrorists were forced to go back and almost came out in the backyard of the building they originally used to construct the weapon. Al-Wahhad pulled his girlfriend down by the arm when he recognized they were so close to their original building, and the pursuing American soldiers still searching the interior of their building for them. Al-Mutairi dropped down when he noticed al-Wahhad and Leila drop down to a knee and hold up.

Al-Mutairi cautiously crawled over to Abdulaziz al-Wahhad's side, struggling with the extra weight of the nuclear weapon weighing him down. The moment he was at the terrorist leader's side, he asked the leader of the group with much concern lacing his tone of voice. "Shabbah, how have we foolishly worked our way back to this foul god forsaken place we fled earlier? There are too many people here who want to kill us, for us to survive for long in this area. I suggest we go off in another direction quickly, before the hated ones pour out of that foul building, and they discover us hiding so near the fools. You know the moment the evil soldiers see us, they'll kill us, no questions asked."

"Why is it you think I need the council of a fool like you, to help guide me over what I must do, to survive this little game of death we're playing with these worthless fools from this evil nation? I shall give the orders and you'll follow them out faithfully, or you'll feel my unfettered wrath fall upon your cursed shoulders. Al-Mutairi, I must ask, what is it you must do to make your device fully operational, and ready for use against the evil enemy of Allah? I am growing extremely tired of running all around this evil land like an arse. I say I shall not run one more step further away from these hated American soldiers sent out to destroy the faithful followers of Allah's sacred words.

"With your weapon of freedom and revenge, I shall blow up their quest to destroy us, along with half of their precious Washington, along with the worthless leaders and law makers right in their foul faces. I believe the all-knowing Allah has decreed this is where I shall make my last stand against the evil Satan that rules this cursed country. Whatever you must do to make this weapon ready for detonation, I order you to get it done quickly, and then we shall end this fracas now." Al-Wahhad demanded from his fellow terrorist.

"Shabbah, I must make a detonation trigger to cause the weapon to explode. I have the foul detonator close to working as it is. All I must do is to hook up a few loose wires to the detonation charge. Then I must hookup the battery that caused me the delay problems needed to cause the spark that'll set the detonation sequence in motion of the foul weapon. It should take me no longer than ten minutes to accomplish this feat, and finish what I have to complete to make the weapon operational." Al-Mutairi offered, speaking quickly to the leader.

"That is good, get on with what you must do to this foul weapon to make it operational, and I and Leila will afford you the cover fire in case the worthless American soldiers come out of that foul structure, and detect our presence and they open fire against us. You must worry about making that weapon operational for me, so we can carry out Allah's sacred will and destroy the great land of Satan. Begin your work while Leila and I prepare to fight off the forces of Satan." Al-Wahhad and Leila took defensive positions and checked their weapons to make certain they were ready to engage their enemy if they dared to attack them.

Al-Mutairi did not want to dare inform al-Wahhad the true reason why the weapon was not ready to detonate. It was because he messed up the battery needed to set the spark to detonate the weapon while originally working on the device. He was banking on finding a safe place where he could continue his work and place a second battery system inside the weapon to cause the detonation. As he thought, he was starting to feel sorry he joined this man and his evil quest to destroy so much of the United States with this weapon of the hated devil. In the back of his mind, he did not want to make the weapon operational, taking in the deaths it would cause to the civilians of this land.

Both Al-Wahhad and Leila covered the doors leading out of the factory to the large back parking lot of the building they used for a safe structure just minutes ago. He could only guess one of his fellow terrorists from their safe house was captured alive, and that one had betrayed their position of safety to the American soldiers who discovered where they were working, so quickly. The small group of Arab extremists could hear the American soldiers as they did whatever they were doing inside the massive warehouse while searching for them. Once the terrorists were comfortable with their defensive stance, al-Wahhad looked over his shoulder to make certain al-Mutairi was still working on completing the weapon for him. Seeing the man busy removing a cover from the small nuclear device, he turned back to the enemy soldiers inside the structure and prepared to open fire on them if they came pouring out of the building and started searching for them.

Al-Mutairi was just going through the motions of making it look like he was really working on completing the small nuclear weapon. He knew he would have to engineer the entire weapon down completely back to where he would be able to place the original set of batteries in to set off the device. He had welded the plate over the battery section, so there was no real safe way to get that deep in the weapon, without destroying it first. He was also fighting with his conscious, because the more he thought about what al-Wahhad was planning to do against the United States, the more he did not want to detonate the device. He wanted to kill, but he did not want to kill so many innocent people with one blow.

Inside the building, Captain Robert Walker was informed the cleanup teams were released by the roadblock detachment, and they were quickly closing in on the structure. He drew in a breath and then growled at the rest of his troops either checking out the structure or hanging around waiting for further orders. "Okay people we did everything we can possibly do in this here stinking dump. Roach, you're in charge of our fucking prisoner, keep him alive until the damn cleanup teams get here, and you can dump his fucking ass off with them guys to keep watch over the dopey fuck. Then you're ordered to get out there along with us while we hunt down the rest of this pack of shit. We know Toll Booth North already tangled with and killed two of these missing shits, so the rest of the lousy fucks hafta be nearby. Let's get out there and find the shits and end this damn game of hide and seek."

The specialized soldiers inside the building attacked the doors to the back of the building in force. Leaving the building, the troops immediately dispersed to make themselves harder targets for the terrorists to hit in case they set up in ambush against them outside.

The moment al-Wahhad picked up the enemy soldiers pouring out of the building he snorted at the other terrorists with him. "Be ready, the evil ones are coming to try and destroy us. Al-Mutairi, you must complete your sacred work for Allah on that cursed weapon as quickly as possible. Because I don't know how long I'll be able to hold off the worthless non-believers coming to attack us. There are more of the cursed lowly infidels than I had first thought searching for us. When you have the device prepared to detonate. Don't wait for any reason or an order from me, you will detonate it and destroy the evil that control the great land of Satan. It's our sacred duty to die for the sake of Allah. Allahu Akhbar, Paradise awaits her Martyrs."

Anger built up in the chest of al-Mutairi, because he did not like al-Wahhad telling him to prepare to die and kill countless innocent people with his death. Resenting ever working with al-Wahhad in the first place, he in his defiance of the terrorist leader caused him to stop any further work on the small nuclear device. With his anger building he rose and then he began waving his arms while calling out to the enemy soldiers, giving away his presence to the ones searching for him and the others.

Buckethead was the first soldier to notice the man jumping up and down and waving his arms wildly and calling out to them. He whistled three times to get Walker's attention, and when he had it. He pointed towards the crazy acting man with his chin. The captain did not hesitate for a second as he fired three rounds at the man trying to be noticed.

When al-Wahhad heard the commotion al-Mutairi was creating behind him, he turned and when he realized what al-Mutairi was up to. He quickly raised his weapon to his shoulder, but before he could fire at his fellow terrorist. His body suddenly jumped awkwardly from the three rounds ripping into his body that Walker fired at him. Al-Mutairi's body dropped and then disappeared fully in the thick underbrush of the field they were trying to hide in.

When al-Mutairi's body disappeared, al-Wahhad got low and growled savagely at Leila. "Al-Mutairi has chosen to betray us to the evil soldiers who hunt and want to kill us. It's now up to us to kill as many of the cursed American soldiers of this foul country of Satan as we can before they kill us. When we engage the evil ones, continue firing at the fools until your weapon is empty, and they killed us. Take comfort in the fact the next time we're together, it'll be in the presence of Muhammad and the Almighty Allah. Good luck my faithful sister."

Al-Wahhad was the first one to open fire on Walker's troops. He fired seven rounds before Walker's troops responded with heavy weapon fire aimed at the one shooting at them. The terrorist leader's fire drew a flood of return fire directed at him and Leila. Thirty-six soldiers dropped down and immediately returned fire at the person firing at them. Within seconds, the area where the two Islamic terrorists hid was being torn up by the heavy weapon fire. Walker allowed the soldiers to continue to fire for a few minutes to make certain they killed the few missing terrorists from the group, before he started to shout at his troops.

"Cease fire, hold your fire. I said hold your fucking fire, not even a stinking grasshopper coulda lived through that crapshoot we just unleashed against these lousy little scumbags. Buckethead, you spotted the first fuck so take four troopers with ya and get the fuck up there and see if we got all the missing scumbags. I'll take four uther soldiers with me and work our way around where the shits were firing from. Keep your eyes open, those scumbags might be just playing possum against us. If we got all three of the sonofabitches, the damn weapon must be with these slugs. Take control of the fucking device, and we'll give it to the cleanup shits for immediate disposal. Move out."

Walker watched as Buckethead, and four other soldiers cautiously worked their way out to where the weapon fire was coming from. He and the few soldiers he wanted with him, started out with the four others, but when he looked behind him. He noticed every soldier assigned to his command, was moving up as one along with the other soldiers without being ordered to do so. They all wanted to see if they killed the missing Islamic terrorists, and if they had the nuclear device. The proud Captain shook his head and smiled to himself, because he was that pleased of the elite troops and their actions.

Buckethead and four other Tier One no fail soldiers cautiously reached the bodies of the dead terrorists. They quickly checked out the bodies to make certain they were dead, and they did not have any booby traps on their person. By the time Walker and the other soldiers got up to where Buckethead and the other four soldiers were working on the dead terrorists. Buckethead already had the bodies stripped of clothes, and his troops were checking the terrorist's weapons and belongings, and anything else they had on their person.

The exhausted Captain stopped where the two terrorists were lying on the ground. Then he headed the fifteen feet or so separating the terrorist he killed from the other two. He noticed the small nuclear device resting a foot away from the body, and he immediately stopped the other soldiers from gathering around the deadly weapon, in case the weapon was emitting any dangerous radiation.

Walker then called out for a Geiger counter to be brought over to him. A second soldier rushed up to his side and handed him the portable counter. He flipped the machine on and smiled because he was right. The gauge on the Geiger counter was pegged at the top of the machine. That meant the weapon was emitting over five hundred Mili-Renkins per hour, which was much too high for anyone without protective gear on, to be anywhere near the poorly constructed makeshift nuclear weapon.

He dropped back where the other terrorists were lying on the ground, and the rest of his soldiers gathered around the two dead terrorists. He barked at the soldiers to get out of the area for their own safety, and then he instructed Buckethead and his group to leave the terrorists and their stuff where it was. He moved the rest of the soldiers back to the commercial building and had them go inside the structure for extra protection from the radiation the poorly constructed device was emitting. Once inside, Walker grabbed a cleanup member and informed the Sergeant he found the missing nuclear device, and it was emitting dangerous levels of radiation.

The cleanup member informed Walker he would send a few of his workers and secure the weapon, and then the Sergeant called over a few of his helpers, and they quickly left the building to secure the weapon and place it in the heavy lead lined container resting on the back of the tractor trailer they used to get up to the commercial building with the other soldiers. Walker was starting to relax when his radio suddenly squawked on him.

"Dragon Lair to Dragon Fire. Come in. Over."

"Dragon Fire here, go with your traffic. Over." Walker replied in an exhausted tone.

"You sound dead on your damn feet, Captain. Nevertheless, you must see this damn thing through to the fucking end. What's the status of your operation, mister? Over?"

"I am dead on my feet Colonel. The status of my operation is classified as complete, Dragon Lair. We ended the operation with the death of all subjects in question with one alive and in custody, and we took command of the item in question, Colonel Leadbetter Sir. Right now, the baby's being placed in the crib, and then the cleanup crews have work on their hands, and once they clear us for travel. I'm gonna send my people over to Andrews for disposition. Dragon Fire Leader signing off. Out."

"It's not that fucking easy, mister. You're right to want to get your people the hell out of the damn incident zone as quickly as possible, Dragon Fire Leader. I don't need your people getting caught on film by any nosy news reporter and later identified, and you become compromised and of no further use to future covert operations. Right now, we're still an invisible operational force, and I want to keep it that way, Captain. You and your people need to operate in the shadows, or your units will be no worth to the security of our nation.

Arrr…make certain you call in your Vipers (Snipers) and gather the rest of your troops before you consider moving out of the incident area, sir. I'm going to leave the Toll Booths set in place where they are currently stationed, and they'll continue with their orders not to allow anyone to enter this incident area, until that fucking item is secured, and the cleanup crews have completed their damn orders and cleaned up any crud they come across in the field, Captain. I'm going to keep a security net over the entire fucking area until I'm absolutely certain your people are out of the area and that baby is secured.

"Walker, you're absolutely correct with wanting to move your troops the hell out of the damn area as quickly as possible, and once you're on Joint Andrews Airforce Base waiting transfer out to our main base of operations at Lejeune. No one will be allowed in the incident area until

General White gives the final okay to remove the damn security Toll Booths and allow the displaced civilians back in their homes. I understand some weapon fire caused a few minor fires and slight damage to some homes and parked vehicles in the area, and that's tough shit for the damn civilians whose homes are burning.

"I'm not going to allow any emergency personnel to enter the incident area, until I know for certain our item is secured and cleanup operations have been completed. I'm aware you have several police officers operating with your Units. Dragon Fire Leader, I'm ordering you to have those officers' takeover the security of the incident area from your troops, along with orders no one is allowed in the area, under orders from the President of the United States.

"Walker, you're to inform the police officers not even their people are allowed to cross the lines of security once they have established said lines. Dragon Fire Leader, once you're on our main base of operations. I'm going to flood your flaming assholes with a sea of cold beer, and enough steaks to stuff them full for a fucking week. You people done well, very well on this operation. I'm damn proud of the troops I trained for doing their work so well, Captain. I'll linkup with you at Andrews. Give your people a well done, Captain. Dragon Lair, out."

Walker did not bother to end the conversation with Colonel Leadbetter as he grabbed a cigarette from the Mutt and took a good pull, as he let out his breath in an exhausted sigh, and then he relaxed a little and let down his guard for the first time since he started this operation. He issued the last orders he intended to give until the next operation he and his troops were ordered out on.

"Mutt, order in our Vipers and have our people assemble inside this fucking building A-SAP. We're gonna have the police open us a lane of travel, and then we're gonna get the fuck outta here and head for Joint Andrews Airforce Base undercover the police will offer us. Get it done. I'm gonna suck in some air and take a stinking break for myself."

When Walker finished speaking with his fellow soldier, Sergeant Dorothy Ramirez moved in and lightly rested her hand on the shoulder of her soldier, she smiled and spoke. "I love you, Robert."

www.ingramcontent.com/pod-product-compliance
Lightning Source LLC
Chambersburg PA
CBHW062100290726
48975CB00001B/54